I0822778

THE SEAM TRAVELERS

The Complete Series

RAY WENCK

JASON J. NUGENT

raywenck.com

jasonjnugent.com

ISBN: 9798985882018

Dedicated to Terry, Molly and Angela for loving my kids despite their crazy dad.
-Ray

I'd like to dedicate this to my readers.
It's been awhile. I hope you enjoy!
-Jason

Contents

Escape

THE SEAM TRAVELERS BOOK ONE

RAY WENCK
JASON J. NUGENT

ESCAPE

THE SEAM TRAVELERS
BOOK ONE

Chapter 1

Phetrix raced through the dark stone halls of the castle, his gray woolen robe trailing behind him. The invasion from the usurper Mortas Frost had begun and his duties to the prince and princess were paramount. They must be saved at all costs.

Shouting men in black armor and dying soldiers surrounded the castle. Flaming arrows streaked the sky and landed inside the castle, striking royal soldiers and igniting wood and clothing. Shouts for medical aid were called to Phetrix, but he ignored them. It pained him to let the injured go unattended. His obligation was to the children. If Mortas Frost gained access to the castle, all hope was gone.

Phetrix slipped on the cold stone floor when he turned a corner, his sandals losing traction in the fray, and nearly slammed into the wall. He righted himself and hurried to the nursery at the end of the hall.

"Are they safe?" he asked the guard stationed outside. He was a large barrel chested man named Wibar. Standing stoic with a sword at his belt and the white stag of King Artus on his armor, he dared anyone to cross him.

"Aye, they're safe. None have come through here but you. Come, inside quick."

He opened the large wooden door to a room decorated in bright paintings of mythical animals. Unicorns and dragons adorned the paintings, most crude interpretations colored by the children Erthic and Elysande, the two-year old twins of King Artus and Queen Gresilda.

"Erthic. Elysande," he said breathless, "Come. We need to go."

Elysande pouted. "No." She turned her back to him, facing an image of a griffon.

"You'll have time for disagreements later. We leave, now."

"No."

Erthic smiled, ready to join the fun. "No," he mimicked.

"We don't have time for this." Phetrix snatched each child into his arms and hurried out the door.

"Wibar, come. I will need your assistance. We must make sure the children are safe."

"I'm yours, mage. Nothing will happen to them as long as I live."

Phetrix entered the hall with the children in his arms and Wibar behind him.

Elysande squirmed and kicked.

"Cut that out! If you—"

She dropped from Phetrix's arms and ran, hurrying for the hallway ahead.

"Come back! Elysande! Don't run!"

He and Wibar ran after her, Erthic giggling at his sister's escape.

By the time they reached the intersection, she was gone. "Elysande! Where are you? This isn't a game! You're in danger!"

The girl giggled and stepped out from an open door on the right. She stuck her tongue out at him and ran back in the room.

"Infernal girl! Come back here now!" He marched toward the door and turning inside, found her with one of Mortas Frost's men, the large white snowflake adorning his black armor giving him away.

"Let her go!" he demanded.

"Ely!" Erthic said, twisting in Phetrix's arms.

The mage set him down. "Stay behind me, do you understand?" The boy nodded.

"I'll be taking him, too," the soldier said. "Mortas will pay dearly for these two."

"He will get no satisfaction. They're under my protection. Touch one hair on her head and I will kill you."

The soldier laughed. "You? Kill me? With what? Wave of your hand and a magic word?" He ran a gauntleted hand through the girl's hair.

"Touch her and die," Wibar said, stepping out from behind the mage with his sword drawn.

"I warned you!" Phetrix said. The mage circled his hands in the air as though kneading dough and a bright ball of light appeared. He pushed it forward, enveloping the man's face.

"Stop that! I can't see!" he screamed. He uselessly fought the light.

"Elysande, hurry! Come quick!" The girl ran to him. "That's it, let's go before the spells wears off." She'd started crying and he held her close. "Wibar, finish this man."

The guard stepped around Phetrix and thrust his sword forward into the man's neck. He howled in agony, clutching at the sword, then let go and fell to the floor, his blood spreading out around him. Wibar wiped his sword on his trousers.

"He won't be bothering anyone again," Wibar muttered. Phetrix turned from the dying man, forcing the children to look away.

"Erthic, follow me! Stay close and don't linger!"

Smoke filled the corridors as Phetrix led them, grumbling about the prophecy. The tapestries on the walls were obscured by the increasingly heavy smoke. The children fell into a fit of coughing.

"I'm so sorry. We'll be out of this soon," Phetrix said. He placed a hand over Elysande's mouth, hoping to shield her from the smoke. She and her brother needed to survive at all costs.

Shouts ahead announced danger.

"There they are! Grab 'em before they escape!"

Wibar shoved them aside to get in front, and reached for his sword.

Black armored men with the snowflake of Mortas rushed them.

Wibar rushed forward, slicing down with his sword. "For the King and the children!"

He caught one enemy in the arm, but his armor protected him enough to deflect much of the blow. Wibar's weight in the blow made him stagger and one of the other soldiers rammed a dagger into his back. The large royal guard cried out, then the rest of the enemy soldiers were on him, swords and daggers piercing him mercilessly.

The children wailed but it was too late for Phetrix to help the man.

Reaching inside at the power he held, Phetrix created another, larger ball of light, and forced it toward the men. They shrieked in horror as the light approached and touched them.

"By the gods," Phetrix whispered. The men were engulfed in a fiery death, the intense heat from the light incinerating them as it moved forward until it dissipated leaving charred remains of four soldiers and Wibar smoldering on the ground.

Both children were hysterical, crying and barely able to control their emotions.

"Dead?" Elysande asked, the word difficult to hear in the chaos of the attack.

"Gone," Erthic said.

"No time. Come children," Phetrix said, carefully stepping through the blackened bones and burnt flesh. He approached another intersection and on both ends of the hall, black armored enemy soldiers faced him. They were trapped.

Nordon, the king's armorer, stepped into the hallway from a door midway between Phetrix and the enemy soldiers on the right, a massive warhammer held tight in his hands. Phetrix noticed a girl in the room where he came from, cowering and shaking.

"Nordon! Hold them off. I need a moment," Phetrix said. The large man nodded and grinned as he turned to the soldiers on their right.

"Let's do this," he growled. He raced toward them, swinging his mighty hammer with a deadly force. The sound of men screaming in agony and the hammer crashing through armor followed. The hall was filled with men and Phetrix didn't know if Nordon was winning or dying. All he knew was that it gave him the time to create the seam.

Samuel, I hope you're ready, Phetrix thought. He closed his eyes and focused. Men were dying around him. The serving girl was crying in the room. The children clung to him.

Phetrix reached deep within himself and conjured the spell he never imagined he'd ever have to use again. It was always a last resort if the castle was ever attacked. It was one of the few places he could perform such a feat.

When he opened his eyes, the hallway shimmered and distorted. It was like looking through water in a glass. Then sound quieted and motion slowed. He saw Nordon finish the men at his end of the corridor before he turned to run back toward the children. The enemy soldiers on the other side approached slowly, their way obstructed by Phetrix's powerful spell. Blood ran down Nordon's arm and his armor was stained with it.

Phetrix pushed harder and the distortion grew worse.

Nordon slowed, lowering his bloody hammer.

"It's our way out!" Phetrix called, noticing the large man's hesitation. "Hurry, I can let you pass. Bring the girl!"

Nordon's eyes widened.

"Now!" Phetrix yelled.

Nordon obeyed. He slid the warhammer into its sheath on his back and lifted the girl from the room, setting her down in the hallway. "This way Nadina," he said holding out a hand to pull her toward him.

Phetrix grew anxious. "If I don't make it, I need your oath Nordon. Swear to protect them. They cannot be found and if they are, they must be protected. The prophecy depends on it. Swear it!"

Nordon cocked his head to the side in deep thought then finally replied, "I swear."

"Hurry into the light, it won't hold for long."

Nadina timidly stepped forward near the bright slash of light.

"Go with her," Phetrix said to the children. Erthic grabbed her hand, Elysande stood next to her.

"Go through. The mage Samuel will guide you. I wish you the best. We will meet again."

Erthic walked with Nadina into the blinding light followed by Nordon. *Where was Elysande?* He thought.

"Ely! Where are you girl?"

The enemy soldiers were closing in, two of them entering the light.

"No!" He screamed. He had to close the seam. The boy would have to be safe with Nordon and Nadina.

He'd find the girl.

Phetrix waved his hands and the light vanished, leaving a faint echo in the dark corridor before winking out.

May the gods save you boy, he thought. He hurried away while the remaining enemy soldiers were disoriented. He had to find the girl before Mortas.

Chapter 2

The attack on the castle lasted well into the night as did Phetrix's search for Elysande. If Mortas abducted her, or worse, killed her, their world was in trouble. At least he saved the boy. Saving one of them might have to be good enough.

Mortas Frost intended on plunging the kingdom into darkness and terror. Murdering the royal family was his only way to secure the outcome.

When Phetrix was younger, he served Mortas faithfully for close to ten years. The man was a monster.

Once, when they were on the march against King Artus's uncle Prince Willem, their army descended on a small village called Whispercross.

"Plunder all you want, kill any who oppose you. Do what you will with the women. We aren't staying long and none of them must be left alive," Mortas commanded them. Phetrix was in horror when he witnessed the brutal slaying of a young boy by one of the soldiers, all because he tried to save his sister.

That was when he realized the evil Mortas had become.

He knew the man was loose with his morals, but this was too much. While on the march toward Prince Willem's castle, Phetrix used a spell known to only a few of the most powerful mage's of the order and created a traveling tunnel to escape the terror. When he did, he stumbled onto something far more important.

Phetrix entered the tunnel, an immense blinding light that tore a seam in the fabric of time and space, but instead of finding himself closer to Willem's castle, he entered a world he'd never seen before.

Mechanical chariots, impossibly high buildings, and noise greeted him. He stood between two tall buildings with more glass windows than he'd ever seen in his life. People walked past him wearing odd clothing and unusual footwear and they stared at him, pointing and insulting him.

"By the gods! Another lives!" a man said to him. Phetrix was too stunned to reply. The man had come from one of the tall buildings.

"Come quickly! Are there more of you? Have you brought the king or Mortas?"

The man grabbed Phetrix by the hand and led him to one of the large buildings. They entered a door made of material he thought was metal. The man ushered him inside and led him to another door which opened to a small room.

Furniture unlike anything he'd ever seen before lined the walls. A box on a table caught his attention. Moving pictures flashed across the box, the sound screeching through it.

"What kind of sorcery is this?" Phetrix asked, pointing a long boney finger at the box.

"I have too little time to explain. I'm Samuel, faithful servant of King Artus."

Phetrix nearly fell over. "You're who?" He knew the name, the entire Order knew who he was.

"I thought you were dead? I was told you disappeared on the battle field."

Samuel nodded. "In a way, yes. I performed the same spell you did. It brought me here," he said waving his hands.

"Where is here?"

"Another dimension. Another world we never knew existed."

"But . . . I don't understand."

"It's not for us to understand, but to embrace. When King Artus learned of this, he instructed me to silence. He feared Mortas would push his evil across our land and he'd need an escape."

"Mortas?" Phetrix asked.

"Now I ask you again. Do you serve King Artus or Mortas?" Phetrix realized the man held a large dagger ready to strike.

"I serve--" He wasn't sure how to answer. He *had* been with Mortas, but the only reason he was here was because he'd fled the evil Mortas had become.

"I am Phetrix. I serve King Artus."

Samuel sheathed the dagger. "By the gods! We will survive this after all! Come, there is much to teach you."

Samuel went into the kitchen, banging items together. Once he was done, he produced two mugs of a dark liquid. "Have a seat Phetrix," he said nodding toward a table. Phetrix, still overwhelmed by his new surroundings, slowly approached the table and sat. Samuel handed him the mug, its warmth radiating outward.

"What is this?"

Samuel smiled. "They call it coffee. You'll like it."

Phetrix waited, wary it was a trap.

"It's fine, I promise." Samuel took the mug, sipped, and handed it back.

Expecting the man to get ill, Phetrix watched him carefully as he spoke.

"We are in a different world, a city they call Chicago. It's in a land called Illinois. Quite a loud place too." Samuel sipped from his own mug and continued.

"When you crossed the seam, you triggered an alarm. You tripped a spell really. It alerted me to the presence of one like me crossing the seam from our world to this one."

"Are you mad?" Phetrix whispered. Samuel chuckled.

"Mad? No. Cautious and prepared? Yes. I had no idea if that no good Rhoden Noster would discover the spell to cross the seam and I had to know whoever was coming across was friend or foe."

"How do you know I'm not an enemy? What makes you so sure I'm on your side?"

Samuel leaned in close. "Are you? On my side? On the side of King Artus? If you plan on returning home anytime soon, you'd do well to tell me the truth."

Phetrix sipped his drink, intent on showing Samuel he trusted him and he meant what he said about serving the King. "I was in the service of Mortas. I thought he was an honorable man. Until . . ." he trailed off, the memory of the looted village fresh in his mind, "Until he ordered a despicable act upon innocent people. I was awakened from my stupor and sought my way out."

Samuel leaned back. "So. You served Mortas," he said slowly, "but yet you claim allegiance to the King."

"King Artus is the rightful heir, I know that now. I've studied in the Order for years. I understand what's at stake."

"Then you know why it's paramount we preserve the King and his heirs."

"I do."

Samuel emptied his cup, went into the kitchen to refill it and sat back down. "A day," he said as he settled in.

"Excuse me?"

"A day. Give me a day where I can show you this world and I'll show you how to get back to ours."

Phetrix considered his request. "Fine. A day. Then I'd like to get back home."

"In the morning, we'll go out and I'll show you around. Then I'll share how to get back. Tonight, you can sleep on the couch."

"The . . . couch?"

Samuel smiled and pointed in the other room. "That over there. I'll get you some clothes in the morning so you don't stand out like you do now."

Phetrix barely slept that night, worried if he was being set up by Samuel.

Chapter 3

Phetrix awoke when Samuel dropped a pan in the kitchen.

"Sorry about that! Just getting some breakfast before we go out. I've got pants and a t-shirt on the chair over there. I guessed your size, I hope they work."

The white haired older man busied himself with the pan, swirling eggs and frying bacon, a scent Phetrix knew all too well from home. He changed into the clothes provided and stared at himself in a mirror he noticed in the bathroom. He wore dark blue pants that were thick. The shirt had the sigil of some local lord.

"What is this? What lord do you serve?" Phetrix asked pointing at his shirt. If he was going to be in public, he wanted to know what lord he was with. He couldn't be too careful.

Samuel laughed. "It's not a lord, it's a team. A baseball team to be exact. The Cubs."

"A . . . baseball team?"

"It's a sport in this world. In this city, the Cubs are one of their local teams."

"Oh." Phetrix let it go, figuring wearing the sigil of a team wasn't as bad as a rival lord.

After breakfast and more of the coffee drink, Samuel took Phetrix out to explore their surroundings.

Samuel tried his best to offer commentary as they walked.

"Chicago is one of the largest cities in this country. It's in the center of the nation and has a busy airport, which may come in handy if we ever have to escape."

"An airport?"

"You see those," Samuel pointed upwards at a slow moving bird with white smoke trailing behind, "those are airplanes. They've figured out how to put people in the air. Quite a remarkable achievement if you ask me."

Phetrix stared at the airplane above, oblivious to the throngs of people walking past them.

"Come, we've got more to see." Samuel nudged him and they joined the flow of people.

"Just outside my apartment where I found you is one entry point to this world. There's another by a parking garage on the southside. Beyond that, I don't know of any other places where a seam can emerge."

"What's a parking garage?"

"Do you see where those cars are going over there, that's a parking garage. Think of it like a . . ." he paused then lit up as the analogy occurred to him, "think of it like a stable for these wheeled chariots they call cars."

Phetrix nodded his understanding. To be honest, the sounds, sights, and the constant smell of something like the lavatories back home overwhelmed him.

"Why are you here Samuel? Why not try to work back in Chevalon? Wouldn't you be more helpful there?"

The older mage turned to him. "There are too many who know me or about me back home. Mortas has been after me, hoping to force me into his service like he's done with Rhoden. Since I refused, he wants me dead. Did you know Rhoden was a student of mine? He's more powerful than you can imagine. Do not underestimate him. Ever!" Samuel punctuated his words with a finger to Phetrix's chest.

They walked around the busy city for hours, Samuel droning on about something called pizza and beers, though Phetrix never saw any. Finally, he'd had enough.

"Samuel, I appreciate the tour, but this is all too much for me. How did this world exist without us ever knowing? What does this have to do with the King and his heirs?"

Samuel stopped, his eyes darting back and forth, then he spoke in a quiet voice. "If Mortas ever comes for the heirs, they'll be safe here. We can protect them within the confines of this city. They'd be anonymous here. No one knows how to travel the seam other than you and I. We need to keep it that way."

Phetrix wondered about the viability of leaving their world to remain in this one, but Samuel seemed convinced. He didn't bother to try and change his mind. King Artus was in no real danger, no matter how much Mortas harassed his smaller lieges. Mortas was wicked, but he didn't seem to have the resources to carry out his overthrow.

"Say, where were you when you travelled the seam? There were only two places I knew of that opened to this world."

Phetrix closed his eyes and recalled where was the moment he opened the seam. "I was near Whispercross."

"Whispercross? That little village? I'd never have found that!"

"I fled Mortas and his army, opening the seam right there. I had no idea it was dependent on a particular place. I just used the spell and found myself here."

Samuel's eyes widened and he spoke in hushed tones. "The location has everything to do with where you go. This is the third world I visited."

"What? No. How does that make sense?"

"Look around, Phetrix, none of this makes sense when you think about it. But yet, here we are. Remember Whispercross. That will get you back here. So will the King's castle."

Phetrix was confused.

"Don't worry. I discovered it long ago. It's quite handy if ever under attack." He winked and slapped Phetrix on the arm. "Come now, I assume you'll want to get back home."

They retraced their way, returning to the building where they started.

Phetrix was exhausted and slowly slipped back into his robes, the familiar feel comforting him.

Samuel led him to another room in the apartment. Inside it was dark. He lit several candles revealing walls covered in writing Phetrix recognized from spell books.

"Stand there," Samuel said pointing at a large X painted on the floor.

Phetrix did as he was told.

"When you return, visit the library in King Artus's castle. Hidden behind the potions books is a trap door where you'll find an exact copy of this spell. Learn it. If you ever return, you'll need it to get back. I might not be here next time. I've also listed the other locations to enter the seam."

Phetrix nodded, still unsure if this was all a dream or something worse.

Samuel opened a book and started reading the spell. Soon the room erupted in a brilliant white light that consumed Phetrix. He shielded his eyes to it and when he opened them, he stood outside the walls of the king's castle.

Before he'd sent Erthic to the realm, that was the only time he'd ever been there.

Chapter 4

Samuel waited, his impatience showing in the form of his muttering and pacing. The three men with him, all former guards of the now deposed king, stood calmly awaiting his orders. Each man wore a dark suit and sunglasses, giving the appearance of being professional bodyguards. In fact, once Samuel figured out the new world, he had them all trained for this very purpose. They stood positioned to observe anyone approaching from any direction.

Samuel stopped his pacing and whirled on the eldest of the three guards, a one-time captain named Trenton. "Are you sure your source was reliable?" he asked for the fifth time since they'd taken up their vigil.

"Yes. He is reliable. The castle *is* under attack and *does* look like it has fallen."

Samuel eyed him, ready to snap at the man for his insolent tone. Instead, he pivoted and began pacing once more.

Samuel had also traded in his lavish robes for a tailored suit. The expensive wardrobe fitted his economic standing. He'd done well in this new world--well, not so new now. The discovery that his magic still worked had a lot to do with his success.

He reached the end of the unofficial path and pivoted for the return. *Where was Phetrix? Had he died in the battle?* He prayed not. If the mage fell, all was lost. If Phetrix was unable to get the King, Queen and the children out of danger then all hope of saving the kingdom was gone forever. Mortas Frost would rule until his death, which could never come soon enough for the people of the land. He was a brutal tyrant, who took pleasure in other's agony. He would make the people suffer greatly.

If the castle fell, the only chance they had of recovering it was if a member of the royal family survived the assault. However, even if they did, Mortas would hunt them endlessly until they were found, torturing and executing any he thought who might be harboring them. Oh, this was bad. So very bad.

A sudden sound caught his attention, like that of an electrical current followed by a tearing of heavy fabric. He spun to face the noise. The three guards took defensive stances all now holding guns.

A dark line appeared head high, stretching across the open air. The location of the seam was not ideal. When he'd first discovered the seam years before, it was in an alley that blocked the view of its strangeness. Since that time, one of the buildings had been demolished in a nuisance abatement sweep. Nothing had replaced the structure which left the seam open on one side. Though not many people walked this section of the city, a lot of cars passed. Anyone could see the seam, although not many would understand its purpose. However, if they spotted people appearing out of thin air, it might be another matter. Especially with the wide use of their communication devices.

A hand reached through pulling on the fabric of the world and made it wider. Samuel and Trenton stepped closer as a toddler was lowered from the gap. Trenton took the terrified boy and handed him off to one of his men. Next came a young woman, equally as scared as the boy. Trenton took her around the waist and lowered her to the ground. The second guard came forward and ushered her to the side. Her face drained of all color as she scanned her new home. She fainted and the guard was forced to lift and carry her toward the waiting van.

The last figure through was a hulk of a man. He stepped through, but no amount of assistance would help him to the ground without causing injury to the assister. The man jumped down. He carried a large warhammer on his back. His massive arms made him appear like something out of the comic books the men were always reading.

"Quick, get them to the van," Samuel commanded.

The two guards took the new arrivals while Trenton and Samuel waited for others. When none came, Samuel levitated to the seam and peered through. The hallway was filled with smoke making it difficult to see. Then, a face came into focus. It was Phetrix. He felt his heart lighten, knowing the mage was still alive. They locked eyes for the briefest of moments. Samuels eyes asked the question, 'What about the King, Queen and the girl?' Phetrix shook his head and shrugged. The seam closed as if a zipper had been drawn. It winked out with an audible pop.

Samuel hovered above the ground lost in thought and sorrow. Were they only able to save one of the four? "This is bad," he said to himself.

Trenton stepped forward and placed a hand on Samuel's arm. "Whether we're staying or leaving, you must not stand out to bystanders."

Samuel looked confused for a moment, then understood and lowered himself to the ground. he had to think. What needed to be done? He grabbed Trenton's arm. "If the boy is the only survivor we must protect him. No harm can come to him or all is lost. Leave one of your men with me and take the others to the house we bought for them. Tell the big man to help guard the boy. Let the woman take care of the boy. You stay with them. Send the other guard back with the van, but only once you're sure all is secure. Keep him safe, Trenton."

Trenton nodded and jogged to the van. One of the guards, Darden, he thought, he could never keep their names straight, shoved the side door shut and the van drove away. He then moved toward Samuel keeping his distance to better take in the surroundings.

Samuel looked around. He had to find someplace to watch from. Standing here for hours would draw attention and that was the last thing he needed. He walked toward the street. he didn't need to speak or motion to the guard. The man would follow. Protection was what he was trained to do and Darden was good at his job.

They walked across the street and entered a three-story parking garage. There, Samuel took up his stakeout. He prayed his vigil would bear fruit and Phetrix would find and deliver the rest of the royal family. He had been happy to discover Phetrix was still alive. However, now that he knew he only managed to save one of the four he was charged with protecting, Samuel cursed him.

How could he not have been prepared for this outcome? The man bungled the job. The only job he really had. He was happy his fellow mage was alive, but if the King, Queen and daughter were dead, the man had a lot to answer for.

Chapter 5

The van returned two hours later carrying Trenton and the other guard, Mathu. It stopped and Trenton got out.

"Samuel, you should go. Get them set up. Explain what you need to and set the wards. I will stay here and keep watch. I'll call you if anything happens."

Samuel wanted to object, but Trenton's words made sense. Besides, if the boy was the only royal member to survive, it was important he got him secured as soon as possible. He nodded, got in the van and was lost in thought.

The drive was a good thirty minutes to the old residential neighborhood. He had purchased the house days before, paying cash at a well below market price. He chose the location because it was an established neighborhood, with residents who, for the most part stayed out of other people's business. He could have set them up in more luxurious quarters, but until they were familiar with their new world, he didn't want to risk them coming under scrutiny.

The house was a two-story, aluminum sided structure with a walk-up attic and full basement. It was within walking distance of stores, schools and a park. It was also less than a minute from an expressway in case the need for a quick escape arose.

Mathu pulled up to the curb in front of the house.

Samuel exited and climbed the stairs. Mathu followed eyeing the street as he went. Samuel knocked and after a bit of hesitation, the door was opened by the huge man. He held the heavy warhammer in one hand, ready to strike. Samuel had no doubt the man knew how to wield the weapon.

The woman and child sat on a sofa. She looked more anxious than the boy did. A little color had returned to her cheeks since she'd stepped into the new world. He studied them each for a moment, then said, "I am Samuel. I will be your contact here. If ever there is an emergency of any sort I am the only one you contact."

Her voice frail and shaking, the woman said, "You mean, you're going to leave us here alone?"

"You'll hardly be alone, dear girl. You will have each other. But, not to worry. I will not leave until I'm satisfied that you can survive and flourish here. You have so much to learn. There's so much to tell you, I barely know where to begin. It will be overwhelming at first, but you'll catch on."

"Are we to stay here, then, sir?"

"That's right. It wouldn't be safe for you to go back now. It appears as though Mortas Frost has taken control of the castle. That may mean this little man's family is no more. If that is the case, it is up to us to protect him until such a time as we can take our lands back."

Samuel sat in the rocking chair opposite the sofa. He would have asked the big man to sit as well, but he feared the sofa might not hold his weight.

"First of all, tell me your names."

"I," the big man put a fist to his chest in case Samuel didn't understand which I he was referring to, "am Nordon. I was the castle's blacksmith."

That explains the muscular arms, Samuel thought.

"My name is Nadina. I worked in the kitchen."

"And this little man is Erthic." He smiled at the lad, but the boy just stared at him, not comprehending everything.

"This is a modern world, full of all manner of people and strange ideas. This house alone has so many magical items as to be called a wizard's keep. It will take time to explain them. Some you will need to know while others you can learn for yourself.

"Let's start with the names. From now on, you are Don and, uh, Dina. We'll figure out a surname later. The boy will be known as Eric.

You are to pose as husband and wife. Eric is your son. Your primary function is to protect Eric at all times and at all costs.

"Nordon, you come with me. I need to show you the houses defenses. Mathu, why don't you take Dina into the kitchen and show her how things work."

Samuel rose and started for the stairs. Nordon followed, Dina stood and went after Mathu.

"Stop!" Samuel shouted. "You have already failed in your duty to the prince." His angry eyes swept from Dina to Don. "One of you must be with the prince at all times."

Dina shuffled to the sofa and scooped the boy up in her arms.

"Don't forget again," Samuel warned.

Over the next several hours and going deep into the night, Samuel gave explanations and lessons in the use of the various safeguards and features of the house. Most were modern technology, some were magical enhancements. All would take time for the two new residents to understand.

Late into the early morning, they took a break. Eric had been asleep for hours. Dina had drifted off an hour ago. Samuel could see the exhaustion drooping Nordon's face, but knew the big man would never complain. Samuel told him to catch some sleep and they would start again at sunrise.

Tired as well, Samuel could not sleep until he checked once more with Trenton. Still no sighting of the royal family. He sent Mathu to relieve the other two and went to sleep. He was up early. Darden was busy in the kitchen showing Dina how to use the stove. Twenty minutes later the entire household was seated at the dining room table having breakfast.

Samuel had just taken a bite of a piece of bacon when his phone rang. He dropped his fork with a clatter on the plate and snatched up his phone.

"What news?" He listened. Then said, "I'm on my way." He stood. "Nordon, you're in charge. Do not leave the house and don't let anyone in other than the people you've met here. Mathu, we need to go."

Mathu jammed three pieces of bacon into his mouth and rose. They hustled out the door and to the van. They arrived in record time. No sooner had the van pulled to the curb, then Trenton ran from the parking garage with a young girl in his arms. Deardon followed, his arm around a tall woman.

They hopped into the back of the van and Mathu had it moving before everyone had settled into a seat. Trenton handed the princess to the woman and pulled his weapon from the shoulder holster he wore.

Samuel said, "Is that it? No King or Queen?"

"No, sir. When they came through, Phetrix said, 'The castle is lost and the KIng and Queen have vanished.'"

Samuel sighed and faced the front. If the King and Queen had vanished, perhaps they escaped. There would be word if they had been captured by Mortas Frost. And everyone would know if they had been killed. Well, nothing they could do about it. They had the prince and princess. It was his job to make sure they survived and grew to an age where they could lead a rebellion.

"Take us to the second house. I don't want them living together."

He had much to do. He needed Id's for the kids and their guardians. They would need a crash course on survival skills for this world. He needed to set the magical wards that would keep them hidden from any who might follow and just so many more details. But he was good at details. It was one of the reasons he'd thrived in a world so beyond his imagination as to never have been a notion.

Samuel would see to everything and when they were ready, he would lead the prince and princess back to their world to reclaim the throne. It was only going to take time and that, thanks to the efforts of Phetrix, they now had.

Chapter 6

Phetrix scoured the castle, losing hope of ever finding Elysande. He feared she might be dead. Dead royal soldiers lay in heaps at nearly every turn. Smoke wafted through the corridors. Mortas brought death in his wake and if that little girl was caught in it, Phetrix was prepared to cross the seam and share the word with Samuel himself. At least Erthic was safe, as far as he knew.

Phetrix turned a corner near the kitchens and listened as he thought he heard a faint sound.

"Ely? Elly is that you dear?" He drew on his power, ready to unleash it on any enemy soldier that might have the unfortunate distinction of harming the girl.

Shouting men from his left startled him, but they were too far off for the moment.

"Ely? Come out dear. It's me, Phetrix. I can take you to your brother." He waited, listening for the sound he heard moments earlier.

The shouting soldiers seemed to be closer, their voices carrying a touch of mirth. He slipped into the kitchen hoping to avoid detection, unsure how large a group was headed his way.

Hope waned.

Then, he heard it again and it was nearby.

Opening every cabinet and every scorched door, he moved silently throughout the kitchen. The place had been burnt in the attack the previous night and looted already. Pots and pans were tossed about the kitchen, a mess the cook would never have allowed to happen had she been there . . . and alive.

Then he found her.

He heard her crying softly and followed the sound to a slightly tilted cupboard door.

"My dear, I've found you!" he said when he opened the door to the hysterical child inside. "Come, I can save you yet." He reached his hand out to her and at first she slapped it away, then realizing who he was, she accepted it. "That's it Ely. Hurry, your brother awaits." She crawled out from the cupboard and clung to him.

The soldiers seemed to have passed as their voices carried toward him from the opposite direction he heard earlier. Carefully, they left the kitchen when they heard a woman's scream from another room.

"Quiet Ely, I need to check on this."

He considered leaving the girl, whoever it was, but her screams called to him. If she were in trouble, he had to do something. He left Mortas' service because of horrific actions like this. Now was the moment to act, even if it meant putting the princess in harm's way.

Channeling a small stream of power, Phetrix turned to Ely. "Stay here. Watch me, but stay here. Got it?" The girl crossed her arms and scowled. It would have to do.

Phetrix crept closer to the open door and peered inside to see a servant girl being fondled by one of Mortas' soldiers.

"Come on wench, stop yer fighting," the man said. Phetrix noticed the black armored man's sword in its scabbard still attached to his belt lying on the floor. His pants were around his ankles.

"Your gonna die soon anyway, so, why are ya giving me a hard time?"

That was enough. Phetrix let loose a tiny bolt of light. It was dark purple and bore through the soldier, melting a hole in his armor and coming out the other side. He turned to look at the hole now punched through him, and fell down on the girl. The servant screamed when the dead man fell on her.

She cried, thrashing until the lifeless man fell off her. That's when Phetrix realized who it was.

"Alyanna? Alyanna, you're safe!" he said.

"Phetrix?" she asked, wiping her eyes. "You have the princess!"

Elysande ran to her, a woman she'd known since birth.

"Alyanna, you've been around the children since early on, right?"

She nodded as she wiped at the tears on her face. The man had ripped her tunic and was trying to grope her when Phetrix came upon them. Fortunately he did, as it presented a new opportunity for him.

"I was their first nanny. I'm still one of many that help raise them." She squeezed Ely, her arms clinging tight to the girl. Watching Ely's face light up within Alyanna's grasp, he knew it could work.

"I don't have much time. The castle is in ruins and the King and Queen are missing. I need a favor." He wrung his hands. He was taking a massive risk with the child, but he had little recourse left. Erthic had already been sent through the seam and should be with Samuel by now. He had to send Elly through as well. It was the only way he could think of to save her.

"I need you to flee with her. Now." It wasn't ideal, but he trusted Alyanna and more importantly, so did Ely. He could only hope they connected with Samuel and eventually Erthic when they got to the other side. He had no time to train her in the ways of the new world and she'd have to cope with the massive change as best she could. It was far too late for a different plan.

Phetrix didn't wait for her reply, but instead spoke the words that created the seam. The white light illuminated the room.

"What is this?" Alyanna asked.

"Your salvation. It's the only way out. You'll never leave the castle alive if you don't go through. Mortas' men are everywhere. They searching for her," he said pointing at Ely, "and if what just happened to you by that solider is any indication, it is quite likely more will try and do the same. Mortas encourages that kind of behavior. You'll be safe. Take Elysande. Erthic is already there. He's with Nadron and Nadina. Find Samuel and live. Hurry, before more of them come."

Elyande tugged at Alyanna. "Brother," she said.

Men shouted in the corridor outside. "Hurry Belam! We want our turn with her too!"

"Go now!" Phetrix urged. Alyanna looked to the door and then to the light.

"But, I don't know—"

"Now!" Phetrix pleaded with her. Elysande held her hand tight, urging her forward. Then, the princess stepped through the light and Alyanna reluctantly followed.

Chapter 7

Mortas Frost sat atop a black steed overlooking the burning valley below. A wicked grin flashed across his face.

"Well done," he said to himself. "Well done indeed."

In the midst of the valley lay the remains of King Artus's castle. It would have been better to secure it instead of razing it, but he wanted the people to know who was now in charge.

Somehow, that mage Phetrix had whisked the children away, but they'd be found sooner or later. He'd dedicate as many resources as needed to find them. As long they lived, his reign would be threatened. And he wasn't accustomed to that.

A horse drew up behind him and a young soldier dropped from the saddle, kneeling on the ground. Mortas waved his hand upward for the man to stand.

"Sir, the royal family is missing. We've yet to find them."

Mortas' anger flared. He reared his horse, and the animal brought its hooves down inches from the frightened man's head.

"I will not tolerate incompetence. Locate the family and bring them to me. Failure to do so will not end well for you."

"Yes sir." On shaky legs, the soldier climbed back atop his own horse and raced toward the main camp.

"They must be found at all costs. I cannot have them running around alive, offering hope when there is none to be had." He patted his horse and turned from the ledge, satisfied at the destruction below.

SEVERAL DAYS PASSED and still no word on the family. Mortas had executed three soldiers who dared tell him the family could not be found. His patience was gone, replaced by an unending foul mood that had everyone scampering from his path. Further delays were not acceptable.

Mortas rested inside the massive tent in the center of the camp. His men were securing the kingdom and scouting for a suitable location to build his grand castle.

"Sir, your mage approaches," a guard at the tent door called inside.

"Good! I've had need of Rhoden Noster."

Mortas sat up and adjusted his shirt, buttoning it closed after his serving girl had unfastened it earlier. Rhoden pushed aside the tent flap.

"My liege, may I come in?"

"Rhoden! Come, come. It's been too long. What word do you bring?"

"I've come about the family."

"Of course you have. Please, have a seat." Mortas motioned to a small stool in the corner.

"Now. What about them?"

Rhoden fidgeted, intertwining his fingers together. "Sir," he began, "I have interviewed both our soldiers and various members of King Artus' staff when they were taken prisoner. There was much smoke and confusion, but from the information I gathered, I have reason to believe Phetrix used a spell unknown to most like me. It's a spell only the most powerful can replicate."

"So? What's that got to do with anything?"

"Everything, sir. I believe he used it while in the castle to whisk away the children."

"To where? What proof do you have for this claim?" Mortas dragged a stool in front of Rhoden and sat, leaning closer with his hands on his knees.

"Where? I don't exactly know, sir. It's hard to explain. My old master Samuel knew of such powerful magic. It's called traveling magic. He tried to teach me once, but I got bored of his ramblings and never paid much attention. I preferred more aggressive forms of my art. But from what the soldiers described of the incident, I feel certain that's the spell Phetrix used."

"Well, what does it do?"

"It opens a portal, sir. A passageway to another world."

Mortas stood and circled around the tent. "Another world? What kind of nonsense are you speaking?"

"None, sir. It's a powerful spell known only by a select group of mage's. Most of them long dead.

"It is an ancient art form with its roots in the very creation of our world. At least that is what I've been told."

"What is this other world? Where is it? If he took the children there, we must track them and end this."

"I agree, sir. However—"

"However what?" Mortas growled.

"No mage known can do such a thing."

"You mean other than Phetrix?"

Rhoden hung his head. "Correct, sir. I know if I had the time, I'd be able to learn it. My powers are stronger than Phetrix's."

Mortas rushed to the mage and leaned in close, his finger pressing against his chest. "Do not fail me in this! Finding those children is paramount. Do you understand me?"

"Of course, sir. Your victory will be secure when we do. I realize the importance of this. I shall discover this spell and we will soon have the power to find them."

"I expect victory, Rhoden. Nothing less."

The mage stood, bowed, and left the tent. Mortas paced around the tent with his hands clasped behind his back.

They scoured the castle after taking it and there was no sign of the children or Phetrix. Artus and his nagging wife were missing as well. Most likely they were in hiding, though they'd never outlast his desire to seek them out. He hoped they'd be found alive so he could make a vivid example of them with a public execution. His hold on the kingdom would only be strengthened by it.

"One day, all of this will be mine. No one will dare oppose me, not when I rid this land of that foul family. Soon. Very soon my hold will be complete."

Chapter 8

F*ifteen Years Later*

WITH A SIMULTANEOUS BURST, they sat bolt upright in the bed, a mix of shock and fear playing across their faces.

"Oh, God!" she said. "They found us."

Intermittent amber lights flashed in their room. A magically enhanced alarm tone, unheard anywhere else in the house, beeped in frenzied repetition. After all this time, the enemy had found them.

"Check the monitors," the large, balding man said. "I'll see to the boy."

They started to move, but the man grabbed her arm and held tight. "Nadina," he said in a firm voice. "Remember our mission and your training."

Her face relaxed. The worry wrinkles along her forehead and temples, disappeared. As if by magic, a different woman gazed back. A look of control and power filled her now narrowed eyes. He gave a reassuring squeeze and let go. She nodded, rolled off the bed and disappeared beneath. When she reappeared, she held a short sword and an Uzi—a modern medieval warrior ready for battle. He stood and armed himself with a weapon large enough to need both hands to hold. However, his well-muscled arms held it outward in one steel-gripped fist.

He did not know the proper name for the massive gun. It had been given to him years ago for just such a purpose. It shot 7.62 caliber rounds out of one barrel, shotgun shells out of another and an experimental, heat seeking grenade from a third. When asked questions about the weapon, the man who gave it to him said, "The bullets go in there, there and there and come out here, here and here. That's all you need to know."

He left the room and Dina raced toward the bedroom closet. She opened the door and shoved the hangers aside, revealing a second door. This one led to the walk-up attic. She entered and climbed the stairs. The attic featured an assortment of monitors, electronics, weapons and storage trunks.

She pushed a button on a console, shutting down the alarm, then examined the four small monitors. Each one showed dark, infrared images from the four directions of the house. At the moment, no pictures were displayed. Each screen showed only the empty, dark night.

A tiny red light pulsed on the monitor responsible for the alarm. Dina tapped a few keys on the portable board in front of that monitor and sent the picture to a larger, central screen. She leaned close, but no matter how hard she strained to see, no threat appeared. A few more key strokes and the pictures ran in reverse. She guessed at the amount of time passed since the alarm sounded, then switched to forward. The recorded scene began to play.

Two minutes later, the reason for the triggered alarm came into view. The sight unnerved her enough to seek the support of a chair. The ghostly image of a Seeker floated past, ten feet above the roof lines of the neighborhood houses. "Oh, saints preserve us."

As she studied the image, her fingers caressed the gun like it was a support animal. She'd only heard of such things, being told stories in her youth but she always thought they were tales made up to scare children into good behavior. Now, she knew those tales were real. After fifteen years of peace, those who searched for them had found an opening into this world. Dina watched the replay through once, then rewound it and scanned again. The Seeker, part creature, part spirit, floated past without paying attention to their house. It would be tuned to the special frequency the boy emanated, but wards had been set to prevent that from happening. They appeared to be working, but wait. Was that a hesitation?

With nimble fingers, she reset the recording and ran it through again, then enhanced and enlarged the image and played it in slow motion. Yes, right there. The Seeker turned its horrendous head toward the house, pausing for just an instant in its methodical side-to-side sweep. Whatever it felt had not been sufficient to warrant a closer look, but it had sensed something. Samuel, the contact for this world, had to be notified. The enemy had entered this world and was actively searching for the ward they had been entrusted to protect.

Dina set the weapons down and reached for the dedicated encrypted radio, surprised to find her hand shook. She pulled it back, cupped it in the other hand and said a quick prayer to buoy her courage. She did not have to dial, punch in, or speak a number. Once the headset was lifted from its cradle, the call was activated.

A voice on the other end, said, "Yes?"

"They're here."

Silence weighed heavy on the other end. "You know what to do. I'll be in touch." The disconnect had an eerie finality to it. Dina set the handset down gently, released the breath she'd been unaware she held, and got up.

Downstairs she found Nordon, in front of the boy's bedroom door, a lethal protector, ready to give his life for his charge. He tensed when she appeared, an unspoken question in the one lifted eyebrow. She nodded. Her body deflated. She leaned forward, placing her head against his massive chest. "Oh, Nordon, what are we going to do?"

"What we were trained for." He put an arm around her to comfort her as well as himself. "What we were trained for, my love," he repeated. "And may the Gods be with us."

She added, "I hope they can find us in this strange world we now call home."

Chapter 9

Nadina watched Eric through the front picture window as he raked the leaves that had fallen from the tree in the front yard. A cup of steaming coffee was held firmly between her still trembling hands. The poor boy had no idea the dangers that now lurked, searching for him. But he also had no idea who he really was.

Nordon had left early in the morning before Eric had risen, to meet with Samuel. She hoped he came back with a plan that allowed them to continue their lives in peace. She paused the cup inches from her lips as an alternate thought came to her. She hoped he had a plan that allowed them to continue living, period.

Eric was a good boy. They raised him as a mission initially, but along the way, fell in love with him as if he were their own. He seldom gave them trouble of any sort. He did his chores with no complaint, was a stellar student and amazing athlete, even if he wasn't allowed to participate in any sports at school.

He was tall, and though slender, had a strong toned frame that promised to fill out in a most alluring way. His handsome features, dark-blonde hair, and brilliant smile drew much attention from the girls at school, as well as the local MILFs and cougars. He was a splendid male specimen who had a great life ahead of him, providing he lived long enough to realize it.

She consummated her sip, the taste, warmth and aroma invigorating her. She remembered the first time she'd been introduced to the then, vile liquid. It was bitter and strong and made her stomach heave. Now, she could barely function without at least two cups of the beverage each morning.

It was amazing what she learned to enjoy over the past fifteen years. Fifteen. Had it really been that long since Nordon and her were thrust into this new world and given the task of protecting Eric, then known as Erthic? She was but a girl herself, unmarried, naive and frightened. But the mage found her in the lower chambers and forced a pledge of protection from her. Then, he'd pushed her through an opening between worlds with the then three year old boy and a man she'd never met, and had entrusted her with the future of their world. My God, how far they'd come.

Samuel found them and set them up as Don And Dina. Nordon and her were forced to live together, complete strangers, in a strange place that moved much faster than either of them thought possible. In those first few months, they barely left the house for fear of having to interact with the people.

Eric piled the leaves, then moved on to rake another area of the lawn. He wiped his sweat coated forehead on a sleeve and caught sight of her standing in the window. He smiled, waved and went back to his task.

She waved back even though he was no longer watching. Warmth spread through her in a far superior and more intense form than the coffee ever could. He might not be hers, and perhaps she'd never have any of her own, but she did love him deeply and that love was enough for her to lay down her life to protect him.

With that thought in mind, she climbed the stairs to check the monitors again, praying she would never see a threat of any sort. The monitors were clear, the wards silent. Loathe to leave Eric out of sight for too long, she tucked a handgun into her slacks at her back and lowered the heavy sweatshirt over the weapon. Though warm for this time of year, the constant bone chilling iciness she felt made the sweatshirt necessary and not just to cover the gun.

Downstairs, she took a look out the front window to make sure Eric was still there, then refilled her mug and sat on the front porch. As she watched him work, a warmth spread from her core melting her chill if only for the moment.

Eric hummed. His body perspired from the effort, but the work wasn't strenuous. He enjoyed toiling outdoors. He stopped for a minute and closed his eyes as a slight breeze against his damp skin seemed to invigorate him. The wind lifted his hair from his head and dropped it back out of place. He ran a hand down it's length to plaster it to his head.

He finished another pile of leaves and started on the last section of lawn. From across the street, Madeline, the cute and curious three year old, who lived in the two-story house two down on the opposite side, called out.

"Hi Reric."

She couldn't quite say his name. Her long brown curls bounced as she walked and waved.

He smiled and waved back. "Good morning, Madeline. How are you today?"

"I'm good," she said in a sing-song voice.

She turned down the apron of the driveway directly across the street. Eric shot nervous glances down both directions of the street. Dina fired one toward Madeline's house looking for her mother. Sissy was a nice girl, but she was only a few years older than Eric. Addicted to her cell phone, she often lost track of Madeline. She felt sorry for Madeline, knowing she was left on her own to entertain herself much too often and for way too long. Dina also worried, since she wandered the neighborhood on her own on a daily basis.

They lived in an older area of town called the North End. The streets were lined end to end with one and two story homes built in the early to mid nineteen hundreds. They had little street frontage and were set close to the road. Cars were parked on each side of the street forcing traffic down to one lane—a problem when cars came from opposite directions at the same time.

It was not a poor neighborhood, but at the same time, it was a long way from being a wealthy one. Most of the properties were well kept and turnover was low, but as the older owners passed away or moved to smaller retirement dwellings, many of the homes were purchased by landlords, or younger couples who did not spend as much time on upkeep as a house demanded. In the few years they'd been there she'd witnessed a drastic change.

"What are you doing?" she asked, stopping at the edge of the street. Her body swayed as she watched Eric.

"I'm raking leaves."

"Oh. Is it fun?"

He chuckled. "No. It's just something that has to be done."

"Can I rake leaves with you?"

He stopped, leaned on the rake and glanced toward Madeline's house. Missy was sitting on the porch, her feet propped on the brick half wall with her head down in typical cell phone using position.

"Ah, no thanks. I'm almost finished."

"Ohhh!" Her voice had a whine to it, as if ready to cry.

Eric had a soft heart. He wouldn't want to make Madeline cry, but also didn't want the responsibility of watching her. That was her mother's job, even if she was incapable of doing it.

"I'm sorry. Maybe next time you can help me. Okay?"

"Okay." But it clearly wasn't okay. Her lower lip stuck out in a pout, far enough for Dina to see from the porch.

Eric went back to raking trying to finish before she cried. He worked fast perhaps hoping to finish before Madeline cried. Dina smiled and sipped her coffee only vaguely aware of the screeching tires and racing engine from down the street. The roar of a mufflerless engine drew her attention when it was half a block away. She glanced in its direction fearful the vehicle was a threat to Eric. Dina dropped the mug and launched from the chair. Her hand reaching for the gun.

Eric stopped to watch as the car flew closer. Dina reached the steps seconds before Missy screamed, "Madeline!"

Dina glanced toward the little girl and horrified to see her stepping into the street between the two parked cars on either side of the driveway. *Oh God, no.* Eric tossed the rake aside as the entire world went into slow motion. He broke into a sprint, his powerful legs pushing to full speed in two strides. She heard him shout, "Go back, Madeline," but it came from somewhere in a hazy distance.

She tried to reach him, still afraid the car was meant for him, but he was too fast and out of reach within two of his long strides. "Eric," she called, but his focus was locked on Madeline.

Adrenaline laced fear spiked extra speed from her, but even as she missed him and understood his intent, in her heart she knew he would not arrive in time. He raised his hands and waved them above his head in a frantic attempt to catch the driver's attention. Unaware of the danger, the driver barreled forward. Dina noted he wasn't paying any attention to the street ahead. His eyes were riveted on the rear view mirror. She stopped and raised the gun thinking to fire a warning shot, but unsure of where to place it. The sound of sirens gave her pause and the reason for the driver's distraction and the speed. He was fleeing the authorities. Dina lowered the gun helpless to do anything to prevent what was about to occur.

With all his strength, Eric focused on Madeline, intent on somehow getting to her before the car slammed her into eternity. The car closed. Too fast. She knew he would not make it in time, yet still he pressed on.

"Eric," the word ripped from her soul.

Three things happened simultaneously. Madeline emerged from between the cars, the front bumper moved to within three feet of her and Eric shrieked, "Nooooo!"

Then the world went crazy.

Chapter 10

Nadina sat on the edge of the chair in the hospital room that held her son. The fact he wasn't really her son, made no difference to how she felt. Having raised him for the past fifteen years, she felt she had the right to the claim. Besides, everyone they knew in this world thought Eric was her son, and she saw no reason to dissuade their beliefs.

She rocked back and forth, elbows on knees, hands folded. She stared at the comatose boy. The doctors had been in, three of them. None had answers, but all wanted to run tests. So far they'd taken blood and had an EKG done. Eric was scheduled for an MRI next.

She didn't know what to do. Reaching him after the collision and finding him unconscious, lying in the driveway, with the little brat from across the street wailing in his arms, she was at a loss, frozen, as fear clutched her heart. The police were there in seconds, already giving pursuit to the driver. They called for an ambulance, but were confused about what occurred.

The two officers had witnessed Eric's bravery, darting in front of the onrushing car to save the girl, but were baffled about how the car made such a sudden, sharp ninety degree turn, slamming into an old oak tree, fifteen feet off the ground.

The little brat's mother ran over, suddenly all concerned about her baby. She screamed at Eric even though he was unconscious, blaming him for hurting her baby and threatening a lawsuit. Nadina clenched her fists, but held herself in check, until the young woman drew her foot back to kick Eric.

Nadina stomped her foot down on the woman's leg in mid-kick, blocking the strike. A red fire, born of fear for her son and rage at the woman, burst behind her eyes. A powerful hand shot forward clutching the woman by the throat. She yanked the frightened woman to within inches of her face. "You ever try to hurt my son again, I'll rip your throat out and your daughter will be safer for it. Now go see to her scrapes like a real mother would." She gave her a shake and shoved her backward. Between sobs, she issued legal action threats.

The officers rushed to separate them. The one holding Missy told her to clam up. "If it wasn't for that boy you were about to kick your daughter would be dead. He saved her. You owe him gratitude and then some, instead of threats. And just so you know, Officer Petry and myself will testify on his behalf. He's a hero. Now take your daughter home."

The ambulance arrived and Nadina called Nordon. He did not answer so she called the number she was instructed to memorize and never use unless it was an emergency. She judged this fit.

A man answered. "Yes."

"There's been an accident."

"What?" the tone more concerned now.

"He's hurt." She remembered she wasn't to use any names. "An ambulance has come. They're taking him to a hospital."

"You can not allow that to happen."

"But—but he needs medical attention."

"Did you call the ambulance?" the voice was angry.

"No. The police did."

"Police?" The voice rose an octave. "Did you call them?"

"No. They were already on the scene."

Silence.

"Okay. It's too late to stop it now without drawing attention. Let me know what hospital and I will deal with it. Go with them and try to stall any tests or treatments."

"Okay. I have to go. The ambulance is leaving."

"Go, but don't let him out of your sight."

The line went dead.

Upon arriving at the hospital, they were rushed into an examining room. Nadina was told to wait outside, but she stayed close enough to hear the conversation between the EMT's and the Emergency room doctor.

"I'm telling you, doc, we didn't find anything. His heart rate is low but nothing drastic. His blood pressure is slightly elevated. He was unconscious when we got there but could find no obvious cause. He has a few bumps and scrapes along his arms, consistent with diving on cement, but nothing severe. No lump or soft spot on his head. We didn't find any obvious spinal injuries, but boarded him anyway."

"Okay. Make sure the paperwork is complete," the doctor said, then he started ordering tests.

Nadina knew she should stop them somehow, but her contact wasn't there. He didn't see Eric's condition. She didn't want to disobey, but she was worried about Eric. What if he died because she refused to let them do their tests? She couldn't live with that. And since she was the only one there, she decided to say nothing.

She dug out her cell phone, an object she thought magical years earlier, but now felt as comfortable using as if she was one of these people. Dialing Nordon's number once more, this time she left a detailed message. Finished, she drew in her courage and called the secret number again.

"Yes." The same voice answered.

"We're at St. Rose's hospital."

"Did you stop the tests?"

"I wasn't allowed inside." True, but not completely.

"I'll handle it. You stay in position to protect him."

He hung up. For a moment she stared at the phone as if it were an evil entity, then, her hands began to shake. It spread to her entire body and the tears welled. She fought them, but in the end lost the struggle and she buried her head in her hands.

An hour later she was in Eric's assigned room watching, waiting and praying. Although she wondered if the Gods she prayed to could even hear her in the strange world.

Chapter 11

Twenty minutes later, a slightly short, round man in a light gray suit, entered the room. She recognized him. His name was Samuel and he was the man they first met upon crossing over into this world. He'd gotten them set up, instructed them in how to survive in the new world and trained them how to use the strange weapons and to protect Erthyic. After pronouncing them ready, he left them to fend for themselves. At first he checked in with them a few times a year, but when he stopped coming, Dina wondered if he might be dead. She hadn't seen or heard from him in more than a decade.

He nodded at her, and moved straight for the bed. He placed a hand above Eric's head and closed his eyes. His lips moved but whatever he said, perhaps a prayer, was too low to hear. Her eyes widened as his hand began to glow, first yellow, then like a sunset, eventually turning a bright red.

She stood, awed and afraid, yet ready to move to protect her charge. What was this strange little man doing to her son? She moved forward, but even with his eyes closed he was aware of her. He held up his non-glowing hand and she stopped.

His hand drifted down Eric's body and the red glow dimmed to a soft amber, before fading out completely. Samuel's eyes fluttered open. For a moment he appeared weak and had to grab the bed to keep from falling. He bent over the bed and shook his almost bald head. His scalp reddened almost as bright as his hand. Minutes later, he straightened and turned toward her.

"Tell me what happened and what has been done here, so far."

He offered his hand and Nadina thought it was to greet her, but once his hand surrounded hers, he placed his other hand over hers and held it tight. He pulled her closer. His eyes darkened and bore deep into hers. She gasped.

"Now, speak child."

She relayed the story, but as she spoke she saw vivid images of the events playing in her mind. The vision was so real she could feel the emotions of the moment and hear the sounds from voices to backgrounds noise of birds and traffic. When her tale was finished, he held her hand a moment longer as if searching for something deeper within, perhaps details she'd forgotten or refrained from mentioning. Satisfied with what he saw or didn't see, he released the hand.

"You did well under the circumstances. Nordon is home checking the monitors to ensure this wasn't an attempt by our enemies to do damage to the rightful heir."

That thought hadn't occurred to Nadina. "You don't think they'd try to kill him, do you?"

He shrugged. "How can I know what goes through their evil minds. They really only need one of the heirs. The other is expendable. Perhaps they found the other one."

"Other one? Did his sister come through, too?"

Samuel pursed his lips as if realizing he'd said too much. He drew in a deep breath and eyed her as if coming to a decision. Then he said, "Yes, his twin sister, Elysande was saved, too."

He picked up a chart and scanned it. "Stay here and watch over him. I'll deal with the tests."

He left and Nadina sat down. Her mouth remained open since hearing Eric was not the last heir. His sister had been found and saved. She wondered why she had never been told. Maybe they saw her as a threat to their security. A weak link in their defenses. Well, they might find out how resolved she was if the threat to her son was real. She would fight to her death to keep him safe. She prayed it would never come to that, but knew the truth of her convictions deep in her soul.

SAMUEL TOOK the elevator down and followed the signs for the lab. He found it after several turns and long hallways. He glanced through the long narrow window in the door. The room was busy. It was a third full with patients waiting to have blood work done. He spied at least half a dozen staff, perhaps more behind the doors. The lab was through a door inside the room and to the right. There'd be less people in that section, but getting to the samples he needed without being discovered would be difficult.

He entered and took a chair along the wall to the right, not eight feet from the lab door. Scanning the room, he found what he needed, then closed his eyes and called up the words to a spell. His eyes fluttered under the strain. Twenty long seconds later, someone gasped.

"Is that smoke coming from that vent?"

Voices rose, then became panicked. Someone got up and rapped on the thick translucent pane of glass on the sliding window to the receptionist. The window slid open and an unpleasant woman with a severe frown looked out.

"There's smoke coming from the ceiling," an older man said.

The woman's demeanor changed in a heartbeat. "Oh, my." She stood and pushed her large frame through the window far enough to be seen by all. "I'm not sure what it is, but to be safe, I need everyone to remain calm and evacuate the office. Please do it in an orderly fashion. Do not panic."

Everyone stood and walked toward the door. Samuel stayed seated. The waiting room cleared, but none of the staff left. *There must be another exit for them.* He waited another minute and when no one appeared, rose to try the lab door. Locked. He waved a hand over the door knob and tried again. This time the door opened.

Samuel stepped inside and closed the door behind him. The room looked and sounded deserted. He hurried toward the back and began searching for Eric's blood samples. He heard voices approaching and realized someone was coming through a side door. He stopped what he was doing, concentrated and chanted. Once again smoke curled out of the vents.

"Oh, man, I think it's spreading."

"Let's get out. The fire department's been called. They should be here in seconds."

The smoke grew thicker, now beginning to hinder Samuel. He

continued his search with less concern now about leaving evidence of his presence. The door opened again.

"We've got thick smoke in here but no heat."

"Maybe a motor is going bad in one of the air conditioning units," a second voice said

"Could be, but there's no smell. Usually if something like a machine is burning out you get heat or that burning rubber smell."

It was harder for Samuel to see. He found a rack with four tubes. He picked it up and held it close to his face. The labels read, Eric Smith. Yes. He found it. He slipped the tubes from the stand, placed them in a jacket pocket and set the rack down, but in the smoke he misjudged the distance to the counter. The rack fell with a loud crack. He froze, his heart racing.

"Did you hear that?"

"Yeah, it came from back there."

"Is anyone in here? Call out. We're firemen. Will come get you."

"Hello."

Samuel had to make a hasty retreat, but he'd done such a good job on the smoke he had difficulty seeing. In fact, it was getting harder to breathe, as well. He walked with his hand extended. He coughed, the sound was like a beacon leading the firemen toward him.

His hand struck the wall and he slid his fingers along it hoping to find a door. Just as his hand brushed over the knob someone grabbed his shoulder from behind.

"I've got you. Hold on, sir. We'll get you out of here."

Something was pressed against his mouth and he panicked.

"Relax, sir, it's just air. Breathe in. We'll have you outside in a few seconds."

Samuel allowed himself to be led. A minute later, he was standing outside with an oxygen mask on his face. The air felt good circulating through his lungs.

He drew in a deep breath and caught sight of a woman in a lab coat speaking with one of the firemen who rescued him. She turned and made right for him. He noted a security guard right behind her.

"Excuse me, sir. How did you get in the lab?"

Samuel put on a stressed and elderly voice, speaking with the mask on. "I-I don't know. When the smoke started I got confused. I was waiting to have my blood drawn. A door opened near me and I thought it was the way out. I went in and guess I was in the lab. I don't know. I was lost. Thought I was gonna die in there."

The woman eyed him suspiciously. She turned to the guard. "Stay here with him, I want to check to see if anyone exited that way. That door was locked. No way should he have been able to get inside."

She pivoted and hurried away. Samuel wasn't sure who she was going to talk to, but she had the look of a determined pit bull and not likely to let him go until she was satisfied. A check of his ID and the lack of paper work would seal his fate. He had to get away.

He bent as if tottering and ready to fall. The guard stepped forward and wrapped a protective arm around him. Keeping him upright. Samuel muttered something the man couldn't understand. He leaned forward.

"What? Are you all right, sir? You need to sit down?"

Samuel spoke again, then placed a forefinger against the man's temple and a spark jumped. The guard's body twitched in a spasm, then collapsed into Samuel's arms. He guided him gently to the ground, placed the oxygen mask over his face and slipped away, losing himself in the crowds.

Chapter 12

Marvin Grant turned the unmarked Ford into the main entrance of the hospital parking lot and drove around the east side. He pulled up along the curb and stopped a few yards from an animated conversation between a group of people consisting of hospital staff, firemen, and hospital security. Two CPD officers stood listening to whatever was being said, apparently by everyone at once.

Evidently a fire alarm had sounded when smoke billowed from several ducts in the lab area. No cause had been found, as yet, but the fire investigators were still working. That alone hadn't been enough to place a call for Detectives, but when a hospital administrator had detained an elderly man who had been suspiciously in the lab at the time and he'd slipped away in the confusion, security had made the call.

Grant stepped from the car and stretched his six-foot three long form. The day was warm, and the transition from air-conditioned car to outdoor heat had already caused a few beads of sweat to pop out on his forehead. He adjusted his shoulder rig, and hiked up his pants, then walked around the car to the group.

His partner, Jessie Vega, was already outside the car waiting for him. The short, barrel-chested Mexican, popped a tic tac to cover the onions from the Italian sub he hadn't had a chance to finish when the call came in. The former college wrestler still looked as though he could go head-to-head in a college match. He turned to Grant.

"Maybe we should wait until they talk themselves out."

Grant knew Vega was kidding, but he did have a point. He put hands on hips and turned his deep black face to the sun absorbing the warmth. Seconds later, he said, "Screw it. Let's make 'em shut up."

They approached the huddle. The two CPD officers looked relieved. Jackson, a black veteran patrolman who once rode with Grant, looked at his old partner and shook his head. "They called you out for this?" he asked, offering his hand.

Grant shook it and slapped his other hand on top. "Wilton, how you doing?"

"Best as . . ."

"Hear that. Yeah, security called us on a possible arson, but that sounds like a job for our trusted brothers from fire."

"My thinking, too." He nodded at Vega who did the same.

A fire captain stepped away from the now silent crowd. He stuck out his hand. "Marvin. Jessie." After shaking both men's hand, he said. "Looks like a false alarm, or at least there was no actual fire. We're still searching for the cause of the smoke, but there's been no other sightings anywhere else in the hospital. All the patients and staff were let back in about ten minutes ago."

"Good to hear," Grant said.

One of the administrators, a middle aged woman with an angry scowl, walked toward them. Vega held up a hand and went to intercept her. "Miss, if you give us a minute to get up to speed here, we'll want to talk to you in a bit. Thanks." he gave her a gently guiding shove back toward the group and returned.

"They call you for the missing man?" Wilton asked.

"Since there's no real fire here, that'd be my guess." He turned to Dave Scalarra, the fire captain. "Unless you got something for us?"

"Nah. I can send the fire investigators report over, but we don't need you."

"Alright, Wilton, give me what you got."

"The woman over there," he flipped open a notepad and read her name, "Susan Pollard, says an elderly man was found wandering the lab during the alarm. He told her he was confused and got lost." Wilton shrugged. "Coulda happened."

Scalarra said, "A couple of our boys found him and brought him out. Gave him oxygen."

Grant nodded. Vega grunted.

Wilton continued. "She says he couldn't have gotten into the lab. She questioned her staff and no one was working with anyone resembling the man. The only place he could have been was in the waiting room and unless someone lets you in, there's no way into the lab from there."

Vega asked, "Did any of the staff go out that way during the fire?"

Wilton shook his head. "She says 'no.' All staff exited through the back door," he nodded, "right there."

"Okay," Grant said, "but then the man disappeared?"

"Yeah. She had a security guy watching him. The guy over there getting his balls handed to him by his boss and the administrator. Guy says, the old man looked like he was going to faint. He grabbed him to keep him from falling. Next thing he remembers, he's being shaken awake by the chief of security and his wearing an oxygen mask."

Both Vega and Grant were focused with game faces on, now. Grant said, "He doesn't remember, being struck or feeling a jab from a needle."

"Nope. Nothing," Wilton said. "One second he held the guy the next he was being shaken awake."

"Huh." Grant and Vega uttered at the same time.

Wilton snorted. "You two been working together too long."

The chief of security came over, talking into a hand held radio. "Joe Perkins," he said, "Head of security. Don't know if this has anything to do with anything, but one of our patients is missing. An Eric Smith."

Grant and Vega exchanged glances. Grant put his hands on his hips. Vega crossed his arms. Their go-to poses when thinking.

"What can the possible connection be?" Grant said.

"I have no idea. Once they found out he was missing, the head nurse on that floor called the number on the admission form. No such number."

"Wait a minute," Wilton said. "Is that the kid we called in?" he turned to his partner, a rookie named Lynd. "Hey, Rook, what was the name of that kid we called the ambulance for?"

Lynd pulled a note pad from his shirt pocket and flipped through it. "Smith. Eric Smith. Why?"

"Apparently he went missing."

Susan Pollard joined them. "Is this related to my guy?"

"Don't know." All business now, Grant began giving orders. "Why don't we start at the beginning? Mr. Perkins, can you get me whatever info you can from your missing patient. It may be two separate incidents, but I want all the information before deciding that. Wilton, would you go inside and talk to anyone in the lab who might have seen the old guy. I need a description. Ms. Pollard, please tell me what you can."

Chapter 13

Forty-five minutes later, Vega and Grant were driving toward the address Wilton and Lynd had for the missing patient. It was different from the one the boys mother gave at the hospital. It might prove to be nothing, but it was suspicious.

"What do you think?" Vega asked.

"Not sure. It's not against the law for a patient to leave, but the false address and phone number makes it look suspicious."

"Yeah. That and what Wilton told us about the strangeness of the scene. I mean, a car fifteen feet up a tree? Come on. He had to be exaggerating."

"Yeah. Want to see that for myself."

"According to Wilton, the boy is a hero. He dove in front of a speeding car to save a little girl. Not many kids today would do that for their own mother."

"Got that right. Not from what we been seeing over the past five years."

Grant made the turn down a residential street with fifty to eighty-year-old houses, row after row, ten feet from their neighbors. Most were well maintained and cared for, but a few had run their course as livable properties and were boarded up.

"Oh man!" Vega exclaimed. "Look at that tree." he pointed.

Grant slowed and leaned forward to see through the windshield. A good twelve to fifteen feet off the ground the large old oak bore the fresh scars of contact with something big and fast moving. A large crack ran halfway around the trunk, revealing yellowish-white wood beneath. The tree leaned toward a one-story house. It would have to be cut down before the next big wind or that house would have instant air-conditioning.

He pulled up next to the curb across from the house they had an address for. Grant let the engine idle as they observed the house. There was no one in sight, but there was an SUV in the driveway.

After a minute of observation, Grant said, "Well, let's go see what's what."

They climbed the steps to a two story, aluminum sided house and knocked on the door. No one answered. Grant tried again, this time with a little more force. The center of the door was glass so they could see a shape approach. A slim woman in her thirties pulled a curtain aside and studied them. Vega showed his badge and the woman's face went pale. She took a moment to compose herself before opening the door.

"Is this about what happened?"

"Well, yes," Grant said. "We have some questions about that and other things."

She looked from one to the other, than stepped outside and partially closed the door. "My son's sleeping, so we can talk out here."

"Is he all right?" Grant asked. "We hear he's had an eventful day."

"Yes. To say the least. He's fine. He suffered some bumps and bruises, but he'll be fine. He's just exhausted. When the fire alarms went off at the hospital, the nurse helped us down the elevator but then went back inside to assist others. Eric, my son, wanted to sleep, so I just brought him home."

"But you didn't tell anyone you were leaving?"

"Ah, no. I know that was wrong, but everyone was busy getting patients out of the hospital. I didn't want to bother anyone and frankly I also didn't want to be talked out of going home. When you knocked I was just looking up the phone number to call them. Guess I should have done that earlier." She jerked and put a hand to her chest. "That's not against the law, is it. Leaving?"

"No, but giving false information might be."

She cocked her head and knitted her brow as if confused.

"The address and phone number you gave were wrong."

“They were?” She acted surprised. “I wonder if I gave our old address. I was a bit out of it. My son was unconscious in the hospital. I wasn't thinking too well. We haven't lived here that long. I guess I got confused.” She offered a smile that lacked sincerity.

“Can we look at your son to make sure he's alright?”

“Ah, he's asleep. I don't want him disturbed.”

“Won't take but a minute, Mrs. Smith. I won't wake him. Just a quick peek inside his room to make sure he's okay. That's procedure,” he lied, “You know, in cases where a parent takes a child from the hospital without doctor’s permission or signing him out.”

“Oh, ah, okay, I guess. But just one of you.”

Grant nodded. She opened the door the rest of the way and the tall detective followed her upstairs to Eric's room. She pointed and Grant cracked open the door before glancing in. He made sure the boy was breathing and didn't seem to be under any stress. Satisfied, he closed the door and went down stairs.

Back on the porch, he said, “You should call the hospital. They were in a panic when they couldn't find your son. People there could get in trouble for losing a patient.”

“Oh my, I hadn't thought about that. I'll call right now.”

“Okay. Good day, Mrs. Smith. You take care of that boy now. I hear he's quite the hero.”

'”I will.”

Grant walked down the steps and toward Vega who was examining the tree.

“What do you think?” Vega asked.

“Not sure. There's something off here. Can't say what.”

“Yeah. Got the same feeling.” They stared up at the tree. “What could make a car jump that high? I mean, look. It's not like there's a ramp here. How could it get that much elevation?”

“Beat's me,” said Grant.

“Ah, forget it. I want to finish my sandwich.”

Chapter 14

F*ifteen Years Earlier*

PHETRIX PRAYED to the gods for the children every day since the destruction wrought by Mortas Frost. He hoped Samuel and the guardians he entrusted with their care would keep them safe. As long as Mortas had no way of finding them, they should be fine. Eventually though, they'd have to come back and reclaim the land. Until then, he'd be as careful as needed for the sake of the kingdom.

Leaving the city Mortas now controlled, Phetrix hunted for the nearest seam back to the strange world. The castle which Mortas destroyed actually housed one of the few places in Chavalon that a mage could open the seam. According to the journal Samuel left behind, there was another obscure location. It was located northwest of the village of Ulti, far to the north of where he was currently.

Remaining hidden within the forests, Phetrix remained in the shadows as much as possible. Mortas ordered Seekers to scour the land, looking for any and all who had been loyal to King Artus.

A small camp lay ahead, its fire a beacon in the waning light of day. Worried it was one of Mortas's search parties, Phetrix approached it carefully.

He crept closer, trying to stay as quiet as possible. Weaving a spell to enhance his hearing, he listened to the group. There were four men and two women, but they weren't what he expected.

"We'll give Mortas a taste of his own medicine," one of the men said.

"Aye, Grynd, we'll make sure he pays for what he's done," one of the female voices said.

Loyalists? Mortas didn't kill them all!

With courage strengthened by the conversations he eavesdropped on, Phetrix revealed himself to the party.

"Hello! I come in peace!"

The group clambered to their weapons and held them in a defensive manner against this new intrusion.

"Who goes there?" It was the man he heard moments before, Grynd.

"Are you loyal to Mortas or the King?" one of the women asked. She had long red hair and cuts on her arms. Her tunic was torn on the side, a bloody bandage peeking through.

The two men with Grynd stepped closer, a madness in their eyes which worried Phetrix. They were both taller than Grynd. One had a bald head and the other wore short brown hair. Long beards adorned both their faces.

Judging by their garb with the white stag embroidered on their tunics, he knew their loyalties.

"I'm with the King. I'm Phetrix—"

"The mage?" the red-haired woman inquired.

"That I am. I am for the King. Does he live? Have you seen him?"

The bald man spat. "Would be nice to know, but tis not our luck."

"You can drop your hands mage. Make a false move and Matildis will gut you." The red-haired woman smiled, spinning a knife in her hand.

"I don't doubt she will. You can be assured I am not one to cause trouble."

"What of the heirs, have you seen them?" It was the other woman. She brushed her long blonde hair to the side, revealing delicate features. Worry flashed across her face.

Phetrix shook his head. "I have not. I can only hope they were taken to safety. Mortas was determined to exterminate the royal family."

The blonde woman sighed and turned, walking to the fire by herself.

"She was a nanny for the children," Grynd said in reply to Phetrix's unvoiced question.

"This here is Gerbald," he said pointing to the bald man. It made Phetrix chuckle but the man didn't seem to see the humor in it.

"And this is Wymar. The nanny is Ancrett. We found each other in the forests after the attack and banded together. Our intent is to mount a counter to Mortas. You'd be an excellent addition to the cause, if you are who you say you are."

Phetrix waved his hands in a circular motion and created a ball of green light. He lifted his hand and it floated upwards, illuminating the camp in a murky-green glow.

"Does this answer your question?"

Matildis nodded. "Works for me. If you turn out to be sent by Mortas, no green glob of light will save you from my blade. I promise."

"Well noted."

"Now that we're all acquainted, maybe we can share our stories. I'd love to hear what you you've gone through, mage," Grynd said.

Wymar and Ancrett went to work preparing a meal for the group. The smell of roasted rabbit made Phetrix's mouth salivate. He hadn't had a decent meal since the attack.

While they were seated around the fire enjoying the meal, Gerbald started the conversation.

"How come none of us know of you, mage? We all worked in the castle for years, serving King Artus and his family. Surely we would've noticed you." Phetrix noticed several others nodding their agreement.

"The duty of mage kept me far from most servants. There were several I knew well. Nadina, Nordon, Alyanna, and others—"

"Nadina? I know her," Ancrett said. "She and I entered service about the same time."

"I knew Nordon. Big fella. He could pound down the ale!" Gerbald said.

"I saw them in the castle as the attack grew worse. I helped them escape." The group looked at Phetrix with wide eyes.

"They live? Where are they? We can grow our company larger with their help!" Grynd said.

Phetrix shrugged. "I don't know where they went. It was chaos. The last I saw, they were running from Mortas's soldiers through the halls. I can only assume they made it to safety. Hopefully, with the King and Queen."

Wymar raised a wooden mug of ale. "To the King! Long live King Artus and Queen Griselde!"

The rest of the group joined in his toast. Phetrix relaxed. He was among like-minded people intent on making things right again. He wondered if he should tell them about the seam and the other world. Though they might fight for the king, would they understand what he did?

Chapter 15

Grynd kept the group loose and relaxed. Considering the circumstances, Phetrix was more than fine with it.

It had been five days since joining the group, and close to three weeks since the attack. Word had spread about a growing rebellion to the north, but that Mortas had also known about it. Whether from Seekers, those black spirit-like entities, or some other means, Phetrix didn't know. He still hadn't told the group about the seam and he was anxious to get to the farm, though the group had no intention of traveling in that direction.

Matildis stepped next to Phetrix who had been lost in thought, wondering what his next move was.

"Mage, you ever kill a man?"

Phetrix scrunched his face. "Yes I have. During the attack. I had to protect the heirs."

Matildis nodded. "Good. We might need more of that if it comes to it. Grynd got word today that a large group of loyalists have gathered in the forests around Whitemoore."

"Way up there? Does Mortas not control all of Chevalon then?"

"He does, but his hold in the north is weak. Whitemoore has sworn to him, but they look a blind eye at the loyalists. It wouldn't surprise me if it soon becomes the center of resistance to Mortas."

Phetrix stroked his long beard. Convincing the group to join those gathered near Whitemoore might help him get to the seam faster. Each day that passed felt like another day wasted. What if Samuel didn't have the children? What if their protectors failed?

The heirs had to live at all costs. Without them, the land was cursed. The prophecy of old dictated their lives, yet Mortas destroyed that. He knew little of what he had done, but Phetrix understood the significance.

"Are we going north then?"

Matildis clapped him on his back. "We sure are! We leave in the morning."

As day broke and the camp packed up, Phetrix beamed with excitement. He packed his gear and helped the others with their own. When they were ready, Grynd led them to a nearby road heading north.

"Keep your eyes open. The road should be fine, but the Seekers are out there. All we need is one to spot us and we'd soon be in danger."

"Come on Grynd, what are you afraid of?" Gerbald chided. "We haven't been in a proper fight for weeks. My blade would like to taste blood again."

"Ever seen a Seeker? They don't have blood to spill!"

Phetrix recalled when he had seen one of those creatures, and Grynd was right. They were ephemeral beings controlled by the whims of their master. Mortas had no reservations in employing them to do his will. They were much more efficient than humans.

They passed several other travelers on the road, but none seemed to mind who they were. The group had hidden their white stag livery under tunics to help keep their identities hidden. They neared a small village and that's when Wymar spotted it.

"Up there, look!"

The group followed his hand to the sky and there it was, a Seeker. It streaked across the sky scanning the village and all roads into it.

"Don't run now, it'll spot us for sure," Phetrix said. "Just move naturally. It might not notice who we are."

They moved cautiously trying not to draw attention their way when the Seeker swooped low, right above their heads. Wymar ran.

"No!" Ancrett called out, running after him.

"Both of you stop!" Grynd cried, but it was too late.

The Seeker spun in the sky and darted for Wymar. The man foolishly tried to outrun it, but couldn't. The Seeker flew in front of him, making him fall over.

Guards from the village came running toward them. The travelers that were nearby scattered.

Ancrett helped Wymar back to his feet as the guards rushed in.

Phetrix swirled his hands, readying a spell. It would expose him to the guards but he had no choice. He had to try and save them.

Phetrix created a ball of white light and shot it forward. It streaked past Wymar and Ancrett, boring a hole through the Seeker before dissipating.

Grynd, Gerbald, and Matildis rushed toward the guards, weapons drawn and yelling.

The guards drew their swords and the three of them clashed with the three loyalists.

Gerbald swung and missed, one of the guards piercing him in his back. Matildis swung down at the guard's arm, severing it.

Wymar and Ancrett both produced weapons and joined the melee. Phetrix was unable to do much as the guards were too close to the group for him to accurately strike them with his powers. He moved around the fight, looking for ways to intervene.

Matildis was thrown to the ground, exposing one of the guards. Phetrix quickly shot a beam of fire at the man. The thin streak of flame pierced the man's chest and he fell over dead.

Wymar swung a short sword at a guard, who blocked it and countered, his blade slicing into Wymar's sword arm. He dropped his blade, clutching at the wound, when Matildis jumped in, knocking Ancrett out of the way. She parried with the guard who looked to be getting the better of her. As she tried to protect Wymar, the guard pushed the fight and nearly pierced her with his sword. Ancrett swung to the side and then lunged at the guard with her knife. She struck him in the side, the blade sinking deep into his flesh. Matildis added her own sword to the man's body and he fell over dead.

Grynd was fending off the other guard, though he seemed to be losing ground. The guard was larger and faster than him. Grynd tried to parry the strikes, but his injury made it difficult. Lines of blood ran down his injured arm, spraying on the ground.

Matildis joined Grynd. "You're no good with that arm of yours," she growled, knocking him out of the way. The guard swung his sword at her, not seeming to care who his opponent was. Grynd fell to the ground and Matildis struck at the guard, forcing him back from her injured friend.

Phetrix raced to the injured Wymar and Gerbald, hoping he could heal their wounds.

"Ancrett, hold your hand here," he commanded, placing her hand on Wymar's wound.

She did so and he channeled energy into the bloody cut. Soon, it closed enough to stop the bleeding.

"Now to Gerbald!" They took a few steps over to the other man, but as soon as Phetrix laid his hands on him, he knew it was too late.

"Aren't you going to do something?" Ancrett cried.

"I can't. Not now. It's too late."

Ancrett pounded on Gerbald's lifeless chest.

When Phetrix turned to the remaining guard, he watched helplessly as he fought with Matildis and parried her sword. He knocked her back and turned, thrusting his sword through Grynd who had been on the ground and hadn't moved quickly enough from the fight.

"No!" Phetrix cried out. Channeling his energy, he prepared to take his rage out on the guard, but Matildis had been too quick and in her rage, sliced through the guard's throat.

When the fighting ended, only Ancrett, Matildis, Wymar, and Phetrix remained. A commotion from the village stole Phetrix's attention.

"More guards. Hurry, you need to run!"

"What, we can't leave them!" Ancrett cried out.

Phetrix pointed a shaky hand at the guards coming their way. "They will kill you! Leave now!"

Matildis pulled on Ancrett. "Come on, he's right. We can fight another day."

"We'll meet again, I swear."

"We better, mage." Matildis ran into the forest with Ancrett and the others at her side.

Phetrix wove his hands in a complex pattern then forced a stream of fire at the guards. They lunged out of the way, giving Phetrix enough time to run away.

Chapter 16

After the attack, Phetrix hid from prying eyes. Always with a look to the sky watching out for the Seekers, he roamed the shadows of Chevalon. Too many had died already and still he was no closer to finding the King or venturing across the seam to unite with the heirs.

Hidden within a cave in the eastern wildlands of Chevalon, he built a small fire, igniting the wet wood with his powers.

Four weeks had passed since the attack, but the memory burned within him, giving him fitful nights of sleep and anxious waking moments.

Huddled near the fire under his cloak, he desperately tried to remember the prophecy of the heirs.

According to ancient legend and secured through the centuries by the order of the Mage, heirs of the first ruler of Chevalon, King Galterius, were the rightful and anointed rulers of the land. For the most part, those rulers have been benevolent and just, ruling with peace and general harmony. There were moments of discord, such as when Prince Hemeri and Princess Ninon almost brought the kingdom to civil war, but Chevalon prospered for much of its history.

The Order of the Mage kept a secret history, a prophecy unknown to the descendants of Galterius.

Galterius's mage Edalf, known within the order as Edalf the Black, cursed the royal family. As Galterius's mage, he was a trusted advisor and confidant. At the urging of the King, Edalf produced a special blessing for the royal family, swearing that one day, royal blood would produce heirs with the ability to wield magic and when they did, they'd produce a dynasty that would last forever.

That was as much as anyone knew about Edalf outside the Order. The truth was much darker.

Edalf had fallen in love with the Queen and Galterius found out. For three days the two fought and argued with Edalf hoping to stay within the King's service, but the King, fueled by jealousy and disappointment, declared Edalf a traitor and set an execution date for him. The Queen plead with Galtarius to spare his life, and against his better judgement, agreed to banish him from the land.

Bitter and heartbroken, Edalf amended his blessing and swore that if magical heirs ever lived, they could be killed and the royal line would die with them, the land forever plunged into darkness.

His first attempt at bringing this to fruition was to pit the son and daughter of Galterius against one another. When Princess Ninon accused her brother Prince Hemeri of trying to steal her prized horse, she gathered a large following intent on crushing him. Edalf orchestrated the entire situation and the Order fought behind the scenes to restore order and reduce the damage caused by him.

Knowing what Edalf set in motion, the Order kept close to the royal family for centuries until the birth of Erthic and Elysande.

Phetrix was the first to spot their ability, the memory clear in his mind.

"What are you doing?" he remembered asking Erthic. The boy had waved his hands, a ball of tightly woven yarn he'd been given to play with spinning in the air above him.

"Ball!" the boy replied. He was barely able to speak but Phetrix remembered the word and the floating orb vividly.

"How did you do that?"

The boy moved his hands, making the ball spin faster. He giggled and lost control, the ball falling to the floor.

Phetrix kept a close eye on him, watching for more signs, though he didn't spot any until Elysande did something similar.

The little girl was in her crib and Erthic was with her, cooing and squirming. The nanny, Alyanna, had called for the mage because of something she witnessed.

"Watch, she'll do it."

Phetrix waited, knowing the boy had been capable of wielding magic and was curious about the girl.

They watched for several minutes before Elysande moved her hands and the blanket wrapped around her slowly rose from the crib and danced. She waved her little fingers making her brother giggle at the display. When she was done, the blanket fell softly on to the mattress.

"I told you! Did you see that?"

"Alyanna, say nothing about this! Do you understand me?"

"Why not?"

"It's important none shall know. I must have your word!"

"Fine, fine. I will say nothing."

Phetrix left and a growing knot of dread filled his belly. The prophecy had come true. If Elysande possessed the ability too, then they were in deeper trouble. Both would need protection. As long as one of them lived, he was certain the curse would not come to pass. He swore that day to never let anything happen to the children.

The fire crackled, forcing his memory to flee, returning to the present. Somehow, Mortas knew about the curse. The Order must have betrayed the King. Someone inside allowed the truth of the curse to escape their lips.

"Rhoden. Rhoden Noster." The name dripped evil. He was a rogue Mage that fled the Order and had gone silent for years. The last Phetrix had seen of him, he was at Mortas's side during the attack. It had to be him!

Phetrix stood, stretching his legs. It was no good dwelling on the past when all he could control was the present. At least for now, the children were safe with his old mentor Samuel in a land far different than their own. Hopefully they lived and hopefully Samuel could train them in the ways of magic. They'd need it to return and claim the kingdom. Until then, he'd bring the rebels together to create a force to repel Mortas.

Chapter 17

Phetrix climbed down from the mountains to the market in the village of Ulti where he frequently begged for food and listened attentively to the gossip of those selling and buying.

Phetrix hid among the southern mountains, living a life of solitude and contemplation. The black clad, snowflake patrols, as he had begun to call them, had concentrated their efforts to find the King and Queen to the north, making it impossible to find a way through. He didn't want to risk capture, nor did he wish to inadvertently lead Mortas' troops to the King. After the attack from the guards and the Seeker outside the village, he didn't want to get anyone else hurt. The best and safest course of action was no action at all. He found the cave and made it his home until such a time when he deemed it safe to continue his search.

For years, he waited and hoped for word that the royal family was alive, or for any sign from the other world to let him know the children were safe. The not knowing drove him to near madness in that first year, but as Mortas tightened his control on the land and more of his troops set up barracks in the town and villages, he knew his decision to hide was right.

It had been close to fifteen years since the children vanished and not a day went by that Phetrix didn't think of them or how to bring them back and reclaim the throne for the rightful heirs. Samuel would take great care of the children, as would those he thrust into their care; Nordon and Nadina for Erthic and Alyanna for Elysande. They were loyal to the King and above all else, willing to go to a far away land, to a place alien to that of their home of Chavalon.

Rain fell in cool drops and the wind blew harshly against his face. Phetrix pulled his cloak up over his bearded face to protect from the elements. Carefully, he joined the throngs of people vying for space in the market. Many arrived daily expecting deals for sale or trade and most left with neither.

Black clad guards patrolled the streets, the snowflake of Mortas emblazoned on their armor. Phetrix avoided them as much as possible. He doubted after all this time any would remember what he looked like, but why take the chance?

"Stop that boy!" one of the vendors yelled, pulling Phetrix's attention their way. A boy close to twelve years old pushed his way through the crowd carrying an apple. Two guards soon joined the chase, closing on him fast.

"Stupid people," Phetrix grumbled. Mortas had controlled all food and wares throughout Chavalon and artificially kept the prices high, forcing many families into servitude to pay off their debts. No doubt the boy was from one of those families. Almost everyone was.

Under his cloak, Phetrix waved a hand and cast a spell toward the guards, making a basket of rotting plums fall in front of them. They tripped over fruit-filled weavework and fell, slamming hard into the packed dirt ground. The boy turned back and laughed, but then slammed into another guard who had joined the pursuit from the opposite direction.

"Damn," Phetrix whispered. It was too late to save the boy without giving himself away. He had to let the guards take him. They'd probably beat him and add another five years of service onto his family, which would earn him an extra beating from his parents.

It was against this evil he hoped to one day fight. If only he could bring the children back, if they were ready to lead and if they still lived.

Hope gave him a reason to wake every day. It forced him to pray, to believe, to move forward as if Mortas would one day be overthrown.

Phetrix shook his head and made his way toward the corner he claimed for himself to beg for alms.

The rain came down harder making it difficult to see. Phetrix inched his way closer to the small store front at the corner hoping to stay as dry as possible while still able to see people walking his way.

"Alms, alms for the poor," he called out. He had a small wooden bowl he used for money laid out at his feet. At the moment it contained rain and a small coin he had placed there to seed the pot.

"Alms, alms please."

Years ago he was a master mage in the service of the king. Reduced to begging, he clung to those memories filled with hope. His abilities with magic were stronger than ever, but alone without the heirs, he had to force his desire to use them deep within himself. Unlike earlier when he tried to give the boy a chance in the market, he rarely used his abilities outside his mountain lair. Within the cave, he was safe from prying eyes. He studied and practiced his craft relentlessly, waiting for the day when he'd use it on Mortas to bring the evil man down.

To enhance his magic, he created magical talismans where he could store magic. If the time came when he needed to fight he wouldn't have to worry about depleting his energy and strength. It was a long exhausting process, but would be worth the effort when the time arose for its use. So far he had a rod, a small ruby and a ring. He never carried those items with him to the village. If a guard ever confronted him he didn't want to risk losing them. Not to mention the chance of having them stolen by any of the number of pickpockets and thieves that roamed the village. He hid the items in the cave behind protective wards only discernible by another mage.

The day passed and the rain subsided, leaving muddy streets and an empty bowl. It was getting late. Phetrix grabbed the bowl, stuffing it inside his cloak, then left the village, headed for the narrow pass leading into the mountain and his home.

As he left the village, a small pinpoint of light emerged in front of him. Resting about the height of a man and close to five horses away, it was a vibrant blue orb.

"What is this?"

Phetrix looked to either side, expecting one of Mortas' mages to appear and trap him.

The darkness around him gave him no indication who was there, if anyone.

Phetrix moved closer to the light, wonder and anxiety growing within him.

As he stood about an arms length away, the orb appeared about the size of his head. It glowed with a bluish hue and gave off a warmth. He peered closer and something moved inside.

"What sorcery is this?" He stepped closer, wary of what he might find. He swore he saw Samuel flash by within the orb, followed by images of a boy and a girl, both about the age of what Erthic and Elysande would be.

"Is this . . . could this be . . . Samuel?"

Phetrix shook with anticipation. Should he touch it? Where did it come from? Curious as to what it was, Phetrix reached out his hand and slowly inserted it into the orb. It rippled from where his hand entered, but he felt nothing other than a warmth spread over him.

Then, he pushed his face into the light.

Chapter 18

Inside the ball of light, strange visions bombarded Phetrix. Immediately he yanked his face out and the warmth fell from him. He breathed erratically, trying to make sense of what he'd just seen.

"This . . . this must be from Samuel."

Some of the images he saw reminded him of the time he crossed over long ago. Buildings looked similar and the wheeled chariots were like before. But the noise . . . the massive amounts of people . . . it overwhelmed him.

"This had to have been sent for a reason. I must discover its meaning."

He checked around him in the forest, wary that a trap had been set by Mortas and his wicked mage Rhoden. If he ever caught that man, he'd unleash a fury of spells on him unlike any he'd ever known. Turning his back on the Order and his mentor was a sin Phetrix wasn't ready to pardon.

The dark of night would not let him discern if anyone were nearby. The ball of light moved, scaring Phetrix.

"No! Don't leave! I've not seen yet!"

Tossing caution to the wind, he plunged his face and this time his entire body back into the warm light.

Massive buildings screamed by, the blurry motion sickening him.

Overhead, blue skies dotted with white clouds were broken by objects cutting their own white lines. Below, chariots blared and people yelled. It made his heart beat faster, worried that he'd been dropped into some sort of strange battle.

The sickening motion stopped and he was left to drift lazily to the ground below.

He landed outside a large building with a red cross painted on the side with words he didn't understand. People in blue and green matching uniforms raced in and out. One of the chariots hurried past him with blue and red flashing candles on top and the same painted cross on the side. The people in green uniforms rushed to the chariot, opening the walls, and pulled out a man covered in blood laying on a moving table.

None of the people seemed to notice him. His garb was considerably different than theirs; a black, dirty robe tied around the waist with a length of rope. His scraggly beard and long stringy hair much different than the closely cropped hair and beards of the men he watched. The women wore the same uniforms. The way they attended the bloody man made him think they were some sort of mages, healing the sick and injured.

Am I at a shrine? He thought. Carefully walking, no, floating toward the moving clear doors of the shrine, he entered.

It was just as noisy inside as out. Men and women shouted at one another in words he understood. It was a different dialect than back home, but they were familiar.

Then to his left, a man he recognized ran through the shrine and headed for two metal doors. He wore a uniform of gray and pushed something on the wall and the doors opened.

"Samuel! Samuel, it's me Phetrix!"

The man never deviated from his task. Phetrix ran to him and entered the small room as the doors closed behind him. Samuel stood next to him nervously looking up at numbers that flashed on and off.

"Samuel, it's me. Don't you recognize me?"

Samuel acted as though no one was there. Phetrix reached out to grab his shoulder but his hand went through him like a spirit.

"It's but a vision. Is this real? Has it happened already? Is it a portent of things to come?"

The room came to a halt and a ding sounded. Samuel walked right through him and entered another hall in the shrine. Phetrix ran after him, willing to see the vision through.

Samuel turned a corner, spoke to a woman seated at a desk, and followed her to a room on the far left. He nodded and the woman went back to her desk.

Samuel watched until she sat back down and then entered the room. Phetrix followed closely behind. He waved at a woman in the room to stay seated, then moved to a bed. A young man lay on the bed, eyes shut, a strange tube attached to his arm. Samuel moved straight for the bed. He placed a hand above the boy's head and closed his eyes. His lips moved but whatever he said was too low to hear. His hand began to glow, first yellow then turning a bright red.

Phetrix glanced back at the woman as Samuel placed hands on the man and mumbled words for a spell. Something about her was familiar. It hit him like a slap. It was Nadina. "Nadina," Phetrix whispered. What was she doing here?

More mature now, the young woman had grown into an attractive lady. But if seeing her now was like a slap, the sudden connection he made was a gut punch. He gasped and drifted to get a better look at the man. Then he saw him. Lying on the bed with a white sheet draped over his body.

"By the Gods! Could it be? It had to be Erthic. It must, or why would Samuel send the globe of light, or be examining the body? Body. Did the boy still live? He studied the boy, now a grown man.

Samuel spoke to Nadina. "Tell me what happened and what has been done here, so far."

The conversation lingered but Phetrix ignored it, moving closer to the man in the bed. He stepped to the right side, moving past a table with a screen similar to the one he'd seen when he first met Samuel in this strange world, but this one was black with green lines bouncing on it.

Leaning over, he realized the man was alive. Then he opened his eyes and he knew—it was Erthic! The boy lived! Hope was alive!

Then with a flash, he was ripped from the room, pulled through the shrine's walls, and back into the sky until he fell on the hard ground in the black forest.

The ball of light vanished, leaving nothing in its wake.

"No! Come back! I have so many questions!"

The sounds of the forest echoed his cries, but the vision was lost. Whoever sent it wanted him to know, the prince lived. Now, it was time to find the King and Queen and let them know their children were alive. The end of Mortas was at hand.

Chapter 19

Rhoden Noster walked amongst the strange inhabitants of this amazing world as if he belonged. Dressed in a suit he'd purchased from a massive store, a department store he learned it was called, using a stolen charge card, he took in his surroundings, mentally marking certain standout landmarks, to find his way back again.

Since discovering the seam, a task he'd spent the better part of fifteen years searching for, this was his third excursion into this new world. He'd learned a lot in those previous trips. Using his magic he'd been able to gain information from some of the denizens, thus understanding the process for purchasing his local attire. He blended in with the throngs of people that wandered the streets of what he now knew as a city named Chicago.

Everywhere he looked people bustled around with no apparent purpose. Many kept their heads down averting their gaze from those around them. They stared or spoke into strange magical boxes, small enough to carry in one hand or slip into a pocket. Rhoden still hadn't fathomed their purpose, but had a feeling they had some magical property. Perhaps a form of magical protection from meeting the gaze of others on the street.

With that in mind, he set his own magical barrier to prevent an assault. His mission was too important to be sidetracked. He stepped down a few inches onto a wider pathway and was startled by the blaring of one of the metal beasts the denizens of this world rode. He started and raised his hands to unleash a magical attack, but refrained at the last moment. As the beast sped past, the rider sent him some sort of magic in the form of hand gestures he did not recognize.

This was truly a dangerous land. Despite gathering basic information, he had much to learn and understand, but so little time. His mission came first. Rhoden vowed that when all was complete and secure, he would return to this amazing world to study it in more depth. For although danger lurked everywhere, he was intrigued and awestruck by the sheer size. The unending amount of people, the shape and size of the structures, the unimaginable products displayed and sold at the various vendors' shops as well as the strange food stuff the people shoved into their faces. Yes, this world frightened him a bit, but he was determined to understand it and eventually become its master.

Because of his plans, he had yet to inform Mortas of his discovery. He would be forced to disclose that knowledge upon producing the heirs, but until then, he kept the secret. He needed contacts here. Minions to do his bidding and teach him about surviving here.

Nothing and no one could stand in his way if he controlled the resources of this world, not even his lord and commander, Mortas Frost. At least for now. He smiled, imagining the look on the man's face when he, Rhoden dared challenge him, bringing the full might of this world down on him. Yes. It was a vision he could almost touch. But first things first. He had to find those two brat kids and return them to their own world. Which was the reason for his sojourn into this world. One of the Seekers he sent forth had spotted one of them.

Because of those previous trips, he had an inkling of what to expect. Hence, the clothes. He needed to fit in and his robes made him stand out, worse, to become a target. He feared the unknown even though he was fascinated. Until he knew more about their abilities, he didn't want to test his own skills against theirs in case their power was superior. For now he was content to walk among them and keep his head down.

He crossed the wider surface and stepped up on the opposite side. The sections of buildings soared into the sky and looked endless. He had yet to see the end of this fortress. According to the signal he received, the Seeker was still a long way off. He stopped, ducking into a recessed doorway. With a wave of his hand and a few muttered words, Rhoden connected with the creature seeing through its eyes. It had little will of its own, serving at the bidding of the one who conjured it. The almost mindless creatures did what it was instructed to do and little more. However, they were the perfect minion. Silent, nearly invisible, extremely deadly, almost impossible to kill and when given a task, continued on until success or told to cease.

This Seeker hovered over an enormous section of smaller buildings. Though similar in structure with their slanted roofs, green pastures in front and back and a metal beast sitting idly by, each had differences, their own individual look. Some were taller, some wider and in an assortment of colors, many of which Rhoden had never seen before.

The house the Seeker focused on was smaller, white and had two metal beasts next to it. Rhoden wondered if the pasture was how the creatures were fed. He sent a mental command for the Seeker to move toward the rear of the building. It did so and the sight of two people sitting on a flat surface came into view. He dared not send the Seeker lower for a better look. Although almost impossible to see at night, their translucent form did have a few observable features during the daylight, such as their black eyes, gray shaded brain and dark red heart.

The Seeker stopped directly above the two forms, he recognized as the women of this species. One was older, both wore trousers as he did, but they were short enough to be smallclothes. Their white legs were bared and the shirts they wore exposed enough skin to be scandalous back home.

He studied them for a moment, then instructed the Seeker to zero in on the younger woman. From this angle and distance Rhoden was unable to make a determination whether she was the one he sought, but nor could he rule it out. They had no description to use since they were babies when they were whisked away. They did have one telltale distinguishing feature that would make identification possible. However, those features lay hidden beneath the clothing, making a positive determination more difficult.

Something slammed into him, sending him reeling backward, and he clutched at his face. His hand came away red. He glanced up to see the offending brute only to find he had walked into a tall metal pole. Without realizing, he had started walking even though his sight was attached to the Seeker. He cursed under his breath, allowed the rage to flow into his fingers and pointed them at the pole. It began to quake and with a screeching groan of protest, bent.

Someone near him gasped. Another watcher said, “Look at that.”

A third said, "Is it an earthquake?"

"No, I think that man is doing it."

With sudden realization that he was causing a scene, the very thing he wanted to avoid, Rhoden released the energy, stuck his hands in his trouser pockets, and with head down, walked swiftly away. He heard murmuring behind him, but closed his mind to the words, wanting to get as far from there as possible. It was a mistake, revealing his power to these strangers. He still had much to learn about them before allowing his true nature to be known.

Rhoden hurried on, now unsure where he was going. The link with the Seeker had been severed with the collision. He had to be more careful and must learn to keep his temper in check, at least until needed.

Chapter 20

Rhoden walked until the larger, newer buildings gave way to older more run down and mostly abandoned structures. He noted less people and the ones he did see dressed less fancy. He likened them to the low born back home. The poor and destitute that clogged the streets with their unclean bodies and ever extended palms.

With the paths less crowded, he stopped to reconnect with the Seeker. Once the connection was reestablished, he found the younger woman had gone and one of the metal beasts was missing.

"Show me where she went," he commanded the Seeker.

It veered from the house and flew with amazing speed, over rooftops and paths. The woman was inside the beast, turning into grounds that held a long, massive building. She stopped in a row of other rides and exited. She wore strange garb. A short skirt of alternating green and white panels and a tight white top with a large green W on the front. She went through a door and was lost from view.

This was getting difficult. How could he find out if she was the lost princess if he couldn't catch up to her? He had to learn more about this world to get around it faster.

"Inform me when she leaves," he said. The Seeker made no reply. It had limited speech, most of which was a high-pitched series of screeches when excited.

Once the connection was broken, Rhoden scanned the area

searching for someone or something from which he could extract information. He walked on with little idea of what to look for or to do. Then, a tall dark man stepped from a narrow path between two run down buildings. He stood eyeing Rhoden with a curious and somewhat unnerving gaze. Rhoden felt obligated to do the same.

"I think this dude's lost," he said.

Rhoden had no idea what a dude was, but had the feeling it was him. He eyed the man with curiosity. The responding voice behind him took him by surprise. He jumped and whirled. Two more dark men stood behind him, both with wide grins. Whatever they thought was funny was not apparent to Rhoden.

The taller dark-skinned man behind him, said, "Well, maybe if he pays us we can direct him to where he wanna go."

The man in front had hair knotted in rows on his head like some sort of crop. He said, "Now, there's a good idea. It benefits everyone. We get money and he gets where he wanna be. How's that sound to you, man?"

Rhoden realized he was about to be accosted. The thought made him smile. Good. Now he would have a chance to try out his skills against someone from this world. Having already experimented on the other two trips, Rhoden knew his magic worked on this world. In fact, if anything, his magic had more power. Although, the reason why escaped him.

"What is it you want?" he asked.

All three men laughed. The one in front said, "That is an interesting question. Let me think on that a moment." He mocked thinking by putting a hand under his chin and glancing skyward. "Ah, I got it. We want your money."

"Money?" Rhoden was unfamiliar with the word, but understood the meaning. They wanted gold and silver, which he had not brought with him. But a thought came to him. He had learned a new word and might be able to learn much more by engaging the men in conversation.

" I carry no, ah, money, but I will pay you later in exchange for information."

The man in front bobbed his head once and pulled back, giving Rhoden a look of disbelief. "Information? What? We look like a public library? What kinda information you want?"

"As much as you can give. I want to understand your, ah," unsure of what to call it without giving away he was from elsewhere, he settled for, "this." He spread his arms to indicate the surroundings.

"Well, sure. Sure. We can give you all the information you want, but like I said, we needs be paid. And first."

"Like I said, I did not bring coin with me, but I will owe it to you on my next trip."

"Oh, you gonna *owe* it to us? You gonna give us your handwritten IOU?" To the men behind Rhoden he said, "Now he think we a bank or something."

The taller of the two men behind him, said, "I don't believe a man who dress in a suit don't carry no money. Let me see your wallet. No, screw that, I'll look for it myself."

He stepped forward, grabbed Rhoden's jacket and thrust a hand into the inner pocket. Anger rushed through him. His face clouded, then contorted into a mask of rage. He snapped his arm down and out of the man's grip, then shoved him backward with both hands. The startled man gave a shout as he fell back on his butt.

For a few seconds, all three men stared in amazement. Then, one by one, angry eyes swung toward him. The man in front stomped toward him, fists clenched, ready to do damage. "Oh, you asking for it now."

The upright man behind, helped his friend up. The assaulted man said, "You gonna pay for that, man." He pulled out a knife, flicked his wrist and the dulled finish of a well used but uncared for blade popped open.

This time Rhoden was prepared for their attack. His hands moved in intricate patterns. He spoke long practiced phrases and extended his hands toward the first man. An unseen force flew from his hands striking the unsuspecting man and sending him flying twenty feet in the air before crashing into a blue metal box with a curved top. The collision knocked the wind from his lungs. He dropped stunned.

Rhoden turned toward the remaining two. Both stood with jaws agape seeing their airborne friend. The man with the knife was first to recover. He lunged at Rhoden hoping to impale him, but the knife and his entire arm stopped moving as if the scene had been put on pause.

"What the . . ." the man said, as the blade turned upward and back, moving toward him. A great strain appeared on the man's face as the blade made slow but steady progress toward his own body. He placed his other hand over the first and with every bit of strength he possessed tried to divert the blade's path, but with a sudden surge, it closed the gap and pounded into his chest. His eyes went wide, his mouth opened to emit a scream, but it seemed to catch in his throat. The third man, glanced from his friend to Rhoden, then turned and fled.

Rhoden reached out and with invisible fingers, lifted the man with the braided hair and flung him into the wall. He went limp, but Rhoden drove him into the wall once more. A sickening crack and wet smack followed and Rhoden released the body. It slid down the wall and landed in a bloody heap.

Across the path, a dark-skinned woman pointed a small rectangular shaped item at him. At first he feared it was a weapon, but when nothing happened, decided it was a personal defensive ward to protect her against Rhoden. Since she stayed on her side of the path and offered no threat against him he ignored her. She moved on, all the while keeping her ward held in front and between him and her.

The man he sent flying groaned, drawing his attention. He surveyed his handiwork with satisfaction, feeling more confident in his ability to survive and thrive in this world. Rhoden squatted in front of the still stunned man. He shook him gently, then harder when he didn't get an initial response. He moaned louder. His eyes opened in small increments, then shot open. "Nonono," he said, trying to crawl away backward. He bumped into the metal box and with nowhere to go, held his hands up in front of him like a shield. "Okay. You win. No more flying."

Rhoden was amused.

"Now then, as I said, I need information and I think you are the perfect one to give it to me."

"No problem. I'm your man. I'll tell you anything you want to know. Be happy to help." The words rushed from his mouth like water from a collapsed dam.

"Yes, I'm quite sure you'll tell me everything."

Chapter 21

Rhoden had been right. The man, DeWayne, was a wealth of knowledge. So much so, he not only kept him alive, but offered to pay him for his service.

The things DeWayne told him left him dumbfounded. This world was more advanced than Chavalon. The metal creatures ridden on the hard paths were not creatures at all, but machines known as cars. Drivers controlled them and evidently, gave them the ability to move fast and go long distances in short times. After gathering as much information as his overwhelmed mind could hold, he reconnected with the Seeker and had DeWayne drive him to the location.

On the way, Rhoden studied his surroundings, taking in the structures, the people and the other vehicles on the road. He was surprised with the speed and agility of the car. "Why do you stop and sit. I need to be somewhere."

"Ah, I have to stop. It's a red light."

DeWayne gave him a funny look. "You do know what a red light is, don't ya?"

"Of course. It's that." He pointed at the traffic signal. "But why do you stop?"

"It's the law."

"Ah! The law of the land. Stop at red lights. That's annoying when you want to get someplace fast."

"Yeah. It can be. But it also keeps you from getting into wrecks with other cars. The light controls who goes and who stops."

"Who controls the lights?"

"They're automatic. You know, on timers. No one controls them. You set it, give it power and it works on its own."

"Like magic?"

"Well, yeah, I guess it is sorta like that."

He pointed at a massive building. "What is that?"

"That's a hospital?"

Rhoden had no idea what that meant.

DeWayne explained further. "It's where sick people go to get better."

"You have healers?"

"Yes, we call them doctors."

"Doctors," Rhoden repeated. "But such a large building. Do you need it that big to accommodate all of your sick?"

"Yeah, and there's three more in the area about the same size."

"Truly? You have that many sick people? Why doesn't your ruler just eliminate all the sick? The buildings could be used for some other purpose. The sick only pass it on and perform no function. Best be rid of the sick and weak."

DeWayne glanced at him with wide eyes and open mouth. "You're kidding me, right?"

"Kidding?"

"Never mind. I think I'd like living where it is you're from."

"That which I seek is in that direction."

DeWayne kept driving and Rhoden grew annoyed. "I said that way. Why didn't you turn and drive that way?"

"What, through those yards? We wouldn't get very far. A lot of them have fences. We'd never get through. Besides, someone would call the po-po. I have to stay on the streets. See, I'm turning here. At the corner."

"What is po-po?"

"The po-leese."

"Po-leese."

"You know, coming from you I think it's better you just say police. That's the law. You hear their sirens or see the blinking lights, you best get your tail running."

"Are they your ruler's army?"

"In a way, yeah. They uphold the law. You drive across someone's property and the police come and take you away."

"Make a turn here. At this street."

DeWayne followed the directions making several wrong turns because of Rhoden's lack of understanding on how to direct him.

"There," Rhoden pointed. "That is where I need to go."

DeWayne parked in a lot full of other cars.

"How many people live in this world?"

"Heck if I know," DeWayne said, "but it's in the billions."

"Billions?" Rhoden was unfamiliar with the word, but accepted that the number was great. "What is this place?"

"This is Whitford High School."

"High school?"

"Man, where you from? Don't they have schools?"

"Yes." He eyed the massive building. "I'm looking for a, ah, someone who went inside."

"Then they're either a teacher or a student. Is this person old or young?"

"Young."

"Then they a student."

"Is entering permissible?"

"Yeah, but you have to go through security and the office and tell them why you're there and who you're looking for."

That wouldn't do. "I wish to examine this school from the outside. Come."

He got out. DeWayne hesitated, but followed. They walked toward the rear of the school where a large fenced area blocked their path. The grounds held a series of fields Rhoden took for training grounds. "Explain these."

"You don't have sports where you from?"

Rhoden gave him an impatient look.

"Okay. Just asking. In front of us is a track, you know, where people run races. Over there, to the right are tennis courts. Next to that is a baseball diamond. I used to be pretty good at that and basketball. The big one to the left is the football field."

As they watched, a bell rang throughout the school. Within seconds the doors were thrown open and a wild horde of young men and women poured out. Thinking he'd been discovered and about to be assaulted, Rhoden went into a series of hand gestures ready to meet the attack head on.

Chapter 22

Grant unfolded his body from the passenger side and stepped onto the sidewalk. It had been Vega's turn to drive. They alternated daily. He didn't mind being the passenger, but Vega had a heavy foot at all times. On a call, he was a NASCAR driver, often taking chances where none were necessary. At those times, Grant often closed his eyes, praying they made it to the scene and didn't become one of their own victims to investigate.

They got a call out when the bodies of two black males were found on a city street. It had been called in by a woman who stated she'd taken a recording of the assault. He expected the men would be the latest victims in the gangland violence saga the city had been in for the last decade. It got worse every year and the powers that be were at a loss as to how to solve the problem. However, when he got there, he discovered the men had not been shot by some drive-by opposition gang. Their bodies had been beaten to death. One man had his head crushed.

He stepped under the crime scene tape and held it up for Vega. The two men surveyed the grounds. The bodies had been covered. The crime scene team was not done with them yet. Grant turned to one of the officers, a veteran named Suarez. "You first on, Daniel?"

"Yes sir. My partner and I secured the scene. Reggie's over their with the witness. Interesting viewing. Makes it pretty cut and dry, except for one thing."

Grant waited, but Suarez made him ask. "Such as . . .?"

"Oh, no. Those words are not going to come out of my mouth. You go see for yourself."

The comment piqued Grant's curiosity. He gave Suarez a sideways glance and ducked back under the tape. Suarez's partner, a rail thin black man named Reginald Pierce, was standing with a middle-aged black woman, next to a metal shopping basket. The perturbed look on her face told Grant she wanted to be anywhere but here.

"Detective Grant," Reggie said, "this is Tanya Forest. She witnessed the assault and recorded it on her cell phone."

"Hi, Ms. Forest, nice to meet you. Thank you for doing this. It will help us capture the killer of those two young men."

"If I'd a known it was gonna take this much time I'd a never called in."

"My apologies for the delay. Once I hear your statement, I'll have officer Pierce take you to the market."

"Oh, hell no! I can't be seen getting out of a cop car in this neighborhood. I'll be a marked woman. And don't be talking 'bout those two like they was saints. They was bad boys to be sure, but they didn't deserve to die. That old white man tossed them around like they's nothing. Never saw such a thing."

"Can you describe him?"

"Oh, honey, I got much better than that." She lifted her phone and tapped a button. A video came to life--one that showed three black men accosting an older man in a suit. It looked like a typical mugging until one of the black men went flying backward, smashing into a mailbox. What made that interesting was the mugger took flight apparently without contact with the muggee. But if that was strange, the next sequence was mind-boggling. The second mugger, now wielding a knife, had the knife turned back on him. It plunged deep into his chest, but the older man never touched him. It was as if the man drove the blade into his own chest.

The third man was lifted from the ground and slammed into the wall. The second contact was responsible for the damage to the man's head. The blow that took his life.

The picture began shaking when the first man went flying. By the time the third man met his demise, the picture shook so bad it was hard to follow, but enough came through to understand the strangeness of the encounter. The woman hid at that point. She ducked behind a parked car. The picture was lost. However a minute later she got up the courage to lift the phone over the hood and continue filming. Only a portion of the scene was in view, but what could be seen, was interesting.

The older man had an extended conversation with the first victim, before walking off together. He could not see where they went, but had a face to work with. He sent the picture to his phone, then informed Ms. Forest her phone was to be held as evidence, which did not go well.

After another five minutes talking with the crime scene techs, the two detectives left. While Vega drove, Grant watched the video several more times. It reminded him of a live magic show he'd once seen. The more he watched the fight, the more he wondered if the entire thing hadn't been staged. Well, except for the two bodies.

He shut the phone off and leaned back in the seat, eyes closed. He'd hand off the phone and hope facial recognition could put a name to the two faces. He didn't understand how the old man did what he did, but he wanted very much to meet him and ask that question.

Chapter 23

"Whoa!" DeWayne said. "Man, school's just letting out for the day. You ain't got to do that voodoo stuff. Just watch."

Rhoden did, but never released his power, ready to cast a spell that would easily take out the front row of the advancing horde, though the expenditure would take a heavy toll on his energy. Sure enough, the loud stream of evacuees, did not move toward him, but instead went to the cars. In minutes a long line of vehicles waited their turn to exit.

From a spot halfway down the building, a door was flung open and armor clad warriors burst out. Rhoden watched with curiosity. They moved toward the football field and began going through a series of warm up maneuvers, preparing for their battle training. Learning how they prepared for battle would be important knowledge.

He moved down the fence to get closer. The warriors formed a square of neat lines, then began doing organized exercises.

"Where are their weapons?"

"Weapons? Ah, if you mean their gear, it's probably stored in that shed." He pointed at a building where two green shirted men were unlocking double doors.

The door opened again and a group of women exited all wearing the same outfit he witnessed his quarry wearing. Were they warriors as well? In the princesses' case, he could understand that. Perhaps they were the ladies of court.

His heart raced as he spotted her speaking with a tall dark-skinned woman. Whatever the princess said caused the dark-woman to bark out a loud laugh. They moved on to a grassy area outside the field the warriors worked on.

Rhoden had to get closer. He had to know for sure if it was her. But how?

DeWayne leaned in close to him and whispered. "Hey, man, you got to be cool."

"Cool?"

"Yeah. You can't be staring at the girls like that or someone will think you're a perv and call the cops."

Rhoden pointed at the blonde. "I need to see her up close."

"Ah, define 'up close.' You ain't thinking some sort of sex thing, are you?"

Rhoden stared at him, confused. Then understanding dawned. "No, that is not my intent. I need to make a positive identification. But the only way to do that is to see her up close."

"It might look strange if we get closer and stare at them. What do you have to see to make this identification positive? You ain't got a picture or something?"

"No. No one has seen her in fifteen years."

"Then how . . .?"

"She has a mark on her side."

"On her side. You mean like underneath her clothes. How you gonna see that without getting her undressed? I didn't sign on for anything like that."

Rhoden continued to observe the young women as they did their own form of warm ups. Forgotten were the warriors who had now broken into smaller groups to work on skills alien in nature to him, but which revolved around an oblong ball.

After their exercise period a few of the girls walked to the fence and removed their heavy outer garments, hanging them from the fence. He slid closer. The tall dark-skinned woman blocked his view as she pulled the garment over her head. He moved away from the fence fast and was in time to see the princess raise her arms to do the same. The undershirt she wore rode up but not far enough to see what he needed.

As the outer garment cleared her head and before she lowered her arms, Rhoden cast a quick spell and with the flick of a finger sent it toward his target. The undergarment billowed as if from a strong breeze and lifted half way up her torso, exposing her midriff. He was only able to get a quick glimpse as the Princess was quick to cover herself, but what he saw caused a gasp loud enough to be heard.

The women turned to face him, all giving him the scrutiny of an outsider who did not belong.

Rhoden averted his gaze. He walked back toward DeWayne.

The taller woman said, “Was that perv eyeing us?”

The other girl, the one he now was sure was the Princess, said, “I didn’t see him. What was he doing?”

“He was watching us take off our sweaters. Guess he thought he was going to see some skin.”

They moved away from the fence and joined the others.

Rhoden did not look back, passing DeWayne and heading toward the car. Once inside, he said, “I have seen what I needed. Drive.”

“Okay, where to?”

“I will direct you, as I am unfamiliar with your paths.”

“Roads.”

“What?”

“They're roads or streets.”

Rhoden nodded. Of course. He knew that. They had dirt roads back home, but he wasn’t sure they were called the same thing here. He ignored the man's chatter. He had found one of the heirs. Mortas would be appeased for now, but it would not last. Once he delivered the girl, he would have to task the Seekers to find the boy. Once they were both delivered he would stay in this world, learn its ways and find a way to become its ruler. Mortas could have his world. Rhoden liked this one.

Twenty minutes later they arrived at a location a block from the seam. “I will need you to return to this spot each day. Sit and wait for my return.”

“What time?”

“From morn to dark.”

“That's a lot of time to be sitting here waiting for you.”

“It is your task. Do not fail me. You will not like the outcome.”

“Okay, sure, I'll be here. Just like you said, but didn't you say something about paying me?”

Rhoden eyed the man, then dug into a pocket. He had one coin hidden in an inner jacket pocket. He removed it and flipped the coin to him. DeWayne snatched it out of the air and studied it. “Hey, what's this?”

“A silver. Keep up your assistance and I'll reward you with gold.” With that, Rhoden got out of the car and walked down the street.

“But, hey wait. This ain't real money. How am I gonna spend this?”

Rhoden continued walking.

“Dee man, what you got yourself into, now?” Dewayne said to himself. He looked at the coin and wondered if it was real silver. If so, maybe this was worth more than he thought. He knew a guy who might know a thing about coins. He looked up and to his surprise, his new boss was gone. He looked around the wide-open space, but he was nowhere to be seen. “What indeed, man?”

Chapter 24

Days after the strange vision, Phetrix beamed with excitement. He'd barely slept since then, the possibilities now endless for the future.

The sun rose in the bright blue sky and he ventured into Ulti to the corner he frequented when begging for alms. Today, his thoughts weren't on his begging or listening to pick up gossip. He was more concerned with King Artus and Queen Gresilda. He needed to find them. To let them know their children lived. But the question was, did the King and Queen still live? After all, it had been fifteen years since the fall of the kingdom. They'd been on the run for a long time.

Phetrix was confident that, if they had perished, it hadn't been at the hands of Mortas. He would have heard. Mortas would have announced to the entire kingdom of their deaths. He would have paraded their bodies through the streets of every town and village. No, Mortas had not found them.

Someone dropped a coin into his bowl. The thunk brought his attention back to the here and now.

"Alms, alms for the poor," he called out. People dressed in fine clothing dropped coins into his bowl but none bothered to look at him. Guards passed, eying him carefully as though he were a criminal. He averted their gaze, worried they might recognize him after all these years.

"Give to the needy! Please help, I have nothing."

A fellow beggar he'd known for years stumbled his way, reeking of stale ale and dung.

"Pendra, how's things?"

Phetrix acknowledged him with a nod.

"Fine, Kol. How are you?"

Kol staggered when he stepped close, his rank breath forcing Phetrix to step back. "Much better since I had me some ale. Compliments of some guard or another. I don't really care who."

Phetrix smiled. "Glad to hear it. I do hope the day is good for you."

Kol grinned, two of his bottom teeth missing. "Always when I got ale."

"Say Kol, you were one of King Artus's guards weren't you?"

Kol snapped to attention and his swimming eyes focused on Phetrix. He put his hands on Phetrix's chest and swept his gaze around them. Leaning close, he whispered,

"Don't say those words out loud if you want me to live." He did another sweep, double-checking that they were alone. "Frost has ears everywhere." He made a grand flourish with his hands to emphasize his point.

"But you were in his service, were you not?"

Kol's eyes widened as he scanned the area around them again. He nodded.

"Do you know where he's hiding?"

He eyed Phetrix with suspicion and scratched at the stubble on his chin. "Dead. They're all dead. King, Queen, the children . . . those poor little children . . . all dead."

Phetrix knew it was a long shot asking this man for information, but he had to start somewhere.

"Why this sudden interest in the King's whereabouts?" Kol asked, his eyes suddenly more focused.

Phetrix hoped he hadn't made a mistake broaching the subject with this man. If he spoke of this conversation during some drunken stupor, word might get to the wrong people and he would be forced to flee. He thought that time was coming soon anyway, but he wanted it to be at his choosing and not when being pursued by guards.

"I'm getting old, Kol. Sometimes I sit here and my feeble mind wanders. I remember the old days. I recalled seeing the King riding through the countryside, ahead of a large assembly of knights. It was quite a sight. That's all. Just an old memory."

Kol nodded. Whatever control it took to keep his eyes clear had faded. "Well, old friend, best to keep those old memories up here," he tapped Phetrix's forehead, "and don't let them escape your mouth." He laughed, then belched.

"Thanks anyway. I was under the impression the King and Queen still lived. But rumors are never quite accurate, are they?"

"No, no sir they aren't." Kol hiccuped and caught himself from falling by reaching out to Phetrix.

"Pendra, you best not share thoughts like that out loud. The ears! The ears will hear and then," he made a motion across his throat with his finger as though with a knife.

"I understand. Thanks my friend. Good day to you Kol. Maybe you've had enough ale for the both of us!"

Both men laughed and Kol stumbled away, scaring a little girl walking with her mother. Not far down the street, two guards accosted him and dragged him kicking and screaming to the magistrate where they no doubt would have him rest off his drunkenness. Eventually he'd be put into service for Mortas.

"Drunkard," he mumbled.

The day grew gray and a chilled breeze swept into the town. The amount of travelers and market-goers dwindled. Phetrix received few coins and his stomach growled. If it weren't for the Seekers, he'd use his abilities more, but it was impossible to know when they might pass. Though he hadn't seen one in a while, he knew they were still searching. Even after all these years, Mortas continued to oppress the people as he sought the heirs, decreeing constant vigilance by the Seekers.

Two years ago Mortas held a massive assembly at the building site of his new castle in the central part of Chevalon. Over three hundred men and women from all over the land attended the spectacle. Phetrix traveled to witness the ceremony as well, though in the guise of the destitute Pendra. Seekers circled the assembly above, their dark shadowy figures swirling and intertwining with one another.

Mortas stood on a wooden platform with Rhoden at his side.

"Thirteen years ago, I deposed a wicked ruler and his family. Today, we celebrate my grand new castle, the seat of your liberty!"

The invited gave a rousing cheer, but the crowd of commoners returned cautious applause.

"That despot is rumored to still be alive." Someone in the crowd booed, a few others joining. "The time has come to end this charade. I will give any of you who find Artus and Griselde a castle and land of your own. If my Seekers find them first and you come in to claim the prize, you will be exempt from taxes for ten years if you bring them to me." A loud murmur rose amongst those gathered. Phetrix raised his eyebrows. Ten years of no taxes was a huge benefit. Mortas had claimed more money from the people than any other ruler he'd known.

"Finally, if those children are found, and brought to me alive, I will bring the captor into my family as an adopted son or daughter, with all the rights of a blood-born child."

This last decree shook the crowd and Phetrix felt a certain energy rise up. It frightened him. The rebellion had grown considerably over the years, though still in hiding. He'd had contact with a few of them over the years, choosing to remain on his own rather than live amongst them. To him, it was a safer choice.

Mortas said something to Rhoden. The evil mage lifted his head skyward, raised his hands, then spread them wide. The Seekers cried out above the assembly and they suddenly burst from their circle and sped out in all directions. The display was a message to the audience of how serious Mortas was about the capture of the royal family.

Mortas brought the attention back to himself.

"The Seekers have gone, searching for my prey. Go, beat them to it and hold me to my word!"

Mortas raised his hands and Phetrix gasped. His hands . . . glowed. Though faint, he caught the sight. Did Rhoden do that? Or . . . did Mortas now posses the ability to wield magic?

He quickly left the assembly, worried that the fight was going to be more dire than he imagined.

Now, as he marched his way through Ulti, he periodically checked the sky for the dark shadows. He hadn't seen any this day, but they were always there. Somewhere.

Chapter 25

Several weeks passed and Phetrix carefully questioned the other beggars in Ulti. As undesirables under Mortas's reign, he reasoned they had little to gain from turning him in. Even if they did, they'd face a severe punishment from Mortas for being homeless beggars interfering with his loyal subjects. They were often transient and never stayed in one town for too long.

No one seemed to know anything about the King or Queen. At least if they did, they weren't sharing the information. Maybe they thought he was a spy and would turn them in? He tried hard to convince them otherwise, but still . . . it could be holding them back.

Hope was fading and he grew desperate. It had been a long time since he'd met with anyone from the rebellion. He worried that maybe they no longer believed they could win. If they'd lost that hope, then Mortas truly did win, no matter if Samuel kept the heirs alive or not. He wouldn't believe it. He couldn't give in to despair. Artus and Griselde were alive, somewhere. They had to be.

Phetrix tried a different tactic. He listened for clues from passersby, hoping he'd hear something that would give him a glimmer of truth that he'd follow to the end.

If they were alive, they were never spoken of. Most likely he'd have to find someone to pay for information so he saved everything given to him, resorting to stealing food when hungry, hoping the guards never caught him.

When he figured he had enough coins saved, he went into the village tavern—the Winking Bear—and cautiously waited for some drunk guard or traveler with a loose tongue.

The first night he went, he discovered nothing. The tavern was subdued more than usual and very little information was to be found. The only bit he did discover was that Mortas had directed his Seekers to the west as rumors of the heirs had spread. It was impossible since they were with Samuel in the other world, but at least it directed Mortas away from the truth.

For the next several nights, nothing of importance bubbled to the surface of the conversations he had with strangers. He pried, he bought more ale, but nothing was shared.

About a week after he started, he was running out of coins and patience. It was a weak plan, but he hoped for more than what he got.

He bought a mug of ale and watched the crowd inside, looking for anyone who might help him with what he wanted. Across the room, a man he didn't recognize sat against the wall with a large brimmed black hat pulled low over his eyes. Several people approached him through the evening and Phetrix watched more than one drop a few coins on the table for him. Hoping that he might have information to help, Phetrix approached the man.

Before he could say anything, he felt a tug on his arm. He turned and Kol smiled at him.

"Pendra, come over here. It's been awhile."

Annoyed at his interruption, Phetrix reluctantly agreed. He watched as more people approached the man who barely spoke a word to them, but nodded as they dropped coins on the table. He'd grown quite a large pile already.

"Kol, I was about to talk to that man. What is it that's so important?"

"Keep your voice down. You don't want to go anywhere near him. He works for Frost. He'll slit your throat before you get your question out."

"But how did you—"

"Listen to me." Kol grabbed Phetrix's cloak and yanked him close. With Kol's lips touching his ear, he whispered, "The King—?"

Phetrix opened his eyes wide. "Yes?"

"He lives."

The words rang louder than any bell or explosion he'd ever heard. The destruction of the castle on the night of the attack was nothing compared to those two words. *He lives.*

Phetrix grabbed him by the shoulders and shook him. "Are you sure? How can this be? How do you know?"

"Be quiet! If anyone hears this, we're both dead men!"

Something nagged at Phetrix and a cold descended over him. He searched deep into Kol's eyes. "I thought you were taken by the guards."

Kol ran a hand through his hair and looked down, speaking quietly. "I was. I paid the price."

"What price was that, old friend? Did it happen to involve selling me out?"

A look of shock, then fear ran through Kol's eyes. "No. No, never. I would never give those bastards anyone. No, I paid," he lifted his tunic, "with blood." Several ragged, red puckered scars lined his chest. "They held me down and had their fun carving on me like I was a roasted wild boar. Believe me, I wouldn't give them anyone. Once they were done with me they took me out back and dumped me in a pigsty." He lowered the shirt. "You have nothing to fear from me, Pendra. My hate for them is far too strong to ever take their coin to sell someone out."

Phetrix was shocked at the sight, but did not allow the scars to satisfy his query. Instead, he bore deep into the man's eyes, and found no sign of falsehood. He relaxed.

"But how do you know about—" He wanted to say the words but they were not in a place to speak freely. What did Kol know that he didn't weeks ago? How did he come to this conclusion?

"Come with me. It's not safe in here." Kol turned and walked out the door with Phetrix at his heels.

As they passed the table where Mortas' man sat collecting coins, Phetrix thought he detected a slight alteration in the tilt of the man's head, as if his eyes followed their exit. The thought tightened a band across his chest. The angst did not release him easy. There was something sinister about the man. Phetrix was determined to stay as far away from the man as he could.

Chapter 26

Phetrix nervously walked next to Kol as the man led him to a dark alley behind the tavern. Guards were no where to be found and Kol waited as a few drunks stumbled out of the tavern. Once they were out of earshot, he began.

"You asked about the King?"

Phetrix nodded.

"When I was locked up, there was another prisoner with me. He sat in a pool of his own vomit and reeked of ale and tobacco. Not that I was much better."

A man walked by the alley and Kol waited, his eyes darting back and forth looking for trouble.

"After several days of sobering up, he and I got to talking. Nearly two months ago, he'd been in the forest west of Ulti living off the land when he stumbled across a small camp. Hungry, he snuck in at night and stole bread and ale. As he was leaving, he tripped on a log he hadn't seen in the dark and fell into one of the tents. Inside the tent was an older man who was built like a boulder. Well, it didn't take long for the older man to beat up my new friend. Bloodied his lip and gave him a swollen eye he did."

"What's this have to do with King Artus? Is there a point to your rambling?" Phetrix leaned close but didn't smell ale on Kol. He'd cleaned up quite a bit since his imprisonment.

Kol glared at him, then continued.

"The man alerted the rest of the camp and soon my friend was surrounded by three other men and a woman. They questioned him, worried he was a spy sent from Mortas. As they were about to kill him, one of the men—at the urging of the woman—put a halt to the proceedings. He declared, 'Spare this man. Let him be. He's done nothing we wouldn't do in his situation. It's clear he's not allied against us. Mortas has not sent him.'"

"Are you implying that was the King? That's not enough evidence to convince me!"

Kol brushed off the insult and started again.

"The woman there came to the man's side. 'Artus, you are wise in letting him go. He poses no threat. The more we can show mercy to, the better we will be when the time comes. Mortas would never be as gracious as you.'"

Kol fell silent, letting the speech sink in.

"So you're telling me you believe the King is alive based on the testimony of a fellow drunk who you happened to be in a cell with?"

"That's exactly what I'm telling you. Why would he lie to me? What's to gain? We were both locked up and awaiting judgment. You asked me a while back if I heard anything and I hadn't. I've stayed far away from those rebels to the north. But since we last spoke . . ." he trailed off, looking down. His hand moved across his chest. "We need to restore the rightful heirs. The reign of Mortas has done much harm to our people." When he looked back up, his eyes glistened.

"Kol, what happened to you? Who were you before you became like me, a poor man trying to live off the mercy provided by others?"

Kol rubbed his hands together and thought about the question before answering.

"At one time, I was a young squire in the King's service tending to horses and the stables. After a few years I rose to the level of King's Guard. I was so proud to wear his colors. To be considered one of the elite." The gleam in his eyes faded, his gaze drifted down. "Now look at me. I'm nothing. A homeless beggar. A no-one who guards feel free to carve up without recriminations."

When he looked up, tears filled his eyes. "I was there, Pendra. Fifteen years ago, I was there. Do you know what it was like to see all those people murdered because of Mortas's ego? He had no claim to the throne but his evil knew no bounds. Amongst the slaughter many of my fellow guard fled. I called them cowards and urged them to stand and fight to the last man. But none listened. I found myself alone. As the enemy streamed into the castle, I took a look around me and knew in my heart all was lost. Then, to my never-ending shame, I . . . I ran from the destruction and certain death, too. I was weak and knew no better than the others who ran. What makes it worse is I never saw what happened to the royal family. My fear and desire for my own self-preservation won out over my pledge to protect the King and his family at all costs."

He wiped the tears away with a violent swipe of his arm. His voice found steel. "Don't you see. I was a failure. A coward. But no more. If the King still lives, he shall have my sword again and this time I will not fail in my duty."

Phetrix inhaled deep. There was much to Kol he didn't know and this revelation was stunning.

"You were at the castle when the attack came? Do you know what happened to the children?"

"Erthic and Elysande? No. I've always hoped they made it out alive, but I never found out their fate."

Phetrix wondered how much he'd be able to trust Kol. Did their mutual bond of poverty give them enough to go on?

"What was it about this story this friend of yours told you that makes you believe him?"

"The way he described the man and woman sounded exactly like King Artus and Queen Gresilda. I could picture them in my mind, older of course."

"I'm still not convinced."

Kol's face flashed anger. "I didn't come here to argue with you! Again, when you asked me about the King before, I had nothing. I've since discovered what I believe to be a fact and my first thought was to share it with you. I've been looking for you ever since I got out yesterday. Believe me or not, I don't care. I've done what I came here for. I hope the information is useful. If not, then I've wasted my time. It doesn't matter. I intend on finding the King. I'm leaving this village and going west into the forest. If I die searching for King Artus, then at least I died doing something. I'm done with begging because the reign of Mortas has forced me to it!"

Kol stormed off, muttering something about heirs and life. Phetrix considered running after him to tell him his story, but then backed off.

If Kol was right and this tale told in a dungeon was true, then it was best he soon figured out how to contact Samuel. It had been years since he attempted to enter the other realm, fearing he'd lead Mortas to the heirs and all hope be lost. Maybe now it was time to bring them back and reclaim the kingdom.

Chapter 27

Four men in suits stepped out from nowhere onto the road. A sharp blast of a horn startled them and a car veered away. Three of the men were ready for battle, but Rhoden lifted a hand to restrain them.

The car bounced over a curb and stopped, the irate driver got out screaming and shaking a threatening hand. He was large both in height and girth. He advanced on them and Mortas eyed him with curiosity.

As the man drew closer, Mortas nodded to one of his large companions. The man moved to intercept. Seeing him approach, the driver halted. The coloring of his face altered to a brighter red. He sputtered something, pivoted and hurried back to his car. Once inside, he sped away.

"What strange world is this?" Mortas said.

Rhoden smiled. "As they say here, you ain't seen nothing yet. But, let me remind you, we need to keep to ourselves. That means as little interaction with the locals as possible. Let me do the talking."

Rhoden had returned two days in a row spending time with DeWayne, learning the local customs, terms and items. He was far from expert, but had a better understanding of the people and the geography. On the second trip he gave DeWayne a list of items they would need including, purchasing clothing for the men. They guessed at the sizes and Dwayne placed the orders after taking several gold coins to an exchange shop. The value of the coins was near six thousand dollars, however the owner paid a mere two thousand and that after a lot of haggling. After paying for everything Rhoden required, he still had a few hundred dollars left, not counting the two gold coins he'd kept for himself.

Rhoden appeared the next day, collected the clothes and disappeared back into his world. An hour later the four men entered the new world.

As prearranged, DeWayne arrived driving a van. Rhoden opened the passenger door and climbed in while Mortas and his two henchmen eyed the vehicle with uncertainty, before getting inside.

"Do you have the information I requested?"

"Yeah. She's at the school right now getting ready for the football game."

"Take us there."

"You got it, boss."

DeWayne drove and Rhoden watched the other men's reactions. Even Mortas's eyes widened as the car accelerated. He remained amazed as the surroundings passed by. But though his curiosity might have been stimulated, he made no comment.

"These machines are the horses of this world," Rhoden explained.

Mortas did not reply, but took in the details. After serving Mortas for many years, Rhoden recognized the man's looks. The one he saw now, was the smug 'I can conquer this land,' look. That bothered Rhoden. He needed to get a foothold in this new land before Mortas had the opportunity to invade it himself. If Rhoden could find both heirs they would keep Mortas occupied for a while, giving Rhoden the chance to make his move. His main advantage was that Mortas had no idea how to create the seam. Though he'd taken to practising magic over the past few years, his skill was low and his patience for the preciseness of the art was lacking. He tended toward the more powerful destruction spells rather than ones requiring finesse.

They parked in the crowded school lot and walked toward the football stadium. DeWayne paid for five tickets and they entered. Rhoden scanned the grounds for what he now understood were cheerleaders and this was a football game, a contest of strength and speed and shear brute force. From the little he'd seen so far, he thought he'd enjoy watching this football.

He spied the princess and climbed into the bleachers directly in front of her. They sat and watched for a while, before Mortas said, "Why have you brought me here?"

"The girl on the field in front of us. The blonde with her hair pulled back into what they call a ponytail, is the princess."

Mortas narrowed his gaze and leaned forward. He studied her for a moment. "How can you be sure?"

He held a hand out and DeWayne placed binoculars in the palm. He lifted them to his eyes and focused them on the girl. Once adjusted he handed them to Mortas.

"She bears the mark."

Mortas placed the glasses against his eyes and jumped in his seat. His hand extended as if trying to touch the image in front of his eyes. His fingers brushed the hat off the head of the man sitting in front. The man spun angrily.

"Hey. You looking for trouble?"

Mortas gave an evil smile. "I'm always looking for trouble."

"Oh yeah? Well, you found it, buddy."

He stood, fists clenched, ready to fight. The two men Mortas brought with him stood as well. The man on the right growled. The offended man froze seeing that both men were bigger than him.

DeWayne said, "They're not from here. It was an accident. He didn't mean anything by it."

The man looked down at Mortas, who flashed a wicked smile. He looked from the twin towers and said, "Well, okay then. As long as it wasn't done on purpose." He turned around, picked up his hat and moved several rows down.

The teams took the field and the cheerleaders broke into a chant. They bounced up and down, kicked and leaped. After the kickoff, as the cheers died, the princess set her fluffy flower like things down and reached up to adjust whatever held up her hair. The shirt with the big W on the front rode up exposing her firm flat stomach. However, it did not show enough to see the identifying mark.

As he had done on the first day, Rhoden cast a spell and the heavy shirt lifted high enough to cover her face, exposing much more than intended. On her left side was a light brown, semi-circular shape, about six inches wide.

Trying to get a closer look, Mortas leaned forward. He gasped and stared harder through the glasses.

"Have you seen the mark up close?"

"No sir, only from a distance, but I'm almost positive it's the mark—the half crown."

"We need to get up close to be certain."

A roar went up from the fans as the home team ran to the far end of the field. Rhoden didn't understand the game, but loved the full contact action.

Mortas stood. "We'll take her now."

Rhoden grabbed his master's arm and held tight. The man fumed at the touch. Fire flamed in his eyes.

"My Lord, this is a different world than ours. We cannot just march down and take her. The people here will react and stop you. It is better to take her when no one else is around."

"These peons cannot stand before my power."

"Possibly so, but look how many you'd have to take out before you got free. Is it worth the risk of failure? We don't know enough of their capabilities. Look at how many might descend upon us."

Mortas scanned the crowd. "What do you suggest?"

"I still have the Seeker overhead watching her. We follow her home and take her there, where fewer people will raise a hand to protect her."

Mortas looked at the princess once more. "That will work."

"Hey, buddy, you want to sit down so the rest of us can see."

Mortas shot the man a withering glare. A second man and a woman added their voices to the complaint.

DeWayne nudged Rhoden. "We should leave before this gets ugly."

"What does one's ugliness have to do with this?"

"Cause there's all kinds of ugly and one is when a crowd turns on you in such a way as to beat you ugly."

Rhoden looked at the angry faces around him. "We should go make preparations, my Lord."

Mortas took one more look at the princess, nodded and handed the glasses to Rhoden. He passed them to DeWayne. The four men walked down the bleachers leaving DeWayne to follow.

Chapter 28

They reached the van as another loud cheer rose from the stands.

"Where to, boss?" DeWayne said.

"Drive, I'll direct you," Rhoden said.

Rhoden connected with the Seeker and followed it to the neighborhood where he'd first discovered the princess. He instructed DeWayne to park several houses down from the target property. Lights were on inside the home.

"We should get inside before she comes home," Rhoden said. "We can take her in private then move her to the van."

DeWayne parked. Rhoden turned to face Mortas. "Sire, I'll take one of the men and secure the house. Once that's done we'll wait for her arrival. The driver can pull the van up and we can transfer her."

Mortas eyes narrowed. Rhoden spoke in a hurry to avoid the confrontation he knew was coming. "Sire, I'm trying to protect you. Although I am more familiar than you about this strange world, I still do not know what to expect. I have no idea of their capabilities. I would prefer to handle this first to keep you from danger."

Mortas gave an almost imperceptible nod. Rhoden turned to DeWayne. "When you see her arrive, move the car forward. Be ready to leave as soon as we're inside."

"Yes sir."

Rhoden exited and one of the bodyguards followed. As they

reached the house, the lights went out. He froze afraid they had been sighted. The house next door had a line of bushes at the front corner of its property. Rhoden ducked behind them to observe the house. Nothing happened for several minutes, but something about the scene looked wrong, though he could not put his finger on what. Without a word to the bodyguard, he crossed to the side of the house, then to the fenced yard behind. He scaled the fence and heard the bodyguard as his bulk made the fence squeal.

Rhoden was about to step toward the rear door, when the hairs on the back of his neck rose. His skin tingled with alarm. He called up a basic discovery spell and swept his right arm in an arc over his head, sending the energy outward. A fine green hue formed in horizontal lines along the house.

He shook off the momentary surprise, understanding now what had made him on edge. There were others in this world capable of magic. Or was this the work of one man? Of course Phetrix would set up protection for the young royals. Well, the old magician was no match for his skills.

Rhoden strode to the middle of the yard, scanned the entire width of the structure and spoke words in a language long dead, calling forth energies only few knew existed. Though this world's sources were weaker than at home, he was still able to draw what he needed.

Swinging his arms in opposing circles, joining the wrists at the completion of the move, he gave the words volume, then yanked his arms apart. Though unseen to the normal eye, the wards protecting the house were ripped open, leaving a large gap surrounding the glass doors.

Satisfied with his work, Rhoden stepped forward and tried the door. Locked. Opening a lock was child's play compared to dispelling a ward. But the effort it took to pass the wards took their toll. Rhoden was forced to rest a moment before opening the door. Not that it took much energy, but if he faced more magic inside, he wanted to be able to respond with power. He spoke the words, and reached for the handle. A spark lit, burning his fingers and repelling him backward.

Shocked and confused, he studied the structure while cradling his injured fingers, wondering what he had missed. With another wave of his arms he sent out another discovery spell, only to find the wards had re-established their position around the house.

The sight angered him. Phetrix was not in the same class of mage as he. His spells did not have the power nor complexity to stand before him. The thought was unthinkable. Once more he dispelled the wards and once more was repelled at the door. Whoever set these wards had superior knowledge and ability. Perhaps this world had mages of its own.

Shaking his hand, he once more found the wards had regenerated. This was impossible. He refused to accept Phetrix was his superior in anything.

"I'm going to cut the wards off. As soon as I do, you need to get inside the house by whatever means necessary. Understood?"

The big man nodded.

Rhoden prepared his spell and cleared his mind. This would take more effort than he predicted and may leave him drained. He made the gestures, but when it came time to pull his arms apart to cast the wards aside, this time, he held his arms wide to keep them apart. He strained from the effort. His muscles protested as if he were holding a heavy weight. The bodyguard picked up a chair and pitched it through the glass doors.

He then stepped through as Rhoden released his grip. Once an opening was made the wards would only cover to that point. He started forward as a violent explosion came from within the house and the bodyguard flew backward out of the building.

Rhoden paused staring open-mouthed at the bloody heap off mangled flesh at his feet.

"They told me you'd come."

The voice startled Rhoden almost as much as the explosion. He looked up to see a woman standing in the doorway brandishing what he assumed was a local weapon of some sort. Wisps of smoke curled up from the twin cylinders, their dark openings aimed at him. Without knowing what the weapon did, Rhoden dove to the side as another explosion occurred. A stinging pain ignited in his leg.

He rolled, coming to one knee. The weapon was bent in half, the woman worked with frantic movements jamming small cylinders inside the chambers. He had no idea what they did, but did not wish to find out. Unsure he had adequate power left to cast a spell strong enough to stop her from hurling the fiery bolts at him, he switched to the stored power in his ring, aimed it at her and spoke the word that released the energy. Two vivid red streams raced outward, catching the woman as if in a net and hurtled her back inside the house.

Rhoden raced forward, leaped over the blood-soaked mutilated body, across the threshold and went inside the dwelling. He slid a knife out from within his jacket. The house was dark, but something moaned and writhed to his left. He snapped his fingers and a small globe of light formed in his palm. He lifted his hand and pushed it forward, revealing the woman pinned against the wall, held in place by the red strands.

Her wild eyes went wider as he approached her. She struggled in vain, kicking her legs, but the harder she fought the tighter the bands became. She gasped for breath and ceased moving. She eyed him with mixed hate and fear.

"So, you are the guardian of the princess."

Before he could say another word, a light shown from outside the house. He stepped to the front window and spied a vehicle on the path next to the house. A sinister smile spread across his face as the princess got out.

"Too bad you failed in your duty."

Chapter 29

The door rattled as a key was inserted. The woman tried to cry out, but Rhoden silenced her with a backhand swipe, sending another red stream that slapped across her mouth. Her head bounced hard as the band stuck her to the wall, serving the dual purpose of knocking her out.

Rhoden stepped back into the shadows of the darkened house. The door opened and excited voices talked over each other. The princess entered, followed by a tall slender dark-skinned girl. The same one he had seen her with before.

"I know, right?" the second girl said. "He's so big and girl, those muscles."

The princess laughed, then froze, steps from the door. "Why are the lights off?" she asked.

"Was there a power outage?" the second girl said.

"Maybe. Mom. Are you here?" She reached for the light switch and flicked it on. It took a moment for her eyes to adjust, but the sight of her mother stuck to the wall two feet off the floor left the terrified girl speechless.

The other girl said, "What the ..."

A man stood in the door frame. In an instant he understood the danger and moved to enter. Rhoden swept his arm out and the door slammed shut behind the girls. They jumped and screamed. The man pounded on the door further exciting the girls into near hysteria.

Rhoden stepped forward. He grabbed the princess by the arm and pulled her roughly behind him.

"Wait. Who ...? Help! Shree."

Shree ran forward, grabbed Rhoden's fingers and ripped them back with such force one cracked. He howled in pain, his grip broken. The two girls ran for the door, as it burst open, slamming against the wall. The man stepped in, fire in his eyes and fury in his massive fists. He eyed the stranger in his house and without looking at the girls yelled, "Run!"

He advanced on Rhoden. Still fighting the pain and with his finger bent backward, casting a defensive spell would be difficult. He reached into a pocket with the uninjured hand and pulled out the amulet he usually wore around his neck, but before he could activate the power stored within, the man was upon him.

A fist struck with blinding speed, shattering his jaw and sending him sprawling. He tumbled in a heap beneath the woman's feet. The amulet flew across the room. The man paused, shocked at the sight of his wife hanging on the wall, her head lolled to the side, like some grotesque piece of modern art. Then the shock morphed to rage and he advanced with murder in his eyes.

Rhoden was too stunned to react. He attempted to crawl away from the crazed man, but he had nowhere to run. His hands extended for him and he whimpered in defense. But just as he feared the end had come, a savage blow was dealt to the man, driving him to his knees.

Behind him stood the second bodyguard, a man equal in size and ability. But, as he moved to deliver the killing blow, the guardian shot a foot back, connecting with the bodyguard's knee, driving it backward. The bodyguard let out a shrill shriek and dropped hard to the floor.

The guardian stood, shook his head once and kicked the guard so hard in the face it lifted him off the floor and slammed him down on his back. He paused over the man to ensure he wasn't getting back up, then returned his attention to Rhoden.

Rhoden crawled into a corner, curled his knees to his chest and cried out in despair. He wanted to close his eyes, to not witness what was about to be done to him, but they refused to obey. His panicked mind raced for a spell he could use without the use of his fingers, but none came to mind. In desperation, he lifted the hand with the broken finger and the ring. The guardian stormed forward, glancing once at his mate hanging from the wall and lifted his mammoth boot to stomp the life out of Rhoden. However, before the foot descended, a blinding white bolt of light, sharp as a physical sword, pierced him from behind. The tip protruded from his massive chest. He arced backward, his face contorted in a mask of agony. He emitted no sound other than a faint gurgling deep within his barrel chest, then the magical blade vanished and the guardian fell to the floor with a heavy thud, revealing Mortas, an evil sneer on his dark face and a glow of triumph in his eyes.

For a moment there was only silence, then, from the outer door, screams filled the house. The two girls stood on the porch, their hands bound by something unseen. Their faces contorted in horror at the fallen guardian. DeWayne stood behind them, his mouth agape, his face ashen.

"Come Rhoden," Mortas said, in a voice so deep and different from his own.

Rhoden wondered what demon Mortas made a deal with to wield such raw and powerful magic. Or perhaps he *was* possessed by some demon. One thing was sure. Rhoden had underestimated his king's power.

Mortas said,"Let us be away from this place."

Rhoden regrouped his runaway emotions and bottled his fear. He had never been hit so hard before. His jaw hurt, his finger ached and his body was drained. Standing, he clutched the injured hand and walked to the door. DeWayne was already pushing the girls toward the street. Mortas bent over his bodyguard, whispered a few words and snapped his fingers. The man's eyes shot open. He stood in a stiff manner as if someone else controlled his strings.

They reached the van and a strange new sound filled the night.

DeWayne said, "Someone called the cops, man. We gotsta go." Rhoden climbed in the front. The bodyguard sat in the back with the two captive girls, but Mortas, with a fire still lit in his eyes, stood waiting to see what would arrive.

"Sir," DeWayne said to Rhoden, panic replacing nervous. "He don't want to be messing with the police."

Rhoden leaned out the window. "Your highness, we have what we came for. Let us be gone."

Mortas blinked twice as if coming out of a trance. Without a word, he entered the van and DeWayne sped off, the sliding door still open and Mortas' head hanging out to see what was coming. Sirens growing in volume, the reflection of the police lights bouncing off houses on the next block, DeWayne made a sharp, angled turn at high speed, that rocked everyone back in their seats.

The girls screamed at the top of their lungs until Mortas grew annoyed. He looked at the zombie-like guard and mumbled something while he snapped his finger. The guard wrapped an arm around each girls' head and clamped a massive hand over their mouths.

Mortas faced the girls and waved his hands. He spoke several words and their eyes glazed over. The guard lowered his arms and sat back. They now had the same zombie expression on their face.

Rhoden pushed aside his pain and reflected on what he'd learned tonight about his king. The man had obviously been practicing dark magic. Creating a zombie took the skill of a higher-level mage. If Mortas could do that, he'd progressed much farther than Rhoden thought. What else could Mortas do? And what did the discovery of this new ability mean for him.

As the car raced toward their escape route, Rhoden wondered if he'd let slip his plans somehow. Clearly, the king had been developing his magic without Rhoden's assistance, or even discussing it with him. The thought gave Rhoden more than one bad feeling. He'd have to tread easy for the next few days and try to decipher what it all meant.

Chapter 30

Phetrix struggled with the knowledge Kol shared. Was it real? Did it matter where he gained it? He desperately wanted it to be true, but now he had a choice to make.

Would he chase after a rumor and seek the King and Queen or would he return to the seam and the other dimension to rejoin Samuel and bring the heirs back?

The choice was maddening. As he blindly walked along the hard packed dirt streets, he barely registered the commotion happening several blocks away. It wasn't until a wiry man slammed into him, knocking him over, that he realized what was going on.

"Sorry mister!"

The man, dirty with his ribs showing through a tear in his shirt, scrambled to his feet and ran away.

"Get back here you filthy rebel!"

Two guards dressed in black with the white snowflake emblazoned on their chests chased the man. Overhead, a Seeker flew across the sky.

Phetrix grumbled. The man might well have been a rebel, but he doubted if the man knew anything about the King and Queen. Their cause had attracted a great many people, mostly those who were crushed under the weight of Mortas's reign.

The guards followed the man around a corner. The Seeker screeched above and darted downward.

"Poor soul. Be free my friend."

Phetrix hoped the man wasn't caught, but felt the outcome was a foregone conclusion.

Returning to his thoughts, he wondered what to do with Kol's information.

He'd spent his life with the knowledge of the prophecy. When he discovered Erthic's ability, it was stunning. Never had he imagined he'd be the one to shepherd the chosen ones to maturity. Elysande's ability sealed their fate. He knew then they were in grave danger. Not that he knew an attack was imminent, but there had always been an undercurrent of discontent in the kingdom, it manifesting in the attack lead by Mortas.

"Whenever there is more than one person gathered together, there is always a chance of people getting angry," Samuel was fond of saying. It was his way of soothing Phetrix's fears that an uprising was imminent. As it turned out, it was, but with Mortas leading the way, it took on a more sinister tone.

"Mortas Frost," Phetrix mumbled. He'd made his way through Ulti and was on a lonely road which led to the mountains and his home within their slopes.

Mortas was an angry man and had always been for as long as Phetrix remembered. Serving within his army felt like the right thing until the evil side of Mortas reared up. When he looked back on his time with him, it was a wonder he hadn't seen the darkness earlier.

Phetrix risked drawing attention to himself and created a small ball of flame to light his way. He'd grown tired of traveling in darkness. Loneliness was a constant companion he wanted to be rid of.

The road wound through the forest, the darkness of night oppressive. Eventually, the road narrowed until it fell away to the foot of the mountains. Only those familiar with the path would notice it. Phetrix had used his powers to cover them as best he could without losing the path himself.

An owl sounded in the distance. Twigs snapped, making him spin toward the sound. *Did the Seekers spot me?*

Forcing the ball of flame to grow larger, he saw the source of his fear. A small raccoon scurried across the forest floor, chittering at his bright light.

Phetrix clutched his chest, letting the deep breath out he didn't realize he was holding in.

"I need to make things right. It's far past time I fixed what Mortas destroyed. The heirs are ready. They'll have to be. The rebels will need guidance, and I can do that."

He turned from the raccoon and found his way back home.

Inside the cave, he covered the entrance with a bearskin and ignited a torch. In the far back corner he'd hidden the journal Samuel left for him. Inside were spells and information regarding the other world. Phetrix dug out the book and sat next to the torch to read.

The rebels need guidance. They need hope. They need the heirs. If I could find the King and Queen, maybe I'd be able to find the other seam and take us all through it. With Samuel waiting, we'd have the power to overcome anything.

Phetrix opened the book, but the vision of the man running from the guards returned to his memory. He had to do something now to make things right. He had to act with an urgency he'd lacked for years. What good would the heirs be if there were no people to lead?

Tossing the book against the wall, Phetrix pushed his face into his hands. He'd had the ability to stop all this, if only he would've tried. With the powers he possessed, he should have been able to do more than whisk away the children with a few caregivers he forced into service.

Did he do the right thing? Had he miscalculated the lengths by which Mortas intended on securing his reign? Thinking of the rebel running from the guards, clinging to the hope that one day the nightmare would all be over, made him angry. Mostly at himself. He was better than that. He'd need to be to set things right.

Chapter 31

The day after Kol's admission, Phetrix awoke with a pounding headache. A thunderstorm erupted outside the cave, the thunder doing nothing to help his head. Rubbing his temples, he wove a spell of healing on himself that dulled the pain. Had another mage done the same to him, it would've rid him entirely of the throbbing.

However, it had been close to five years since he met with anyone from the Order. As far as he knew they were all dead, executed by Mortas.

Mortas decreed they be disbanded and labeled as traitors, with Rhoden the lone exception. Phetrix was in Ulti the day he heard the news, begging for alms and attentively listening to the crowd.

At first he heard it in passing.

"Did you hear Mortas has outlawed the Order?" one woman said to another as they walked by, ignoring the haggard looking old man Phetrix portrayed himself to be.

"But they've protected Chevalon since as long as anyone can remember," the woman replied.

"I know, but they've gone afoul of his ways."

Their conversation followed them, their words piquing his interest.

Another couple walked by, dropped a coin in his bowl, and were discussing the current situation.

"Can you believe it? He actually did it," the woman said to the man.

"He's gone mad with his own power. It's amazing what—"

Phetrix lost the rest of their words as others walked by, a concerned murmur rising amongst them.

He never thought it possible that the Order would be subject to the whims of a ruler. They were above petty political differences. That is, until Mortas disrupted the entire world order.

Even during the near civil war caused by Prince Hemeri and Princess Ninon, the Order remained neutral. They were above the fray and they were responsible for rebuilding what those two tried to destroy.

To hear rumors of its demise was disheartening.

Phetrix picked up his bowl and left his corner, seeking to validate the claims he'd heard.

Near the town center, a large group of people gathered as a crier sent by Mortas repeated his decrees.

"By the order of Mortas Frost, rightful ruler and sovereign of Chevalon . . ."

The crowd groaned at the words, forcing a grin on Phetrix's face.

"The Order of Mages, commonly referred to as The Order, is hereby banished and outlawed from the land. Furthermore, any who dare assist or openly aid the Order will face immediate punishment up to and including execution by hanging. The Order is an enemy of the Crown, and our benevolent leader Mortas Frost shall rid the scourge from Chevalon."

Phetrix pushed his chin back in place, his mouth opening wider as the man spoke.

"How could this be?" someone in the crowd said.

"What about Rhoden?" another countered.

An unease he'd never seen before rippled through the crowd.

"Mortas has lost his mind!" a man yelled, forcing the crier to stop repeating himself. Three guards rushed into the mass of people and dragged him away. The crowd grew silent and worried, their feelings evident in their scared faces as they watched the man pulled across the dirt street.

Clearing his throat, the crier began again. "By the order of Mortas Frost, rightful ruler…"

Phetrix shook his head and walked away, unwilling to concede the fact that Mortas crossed a line none had ever dared to cross. The Order was always there. It had protected Kings, Queens, and the common people since its inception. How could one man disrupt it all?

The reign of Mortas grew more worrisome by the day and the need to repair the damage done more necessary.

When he left the town center, he passed an old woman who winked at him. *Odd*, he thought, but continued on. At the next corner, she was there again, this time waving him toward her. He ignored the old lady and turned the corner, heading for the road out of the town.

When he got a block away, she was there again.

"Who are you?" he asked. "Why do you follow me?"

She approached him slowly, then her eyes flashed a bright blue.

"What?" he mumbled.

"Phetrix, come with me."

She turned abruptly and walked to a nearby house where she entered, leaving the door open. Hearing his name spoken aloud almost made him jump out of his skin. No one knew who he was, he was certain of it. Whoever she was, he had to find out what she wanted. Grasping a small amount of magic to protect himself, he followed her inside.

The door slammed shut behind him and a torch ignited to life.

"What's going on here?"

"Relax mage, you're safe here." The woman turned to him and her wrinkled face smoothed out, revealing a younger version of the woman. Her hair turned from white to dark brown.

"Who . . . who are you?"

"Mathilda, from the Order. Have you heard the blasphemy of Mortas?"

He slowly nodded, unsure what to think of the current situation.

"The Order has gone in hiding. You will do well to follow suit. You've been in the mountains, right? Good. Remain there as long as possible until we can sort this whole thing out."

"What 'we' are you referring to? Who are you Mathilda?"

"I serve the Grand Mage, Samuel. I hear you know his whereabouts?"

Phetrix gasped. He never realized Samuel would have more contacts back in this world. It made sense and he should have seen it sooner.

"I do. I met him once."

"Then you know the heirs are safe."

He nodded. At least he hoped they were safe.

"Our situation here is dire. The need for the King to return is greater than ever."

"Is he alive?"

"We . . . we've yet to find him. We have turned our hope to the heirs. Only they can repel the evil wrought by Mortas. We can help them."

"By sticking our heads in the ground and doing nothing?"

Mathilda stepped closer, her bright blue eyes piercing him. "By staying alive until the day comes."

When Phetrix finally left that meeting, his mind found it difficult to wrap itself around the current situation. The Order was aware of the heirs. They were now outlawed by Mortas. They wanted to stay hidden for what . . . a time in the future?

Thinking back on it now, it made his head throb harder. Though Mathilda was the last of the Order he'd met, he sure could use her power to rid him of the pain rattling inside his head.

The thunder boomed again outside and he closed his eyes, trying to will away the memories.

Chapter 32

Phetrix went into Ulti, preparing to take his street corner and beg for alms as he'd done for some time now, when he noticed guards harassing a couple. Initially he walked past, not wanting to engage them, but the further away he got, the more guilt crept in and forced him into action.

It had been a couple days since he met Mathilda, but he learned a couple valuable things from her. The first was that the Order remained alive, in one form or another. They were hiding in plain sight. Who knows how many he'd seen over the years? They were actively trying to find the King and knew about what he did with the heirs. No doubt Samuel played a major role in all of that.

The second thing he learned was how to disguise himself. Mathilda's magic fooled even him, and he should've known better. When they were talking, he studied the remnants of the spell and dissected them until he could cast it himself. Feeling he had a good grasp of it, he ran behind the nearest building into a deserted alley and cast the spell on himself, turning him into a younger man without a beard.

Once he felt sure it worked, he stepped into the street to confront the guards. More to test his magic than anything else, though helping the couple just made sense.

"What are you two doing to these people? What did they do wrong?"

One of the guards turned to him. "Leave us be! This is none of your concern!"

The woman looked at him with terror in her eyes. Her companion wasn't a large man and he seemed overwhelmed by the guards.

"I asked you two idiots a question. What crime could they possibly have committed that you fools felt the need to bother them?"

"Fools? Your tongue is gonna get you in trouble!" the other guard said. He was taller with a scar across his face.

"I won't tolerate your ignorance. Why are you messing with them?"

The guards tossed the couple to the hard dirt road and turned to him.

The shorter guard cracked his knuckles. "Ignorance? Mortas will not be pleased that we have people questioning his servants."

"I don't really care. What I do care about is why you find the need to bully these people. As far as I can tell, they've done nothing wrong."

He felt a surge of adrenaline course through him. It had been a long time since he found himself in a physical altercation. He didn't intend on this turning into one either, but the possibility made him ready just in case.

"That's our decision to make," the tall guard said. "Now you get to come with us!"

The guards moved quickly toward him, but Phetrix waved his hand and caught them in an invisible grip.

"What the--" the tall one said, "We've got a mage! Outlaw! You belong on the gallows!"

Phetrix waved his hand and stuffed both their mouths with air so they couldn't speak.

Turning to either side, he used his power to push the guards out of the street and into the alley. He turned to the couple.

"I suggest you two leave. The rebellion is alive. The heirs are returning. Quickly now, go! Spread the news. The heirs are coming!"

The pair picked each other off the ground and stared at him with wide eyes.

"The heirs?" the man asked. His question made Phetrix pause. Everyone knew them, didn't they?

"The children of King Artus and Queen Griselde? They live! They will restore this land to its former glory. Mortas will be vanquished."

The guards struggled against his magical grip, but Phetrix held firm. Fortunately no one else had come near them.

The woman seemed to understand him. "The heirs. Erthic and Elysande. They're alive? That means—" She slapped her partner's arm. "They live!" Hope flashed across her face.

"No go before more guards arrive! I'll take care of these two, but you have to go. I can take care of myself. Hurry. Spread the word. The heirs shall return!"

The couple nodded and ran off. Phetrix turned his attention to the guards.

"As for you two, I think you need to learn a lesson."

As he was about to let loose all his frustrations, he felt the concealment spell waver. *Oh no*, he thought. If his disguise vanished, he'd have no way of returning to the town later without being noticed. He had two choices.

He could dispose of the guards, killing them so they'd never be able to reveal his true self, or he could flee. He considered killing them the better option but before he could weave the spell to do so, a family walked by the alley and stopped, noticing how the guards were in a state of frozen movement. They had a young girl with them that pointed at Phetrix.

"Mage?" she asked in a sweet voice.

Her father glared at him, then yelled loudly. "We have someone from the Order! Guards! We have a traitor!"

Phetrix cursed to himself. He was there to help them! Mortas would never be the ruler they needed! He was a monster and must be stopped, why can't they see that?

He ran from the alley while the father raced after him, shouting and calling attention his way. Phetrix spun, cast a spell to trip him up, and ran away. The man fell to the ground and rolled to a stop. Guards ran after him, but he turned through narrow alleys and winding streets, eventually losing his disguise. He slowed his pace and stooped like an older man. Rounding a building, he took up position on the corner like he normally would and nervously waited as the guards ran past him.

He breathed a sigh of relief when they didn't recognize him and scoured the streets searching for the younger man he no longer was. It had been an interesting experiment, but he cursed himself for going too far. He should have known better. After fifteen years, many had given up on the return of the King and Queen. There were also those too young to remember a time without Mortas as the ruler and still others who had been under his rule for so long, the King was no longer relevant. A large portion of the population held King Artus to blame for their current situation. They felt abandoned, left to the mercy of Mortas and his minions.

As Phetrix settled into his begging position, he wondered if there would be enough support for the King to return. If the support had been there years ago, why hadn't he made the attempt already? Maybe the real reason was the people no longer stood behind him and accepted him as their rightful ruler.

All I wanted to do was help. Have we become so jaded that Mortas seems like the right choice for us? The rebels have been in hiding too long. The Order has lost its luster. Something has to be done. The heirs must come back to make things right.

Alone, he couldn't force the change Chevalon needed. With others, he'd be able to bring back the glory of the kingdom. He only hoped it wasn't too late.

Chapter 33

Three days after he attacked the guards, Phetrix returned to Ulti and the street corner he frequented. The day was warm and not a cloud drifted in the sky. It was almost enough for him to forget the dire situation the kingdom was in.

Then he heard the crier.

"Mortas is coming! Mortas is coming! Gather in the town square. Mortas is coming!"

People ran past him, jostling with one another to get as close to Ulti's central square as they could. Children cried as their parents dragged them through the throng of people. Mothers scolded their little ones, fathers laid swats to their bottoms.

Phetrix watched, anxiety growing as the crowd grew. *Why would he be here today?*

Ulti was a small town never gaining the eye of any ruler as far as he remembered, which is why he chose the place. It was far enough from the capital to avoid detection and other than the market, it wasn't of significance.

A shadow raced across the ground and Phetrix looked up. Five Seekers streaked across the sky, their black wispy forms a stain against the azure sky.

Oh no, are they here for me?

The thought of his actions against the guards causing all this worried him. Mortas was unpredictable and ruthless. If what Phetrix did brought his ire . . .

He packed up his bowl and joined the throng of people, pushing his way closer in order to hear what was to come.

The crier continued his calls. "Mortas is coming! Mortas is coming! Gather in the town square. Mortas is coming!"

Moments later, the Seekers swirled above the crowd, silencing them. Phetrix felt a nervous calm growing within the assembled people. They were just as worried as he was.

The guards sliced through the crowd to open a path. People cursed and shouted back at the guards who pushed them out of the way. Phetrix focused on the opening the guards held. It took several minutes before anyone appeared.

Then he saw him.

Mortas.

Clad in black armor, the white snowflake blazing bright on his chest, the sigil of House Frost. They were an old family from the far north. They claimed ancestry to the same lineage as King Artus though the connection was never substantiated. The Order kept identical records as those that were housed in the castle before Mortas destroyed it. Phetrix spent many days studying the unbroken line that connected to Artus and then the children. House Frost was never part of it. They weren't even married into the family as far as he could tell.

Mortas smiled and waved as he marched through the crowd. His massive black stallion, had the same arrogant air as its rider, it's sheen so glossy as to appear oiled. The people were quiet, a low rumbling reverberating amongst them as shock registered on their faces. Mortas stopped in the center of the crowd and coaxed his beast into a complete circle so he could view the crowd from his superior position

A cart was pulled in place by two horses and Mortas dismounted on to it. Once there, he raised his hands high and the anxious murmuring within the crowd ceased.

"My lovely subjects, it is my honor to visit your beautiful village." He paused and tepid applause greeted him. He continued, unphased by the response.

The smile faded for an instant, then he recovered. "Very well then. Let me get straight to the matter at hand."

"The King lives!" someone cried out. Phetrix whipped his head in the man's direction and watched as guards rushed at him and dragged him from the assembly. He screamed as they pulled him away. "The King lives! Mortas is a fraud! The heirs will return!"

The poor man. They'll kill him for sure, Phetrix thought.

Mortas grinned as they hauled the screaming man away.

"My subjects," he cried out, stealing their attention away from the man, "It has come to my attention that one of you is from the Order. One of you is a traitorous mage." A murmur rose amongst the assembly, people turning to their neighbors unsure what to think or do.

"I have decreed the Order to be a subversive organization that shall not be tolerated within my lands. You have heard the law spoken to you plainly. Because of this act, I have come here to snuff out this traitor and restore proper order to your town and my kingdom. If you do not produce this deceiver to me and my guards within a week, I will have no recourse but to garrison this town with my followers and enact martial law. I will not tolerate disobedience. I will not allow such sedition to go unchecked."

He paused, the words sinking in the crowd.

Phetrix felt ill. This calamity was his fault. His rash actions brought this punishment to innocent people.

"We'll find the mage," a woman cried out. Several others agreed, but not as many as Phetrix assumed would. Maybe they were ready for the heirs to return? Maybe they understood the evil Mortas to be.

Soon, others echoed the woman and swore to flush out the mage, making Phetrix's earlier optimism drop with each added voice.

Mortas raised his hand, quieting the crowd.

"I expect to find this traitor with your help. We cannot let this mage run amongst you freely. Whoever it is, they are dangerous and seek to pit you against me. They must be stopped."

He climbed down from the cart and followed his escort through the crowd.

Phetrix shook his head. How could the people buy his logic? Mortas was evil, how could they not see it?

As he left the assembly, Phetrix overheard several people talk amongst themselves.

"I'd never turn in a mage to that fool Mortas. He's done more harm than any ruler I've ever know," one man said. His companion, an older man agreed.

"The Order has always been looking out for us. I trust they're doing the same now."

A woman on the other side of Phetrix spoke to her children in a quiet voice. "You see a mage, you tell me. Don't share it with the guards. You hear me? They are good and honorable people protecting us from harm."

"Yes mother," the two girls replied.

Phetrix left the assembly with a renewed spirit. Whatever Mortas had done to try and crush his opposition was creating a different effect. If Phetrix could finally bring the heirs back, he'd have support for their cause. Time was running short. Action needed to be taken.

Chapter 34

Two weeks after Kol revealed his information, Phetrix decided to attempt crossing through the seam. It had been years since he had tried and there were few places left within Chavalon where he could perform the feat. The old burned ruins of the castle were no longer feasible, but a farm outside the city proper housed a location he could enter.

When he studied the book Samuel had him read, there were five locations within Chavalon where the older mage documented seams that led to alternate worlds. It was a three days journey from where he lived. Packing his belongings in a tattered leather bag, he slung it on his shoulder and left.

Seekers were a constant threat. Rhoden and Mortas forced the creatures to stay on constant vigilance. Until Mortas's appearance, he hadn't seen one in months, but he also stayed far away from most clusters of people as he lived within the wild mountains.

If he knew where the seams were, maybe Rhoden did as well. The wily mage wasn't as proficient as he with his powers, often resorting to storing energy within objects to assist him when he needed it. Phetrix had no need of such tricks. His power and knowledge were so great, he had all he needed. However, as late, he too had been storing magic, especially as he learned new spells he wasn't as used to casting on a more regular or practical basis.

Setting off at daybreak, Phetrix hiked down the mountain and entered the forest to the west of Ulti. He worked his way through thick brush and forest overgrown with thistle and vines. It was an unforgiving place, but afforded him the protection he desired from prying eyes of stray Seekers.

"Can Kol be trusted? Are his sources true?"

Phetrix spoke aloud, giving himself company along the desolate journey.

Could the drunkard be trusted? Was the King still alive? Maybe he ought to find him first instead of driving headlong into the tear and possibly giving away the location of the heirs.

After fifteen years of hiding, he wanted something different. "I must find them. Samuel sent me a message. I must heed it. What will come of Chevalon if I ignore his call?"

Birds chirped and rabbits scurried across dried leaves. The afternoon sun was hidden behind a canopy of bright green and Phetrix moved with a purpose through the forest.

He didn't fully trust Kol, but something about his conviction made him at least question it. If he was wrong, what did he lose? Living in the mountain cave brought him no closer to reconciliation with the King. If he did something, maybe he'd have a chance to approach the growing rebellion with the heirs.

"What am I doing? Running like a fool to try something that will probably kill me or get someone killed. Pah!"

A nearby squirrel chattered at him when he yelled out.

Ignoring the pest, Phetrix pushed his way through to a small stream where he rested and sipped the cool water.

Scanning the sky above for Seekers and the sun, Phetrix decided to stay where he was for the night. He got about as far as he expected and with nightfall, he dared not press his luck.

When the morning's crisp air awakened him, he set off again on his trek to the farm and the seam with which to travel to the strange world.

"How are we going to rid Chevalon of Mortas? What are we going to do once we bring the heirs back? Will they be ready?"

He hoped so. The entire reason they were whisked away was for their safety and training. As young as they were when Mortas attacked, they didn't stand a chance to defeat him. They were too young to realize the potential of their power. Hopefully over the years, Samuel would have them ready. Somehow.

Near midday of the second day, Phetrix stumbled upon a body.

"What is this?"

Cautiously, he approached the bloated and decaying body. It appeared to be a man much younger than himself. The man had been huge. Though animals and insects had been devouring it, the frame stretched well over six feet.

Phetrix scanned the area and noticed a charred circle nearby and when he looked at the entire area, he realized it was once a camp. Grass and leaves smashed in patterns showed where cots lay and people walked.

"They must have been here for some time. What were they doing out here?"

Holding his nose, he bent closer to the man hoping to discover what caused his death. There were no obvious signs of struggle or trauma other than a single hole in the center of his forehead. At first he thought it was from an arrow, but it was a perfectly round hole and appeared to have been singed on the inside as though from a bolt of fire.

"Rhoden? Mortas? There are few with this kind of power."

Phetrix moved the man's leather coat to the side and gasped.

"The story . . . it is true!"

The man wore a shirt of linen emblazoned with the sign of King Artus—the white stag.

"Impossible," he whispered. The symbol had been wiped from Chevalon by Mortas in the years following his overthrow. This man must have been part of the rebellion, but this far south?

"What if the King was here?"

It couldn't be true, and he knew it the moment he spoke it aloud.

"So who are you? What did this to you and where are the rest of your people?"

A chill went up his spine as he considered his discovery.

Then, a crash in the forest to his right startled him. He crouched, waiting for the intruder. Holding on to his powers, ready to strike at the unwanted visitor, Phetrix leaned closer to the dead, stinking body, trying to use it for cover when a man appeared. Laughing at himself, Phetrix rose.

"Kol? What are you doing here?"

Chapter 35

Kol embraced Phetrix, turning away from the dead body.

"I told you Pendra, my friend's story was true. Look at the evidence!"

"But why are you here? How did you find me?"

"Actually, I wasn't looking for you. I was trying to find the King to pledge my services to him once again, but all I found was this man. And you!"

Phetrix took a few steps away, pondering his next move. Should he tell him who he really was? How far did he trust Kol? Could he possibly be serving Mortas?

"Kol, tell me the truth. Tell me why you're here." Phetrix waved his hand, using a spell he hadn't tried in a long time. If successful, Kol had no choice but to tell the truth.

"I've already said. I'm here to pledge myself to the King." Kol's eyes glassed over as the spell took hold.

"What tavern did we meet in a few days ago?"

Kol cocked his head to the side. "The Winking Bear. Why?"

"Who is Mortas to you?"

"The no good bastard is an evil usurper, killing the royals for pleasure. He wants ultimate power for the price of royal blood. He's not my lord."

Phetrix turned, thought about what he'd do next, when Kol interrupted him.

"Pendra, would you join me? Come with me and we'll find the King. He lives, I know it!"

"Phetrix."

"What?"

"My name is Phetrix."

Kol's face scrunched. "I've heard that name. Everyone has. You can't truly be him. He was a wise—"

Phetrix raised his hand and produced a ball of light that hovered between them.

"Mage? You could say that."

"But how did you escape? The castle burned!"

"I'm not easily killed."

"But the children! Do you know what happened to them?"

Phetrix nodded. "They are safe, for now. At least, I believe them to be."

"Why hide this from me? We've been asking for alms together for a long time now. Why did you never share this before? Why would one of the most powerful mages of all Chevalon be reduced to beggary?"

Phetrix raised a hand to stop the questions.

"I'm in hiding much like yourself. Sympathizers to King Artus are not highly regarded these days. I prefer to keep my head on my shoulders."

"But you have great power! You could easily stop any attack!"

"I'm not invincible nor am I powerful enough to take on an entire army devoted to Mortas."

"But . . ."

Phetrix waved his hand and the light vanished. "I know where the heirs are."

Kol's eyes widened. "You do? Where?"

"Safe."

"Can we bring them to the King? If the rebellion knew they were alive, things might change quickly."

"Since when did you become such a noble supporter?"

Kol hung his head. "I've spent far too long with ale. I've tried to drown my past and run as far away from it as possible. When I was in that cell, something happened to me. Hearing that maybe the King still lived sparked a hope within me I hadn't known for years. Living as we have is meaningless. Living with hope, well that drives a man to do many wonderful things."

"Aye that it does. And that brings us to this place with this man, dead and stinking before us. He bears the white stag. If he wasn't with the King, then he was at least an ally."

Kol walked around the dead man, inspecting him carefully.

"All I see is a hole in his head. What do you think did such a thing?"

"I can conjure a spell producing tendrils of flame capable of doing such a thing. My guess is someone else has that ability as well."

"Rhoden?"

Phetrix nodded. "He's also ruthless enough to murder a man with his powers. I estimate he's been dead about three days. The growth around him and the rot taking over his flesh are no older than that."

"Where's the rest then? If a camp was here, where'd everyone else go?"

"Kol my friend, that is the mystery of the moment. Now, do we try and figure that out or do we seek the heirs and bring them back?"

Kol thought about the question carefully then answered. "The heirs. If the King has hidden this long without detection, he can do so a bit longer. If the heirs can be brought back, we will ignite a rebellion far more powerful than whatever it was that did that to the poor man," he said pointing at the dead body.

Phetrix smiled. "That's what I was thinking as well. Shall we go then?"

"After we bury him. We should respect our dead."

"That we shall. We can take care of our friend here and then we'll be off. Where we're going, you'll be amazed."

They spent over an hour digging a shallow grave with two thick branches they found and gently laid the dead man within. They covered him and said a quick prayer.

"Are you ready Kol?"

"As ready as can be expected. So tell me about where we're going."

"Words will never do it justice. When you see what I've seen, you'll understand."

They left the grave behind and together marched toward the north, toward the farm where Phetrix could open the seam and enter into a world far different than their own. Hopefully when they got there, the heirs would be ready. The vision Samuel sent him seemed to indicate something happened, but what?

Chapter 36

Phetrix and Kol moved carefully through the forest, their gaze constantly going to the sky, wary of Seekers revealing their movement. Kol kept up with Phetrix's pace, and soon they rested for the night, waiting till the morning to travel again. Once the sun rose, they were off, moving closer to the farm and the unknown beyond.

"Kol, how well did you know that person in the dungeon with you?"

"Not well. He and I had been there before, but that's about it. Why?"

"I wonder why you felt compelled to believe him? What was it about his story that made you think, 'Yeah, I can trust him.'"

"The detail of his story seemed too real. We both saw the result of it. He told the truth. That man we left yesterday is proof!"

"It's proof that the rebellion exists, and close to us. What if your friend was a spy? What if he was sent by Mortas to secure more important captives? I still don't buy the entire story, but I have hope the King lives. If not, we must unite the rebels to the heirs and reclaim this land. Mortas has done great destruction to it all."

"He has, huh?" The strange voice made both men spin in the direction from where it came. Two men in black armor with the snowflake of Mortas emblazoned on it were nearby, their swords at the ready.

"Who might you men be?" Phetrix asked.

"We do the asking, not you." The man was large with a stomach to match. His long hair was straight and greasy and scars ran along his face, indicating he'd seen many fights in the past. The other man was thinner, older, and had a gray beard that almost touched the tip of the snowflake. Both looked tired and weary.

"My name is Pendra and this is my companion Harold. We travel in peace, seeking food and shelter."

"Food? Are you daring to defy Mortas by growing your own without his consent? You know the penalty for that, don't you?"

Kol puffed out his chest. "Mortas cannot rule like this! He's not the rightful heir to the throne and his ways are evil. They bring a plague upon the land."

What was Kol doing?

"A rebel, eh? You ready to die for those remarks?"

The thinner man stepped closer. "You might not want to provoke my friend here. His temper is about as short as he is."

Kol stepped even closer. "The heirs will conquer this land and Mortas will be dead."

Oh dear Gods, what has he done?

"An interesting statement from a drunkard. A dark man stepped from behind a large tree. He wore a black brimmed hat and a heavy black cape, but had no emblem on his chest.

Phetrix felt Kol stiffen beside him. A quick glance showed Kol's color had drained. The sight was enough to pale his own face. The new arrival stepped closer. He oozed confidence. The sinister sneer suggested he was going to enjoy whatever was about to befall them.

Closer, Phetrix recognized him as the man from the tavern collecting money, though for what purpose, he still did not know why. Kol's words came back to him. *You don't want him. He works for Mortas. He'd cut your throat before you got your question out.*

The dark-complexioned man rested one hand on his sword and the other one on his belt. "I've been watching the two of you. I think you're up to no good. In fact, I'd go as far as to say you're conspiring to overthrow the King. A traitorous notion that will result in your deaths."

Phetrix tried to avoid a conflict, though he knew it was already too late. "Please, we don't want trouble. As this gentleman stated, my friend is a drunkard. He knows not what he's saying. We're just two beggars on our way to a new town."

Kol objected. "I am not drunk. I haven't had a drink in weeks. And I don't regret my words. You are the real traitors. You overthrew the rightful king."

The man laughed. "What you're forgetting drunkard, is that your king has been gone for fifteen years. Mortas rules now."

"Well, maybe not for long. Isn't that right, Phetrix?"

"Phetrix?" the dark man said. Suddenly he didn't appear to be so sure of himself. He slipped back allowing the two guards to have clearance. If the guards recognized the name they showed no sign.

Phetrix watched the reaction from the dark man and knew he had been outed. He had to stop him. If word got out that he was alive, and in the area, no one would be safe.

The heavier guard rushed toward Kol. Despite his bold words Kol was unprepared for an attack, his rusted sword still hanging from the rope he used for a belt.

"Treason like that deserves death," the guard said, raising his sword for what he surely believed to be an easy kill. "Do you have any last words?"

"I do. Goodbye," Phetrix said. The mage swirled his hands through the air creating a ball of wind and released it at the guards. The powerful blast knocked them both off their feet.

"He's a rebel! One of the wicked spell wielders!" the thin guard cried out. The two guards regained their footing and held their swords out, poised to strike.

Phetrix looked past them searching for the dark man, but he was gone, vanished like a spirit. He turned his attention to the two guards. they stood ready yet reluctant to resume the fight.

"Come with us and renounce your allegiance. If you refuse, we have the right to execute you on the spot," the heavier guard said.

"I doubt they'll comply, Neff," the thinner guard said, "Let's kill 'em now."

Neff, the heavier guard, rushed at the pair. Kol crouched, ready for the man, his rusted weapon ready.

Phetrix waved his hands again, using spells he hadn't touched in years. It was a risk to perform them out in the open like this. If the Seekers found him, they'd be on him quickly. With these two guards, he'd have to make sure they never made it back to Mortas. Then he'd have to find the dark man.

"Stand aside, Kol!"

Phetrix released a bolt of fire that struck the thin guard.

Neff stumbled as he watched his partner burn. "Kreen! No!"

Phetrix waved his hands and another streak of fire released from his hands and engulfed Neff. The large man screamed in agony.

"Hurry Kol, take one of their swords and finish them!"

Kol smashed into Kreen, knocking the burning man over, and wrestled his sword away. Once in his possession, Kol slammed the blade through the burning leather armor into the man, piercing his flesh and killing him instantly. He withdrew the sword and went after Neff.

The larger man fought against the flames, trying to pat them out.

Phetrix prepared another blast, but Kol stepped in his way as he was about to release it. Pushing his hands aside, he let it go above Kol's head, the flames streaking wildly above him.

Kol spun. "Watch it! You nearly—"

Neff struck at him with his sword, catching the man in the back, and making him fall to the ground from his weight. Kol struggled with the flaming man who seemed not to be bothered with the fire surrounding him. His flesh turned black and charred but he refused to stop.

Phetrix waved his hands again, ready to strike, but feared he'd catch Kol in the attack.

Neff struck Kol with his massive fists, blood bursting from his nose.

Releasing the flames, Phetrix waved his hands again and created another blast of air. He pushed it at Neff and it knocked the man off Kol.

Working fast, Phetrix wove a spell of lightning and let it fly toward Neff. It struck his flaming chest and exploded his insides, creating a massive hole where the snowflake was once displayed.

Kol regained his footing, wiping off the blood from his nose on his pants. "You got what you deserved!"

Phetrix wove his hands again, and let a spell of healing settle on Kol. "This might not work the best. My skill in healing was never great."

He watched as Kol registered the magic flowing over him. He could see in the man's eyes that it was working, though he didn't know how well.

When he was done, Phetrix scolded the man. "Don't ever do that again! What if a Seeker had found me? What if that wicked Rhoden had discovered me? We have to be more selective in how we handle them! At least until we get the heirs back. The dark man escaped. He'll be on the road in a hurry spreading word about us. We have to move. Once he alerts Mortas that I'm alive, he will flood the area with Seekers. We'll never be able to move without threat of being seen. "

Kol shook his head. "I know. But the time has come! You saw what happened at the camp yesterday. If those two had anything to do with it, we did a great thing. Even if they didn't, they earned it for who they follow." He took the sword, removed the scabbard from Kreen, and put it on his waist. Leaving the old one behind.

"Let's move. The farm is nearby. We'll be free of this soon and be in a world where my spells might not even work. I don't know exactly, but it's our only chance of making things right again." Phetrix marched off, knowing Kol was following. The man might not be the smartest, but it was good to have a companion. Where they were going, he'd need all the help he could get.

Chapter 37

DeWayne flew down the side streets and turned on the main road that would lead back to where he first picked the strange group up. He wanted to ask about his payment, but after witnessing what he had, thought it best to keep his mouth shut.

He glanced at Rhoden and spotted the finger sticking straight up. The site made him gag. He fought down the nausea, just wanting this nightmare to be over. The man mumbled something to himself, but he didn't want to look, fearing he'd see something far worse than a dislocated finger.

The girls were eerily silent considering their predicament. He looked in the rearview mirror and saw both of them staring straight ahead with blank looks as if drugged. A blue light reflected in the mirror. The cops had found them. He still had several miles to go before reaching their destination. "The police are following us."

Rhoden and Mortas swiveled in their seats to look behind.

Rhoden asked, "How much further?"

He accelerated. "Less than two miles." The look showed he didn't understand miles. "We're close."

The flashing lights gained on them. DeWayne could see more than one car pursued them. He swung around the corner, now blocks from his goal. The turn was at such a high speed, he could not hold the line. The van swerved, threatening to tip and roll. It bounced over a curb lifting everyone off their seats. He sideswiped the front of a brick building, sending sparks flying, before righting and driving down the sidewalk.

At the end of the block he veered into the street. With one block to go, the cops made the turn. They closed in fast.

DeWayne hit the brakes hard. With no one wearing a seat belt, everyone flew forward. Rhoden caught his weight by bracing his good hand on the dashboard, but his knees made contact and he cried out. Both girls ended up headfirst in the space between the two front seats. The bodyguard struck the seat in front of him head first, but Mortas appeared to hover above his seat.

"Hurry. Get out. They're right on top of us," DeWayne shouted.

The doors flew open all at once. Mortas glided out and faced the onrushing cars. Rhoden and the bodyguard pulled the zombie-like girls from the car and guided them toward where ever they were going. DeWayne watched in fascination, his fear subsided for the moment.

While Rhoden made strange hand gestures at the night air, the police screeched to a stop and multiple doors swung open. Shouts rained down on them. Everyone screamed for them to drop whatever weapons they possessed and lay down on the ground.

To Dewayne's amazement, the sky ripped apart. A long tear appeared like Rhoden had sliced through a canvas with a box cutter. He motioned to the bodyguard, who in robotic fashion tossed a girl over each shoulder and stepped toward the tear in the air.

The cops went ballistic in their commands and several broke cover from their cars and rushed forward. Rhoden, with his recovered amulet in hand, shoved his arm out like punching the air and the two cops flew backward. The other cops watched their comrades rolling along the ground in stunned silence. Then, as if an unseen director shouted 'action,' all hell broke loose.

Gunshots erupted and bullets filled the air. Rhoden made more hand movements. Whatever he did, the bullets missed him. Mortas grunted, and glanced at his arm where a stream of blood rolled down his sleeve. He gave it a look of curiosity, then a dark cloud shrouded his face. He shouted something in a voice straight from hell and flung his arms forward.

The first police car lifted off the ground and was flung hood over trunk through the air, landing on top of the second car, smashing both.

One of the police opened up with a shotgun. Rhoden backed up, his features strained with effort.

The bodyguard stuffed each girl through the tear. They disappeared from sight. He stood to the side as Rhoden climbed through, then waited for Mortas. With a one armed sweep, two more police cars went sailing sideways, crashing to the ground twenty feet away. He turned, appeared to levitate, then was gone. Before the bodyguard could step through, a barrage of bullets slammed into him. He dropped to his knees, held for a second, then fell forward onto his face.

DeWayne could not believe his eyes. His fear was so intense, thoughts were too difficult to form. His body vibrated with a violence that rocked the van. It wasn't the noise that shook him from his fugue, but the deafening silence.

The police approached with extreme caution. A face appeared to hang in the air suspended by some unseen force. Mortas glared at the cops. His eyes burned with a fire so intense, DeWayne imagined he felt the heat. The head swung in his direction and the eyes flared.

He screamed, ripped the stick into drive and jammed the pedal down. He was still screaming minutes later when he pulled to a stop, three blocks from his apartment building. He slumped in the seat, eyes still wide with fear and the scream fading like the end of a song track. He became aware of a warm wetness on his seat. At first he feared he'd been shot, then realized his bladder had released at some time during the ordeal.

With a glance at the mirror he discovered the rear window had been shattered at some point, too. His body was racked with a series of violent spastic convulsions. He had a strong urge to curl into a fetal position and suck on his thumb. His mind walked a narrow line between saneness and insanity. Part of his brain wanted to replay what he'd seen, but the other part fought to keep the scene hidden. Then, a new thought came to him. He helped madmen kidnap two girls, watched them kill a man, saw another two die, and was in the middle of a shootout with police—all that and he never got paid. The idea was enough to make him weep.

DeWayne had no idea how long he sat staring blankly, but somewhere, deep in his consciousness, the thought broke to the surface that he had to get up and out before the police found the car. As he sat up, he felt something stuck to his cheek. He brushed it off and it bounced on the seat. It caught his eyes and he gasped. It was a gold coin. He snatched it up and stared open-mouthed. He glanced down and found two more coins and something else—a stone of some sort that looked like a gem he'd never seen before. Not that he had much experience with gems of any kind. He held it eye level and stared mesmerized. It winked at him. A smile spread across his face.

He attempted to wipe the car down, but decided it wasn't worth the trouble. He left the keys in the ignition. It would be gone by morning. He zombie-walked home, praying he never saw Rhoden or, that crazed demon from hell boss of his ever again. Then, he focused on the gold coins and adapted his prayer to at least not for a while.

Chapter 38

Marvin Grant left his favorite after-work hang out, a cop bar called Fuzzy's. As a bachelor, most nights he ate dinner there and some nights imbibed a few more drinks then he should. Tonight was one of those nights. Though not drunk, at least to his definition, he might struggle to pass a field sobriety test.

He slipped into the car and started the engine. As he was buckling his seat belt the radio squawked requesting all available units and announcing a homicide and chase. He noted the location of the chase as the various cars answered the call and took up pursuit. It wasn't far from where he was at the moment. Although he wouldn't get involved since he'd been drinking, he decided to follow in case of an emergency.

He pulled Vega's Tic Tacs from the console and popped four, then did a u-turn away from the curb and headed in the direction of the chase. He drove fast, but not at pursuit speed. Ahead, a car raced past. He guessed it was the suspects vehicle. By the time he got to the corner, four squad cars whizzed past. He let them go, then made the turn. He didn't want to add his lights to the color display unless necessary, so he followed at a distance.

The squad car's brake lights flashed on in unison. Officers leaped from barely stopped vehicles. He pulled to the side of the road a quarter of a block away. The sound of gunshots echoed off the buildings. Grant unbuckled his seat belt, slid his service weapon from the holster and opened the door.

He had just placed a foot on the street when a squad car lifted into the air and crashed atop another one.

"What the hell was that?" he said, ducking to avoid stray bullets and other flying vehicles. He jogged to the sidewalk and crept closer, using parked cars for cover.

A police officer went flying through the air and smashed into a building. He hit hard and slid down the wall, landing in a sitting position before toppling over. More gunshots followed, including several shotgun blasts. Grant moved to where he had an angle for a shot. He didn't want to discharge his weapon especially having been drinking, but his brothers were in trouble. He took aim at a man who appeared to hover above the ground. He was so astonished by the sight he held his fire until the man disappeared into thin air.

A second man levitated off the ground. Grant took aim, but before he could pull the trigger, the two remaining squad cars skidded sideways, colliding with each other. The officers scattered to avoid being crushed. The second man disappeared, leaving the biggest man alone. He reached up to what looked like a tear in the air. A hand reached out of, what? To help the man up. Grant could not let the man escape and his fellow policemen were no condition to stop him.

He aimed his weapon, a gun he'd never fired outside the shooting range, and pulled the trigger three times. The body jerked, took a step and dropped to his knees. A face that floated in midair, sans torso or legs, glowered at him. Then with a sudden flash, was gone like some illusionist vanishing from a stage.

A car, the one that transported the disappearing men, raced away from the scene. Grant raised his gun, but the car was around the corner before he had a chance to sight. He stood and walked dumbfounded toward the fallen man. A few other policemen got up. They challenged him, ordering him to drop his gun, until he showed his badge. He stepped over the body of the man he shot, kicked away the gun lying next to him and bent to check for a pulse. He found none. Fifteen years on the job and the first time he had to use his weapon he killed a man.

There would be all kinds of investigations, not only into the events that transpired before they got here, but also with all the bizarre things he'd witnessed, along with the shooting. If he feared being busted for drinking, the things he witnessed had long ago shocked him sober. He holstered his gun and went to assist the injured. It was going to be a long night.

Chapter 39

It took two days for Phetrix and Kol to reach the farm. He'd not been there before, but Samuel's instructions were clear. The farm looked exactly like how he described it in his journal, all the way down to the dark orange color of the barn.

"Phetrix, are you sure about this? What you say sounds unreal."

"Kol, I know it can be difficult to understand, but I swear to you it's real. I've seen it. I've been there once. The heirs are there. By now they should be . . . eighteen years old? If I'm figuring things correctly that is."

Kol shook his head. "It's too much to grasp."

"You'll see. And then . . . we'll have work to do."

They marched through tall grass and headed for the northwest edge of the farm where a boulder jutted from the ground.

Kol seemed nervous, maybe even worried about what was to come.

"Phetrix, why don't we just connect with the rebels and fight Mortas? With your powers, surely we could cause damage."

"Without the heirs, it's meaningless. The prophecy—"

"Don't tell me you believe those old stories?"

Phetrix stopped and regarded the man.

"Of course I do. It's why I've done everything I have. It's the *only* reason I still breath. Have these past years not proven how true they are?"

"These years have proven how inept Mortas is. It proves how corrupt a man he is, but it doesn't prove the prophecies are true."

Phetrix shook his head. "Then stay here. Go fight your meaningless battle and lose your life for nothing. I choose to fulfill the prophecy and bring back the heirs. Only once they return can we defeat Mortas and restore the land. Believe me or not. Help me or stay. No matter your decision, I will continue on to fulfill my duty."

Kol waved him off. "I have no connections here. If you believe so strongly, I should at least hang around to see if it happens. What's the difference between a fight here or a fight at this other place you say exists?"

Phetrix smiled at the man. He had a point.

"I promise you won't be disappointed by the strange world we're about to enter. It's like nothing you've ever seen."

The late afternoon sun hung in a blue sky streaked with clouds. It was a cool day and the birds in the far off trees sung softly. For Phetrix, it was an ideal afternoon. What he was about to try would change the world he knew forever. He'd either succeed in his quest, or he and Kol would die in a foreign land as defeated foes. He stopped and closed his eyes listening to the birds. He might never make it back here and he wanted a memory to cling to.

"Are you alright? What's wrong?"

"Nothing at all. I wanted to grasp Chevalon one last time, just in case."

Kol shielded his eyes and scanned the fields around them. "A farm. Your last memory might be a farm. Too bad it wasn't a tavern or something with a bit more atmosphere." He smiled and clapped Phetrix on the back.

They moved closer to the boulder. "This is the place. Are you ready Kol?"

"No. But don't let that stop you."

Phetrix closed his eyes and swirled his hands in the air, remembering the motions he used many years ago to open the seam while in the castle. At first, nothing moved. The air was still and the birds went silent. Then, with a loud crack and a bright flash, a line of light emerged. It stood taller than either of the men. It shimmered and then expanded, opening wider.

"By the gods," Kol said softly. "What is that place?"

Phetrix opened his eyes to see a bustling city with buildings much larger than anything he'd ever seen in Chevalon. Wheeled chariots raced across streets that were smoother and cleaner than those within their cities.

"What is that place?"

"It's a strange world, unlike ours. There are more people than you can imagine. The heirs are hidden there."

"What's the name of the place?"

Phetrix smiled, recalling the name scrawled in Samuel's journal. "That place is called Chicago."

Phetrix released his spell and the seam wavered, but held strong. "We need to go through. Stay close to me once we do. I've been there once and it can be overwhelming. We'll need to find different clothes quickly. We won't fit in looking like we do."

"Yeah, sure," Kol replied absently. His eyes were fixed on the scene showing through the seam.

"Shall we?" Phetrix stepped into the seam and his foot set down on a hard surface made of what looked to be stone but was wider and flatter then any he'd known. He turned around and Kol was still on the other side of the seam.

"Kol, come on! It won't stay open for long."

The man looked like he was about to flee.

"Hurry Kol! It's the only way!"

Kol sighed and closed his eyes, mumbling something Phetrix couldn't hear. Then he looked through the seam at Phetrix.

"I'm ready."

Kol walked forward, but the seam started to shrink and narrow.

"Oh no! Kol, the seam is closing! Run! Get through before it closes!"

Kol ran and tripped over something in the grass.

"Kol!"

Fortunately, he landed on the other side of the seam moments before it sealed shut.

He made it.

Chapter 40

Samuel slowed the car at the cross road, peering down the street to the house where Princess Elysande and her guardians had been living. Police cars and emergency vehicles swarmed the area. Their street was blocked by the mass of vehicles. He had no way of getting inside to discover the amount of destruction and death that had occurred.

Two men guided a gurney down the front walk toward a waiting ambulance. The body was not observable, being inside a black bag. Judging by the mound the body inside created, the deceased was quite large. He thought of Markus, the guardian he had coerced initially into protecting the princess, and prayed he wasn't the victim.

Two men in suits stepped out onto the front porch. One was short, stocky and black. The second man might have been the first's brother, in physique and mannerism, except for the skin color. They spoke and the black man glanced back inside the house, while his partner shook his head and dragged a hand over his head. Samuel took the gestures to mean, whatever happened inside had been either inexplicable or grotesque, maybe both.

They stepped aside, to allow a second gurney to descend, this one also carrying a bagged body of an approximate size as the first. His fear grew. Markus may not have survived the encounter with whoever came calling. Were the assailants from this world or the other? He wasn't sure why he held onto that hope—that it might have been a break-in gone bad. In his heart, he knew the truth. The princess had been discovered. The only question left was whether she was there when the attack occurred or elsewhere. He had to find Alyanna, the other guardian.

As if on cue, she was led out by a male and female EMT. Samuel let out a long breath of relief. But if she was here, where was the princess? She was never supposed to be out of their sight, even if the girl was not aware of their scrutiny. Did that mean she'd been here? For once, he prayed they had allowed the girl to go out unprotected. He studied Alyanna. She looked shaken and leaned on the EMT's for support, but otherwise appeared uninjured. Her head hung as if incapable of holding it erect. Perhaps it was from the knowledge she failed to keep her charge protected.

The black detective stopped them for a moment, said something, then motioned for a uniformed officer to accompany them. They climbed into the back of a waiting ambulance. Minutes later, the EMS vehicle drove off. Samuel followed. He had to speak with Alyanna. He had to know what he was dealing with.

He parked in the hospital lot and watched as Alyanna was placed in a wheelchair and taken inside the emergency room entry. The cop followed close behind. Samuel worked up a plan and exited the car. He rushed through the doors in time to see Alyanna wheeled through double doors at the rear of the room. He went that way to catch them, but a nurse stepped in front of him.

"Can I help you, sir?"

"Ah, they just brought my niece in. I was trying to catch them."

"She's being taken for examination. If you want to sit in the waiting room, someone will let you know when she's through."

"But . . ."

"Sir, there's nothing you can do for the moment. You are not allowed back there right now. Please, take a seat." She pointed behind him to the rows of mismatched seats and gave him a look, that said, 'Don't challenge me.'

His shoulders slumped. He turned and walked, glancing over his shoulder. The nurse had been expecting something and stood with arms folded and an 'I dare you,' look. He sat.

More than two hours later, the nurse came over and said, "Your niece has been taken to a room. They're keeping her for further evaluation. She is in room three twenty-two. You may not be able to see her yet, but you can check in at the nurses station and wait upstairs."

"Thank you."

Samuel found the elevators and rode to the third floor. He ignored the nurse's station and hunted for the room. He didn't have to look hard. The cop stood guard outside her door. He hesitated, then proceeded. It was perfectly normal for a relative to be here and want to see the patient.

He nodded at the cop and turned to the door. The man extended an arm to block his path. His other hand slid to his weapon. "I'm sorry, sir, No visitors."

"But, I'm her uncle."

"I understand, sir. But for the moment she is off limits to everyone including family until the detectives can speak with her."

"This is outrageous. She's my niece and I want to see her."

"I understand, sir, but no matter who you are, I'm not letting you in. You need to lower your voice and go sit down in the waiting room. Someone will inform you when she can have visitors."

Samuel stood gaping at the man, not sure what to do next. He could get into the room with ease if he wanted, and he did. With a glance up and down the hall, he quickly formed a plan. He went to the waiting room, found a red plastic chair and carried it back. The cop stiffened when he saw him approach.

"Sir, you don't want to make this a problem."

"Not at all."

He set the chair down against the wall next to the door.

"You can't sit here, either."

"The chair's not for me."

The officer's brows knitted. "Who's it for?"

"You." Samuel smiled.

Whatever the cop saw in that smile caused him to reach for his weapon. Samuel mumbled a few words, waved his hand in front of the man's face as the gun slid from the holster, but before he could bring it up, his head lulled to the side. Samuel caught the man before he collapsed and dragged him to the chair. He sat him down, then holstered the gun. With another quick glance down the halls. He entered the room.

Chapter 41

He closed the door and stood studying the woman in the bed. He wanted to feel compassion, to comfort her agony, but the princess might be in danger and this woman was to blame. She cried softly, unaware of his presence. He stepped closer to her until she noticed. Her head turned. Within seconds of recognizing him, she burst into tears. He advanced to calm her. Sobs racked her body. The heart rate rose, the intervals between beeps decreased.

"Oh Samuel," she extended a hand to him. He let it hang, angry with her failure. "They have her."

"Who has her?" his tone harsh.

She pulled her hand back. "The mage came for her. They killed Markus," she screamed his name.

He stepped to her bed and glared at her. She cringed and withdrew to the far side, wincing from the effort. The pain made her gasp. She clutched at her side. A red welt stretched across her face. Her chest was bandaged, perhaps indicating broken ribs. She had at least put up a fight.

Samuel allowed some of the anger to drain. She would have been no match for Rhoden. Their best hope of defense had always been not being discovered. He trained the guardians as best he could, but in the end, it was never going to be enough. He blew out a breath allowing the hostility to go with it.

"Tell me, Alyanna. What happened?"

She explained adding how she killed one of the bodyguards. But once Rhoden entered, he incapacitated her. Unfortunately, she had been rendered unconscious and never saw what happened to the Princess. Had Rhoden managed to escape with her or was he still in this world? He needed to go. To plan for either contingency.

"You did the best you could, Alyanna. Rest. Get well." He turned to go.

"Samuel, Markus is dead."

He didn't respond, nor did he look at her.

"We gave up everything for you. Our homes, our futures. Our lives."

He spun now, anger driving his words. "You gave up nothing. You would have been killed or enslaved had you stayed. I gave you a life, a future. Am I upset Markus is dead?" He paused, his voice softened. "Yes. But I have to find the princess. If I succeed, there will be time to mourn him later. If I don't, it won't matter since I will have joined him." He opened the door. "Be well, Alyanna."

MARGARET STERLING WALKED out of the conference room and down the hall toward the lab. She just finished yet another long explanation of what happened the day of the so-called fire. Still no cause had been determined, but fortunately, neither had any damage. She was tired, not just physically drained, but mentally exhausted and fed up with having to explain her actions. It wasn't her fault some old geezer got into the lab. *She* certainly didn't admit him.

She made a turn and ran into a man.

"Oh, excuse me," she said stepping away.

"My fault entirely," the older man said. "Pardon me."

He moved away from her down the opposite direction. Clearly something pressing was on his mind. She made it two more steps before a nagging in a far corner of her brain slowed her steps. She was brought to a halt three steps later as the nagging notion took root and fought to the surface. Five seconds later she had it and whirled to give pursuit. She raced through the door dodging past incoming and outgoing patients and finally stood out front scanning the parking lot.

"No, I'm not letting you get away this time," she muttered, determined. Still, not finding him, she pulled out her cell phone and dialed the number of the detective who'd given it to her. She expected it to go to voicemail, but to her surprise was answered on the third ring.

"Grant."

"Detective, I don't know if you'll remember me, but this is Margaret Sterling from City Hospital."

"Sure, Ms. Sterling. I remember. what can I do for you?"

"That man came back. The one who was in the lab the day of the fire. I just saw him leaving."

"Can you see him now?"

"No, but he only just left."

"I'm close. Where are you?"

"Out front."

"Wait there."

SAMUEL SAT in the car contemplating his next move. He took out the cell phone from a jacket pocket and stared at it for a moment. Such a strange item. Had he not been forced to live in this world for all these years, he never in his wildest dreams would have thought of such a thing.

He typed in a number from memory. Dina answered on the first ring.

"Tell me you still have the prince."

"Yes. Why?" A note of panic crept into her voice. "What's happened?"

"They found and took the princess."

"Oh no. Did they cross back with her?"

"Unknown. I'm going to find out, but I need you to put the emergency plan into effect. I can not be sure they have not discovered you, too. Go to the safe house, use the security I showed you. If you do not hear back from me. You are on your own."

"Understood." She hesitated and he could hear in the silence she had something more to say. "Speak, Dina."

"Don't you think it is about time the prince knew the truth?"

"If I do not come back, use your best judgment as to what you do or what you tell the prince." He was about to disconnect when he changed his mind. "No, get him out of town now and then tell him.

Tell him everything, then increase his training. It will be better if he is involved in his own defense."

"Samuel."

"Yes?"

"Good luck."

He disconnected. If Rhoden had already secreted the princess through the seam, he would need a lot more than luck. He drove out of the lot as a police car approached, lights flashing, siren wailing. He braked, let the unmarked car pass, then drove on.

Chapter 42

Grant screeched the car to a stop in front of Margaret Sterling as she waved her arms frantically over her head. He hopped out of the car and ran to her.

She ran to meet him, pointing toward the street. "You just missed him. He just left the lot. He turned left."

"Did you notice the type of car?"

"It was a green four door. I think a Buick. You should still be able to catch him."

Grant didn't reply. He whirled back into the car and sped away. Once he reached the street he lit the light and made the turn. The green car was not in sight. He doubted success, but after the night he'd had already, he needed a win. Ten minutes later, he pulled to the side of the road and pounded the steering wheel.

SAMUEL MADE a stop at his apartment and gathered the items he had both saved and collected should he ever have need to cross through the seam again. In truth, he'd been back several times, to keep in contact with those still loyal to the crown, but none of those trips required him to do what this journey called for.

He was getting older and was sorely out of practice. He wondered if he still had the ability to deal with this threat or if his time had finally come to an end.

The car nosed up the ramp of the parking garage. He parked on the fourth of six levels, to the far right. He stripped out of his suit and shoes and replaced them with his robes and boots. The clothes and other items of this world were locked in the trunk.

GRANT MADE A U-TURN, frustrated and thinking about going back to Fuzzy's. He no longer wanted to face sleep sober. He debated going back to the hospital, deciding instead to report his failure to Margaret Sterling by phone. At a stop light, he slid the phone from his pocket and glanced down to find the number. When he looked up, a green car had made the turn on the road out in front of him. It could be the same car, but it was going in the opposite direction. Still, wanting something to go right today, he decided to follow. He put the phone down on the passenger seat and turned on lights and sirens. He was the third car in line and had to wait for the cars in front of him to move to give him the room to go around them in the oncoming lane. The maneuver cost him several precious seconds. It took him a moment to find and lock on the green sedan, then it was all out pursuit.

He cut the distance in half and spotted the green car turning into a parking garage.

SAMUEL STRODE to the partial wall. This was the tricky part. The top half was open and he now faced a twenty-story office building. Normally he would wait until dark, but he could not afford to delay. If the princess had been taken, he had to get to her as fast as possible before that monster, Mortas got a chance to play with her and create a royal minion that would sway the people to give up the rebellion.

He dared not enter through the original seam, knowing Rhoden would have an ambush waiting for him. Through the years he'd searched for another path across. It had taken a long time and cost a lot of energy and strain on his brain and heart. There had been two false paths, one leading to a desolate world of harsh winds and torrid heat, the other an icy world so bone chilling his face numbed just peering through the seam.

However, he did find an alternate route, six of this world's miles from the original entry point. He used it once. The only other person with knowledge of the seam was Phetrix and an old man who lived on a farm not far from where he would enter. That man was his conduit to the rebels loyal to the king and queen.

As he took one long last look around the garage and the world he could see beyond, he heard from somewhere on one of the lower levels a car was coming fast, the tires squealing in protest. He then began the spell that could lead to his death. As the seam opened, his gaze rested on a window seven floors from the ground in the office building. A woman stood watching him, a mug of something in her hand.

She waved at him, evidently thinking his gesticulations were the like. He gave her a quick wave, stepped up onto the concrete wall, and stepped out into open air. His last sight of this world was the woman's horrified face, perhaps thinking he was about to commit suicide. As the seam closed behind him, he wondered what she thought now.

Grant found the car on the fourth level. He'd entered sans lights and siren, not wanting to spook the driver. He braked and scanned the garage, but the man was nowhere in sight. Had he changed cars and escaped past him? No, he didn't remember a car going the opposite direction. The only other choice was if he went up. Two more floors lay above.

He started moving and then slammed the brakes fast as he caught sight of the man standing on the edge of the half wall.

"Oh, don't tell me he's gonna jump." He slipped the stick into park and got out, mumbling "can this day get any stranger?"

As he ran the man waved to someone in one of the office buildings. He didn't have the angle yet to see who. In front of him, just beyond the wall, trees appeared, then he saw a what looked like a very old barn. They appeared out of nowhere and seemed to float in the air. What the hell was going on?

Grant ran around the green car and toward the man who looked oblivious to his presence. The man calmly stepped off the ledge. Grant screamed, "No!" But he was too late. The man was gone. He reached the wall and looked down. No body was in sight. He leaned further for a better angle. Nothing. Where did he go? he looked out straight off the wall looking for the tree and barn, but they had disappeared as well.

"I'm losing my mind."

He glanced up and spotted a woman pressed against the glass of the building across and above him. He lifted his arms in a shrug. She shook her head and returned the shrug. Now he regretted asking if the day could get any stranger. It just had.

He climbed back in his car and sat wondering what to do. A car came up behind him and honked. he wasn't ready to move so motioned him around. He sat in the car running through the events of the day. The flying cars, the disappearing men. Now this guy vanished. Had aliens come to the planet?

Finally, he decided to go down and check the sidewalk to verify the man had not plunged to his death. As he drove away a shouted voice caught his attention. Grant hit the brakes and looked for the source. In the rear view mirror, two men came into view in the same place the other man had disappeared. Both were dressed in shabby clothes and looked like homeless men. What caught his attention though was the sword one man carried.

"Oh hell no. This can't be happening."

He exited the car and stared over the roof at the two men. His first thought was he needed a drink. His next was this was going to be a long night.

Capture

THE SEAM TRAVELERS BOOK TWO

RAY WENCK
JASON J. NUGENT

CAPTURE

THE SEAM TRAVELERS
BOOK TWO

Chapter 1

"What the hell is going on here?" Detective Grant said to himself. A minute ago, a man—a person of interest in several cases that may all be connected—jumped off the cement barrier surrounding the third story of a downtown parking garage. Before Grant had a chance to run to the spot and peer down at the remains, two men appeared, *poof!* as if by magic. They were just—there. A horizontal line appeared, like someone had cut the air with scissors. Then the two men stepped through, and there they were, like they'd stepped out of the set of some fantasy movie featuring Hobbits and wizards.

The older man looked stunned. The younger one looked insane. Their appearance suggested they'd been living on the streets for years. Not wanting to deal with homeless men, Grant might have left, except that the man disappeared, and not long ago, he'd seen a similar sight. A line split the world where three men stepped through and vanished, taking with them two high school girls. *Poof!* Gone. Just as the other man had done seconds ago, and now these two. *What the hell was going on?* It was enough to make him want a drink—and he didn't drink.

Grant noticed the two men were armed. Each had a knife on their belt, and the younger man also carried a short sword. Grant slid his weapon from its hip holster and pressed it against the back of his leg. Then with caution, and what he recognized strangely as fear, he approached the vagrants.

The older man broke from his fugue first. Spying Grant, he raised an arm, "Ah, kind sir. We are in need of some assistance."

Grant didn't doubt that. He was thinking the psychiatric kind. They looked like rejects from a fantasy role-playing game. "Are you looking for a Dungeons and Dragons campaign?"

The question stymied the man. "I can assure you I'm neither looking for a dungeon or a dragon. Ha! As if dragons existed."

The other man looked confused. He kept turning in circles, examining his surroundings. He stopped for a moment and placed a hand on the car next to him. He caressed it like it was a living thing. Grant thought he must be on something.

"We're looking for someone. A man named Samuel. Can you direct us to him?"

Is this guy kidding me? "What? You know how many men named Samuel live in a city this size?"

"Oh, I hadn't thought about that."

Then a connection was made. An idea bloomed. "Wait. This Samuel. Is he an old guy, like you?"

"Oh, heavens no. He's much older than I."

A curious response. This guy looked to be sixty. How much older was this Samuel? Grant recalled the details of the vanishing man. "Is he short? With a belly and white hair? Wearing a suit?"

"Yes, he is short; at least shorter than I. His hair is white, and of course, he has a belly. How absurd that he wouldn't! As for the suit, if you mean armor, I doubt it. But if you mean something else, then perhaps."

Grant frowned. This was getting him nowhere. "Where'd you come from?"

The question took the old man by surprise. "From right here."

Something in the man's eyes told Grant he was lying. "You just appeared. I saw you step through a…ah…I don't know. A slice or a seam or something. As if you were entering this world from another." He glanced down as if surprised the words had come from his mouth. "Now I sound as crazy as they look," he muttered to himself.

The old man moved, drawing Grant's attention. A sparkle appeared in the eyes, giving him an intelligent yet mischievous appearance. Instinctively, Grant raised the gun. The old man froze. The glint in his eyes was gone. He glanced from the gun to Grant. "Did you see Samuel, then?"

"If Samuel is the short white guy with the white hair, the belly, and the suit, then yes. He stood on that ledge right there and stepped off into midair. He vanished the same way. Then Shazam! Here you two were."

The old man tapped a finger to his lips, his expression thoughtful. "I see."

"I see, too. I see that something's wrong, here. I need to see your ID."

"My ID? What is that?"

"Are you telling me you have no identification?"

"Oh! You want to know who we are. Very well. I'm Phetrix. This confused man is Kol."

"And I'm just supposed to take your word for it?"

"Of course. Why wouldn't you? We are who I said we are."

"No. That's not gonna fly. If you can't show me some form of ID, the two of you are coming with me to the station. We're gonna have a nice sit down and discuss this Samuel and where you two came from."

"As lovely as a nice sit-down sounds, I'm afraid we're going to have to refuse. We have too much to do and we need to find our friends."

"Friends? You have friends other than Samuel?"

"Yes. And they need our help. We have important information they need to keep the–" He stopped speaking suddenly, as if afraid he'd revealed too much. "Anyway, thank you for your assistance. We must be going."

Grant took up a more defensive position. The gun was pointed at the old man's chest from a distance of six feet. "No. You're coming with me." He reached behind him and unsnapped the cuffs. "You," he said to the second stranger, his voice more commanding, "Come here. Both of you. Turn around."

"Sir, I'm trying to explain. We don't have time for delays. Someone important to us may be in peril."

"You can tell me all about it once the cuffs are on."

The old man shook his head, annoyed. "I'm sorry, but you leave me no choice." The old man mumbled something and made a strange motion with his hand, then –

Grant shook his head as if coming out of a trance. Thoughts ran through his mind in a flash. The two men. He looked. They were no longer in front of him. He whirled, fearing they had gotten behind him. He saw no one. Feeling both panic and fear corral him, he spun in all directions, scanning the garage. How did they get past him? Why didn't he remember seeing them move?

Grant hopped into the car. He made a fast turn, squealing the tires on the concrete, then sped down the ramp. His head pivoted side to side in search of the men he now considered fugitives. By the time he reached the street, he knew he'd lost them. *How had this happened?* Answer: he was losing his mind.

He pulled into the street, swung wide and turned back onto the ramp. He stopped in the same place, got out, and walked to the wall. He felt the space above and beyond. If something was there, it was no heavier than air. *Well, of course not. These people are messing with your mind.*

Grant glanced down. No body lay splattered on the ground. Determined to discover the secret, he stepped up on the wall. His hand pressed hard to the support wall running above to the next level. Again, he felt the air. As if moving with a mind of its own, his leg stretched out in search of the opening to the other world.

Maybe he needed to let go. Perhaps the opening would appear and catch him. He stopped himself from doing such a stupid thing, but only barely. He *was* losing his mind.

In an office building across the street, a group of people was huddled at the window watching him. They pointed and looked concerned. Several aimed phones at him. *Great.* He was about to go viral.

He hopped down, leaned against the wall, and folded his arms. None of this made any sense. Were they being invaded by an alien force? Was the world literally coming apart at the seams? No; more like he was coming apart.

In a last desperate effort to make sense of whatever he'd seen, he scanned the garage for cameras, thinking—no, hoping—he was being pranked.

Chapter 2

"Don," Nadina said, "we need to move Eric someplace safe."

"I understand that, but where could be safer than here?"

They stared at each other for a moment before Dina turned away. Since stepping through the seam and entering this strange world those many years ago and being cast together with Nordon, she'd grown to love the man. Sometimes, however, he could be so bull-headed that she wanted to kick him.

He came up behind her and wrapped his massive arms around her. She was always amazed at how a large, muscle-bound man like Nordon had such a gentle touch. "Now, Dina, don't be like that. Just hear me out."

She pressed her head back against his chest. He was tall enough he could rest his chin on her crown. Her gentle giant. She sighed. He took that as a sign to make his case. "The entire house has magical wards protecting it. Look how well they worked the first time. On top of that, we have more electronic security than the mayor." She pivoted and started to reply, but he held up a hand and touched a finger to her lips. "Not to mention an arsenal the military would be jealous of, and if that wasn't enough, we have two kick-ass guardians."

He paused, waiting for her to comment. When he felt no rebuttal was forthcoming, he lifted his finger.

"Who's the other guardian?"

"Huh?"

"Well, there's me. Who's the second one?"

He gave her a stern look. "Oh, think you're funny, eh?" He put his hands on her hips and lifted her. Dina's head touched the ceiling. She laughed and slapped at his arms.

"Put me down, brute!"

"Brute, is it?" He lowered her until they were face to face, her feet dangling above the floor. His eyes softened. "You know I love you, don't you?"

"Yes, I know. But you're still a brute. And—" her voice took on a more serious note. "I'm scared, Don."

"What? You? You're not 'fraid of anything."

"Not so much for me as for Eric. I'm afraid of failing him, like..." she choked, unable to say their names. "Elly's guardians. We can't let that happen."

He set her down. "No. Of course not. What else did Samuel say?"

"He said that both Rhoden and Mortas were here. They took Elly, Nordon. They took that poor child and she doesn't even know why. She must be so scared. Her male guardian is dead. The female is in the hospital. I wanted to go to her, but Samuel forbade me. He was afraid if someone was watching her, they'd see me and follow me back here. He blames them. In his mind, they don't matter. They're just tools. They failed their mission and have no further value. I don't want that to happen to us. I couldn't bear losing Eric. He is like our real son."

Tears leaked from her eyes and trailed down her cheeks.

"We won't let that happen, Nadina."

She took strength from his confidence. She wiped her eyes and dried her hands on her slacks. "Samuel said to get Eric some place safe and tell him who he is. If Mortas comes for him, Samuel wanted Eric to know why and to have a hand in protecting himself."

"I can't believe after all this time they found us. How? Why now?"

"I'm afraid that's beyond our knowing."

All right. Here's what we do. We stay here for now until I can secure other lodgings. The problem is that unless Samuel shows up, we'll be without any magical protection. In the meantime, we need to sit Eric down and explain his heritage. Will that work for you?"

Dina hugged him. "Yes. Thank you."

"We'll tell him tonight after his fencing lesson."

DEWAYNE SNYDER SAT in his car down the street from what his employer called the seam. It had become his daily ritual ever since meeting the dark and scary Rhoden. He was skeptical at first, but the man's money had proven to be real, erasing any apprehension he felt about what the man did.

The kidnapping of those two girls still made him uneasy. He didn't want to be part of any human trafficking. He planned to tell his new boss that if he ever came through the seam again. Or he hoped to. The dude was seriously not right. But as intimidating as he was, he was nothing compared to his boss. He had never met anyone who could put a chill through him just by being in his presence. A cold evil emanated from the man, like Satan himself had entered the world.

He thought about the money; well, the gold coins Rhoden had given him. At first, he had no idea what to do with them. It wasn't like he could go down to the corner store and pick up a fifth of vodka. Then, he passed a gold exchange place and walked out with two grand. He was sure the man had cheated him, but two thousand was two thousand more than he had before. In fact, it was more money than he'd ever held at any time in his life. He still had four coins left.

After that, he knew he'd show up every morning as his boss requested. Well, ordered. Still, he was determined to let the man know he wasn't going to be involved in anymore kidnapping. He'd done his share of bad things before; mostly mugging people on the streets with his boys. But his boys were now dead. He shuddered at the memory of how Rhoden flung them around like they were weightless. He had to draw the line. Mugging was one thing, but kidnapping? That was some serious time if he got caught.

The past few mornings there'd been a police presence at the sight. Rhoden and his boss did some serious damage to the cops; some had even died. That wasn't good, either. Not that he had any love for the cops, but killing one meant a citywide manhunt. Not something he ever wanted to be a part of.

The street was clear now, but he'd seen no sign of his boss. He didn't want to admit it, but he was relieved. He'd wait another hour, and it would be time to spend some of his new wealth to treat himself to the biggest steak he could find.

DeWayne slumped low in his seat. He was drifting toward sleep when two men came down the street. They moved fast and kept glancing behind them, which in itself was suspicious, but it was their clothes that made them stand out. They might have passed for homeless, except for their medieval attire. They looked like extras from a *Game of Thrones* episode.

Curiosity made him start the car with the intent to follow them, but then thought of his boss. DeWayne didn't want to miss out on a payday, but even more than that, he didn't want to risk pissing the man off.

He turned the ignition off and slumped back in his seat.

Chapter 3

Elly was aware of moving; however, her body was *not* under her control. She struggled to free herself, but her body wouldn't respond. She was being carried on the shoulder of a massive man. The farther he walked, the more scared she became. She wasn't alone, and that both frightened and comforted her.

From the corner of her eye, she noticed Shree. They'd been friends for years, and now they had both been taken hostage by some weirdo who must have hypnotized them. There was no other explanation.

Her anxiety grew as the strange man carried them through a…a… something. She had no words for what it was. It was like the air sliced open, revealing something beyond. It was daylight there and looked to be in the country. She hated the country. Nothing about rural living suited her.

When she tried to protest, her mouth wouldn't move. Sweat ran down her face and she couldn't move her hands to wipe it off. Her heart beat fast. What were they gonna do to them? She'd seen too many movies and read too many books to know how this might end. Most likely she and Shree would be sold off into some human trafficking operation and forced to do horrible things. *Oh God, please don't let this happen! Please help us!* Her prayers escaped her mind but not her lips. The man carried the girls through the glowing slice into the air and dropped them on thick grass on the other side.

"Get up. You two can move now."

The male voice was deep and dark, but the man who had carried them through wasn't the one speaking. This one seemed to be in charge and his dark face frightened her.

Shree looked to her and Elly nodded. Both girls jumped to their feet and ran. They didn't get far when they were grasped by an unseen hand and held in place by an invisible force. It turned them to face the scary man.

"I said you could *move*, not run. Don't make this harder on yourselves than it needs to be. I've searched for you for far too long to let you go now."

"Who are you? What do you want with us?" Shree asked.

"I really don't need you. It's her I'm after."

Elly's eyes went big. "Me? What about me? I've not done anything wrong!"

The man smiled. "No, you haven't. And you won't. Your time is over. I have one need from you, and when I get it, you become dispensable."

"Oh no. You're some kind of pervert, aren't you? Don't you dare touch me!" She felt an electric tingle in her hands, but then it vanished.

The man's evil grin told her what his true intentions were.

"I don't know what kind of insult you're trying to use. That world is strange to me. But this one," he said with a flourish of his hands, "is not! It belongs to me, thanks in large part to your parents and those infernal mages. All of this…mine!"

"My…parents?"

Elly had no idea what this man was rambling about. He spoke about things like she might know them, but she was clueless. Moments ago, she was a cheerleader and hoping the Bears would be good this year. Now…now she and Shree were out in the country.

The man approached them and held out a hand, cupping her chin. "You don't know, do you?"

"Know what? That you're some creepy old man that gets off on young girls?"

"You're sick, man!" Shree added.

"You really don't know, do you? Samuel kept you in the dark all these years. I wonder if your brother knows."

"I don't have a brother, moron! I'm an only child."

"See, you got the wrong girl. Let us go and we'll forget all about this," Shree said. Elly nodded her approval.

"On the contrary. I have the right one."

"That you do, sire," said a third man. The girls hadn't noticed him at first. He was younger than the one talking to them, but he looked just as fierce.

"Rhoden, these two belong in the dungeon for now. There is much to decide before I end their lives. She may be useful to my lineage. When we get to the castle, make sure they find a nice damp home."

"Of course, sire."

"Castle? What the hell are you talking about? Are you all crazy? I don't belong in no castle, and neither does Elly. I'm telling you, you got the wrong girls!"

"Silence! I will not tolerate your speech!" The man waved a hand and Shree put her hands to her mouth as though to rip off something, but there was nothing there.

"Do you want to follow her lead?"

Elly shook her head.

"Good. Stay quiet and I might go easy on you. Your parents were wrong to send you away. Samuel and Phetrix were fools to think they could hide you from me forever. You and I will build a union that will secure my hold on the kingdom for good. I do hope your brother decides to show. It'll be much easier to dispose of you girls by then."

"I don't know who you think I am, but I'm not the girl you're looking for." Panic crept in Elly's mind. The way this guy was talking sounded like he meant to do something really, really bad to her.

"But of course, you're the girl I've been looking for. Do you think Rhoden here would lead me wrong?"

The man approached her and grabbed hold of her shirt.

"Hey, stop! Don't touch me!"

The man yanked it up, revealing the birthmark on her side. "The moon scar. The sign."

She'd had the birthmark for as long as she could remember. As a young girl, she had traced her fingers along the edges, marveling at the crescent moon shape.

"A sign?"

"You are the princess. You are daughter of King Artus and Queen Griselda. Your twin brother is Erthic. Your name," the one called Rhoden said, "is Elysande. Princess Elysande of Chevalon. You and your brother are the last of your line. It's been long past time that your family was wiped out."

The other man smiled. "Take them to the dungeon. We have much to do."

The large oaf that carried them from their home to this countryside grabbed the girls, slung them on his shoulders, and marched across the fields.

Elly was confused and in a state of shock.

Chapter 4

Elly beat on the man's back, hoping to free them. The man didn't budge. She soon gave up and planned her next move.

The journey took several hours. Her body was numb from the position. To her surprise, as night fell, they were indeed brought to a castle.

"Shree, do you see this? Where'd a castle come from?"

"Girl, I don't know. What I do know is that I'm scared and 'bout ready to do something. We gotta get free!"

Not long after, they were taken down a flight of stone steps and along a dark and musty corridor to a jail cell. The thick iron bars reminded her of the old westerns her father enjoyed watching. The door was slammed shut and the girls were alone.

"What the hell is going on?" Elly asked.

"I've got a bad feeling about this."

"Me too. How are we ever gonna get out of here? What do you think they want?"

Something stirred in the cell next to them. Elly pushed herself against the far wall.

"You don't get out of here," a woman said. She pulled back a stained blanket and revealed herself, though Elly wished she hadn't. The woman in the dirty clothes looked old. Like really, really old. Her white hair was caked with what she hoped was mud. Black streaks ran down her face.

"Who are you?" Shree asked.

"'Tis not to question, but to know."

"What?"

"I know I'm a prisoner. Just like you, but you don't know it. You question. Why? Accept and be well."

"I don't know what games you're trying to play, but we don't belong here. I don't even know where here is. Do you?" Elly asked. The woman may have been old and gross, but she didn't give her the scary vibe like the two robed men did.

"Here? Here is a dungeon. Where those who oppose Mortas Frost are tossed away like table scraps to one day be killed or forgotten. Or both."

Elly ran a hand through her hair. "Shree, do you even know what's going on? Like, where are we? Do you think we're still in Illinois? I don't remember any castles near us. I don't remember any castles outside of Europe at all!"

"I wish I knew. I'm getting a weird vibe about this place. I don't know where we are."

"Chevalon. How can you not know? We are in Chevalon."

"What's a car got to do with this?" Shree asked.

The old woman glared at her, waved a hand dismissively, and huddled back under the blanket.

"Shree, I'm scared. I think they've got us mixed up with someone else. Maybe this is some weird cult and everyone is supposed to play a role or something like that. I've seen something like that on TV before."

Shree wrapped her arms around herself and nodded. "Maybe. No matter what, we stick together. Got it?"

"Of course! I've got your back."

The girls waited for someone to rescue them or someone to just check in on them, but hours passed with no one stirring other than the old woman in the next cell who fell asleep, snoring.

Elly curled up next to Shree and the girls clung to each other throughout the night.

At some point, a guard finally arrived. Elly had no idea what time it was. Without a window to the outside, she didn't know if it was light out or not. It felt like they had been there for hours.

"You two, in the funny clothes. Here's your breakfast. Hope you like gruel."

He slid two wooden bowls into their cell and tossed a couple splintered wooden spoons at them. Elly grabbed a bowl and wrinkled her nose at the scent.

"This smells gross. It's like oatmeal, but worse." She dropped the bowl to the floor. The old woman in the next cell cried out.

"Don't you waste that food! If you won't eat it, give it to me!"

"Here, take it." Elly kicked the bowl across the floor and it tumbled into the woman's cell. She didn't wait for the spoon and readily ate it with her hands, licking it off her bony fingers. Elly turned away in disgust.

"Shree, where the hell are we? Do you have any idea what's happening? How are we gonna get home?"

"We'll work it out. I promise. We're smart girls, right? I don't care what they say about cheerleaders." She winked at Elly, softening the harshness of their situation.

A few hours passed and a different guard dressed in the same black uniform with a large white snowflake on the front approached the cells. The snowflake and black outfit reminded Elly of Medieval Times, the restaurant her parents took her to once. She hated the place. She had to eat with her hands and the horses scared her.

"Come on, lady, it's time."

"No, please, spare me! Tell Mortas I'm not with the resistance. I don't know King Artus or Queen Griselda. Their children were never at my home. I swear!" the old woman cried. She begged on her knees for him to let her live.

"Please don't do this! I'm loyal! I swear my life to Mortas Frost!"

"Beg all ya want. It's time. Frost has made his decree. The square will welcome your blood."

He unlocked her cell and she made a feeble attempt to flee. He was much larger and grabbed her with one hand and smacked her with the other. She squealed.

"Let her go!" Elly demanded. "Let the woman go, you ignorant oaf. What kind of man hits a woman?"

The guard turned to her; his thick face creased with a grin. "A guard doing his duty. Stay out of this or I'll be back for you. Both of you. I bet you'd be begging for mercy once I got hold of ya."

The old woman struggled to free herself but he was too strong.

"What are you doing to her? Let her go!"

In Elly's fury, she felt a flicker of something inside her, like a light suddenly bursting with life. Her surroundings were alive; humming. She could sense everything around her. All the cracks in the iron bars, the cold bowl of gruel, the rats racing across the stone floor. All of it seemed alive.

"Elly, are you all right? Elly?" Shree shook her, finally breaking her from her stupor. When she regained her sight, it was just the two of them.

"Where…where's the woman? What happened?"

"I don't know. Your eyes…they went white. Like, all white. You were gone for a few minutes and the guard looked shocked when he saw your eyes. He couldn't leave fast enough with the woman. I think… I think something bad happened to her. She screamed the entire time he was dragging her out of here."

"I don't remember any of that," Elly whispered. "I felt everything in here. I felt…like my body vibrated with energy or electricity. Power." It sounded weird, but that was the best way she could describe it. She felt a surge of power like an electrical current raced through her body.

"Here, let me help you." Shree gently nudged her toward the wall and helped her to sit. "Relax, girl. Whatever happened, I'm sure it's ok. We gotta think of some way outta this place. Things aren't right. I don't know where we are, or what this Chevalon place is, but I don't think we're at home anymore."

Elly nodded, thinking about the burst of energy she held for the briefest moment. It was like nothing she'd ever experienced before.

And it scared her.

Chapter 5

"Phetrix, what is this place?" Kol asked, mouth agape, in awe of everything.

"It is called Chicago. It is a city in another world."

"It is so—big. And-and so—strange." He pointed at the variety of vehicles on the street. "What are those creatures?"

"They are called cars," Phetrix said, annoyed. He had more important things to do than play tour guide to Kol. Though he'd only been there once, he had to locate Samuel. If he had crossed into Chevalon as suggested by the tall dark man, then he had to find where Samuel lived. Valuable information was inside. Information he needed to locate the heirs. His best bet was to retrace the route they'd taken on his last trip to Chicago, though that had been almost two decades before and from the other seam. The problem was Samuel had been there at the seam to guide him the first time.

It didn't take long for Phetrix to realize he was lost. He pulled Kol to the side. The man sought his dagger. "What is it? Trouble? Is it Mortas?"

"No. I need to cast a spell to find Samuel." Phetrix searched through a bag slung across his neck and shoulder until he found a small tome. He flipped through the pages, stopping at the one he needed. After reading the spell, mumbling a few things under his breath, he took out a polished black stone with a tiny arrow attached. It fit in the palm of his hand. With the components in his hand, he uttered the words to activate the spell. Nothing happened. Phetrix knitted his brows. Why hadn't the spell worked?

He tried again, this time increasing the amount of power. It took several moments, but the arrow began to spin. It stopped, pointing out a direction. "This way."

They followed the path of the arrow. It led them to several turns, then suddenly changed direction, pointing at a tall dark-skinned man who passed them. The arrow followed the man.

"Samuel?" Phetrix asked with uncertainty.

The man pivoted and eyed them. "Do I know you?"

Phetrix said, "Apologies. I thought you were someone else."

"Quite the coincidence, if he looked like me and has the same name."

"Yes, isn't it?"

Phetrix turned and walked away. The spell needed more specifics to locate the proper Samuel. Their journey took them around the city. To Phetrix's concern, each time they cast the spell took longer to activate and more power. He was draining fast. Perhaps this world was not conducive to magic. That could prove devastating.

They found eight more people named Samuel, but not the one they needed. Six hours later, exhausted and needing a rest to rebuild his energy levels, Phetrix came across a building that looked familiar. It was one of the tallest buildings he had ever seen. He remembered asking Samuel about it on his first time here.

"I believe we turn here."

Kol's eyes followed the building up to the sky. "How is it possible to construct something so big without it collapsing?"

Phetrix ignored the question and rounded the corner. The spell died out. That surprised Phetrix. It had not been as useful as he hoped, but that it fizzled out concerned him.

Another twenty minutes and a few wrong turns later, they stood in front of Samuel's building. Phetrix pushed through the door. Kol followed, still dumbstruck by the enormity of everything. They took an elevator up, which sent Kol into a whimpering wreck.

"Get ahold of yourself, man," Phetrix chastised. "We draw too much attention to ourselves as it is without you losing your sanity."

Kol straightened and pulled his mouth shut but maintained a death grip on the hand bar. The elevator halted with a bounce, again sending

Kol to the edge of a breakdown. Phetrix exited and Kol leaped after him. Phetrix pulled up next to a door. He hoped it was the right one. It had been so long ago and all the doors looked the same.

He knocked. No response. Twice more, and still no answer. There was one way to know if this was Samuel's door. He swept his hand over the frame. A greenish glow appeared, then vanished. It was protected by magic wards. He had the right room.

From the end of the hall, Kol said, "By the gods and all that is holy."

Phetrix joined him at the window. They stood but eight stories high, but the view was wonderful yet intimidating. While they admired the city skyline, Phetrix gave thought to what he should do—wait or continue the search? He decided to wait, but after an extended time, he opted for a new plan.

The short rest helped him recover some strength. Reaching inside his heavy robe, he withdrew a small tome and a small worn leather pouch from an inside pocket. From the pouch he pulled out a green gemstone. He said a few words and touched the stone to the doorknob. To his surprise, nothing happened. He repeated the process. Either the wards were more involved than he thought, or something was wrong with his magic.

He tried again, this time starting with a dispel spell to knock down the wards. The effort left him weak. He placed a hand on the wall to keep from falling. This was not good. How did Samuel handle using magic in this world?

Sweeping his hand over the frame again still showed a faint green hue. Phetrix once more cast his spell. This time, only a faint green tint remained. Samuel must be much more powerful than he thought for it to take three tries to dispel the wards. He repeated the open spell using the stored magic in the gemstone and the door clicked.

Phetrix pushed the door. It swung open. He took a periphery glance around the interior before motioning for Kol to follow him.

Kol entered warily. "So, this other wizard lives here?

"Yes."

"How is it you know him if he lives here?"

"It was a long time ago. We reconnected by accident. Now please, stop asking questions. I need to rest and concentrate."

Phetrix sat on a plush chair and gazed around the room searching for the most likely place Samuel would have hidden information on the whereabouts of the heirs. Though an experienced wizard with an enormous amount of power and magical storage, he was surprised at how drained he felt after using such low-level spells. Something was clearly wrong. Perhaps Samuel's spells had a draining effect on whoever used magic. He hoped that was all it was; otherwise he might be rendered useless during a battle.

While Kol search manually, Phetrix sat and studied the small apartment while his power restored. Fifteen minutes later, he stood and cast a locate magic spell around the room. Nothing glowed. He entered the sparsely furnished bedroom and tried again. This time he received a faint reddish glow from the closet.

He opened the door and pushed aside the collection of clothes that marked the inhabitants of this world. They were a far cry from his tattered and filthy robes. For a moment he pondered borrowing one of Samuel's costumes to better fit in, but realized the man was much smaller and plumper than was Phetrix.

Unable to visually spot whatever was hidden within, Phetrix used his spell again. The glow came from above. "Kol, use the hilt of your sword to tap the ceiling there." He pointed. The hollow tone gave him hope that a hidden panel existed. No matter how he searched and prodded, however, he could not find the way to open the secret door. That left him with only a magical option left to try.

He lay down on the bed to regain his strength. Feeling depleted was a horrible feeling to someone with his ability. This time he waited thirty minutes before making his attempt. He first had to rid the compartment of any magical protection. With great effort and concentration, it took two tries to accomplish.

Once rid of its protection, the hidden compartment revealed itself quickly. A panel dropped down showing a recessed two-by-two-foot space. Inside was an ancient ornate wooden box. Phetrix knew its purpose. The box was actually a puzzle. To open it, you needed the right combination of things to happen in the proper order. Otherwise, bad things might occur. The box could burst into flames, taking with it whatever treasure was hidden within. Or, it could cause serious damage to the person opening the box. Phetrix knew whatever was inside was too valuable to attempt to open the box without proper study. That took enormous amounts of time. Time he did not have to spare.

Chapter 6

He left the box alone and pulled down several tubes, the kind used to protect ancient parchments from long lost spells to maps of the unknown lands of Chevalon. After first checking for a defensive spell and finding none, Phetrix pulled the cap off one tube and upended it. A dozen rolls of fragile parchment dropped out. They were in such delicate condition, Phetrix was loathe to handle it for fear of damaging something of great value.

Because the pieces were so old, Phetrix believed it was not what he was searching for. Anything that showed the whereabouts of the heirs would be no older than fifteen years. Unless Samuel scribed the information on an ancient parchment, these were of no help. He slid them back into the tube, replaced the cap, and stuck it back in its spot. The parchment in the second tube was in much the same condition as the first. However, inside the final tube was a heavier stock; newer than the others. The pages still held a yellowish hue but did not look or feel old, and they unfolded with ease. The ends curled up, but the paper unrolled and lay flat.

Phetrix leaned over the page. It was blank. He turned the page over, but the other side was also blank. That confused him at first. Why would Samuel go to such trouble to hide something that was blank? The answer came quickly. He wouldn't.

That meant magic was involved.

He again called up his dispel magic to counter any spell. But before he released its energy, he halted. If the parchment did not have a protection spell on it, he risked erasing what was hidden. He sat and pulled out his tome. The pages were tattered from years of use. So much was written there over the past fifty plus years that he'd forgotten more than he remembered. Of course, that was the value and the purpose of the book.

It took time to locate the proper spell. It had been so long since he last used it. He'd even forgotten the name, simply titling it, reveal message. He studied the ancient words in the long-lost language of ancestors gone for centuries for a long while until he was sure he had the words and the proper incantation down. Then he pulled out a small compartmentalized box from another deep pocket in his robe. Each one of the eight sections held a different colored powder. He chose a pinch of a dark yellow powder that was a shade darker than the parchment.

Phetrix stood and placed a book on each corner of the parchment to keep it flat and still. Then he spoke the words to activate the energy and sprinkled the powder over the page. He repeated the magical phrase until the powder began to swirl. It spread out above the page in an aerial rectangle the same size as the parchment, then settled. Within seconds of contact, lines revealed themselves. As they filled in, Phetrix could see it was a map.

It took a time for it to complete. Afterward, Phetrix was baffled. No landmarks or notes gave any hint as to the location the map depicted. However, a number one lit the top right-hand corner. Did that mean page one, or was it telling him something different?

He lifted the end of the map to see if there were sheets of parchment stuck together, but he only found the one page. He flipped the parchment over. It remained blank. Phetrix decided to try the reveal spell again and repeated the process. This time a different map was shown. This one had the number two in the upper right-hand corner. However, this one also had a glowing blue dot halfway up the page and two thirds to the left. Excited by the discovery, he lifted the page to study it closer. To his frustration, no other signs or clues came to light.

He walked toward the bedroom window, hoping more light might reveal something else. Nothing happened. Did the blue dot represent one of the heirs? If so, why was the opposite side without a dot? He was sure the heirs had been separated for their own protection. Had something happened to one of them?

No, wait. Something did happen. The map had switched sides. The blue dot was away from him as he moved toward the window. Now it was closer and had flip-flopped sides. To test a theory, he kept the map in the same position and turned around. At first, nothing happened. Then the lines faded and reformed back to their original direction.

Phetrix all but ran into the other room where Kol stood mesmerized by the Chicago skyline. "I think I found them…well, at least something that will lead us to them. Come. Let's test it and see if it works."

"What is that?" Kol asked.

"A special map I'm hoping will lead us to the heirs. Since we can't find Samuel, I'm trying to find them."

Because Kol had been too traumatized by his first ride in the elevator, they hurried down the eight flights of stairs to door leading to the lobby where they entered the building. They exited through the glass doors. Phetrix held the map in front of him and turned left. The map changed, placing the blue dot closer to his body. He pivoted left and the map righted. "This way," he said.

It guided them block after block through the hordes of people and across the streets filled with strange horseless vehicles. Kol led the way to prevent Phetrix from running headlong into people or obstacles. They traveled deeper into the city across a bridge over a wide river. The map shifted every time they made a wrong turn. More than three hours later, they were still walking and felt they had not made much progress.

They stopped to sit on a bench for a breather. They were hungry, thirsty, and near exhaustion. After several minutes, Phetrix glanced at the map and leapt to his feet.

"What's the matter?" Kol asked

"The lines are fading. We must hurry before we lose it completely."

They took off at a faster pace, but several minutes later, Phetrix slowed.

"Is it gone?"

"No. To the contrary. The lines have become more visible. I guess we have to keep moving or the map fades."

"I hope we find it soon. I'm not sure how much longer I can keep going."

Phetrix didn't respond, but his body was telling him the same thing.

They trudged on; each step heavier than the previous. The buildings became shorter here. The area was filled with dilapidated, rundown, and ill-kept structures. Fewer people were on the streets. The massive buildings that reached into the clouds were gone, replaced by smaller one and two-story constructs that resembled the hovels of the townsfolk back home, only these were large enough to house four families. Two hours later, Phetrix stopped again. He stared at the map. At the bottom of the page a tiny red dot had appeared. He started walking with his eyes glued to the red dot.

After traveling another length of road, he noted the dot had also moved. He shifted to the blue dot. They were close now. A quick scan of the area showed they had entered a residential area with nicer homes. There was grass surrounding most properties, as if it was farmed there.

He stopped and Kol came up next to him. He wiped his brow with an already sweat-soaked sleeve. "What is it?"

"This red dot represents us. This blue dot is our destination."

Kol understood the implications immediately. "Let's get there fast so I can collapse."

Chapter 7

Samuel stepped through the seam and inhaled deep. The scent of honeysuckle and rain greeted him. Instantly he felt his power restore within, building him up once again.

"How I've missed Chevalon." It had been a few years since he'd been back, the last time to spread the rumor of the heir's existence, and he never met the same people twice.

The gray clouds overhead and wet ground beneath his feet told him it had rained recently, though now the skies were dry. He wasn't quite prepared to sink into mud, but it would do. He was home.

He ran a hand over his clothes. He needed to change so his appearance didn't give him away this time, which was a problem he encountered early on.

"Way to think this through, old man," he muttered to himself.

Walking across the wet fields, his feet were sucked into the mud, making it difficult to travel. If there was one thing he enjoyed about the world through the seam, it was the concrete sidewalks. Chicago stunk at times, but he always had solid footing.

Birds cried in the distance. They didn't sound anything like those back in Chicago. There, he dealt mostly with pigeons and seagulls near Lake Michigan. Here, starlings and jays lived in the large maples and oaks that grew in Chevalon.

A terrible screeching sound startled him and Samuel spun to see a black figure racing across the sky.

"A Seeker," he whispered.

Wretched creatures more ephemeral than physical, Seekers were born of ancient and forbidden magic. The Order outlawed their use over a thousand years ago. Mortas cared not for subtlety nor prohibitions.

Long wispy tails trailed from the Seeker. It darted across the field; no doubt attracted by Samuel's use of magic.

"You won't get me so easily. I'm old, not dumb." Samuel wove a spell so quick and simple, the Seeker never noticed it. The spell masked his true powers, rendering him invisible to the Seeker. "I'd like to see you figure this one out."

Samuel kept an eye to the sky but trudged through the muddy field, intent on visiting the farmer. With a horrific screech, the Seeker sailed away. It would follow some other magic user, not him.

Nearing the weathered farmhouse, Samuel wondered if the old farmer still lived. It had been so long since he'd first met him and he was already old then.

When he first found the location of the seam in the field, Samuel approached the old man who owned the land.

"Hello, friend," Samuel said on that day long ago. "My name is—"

"You're that mage, aren't you? Samuel? From the king's court, if I reckon."

Samuel grinned. "It seems my reputation precedes me even here. Indeed, I am. And you are?"

"Jed. My name's Jed." He stood at the entrance to his farmhouse. A woman appeared from inside and stood next to him.

"This here is my wife, Annabelle. My sons Ambrose and Declan are 'round here somewhere tending the fields. You here about Colla?"

Samuel scrunched his eyebrows. "Colla?"

"Our son. He's with the Order."

Annabelle patted him on the arm. "Jed's been worried ever since he left. Has something gone wrong?"

Samuel waved off their worries. "No, no. I have no knowledge of your boy, but I can certainly check in on him when I return to the king."

Jed stepped forward and narrowed his eyes. "Then why are you here, mage?"

"It's best if we speak in private."

Annabelle laughed. "Have you seen where you stand? We've got no neighbors! You can't get more private than this."

"Still, what I have to share must never be spoken of. Can we go inside? I'd feel safer sharing in private."

Upon entering their small wooden house with its thatched roof, Samuel wove a spell shrouding the entire home in privacy. No one outside would hear them. Satisfied they were safe, he paused. Could he trust these people? Would they ever turn over this information?

"Where do you come from?" Samuel asked.

"Excuse me?" Jed replied. "You were the one to come to us. What do you mean by asking us where we come from?'"

"My apologies. I mean no disrespect. There is something unique in your field. Something…that can be dangerous if found by the wrong people."

"Dangerous? All we got is wheat and barley, and only barely some years. What do you mean, dangerous?" Jed shook his head.

"In your field is portal—a seam, if you will—to another place. It would be most important to keep it a secret and let no others know about it. None but me, that is."

Jed looked past him to the door. "A what?"

"It's a place for me to travel long distances in a short amount of time."

"Oh." Jed settled back into his chair with Annabelle at his side. "So why's it so important?"

"One day, it may be important to the king. I don't know when, but I know it needs to remain hidden until such a time. If any mage comes looking for it, say nothing. Nothing! Let no others inspect your land or try to make you give them information about it. Am I clear?"

"Seeing as how I got no idea what you're talking about, it won't be hard keeping it a secret. What's in it for me?"

Samuel smiled, anticipating he'd have to compensate the farmer for his silence.

"Here, take these. Every year, I'll give you five more." He handed five gold coins to Jed. The farmer's face beamed with excitement.

"Every year?"

"Every year, Jed. Do we have a deal?"

"Colla."

"Excuse me?"

"And I want you to look after Colla. The boy'd lose his head if it weren't attached to his shoulders."

Samuel grinned. "All right, then. I'll look after Colla, too."

Jed extended his hand. "Deal." They shook on it and Samuel left, occasionally visiting Jed and his family to make sure their deal remained intact.

It had been a few years since he'd seen Jed. Remaining in Chicago and watching over the safety of the twins consumed much of his time. Failing to save Elly from Mortas weighed on him, making him angry every muddy step of the way to Jed's house. Everything he'd done to secure her in the other world had failed. Did he trust in the wrong people? Did he give Phetrix too much credit for his powers?

He doubted it was any of that.

Mortas and Rhoden…that wicked former student of his… outsmarted him. That hurt the worst. He prided himself on seeing connections and events long before they happened. Missing this meant he was losing his touch. He'd have to find her soon before Mortas did something horrible.

Samuel approached the old familiar farmhouse. "Jed? Annabelle? Ambrose? Declan, are you here, son? Hello? Is anyone home?" he called. No one seemed to be around. He went to the door and knocked. No one answered. He knocked again. Finally, someone inside stirred. When the door opened, he was caught off guard.

"Who are you?" the man inside asked. Samuel felt magic radiating from him.

"I should ask you the same question."

"What do you want?"

"Is Jed here?"

The man shook his head. "Ma and Pa died several years ago. What do you want?" The man scowled, making Samuel uncomfortable.

"Wait…are you Colla?"

The man peered at him. "Who's asking? Are you one of Frost's men? I told the last one—"

Samuel waved a hand in the air, shaking off the suggestion. "Oh dear, no. Quite the opposite, really. Can we talk in private?"

"Phetrix?"

Samuel smiled. "Not quite, but close."

Colla's eyes widened. "Samuel?" he whispered.

"In the flesh." He bowed with a flourish.

"Come inside, then. I'm sure you have no idea what's been going on."

Colla ushered Samuel inside.

Chapter 8

"Have a seat over there. Let me get a fire going. Do you like tea? Of course, you do. I'll get a kettle on."

Colla busied himself with lighting a fire and preparing a pot of water for tea. Samuel sat at the scuffed wooden table in the middle of the room, the hard-packed dirt floor so unlike the hardwood of his apartment in Chicago. Funny how quickly he'd gotten used to such luxury. When he last lived in Chevalon, the stone floors of the castle seemed the epitome of flooring construction.

Samuel absorbed all Colla shared with him.

"Since the rise of Mortas, Chevalon has been a horrid place. I used to live in town, but its dirty and overrun with crime. It's no place to live. I've seen more than my share of executions, including my parents'." Colla looked down and took several moments before resuming the conversation. "The Order barely exists anymore, and only then in secret. Too much death; all of it done in the name of harmony."

It was difficult to hear him speak about the atrocities Mortas committed in the name of a "more peaceful and just Chevalon." Mortas was cruel. His mage, no better.

"So, your parents died at the hands of Frost?"

Colla nodded. "He figured out they were hiding something from him. Aiding the resistance. They were executed as traitors."

"Your parents were good people. They—" he paused, wondering

just how much Colla knew of the seam. Did he know it existed in their field? Had he seen others come through?

Samuel calmed himself. He'd been preparing for a return to Chevalon since the twins escaped. The personal price many had to pay never occurred to him.

"For their deaths, I am sorry. They died protecting something important. They died not in vain, but in glory. When Mortas Frost is finally defeated, it will be because of them. Have no doubt of their bravery and sacrifice."

Colla stood from the seat by the fire and walked across the room. Samuel worried he had crossed a line with the man.

"I apologize, Colla. I didn't mean to pick at fresh wounds. Your grief is something I cannot fathom. Please forgive me." He thought for a moment. "What about your brothers? Are they around?"

"Dead. Mortas had them killed as well."

"Oh dear. I'm so sorry for your loss."

Colla nodded. "Thank you, mage. Your kindness is appreciated."

Samuel let the moment pass, allowing the tension to dissipate before he spoke again. He was here for a purpose. The guardians failed to protect their charge and though the conversation was helpful, he had more important matters to address.

"Colla, I need to find the princess."

"Princess? She's gone. She and her brother have been gone for fifteen years."

"Not exactly."

The man spun on him. "She lives? How? It's impossible!"

"My return here is because of her. It's because of Frost. She's back. She lives!"

"If the heir lives still, that means—"

"The kingdom can be restored. We can rid the land of Mortas's evil. We can return the kingdom to the rightful heirs and restore what's been destroyed."

"The king and queen," Colla muttered.

Samuel jumped to his feet. "Do you know where they are? Do they live? It's been so long that I thought…I thought maybe they might be gone."

"Rumor has it they hide in the northern forests. A large gathering of the resistance hides in the wilds where not even Rhoden dares to tread. They leave them to themselves in a land none will enter. There are far too many dangers. Eventually, they'll find their end at the hands of a beast or the elements. One or the other will take them all."

"If the royal family lives, maybe we can bring them all together. Can you imagine how the people would respond to the royal family whole again? Mortas wouldn't stand a chance!"

Hope sprung in Samuel's old heart. He never imagined King Artus and Queen Griselda still lived. He assumed they died years ago and the rumors were continued in order to keep Frost guessing. But if they were alive, that would change everything.

The water boiled and Colla took it from the flame. He poured some into two wooden cups, then added a small cloth bag filled with tea to each. He let them steep for several minutes before handing a mug to Samuel.

"Thank you."

The men sat opposite each other at the wooden table, an awkward silence growing larger as they sipped. The fire snapped and popped. Outside, birds rang out the last calls of the day. Finally, Samuel spoke.

"Colla, what do you know about your land?"

"Wheat doesn't do well most years, but neither does anything else."

"No, not that. What do you know that's special about your land?"

The man set his mug on the table and crossed his arms. "Maybe something."

"Have you had other visitors? Were they dressed strangely?"

He seemed to touch a nerve. Colla scowled at him, words on the tip of his tongue, but before he could say a thing, they heard a terrible screech outside. Colla's eyes shot to the ceiling.

"Seekers!" he cried.

"Relax. They can't see my essence. I cast a spell on the place when I entered."

"You did what?"

"It's a simple thing, really. No matter, they cannot—"

The roof suddenly burst open, the thatch erupting into the air. The loud crash deafened Samuel for a moment. Through the hole, three Seekers crashed into the home, swirling around them.

Samuel let loose thin tendrils of lightning.

"Colla, run! I'll hold them off so you can escape!"

Samuel didn't have a chance to see if the man listened or not. The Seekers closed in on him, the lightning boring through the ephemeral bodies. They screeched madly, as though in eternal torment. Their long black robes drifted on unseen winds.

"You rotten creatures! Go back to the pit that spawned you!"

Samuel created larger bursts of white-hot flame and flung it at them. He'd never have been able to do that back in the other world. His powers were limited to what he could store. Here in Chevalon, it surrounded him like a comforting blanket. It penetrated deep into his bones.

The Seekers slammed into pots and pans, knocking the wooden table over, busting the chairs. One of the chairs fell into the fire and ignited quickly. Soon, the side of the house burst into flames, the fire growing fast and hotter.

Samuel didn't notice if Colla was still there or not. The Seekers tried desperately to attack, though Samuel held his ground. He fought with a fury he hadn't touched in years. The feeling of power flowing through him was amazing.

"Die, you wretched things! You have no business here!"

The flames grew taller. Samuel had to get out before he was caught in the inferno.

Summoning as much strength as he could, Samuel created a massive blast of lightning, and pushed it out from him. The effort strained him, but he forced it farther and farther away from his body. Flinging his arms wide, the wall of lightning radiated outward in all directions. A loud boom of thunder followed, rattling everything inside the flaming house. The Seekers howled in agony and fell silent.

They were gone.

Still trapped in the burning house, Samuel pushed his way through the smoke.

"Colla, are you here? Where are you?"

He listened but heard nothing. The flames raged higher and hotter, forcing him to abandon the house.

Samuel cast a small spell to push away the smoke and found the door. He ran to it, rushing to the outside, where the clean air filled his lungs.

When he got his bearings, he looked around the home but didn't find Colla anywhere.

"Dear boy, I hope you got out safe. I swear, if Mortas caused your death because of me…I'll strangle the man myself."

Chapter 9

Grant was beyond annoyed. He was downright pissed off. He didn't understand what was going on and when that happened, energy built up inside him to the point of exploding. Before that occurred, he needed to work some of the pressure off. However, this case, or lack of one in this instance, would not allow him to step back and get some recuperating distance. It would not release its hold on his mind.

So he found himself on the street where the shootout had taken place. He stood staring at the mysterious area where the men and kidnapped girls disappeared. How could it have happened? He sure didn't have the answers. No one in the department did. There was talk of bringing in experts, whoever they might be. Grant thought they needed a wizard, magician, or voodoo witch doctor to figure out how they magically vanished.

He crossed the street and approached the approximate location of the rift. If something existed there, he couldn't see it. With a tentative reach, he extended his hand to feel for any abnormality. He flinched back twice, fearing his hand might disappear. Frustrated and annoyed at his own cowardice, he thrust his arm straight out. Nothing happened.

He placed his hands on his hips and stared hard, searching for a seam or anything unusual that might offer answers. After a minute he scratched his head and turned around. As he walked back toward his car, he glanced down the street. He wasn't sure what drew his attention to the parked car two blocks down, but curiosity piqued, he walked toward it.

By the time he covered the first block he realized the dark shape he saw through the window was a person. He advanced faster, an excitement latching onto his heart, making it race. By the time he was half a block away, the gun was in his hand. He had no recollection of drawing it from the holster. It was clear now that the shape was a man. A black man with hair piled high on his head the way the kids did nowadays leaned against the window. *Was he dead?*

The thought rose goosebumps up his arms. The chill made him slow his pace and glance around to ensure he wasn't walking into an active shooter scenario or an ambush. He made a complete circle with his weapon up before continuing toward the car.

The man appeared to be alone. He showed no sign of injury and the car did not have any broken windows or recent exterior damage. Gun aimed at the man, he stopped three feet from the door. He saw no rise and fall of his chest.

A thought came to him. Hadn't there been a report of a black man assisting the kidnappers? Maybe the kidnappers had no further use for the man and killed him. He stepped closer and tapped the barrel of the gun on the driver's window. The man stirred, then jumped. He smacked his head on the interior, then seeing Grant with his gun aimed, jerked sideways across the front seat.

"Open the door and get out of the car," Grant commanded.

The man stared wide-eyed back at him but did not make any effort to move.

"I'm not going to say it again. Open this door and get out, or –" *What?* He realized he had no idea of what he would do if the man did not comply. But he feared his already high level of anger might make the or something beyond his control.

"Okay. Okay. Don't shoot. I'm coming out."

Grant was relieved the man responded. He feared the alternative; not for himself, but for this man. What if he was innocent and had just fallen asleep? Perhaps he'd been drinking all night and chose to sleep in the car rather than drive home? Even if that was true, he still needed the man out of the car to determine his course of action.

The man reached for the door and pulled on the handle. The door opened a crack.

"Come out of there slowly and with your hands where I can see them. They'd better be empty, too."

Grant stepped back and to the right to give himself distance and a clear line of fire if needed. The man unfolded in slow motion. He was tall and lanky. His dark skin glistened.

"I-I'm sorry. Guess I just fell asleep," he said with a nervous edge.

A sudden gust of air hit Grant from behind. Not a breeze. Not cool. More stale, like the opening of something long sealed. A curious thing, but not one demanding his immediate attention, especially with a suspect under his gun.

"Very slowly pull out some ID."

The man hesitated. His eyes glanced past Grant. Grant stiffened. He knew the man was trying to divert his attention. But for what purpose? To attack or run? The suspect might be able to outrun him—the emphasis on might—but to attack, no way. He'd be dead long before he reached Grant.

"Okay. Okay. I'm getting my wallet out. Don't shoot."

He reached behind him for his wallet. Or a gun? There it was, that look again, as if someone was behind him. Despite believing it an obvious ploy to get him to turn his head, the hairs on the back of his neck stood on end. A chill raced up his vertebrae and his finger tightened on the trigger. Then, something hit him from behind, lifting him from the ground and tossing him like a doll. The gun fired. The suspect dove. Grant flew over the car, hit the ground, and crashed into a light pole. He hit with such force that the wind was knocked from his lungs and the lights went out.

The light returned in increments. Consciousness was slower in recovering. Grant had no idea how long he'd been out, but there was a lot more traffic on the roads now. He sat up, groggy and with a headache. He leaned back against the light pole, drew his knees up and closed his eyes. He took a slow mental assessment of his injuries. They appeared to range from scrapes and bruises to a laceration on his forearm that had bled enough to leave a pool on the sidewalk and now had crusted to slow seepage.

The worst of it was in his side where he'd struck the pole. The sharpness of the pain indicated he may have a broken rib or two. He winced. As the pain subsided, he opened his eyes. The car was gone.

He swept his gaze over the area. So far, no one paid him any attention. Perhaps they figured he was another drunk sleeping it off on the streets.

Grant tested his legs and attempted to stand. His body thought differently of it, though, and he was forced to stay seated. He regrouped and tried twice more before making it to his feet. He stretched, groaned, and stretched some more. It was then he noticed his holster was empty. Panic pushed pain aside. *No!* He couldn't lose his service weapon. That was a major mark against any officer. He scanned the ground around him, finding the gun on the grass ten feet away. He exhaled with relief and felt instant pain. He needed to get checked out. But first, he had to make a report.

Chapter 10

DeWayne had been scared. He thought that detective had him. He envisioned being locked away for a long time for being an accomplice to the double kidnapping. But then, Rhoden, his boss from another world, appeared and saved his bacon.

He drove too fast away from the scene, making multiple turns and tossing his passenger around. Though Rhoden gave him a sour glance, he said nothing. Once a few miles distance from the scene and no sign of pursuit, DeWayne slowed the car. His face was wet with perspiration. His shirt was soaked. But now that he had time to think, some of the adrenaline and elation wore off. *Had his boss killed that cop?* He had no love for cops but killing one put you at the center of a manhunt. If he thought being an accomplice to a kidnapping was bad, he was close to hyperventilating over killing a cop.

"You may slow down now," Rhoden said.

"Oh yeah, sure." DeWayne eased from the gas.

"You will need the bigger car. The van, you called it."

"Oh, ah, yeah. About that. I don't think it's such a good idea to be using the van again. I'm sure the cops have a description. I'm not sure what you're planning, but it might not be a great idea to kidnap anyone else so soon. Cops be looking for a white van. Might mess up your plans." He shot a nervous glance at his boss. "If you don't mind my asking, what are your plans?"

Rhoden ignored the question. "If what you say is a concern, you will need to obtain another such vehicle. In short, men will be entering this world. We will need transport. Let us find it now."

DeWayne was annoyed. The man obviously thought finding a vehicle—any vehicle, let alone a van—was as easy as taking it. Well, actually, he supposed it was. *The best way to get exactly what you want is to buy it.* He looked at Rhoden. The man was smiling.

"Actually, the best way is to take what we want."

Did the dude just read his mind? Oh, man! Is he in my head now? How much had he heard? DeWayne began to sweat again. "Ah, yeah, sure. There is that way, too."

They drove on, scanning streets and parking lots. "There," Rhoden said, pointing.

DeWayne followed the extended finger. Parked in a restaurant lot was a black passenger van with the extended rear. It would easily fit eight people.

"Let's take that one."

"Ah, sure. I'm a little out of practice boosting cars, but I'll give it a shot."

Rhoden turned his gaze on him. The hard, dark orbs narrowed. DeWayne felt them penetrate deep into his brain. "No. You will succeed."

DeWayne found it difficult to swallow. He pulled down a side street and parked in front of a duplex. An elderly couple sat on the porch. He watched them for a few seconds, wondering if they'd call the cops on him for parking in front of their house for an extended period. He spun in his seat and scanned the back seat for anything he might need. He had a few tools in the trunk but nothing he couldn't live without. He dug into the glove box and pulled out things with his name on it. With those pages tucked into his back pocket, he got out of the car. Rhoden made no effort to get out.

DeWayne leaned inside. "You know, whoever owns that van might come out at any time. It'd be good to have a watcher to warn me."

"I have complete confidence in your ability. I know you won't let me down. You should know better than to let me down."

The chill ran laps up and down his spine. He closed the door and popped the trunk. After rummaging around inside, he pulled out a screwdriver, a Slim Jim, and a crowbar. He pressed them against his thigh out of view from the elderly couple, then walked toward the restaurant half a block away. As he neared the van, he checked the restaurant door. A man and woman exited. He walked past the van. The couple turned in his direction. For a moment he feared they would get in the van, but they entered a Honda next to it and drove away.

DeWayne circled around the lot, coming in from the front entrance. He ducked to the side of the van farthest from the restaurant door and went to work on the passenger side. He slid the thin flexible tool down the outside of the window. It took him three tries to hook the lock and pop it open.

He dove across the seat and closed the door behind him. He didn't want to get into the driver's seat until he started the engine. With the tip of the screwdriver wedged into the column, he gave smacked the handle with the crowbar and pried the compartment open. DeWayne had just placed his hands around the wires to pull them free when the driver's door opened and a large black man appeared.

"What the —"

DeWayne tried to retreat but the man reached in, clamped strong hands around his head and pulled him out of the van. His legs fell off the seat. His feet hit the doorstep and his knees banged on the blacktop. Before he could cry out from the pain, a massive fist connected with the side of his head and sent lights flashing and pain everywhere.

The man lifted him, tossing his body against the van, and wound up to drive his face out the back of his head. Dewayne threw up his hands in a weak countermeasure, but the punch never landed. The man was lifted off his feet and slammed headfirst into the van with enough force to leave a dent. The man went limp. DeWayne looked up to see Rhoden approaching with his arms extended in front of him. He moved them back and forth like he was tossing a heavy load. The man crashed into the van again, and this time Rhoden released him and he slid to the ground face first, unconscious.

Rhoden shoved past Dewayne and climbed inside the van. DeWayne stared from the unconscious man to Rhoden. His boss motioned at DeWayne with his fingers. DeWayne dropped to the ground, found the keys, and climbed inside.

The van's engine roared to life. He backed out of the parking spot, clipping the bumper of a car across the lot. He whipped the wheel around and barreled out onto the main street, narrowly avoiding a collision.

Breathing still ragged, DeWayne maneuvered through traffic until he was miles away.

"Make your way back to the seam," Rhoden commanded.

DeWayne didn't hesitate. He had no intention of pissing off his boss. He stopped two blocks farther down than he had been in the car.

"You must get closer."

"Not a good idea. The cops have this area staked out."

"Who are the cops staking?"

The question confused DeWayne for a moment. "No, not staking, like killing vampires. They're watching the area to see if anyone comes back. As soon as I see your people I'll drive up. If we get too close, they might spot us. If that happens, your men could get taken down before they have a chance."

Rhoden appeared to ponder DeWayne's words. "Very well. We'll do this your way. You need to drive past the seam and return here. But cops or no cops, we will get my men."

DeWayne did as he was ordered. As they passed the lot where the seam was, Rhoden made hand gestures and spoke in some strange language. He caught a glimpse of the seam opening as he passed. They rounded the block and stopped in the same spot as before, almost four blocks from the seam.

"Wake me when they arrive." With that, he leaned back in his seat and closed his eyes.

"Ah, sure, boss. Whatever you want."

Chapter 11

Samuel set a ward near the seam in the field and took a long look back at the burning home. Whatever had been happening in Chevalon since he left, it was clearly more dangerous than ever.

He left the muddy fields, his feet soaked and dirty, and trekked north.

Even before Colla's admission about a resistance group in the north, he'd heard rumblings of it over the years while he tried to remain hidden in Chicago. Whatever was up north, it was the best place to find others to aid in the search for the princess.

Samuel kept an eye skyward for Seekers. He'd seen at least three more since the encounter at the farmhouse a few days ago. Mortas seemed to have them at his disposal, and that angered Samuel.

Seekers were strictly under Order control; no person without Order approval had the ability or permission to dispatch them. Mortas must have used Rhoden to secure them to his cause. They were mindless, wretched things anyway, but yet they should never be in the hands of someone like Mortas.

The air grew chillier the farther north he travelled. It reminded him of a trip he'd made in the previous world when following the prince to Wisconsin on a field trip.

He scolded the guardians for allowing it, but Nadina wouldn't hear it.

"He's a boy, Samuel! How's he supposed to learn anything if we don't allow him to experience new things?"

"As a guardian, your job isn't to give him fun experiences. It's to prepare him for a return to Chevalon. He has a duty to fulfill and a land to save."

Nadina rested her fists on her hips. "He's going."

Nordon laughed. "I'd let it go, Samuel. I've been on the wrong side of that scowl one too many times."

"Your only function in this world is to protect him. You were placed here by Phetrix, and I wonder about his judgement when things like this happen."

The mood turned sour. Nordon stood and cracked his knuckles. "We didn't ask for this. The care of the prince was thrust upon us and we're doing the best we can under these circumstances. If you don't like how we handle our duties, find yourself other guardians."

"He's going. Eric needs to get out more. The boy will go crazy if he stays here all the time."

Samuel looked at the two of them and threw his hands in the air. "Fine! But I will not let him out of my sight!"

The following week, he drove behind the yellow school bus as they visited a Christmas tree farm just beyond the border of Wisconsin. At first angry with the guardians for what he perceived as their neglect, he simmered down on the drive and enjoyed the brisk early winter day.

The atmosphere around him now felt much the same. A growing anticipation of what was to come was tempered by the calm coolness of the air. He chuckled to himself for getting so angry at the guardians before.

Samuel let the memories fade and returned his attention to the task at hand. So far, he'd been able to bypass several small houses and a wagon carrying straw. His clothes weren't near warm enough, but the need for secrecy outweighed everything else.

It was on the fifth day away from the farmhouse when he had the first real opportunity to steal someone's clothes.

Near sunrise, he approached a small home. Smoke drifted upwards from the stone chimney. Hiding behind a tall oak tree, he watched the house, waiting for movement. Finally, he spotted a man close to his size leave the house. The man had a bow and a quiver full of arrows slung over his shoulder.

"Out for the hunt? This will be perfect!" Samuel muttered to himself. He waited until the man crested a small rise to the west and carefully crept toward the home. Then his plan was ruined.

"Hello? Who are you? What do you want?" a woman's voice called from inside the home. Samuel hadn't seen anyone else as he spied the house and her voice shocked him.

Reacting in fear, he cast a spell to immobilize her. He waited a moment, then opened the door, hoping the spell worked.

Inside, a small woman much older than himself was frozen in a statuesque pose. Her hand was poised to open the door and one foot was inches from the floor. Had she been any closer to the door, he would have hit her with it. The spell only stopped movement, so she'd still be able to realize what was going on, but until the spell wore off, she couldn't do a thing about it.

"Hello ma'am. Sorry to bother you. You'll be fine soon, I promise. I needed some clothes, that's all."

Samuel carefully maneuvered around her for heavy wool pants and a shirt, and then grabbed a black wool robe. The fabric was rough and scratched his skin. "Too used to the finer materials in the other realm," he chided himself. When he was dressed, he stepped around the woman and left, turning back as he closed the door.

"Say nothing. I promise you, I will repay my debt."

A few feet from the house, he dug a shallow hole and buried his clothes.

Now somewhat protected from the elements, Samuel could travel more openly and approach villages on his path. Random travelers no longer forced him to hide. His trek was north to the rebellion. To the people that could help him rescue the princess and avert further calamity.

If only he wasn't too late.

Chapter 12

On the second day after acquiring clothes, Samuel stumbled upon a small village. He didn't recognize the name but it was old and secluded. The homes were weathered. Frozen mud covered holes and cracks. There was an inn near the central square that caught his attention. He had no money, but he also was tired of the cold. Whatever it took, he'd get a room and a warm meal.

The sign outside the inn was faded, the letters barely legible. *The Bear Trap*.

"Great. Let's hope the inside is better."

Samuel opened the rickety door and was hit with a pungent stench of mold and…death? It was dark inside.

"Hello?"

He waited for a reply. "Hello? Is anyone here?"

When he entered the inn, he expected a roaring fire and at least a few people in the common room. Instead, he found a deserted and dusty shell of what promised to be a good place to stay.

"Where is everyone? What is that awful smell?"

Taking a chance on being discovered, he created a small orb of light to guide him. His breath came out in tiny puffs, the chill penetrating his woolen clothes.

The place was a wreck. The counter was covered in dust. Mold grew along the back wall; long streaks of black racing upwards. The fireplace looked like it hadn't been used in a long time.

"What happened here?"

In comparison to the ever-present mass of humanity in the city, this was eerie.

The floor creaked when he walked to the counter.

"Hello? I'd like a room, please."

He walked past the counter, the hairs on the back of his neck standing up. Nothing felt right about this. The door to a room behind the counter stood ajar, and carefully, he pushed it open.

The smell overpowered him and he cupped a hand over his nose and mouth. When his eyes adjusted, he saw the source of the odor. Two bodies lay intertwined in a grotesque scene of death. An older man and woman were locked forever in an embrace. They seemed to have been tortured, from the looks of the wounds on their frozen flesh.

Samuel inspected them for a moment, hoping to discover the cause of their demise, but the overwhelming funk cut his inspection short. He turned to exit the room when something caught his eye. In the far corner, there was a mass of black fabric with something distinctive on it folded and shoved behind a chair. Part of it leaned out.

"What is this?"

Avoiding the bodies, he slunk along the wall to reach it. Unfurling it, he recognized the sigil immediately. The White Stag of King Artus.

He spun, looking at the couple again. Were they the King and Queen? He shook his head, knowing it wasn't true the moment the thought came to him. They were too old, even after fifteen years.

Samuel tossed the flag back to the floor. Whatever happened to the couple, he expected it had to do with the resistance. It still didn't explain why the inn was deserted.

"Wait…"

He raced out of the room and back to the street. It hadn't occurred to him earlier, but the village was empty. No lights were on in any house. No smoke poured from the chimneys. It was close to nightfall and not a single sound could be heard.

"Mortas, I swear you'll pay for this! Nothing good will come of your actions."

It had to be Mortas Frost. There was no other explanation for it. The people must have been part of the resistance, or at least sympathizers, and they were all killed because of it. He assumed behind every door would be another gruesome scene like at the inn. How long ago did this happen? If he'd have returned with the heirs instead of biding his time and losing one in the process, could he have prevented it? Those were questions he couldn't answer. All he could do was push forward, try to fix the situation, and rid the world—both worlds—of the grip of Mortas Frost.

"There goes my comfy night."

Samuel walked slowly through the village, careful to inspect each home along the way, hoping for a sign of life. By the time he reached the edge of the village, he found nothing. Not even a stray pet. The entire village was just…gone.

"I could use a shot of malort right about now."

Pulling his hood closer around his face, he left the village behind to take his chances in the wilds beyond. He considered creating another small orb of light, but if the Seekers were out, they'd spot him a mile away.

His mission was more crucial now than before. If Mortas was destroying villages no one knew about because their sympathies were with the rightful rulers of Chevalon, what other atrocities was he capable of? It pained him to think he could've done something sooner to stop this. If maybe he brought the heirs back when they were of age instead of waiting until they were older, he could have prevented this. How many more people died because of him?

The image of the couple intertwined in death haunted him. Their twisted bodies mocked him. They accused him.

"You'll get yours, Mortas. You and Rhoden both. The people deserve better, and I'll make sure they get it."

After leaving the village behind, exhaustion crept up on Samuel. He needed rest. He'd been going for several days with little down time. At his age, it wasn't wise to taunt the fates, and years of polish sausage didn't help, either.

A pine tree nearby looked promising. He carefully inspected under the branches, and when certain he was safe, cast a spell obscuring his magic and then set a ward against intruders. It took a while, but he finally got to sleep after creating a small floating flame under the tree. He allowed it to burn out before closing his eyes for the night.

Chapter 13

Grant went to the station after spending the last few hours in the hospital getting his broken and bruised ribs x-rayed and bandaged. He was not in the best of moods to begin with, so when traffic slowed then stopped, he was ready to explode all over someone. As the traffic inched forward, Grant found that someone. Two someones, in fact.

The two men who'd escaped from him in the parking garage were crossing a street. The older man held either a newspaper or map in front of him. Grant passed them. He could have put on the lights and siren and got out, but that would announce his presence and spook them. He was in no mood or condition for a chase. He drove down the street and around the block.

He sped down the first block, afraid they'd pull another disappearing act on him, but his luck held. He spotted them two blocks down crossing the street and entering a residential neighborhood. These were nice homes on smaller lots in a respected older neighborhood a mile outside the city.

Grant wondered what they were doing here. He toyed with the idea of following them but decided he'd rather have them in cuffs and an interview room instead. As they turned down a block still following their map, Grant pulled to the curb and got out. He quick-stepped on his toes to get to them fast with as little noise as possible.

In a booming voice, he shouted, "There you are! Now you're mine!"

Without hesitation, he whipped out cuffs and moved to the younger man. Taken by surprise, the man was frozen to his spot. That didn't prevent Grant from body checking him into a streetlight pole. Pinned there, Grant snapped a cuff on one wrist.

"Hey!" the man said.

Grant ignore him. He dragged the cuffed hand down toward the older man who looked exhausted to Grant and tugged his hand from the map. The paper rolled up as he cuffed the men together. Once secured, he removed their weapons.

"Now, I'm going to get some answers from you two." Neither man responded. The younger man stared dumbly at the cuff. The older man did not look well. His already pale skin whitened to a ghostly pallor. Grant stooped before him. "Are you all right?"

Phetrix gave a faint nod. "Just overextended my power. Not used to using so much anymore. Out of practice. I'll be fine after some rest."

Grant didn't understand much of what the man said, other than that he'd overexerted himself and was now weak. "Okay, let's get you off the street and out of this heat." He guided the two men toward his car and opened the rear door. He told the younger man to get in, then assisted the older man inside. He closed the door and walked back to retrieve the knives, the map, and the sword, and placed them in the trunk. After waiting for traffic to clear, he slid into the driver's seat and turned to face the men.

"Are you well enough to answer some questions?" He'd already made up his mind he was asking them, regardless of the man's response.

"Fine, but please hurry. We may have to leave fast."

"Oh? Someplace else to be? Where's that?"

"I don't know yet. We were following the map."

"To where?"

"That I'm afraid I will keep to myself."

"Well, the sooner you answer my questions, the sooner you can get back to whatever you were doing. Let's start with your names. You couldn't offer ID before, so I'm guessing you don't have any.'

"I am Phetrix. This is Kol."

"And where are you from?"

"Chevalon."

"Chevalon? Never heard of it. Where's that located? Is it a city?"

"It is the kingdom we hail from. It has since fallen into the hands of the usurper, Mortas Frost. We are here to restore the rightful heir to the throne."

Grant's jaw opened. He stared from one man to the next. "Is this some real-life fantasy story? Sorry. I'm not playing. What are your real names?"

"Sir, those are our real names. We can't give you what we do not have."

"Well, you're going to be late to wherever you're going, because I'm taking you in for questioning." He spun in his seat, shifted into drive, and pulled into traffic. A short time later Grant pulled off West 14th Street into the twelfth district parking lot. He parked and opened the rear door. "Get out."

The two men obliged. Grant noted the older man, Phetrix, looked somewhat better. Some color had returned to his face.

"Sir, it is of the utmost importance that we are free. We must be able to reach the heirs. To do so may mean the difference between life and death for them. The lives of every man, woman, and child in our kingdom depends on whether we find and return the heirs safely."

"This is the real world and the real time. I'm not involved in your storyline, so save it for someone who is. Now, move your feet. You're not going anywhere until I'm satisfied with your answers."

Grant pushed them toward a door. Officers entered and exited the building in an almost steady stream. He led them through the lobby. One of the men at the front desk said, "Heard you had a rough day, Grant. You need help?"

"No, Pops. I've got this, but thanks."

With a hand on each man's back he pushed them into a loud and busy room. He maneuvered them down an aisle and plopped Phetrix into a wooden chair. He reached across the aisle and snagged a second chair from another desk and shoved it under Kol. Grant sat with a wince as pain shot through his ribs, reminding him of current events.

"Have we done something wrong to be taken into your custody in such a fashion?" Phetrix asked.

"That remains to be seen. Since you weren't cooperative last time, I'm ensuring your cooperation this time. You have no ID. You say you're from some foreign country I've never heard of, which makes me think you're illegals. And you refuse to answer my simple questions. At this point, I'm holding you on suspicion."

"Of what?" Phetrix asked.

"Suspicion of being suspicious. How's that?"

"We'll be glad to answer your questions to the best of our abilities, but perhaps you can also help us."

Grant blinked in rapid succession. "Wait. How's that? You trying to negotiate with me now?"

Undaunted by Grant's tone, Phetrix continued. "We are here searching for the heirs of the throne to our kingdom."

"So you said. And I said I'm not playing your game. Now, answer my questions or I'm going to find a nice cell to lock you up in until I can find what looney bin you escaped from."

Phetrix jolted erect. His eyes widened and he stood. Grant stood fast and backed a step, hand finding his weapon.

"The map. Where is the map? I must see it before the lines fade. We must go."

"Sit your butt down is what you must do. You're not leaving here until I say so."

"Sorry, sir, but we must. Come, Kol."

Kol stood. Grant's voice rose above the din. "Sit your butts down *now*."

Phetrix pointed at the cuffs and mumbled something Grant could not hear. To his shock the cuffs tumbled to the floor and bounced under his desk. As the two men made their way to the door, Grant shouted, "Freeze!"

The entire room went quiet. All over the room, men jumped from their desks, ready to respond. Several had hands on weapons. Grant already had his in hand.

Chapter 14

Phetrix stopped and scanned the room. There was no way to get out of there without interference. Best to deal with it now and all at once, rather than each man independently. But his magic had been suspect since entering this world. Could he trust it now? He had no choice.

He lifted his hands over his head and turned in a circle, chanting something over and over. He turned faster, putting everything he had into the spell as men approached to apprehend them. Just as three men converged on him, a powerful wind rushed through the room, scattering paper. The sheets were lifted and flew in a circular fashion at a potentially hazardous speed.

The three men were pushed back. Chairs moved across the floor. Phetrix continued to circle faster and faster until the gale force wind prevented anyone from advancing toward him. Most men were pushed backward, losing the fight to gain ground. Standing in the center of the storm, Phetrix and Kol moved with ease toward the door. Someone fired a shot, but the bullet had no effect, if it even reached them at all.

Phetrix followed Kol out the door and into the lobby. The two cops at the front desk moved to intercept them. Kol knocked one down. Phetrix blew the second man back with a blast of wind. They exited the building. Kol ran. Phetrix called after him. "I need the map."

"We can't wait. There's too many of them. We'll come back for it later."

Phetrix sighed at the loss but ran after Kol. His energy was not completely restored, so the spell would not last long. They had to make good their escape before they were caught. They reached the main road. Phetrix pointed. "That way."

They ran down the road. Ahead of them a large vehicle with its back end open made its way down the road. It stopped for a moment under a red light. Kol reached it and climbed up and inside. He leaned down and stretched his hand out for Phetrix. Their hands locked as the car jolted forward with a groan. Still weak, Phetrix was hauled inside. They tumbled back onto a pile of assorted metal items. It was far from comfortable, but it beat running. At least for the moment, it was going in the direction they had traveled previously.

THE WAIT WAS UNBEARABLE. While Rhoden slept, DeWayne kept watch. He grew more antsy by the minute. This was not what he wanted to be doing. He had some money now, though not nearly enough. He could leave town and never come back. This was not his thing. Too many cops, too many crazy people, and way too much weird stuff going on, like the seam. What if this was an alien invasion and he was helping them to take over the world? That made sense. They came from another world. It certainly wasn't anyplace he'd ever heard about. And what was all that magic stuff they did? They tossed the cops and their vehicles around like they were nothing but Matchbox toys.

He cried out and jumped in his seat at the sudden grab of his arm. The grip tightened until he settled down. He looked at Rhoden and saw the man's eyes were still closed. For a moment he feared the man had been reading his mind. Then he spoke. "They are coming. Get closer. It will be best if they are not seen."

DeWayne started the van. The hand continued its grip on his arm, releasing only after the van moved. DeWayne drove slowly. So far, he saw no sign of the opening.

"Use the van to block the area."

"Okay." He passed the location of the seam and did a U-turn. He stopped next to the open lot. Ten seconds later, the zipper pulled back and the other world opened up. A head poked out, but it didn't look human. It did a scan of the area, stopping on the van. Rhoden gave a nod and the first man stepped out.

DeWayne watched in horror as each man that followed appeared bigger than his predecessor. The six muscle-bound hulks walked in an army formation, their movements awkward and wide. As they entered the van, it tilted until the first two were seated. The back end of the van was so low, DeWayne feared the shocks would give way.

"Drive," Rhoden said.

"Where to?"

"Just go. I'll know more soon."

DeWayne kept the speed down, not only to avoid notice, but for fear of hitting a bump at a higher speed might bottom out the rear end. He had never seen such big men before. He glanced in the mirror. They all sat stone-faced, their black eyes looking forward, never moving. They barely blinked. DeWayne was reminded of some science fiction movie he once saw where the invaders were all clones. Rhoden was strange and scary, but these dudes were weird. Maybe it really was an alien invasion.

They drove on for several miles before Rhoden said, "Turn here."

DeWayne obeyed. A few more blocks and another command to turn. Then, "Stop." The word had come with such suddenness and force that DeWayne stomped on the brakes, sending the six clones forward into the seats in front of them. The man behind DeWayne's seat hit the back hard enough to toss him into the wheel. It took a few moments for the van to settle.

"You will wait here. One of my men will guide you when it's time." He opened the door and stepped out.

Darkness had fallen. Rhoden picked an unlit area near a deserted and desolate portion on the outskirts of the city. The headlights caught movement. A nearly transparent form landed ten feet in front of the van.

DeWayne's jaw gaped as Rhoden approach the creature. It was difficult to make out details, since much of the light went right through the creature, but a few dark spots inside the frame of its body gave some definition. It had wings and looked like a ghost. It squatted on two legs.

Rhoden appeared to be conversing with the thing. Then, to DeWayne's surprise, Rhoden climbed on the creatures back and sat between the wings, and it took flight. One of the men from the back opened the sliding door and got in the front seat. The van rocked under his weight.

Dewayne looked at the man. He made no comment, only staring straight ahead. Unsure of what to do, he said, "Am I supposed to follow him or stay here?"

There was no response or any indication his words had been heard. He sighed and sat back. As the minutes ticked away, he grew restless. He wanted to get out and stretch his legs. He also needed some fresh air. The van had taken on a foul odor. He swished his hand in front of his nose. "Whew! One of you needs to step outside if you're gonna be all gassy." No one moved.

DeWayne reached for the door. As it opened, the man next to him growled. It was a deep rumbling sound that left no doubt in DeWayne's mind that the growler was not happy with his decision to leave. He glanced at the man next to him. Though DeWayne was not looking at him, the man's face had altered in appearance, making him look more animal than a human. He closed the door. As soon as it shut, the growling ceased. "Okay, don't go getting all ferocious. I just wanted some air."

He looked at the man, whose gaze was still focused ahead. A look in the mirror showed the others were in the same position. With them paying him no attention, he took the opportunity to study them. Large round heads; slightly bulging eyes like all the weightlifting had pushed them forward in their sockets. Protruding foreheads with plastered black hair. A slight greenish tinge to their skin that reminded him of an alligator. *And what the hell was that?* Down the back of the necks were reptilelike bumps and ridges. The sight made him queasy. These were not humans. He had no idea what they were, but he thought of them as reptile men. He sat with his back pressed against the door, wanting distance from whatever these things were and access to the door handle, should the need arise for a fast getaway.

As if understanding his thoughts, the reptile man sitting next to him turned his head and looked at him. The eyes changed from round pupils to slanted, then back again. His body began to shake uncontrollably. He looked away to calm himself, but a voice said, "Go. Now."

Had there been a hiss in those words? He looked at the beast, surprised it could speak. The eyes and the face looked normal. Had he imagined the whole thing? Was the darkness playing tricks with his overactive imagination?

"Okay," he managed. "Where?"

The man-thing flicked a massive hand toward the windshield. "Go. Now."

Happy to be moving, Dewayne put the van in gear and drove, praying this night would end soon and he'd be alive to see the morning.

Chapter 15

Samuel left the village behind and tried to forget the horrors within. It was too much, and his guilt didn't need the anguish. The early morning sun was soon obscured by dark gray clouds.

"The last thing I need is rain."

He grumbled and pulled his robe over his head, waiting for the heavens to open up. For most of the morning, he was spared the inconvenience, much to his delight.

Near the noon hour, he heard the screech of a Seeker and scrambled to hide under a tree. He watched as it circled above as though it had caught his scent. He cast a quick spell to hide his ability, and the thing howled at the lost trail and darted to the west, hopefully gone for good.

"Fancy bit o' cover up, eh?"

Samuel nearly jumped out of his skin at the voice behind him. Instinctively he drew in a huge amount of power, ready to unleash it on his interloper.

"Whoa! Whoa there, fella. No need to do that." The man held up his hands in a gesture indicating he was not a threat. He was tall and skinny and covered in thick gray furs. His smile was unnerving. One of his bottom teeth was missing and his tongue poked through. Samuel forced a grin.

"What's funny, old man?"

"Nothing. Sorry. Please forgive me."

"Who are you? Whose side are you on?"

Samuel froze. *What was the correct answer?*

"What are you implying?"

"Whose side do you support? Mortas or the resistance?"

Samuel considered his options. The man seemed to be alone. If Samuel gave him an answer he didn't agree with, he might have to fight his way out of this. Not that Samuel presented a physical challenge to the man, but with his powers restored fully since returning, he'd have no problem dispatching him. If the man had accomplices, then the situation would be more dire than expected.

"Who do you think I support?"

"By the way you fooled that Seeker, I'd say you belong to the resistance. Is that right?"

The man shifted his feet and slid out a dagger from under his thick coat.

"You are an observant man. I am what you say."

Samuel prepared himself to unleash a blast of electricity at the man. A few tense moments passed and the man sheathed his dagger.

"Only a fool would make that claim." He grinned and slapped Samuel on the shoulder. "I figured you were one of us!"

Samuel released the energy and relaxed. He'd found the resistance!

"Name's Charkra, but you can call me Char. Most do anyway, so it's no problem."

"I'm…" Samuel hesitated, unsure if he should reveal his identity just yet.

"I'm Lemmox, from a village to the south. Pleased to meet you." He extended a hand and Char paused before grasping it.

"Well…Lemmox? Nice to meet you. I guess you heard the call. We've gathered just beyond that ridge."

"The resistance is here? What about…what about the King?"

"I think it best you ask your questions to our leader. She can answer you better. But, if I'm gonna take you there, I gotta blindfold you."

Samuel turned his head to the side. "Huh?"

"You expect me to trust that you're some good-hearted old man who wants to fight on our side? How do I know you aren't one of Rhoden's men? How am I supposed to know if you are telling the truth?"

"I guess there's no other way."

Reluctantly, he allowed Char to cover his eyes and tie the fabric behind his head.

"Try anything stupid, and that dagger will slit your throat. Am I clear?"

"How do I know *you* aren't the one lying to *me*? For all I know, you might be one of Mortas's men, here to lead me to my death."

Char laughed. "That's a good point. It's not gonna change our situation, but I guess you have a right to be scared."

Samuel attempted to use a spell to see outside of his body, to get an idea what was going on, but it was no use. He hadn't used it in so long, he couldn't remember the details. Besides, he didn't want to give away any more of his magical powers than he already had. The element of surprise was better if left as such. He'd be ready for anything if the time came.

At least he hoped so.

Char pushed him forward, causing him to stumble. "Come on, old man. This way. Don't worry. I won't let ya fall."

Samuel cautiously stepped forward, moving slowly in hopes of avoiding a branch or other obstacle. Every once in a while, Char would turn him a different direction, making him wonder if he were being pushed in circles.

"Are we there yet?"

Samuel giggled when he said it. The phrase reminded him of the princess and the story told to him of how anxious she got when her guardians drove her to St. Louis to see the Arch. They shared of how she asked them over and over, "Are we there yet?" so much that Markus nearly pulled off the side of Interstate 55 just north of Springfield to let her out.

Now, Samuel wondered where in Chevalon she was. Reuniting her with her parents was all he could do now. Rescuing her from Mortas had to be part of the plan. She couldn't be left with that man.

"Are we what? I'll tell you when we are."

Char pushed him roughly, obviously not seeing the humor in his question.

Samuel relaxed and allowed the man to guide him, trusting that he wasn't making a mistake.

After nearly an hour, Char stopped pushing him.

"We're here. I warn you, try anything stupid and you will die." To emphasize the point, he poked him in the back with the dagger.

He ripped off the blindfold and Samuel drew a tremendous amount to power, ready to strike.

When his eyes cleared, an older woman smiled back at him. Her bright blue eyes were striking.

"Welcome. We've been hoping you'd return, Samuel."

His heart quickened. "Who are you? How do you know my name?"

She smiled wider. "Don't you recognize me?"

Slowly, her face turned from that of a wrinkled old woman into a young woman with brown hair. Samuel gasped.

"Mathilda?"

"In the flesh!"

Chapter 16

Samuel could hardly take his eyes off the young woman in front of him. Years had gone by since he last met her, and she appeared not to age a bit. What the people in the other realm wouldn't do to get her secret!

Samuel noticed they were in a small room with dark wooden walls. The glow of candles lit the room.

"Where are we? What are you doing here?"

"Nice to see you, too, Samuel."

He had no time for games. If he was at the resistance camp, then the royals should be nearby.

"I'm looking for King Artus and Queen Griselda. Are they here?"

As expected, he got no answer. He debated how much to tell, but since she already knew who he was, he added, "Their daughter, Princess Elysande, has been brought back by Mortas and his men. I assume he intends to make a public display of her death."

Mathilda cocked her head to the side. "I thought you were protecting them in this land…Chicago, is it?"

Samuel's face flushed deep red. "We were. We had them hidden—"
He turned to the side, considering her words. Char shifted behind him. "How did you know about the other place? Who told you?"

Mathilda causally walked around the room; her finger pressed to her lips in thought. They were the only ones in the room besides Char. Outside, men were shouting about Seekers.

"We have visitors. They must have followed you!"

Mathilda pointed a bony finger at him. "If you brought them here after we've been hidden for years, I swear…"

"Who do you think you are, Mathilda? All of this…the resistance, the traveling, everything…is my plan. None of this is possible unless it was from me."

"Then maybe you should have returned sooner. How many murders have you witnessed? How many of the Order did you watch get hunted down and tortured by those Seekers?"

A woman burst into the room. Char reached for his dagger in anticipation.

"Mathilda, Seekers fly overhead!"

"Are we hidden? Have we moved everyone into cover?"

"I think so, ma'am. The Seekers haven't scoured the camp. They seem content to continue flying."

"Report to me if they get too close. Thanks for the update."

Samuel's anger grew hotter. Who were these people to deny him? They had no right! All of this was his plan from the beginning.

"Do you know where the royals are? Do they live? Are they here?"

Mathilda shook her head. "It is not the time to discuss such matters as our people cower from the Seekers. Let the danger pass and we can discuss the situation over a warm meal." Mathilda turned to leave. "Oh, you can have free reign of the camp. Char, make sure no one bothers Samuel. He is, after all, the man behind our cause."

Char nodded.

"No! I demand answers now! I've seen what Mortas will do to wipe out the past and kill the royal family! He traveled across the seam to a world I thought safe from his touch. He's killed good people. I've travelled far and been through dangers. I will not budge until you give me the answers I seek."

"No."

"*No?* No…what? They aren't alive?"

"No, I won't tell you now. Get over yourself, Samuel. You acted like a coward when you chose to flee instead of fight. I've been left here to pick up the pieces. We've struggled to maintain a resistance, but we have maintained it. Many lives were lost in the process. You don't get to come in here demanding anything. The Order is no longer. The previous hierarchy no longer exists. We've done what we had to for our survival. I know Phetrix was here for years, but now he is gone Whatever you have him doing, I hope it leads to a resolution quickly. Your plan so far hasn't been the best. We'll talk later." She exited the room, the tension of the moment lingering.

Who were these people to act in such a way? If it weren't for him, they'd all be dead. Their job was important because he made it important. Ungrateful!

Char left him alone, the tall man slinking out of the room and into the camp outside. Samuel did the same, preferring to find answers instead of waiting for them.

The moment he went outside, he spotted the Seekers above. They cried out but were already moving past the camp.

Tents and a few shoddily built wooden structures dominated the valley. There were far more people than Samuel had expected. It gave him hope that this many defied Mortas and banded together. He might yet pull off the insurrection with these people at his side.

Samuel glided through the camp, inspecting the people and looking for any sign of the King and Queen. The longer he went without seeing them and without any sign of their existence, the more concerned he grew.

"A beast! Gather arms! We have a pod of beasts!" A woman screamed. She was near the food tents about fifty yards to his left.

"A beast? A snowbeast? They exist?"

Samuel heard the rumors before he left. They were similar to what they called a Yeti in the other world. Like in that world, he didn't think they were real.

Men and women raced by with spears and bows. A few men had swords that had seen better days. A great gathering assembled near the cook tents and Samuel drew closer, intending to learn whatever information he could.

"We all knew moving here was dangerous. These lands hold creatures the rest of Chevalon dares not believe in. It has created a natural barrier to Mortas's forces. Other than the Seekers, we've been safe. The time has now come for us to defend ourselves. Snowbeasts do not distinguish between leaders or followers, or between rich or poor. They're ruthless killers," the woman said.

Samuel followed the crowd, hoping to catch a glimpse of the beasts. The woman continued her lecture. "Before Mortas stormed the castle, evil like this didn't roam Chevalon. Destructive creatures were held in check, as though some cosmic force was at play. Since Mortas claimed the throne, more and more creatures like this were given a freedom they never should have had." The situation had grown dire, indeed.

"Over there!" a man shouted. The crowd turned to the left and four giant snowbeasts scrambled toward them.

"What in the world…" Samuel said. The beasts were taller than any man he'd ever met, and that included those men in the other world that played basketball. They were thick and their white fur protected them from the cold. With long fangs and blood-red eyes, they looked like something out of a horror movie.

They roared and rushed at any movement. One man was too close and the snowbeasts ripped into him, shredding his clothes and flesh in a matter of moments. A hush fell over the crowd.

"Do not give up! We must repel them or face more!" the woman organizer shouted. A group of archers spread out to either side of the pod and fired arrows into their midst. By their howls, Samuel could tell they had found their mark.

Still, the creatures persisted and pushed forward.

The efforts of the crowd seemed to falter. Nothing worked. Samuel decided to act.

He stepped in front of the crowd as the snowbeasts barreled down on them. Drawing in a significant amount of energy, he shot the beasts with destructive bolts of lightning. The people nearby covered their ears. He struck the foremost beast and it flew backwards from the blow, landing lifeless on its back.

The other beasts didn't flinch and continued their bloodlust. Samuel followed his initial surge with a more powerful one, striking the remaining three beasts. The lightning bore a hole through their bodies, shattering bones and singeing their fur. The three collapsed to the ground. Several from the crowd ran to them to check for signs of life. All three were dead.

The crowd turned to Samuel, a hushed anxiety rising up amongst them. Mathilda strolled from the back.

"Is everyone ok? Anyone hurt?" Her eyes fell on the mauled man and she bowed her head, mumbling words no one understood. When she looked up, she turned to Samuel. He'd recovered from the magical blast and was stretching his hands.

"So, you've come to actually do something? It's about time."

Samuel let the power leave him and focused on Mathilda. "I did what I thought was best. Mortas was more devious and powerful than I had imagined. He let his mage create things that shouldn't be. I didn't expect one of the Order would betray us all."

"Everyone: prepare to move again. The Seekers will surely have noticed a display of power like that. We must remain on the move until we can settle again."

Mathilda glared at Samuel. "Come with me." She turned and stalked off toward a tent. Samuel considered leaving. Nothing here was what he'd expected. He began thinking the King and Queen were dead and he was wasting his time, unless he could get someone to help him rescue Elly. She was now the most important focus. She had to be. If Mortas had his way, she'd soon be dead if she wasn't already. Chevalon deserved better.

Chapter 17

Nadina prepared one of Eric's favorite meals: pork chops with fried apples, mashed potatoes, and fresh corn. She wasn't sure why she had put forth so much effort, other than a hope to put him in a receptive mood for the discussion they needed to have later.

Talk at the table was light, revolving around Eric's enthusiasm over being selected to represent the fencing club in an upcoming tournament. He spoke with excitement, pleased with the honor and the chance to show his skill to a larger audience.

Nadina didn't have the heart to tell him the tournament would not be happening for him. She watched as he ate with gusto. The sparkle in his bright blue eyes and the glow on his face was everything a mother wished to see in their child. And though she never forgot who Eric was or her own purpose in this world, she did think of him as her own. It was her right. After all, she had raised him; given up everything for his well-being. His real mother had only two years with him. Dina doubted the queen would even recognize her own child after all this time.

She thought about that. If the roles were reversed, how would she handle not being able to see her child for nearly sixteen years? It would drive her crazy with fear and worry. Her thoughts drifted to the queen. She was nice enough, though Nadina had only passing words with her. She had been nothing more than a castle servant. The queen most likely never knew her name. Was the queen even still alive? The thought both excited and saddened her. Eric was just as much hers as he was the queen's. Would she be able to give him up? She was not looking forward to destroying Eric's version of the world.

"This is really great, Mom," he said.

His voice broke the spell of memories. All she heard, all she ever needed to hear, was the word mom. She looked at her son and could not stop the explosion of tears. She stood in a rush and left the table.

"Mom?" His voice followed her. She knew he'd be concerned. He was such a great boy. But she couldn't face him now. She had to compose herself. She had to be strong, because after their talk, Eric would never again look at her the same way. He'd never again call her Mom.

GRANT WAS FILLED with rage as he left the captain's office. He'd taken a major chewing out for what the old man did to the station. He got shouted at for not searching his suspects more thoroughly. It was obvious the man had some sort of mechanized weapon on his person under that robe. Otherwise, how could he explain the damage done?

Though Grant took the dressing-down, he was certain whatever the old man had done was not a form of mechanized weapon or terrorism. The entire ordeal was surreal. It was as if the man waved his hands and made the tornado happen, Just like magic. He dared not utter that word in front of the captain, but whatever had happened...whatever *had been* happening was beyond any explanation he could give besides magic.

Regardless, he was going to find those two rejects from a fantasy role-playing campaign and make them pay. He ignored the glares from his colleagues, most still picking up the scattered paperwork around the room and made for the door. Once outside, he paused to unleash his pent-up anger in a roar of frustration and went to his car.

Before he got in, his partner Jessie Vega trotted up. "Captain says you're going to need some assistance."

Grant stared at him for a moment. The captain was having him watched. Maybe it was for the best. Whatever happened now, there'd be another witness to attest to the events. He nodded, got in, and buttoned the passenger door open.

Vega slid in. "Strange goings on, huh?"

"You got that right." He started the engine.

"So, what do you think caused it?"

So the captain wanted Vega to pump him for his thoughts. He wasn't that easy, nor that naïve. "Haven't a clue. But I'm going to find out."

He pulled out onto West 14th Street. One of the officers entering the lot during the escape said he saw them running in that direction. That was where he'd start. They were on foot, so couldn't be that far ahead. Their description had been sent to all units. Their appearance should make them easy to spot. So far, however, they'd evaded notice. That worried Grant. If this man did have some strange magical ability, perhaps one of his skills was invisibility.

Grant glanced at Vega. The man was studying him. He dared not voice his theory for fear of ridicule and being sent to a department shrink for analysis. He stopped at the next intersection and tried to determine the best route. That no one had reported a sighting made him think they'd stayed off the main roads. A thought came to him. They were dressed like homeless men. The homeless had usual routes and hangouts where they knew they wouldn't be pestered and could find food and lodging. He turned toward the nearest one.

Though he'd been up for the better part of a day, sleep was far from his mind, as was the broken rib. He wanted to find those men and wouldn't stop looking until he had them locked away.

IT WAS DARK. Phetrix had no idea where they were but thought they were still on the right course. The truck turned off the path quite a while ago, putting them back on foot. With no idea how much further they needed to go, Phetrix could only hope to find the location without the map before being discovered again.

The constant focus and travels left him exhausted, but he dared not release the slim hold he had on finding the heirs. They plodded on, strides getting shorter and steps taking longer.

They passed under a bridge. Above them, the rumbling of this world's magical carts echoed. Something stirred to the right, up a slope leading to the bridge. Three men descended and planted in front of their path. Phetrix continued forward, but Kol stopped.

"Excuse me, sirs." He attempted to pass, but one of the men blocked his way.

"This here's what's known as a toll road," the tallest man said. "You got to pay a fee in order to pass."

"We have nothing to pay with," Phetrix said.

"Well, that's a shame, but forgive me for not taking your word. We're gonna have to search you."

Two of the men stepped forward. As they grabbed Phetrix, Kol ran up on the right and punched the man. He went flying, hit the ground, tumbled, and rolled to a dazed stop. The man giving the orders flicked open a knife and swiped at Kol.

Phetrix muttered, "We don't have time for this," and punched the man on his left in the eye. The man released him and howled, covering the injured eye with his hand. Phetrix stomped down on his foot. The howling increased. The man hopped on one foot while still holding his eye. Phetrix stepped forward and shoved the man's chest. He toppled over.

Kol managed to snag the knife wielder's wrist. He gave it a vicious jerk and something snapped, followed by a high-pitched keening that hurt the ears. Kol took the knife from the man's hand and shoved him backward. He examined the blade. Satisfied with its potential, he slipped it into his rope belt.

Phetrix announced, "We have to go that way." He pointed.

"Let's go, then," said Kol. "But I got to warn you, I'm beyond exhaustion. I'm not sure how much longer I can go."

Phetrix sighed. He walked on with no idea where he was going.

Chapter 18

Rhoden melded with the Seeker, utilizing its superior senses to search for signs of magic. Whoever was protecting the heirs was good. The signs were undetectable, unless you were better than the wizard who set the wards. Once triggered, they gave off the faintest hue of magic. It lasted but a few seconds. If he didn't pick up the thread right away, it would be lost.

He guided the Seeker in a pattern that enabled him to scan three blocks at once. He was still amazed at the size and number of houses here. Dreams of conquest returned. After he found the second heir, he would disappear into this world and begin his planned takeover. Once complete, he would lead an army back through the seam and destroy Mortas Frost.

Below and to the right, a faint tone sounded like that of a tiny bell. He turned the Seeker hard and into a dive. The creature screeched at the sudden move, but Rhoden silenced it with a slap to the side of its translucent head. The tone faded. "No, not yet."

But it was already too late. Still, all was not lost. He narrowed the hunt down to the middle of one block. Ten to twelve houses. He would just have to search them all.

"Come, now," he sent out the command for his men. While he waited for their arrival, he sent the Seeker lower until it was ten yards above the rooftops. Sweeping back and forth, Rhoden scanned for signs that at least might eliminate some of the houses if they didn't lead him to the boy.

"I DON'T UNDERSTAND, Dad. Did I say something to upset her?"

Eric looked confused and hurt. Nordon sighed and pushed back from the table. "No, son, it's not you. There are things in play at the moment that have us both on edge; things we planned on discussing with you tonight after dinner."

"Things? What things? Are you or Mom in some sort of trouble?"

"These are things that will have an impact on all of us but will affect you more than us."

"Wait! What are you saying? You're not going to tell me I'm adopted or something, are you?"

Nordon studied the boy. He was such a good boy—no, strike that--young man. So smart, kind, and caring. He had a big heart. He was a son to make any man proud, yet, he was not his son by birth. He might have raised him, but in truth, he was nothing more than a placeholder or a guardian.

"Seriously? Is that it?"

"In a way, yes. But Eric, there is so much more to the story and you need to hear it all to understand not only who you are, but how your life is about to change."

In a sudden eruption of sound and light, the alarms went off. Though tuned for Dina's and his ears, the boy reacted. "What is that?"

Nordon stood, his chair toppling backward. Eric stood as well, a look of confusion and fear creasing his face. Nadina ran into the room. "We're too late."

"I'm sorry, Dina. You were right. I thought we'd have more time."

"Can't be helped now. We must protect Eric. Get to the monitors. I'll get the weapons."

Nordon raced for the stairs.

Eric said, "Protect me? From what?"

No time now," Dina said. "Follow my directions. Do not question or argue. Your life may depend on how fast you react."

"But--"

She shoved him from behind. "Move. Get up the stairs. Now."

Dina burst ahead of him, taking the stairs two at a time. She entered her bedroom and slid on her knees to the side of the bed. From underneath she pulled two large cases. Eric stood behind her as she opened the smaller case and pulled out a machine pistol, a handgun in a holster, and a combat knife in a sheath.

"Grab that case and take it upstairs to your father."

"Upstairs? Where's there an upstairs."

"Eric, pick up the case."

He did so and followed his mother into the closet. A row of hanging clothes was shoved to one side, revealing an open door and stairs leading up.

"What the..."

"Move, Eric. We can discuss all of this later if we survive."

"Survive?"

She didn't wait for him and bounded up the attic stairs. She heard him follow.

Nordon was seated at a table with five monitors mounted above it. The room was swathed in a reddish glow. As she approached, Nordon tapped some keys and the larger center monitor's image changed.

Dina leaned over his shoulder to get a look. "Anything?"

"Nothing yet, but...there!" He pointed at a lower screen, tapped a key, and sent it to the larger central one. An image of a man riding a Seeker flashed. The camera followed the creature for a few seconds before it flew from view.

"Which camera?" Dina asked.

"The back."

She turned, but Nordon grabbed her arm. "You handle this. I'll go." He stood and moved from the table. Dina took his arm. For a moment they exchanged knowing looks, but neither spoke. Then, in a tender move, Nordon patted her hand and the moment faded. He moved to Eric and took the case from his hand. He set it down, opened it and withdrew a massive weapon with three barrels. He closed the case, picked it up and stood. Eric's face paled. His mouth hung open. "You stay here. Do what your—mother tells you." He hastened down the stairs.

"What is going on?" Eric asked. "What's with the guns and all this cloak and dagger stuff? Please tell me we're not terrorists."

"I'll try to answer your questions, but it's important I keep watch. And no, we're not terrorists."

Eric stepped closer to get a better look at the monitors. "What is it you see?" Something flashed across a monitor. Eric stiffened and stepped back. "What was that? It looked like someone riding a dragon or something."

Dina worked the keys. The Seeker was no longer in view but was now in front of the house. That worried her. It wasn't moving on. It was as if it was narrowing a search grid. A thought struck. *Was it tuning into the wards?* Her fingers flew across the keyboard and the reddish glow and the alarm ceased. To her dismay, the creature returned and hovered in front of the neighbor's house. The rider turned his head from side to side as if trying to determine which house they were in.

She didn't know how, but the rider knew they were there, someplace. He might not have zeroed in on the exact location, but he knew they were close.

Dina took out her phone and called Samuel. It rang and she left a message. "I think we've been discovered. We need help."

"Mom, talk to me. What is that thing?"

"It's called a Seeker. It's looking for you."

"Me? Why me?"

Dina's shoulder's sagged. "I didn't want to tell you like this. It's from another world. The world you come from. It's been hunting for you for fifteen years."

"The world I come from? What are you saying? I'm some sort of alien?"

"In a sense, yes. You are heir to the throne of a world called Chevalon. The castle was attacked and you were forced to flee. We have kept you safe for all these years, but for whatever reason, they have discovered you."

Eric could only utter sounds. He cleared his throat, which felt suddenly parched. "What happens if they find me?"

Nadina turned her worried face toward Eric. "Nothing good."

Chapter 19

As they crossed the now bustling camp, Mathilda spoke to Samuel. "I don't mean to be so harsh. We've been through a lot. It crushed my soul to see the Order decimated like it was. There are very few left. I dare say you, Phetrix, and myself are the remaining members. And Rhoden, but…we both know what he's turned into."

"I've been under similar stress trying to keep the heirs safe in a dimension so unlike ours. Have you ever seen a baseball game or deep-dish pizza?"

Mathilda looked at him with a confused expression. "What are those?"

"There are so many unique and wonderful things to experience in the other realm. They call it Earth. There's a lot of problems there, but it's fascinating all the same." He rubbed against the stubble that had grown on his face since returning. He chuckled, knowing if he were back in Chicago, he'd have shaved days ago. The long beard he used to sport no longer felt necessary.

"No matter. My apologies for my actions. I meant no disrespect. You did create this plan. It's been a good one, at least as good as it can be, considering how ruthless Mortas turned out to be."

"Mathilda, what about the King and Queen? Is there hope yet? Are they still alive? Please tell me they're ok. If not, we must find Elly and save her. Mortas will surely kill her."

Mathilda stopped and took his hands in hers. "Samuel, the King and Queen—"

"Attack! To arms!" a man shouted.

Samuel and Mathilda turned toward him. "Oh no," Samuel whispered. A Seeker had dropped from the sky and circled the man who screamed for help. Others ran to him, but then more Seekers appeared from nowhere. Seekers harassed the entire camp, tearing into the men and woman as they raced by.

"No! They must have homed in on your magic!"

Guilt overpowered Samuel. He didn't mean for this to happen. His anger got ahold of him. "Then I have to stop them."

"Not alone." Mathilda stood next to him and he felt her grasp the power around them. He did the same, withdrawing a vast amount of power. He had no fear of weakening or losing the stored magic.

"It's too late to stay hidden. Mortas has found us! Do what you can to stop them and save the people!"

Mathilda nodded and ran to one side of the camp, her power radiating from her.

Samuel gazed at the Seekers nearby and marveled at how they terrorized at will. "Rhoden, what have you done?"

Samuel pushed his hands forward and white fire erupted from his fingers. It streaked across the camp, boring into the nearest Seeker. The horrid black creature cried out in agony, but Samuel didn't wait. He unleashed another quick spear of flame, it, too, finding its mark. The Seeker howled, forcing Samuel to cover his ears. When the screams died, Samuel continued to hear echoes of its pain in his head.

The Seeker swirled around the camp, crying out. Then, behind him, Samuel stared at a small force of soldiers all dressed in black armor with the snowflake of Mortas Frost on their chests.

"No!"

The soldiers swung their heavy swords, slicing into anyone they could find. The cries of the people rose higher than the screams of the Seekers.

Mathilda's power blossomed and he watched as she fought off a Seeker, but she seemed unaware of the soldiers.

A Seeker cried out, pulling Samuel's attention away from the soldiers. He spun in time to catch the Seeker slamming into him, knocking him breathless to the ground.

Chaos erupted around him. Soldiers fought against the resistance, their superior weapons handling everything thrown at them. The Seeker swung back around, screeching and diving for him.

Samuel struggled just to breathe. He was too old for this kind of fight. The Seeker raked its deadly claws across his arms, and it was like molten iron running across his flesh. Samuel squirmed on the ground for what felt like an eternity, finally able to breathe again and rose slowly to his feet.

The soldiers had cut a swath through the disorganized resistance fighters. Bloody bodies lay strewn across the camp. Screaming, crying, and shouting people added to the already confusing state of affairs.

Samuel pulled in his power and unleashed a torrent of white fire at the soldiers in black. He collapsed to his knees, the strain too much. When he looked up, several of the soldiers were lying on the ground. Far too many still stood. He hadn't done enough. They continued to attack the resistance, who by now, was organizing some sort of counter.

The Seeker cried out, forcing Samuel to find it in the sky. He drew in the power and fired a thin strand of lightning at it. The bolt struck the Seeker and it exploded in a burst of ash.

Mathilda was across the field. She'd fought off two of the Seekers, but one remained. The resistance around her formed into straight lines, ready for the soldiers that attacked from Samuel's side.

"Come on! Get up, old man!"

Samuel looked up at Char. He'd raced across the camp with two others, fighting the soldiers until they got to him.

"Save the King. Save the Queen," Samuel said in a weak voice.

"What are you talking about? Get on your feet and come with us!" Char replied.

They yanked him up, his legs wobbly and weak. The soldiers approached and Samuel pulled in more energy than ever. Just as he felt like his body would break, he let it fly toward the soldiers. The white explosion created a massive boom that echoed across the camp. The soldiers flew backwards, their bodies ripped apart by the blast. Samuel fell down again, far too weak to continue.

Char and the two men with him chased after the remaining soldiers, screaming as they ran. Samuel heard the clang of sword on sword, followed by the victorious shouts from Char.

Mathilda followed his lead and fired a thick lightning bolt at the Seeker. When it struck, it vaporized the black creature, ending the fight.

Groans from the wounded broke the eerie silence. Samuel's ears were ringing from the explosions. Slowly, he stood and surveyed the damage.

Wiping his face, he realized how terrible the attack had been. Well over half the resistance, or close to it, lay dead. He could not summon enough healing spells to fix all the wounded. And there'd be more dead soon.

"How? What happened?" he said in a weak voice.

Char returned and the two fighters with him each lifted Samuel up under their arms.

"It's ok now, old man. The enemy is dead."

"For now. How long until they send more? We…we need to end this. We need to get the princess."

By the time they met Mathilda in the middle of the camp, Samuel found it difficult to cling to reality. The dead surrounding him was too much. The vile actions of Mortas Frost stared at him with dead eyes.

"Samuel, are you all right? Are you hurt?"

Mathilda wove a spell over him and he felt the healing begin.

"I live. More than I can say for your people. How did they find us?"

He knew the answer when he asked the question, but he didn't want to believe it.

"We'll regroup and continue on. We can never let Mortas win. The time for the resistance to rise is now."

Samuel hoped she was right. He didn't have the answers yet.

Chapter 20

"There," Phetrix said. "I felt it without the spell. Someone is using magic. It is strong enough to feel. That can't be good. We have to hurry."

The two men increased their pace, but even with an adrenaline boost, neither was in condition to keep up a fast pace for more than a few minutes.

Between gulps of air, Kol said, "Do you know how far away?"

"No. The signal is strong but that could because of the spell I cast. Either it's close, or whoever is using the magic is powerful."

"We need to find a faster way to get around this town."

Phetrix had the same thought. If only he knew how to manipulate one of the cars. They hustled around a corner and found themselves on a main thoroughfare. Twin lights played over them in a steady cadence of passing cars. Buildings were smaller and ahead gave way to the smaller structures Samuel had called houses.

His chest pounded from the strain of their pace. Air was difficult to find. He didn't know how much longer he could go, but the thought of losing the heirs drove him onward.

Lights caught them in their beam. The car swerved to the side of the road, keeping them in the spotlight. Both doors swung open and two voices shouted, "Freeze! Police!"

Startled by their sudden appearance, Phetrix did halt, but only for a second. "We do not have time for this. We must be on our way."

"If you don't stop right now, I will shoot."

"Shoot?" Phetrix stopped again. Next to him Kol withdrew the knife he had taken from the attacker.

One of the men moved forward, but Phetrix could not distinguish him with the lights in his eyes. He put up a hand to shield them.

"He's got a knife, Vega."

"Drop the knife," Vega shouted, swinging toward Kol. "I'm not going to tell you again. You want to die?"

Kol looked nervous. This was all too much for him. He was completely out of his element. Phetrix said, "Put down the knife, Kol. Don't get killed. This may be the break we needed."

Kol thought for a second, then bent and dropped the knife. The two men approached aiming strange metal things at them. As the taller man got closer, Phetrix recognized him. It was the local sheriff. Detective Something.

Phetrix was grabbed roughly and shoved against the car. His arms were yanked behind him and he felt a hard pinch on his wrists. "Please sir, we must be free. Someone's life depends on us."

"Yeah, let me guess. Someone's about to be eaten by a dragon and you have to cast a spell to protect them."

"That's not be far from the truth, although not a dragon. I may be the only person who can save those in trouble. Please, just take us to where I need to go and you'll see for yourself."

"And where is this person who's in danger?"

"I'm not sure, but we were following the thread when you arrived. Please, this is most important."

"Yeah, well, I've got important things to take care of, too. Like hauling your butts back to the station where I can lock you up for a while."

"No. That cannot happen. We must be free. The safety and future of our entire world depends on my saving the heirs."

Vega said, "I think these two need psychiatric care."

"I agree. Let's get them processed then make some calls."

The rear door was opened and Kol shoved inside. The door slammed. Detective Something guided Phetrix into the street and to the opposite side. His door was opened, but Phetrix did not enter. "You must listen to me."

"Must I?"

Phetrix felt something strike the back of his knees. His legs bent and he was pushed into the car sideways. The door slammed shut. Once in his seat, the tall dark-skinned sheriff ignited the car. "You've made this a very long day. I'm going to be so glad to get you behind bars so I can catch some zees."

"You're making a terrible mistake. I insist you release us."

"Oh? Do you, now?" He laughed.

The other man spun in his seat to look at Phetrix. "In the immortal words of Ricky, *You've got some 'splaining to do.*" He faced forward and laughed.

The car moved. Phetrix was angry. He had little time to deal with these fools. Though his power was still low, he was determined to get to the site of the magic. The thread was fading. It might start again, but if not, he had to lock onto it now or lose it altogether. He scooted forward, closed his eyes, and concentrated on the shackles that held his arms behind him. He placed a finger on each bracelet and muttered something. The clamps opened.

He opened his eyes and noticed the shorter man eyeing him suspiciously. "What did you say?"

Phetrix smiled. "It's not what I said, but what I'm about to say that should concern you." He lifted his arms to his sides.

"Hey!" Vega shouted and reached for his weapon.

Phetrix completed the spell before Vega could threaten them again. The power flowed from him with ease, surprising him. The shorter man was thrown against the door as the car made a sudden sharp turn, cutting across traffic and narrowly missing four or five other cars. Horns blared, voices were raised, tires screeched. The car made contact with another one but continued on after scraping along its length. It completed the U-turn and moved in the opposite direction.

"What are you doing?" Vega said, his voice higher pitched.

"I'm not doing anything. The car won't respond. It's doing its own thing." Grant groaned with effort trying to get the wheel to react.

Vega saw the strain on Phetrix's face. "I think the old guy is doing something."

"Doing something? Like what?"

"I don't know. His face looks like it's about to explode. Maybe he hacked the system."

"Well, stop him."

Vega yanked his gun free and aimed it over the seat. "Stop whatever you're doing, or I'm gonna stop you."

Kol lunged forward and rammed his head into the side of Vega's face. The gun discharged, punching a hole through the roof. Stunned, Vega slumped in his seat.

"Stop whatever you're doing before you get us killed."

"I asked nicely, but you refused to listen. Take us where we need to go and I will stop." In truth, Phetrix could not keep up the control spell much longer. The strain was unbearable. His body shook from the extreme effort it took to keep the spell powered.

"Okay. Okay. Release the car and I'll take you."

Phetrix let the energy go and slumped back in his seat. Exhausted, he fought to find the thread. "Straight ahead." His voice was weak. He feared he might faint before they reached their destination. "It's not much further, but please hurry."

Chapter 21

DeWayne turned the corner where the reptile man directed. They were in a residential neighborhood of older homes. He drove a half block before hearing, "Stop." He braked in the middle of the block, not sure what to do or where to go. A minute later the doors opened and the six man-beasts exited, leaving him alone with no instructions.

After they left, he thought about escaping, but fear that his boss would find him made him stay. Instead, he moved to the side of the street and parked.

He watched as the six massive forms lumbered down the street. They stopped several houses away and stood waiting. A car came down the street from the opposite direction. It slowed and honked at the beasts, but they did not move. The car inched forward until it was only a few feet from the horde. The driver honked twice more, then stuck his head out the window and began yelling at them with colorful language.

Two of the beasts lifted the front end of the car walked it around so it was facing the other way and dropped it. The car bounced. The driver did not hesitate. As soon as he had traction he sped off.

Five minutes later, Rhoden descended on the strange creature. He leaned forward and spoke to them, then lifted off again. The beasts spilt into two groups, each moving to a side of the street. There they spread out until they were in front of six houses. Whatever or whoever they were searching for was obviously in one of those houses.

DeWayne tried to envision how the scene would play out, even if they found the right house. If they broke into all six, someone was bound to call the cops. He looked around the street plotting out his escape. With or without Rhoden and his men, he was leaving before the cops arrived. He only wished he'd asked for payment in advance. Of course, the money didn't matter if you were in jail.

"NARDON!" Nadina called, panic now obvious in her voice.

Nardon's thundering footsteps shook the attic floor. He pounded up the steps, face sweating and stern. "What is it?"

"We've got company." She pointed at the main screen. In front of the house stood an enormous man. He stared forward but did not move.

"Oh, by the gods. It's an amphoid."

"A what?"

Half man, half reptile. They're created with dark magic. That man riding the Seeker must wield dark magic. We're going to need Samuel, and fast."

"I've called. He doesn't answer."

"This could turn bad. Move the camera view to the sides."

She did. The lens picked up an amphoid on each side of the house.

"Three."

"Can you handle them?"

"Aye, if my aim is true and they don't all rush at once. I need to go down and catch them before they get inside." He turned, coming face to face with Eric.

"What do you need me to do?"

Nordon wanted to say *Run!* but he knew Eric wouldn't leave them, no matter what the risk to himself. He reached behind his bulk and came back with a handgun. "You think you can use this?"

Eric looked at the proffered weapon and swallowed. He nodded. "If need be."

Nordon racked the slide, flicked off the safety, and handed it butt first to Eric. He took it tentatively. "If anyone other than me comes up those stairs, you shoot. Aim for the chest to slow them down, then walk the bullets up to the head. Head shots are the only way to kill them."

Nordon went down the stairs. He shut the door. On the other side, they heard hangers moving.

Nadina said, "Don't worry. If it gets that far, I'll be right there beside you."

Eric nodded, then moved to a position that allowed him a straight-on line of sight at the doorway.

"Oh dear," Dina said.

"What?" asked Eric.

"The rider landed. He is giving directions. Three more amphoids crossed the street. We now have six to deal with. I don't think he knows which house, but he's apparently narrowing the possibilities."

"Oh no! He gave a signal. They're coming."

As they watched, three amphoids raced forward, each at a different house. One to the left, one to the right, and theirs. They waited an eternity for something to happen, then an explosion rocked the house. Automatic weapon fire followed. Dina stood, grabbing her weapon. She reached the stairs.

"I'm going down to help. You stay here and cover our retreat. No matter what you hear, do not come down after us. Make sure it's not us before you fire." Another explosion shook the house. "If we don't come back, do not stand and fight. You are not ready yet. Run. Save yourself. A man named Samuel will find you. Do what he tells you." She started down the steps, halted, and looked at him, tears welling. "No matter what, know that we love you with all our hearts." Then she was gone.

She exited the closet and made sure the clothes covered the door. Then she moved to the bedroom door. A fierce gun battle waged below. She couldn't let Nordon face it alone. They were brought into this strange and wonderous new world together, and if need be, they would go out together, doing what they'd been trained to do: protecting the heir to the kingdom.

She entered the hall, crept down the stairs, and immediately opened fire. One of the beasts was down, but now that the wizard knew where they were, he commanded the others to the attack. Nordon grappled with one in a fierce struggle of powerful muscles. Dina targeted the next one through the door. Some of the rounds did little damage; others bounced off the tough skin.

The creature zeroed in on her and rushed forward. Dina emptied an entire magazine, dropping the beast not four feet from her. She quickly changed out mags as the next one came at her. She only had two more. She had to be more proficient with her shots.

OUT ON THE STREET, DeWayne, who had slumped in his seat to be less noticeable, bolted upright as the first explosion rocked the quiet neighborhood. "Oh man, they started a war," he muttered to himself. He reached for the key to start the engine. In the side mirror he spotted headlights. A car was coming. He'd wait until it passed before driving away.

As it neared, it slowed as the second explosion happened. He sunk lower in his seat but risked a glance at the car. Once he saw the driver, he dove for cover. It was the cop who tried to arrest him earlier today. That settled it. As soon as the car went by, he was gone.

To his dismay, the car stopped abreast of his door. "Oh man. Not good. Not good at all."

Chapter 22

They had no sooner made the turn than an explosion lit the night. The blast came from midway down the block on the left. Vega was just coming around when it happened. The sound cleared his mind in a hurry.

"You see?" Phetrix said. "I told you. Those people are in trouble. Let me out. They need my help."

"You seeing this?" Grant asked Vega.

"What the hell have you gotten us in to, old man?" Vega said.

A second explosion shook the car. While Vega picked up the radio to call whatever this was in, Grant opened the door and pulled his gun.

"Sheriff, please. Let me out. I can help."

"I don't think so. I'm not putting civilians in harm's way."

Grant got out and shut the door. He stared ahead, not sure of what he was witnessing. A sound and rush of air made him lower his head against the sudden gust. It buffeted him twice before receding. He looked up in time to see a creature with a man riding on top ascend. He stood staring until Vega came up to join him.

"Did you see that?" he asked.

Grant merely nodded.

"Oh, thank God," Vega said.

Gunfire erupted in one of the houses. Large men were assaulting it.

If the others were as large as the man standing in front of the house, it would be a formidable force.

"What should we do?" Vega asked.

"What we're paid for. Protect and serve." He lifted his weapon and advanced. They separated by about ten feet. Whatever was happening inside the house sounded like a war zone.

Grant approached the large man, who so far had yet to notice his approach. He got to within thirty feet before he moved, and then only to raise a buckethead toward the sky. The man and he creature still hovered there. He couldn't make out what the creature was. His first thought was dragon, which sent his mind back to when he asked the old man if he was playing dungeons and dragons. *Could this be real?*

The massive man turned his dark recessed eyes toward Grant. Before Grant could issue a warning, the man charged. He roared forward at surprising speed, head down like a bull trying to gore him. "Police! Freeze. I will fire." But the man did not slow. If anything, he got faster.

Grant squeezed the trigger. The round struck but did little to slow him down. He fired twice more. Other than twist him to the side, the bullets had little effect. Panic began to take root. He forced himself to hold his ground. He pulled the trigger in rapid succession until the slide locked back. Still, the beast—he could no longer consider him a man—barreled down on him.

From behind him a blast of jagged light lit the night, leaving sizzling air behind. It struck the beast in the chest, slowed, then made the thing dance before it exploded all over the street. Bits of flesh, bone, and assorted fluids pelted Grant. He ducked to cover up but was already coated.

He whirled as someone came up next to him. It was the old man. "The only way to kill them is by magic or to penetrate their small brains. Target their eyes. The brain is between them."

The old man moved past, leaving Grant on the verge of blathering.

Ahead, Vega closed on the house. He moved toward the front steps, gun up and ready, when something pierced him from above. He toppled, falling face first on the cement. The sight spurred Grant into action.

He pulled out his radio and called, forgetting all protocol. "Officer needs assistance! Officer down! We've got a freaking war going on here.

Send all the help you can." He shoved the handheld into his pocket, changed magazines, and advanced after the old man.

As he neared the house, he saw that the old man was in some sort of hand gesturing battle with the guy riding the thing. He had no other names or words at the moment. Grant left him to whatever he was doing and moved toward Vega and the house. Another large beast ran through the door and leaped off the porch directly at him. A scream escaped his lips. Despite his fear, he kept his composure and fired one shot after another at the large recessed eyes.

He lost track of how many rounds he'd fired, but when the man-thing landed, it was face first three feet from him. "Sweet Jesus, what are these things?"

Inside the house, the battle sounds faded. The body of another man-thing lay on the porch. The door was busted open. He moved to the steps. Sirens filled the night from every direction. Overhead he heard the rotors of a helicopter. He wanted to wait for backup. He prayed it would arrive fast but feared for the inhabitants of the house.

He changed out magazines as he climbed the front porch and stopped at the door. A fourth thing body was in pieces and splattered all over the floor, walls, and ceiling. A large man was in a death match with a fifth creature while a woman threw powerful skilled but largely ineffective punches and kicks at a sixth.

Coming down the stairs was a young man carrying a gun. Grant lifted his weapon and pointed it at him. "Drop the gun, son. I don't want to shoot you."

He didn't appear to hear the words. He stared in horror at the struggle between the woman and the man-thing. A closer look showed dinosaur-type ridges running down the thing's spine. Its neck appeared to elongate. His mouth opened beyond human potential and razor-sharp teeth snapped at the woman.

If he didn't do something fast, she was going to be chomped in half. He moved closer, but before he could shoot, the boy vaulted the railing and landed feet first on top of the creature. The force of the blow sent the beast backward, plowing into Grant and knocking him down. The boy let out a warrior's cry and went all-out crazy on the thing. He kicked it off Grant, then went into a flurry of punches and kicks that had damaging effect.

Regardless of the punishment, the beast rose and attacked. The woman, having recovered her weapon, stepped in front of the boy and fired a full automatic burst into the thing's face. It dropped like a boulder. Grant felt the aftershocks through his feet as he tried to rise.

The large man was rolled onto his back. Muscles straining, he tried to keep the beast's teeth from clamping down on his face, but he was losing the battle. Grant walked up, placed the gun against the side of the thing's head, and fired four times. The beast rolled and fell, leaving the man unencumbered and sucking air in deep, ragged drags.

A cacophony of sirens and screeching vehicles echoed along the street. Men were shouting and running. The old guy came to the door followed by his companion. He rushed forward. "Is that the heir?"

The woman closed protectively in front of the boy, gun up. The old man stopped. "I'm a friend of Samuel's. I'm here to help. We need to get out of here before Rhoden brings others back."

The massive man got to his knees, then to his feet with the aid of the young man.

"You may not remember me, Nadina, but I am Phetrix. I'm the one who sent you here fifteen years ago."

Relief flooded her face. "Oh, thank the gods."

Police rushed up the stairs, guns drawn.

"Come, we must leave now," Phetrix said.

"Whoa! Whoa. Ain't no one going nowhere, 'til this gets sorted out," Grant said.

"I'm sorry, Sheriff. I thank you for your assistance, but we have no other choice. Perhaps we will meet again and I can explain. For now, we must be away." With that, he cast two small pebbles down. Upon contact with the floor, they burst into a stinking cloud of smoke. As other cops came into the house, the overpowering sound of gagging and vomiting was heard. Forced to clear out or pass out, seven cops stood on the sidewalk trying to get clean air into their bodies.

Twenty minutes later when the cloud dissipated, Grant led them back into the house to find all survivors gone. He looked around the house at the bodies and the damage and wondered how he would explain this one.

Chapter 23

Grant gave descriptions to the officers and sent teams in search of the survivors. He radioed in for a crime scene team and morgue pick up. Half the block was a crime scene. One of the patrolmen came downstairs and called, "Yo, Detective. You gotta see this."

He scanned the main floor again, wondering again how he was going to explain all this to his boss, then followed. He entered a bedroom. On the bed was a hard case. The foam inside showed the shapes of two guns, but neither was there. Impressions in the foam suggested other items had been stored there as well.

"This doesn't look like the case of some ordinary bad guy," the officer commented.

"You suggesting it's a pro?"

The man shrugged. "Just saying."

Grant nodded. "Anything else?"

"Not yet."

Grant walked around the room studying everything. It was a typical bedroom. Though small, it had a king-size bed and two dressers. The man and woman slept here, he assumed. "Are all the bedrooms about this size?"

"No. Two are, but the one next to this one is larger. It looks unused."

He looked around the room again. "Why would they use the smaller room? Did you get a look at the man?"

"No. I was coming up the steps when the cloud hit."

"He's about the biggest human I've ever seen. Why cram all this stuff and his big body into a smaller space?" His eyes looked for things that weren't there, like photos. "Do the other rooms have any family pictures?"

"Not sure. I'll go look." The officer left the room. Grant continued to survey the space, stopping at the cracked closet door. He moved toward it, opening the door all the way. It was a decent-size space. Shelves lined three sides above racks of hanging clothes. It was a do-it-yourself job. Shirts hung from the top bar and pants from the lower one. He noted they were all men's clothes.

Grant moved some aside to see if anything was behind them. He found full shoe boxes. On the left side, the three boxes sat on a narrow shelf barely above the floor. *What was this for?* He picked up a box. It held gym shoes. As he went to set it back in place, he spotted a seam. He followed it up, pushing the hanging clothes aside. There was a door.

He stood and pulled his weapon. The officer came back. "Hey, I didn't—"

Grant put a finger to his lips. He pointed at the door. Seeing Grant's weapon out, the officer pulled his own. Grant motioned for him to come. He nodded at the door and the officer leaned forward. His eyes widened.

Grant touched the knob, but before turning it, he moved the clothes behind him aside so not to be in the doorway if shooters were waiting on the other side. He stepped back and pulled the door open, using it for cover. They led with guns, then glanced inside. No shots erupted. No one cried out. No footsteps sounded in rushed retreat.

What they found was a stairway leading up.

Grant slid around the door and placed a foot on the first step. He leaned in to look up. The rafters were bare. No insulation. The walls leading up were finished with drywall. Keeping the gun trained upward, he took the next step. The board creaked and he kept going. The officer stopped on the first step and kept watch over the floorboards above in case anyone peered over.

Grant ducked as he reached a small landing and glanced around. Two more steps led up. He scanned the floor. There were no people, but the room held a lot of very modern technology. He came to his full height and climbed the last two stairs.

"You good?" the officer said.

"Yeah. You might be right about them being pros."

Grant moved toward two long folding tables. Five monitors were mounted to the constructed wall in the middle of the space. A desktop computer sat on one table and a keyboard and smaller monitor were on the other. Cords ran down the wall and along the floor to an outlet someone had installed for the sole purpose of powering the system.

He glanced behind him, hearing the officer ascend. "You stay here and keep watch. I don't want anyone coming close to this until our people have gone through it."

"Count on it."

Grant walked past him on the way down. He patted the man's shoulder. "Nice work." He exited the room and went downstairs. The morgue transporters and crime scene techs had arrived.

Seeing him, one said, "So, where's all these bodies you needed picked up?"

"Very funny." He reached the main floor and froze. His face fell. The bodies were gone. "What did you do with the bodies?"

"Whoa! Not us. We just got here. The only body out there is Vega, and he's not dead—yet."

Grant raced for the outer door, stopping on the top step of the porch. He looked down the street. Those two bodies were gone as well. Someone was being loaded into an ambulance. He leapt down and ran, getting there before they closed the doors. It was Vega. He whirled. "Hey!" he called out to the dozens of officers on the street. "Who came in here and removed the bodies?" No one spoke. "Seriously? Not one of you saw six three hundred-pound bodies hauled away? What kind of cops are you?"

His boss walked around a car and headed his way. "What are you telling me, Grant? That you lost six corpses?"

Chapter 24

They left by the back door. Nordon led to the back fence. It was locked with a chain and padlock. He hadn't thought to bring the key, nor did he bring the one for the garage or the car. He vaulted over the fence, the cross bar bending under his weight. Nadina and Eric hopped the fence with ease. Kol managed, but Phetrix slipped and had to be hoisted over the fence by Nordon.

Down the alley they ran.

Phetrix said, "I'm not sure how long the smoke will keep them occupied."

"We will need transport or they will find us before we get very far," Nordon said. At the end of the alley, Nordon held up a hand. They needed to cross the street to the alley across the way, but to do so would put them out in the open. Since he carried his huge gun, it was unlikely anyone would stop for them.

From the left a long black van turned the corner. Nordon made a hasty decision and leaped into its path, his weapon pointed at the driver. The black man braked hard.

Nordon motioned for the others to move. Nadina reached the sliding door and yanked it open. Eric, Kol, and Phetrix clambered in. Once inside, Dina held her gun to the driver's head to allow Nordon to get in the passenger seat.

"Sorry for the intrusion," Dina said. "Drive us away from here and you will not be harmed."

The man grunted and pushed the pedal down hard. The van leaped forward with a squeal from the tires.

"Slow down," Dina said. "Keep a nice steady speed."

"O-okay. Just don't shoot me."

"Get us safely away from here and you won't have to worry."

He drove. Dina stayed crouched on the floor between the two front seats. "Any idea where we can go?" she asked Nordon. He nodded but didn't offer an explanation. Dina understood. He didn't want to give the location away in front of the driver.

"It's good to see you again, Your Majesty," Phetrix said. "Although I wish it were under better circumstances."

Eric said, "Excuse me?"

Dina looked back. Eric's face showed his confusion. He shifted his gaze to her. "I promise I'll explain everything once we find someplace safe."

"You mean he doesn't know?" Phetrix said.

"We were just about to tell him when the attack came."

Phetrix gave a sage nod and sat back in his seat. They drove for close to an hour until they were well out of the city, then Nordon had the driver pull over. "I need your phone."

"My phone?" the driver whined. "But—"

Nordon shifted the gun toward him. "Thanks for your cooperation."

The man dug out his cell phone and handed it to Nordon. "Now get out."

"Ah, man!" He opened the door and stepped out. Nordon shifted to the driver's seat. He leaned out the window. "I will leave the van an hour south of here. I'll drop your phone a mile down the road. You'd do well to forget you ever saw us."

Nordon shifted and drove off. A mile later, he hit the brakes and tossed the phone ten yards into a field. At the first cross street, he turned left and headed south. At the first western crossroad, he turned right. Several miles farther, he went north. Thirty minutes later, he turned up a dirt road that led to a copse of trees. Within was a log cabin. As he entered the clearing, bright blinding lights flooded the area.

A man came out the front door holding a rifle. "You best turn that thing around and head back outta here. This here's a no trespassing zone. Duly posted."

Nordon leaned out the window. "Samuel said I should come here if there was trouble."

The man lowered the rifle but still kept it pointed at the van. "And is there?"

"Yes."

He pointed the rifle down. "Move the van into the barn." He walked to a side building and rolled back the door. Nordon drove inside and parked.

"Don, where are we?" Dina asked.

"Someplace safe."

"But how did you know about it?"

"Samuel showed it to me not long after we arrived here. He made me commit the directions to memory."

"Is he from here or our world?"

"Don't know. Samuel said if we needed to run, we could find help here." He opened the door and stepped out. The man was close by, the rifle now tucked under his arm.

"Is Samuel here?"

"No," Nordon said. "We're not sure where he is."

"Well, unload and come in the house. We'll get you squared away for tonight, then decide what to do with you in the morning."

They exited the van. "Wow! Five of you. There's not much room in the cabin, but we'll make do. Name's Tetrin."

Nordon made the introductions, then Tetrin led the way to the cabin. Inside was a thin woman with a mean glare. She held a shotgun and looked ready and willing to use it, should the need arise. "This is my wife, Catron."

They introduced themselves in greeting, but the woman only offered her glare.

"You want some tea?" Tetrin asked.

Phetrix spoke. "I for one would be most grateful for a cup of tea."

"Catron, can you see to the water?"

His wife continued her stare down. "Catron, they are our guests. Samuel sent them."

Samuel's name made her flinch and break eye contact. "Samuel? Well, all right, then."

She set the shotgun down. “Make yourselves to home.” She went into the kitchen.

Chapter 25

DeWayne couldn't believe his luck. First the attack by Rhoden's henchmen, then the police blocking him in. Then, when he'd finally maneuvered the van past the cop cars, he gets stopped by the very people that Rhoden attacked. Now he was out there in who knows where without a car or his phone.

Man, he had never seen a night so dark in his life. Living in the city got dark, but there was always a glow of light somewhere. However, this blackness was so complete that he was invisible.

He hiked down the road toward where he saw the brake lights come on. He wasn't sure why he bothered. He'd never be able to find the phone, but he walked on anyway. What else could he do? At the approximate spot, he stopped. He scuffed the ground with his foot. He moved along the side of the road about twenty yards, then turned and started back. As he turned to make a third pass, his slid down a slope.

He fell to the side to grab anything to stop his descent, but it was mostly long grass and weeds and either slipped through his fingers or tore from the ground. His feet splashed into ankle deep water. "Ah man! Please don't let there be snakes."

He scrambled up the slope, reached the top, and slipped and fell on his hands and knees. A car went by, its headlights not reaching far enough into the darkness to shine on him. He moved forward, waving his arms in a futile attempt to get the driver's attention, but called out too late. That was when he realized he was farther away from the road than he should be. As he fell down the drainage ditch again, he clawed at the ground, snagging enough dirt and weeds to prevent another splashdown. He pulled and clawed his way to the top and rolled onto his back, exhausted.

How was he gonna get back home?

He pushed to his feet and took a tentative step, wanting to avoid falling again. Something crunched under his foot. He froze. A knot formed in the pit of his stomach. In slow motion, DeWayne bent and groped on the ground, knowing what he would find. His hand brushed across the phone and its shattered screen. "Aw man!"

Then the screen lit with an incoming call. "Yes?" He had no idea who it was. The screen didn't show a number, but he eagerly tapped the screen to accept the call, but no green button or arrow displayed. DeWayne tapped the screen multiple times with no luck. He swiped his finger across the cracked screen. Nothing happened. He grew more agitated with each ring and he could not answer. "Aw! Come on, man."

Sure the call would end before he could connect, the screen changed and a voice said, "Where are you?"

He did not recognize the voice. Just his luck, it'd be a wrong number. "Who-who is this?"

"You already know. Where are you?"

It was Rhoden. Somehow the dude had figured out how to use a phone. Strange, though; he didn't remember giving him the number. "Man, I got no idea. I can't see a thing. I'm in the boonies somewhere between Crackerville and the end of God's country."

"Stay where you are. I'll send something."

The line went dead. He stared at the phone. "Did he just say he'd say something?" A chill ran down his spine. The phone fell apart in his hand. "Man!" He flung it to the ground. "Could this night get any worse?"

Then he slipped down the drainage ditch again.

RHODEN GAVE THE SEEKER A COMMAND. It screeched and took flight, leaving him alone. He climbed the hood of a parked car and sat with his back against the windshield. He had a newfound respect for the warriors of this world. They were far more skilled and determined than he'd anticipated. Conquering them would take more thought and planning, but once he ruled them, they would make an undefeatable army.

He'd barely escaped, but his vantage point gave him first-hand knowledge of how they attacked. Their weapons interested him. He wondered if they would work in his world. Perhaps he was going about this the wrong way. Maybe his best course of action was to bring these weapons into his world, create an army, and defeat Mortas first. Once that was accomplished, he could turn his attention to this world.

Instead of returning the heir to Chevalon, he should just kill him. With all hope of resurrecting the throne to the rightful heirs, the people would collapse. He could then lead a rebellion against Mortas, the man responsible for the death of the royal family.

Yes, he liked that plan. He closed his eyes and allowed the scene to play out in his mind. So engrossed was he in his dreams of conquest, he never heard the car stop.

"Sir, what are you doing out here."

Startled by the sudden interruption, Rhoden sat upright and reached for the sword at his belt, the sword he hadn't strapped on for this trip. The man saw the move. His hand lowered to his weapon. Rhoden eyed the gun. He very much wanted to have one.

The officer moved away a step and angled to the side of the car. "Is this your vehicle?"

Rhoden looked at the car as if surprised where he was sitting. "No, it's not. I find these beasts far too limited in their mobility." He slid to the front and sat on the edge, his feet on the front step of the car.

"Let me see some ID, sir." He held out a hand and motioned with his fingers.

"ID? What is that?"

"Stop playing games, sir." The man's voice took on a harsher edge. "Identification. Now!"

"Oh, you wish to know who I am." He balanced on the shiny step. "I am Rhoden, soon to be the ruler of this world. You will soon answer to me."

"Have you taken drugs tonight, sir?"

"Drugs? No. I have been looking at your world from an entirely new perspective, but I have not been drugged." He hopped to the ground, feeling spry and excited. "I would very much like to have that weapon." He imitated the man's gesture, extending his arms and wiggling his fingers. "Be a good minion and hand it to me, please."

The officer stepped back and drew the gun. "Sir, turn around and face the car. Put your hands flat on the hood."

"Tsk! Tsk! Is this any way to treat your king?" he said. "Extractous!" The gun flew from the man's fingers. However, the weapon discharged, the tiny bolt scribing a line along the side of Rhoden's head. He winced at the pain and flinched. The gun flew past his outstretched hand, past the car and landed on the grass beyond.

The officer shook off his shock and raced at Rhoden, who was unprepared for the suddenness of the assault. The man hit him chest high and drove him backward over the car and onto the hood. They grappled, but Rhoden was never much of a physical fighter. He relied on others or his magic to do the damage for him. They rolled down the hood, falling to the ground. The man was strong and managed to maneuver Rhoden to the bottom position as they fell.

Rhoden struck hard, driving the wind from his lungs. His head smacked the hard surface, sending white bolts of light through his eyes. Consciousness began slipping away. He managed to get his hand against the bulk of the man's chest. With all his remaining strength, he uttered, "Eruptus."

The man shook violently before his chest exploded, sending bone, blood, and flesh raining on Rhoden. The gore coated him. He lay still for several moments, fighting off the urge to sleep. He couldn't be found here. He had to move. Rolling back and forth he dislodged what was left of the man and crawled up to the grass. There he collapsed.

Unsure how long he lay there, a sudden wind gust roused him. He looked up to see the Seeker and his minion DeWayne landing ten feet away. Rhoden motioned him to come.

DEWAYNE WAS in shock as the Seeker began to drift toward the ground. A police car was in the street. Its lights were flashing, but there was no sign of the cop. "Man, what have you done now?"

The Seeker settled and Rhoden motioned for him to come. He looked injured. In the back of his mind, DeWayne hoped he might die. Then he wouldn't have to deal with Rhoden anymore. He moved to his side and knelt next to him.

"Oh, dude, what do you have all over you?" DeWayne bent and lifted the man's head. "Oh. Oh. Oh, yuk! Is that—is that blood? I think I'm gonna be sick." He leaned to the side and heaved.

A hand clawed its way up DeWayne's chest and wrapped around his neck. The grip tightened and pulled him down. "I need to leave here."

"I'd say. You need a bath, like real bad."

"You must help me get to the seam."

"Yeah. Okay. Sure."

"Help me up."

Rhoden draped his blood-soaked arm around DeWayne's neck. *Now I'm gonna need a bath.*

"Put me on the Seeker."

DeWayne guided him to the strange creature. It went into a frenzy, perhaps protesting over the smell of blood. DeWayne lifted Rhoden onto the creature's translucent back.

"The weapon."

"The what?"

"Over there. The weapon. I must have it."

DeWayne followed where Rhoden pointed. His foot kicked something hard. He bent to pick up the gun. *This can't be good.*

He took it to Rhoden.

"Climb on," Rhoden said.

"Ah, are you sure? 'Cause it doesn't look like there's enough room for us both."

"I am in no mood to argue. I will need your help to get through the seam."

DeWayne tried to find a place to step up. The creature screeched and snapped its ugly head at him. Rhoden grabbed his arm and pulled him up. Once seated, Rhoden gave the Seeker a command and it lifted off the ground. It was then DeWayne saw the remains of the cop. He leaned to the side and retched again.

A few minutes later they landed near the seam. DeWayne helped Rhoden down. Rhoden uttered some words and the air split open to reveal a countryside. Dewayne hadn't been this close to the seam before. The sight mesmerized him.

"Help me," Rhoden said.

DeWayne lifted the man, aware that every contact with him transferred more blood and flesh to his body. He would have to burn his clothes and scrub his body for a whole week to get the smell off, though nothing could scrub the memory from his mind.

Rhoden slipped through the seam. DeWayne was about to move away, but a hand shot through the gap and snatched his arm. "You must come with me."

"Say what?"

"Come."

The next instant, DeWayne floated off the ground and through the opening. He landed on soft ground in a field. The Seeker followed him through, then the seam closed like someone had pulled a zipper.

They remounted the Seeker and took flight. The creature appeared to struggle under the weight. For a moment, DeWayne thought they were going down, but then Rhoden whispered something in its ear and it got stronger.

It wasn't night here. It was hazy, like the sun might be just setting. It looked like a typical farm back home. Maybe this world wasn't so different after all. Then he spotted the giant hairy abominable snowmen-type beasts.

Dude, you're not in Kansas anymore.

Chapter 26

The four of them sat around a kitchen table in silent contemplation. The lone light above the table gave everything a more ominous feel. Kol snored loudly from the sofa twenty feet away.

Nordon looked as exhausted as she felt. Phetrix sat studying Eric. For his part, Eric sat passively waiting for someone, anyone to explain what was going on. He was so good looking and strong. He deserved to have a life like any other boy his age; not to be strapped and hindered by his blood and duty to a world he couldn't possibly remember. But it was not to be. If they didn't deal with the threat to him now, he'd spend the rest of his life running.

His eyes met hers and held. His implored. Hers watered. She brushed the tears away, cleared her throat but found she was too choked up to speak. His hands stretched across the table and covered hers. "Mom. Just start."

She nodded, wiped away more tears and said, "First of all, know that I love you." Her hand sought Nordon's. She squeezed. He gave her a weak smile. "We love you. We always have and always will." She paused to gather her thoughts.

Eric said, "But—"

"But we are not your parents." Her voice cracked and she broke into sobs.

Phetrix patted her hand. "It's all right, Nadina. I'll take it from here."

"And who are you?" Eric asked, a note of irritation creeping into his tone.

"My name is Phetrix. I am—or was—the wizard in the service of the King and Queen of Chevalon, where you were born."

"Chevalon? I've never heard of it."

"No, you wouldn't have. It doesn't exist in this world."

"So, you're saying I'm an alien? Is that it?"

Nordon said, "Only in that it pertains to you being in a foreign land. You are human, not some space creature. You just come from another time and place, but it is an alternate dimension to this world."

Nadina said, "More than fifteen years ago, you lived in Chevalon when an evil man—"

"Mortas Frost," Phetrix added.

Nadina continued. "… attacked the kingdom. His forces were too strong to repel. When it looked like Chevalon would fall, Phetrix opened what he calls a seam into this world."

"I discovered it quite by accident, but once here I found another wizard thought long dead, named Samuel. He'd been here for years and set up a network of people taken from Chevalon over the years, like Tetrin and Catron here, for the purpose of escape and safety of the royal family.

"However, with the castle being overrun by Mortas' troops, I was unable to get to the King and Queen. So to make sure you, the heir, was safe, I sent you through the seam with Nordon and Nadina as your guardians. You were only two at the time, so you would have no memory of these events.

"We raised you with the intent of bringing you back once the throne could be reclaimed. However, the King and Queen, your true parents, were never seen again, and no organized resistance could ever be mounted to overthrow Mortas."

Eric glanced at Nadina and looked away. Her heart fell. He would never look at her the same way again, as he did when he thought of her as mother.

"I was in hiding for all these years. Recently I'd been hearing rumors that the King and Queen were still alive and a resistance movement was on the horizon. Kol and I searched for them with little success. There has been a bounty on my head since the fall. When I was discovered, we thought it best that I come to find Samuel and update him on the events in Chevalon. We were unable to find him, though. I fear Rhoden, Mortas' wizard, may have gotten to him first."

"So what is it I'm expected to do? Lead a revolution? I'm a high school student. A very confused high school student who has no knowledge or interest in doing battle on a foreign world. My only education in those realms comes from video games." His voice rose. "What do you want from me? I'm no king. No ruler. I haven't even graduated yet. Earlier today, I was a normal boy. Now, my house and family…or the people I thought were my family…was attacked and I'm on the run."

Dina's face crumbled. She stood and ran from the room and the cabin.

Nordon looked at Eric. "Boy, regardless of who we are, do not ever disrespect that woman. We didn't ask to be torn from our world and come to this strange land any more than you did. But we did it gladly to protect you. You owe us both your life…but mostly, you owe her. We may not be your real parents, but we raised you like we were. The love we gave you was just as real. We didn't ask for this anymore than you did, but here we are. As far as we're concerned, you are our son and will always be. At the very least, show some gratitude."

He stood and followed Nadina outside.

Eric sank into himself.

Phetrix said, "This has not been easy for any of us, but you need to understand the situation. Many people are counting on your return to end the brutal reign of Mortas. That may be a lot for you to comprehend, but it is the reality. Whether you choose to take up your proper role or hide here in this world is your decision. No one can force you to take back the throne, but many will continue to suffer if you do not.

"That's unfair."

"Be that as it may, it is the truth. You are the heir to the throne. Now that Mortas knows you are here, he will stop at nothing to prevent you from returning."

"Is there no one else who can do this? You said the King and Queen are still alive. Can't they lead the rebellion?"

"If the rumors are true, yes. But I have been unable to confirm them. It may just be the hope of the people praying to be rescued from the hard lives they were forced into since Mortas' takeover. I don't know."

He let the words hang in the air and searched Eric's face for a reaction. Seeing nothing, he played his trump card.

"As for anyone else who can lead—well, you have a twin sister."

At this, Eric's eyes widened and his eyebrows shot up. "A sister? Where?"

"Up until a few days ago, she was here. I got her out, too. According to your mo—er, Nadina, Rhoden captured her two days ago. I was unaware of this until tonight when she told me. Rhoden would have taken her back to Chevalon for Mortas to deal with. He will make her an example and execute her in public to end all hope of a revolution. However, now that he knows you are here as well, he may delay to have both of you. Your deaths will end the royal line and any hope of a return to the previous rule."

Chapter 27

Grant left the station with the desire to check what was left of his butt. Having it chewed out by the captain and several other superiors for the better part of two hours, he was in no mood to talk, let alone speak to another human for a long time.

Human. The word hung in his mind like an omen. What was he dealing with? How did those bodies simply vanish without anyone seeing them?

Fortunately, enough officers had seen the attackers to corroborate his account of the story and take some of the pressure off. However, it was the dash cam and several body cams that shut up his superiors and kept him from being benched on the case.

The camera footage clearly showed the attack. One angle caught Vega being lifted off the ground and body slammed. He felt bad about that. In all the confusion and yelling, he'd forgotten about his partner. Early reports had him recovering from a wound to his back, broken ribs, a broken arm, and a concussion. Grant was on his way to the hospital now.

However, with all the officers on the scene, not one dash cam or body cam caught the mysterious disappearance of the attackers. The hardest part for the brass to swallow was losing the defenders in the house. Grant left out the part about the car driving itself to the scene.

That he had two of the people involved in the battle in the back seat of his car and still managed to lose them did not help his case.

After he'd taken all the reprimands he could take, he'd been the one to suggest checking the cameras. After viewing them, the brass cooled and he was allowed to stay on, but barely. If he didn't show progress within twenty-four hours, a new team would be assigned and he'd be relegated to gopher duty.

He got in the car and drove toward the hospital. The twenty-minute drive gave him a chance to clear his mind of all the negativity he'd endured and refocus his thoughts. By the time he reached the hospital, he had the makings of a plan.

Vega was out. He had a cast on his arm, tape covering his entire rib cage, and a bandage around the back of his head. Tubes ran to his arm. Electrodes were stuck to the sides of his head and oxygen was snaked into his nose.

He stood gazing at his partner for a few minutes. He gave a silent prayer and said, "Sorry, partner. I'll get 'em for you. I promise. You just get well." Then he left.

Grant drove to the vacant lot, the area that seemed to be in the center of much of the trouble. He parked, got out and patrolled the street in case the young black person of interest was in one of the parked cars. He didn't find him but was surprised to find his gun in his hand. He didn't remember pulling it.

He stopped in the empty space between the buildings where the girls disappeared in front of his eyes. *How was it possible?* It had to be technology of some sort, like a magician making an elephant vanish. Misdirection. Isn't that what they called it? Did that mean whatever occurred happened elsewhere, but they had been duped to look here? Maybe. But in truth, he had no idea, other than the nagging feeling in his detective's gut that something more was at play here; something they as yet didn't understand. But when they did, it would all make sense somehow.

Still, the questions whirled around his brain. Not just the disappearance, but the man who vanished in the parking garage and the two men suddenly appearing. What were those things that attacked them? They sure didn't look human to him. What about that strange gust of wind at the precinct, like a helicopter was landing in the room? And how did the old man get out of the locked car? What weapon did he use to stop that thing in its tracks? It looked like a bolt of lightning. Maybe it was some sort of taser.

Too many questions and nowhere near enough answers.

He returned to his car, started the engine, then had another thought. He shut it off, angled his seat back and settled in to observe. For whatever reason, he was sure someone would return to this spot. And when they did, this time he'd be ready.

ERIC WAS TOO wound up to sleep. How could any of them expect him to after the bombshell they'd dropped on him tonight? His parents weren't his parents. He wasn't from this world. He was some sort of prince in this other world. And people from that other world wanted him dead. Sleep! Right. That's going to happen.

But, perhaps the most mind-shattering announcement was that he had a sister; a twin no less. How could they keep that from him? Then to find out the dude who was hunting him already had her. What was her name? Elysande? Elly, his mother…no, not mother…the pretender said.

What was he supposed to do? What did they expect him to do? Ride to the rescue? It was all too much to absorb. He needed air. He got off the sofa, slid into his shoes, and unlocked the door as quietly as possible. On the porch he sucked in deep breaths of chilled air. The air smelled different out here. Cleaner, perhaps. Definitely more invigorating. And the stars. Where did they all come from? On a good night in the city you could only make out half as many as in this sky.

He stared up at the vastness and wondered if he came from one of those stars.

"Searching for home?"

The voice startled him. He spun around so fast he almost stepped off the porch.

"Sorry. Didn't mean to scare you."

Eric saw it was the old man, the so-called wizard. "I didn't see you there." He thought about what the man said. "Can you read minds, too?"

Phetrix chuckled. "No, but it wasn't hard to figure out. You have had a lot dumped on you tonight. It didn't take a wizard to make the connections."

"Do I come from somewhere, you know, up there?"

"No. In truth, you're from this world we call Earth. You were born in a parallel dimension. I just happened to find a way through the veil at a time when we were desperate to escape. I know it's a lot to take in, but don't blame Nordon and Nadina. They did their best for you and were as much victims of the times as you were. They were strangers forced to live together as man and wife and to adapt to a world far more advanced than their own. They created a family, and from the looks of it, they did an admirable job. You certainly did not lack for care and love."

Eric took that in. He'd been so wrapped up in his own upheaval, he hadn't given any thought as to what his guardians must have gone through. And no, he couldn't argue about that he was loved. Memories rushed through his mind. Tears welled as he settled on those special times that warmed his heart. Then, in a reddish flash they were gone.

He wiped the tears away with an angry swipe of his arm. There might have been happy times, but that didn't excuse them from telling him the truth. He was certainly old enough to have known. It would have been easier to swallow then, rather than to discover the secret while fighting for his life.

He whirled on the wizard, hands clenched into fists at his side. "I should have been told."

"Maybe. But they were under orders not to tell you until you were ready. That time was coming. Unfortunately, life doesn't always follow our plans. You can't blame your guardians for doing what they were sworn to do to protect you at all costs."

He stood and stretched. "It's time for an old man to be in bed. While you're out here feeling sorry for yourself, give some thought about what you will do now. Back home, you would have been a man four years ago. It's time to be a man now. Face the truth as you now know it and accept the role you must play. We all have our burdens to bear. This is yours. Step up, young prince. Step up."

He patted Eric on the shoulder and entered the house. Eric blew out a heavy breath. A fine mist rose up from his breath. "Step up. Ha! Easy for him to say. He wasn't a prince. Heir to a throne." He froze, hearing his own words. *He was a prince! Heir to a throne.* Holy crap!

Chapter 28

They sat at the table the next morning eating a breakfast of scrambled eggs, ham, and toast Catron had prepared when the sound of a vehicle approaching sent Don and Dina to their feet.

"Mage, are you expecting anyone else?" Nordon asked.

"Unless it's Samuel, I don't know anyone else here."

The two guardians had weapons in their hands in seconds. Kol stood to the side holding a knife. Tetrin grabbed Eric by the shoulders and pushed him behind. Catron brought two shotguns out and handed one to her husband.

Phetrix moved toward the window and peeked out. A silver car was parked thirty feet from the cabin. A woman exited and studied the cabin. She made no move toward them, nor did she show signs of aggression. She opened the rear door and came out with a weapon similar to those Tetrin and Catron wielded.

"Whoever she is, she is armed," Phetrix said. "Does anyone know her?"

Dina stepped forward. Don backed away, motioned to Kol and the two men exited out the rear door.

"I don't know her," Dina said.

"Something about her is familiar," Phetrix muttered.

The woman took two steps forward. "Catron, it's Alyanna. Samuel brought me here years ago. He told me if I ever needed a place to hide, I was to come here."

"Alyanna. Of course," Phetrix said. "She's one of the guardians I sent to protect the princess," he said to the others.

He moved toward the door. Before he opened it, Nordon bellowed, "Set the weapon down and back away!"

The woman whirled, aiming her weapon at the voice.

Fearing a catastrophe, Phetrix flung open the door and stepped out. "No one shoot."

The woman spun his way. Nordon's bullet ripped through the woman's shoulder, spinning her around and flinging her to the ground. Her weapon went flying.

"No!" Phetrix yelled. "Do not shoot!" He ran down the steps and dropped to his knees at the woman's side. "Oh, Alyanna!"

She was barely conscious. Voice weak, she said, "Phetrix, is that you?"

"Yes, child."

"They have the princess." Then she slumped back in his arms.

"Move aside, wizard." Catron knelt next to him and took Alyanna in her arms. She pressed her fingertips to the woman's temples and focused, closing her eyes. Seconds later, she opened them. "We must hurry. Tetrin!"

Her husband bounded down the steps, dropped to a crouch, and scooped Alyanna up in his arms. He carried her into the cabin.

"Put her on the kitchen table," Catron said. "Everyone else out of the cabin."

"I can assist if you wish," Nadina said.

"Boil water. Tetrin, bring my kit. Wizard, I need a spell to keep her stable." She turned on the group with fire in her eyes. "The rest of you, begone."

Nordon, put a hand on Eric's shoulder and guided the wide-eyed boy toward the door. Kol was already outside.

Phetrix placed a hand on Alyanna's forehead and mumbled a few words. His hand glowed blue for an instant and then he pulled away. "I didn't want to give her too much for fear she would wake. But she is stable for the moment."

"Then you are no longer of use. Go."

Phetrix left and joined the others on the porch. Ten minutes later,

Tetrin came out. "Catron is a gifted healer. She has saved me numerous times. I'm sure Alyanna will be all right."

"I'm-I'm sorry," Nordon said. "When she whirled on you like that, I thought she was going to shoot. I didn't want to take the chance of getting you shot."

Phetrix put a hand on the big man's shoulder. "There is no blame. We are all on edge. She will pull through this."

Nordon hung his head and walked away from the cabin.

Eric asked, "Who is she?"

"She is like your mother and father. I was able to get you to safety, but your sister Elyande, was always mischievous. She thought we were playing a game and ran from me. I had to find her before Mortas' troops did. It took a while, but when I did, you and your guardians had already been whisked away. I needed someone to care for your sister and found Alyanna. It was deemed better to keep the two of you separated. In case anyone followed, they could not capture both of you together. Alyanna and one of Samuel's men were tasked with protecting your sister."

"But you said this Mortas guy has my sister."

"Yes."

"Then why is she here? If her job was to protect my sister, why wasn't she captured, too, or dead."

Phetrix eyed the boy. A slow anger built within him. "Do not judge others, boy; not until you have all the facts or have walked in their shoes. You saw the kind of forces Mortas has at his control. Not everyone can stand against such an assault. In truth, had I not come along when I did, you may very well have been captured, too, and both Nadina and Nordon might be dead. You may someday be a good leader, if you survive that long. Make sure you don't alienate those who are loyal followers without understanding a given situation."

Phetrix turned and walked away.

Tetrin stepped forward. "A lot of people will follow you once they hear you're alive. Many will give their lives to protect you. To earn their respect, you have to be willing to give respect. That woman in there fighting for her life deserves respect."

Then he left Eric, too. He saw Kol leaning against the cabin wall. "You got anything to add?"

He shook his head. "Not me, Your Majesty. I'm just a loyal follower."

Your Majesty! That was going to take some getting used to. He stepped off the porch and went for a walk.

Chapter 29

Eric lost track of time. He wandered aimlessly through the woods surrounding the cabin. He had no idea how far he'd walked, but when he turned around to get his bearings, he spotted Kol fifty yards off to his left. A scan of the area showed his father—no, guardian—twenty yards to the right. He'd never get used to not calling him Dad.

The sight of the two watchers irritated him. He lifted his arms to the side and shouted, "What? You think I was going to run off?"

Neither man spoke, which angered him further. He tramped back to the cabin, surprised it took so long to get there. By the time he stepped into the clearing, he had calmed. Everyone was sitting on the porch. They stopped talking as he approached. Kol and Nordon exited the trees a minute later.

Eric stopped at the porch. "How is she?'

No one spoke for a moment, then Phetrix said, "She'll be fine."

He didn't know what else to say and felt awkward being the center of attention. "That's good," he said for lack of anything else.

Catron stood. "Since our breakfast was interrupted, guess I'll get dinner started."

"I'll give you a hand," Dina said.

"Pleased for the help," Catron said and the two women went inside.

"So," Eric said. "Now what?"

"We wait," said Phetrix.

"Great," mumbled Eric. He climbed the porch and dropped into a wooden rocking chair. They sat in silence for a while before Phetrix said, "How much training has the boy had?"

"Fencing, archery, hand to hand," Nordon said. "No guns or knives."

"Why?"

Nordon shrugged. "Wasn't sure if guns would work in Chevalon. Knives are personal. Wanted him to know how to disarm an opponent before teaching him attacks."

"While we have some time, take him someplace secluded and teach him to shoot. Kol, you teach him swordsmanship."

"I already know how to use a sword."

"No, Eric, you don't," Nordon said. "Fencing and sword fighting are two different skill sets. You finesse with a foil. A sword fight is much more brutal. Skill is good, but brute force and speed are better."

"Come, Son; we will teach you."

Eric riled at the word *son.* He wanted to scream, *I am not your son!* but swallowed the outburst and followed his guardian. Kol stepped in behind him.

They walked about a half mile deeper into the woods. There, Nordon gave him his handgun and instructed in its components and operation. He paced off twenty steps and used his knife to carve a rough circle in some tree bark. One shot at a time, Eric fired on Nordon's command. The gun bucked in his hand at first and his shots went high and wide, but after half a mag of rounds, Eric began to get the hang of getting his shots on target.

Nordon took the empty gun and showed him how to drop the magazine. He let Eric load it himself, snap it back in place, and chamber a round. He did another mag of single shots. The third and fourth ones were all double shots. For the last one, Nordon carved out two more targets and instructed Eric to rapid fire five shots and pick up the second target. He repeated the sequence with the third tree.

"Good. You have the basics down. Now, let Kol show you some things with the sword and knives."

"Now, Your Majesty—"

"Please," Eric interrupted. "Don't call me that."

"As you wish, Your—ah, Eric."

"I only have a short sword, so it will be different from using a full size one, but I can give you a few basics that will help you."

Over the next hour, Kol gave Eric a detailed tutorial on fighting and surviving using a sword. By the time Nordon called a halt, Eric was sweating and had worked off much of the anger coursing through his veins.

They walked back to the cabin in silence. The table was being set for dinner when they arrived. Dina told him to wash for dinner like she'd done hundreds of times before. It felt and sounded normal to both of them.

They sat to a rabbit stew. He ladled the brown gravy, meat, potatoes, onions, and carrots into a bowl. "I've never had rabbit before." He looked around the table, embarrassed the thought came out in words. "At least, I don't think I have."

Tetrin said, "Get used to it, lad. It's a staple in Chevalon." He forked a large bite into his mouth. Gravy dribbled down his face, absorbing into his beard.

Eric took a tentative bite. He wasn't sure what he expected, but it was as good as any other stew he'd ever tried. He finished and glanced around to see if anyone else was having seconds. Without asking, Dina ladled another bowl for him.

He looked surprised. "I know that look," she said. "I'm sure you're starving. Eat up."

Nordon bellowed a laugh. "Got a healthy appetite, that one does."

"As long as his appetite doesn't make him as big as you," teased Nadina.

After dinner, while the dishes were being cleared, Nordon asked, "So, wizard, what do we do now?"

"I've been giving that some thought. Samuel still has not responded to any of our calls. If Elysande was taken through the seam, it stands to reason he went after her either to rescue her or meet up with the king and queen. I can't be sure, but I think he's there."

He took a moment to look at the group. "I'm going to cross over as well."

Nordon and Nadina began to protest at the same time. Phetrix held up his hand for quiet. "For the moment, the prince is safe. Samuel needs my help more there than you do here."

"What if they come back?" Nadina said. "We barely survived the last attack and that was with your help."

"I understand. My hope is we can keep them too occupied to think about crossing back here. I'd like to take the fight to them for a change.

However, to do that requires me to be there and find the king and queen. I think Samuel knew where to look. I don't."

"Precisely why you should stay. It may take so long to find them that Rhoden has time to lead another party here."

"You'll have to stay hidden. Don't give them the chance to locate you again. Rhoden is not as familiar with this world as are you. He may keep searching in the city, never thinking to look out here."

"I still don't like it," Dina said.

"Nor I," added Nordon. "We can fight a lot of things, but not magic."

They argued back and forth for a few more minutes before Eric said, "I have a better idea. We all go."

Chapter 30

The silence that hung over the table was deafening. Then everyone spoke at once.

"No."

"Not going to happen."

"No way, and that's final."

Eric waited them out. What he proposed was dangerous. He understood and accepted that. What surprised him, though, was how calm he felt suggesting the action. "It would be better to have numbers in Chevalon. It solves having to battle on two fronts, not to mention that it's my sister we're rescuing. I want—no, need to be a part of the solution."

The voices started again. This time, Phetrix spoke over them. "Mortas already has one heir. I am not putting you in a position where he can capture both. That makes no sense and I will not allow for it to happen. Put the thought out of your mind."

Nordon said, "Though I applaud your desire to play a part, Phetrix is right. It is folly to put you within reach of Mortas' army. Just from a strategic move, the idea holds no merit. Believe me, Eric, the time will come when you will have to lead. It's just not yet."

The bedroom door opened. Alyanna came out naked from the waist up, save for the bandages covering her shoulder and a towel wrapped around her chest. "You will not be going without me."

"Alyanna, you must not be up," Catron said. "If you undo my handiwork, I'll make you redo it yourself."

"You are far too weak to travel," Phetrix said. "You stay and regain your strength. You can help keep the prince safe."

"No!" the word flew from her mouth. "They took my girl. They killed…" she choked back a sob, "…Markus. He was such a brave and good man. He gave his life for her. Can I not be expected to do the same? I was responsible for her. I failed her. I have to make it right for her sake. For me. For Markus."

Catron took the woman by the arm. "Nothing will be decided tonight, Alyanna. You need your rest. We can talk about it more in the morning."

"You hear me, old man," she said to Phetrix. "Make all the plans you want. You will not leave without me." The door closed, cutting her off. Catron could be heard hushing her.

No one spoke for several minutes, not wanting their words to drift through the door and be overheard by the wounded woman.

Kol said, "Something I been thinking. What if we put someone near the seam to give warning should Rhoden cross back over?"

"Kol, that's a brilliant idea," Phetrix said. "We cannot spare anyone and if Samuel has others here to help him, I have not met them, nor do I know how to contact them. The best thing to do is for me to set alarms at the seam to notify me if someone uses the portal. That way, even if I'm not here, you can be ready."

As they discussed plans, Eric kept his mouth shut and listened and watched. He understood their arguments for him to stay, but it didn't matter. He was going if he had to go alone. He had no idea who Rhoden or Mortas were, but they messed with his sister. They had to pay. Somehow, Eric would find a way to cross to the other world.

He listened for clues about the location of this seam. So far, he knew it was in the city and on the edge of downtown, which he knew to be immense. He had no idea how he would get there, but he'd figure something out.

As the discussion broke up, Eric went out and sat on the porch. He stared into the sky wondering at the number of stars.

DEWAYNE STEPPED out from the other world, awed by what he'd witnessed. It truly was a different place. A kind of backward country where strange creatures roamed the land and skies, and magic was prominent, though illegal if not through a member of King Mortas' army.

He was treated fine, but like an outsider. Though brought to the city, he was not allowed entry into the castle. Rhoden left him at a tavern, which was fine by him, but the dark heavy stuff that passed for beer, ale as they called it, made his stomach queasy. He asked the barkeep where the bathroom was and the man laughed at him. "Bath? You need a bath, head down to the stream." His other patrons laughed.

DeWayne stumbled out the back door and found a small square shed. The smell told him its purpose. He opened the door. The odor hit him, watering his eyes. He saw the hole cut in the rough wood, heard the buzzing of the flies, and the sound of some creature gnawing at something inside the hole and was cured of the need to go.

When Rhoden returned, he was given new instructions, handed a small leather pouch full of coins, and led back to the seam. As it sealed behind him, DeWayne glanced around, happy to be back in his own time. Then he caught sight of a car parked across the street. The man sitting inside was the cop that had hounded him the day before. From the looks of it, the man had fallen asleep on his stakeout.

DeWayne moved toward the rear of the lot and down the alley. Once he reached the cross street, he was a quarter of a block behind where cop was parked. From there, he worked his way down the street. He had a lot to do before Rhoden crossed over again.

Chapter 31

Elly and Shree continued their vigilance throughout the day after the old woman was taken away. They heard screams and shouts from outside the walls, but they didn't know what happened.

Elly grew restless, itching to find out more about the strange feeling; the power she felt earlier. What was it? Should she be scared? Was it dangerous? She grunted and leaned back against the cold stone wall.

"We have to get out of here. This is crazy. I'm worried they might try and *do* something to us."

"Like what?" Shree asked.

"Like..." She didn't want to say it out loud. She'd never experienced sexual assault before; never had to fight off a man trying to force himself on her. A few of her friends had experienced the horror, and it broke her heart every time. Saying the words felt like an admission of the inevitable, as though they could conjure the terrible reality.

Shree placed a hand on her shoulder. "You don't have to say it. I know. I feel it, too."

"Then what do we do? How are we gonna escape?"

"Girl, you know we won't let them touch us! I don't care if I gotta rip out all their eyes. It won't happen."

Elly giggled. "Damn straight."

A couple hours later, the guard from the morning returned, this time with wooden plates of cooked vegetables. Carrots, radishes, and something green that was either cabbage or lettuce; Elly couldn't decide.

"Here, eat up before the rats do. They seem to be the most well-fed of all down here," the guard said in a gruff voice. "Mortas wants to make sure you got your strength."

"Why? What's his plan for us?" Shree asked.

"I don't question my lord. You'd do well to keep silent, too. I'd hate to see such a lovely as you lose her head."

Shree ran a hand across her throat. "My…head?"

The guard chuckled and left the plates near the cell doors. "Better hurry before the rats beat you to it." He left, his heavy footsteps echoing in the stone hall.

Elly grabbed the plates and handed one to Shree.

"I'm not eating that!"

"Why not?"

"What if it's poisoned?"

Elly inspected one of the carrots. It looked fine to her.

"I doubt they'd poison us. I get the impression they'd be more brutal than that."

Shree gasped and placed a hand over her mouth.

"What?"

"Do you think they cut off the old woman's head? Who are these people? This is barbaric!"

Elly lost her appetite. Shree was right. Nowhere was it right to inflict such terrible punishment on someone. She dropped her plate to the floor. Moments later, a pair of rats skittered to the food, gnawing on bits of radish.

"I can't take this! We must get out of here!"

When she spoke the words and felt her anger growing, Elly felt the power inside her swell like an inflatable ball. Instead of being frightened by the sensation, she embraced it. The surge flowed through her. She fought the anxiety, trying to remain calm, but the feeling ebbed. "No!" she yelled, allowing her anger to reignite.

"Elly, what's going on? What are you doing?"

"I, I don't know. I can feel something growing inside me."

"Oh, girl, you mean like an alien?"

Elly shook her head. "I can feel…I don't know how to explain it. I feel something bubbling up inside me. A power or strength. The more it builds, the more I feel like I'm gonna explode."

"Don't hurt yourself! Please be careful!"

Elly lost control and the power vanished. She reached out to steady herself against the damp wall.

"What happened?" Shree asked.

"I…I don't know. I tried to hold it and understand what it is, but oh, I don't know."

"Hold what? Girl, you're talking crazy. Have these people gotten to you, too?"

"It's just…I can feel my body expand, but not in a bad way. It makes me feel strong sometimes. When I get angry or worked up, it fills me up and I feel this tension building, but I don't know what to do with it. I've never felt anything like this before."

"It's not a like a fever or something like that, is it?"

"No, I don't feel sick. I do feel weak afterwards."

"Can you do it now?"

Elly closed her eyes and tried to make the feeling return. She grunted as she failed to hold the one thing that might help them.

"I'm sorry."

Shree put her arm around her. "It's ok. We can figure this out. Whatever it is you feel, maybe it'll come back."

They spent almost three days in the dungeon with no contact other than the random guards who dropped food for them. It wasn't until late in the second day that the girls, both starving, finally gave in and tried the food. When they both survived the night, they ate what was brought to them after that.

Eating the latest dish of potatoes and leeks, the girls were startled by the arrival of another prisoner. It was an older man missing his left eye. After the guards tossed him into the cell next to theirs, Shree offered him some of her food.

"Hey mister, want something to eat?"

The man shrunk from her.

"It's not poisoned. We've been eating it for two days now and neither one of us has died."

He refused her offer and stared at them with a wild eye.

"Whatever, then. Your loss." Shree finished her meal and the girls leaned back against the bars, watching the older man.

After what felt like forever, Elly stood and stretched. When she did, her shirt raised and exposed her half-moon scar.

A gasp drew their attention. "It can't be!" The man grabbed the bars with shaky hands and pulled himself to his feet. He pointed at Elly's bare midriff. "The mark of heirs! The princess has returned!" the man shouted, scaring both girls to death.

"What the hell, dude?" Elly cried out.

"Yeah, what's that all about?"

He raised a wrinkled hand, extending a long finger at Elly. "The heir," he whispered. "Chevalon will be saved!"

"What is wrong with you? I'm not the heir of anything. I'm just a girl."

"I can die a happy man! Chevalon will be saved!"

It was then two guards arrived. "Gruthe, it's time you faced justice. Come on," one of the guards said. They opened the cell and ripped him from the bars.

"The heir! The heir lives!" he shouted as they dragged him away.

"Hey, what are you gonna do to him? Let that man go!" Shree called out.

They ignored her and dragged the old man away while he continued shouting about the heir.

Shree turned to Elly. "Can you believe him? What's going on around here?"

"I wish I knew. These people are freaking me out!"

Minutes later, they heard the man scream a horrible sound, one so terrible that Elly's anger bubbled up inside her.

"What?" Shree asked.

Elly felt the warming power fill her. She had no idea how to control it, but knew it was something she wanted. She let the sensation fill her until it could find no place else to expand.

"Oh God!" The feeling both excited and frightened her. Her awareness of everything around her heightened. Then her head began to throb. "I think I can—" *What? What could she do?* An idea came to her. She put the thought to the test.

Elly thrust her hand at the cell door and a flash of light burst from it and exploded the lock, forcing the door open, where it slammed against the stone wall. The recoil of the release pitched her backward. She hit the wall and slid to the straw-covered dirt floor.

"Elly! You did it!" Then Shree noticed her friend on the floor looking dazed. "Oh, Elly. Are you all right?"

"I-I think so." She needed help up and then leaned on Shree to prevent her rubbery legs from giving out.

Shree whispered, "Somehow you opened the door."

She had no idea how she created the blast or how she threw it at the door, but it worked.

Though her head pounded, she felt her strength returning. "Let's go. I think I can hold this power for a little longer. It might help us."

With Shree still providing support, Elly walked slowly, afraid if she lost concentration, she'd lose her connection to this power she suddenly wielded.

They got to the end of the stone hall and a flight of steps to their right went up into darkness. "I guess we go this way."

Creeping up the steps, they made it to another floor. A long stone corridor with wooden doors on both sides ended in another corridor that intersected it.

"Hey, what are you doing?"

Elly didn't see him at first, but a guard dressed in black with a large snowflake on his chest was near a door on her right.

"Do something!" Shree whispered.

Elly didn't know what she could do. Should she try and send a bolt of light like she did at the door? What if it killed the man? She didn't want to go to prison for murder!

The guard unsheathed a short sword and ran toward them, his girth keeping him from going too fast.

"Stop right there! Don't go anywhere!" he yelled.

Elly panicked at the sight of the sword and the charging brute. The power increased and she let another blast go. A bright flash of light erupted from her fingers. It struck the guard in the shoulder. He dropped his sword to the floor, the clanging sound reverberating throughout the corridor loud enough to wake the dead. The force of the light tossed the man into the wall, where he slid down.

Shree ran ahead. "Come on, Elly! We gotta find a way out!"

It took her a second to register that Shree was calling to her. Elly raced toward her, hands holding her head. Carefully, stepped past the guard who was moaning and clutching his bloody shoulder.

"I can't believe I did that! I could've killed him!"

"Doesn't matter. I think they're gonna do the same to us if we don't get out of here!"

Shree grabbed her arm and pulled her forward until they were at the intersection. "Now which way?"

Elly scanned both directions, then closed her eyes. She needed to ease the pressure in her skull. Instead, she tapped into the power but didn't know what to do with it. Nothing happened. When she opened her eyes, she knew which way to go.

"Down here!" She led Shree to their right, following the stone floors.

Behind them, guards shouted for them to stop.

"Hurry! They're catching up!"

Elly felt the power surging through her again and quickly spun, sending a blast down the corridor. It struck the ceiling above the men, and the stones exploded, raining debris on the guards. They shouted and cried out, but they were stopped.

"Girl, I don't know what got into you, but don't you ever let that go!"

Elly barely heard, fighting the growing headache.

"This way. I think I see a door."

The girls ran forward to a large wooden door. They pushed on the iron ring and it slowly creaked open, revealing a stone courtyard illuminated by the light of the moon.

"We made it. Now what?" Elly asked.

"Now you find out what real pain is like."

Elly's heart jumped into her throat. Both girls spun around. The one called Rhoden stood facing them, his hands glowing.

Chapter 32

Rhoden cracked a grin and let electric bolts fly from his hands. In desperation, Elly thrust hers forward, her burst of energy creating a shield of light. She had no idea how she did it, only that it appeared. Rhoden's bolt crushed into the shield, creating a loud boom of thunder. Shree covered her ears and Elly fell to one knee.

"Get up! Hurry!" Shree yanked on her arm. Elly felt dizzy and weak, unsure if she could follow.

"Shree…I don't know…"

Shree pulled her up and pushed her into the courtyard. Rhoden screamed something she didn't understand, calling for sea curls. *What are sea curls?* she wondered.

A terrifying shriek caught her attention. Circling above them were two black demons with long shredded robes. The ghostly things howled and cried out.

"Don't let them get away!" Rhoden cried out.

Elly had no idea what the things were but didn't want to find out. She raced after Shree across the stone courtyard. Rhoden was behind them, firing flaming projectiles at them.

"What the hell!" Elly cried out. She struggled to grasp what was going on around her. What were those things and what was this man doing trying to hurt her? And where in the world were they?

Elly fought the dizziness and spun, casting her hands out toward

Rhoden, and let a surge of energy fly from her hands. The power she felt within her was intoxicating. *How had she never known about this before?*

Then she laughed a loud maniacal laugh.

Shree grabbed her arm.

"What's wrong with you, Elly? Are you ok?"

The black creatures cried out again, their loud horrible shrieks piercing her ears.

"This isn't real. It can't be real," Elly replied quietly.

"It sure as hell is real! I'm not fake!"

Rhoden fired a ball of flame at them. It flew straight and true, and just before it engulfed them, it made a right angle turn and it caught a nearby tree on fire. The trunk was engulfed in fiery yellows and oranges as the flames inched upwards.

What had just happened? They were about to be fried to a crisp and the ball of fire danced away like it had hit an invisible shield. She had no time to analyze. Guards poured into the courtyard from all directions with swords raised.

"See, Shree? They can't be real! No one uses swords anymore! It's all guns now. We're in some weird dream."

Elly refused Shree's tug on her arm.

"Elly, come on! Use your power or something. They're gonna get us!"

"I have no power. This is a dream."

"Then if it's a dream, use your fake powers to make these guards go away."

Elly felt a surge within her and then flung it outward haphazardly. She spun in a circle. The light rippled away from her like a stone skipping in a pond, radiating out from her across the courtyard. It struck the guards and they fell down screaming. Swords and shields clanked to the ground. The sound of men dying echoed around them.

"Fun little trick, but you'll need more than that."

Elly spun and Rhoden was only feet away from her. He motioned with his arms and both girls were caught in an invisible rope, unable to move.

"Elly! Do something!"

Elly struggled against the bindings but they were unmovable. When she tried reaching into the power she'd become used to, she struck a wall. She was aware of the power: could almost see it, but a barrier of some sort prevented her from accessing it. The tease was overwhelming. She struggled and fought against it, but nothing worked.

"You're more powerful than I imagined. Harnessed correctly, you could be useful. Mortas doesn't need to know how powerful you are. Not yet."

"Let us—" Shree's mouth was closed by an invisible force and the rest of her words were silenced.

Rhoden slowly walked forward until he was inches from Elly's face. She smelled his musky scent and the wool of his robe.

"Little girl, do you have any idea who you are? Do you know what it means to be the princess?"

"I'm not a princess," she growled.

"Oh, of course not. You're just a girl from another world who likes boys, and what was that called again—football?"

Elly didn't understand him. He spoke in riddles that were beyond her comprehension.

"I just want to go home. I don't know how I got this ability, but it can't be real. People don't just create electricity and fire. This has to be a dream, right? You're in my head. I didn't kill several men just now, either. It's a bad dream. Maybe it was something I ate?"

Rhoden shook his head. "No, girl; this is real. It's more real than you know. Mortas plans something special for you, but I might have a more pressing need of you."

"What…need?" Elly worried that this man was gonna do something terrible to her.

"Guards! Take these two back to the dungeon. Be careful with this one. She's under my power at the moment. After you get them locked up, I'll make sure she can't do this again."

Four guards shambled their way to the girls. All were injured with massive burns on their arms and legs, and angry.

Two guards grabbed her and dragged her forward while the other two did the same to Shree. The girls were still immobilized and could do nothing to fight against them. Elly screamed and was silenced by an invisible gag much like Shree had been moments earlier.

"You two won't be so lucky next time. I underestimated your use of magic. It won't happen again."

Elly screamed in her head. She wanted this nightmare to be over and tried willing herself to wake up.

The guards dragged them across the courtyard. Dying soldiers moaned and fought the inevitable. Elly fought back tears when she realized they were dead, or close to it, because of her. She didn't mean it. She only wanted to escape. If this wasn't a dream, that meant she committed murder. How could she live with herself?

The guards wasted no time pulling the girls to the dungeon where they were thrown inside another cell and locked up once again. Rhoden followed the guards and motioned at Elly.

"That ought to hold you. You won't escape that easily again. Try as you might to reach the power, I think you'll find it unavailable to you. I'll be back."

"Screw you!" Shree yelled.

Rhoden furrowed his brow. "I don't know what you mean, but from your tone, I assume it's an insult. You'd do well to watch yourselves. Especially you. I don't need you. The only reason you are still alive is so I may use your death as leverage to gain the princess's cooperation." He turned and walked away, the echo of his footsteps growing quieter.

"What have I done? What are we gonna do now?" Elly asked. They were no farther away from their fate than they were earlier. And now she was cut off from the only means she had to get them out of there.

"If only I'd wake up, this would all be over."

"This is real, Elly. We're in a lot of trouble. We gotta get out of here. Somehow."

Chapter 33

Elly and Shree spent hours alone in the dark, dank cell. Elly tried desperately to grasp her power, what Rhoden called magic, but every time she tried, it avoided her hold.

"What's gonna happen to us?" Shree asked.

Elly shook her head. "I wish I knew." She paused, afraid to speak the words aloud, but then thought better of it. "Let's suppose this is real. Let's pretend we're in some strange world that's kinda like our Medieval Times. Let's say these people really think I'm some sort of princess—"

"With a brother! Don't forget that."

"Yeah, with a brother. Let's say all of this is true and I do have these amazing powers. What does it all mean? Why would we be here, and why do these people want us? What did we ever do to them? I had no idea I had these abilities until we got here."

The sound of footsteps on the stone floor cut their conversation short. The girls turned to the dark hallway. Into the glow of a torch on the wall walked the man that first took them from their world. The man called Mortas Frost.

"Girls, I see you're adjusting to the dungeon well enough. I heard there was an incident earlier. You killed many of my men. Do you know what the penalty for that is in my kingdom? I would have the right to execute you in public. I'd have the right to let everyone see what the penalty is for disobeying me and causing harm to my people."

"Then do it. If you're gonna talk such a big game, go ahead and do it!" Shree said.

Mortas shook his head and clasped his hands behind his back. He wore a black shirt with a white snowflake on the front with a long black cape draped over his shoulders like a villain from the old comics Elly's dad used to read.

Elly's dad, who was killed by the man in front of her.

"Little girls, why do you fight the inevitable? Do you know how long I've been seeking you, Princess?" He ignored Shree and gazed at Elly. She felt the weight of his stare and fought hard to not turn away.

"I'm no princess," Elly growled. "You killed my father. You brought us to whatever hell this place is. When I get my hands on you, I'll do worse than what I did to those guards of yours out there."

Mortas grinned. "I do like a challenge. You are aware of your predicament, are you not? My mage Rhoden has you completely incapacitated. I, too, have a touch of the power and I can sense how strong his bond is over you. Go ahead, fight it. Wear yourself out. I'd be delighted to watch you grow weak." His eyes blackened like the devil had just possessed him. "And let me remind you." He turned those evil eyes on Shree. His voice reverberated around the stone walls in a deep rumble. He extended one arm toward her and lifted. "I don't need her, Princess." Shree gasped as she was lifted by an invisible hand, her feet dangling in midair. "Defy me and you shall watch her die." Shree gurgled and kicked her feet. Her hands clamped around the invisible force, trying to break the hold.

"Leave her alone!" Elly ran at him, grabbing the bars of the cell. "What do you want from us? Why are we here?"

Mortas looked around the hallway and spotted a wooden stool. Extending his other arm, the stool slid across the floor, stopping behind him, all the while he kept Shree dangling. Her face reddened; her eyes bulged. He took a seat and crossed his arms in his lap. Shree fell to the floor and coughed, sucking desperately for air.

"Princess Elysande, you and your brother are the last of your line. I fully intend on murdering you. Both. Eventually. Although I don't have any use for him, you may still prove useful."

"You can't do that!" Elly screamed.

Mortas shrugged her off. "She'll die, too." He nodded toward

Shree, who was still breathing hard. "I have no quarrel with her, but I have no sympathy for her, either."

"I dare you to touch me. It'll be the last thing you do," Elly snarled. She tried in vain to harness the power, but it was just out of reach.

"The man I killed wasn't your father. He and your mother were nothing more than royal servants forced into service by Phetrix. They were nobodies, if you think about it."

"Shut up! How dare you talk about my parents like that! They were good people!"

"Of course, they were good. But they were servants."

Elly stalked around the cell, her anger flaring white-hot within her. She'd never been so insulted or angered in her entire life.

"The man was weak. He should have watched over you better."

Elly ran to the bars again, trying to reach through and grab hold of Mortas' shirt. He sat just far enough away that she couldn't touch him.

"Little girl, let go of your anger. It will do you no good. I'm in charge here. You will do what I command or die sooner rather than later. Once I get your brother here, all will be over. My reign will be made complete and your family line dies with you."

"What is wrong with you? I have no brother! I am not a princess! My parents raised me in Chicago, and you murdered my father!"

Elly felt something snap inside, like a hair tie pulled too tight. In that moment, she felt a release. Her anger flushed with the incoming power that radiated through her entire body. She absorbed as much of it as possible, pulling in more and more until she felt like bursting.

Mortas's eyes grew wide. "No, no this can't be happening! Rhoden said—"

Mortas jumped from his stool, feebly waving his hands to cast a spell, though whatever he did it had no effect on Elly. She harnessed the power, feeling every nerve on her body buzz with electricity.

Elly directed her anger at the metal bars around them. The door glowed a bright red and melted, dripping molten pools of iron. Then the remnants exploded.

Mortas jumped back, knocking over the stool. "Guards, get down here, now!"

Mortas wove a simple spell of protection to keep the bursting iron bars from reaching him. Soon several black armored guards raced into the stone hallway with swords brandished.

"Stop her! Don't let her out!"

Elly wasn't taking any chances. She failed the first time, and she'd not fail again. Directing her hand toward the guards, she flung energy at them, though she didn't want to kill anyone. She let the power consume their feet and legs, forcing the guards to cry in pain and fall to the floor.

Mortas tried stopping her, but his power, as great as it was when he stole them from her home, seemed to pale in comparison to what she now possessed.

"Come on, Shree. We're leaving."

Elly spun her hands and let the power flee from her toward Mortas. His shield held, but it was a struggle for him to maintain it.

Elly felt the immense power within her and she dared any guard to stand in her way. None would stop her. Not now. Not while her anger-fueled actions pushed her forward. Wherever the hell they were, as long as she held the power, she knew they'd be safe.

Several guards ran toward them, but she pushed them back with a blast of energy that slammed them against the walls and extinguished the torches along the hallway. Mortas used the distraction to make his escape.

"Damn, girl! That power is something else!"

Elly turned and ran down the corridor with Shree behind her.

Tracing their steps back to the outer courtyard, Elly and Shree hurried across the stone walkway. More guards ran from the castle, yelling for them to stop.

Elly turned to Shree. "Go. Run out of here. Let me finish this."

"I'm not going anywhere!"

Elly shook her head. "Whatever, you stubborn thing!"

The guards closed in. Elly pulled in the power, then let it fly. The guards were bowled over like so many pins. Strange, but she no longer felt as weak as before. Though her head throbbed, it was a far cry from the severe headache she felt when using her power the last time. Perhaps her body was adjusting to the strain, or maybe she just needed to be mad enough to wield it without harming her body.

More guards came. Again she pushed the force outward. The moment she expected it to strike the guards, it stopped short, slamming into a shield of some kind. From a second-floor window of one of castle towers, Rhoden stood facing them, his hands moving frantically.

"Damn! He stopped me."

Elly looked to Shree. "I guess we run!"

Both girls sprinted from the courtyard toward the gate. Three guards with pikes lowered their weapon at them. Elly pushed her hand forward and a blast of power knocked them backward. Behind them, she heard Rhoden yelling.

"Shut the gate! Shut the gate!"

The iron gate creaked as it was slowly lowered.

"Oh no!" Shree cried out.

Elly ran faster, using blasts of power to hold back any guards following them. Flaming orbs erupted all around them. Elly chanced a look back to see Rhoden firing at them.

They neared the gate and two guards tried to stop them. One of them sliced with his sword, cutting a deep gash on Shree's arm. The girl cried out and fell down, rolling to a stop.

Elly rushed the guard. She punched him in the chest as the power released. He was thrown back to the stone wall and collapsed in a boneless heap. The other guard stepped toward Shree with his sword raised, and as he was ready to strike the killing blow, Elly shot him with a large bolt of electricity, boring a hole through his chest, and exploding blood and bone out the back. The sword fell from his hands and landed on Shree.

A ball of flame struck next to Elly and knocked her over. Her pants ignited. She rolled on the ground, patting her leg, and tossing dirt to put it out. Another ball of flame struck at her feet, igniting her shoes. She stomped her feet to put the flames out.

"Come on, Shree, we have to go!"

Pulling her friend up, the two girls raced through the gate into complete blackness outside. Guards raced after them, but after a few blasts of air, they were pushed back. They darted for the trees to the right of the castle. Arrows landed around them, but Elly had to believe they were firing blindly. A ball of flame shot into the air like a flare, but it lit the sky in front of the castle and they were just outside its cone of light. They ran hard toward the trees. Shree struggled, but Elly refused to let her fall. Her fiend was hurt and bleeding, but she couldn't do anything for her until they were safe.

Two more fireballs lit the sky like fourth of July fireworks, but by then they were hiding in the dark forest.

Chapter 34

Nordon drove the van back toward the city. They decided to leave at night. Alyanna would be angry, but she needed her rest. Kol sat in the passenger seat with Phetrix directly behind. As they drove, Phetrix worked on the wards he planned to use at the seam. The other two kept quiet so not to disturb him. As he worked, he gave thought to recent events.

He'd been having difficulty generating enough power to enable his spells. Several times he had to recast the spell to accomplish his goal, yet in the heat of battle, he'd been able to unleash fierce lightning bolts at the amphoids with ease. Why? He had to know he could count on his magic if lives depended on him. Had it been a strange phenomenon of this world? Did it take time for his body to adjust, or was it that the magic power lines all wizards tapped into were fewer, inconsistent, or less powerful here?

He had no answer and was determined to find one. He did have a theory but wasn't sure how to test it out. He went back to the work at hand, satisfied for the moment his power was full, but he would revisit the problem later.

BEHIND THE THIRD-ROW BENCH SEAT, lying across the floor of the cargo area, Eric listened to the old man mutter strange words and tones. It sounded like a prayer in some long-forgotten language. Perhaps it was fear or maybe it was knowing he'd disobeyed his guardians, but an uneasy feeling ran through him. His body vibrated with nervous energy. In an attempt to calm himself, Eric breathed in slow, deep breaths and exhaled. It didn't help.

He didn't feel like himself; like he was coming down with the flu or a cold. As the drive continued, he felt worse. He feared his discomfort would give away his presence. Beads of sweat popped on his forehead. He blotted them with his sleeve. He felt feverish and had a hard time breathing.

"We're getting close," Nordon said.

Seconds later, Phetrix ceased chanting. "I'm ready."

For whatever reason, Eric's body began to relax. The pressure he'd felt in his chest dissipated. Though he was strangely tired, he no longer felt ill.

The van pulled to a stop down the street from the seam. Nordon took in the surrounding area for signs of any enemy. "It looks clear," he said to Phetrix.

"This is the original seam," Phetrix said.

"It's the only one I know of," said Nordon.

"It's the one I passed the heirs through those many years ago, but not the only one. Kol and I came through a second one. This looks different than it did fifteen years earlier."

"It is. One of the buildings has been demolished and two others have been erected on the other side."

Phetrix didn't respond. He glanced out the window, then moved to the rear seat to look out the back. Eric held his breath as the old man knelt on the bench inches above him. "Okay. Let's do this," he said.

The van shifted as first Nordon removed his bulk, then Kol exited, and finally Phetrix. The doors shut behind them. Eric waited a few moments before lifting up high enough to see. He spied the three men crossing the street toward a vacant lot. Eric wanted desperately to get a look through this seam just to have an idea where he came from.

As the men stopped in the middle of the lot, Eric cracked open the rear door and slid out. He pushed the door but did not shut it all the way. If he needed to retreat in a hurry, he didn't want to fumble for the handle or to have to open the door quietly. He peered around the van.

Nordon and Kol were stationed on either side of the old man standing guard. Phetrix had his arms up. The long, gnarled fingers of his left hand made a circular motion. His voice carried across the street. The words sounded the same as the ones he'd muttered in the car, only these carried the weight of power.

Eric felt an inexplicable thrumming in his chest. For a moment he feared the ill feeling had returned. It ebbed for a moment, giving him relief. Then, Phetrix began speaking and the words reached him.

Once more the strange sensation swept through him. The discomfort grew with the volume of the old man's voice. He bent at the waist and rested his hands on his knees. His body tingled. Regardless, he could not take his eyes away from the old man.

A tear opened in the air, like someone had unzipped the sky. Phetrix touched several points around the seam. A minute later, the seam was gone. As before, the unease passed, leaving Eric tired and slightly unsteady on his feet. As the three men turned toward the van, Eric slid back in position. He held the van door ajar until he heard the other doors opening. Then, timing the move to blend with the others, he pulled the door shut.

"Will that work?" Kol asked.

"It should, unless Rhoden senses the magic and tries to dispel what I've done."

"Why can't you just seal it closed for good?" asked Nordon.

"I'm not sure if or how I can. Whoever or whatever created the seam wields more power than do I. I will have to study it and its history to get an idea how to accomplish that. My feeling is it will take the power and experience of several mages to close the portal."

Nordon started the engine and pulled away from the curb. Eric risked being seen, lifting up to get a closer look at the area of the seam. He noted the older buildings to the right of the lot and the newer ones to the left and all landmarks that could lead him back to this spot. He wondered if he needed some special ability to unzip the seam. Maybe it needed a keyword.

The van turned and the lot was lost to view. However, Eric was certain that once he returned to the area, he could find the spot.

GRANT WAS STARTLED AWAKE. He couldn't be sure what had spooked him; perhaps it was a bad dream or the sound of a vehicle driving by. Whatever the cause, he was alert now. He rubbed the sleep from his eyes. With a fast doubletake, he spotted three men in the lot. He reached for the door handle and his gun at the same time and stopped.

Whatever the men were doing, they were not going through the slice in the air. They turned and walked away. Perhaps someone had already gone through while he slept. He cursed under his breath. Possibly they were waiting for someone else to come through. That would be worth waiting for.

As the men neared, he slid lower in his seat and pulled out the gun. He recognized the strange old man and his dimwitted friend and the large man from the house during the gunfight. They angled across the street toward a large black van. He had a choice to make. Stop them now or wait to see what happened. He opted to wait.

They climbed into the van. For a while, nothing happened. He swept his gaze from the mirror to watch the van, then back to the lot, expecting someone to make a sudden appearance at any second. To his surprise, the van drove away from the curb, past his position and around the corner. "Huh!" Grant gave them a second to get out of sight before starting his car. It was better to follow the known rather than wait for the unknown. He'd see where they went and call in for back up. If there were more of them, he'd wrap them all up at once. Then his boss could see for himself how weird this case had become.

DEWAYNE DECIDED to steal another van rather than spend the money he'd been given. He'd rather spend it on himself than transportation for his boss. This one, a Ford Transit, stood taller than the black van and only had windows in the rear. It also had one bench seat that could only seat two if they were the size of the last batch. Otherwise, they'd have to sit on the floor.

He pulled down the street wanting to keep well away from the detective, though if he was still sleeping, it might not matter. He hoped the man would give up and leave long before Rhoden needed his services.

DeWayne slouched low in the seat so only his eyes and top of his head were in sight. He had only been there a minute when movement caught his eye. Someone moved behind a black van. He sat upright and focused hard. *Was that the van he stole?* It might be. There was a man standing behind it. No, not standing. Using it for cover. He was watching something across the street.

DeWayne switched his gaze to follow the watcher's. Though too far away to see the entire lot, he saw another man; this one with a long knife in his hand staring out at the street. *Had he just come through the seam?* He shifted to the passenger seat to get a better angle. From there he could make out a second man wearing a long dark robe. He appeared to be doing something to the seam. It glowed yellow for a few seconds, then disappeared.

The two men turned and walked away from the lot. A third man joined them. DeWayne recognized him for sure. He was the man wielding the massive gun and who stole the van DeWayne had stolen. That helped him identify the first two men as the ones who got out of the police car and zapped one of Rhoden's thugs. What did they do? He found himself hoping they had sealed the seam permanently so he'd be free of the madness.

They walked toward the black van. He glanced back and saw the watcher slide back inside like a stowaway. He had been in the van that night, too. A lightbulb popped on in his head. *Could that be the heir they were looking for?* Huh! If so, this information might earn him a big bonus.

The men climbed into the van and pulled away. *Even better. What if he could lead his boss right to them?* This could make him rich. He started the van as the other one rounded the corner. He almost forgot about the detective. Evidently the man was awake now. He drove his car after them. Of course, it wouldn't be that easy. Well, he'd just have to keep them both in view. DeWayne drove to the corner, hesitated to make sure the other vehicles were still moving, then followed.

Chapter 35

"Something on your mind?" Nordon asked the mage.

"Huh? Oh, I was just thinking. Ever since I've been here, I've had trouble with my spells. They either fizzled too fast or depleted my energy level too fast. I was exhausted using my magic to get to your house during the attack, yet once there, I was suddenly invigorated. I'm trying to puzzle out why."

"You didn't have any problems here, did you?"

"No, and not at the cabin when I set wards to warn the others."

"Maybe all this traveling wore you out and adrenaline perked you up?"

Phetrix nodded. "Possibly, but I feel like something else is happening. I don't think magic works the same way here. The energy I draw in to focus the spells might be different or harder to find."

Nordon's phone rang. He answered. "Problem?" He listened. An excited female voice could be heard throughout the van. "What are you talking about? Of course he's not with—" He stopped speaking and jammed on the brakes.

"What's the trouble?" Phetrix asked.

"Dina says Eric is missing."

"What?"

A door opened. The van shifted. Moments later, the rear doors were flung open and revealed Eric's hiding place. "What were you thinking, boy?" Nordon's voice boomed. "What part of *stay in the cabin* was beyond your comprehension? Your mother is worried sick about you."

"I didn't want to be left out." Eric said, swinging his legs out. "And she's not my mother," he said, defiance ringing in his tone.

"Boy, I hope you have a better head on your shoulders than that."

Eric exited and walked to the side of the van. He opened the sliding door and stepped inside. Nordon shut the doors and got back in the driver's seat. He picked up his phone. "Not to worry. He's here. Huh? I don't know what he was thinking. You'll have to ask him yourself." He ended the call in a huff.

No one spoke, creating an uncomfortable situation. Finally, Phetrix said, "You may be the heir to the throne, but without wisdom, you'll not last long in the role. Wisdom is gained through experience, study, and listening to those who have been placed in a position to support you."

"I won't be left out. I want to be involved. If my sister has been kidnapped, I want to be part of the rescue effort."

"Be that as it may, you are not trained yet how to be of value to such an expedition. How effective can the rest of us be if we have to look over our shoulders at you to keep you safe? What good will it do to have both of you captured…or worse, killed? Who does it benefit then? You have no idea what's at stake. An entire world is depending on you to lead them to victory over Mortas. You cannot be their hope if you are dead. To lead means making the right decisions at the right times based on the knowledge and information in your possession at a given moment. We are a long way from that moment. You have much to learn before an attempt can be made. Until then, it is our job to keep you safe until such a time when you are ready to lead. Can you understand or will I be required to have you bound and gagged?"

Eric snorted. "As if."

Phetrix's eyebrows rose. "As if, indeed." He spoke a few strange words that sounded like Latin and made a swirling motion over Eric's head with his finger. Eric squawked as his arms were drawn tight to his body and anchored to the seat. Something pressed against his mouth like an invisible hand and his lips were sealed tight. He could not move or speak other than to make grunting sounds. His eyes widened in panic. Eric whipped his head back and forth to dislodge whatever covered his mouth.

"As I said, you need knowledge and experience to lead. You have neither. Now be quiet so I might think about our next move."

Instead of planning, his mind turned toward the theory he'd been working on. What if the recent resurgence of his power was because he was in the presence of the prince? Even at the age of two, his sister, Elysande, had shown signs of having the ability to cast magic. Perhaps that same ability resided in the prince, but latently. The three times he'd been near him, Phetrix felt the power course through him as it always did. However, when away from him, his attempts had sputtered or faltered. If this was true, all the more reason to keep him close.

GRANT ALMOST DIDN'T STOP in time. He made a quick last-second turn and parked. The van slammed on its brakes. The large man in the driver's seat got out and opened the back doors. A smaller, younger man got out. Grant recognized him from the fight at the house. They had words, then got back into the van. It seemed to Grant that the younger man wasn't supposed to be there. He let the van get more distance in case of another sudden stop, then followed.

They drove for more than an hour, leaving the city on a westbound road and entering farmland. With little traffic on the road, Grant was able to let the distance between the vehicles grow. Ahead, the van made a turn and disappeared. Confused by the sudden loss of taillights, Grant accelerated. As he neared the spot he'd marked mentally, he could find no road.

"No! This did not just happen." He crept onward, but soon realized he'd gone too far and turned around. Down the road, another vehicle was heading toward him. He swung around, having to make the turn in several attempts to avoid driving down a drainage ditch, then drove back.

The other vehicle slowed; then, as Grant edged forward, it sped up and shot past. Perhaps the driver thought Grant was going to carjack him. Moving at only five miles an hour, Grant scanned the area again. If something was there, it was too dark to see it. He swung around again. This pass, he moved a few feet and stopped to look closer. He repeated the move three more times before finding a small opening. He got out of the car and walked toward it. He switched on the light on his cell phone and discovered twin tracks entering a wooded area.

It was decision time again. Follow the tracks now, in the dark where he had little idea of where it led or mark the spot and come back at first light, hoping they'd still be there. No, he wanted this over. He got back in his car and aimed for the tracks. With the headlights beaming directly on them, the tracks were easier to follow. The foliage was close and often dragged across the car, yet Grant plodded onward.

Not sure of how far the road went, Grant didn't want to go in so deep that his lights announced his presence. He shut them off, but within fifty feet he hit a small tree. He could no longer see well enough to continue. Getting out was another problem. A large tree blocked the door. He was forced to climb across the console and exit through the passenger door.

The walk was difficult. The overhanging trees made the darkness more complete. He began to think he'd made a mistake by leaving the car, but then the fear escalated when he wondered if he could find his way back to the car. After nearly thirty minutes of walking, stopping, flashing a quick light and moving on, he caught sight of a light flickering through the trees in the distance.

He stopped, crouched, and slid the gun from its holster. For a long while, he squatted in the dark and listened for unnatural sounds. He moved in a zig-zag pattern until he reached a clearing. A log cabin and two outbuildings covered much of the open ground. The black van was parked next to the cabin. Lights shone in two of the windows. It made moving around easier.

Grant approached with caution. The heavy wooden steps leading to the porch creaked. He froze, then as quietly as he could, moved up on the deck and pressed against the thick logs between the door and the window. The light inside was extinguished. A chair scraped, followed by reverberating footsteps he could feel through the floorboards on the porch.

He tensed to make his move and confront whoever was inside as they came through the door. The inner door opened.

"You make a move and I'll scatter your body parts all over the wall."

The voice took him by surprise. He swung his weapon toward the sound. A heavyset man with long wild hair and a crazed look in his eye stood off the porch, a shotgun balanced on the railing. "Better think twice."

"I'm a cop."

The outer door opened and someone stepped out. Grant couldn't afford to look. He began plotting a shooting sequence. Fire as he dove to his right. Pivot onto his back and shoot at whoever came out the door.

"Bull! Put the gun down or Rhoden will have one less thug."

The name confused Grant. "Who?"

"Yeah, whatever."

"No. He is a cop, if that means sheriff," Phetrix said. The porch light flickered on, casting a dim glow.

"Ah, no way."

"Way," Grant said, pulling back his jacket to expose the badge hanging from his belt.

"Don't care. Lower the gun or you'll be a dead cop."

"Sheriff Grant," Phetrix said. "My advice to you is to drop the, er, gun. I will vouch for your safety."

"You'll forgive me for not feeling secure with that statement."

He heard rather than saw movement to his left. Phetrix came into view. He walked to a position between the two men and stopped. "Now, whoever shoots hits me instead."

"Dag-gone wizards. Always getting in the way." The shotgun wielder lowered the weapon and walked back around the house.

"It's good you are here, Sheriff. I think we will soon need your assistance."

"Oh, is that right? How 'bout I assist you into my car and escort you to jail?"

Phetrix blinked twice and said, "No, I don't think so. Come inside. We will fix you some tea and have a nice chat." He turned toward the door, ignoring the fact Grant still held the gun on him.

"What do you mean, I don't think so? I'm a policeman. If I give you an order, you obey it."

Phetrix reached the door being held open by the big man. "Perhaps another time. We have things to discuss. Shall we?" He stepped inside, leaving Grant's jaw hanging slack

Who are these people?

Chapter 36

Grant walked to the doorway and peered through the screen door. The big man stood to the side and the gun man leaned against the kitchen cabinets. The old guy, his partner, a younger man, and two women sat at a table. His first thought was to go back the way he came and forget all about whatever was happening, but he knew he couldn't. Not just because it was his job, but because the entire case was so bizarre that he owed it to himself to at least get an explanation. In fact, several explanations were due…especially concerning how he managed to take control of the car and whatever it was that shot from the old guy's fingers to take down that brute.

He sighed and opened the door. As it closed behind him with a crack, all eyes focused on him. He realized they were looking at the gun still in his hand that was now hanging at his side, as much as they were at him. He holstered it and advanced toward the meeting.

"Have a seat, Sheriff," Phetrix pointed to the empty one. "Thank you for joining us. We have much to discuss and I fear little time to prepare."

"Prepare? For what?"

"Ah, that is the question. I'm sure what you have seen and encountered so far will pale compared to what Mortas will send this time."

Grant frowned. "And who's Mortas?"

"Instead of asking questions, allow me to give you details that may answer all of them."

"Well, won't that be nice?" He could not contain the sarcasm. This entire affair was out of control.

"Please bear with me for a short while. You will understand better when I am finished."

A copper kettle whistled. One of the women stood to retrieve it.

"As I have mentioned before, my name is Phetrix. I—we come from a land called Chevalon. You have already indicated you have never heard of it. That is because it does not exist in this world."

"Excuse me?"

Phetrix held up a hand. "Give it a moment, if you please." He lowered his hand as the woman brought two cups of hot tea to the table. They were passed to Phetrix and the guest, Grant. "Ah, thank you, Catron."

Grant stared at the liquid, half expecting to see something swimming around in the cup.

Phetrix continued. "Many years ago I discovered a portal that allowed me to cross from our much smaller world to yours. I kept it a secret, but a few years later when Mortas attacked our castle, I used the portal to send the prince and princess here with some loyal guardians. The idea was to keep them safe until such a time when they could return to claim the throne. Unfortunately, that time never came. They were raised here as inhabitants of your world. Recently, however, Rhoden, Mortas' mage—"

"Mage? You mean like magic?" Grant interrupted.

"Yes, precisely. Rhoden discovered the portal and sent his minions into this world in search of the heirs."

"Okay, I think I've heard enough. This fantasy realm you've concocted sounds fun, but *magic*? Really?"

"Of course. Do you not have mages in this world?"

Grant snorted. "No. And before you ask, no, I don't believe in magic."

Phetrix lifted his eyebrows in surprise. "No mages? No magic?"

"Not so much as a hocus pocus. So unless this story has any basis in reality, then it's time for me to leave."

Grant pushed his chair back and stood.

"Please do sit down, Sheriff. You haven't finished your tea."

Grant started to speak, but before the words came out, the cup of tea lifted from the table and hovered inches from his face. "Seriously? Parlor tricks?" Grant glanced over and beneath the cup searching for strings. He waved his hand over the top, expecting to send the cup flying. Nothing happened. He swept his hand under the cup. Again, nothing. "Is this controlled by remote? See, technology…now that I understand, but it sure isn't magic."

The cup settled back on the table. "Sheriff Grant…"

"I'm not a sheriff. I'm a detective. I detect things and I'm detecting a whole lotta bull in this cabin."

"I assure you, no livestock is within these walls," Phetrix said.

Grant looked dumbfounded.

"Told you this was a mistake," the gun man said. "Shoulda just let me shoot him."

"Now, Tetrin, there is no need for that. Detective Grant, please at least allow me to finish. I promise, though it may sound strange to you, it is all true, and I dare say you will have proof in a short time."

"Proof, eh? Okay, I'll listen if only to see this so-called proof."

He sat and kept back from the table in case he needed to rise in a hurry. He kept glancing at the shotgun man in case he went for a weapon.

"As stated, Rhoden sent his people through the portal in search of the prince and princess. Evidently, he found the princess. He took her."

"When you say took, you mean kidnapped?" Grant said.

A door opened and another woman appeared. She wiped at her red-rimmed eyes. "That's right, Detective. Kidnapped."

Grant recognized her. The woman from the house where the bodies were found. She was stuck to the wall by some strange goo that looked like Spiderman's web. Two teenage girls had gone missing.

"I can see on your face you recognize me," Alyanna said. "It was my girl, my daughter they kidnapped. It was my husband they killed." Fresh tears flowed. "Please. Help us get her back."

The woman who made the tea stood and wrapped arms around her. She cried and clutched desperately at her comforter.

"You see, Detective," Phetrix said. "This is all very real."

Grant thought for a moment and scanned the anxious and nervous faces around the table. "So, if the kidnapped girl was the princess, that makes her the queen?"

"No. Alyanna is the guardian I sent with the princess."

The woman still seated said, "She raised her as if she was her own.

Just like I raised my son." She put an arm around the chair of the teenage boy next to her. "We may not have given birth to them, but that doesn't lessen the love they were raised with."

"And this is—the prince?"

"Yes," Phetrix said. "Prince Erthic of Chevalon."

"Is that true?" he asked the boy.

He shrugged. "I guess."

"He has only just learned the truth himself earlier tonight. Under the circumstances, we thought it best he knew who he was. Unfortunately, his sister Elysande was never told. She has no idea why she was taken. But trust me, Detective. Mortas will make her pay, regardless."

Grant pushed back on the chair, rising to the rear legs. The faces looked so earnest. Had they all been brainwashed? What other explanation could there be? He looked around for hidden cameras. Maybe he was being pranked. If so, these were good actors. They all believed what the old man was spinning. Yet something in the story rang true. The kidnapping was real. He knew that for a fact. He'd been there as units converged on the kidnappers. He'd witnessed the cars being tossed around like lightweight props. And hadn't the kidnappers disappeared into thin air? He had a new understanding of that phrase.

"Let's say, I believe even a portion of this story. What is it you expect me to do?"

Before he got an answer, a shrill alarm sounded from somewhere on the old man's person. He shot up, made a gesture with his hand, and the alarm went silent. "I guess we will find out, Detective. Someone just crossed through the seam."

Chapter 37

Elly and Shree huddled close together as they listened to the guards searching for them. They remained hidden under thick brush, trying to stay as quiet as possible.

Shree trembled and Elly wrapped her in her arms, making the other girl wince.

"Sorry," she whispered. The gash on Shree's arm looked terrible, even in the dark. Elly close her eyes and concentrated on the wound, imagining in her mind using her newfound powers to close and heal it, but when she opened her eyes, nothing happened. Frustrated, she clung to her friend as the night wore on. Many hours later, the chill of dawn forced them both to shiver.

"I think they're gone," Elly said, teeth chattering. Shree smiled weakly.

"I haven't heard them in a while."

Elly let go of her friend and carefully stood up.

"Don't! They'll see you!" Shree tugged at her shirt, trying to keep her from revealing their location.

"It's fine. I don't think anyone's here."

Branches snapped behind them. Elly quickly fell back to the ground.

"I told you," Shree whispered.

Elly dismissed her and scanned the forest for the source of the sound.

Another twig snapped. Leaves crunched. They heard the sound of footsteps gaining on them.

Elly reached inside to grasp the power but she clutched an emptiness devoid of anything useful. "Damn."

The footsteps grew closer. A breeze kicked up, the trees swaying back and forth.

Then the footsteps stopped. The forest went silent. Far in the distance, they heard a terrible scream.

"What was that?" Shree asked. Elly turned back to her and the girl's eyes were wide, the fear evident on her face. She clutched her arm where the blood trickled.

"I don't know."

The footsteps returned, racing toward them. Elly tried again to clutch the power within but it remained stubborn and unavailable.

The bushes in front of them shook and a small black bear froze when it saw them. It was about the size of a black lab. It stood on its hind legs, roaring as if to warn them.

The hideous shriek sounded again. The bear turned to the sky then darted away, crashing through the brush.

Elly wiped her forehead. "It was just a bear." When she turned back to Shree, the girl was transfixed on something above them.

Elly followed her gaze.

Circling the trees above them was a demon-like creature. It was black with long flowing robes. It reminded her of the dementors from the Harry Potter movies.

"Where the hell are we? How can those be real?"

Another joined the first and the two of them screeched horribly, their loud terrifying howls echoing through the forest. They circled the trees, darting between the upper branches. They were looking for something.

"I think they're after us. Those things up there. They have to be!" Elly said.

Shree covered her mouth with her hand. She trembled, her eyes never leaving the things.

"Don't move. I don't think they saw us."

Elly tried once again to claim the power within, and for a moment felt a glimmer of hope as she held it, but then it slipped through her hands like grains of sand.

One of the creatures turned toward them the moment she touched the power. When her touch vanished, it turned away.

"I can't do anything to help. We have to stay quiet or they'll see us."

Shree nodded, the look on her face revealing her terror.

The heavy crashing of brush nearby made them clutch each other. A distant voice called, See anything?'

The response was so close both girls shook violently. In her mind she repeated, *Please don't see us. Please don't see us.*

The thicket where they had been hiding parted. From above, an impassive face glanced down at them. The eyes swept over and around them, then the man moved on.

The girls stared wide-eyed at each other. Afraid to move, they waited five minutes before releasing each other.

"Why didn't he see us?" asked Shree.

"I don't know, but I'm not complaining."

"Did you make us invisible?"

"What? No. That's impossible."

"Really? After all we've seen here?"

"Shh! They might hear you."

The black creatures swirled in the blue sky, shrieking and wailing. Birds flew from the trees. Squirrels and other unseen animals raced across the forest as though aware of the danger these things possessed. Elly felt it, too. They radiated a dark, sinister essence. She couldn't have described it to Shree, so she kept quiet, but inside, she could feel their presence like nothing she'd ever experienced.

Shree shifted and a twig snapped. Both creatures spun in the air toward them. They waited in the sky, hovering in place, anticipating something more.

Elly held her breath. Fighting against guards was one thing, but these demons…it was more than she was capable of, especially since she was still blocked from touching the power.

The things waited for what felt like an eternity. Elly wondered if she was dreaming and if she might wake up at any moment. She hoped so. The fear growing inside her was too much to bear.

One of the creatures screamed loudly, the other matching its awful shriek. They turned from the girls and hovered over another part of the forest, their backs turned.

Elly let out the breath she'd been holding. Shree uncovered her mouth.

"Elly, I'm scared. Whatever this place is, it's not home. It can't be. Did you see those things?"

Elly nodded. She'd been thinking the same thing. She didn't want to admit it, but her friend was right. They weren't home anymore. They probably weren't even in the same dimension as before. It sounded crazy when she thought about it, but what other explanation was there?

She now possessed magical abilities. People were using magic against them. Castles, dungeons, and medieval-looking guards. And now these flying demons? None of it made sense, but it was the reality they now faced. If it were a dream, it was a bad one. She'd prefer being out on a boat in Lake Michigan, sunbathing and enjoying the day. But this? It wasn't anything she wanted to experience. As cool as it was to have abilities, even when they allowed themselves to be present, she would much rather be back home.

Elly turned to her friend, the blood dripping from her arm. "Here, let's do something before that gets worse." Elly ripped part of her shirt off to tie around Shree's arm. When she did, her moon scar was revealed. She traced it with her fingertip, remembering the words of the men who took.

Elly paused, then wrapped the strip of her shirt around Shree's arm. "It's the best I've got."

"Thanks. You know, if we're gonna be here a while, we might want to get something different to wear. These clothes are gonna give us away."

Shree was right. Their jeans, t-shirts, and shoes were clearly not from this world. If they were stuck there now, they'd have to fit in.

"Ok, sounds like a plan, then. Are you up for leaving?"

Shree nodded. "Yeah. I don't wanna stay here any longer. What if those things come back?"

Elly helped her up and the girls moved slowly through the forest, not knowing where they were going or what awaited them.

Chapter 38

When she was a girl, Elly often played a game she called Where Are We Now? with her parents. She'd guess from the position of the sun which way they were headed, and given the time from their house, she'd call out a street name or name of a neighboring suburb. It exhausted her mother and her father laughed. As she checked the position of the morning sun in this strange world, the memory made her smile, though it didn't last long when she remembered her father was dead and her mother was hurt somewhere far from where she was now with no way of knowing how to get back.

"How's your arm?"

It had been a few hours since they left the dungeon and the dark forest outside where the black creatures flew across the sky.

"Fine, I guess. It hurts some, but the bleeding stopped. It's gonna be a mess when I take this off, though."

"I'd like to get some water and make sure you aren't infected."

"And clothes. I feel like we've got a beacon on us screaming, Look at us!"

"Yeah, that, too."

Elly led them west, the way she felt they'd come from when they were hauled through the seam of light and deposited here.

"Shree, look!"

"Is that a house? It's so small!"

"We certainly aren't back home. Wherever we are, these people are different. We can check it out and see if we can find clothes. It might help us to blend in."

The girls crept closer to the home. A light flickered inside. It was hard to tell at first since it was early afternoon, but Shree spotted it and pointed it out.

"There. You see that? I think someone's inside with a flashlight or something."

"More likely a candle or torch. Damn, I should've played D&D when I was younger! This world is like something like that."

Shree giggled. Neither girl had an interest in fantasy or medieval history. They were both too busy learning new routines for cheer competitions and worrying about what college they were going to. Shree was smart and wanted to get into journalism. Her eyes had been set on Northwestern a long time ago. Elly would never commit to one field of study. She vacillated between biochemistry and marketing, two fields that couldn't be further apart. She was thinking of going to Loyola or maybe south to SIUE. Time was running short and she needed to make up her mind if they ever made it back.

"Let's check it out first and see who it is."

Shree agreed and they quietly approached the nearest window. The glass was murky like it was made of river water, making it difficult to see through. It looked like an older woman by her shape and the constant cough gave away her feminine voice.

"I think we got lucky," Shree whispered.

"Yeah we did!"

The sound of logs thudding to the ground startled the girls.

"What are you doing?" a man growled.

Both girls spun around, Elly's heart beating a million miles a minute.

"What are you two, rebels? You with the resistance? What are those clothes?"

Elly held out her hands in a pleading gesture. "We're not with anything but ourselves. I don't know anything about this resistance or rebels."

"Then why are you sneaking up on my grandma?"

The man's eyes narrowed. He was huge, maybe six-foot-four, and thick. His arms and legs were like tree trunks.

"Elly, do something with your power!"

Elly closed her eyes and willed the power to come to her, but it remained hidden.

"I can't. It's out of reach."

"Power? Are you some kind of mage? The Order is banned. Mortas wills it and it is so. I'd get a lot of coin for reporting you two." He stroked his chin and grinned. "I need the coin. Save me and Grandma from starving."

"Starving? What's going on? Maybe we can help."

"Elly, what are you talking about?"

"You two can help. When I turn you in as traitors, Mortas will pay me handsomely."

The man bull-rushed them. Shree cried out and Elly yelped. The man grabbed both girls and scooped them up like they were dolls.

"Grandma! Bring me some rope. We have traitors from the Order here!"

"Let go of us! We aren't traitors or anything like that!"

"Yeah, let us go!" Shree added.

Both girls struggled against his grip. Shree squirmed to the side and the man lost his grip, dropping her to the ground.

"Ain't no man gonna take us again!" she yelled. Shree swung her leg and kicked the man in the knee. He fell down, letting go of Elly as he did.

"You ignorant girl!" He swiped at her with his hand, catching her leg and pulling her to him. Shree struggled, kicking and screaming. Elly joined her and leapt at the man, scratching at his face. Thin lines of blood marked his dirty cheeks. He cried out and pushed her away, forcing her to stumble and fall.

"Traitors or not, I won't let you hurt my grandma!"

"We weren't going to!" Shree yelled.

"Shut up!" The man backhanded her, an angry mark blooming on her dark face.

"Leave her alone!" Elly snarled. She felt the power growing into something she could wield. It was strong and intoxicating. She grabbed for it…and connected. She allowed the power to flood her, filling her with its sweet touch.

"Let her go or you will regret it!"

"She's mine. You're both mine, little girl!"

Elly lashed out and struck him with a savage blast of energy so powerful she scared herself, but it did nothing to move him from Shree. His enormous size resisted her blast.

"It's true! You're with the Order!"

The door of the little house creaked open and a small older woman who looked blind and feeble stood holding a length of rope.

"Drent, what are you doing, dear? Here's the rope you called for."

Elly let go of the power at the sight of the older woman. She'd never known her grandparents. They were killed in an accident. Her mom often told her stories of how dedicated they were to their family.

"Grandma, get back inside! We have mages from the Order here. They must be taken in! We'll never starve again!"

"From the Order? They help people, Drent. They do no harm. Please, everyone come inside and I'll fix some tea."

"Grandma, they're the enemy! Mortas Frost has outlawed them!"

"Please, we mean no harm. We only need a change of clothes and we'll be on our way," Elly said. Shree continued to struggle against the larger man, her efforts only serving to tire her faster. Somehow, she freed her hand and gouged him in the eye. Shree dropped from his grip.

Drent howled, a thin trickle of blood running down his face. "You little hag!" He reached to his belt and produced a small dagger, swiping it toward Shree.

"No!"

Elly lashed out with the power and blindly struck him with a jolt of uncontrolled energy. It struck his elbow, cleaving his lower arm off. His forearm and dagger fell on Shree, splashing her with his blood. Drent screamed as though stung by a thousand bees. His grandma didn't know what to do.

"Drent, what's happening? Are you hurt?"

The large man thrashed as he held on to his now-shortened arm. Blood sprayed over all of them. He let go and grabbed Shree by the hair.

"She's sealed your fate!" With the stump of his arm, he smacked her across the face. As he was about to strike her again, Elly's anger fueled her.

She struck out with a surge of power. It ripped through Drent, killing him instantly.

"Oh no!" Elly whispered. She hadn't meant to kill him, only injure him enough to leave Shree alone.

Drent fell to the ground. His grandma grew more anxious.

"Drent? What happened, dear? Drent?"

Shree pushed herself away from the dead man, staring at Elly with large, scared eyes.

"Girls, what happened to Drent? I need him to help me. I can't do any of this on my own!"

Elly held a hand over her mouth. *What had she done?* She'd murdered a man!

Shree got to her feet. "Elly, let's get what we came for and get out of here. This is too much."

"But what about Drent? Where's my grandson?"

"He's right here," Elly said, guiding the old woman to the dead man on the ground. "He had an accident." The old woman dropped to her knees and ran her hands along him. She felt along his body, gasping when she got to the hole in his chest.

"Go ahead, Shree, see what you can find." Shree quietly entered the home while Elly tried to console the old woman.

"I'm sorry, ma'am. It wasn't meant to be this way."

Shree exited the house a few moments later. "These should do." She held up a couple wool robes that looked itchy.

"Drent! Oh, my dear boy, what's happened to you?" The old woman bent over sobbing across his chest. Elly stood and backed away.

Her new powers were helpful when she could touch them, but they came at a cost. She was trying to help, but did she have to go that far?

The girls changed into the thick robes and left the old woman weeping over her grandson. Elly's heart broke thinking of the woman's fate now that her sole provider was gone, and it was because of her. *But he tried to hurt Shree*, she told herself. She was only doing what was right.

One of the black creatures reappeared in the sky above, no doubt attracted by her use of the power. Shree tugged on her arm and pointed upwards.

"Damn," Elly muttered. She gave one long look at the old woman and turned away, determined to use her power with care.

Chapter 39

DeWayne drove past the spot where the cop disappeared into the woods. He braked and looked down the path. Brake lights blinked on several times indicating the car's location. He shifted his gaze to the windshield then the mirrors. He was alone on the road. He unbuckled his seat belt and roamed through the van looking for a marker of some kind. Under one seat he found a spirit towel like fans waved around at football games. He grabbed it, jumped out of the van, and ran to the trees. Using his phone's light, he spotted the trail the cop took. Moving left about ten feet, he tied the towel to a branch and jogged back to the van.

He drove to the first intersection, then stopped to memorize the cross streets. DeWayne drove faster than he should have to get back into the city. He had information; valuable intel that was sure to pay him well. Once in the city, he slowed and followed the speed limits. It took more than an hour to get back to the seam. Not having to worry about the cop made it easier to park closer.

Since Rhoden had been wounded, Dewayne wondered whether the man would be able to return. The last time he saw him, he hadn't looked too good. Did they even have doctors there? Maybe he died. DeWayne tried to decide if that was good or bad. True, he wanted to be out of Rhoden's employ, but now that he had info that might net him a big payday, he wanted the man to show up.

The hardest part about the wait was staying awake. It was a battle he eventually lost. The shifting of the van startled him awake and alert. He found more massive creatures loading through the side door. The passenger door opened and Rhoden sat looking as healthy as ever. DeWayne was sure he'd locked the doors. He quickly dismissed that thought, remembering who he was dealing with.

The last of the men sat and left the sliding door open. He wondered if they didn't know how to shut it or weren't smart enough to know it needed to be closed. He hopped out and shut the door, then climbed back in.

Dawn was less than an hour away. A faint glow lit the eastern horizon. "I have some information you might want," he said.

Rhoden turned to face him, his gray eyes narrowing. "Tell me."

"Last night, that old guy who fought your men yesterday. His friend and a really big guy came here. They stood in the lot by the, uh, seam."

"Did they cross over?"

"No. They just kinda stood there looking at it. The old guy opened the, ah, seam, but they just looked at it, then left."

Rhoden turned his face away. He sat in silence for a moment, then opened the door and got out. DeWayne glanced nervously in the mirror. Six more monsters sat behind him staring straight ahead. He fought the chill coursing through his veins but could not prevent it from creating the shudder.

Rhoden stood near the seam. He made hand gestures at it like he was having a discussion with someone. After a minute, he returned and sat. "Clever. The wizard set wards on the portal. He is aware of our presence. It will be more difficult to find him now."

"I might be able to help with that, too."

Again, Rhoden shifted those cold orbs his way. "Once they were done, uh, setting the wards they drove off. I followed them." Was it his imagination, or did a flicker of fire show in his boss's eyes? "They drove about an hour out of the city. I marked the spot where they're hiding."

No. He did see a flash of fire.

"And you can take me there? Now?"

"Yes sir." He started the engine. He shifted into gear and said, "Oh, and they had a younger dude with them. I think it might have been the prince you're looking for."

He glanced right and saw Rhoden's eyes glow red as if they had caught fire. "Go. Now!"

DeWayne needed no further prodding. He pulled away, not wanting to look at those eyes again.

GRANT STOOD WATCHING as everyone except for the boy was in motion. From all over the cabin weapons appeared as if by magic. Except Grant was sure these weren't magical weapons. They looked like regular guns to him. Well, not the big guy's gun. It was massive, like it needed two people just to hold it and third to shoot.

The old guy barked orders. Everyone listened. Finally, Grant shouted, "Hold on! Wait a minute! I am not letting you bring those weapons into the city to start a war. There are too many innocent people who might get caught up in this madness and get killed. I am not going to have that weighing on my conscious."

"What do you suggest, Detective?" Phetrix said.

"I'll go into the city alone." The drive would give him time to think, to plan, and come up with what to tell his boss. Although he needed to stop the strange invading force, he also needed to deal with Phetrix and his band. "I'll contact my superiors and inform them there's a credible threat of terrorist activity. I'll mobilize as many units as possible and try to convince the captain to deploy SWAT."

"SWAT? Is that a magical weapon?" Kol asked.

"It sure can be. Especially if a battle is looming."

"Detective Grant," the large man, Nordon said. "It would be better to stop them in the city rather than let them come to us."

"I understand that, but it won't be better if a lot of people die to save you. I have to insist you let me handle this."

Shotgun man, the large man, and the woman who'd lost her daughter began protesting at once. It was Phetrix who settled them down. "Very well, Detective. We will give you the chance to handle this."

"What?" shouted the woman, Alyanna.

"You've got to be kidding!" Nordon yelled.

"Shoulda let me shoot him," said Tetrin.

"No, everyone. This is why we took Detective Grant into our confidence. Let him do what he can to stop Rhoden." The moaning continued, but with less volume. "You will fortify the cabin in case they get this far."

"Where will you be?" Nadina asked.

"I am going with the detective."

"Wait a minute," Grant said. "I don't think—"

"I know who to look for. I will be able to stop them for at least a while until you can get your fellow detectives there to finish the job. Can you do that by yourself?"

Grant gnawed at the inside of his cheek. He didn't want the old man along, but he had to admit he was right about identifying the threat. Besides, if he kept the old man close, he wouldn't have to hunt for him later when it was time to make arrests. "Okay. That works. Let's go."

"How will we know if you find them?" Dina asked.

"Give me your cell number," said Grant. "I'll call if something happens." She did and he entered it in his phone. Nordon gave his as a backup.

Phetrix said, "I have to gather some things. You go along and I'll follow in a moment."

Grant had the feeling the old man was up to something, but he nodded and left anyway. Once outside, he'd be able to hear and see any ambush. He walked toward the path he took last night. By the time they reached the city it would be daybreak. He stopped just inside the tree line where he had a view of the front and side of the cabin. Should anyone try to get past him through the woods, he'd see them. The only person he saw exit the cabin was Phetrix.

He waited for Phetrix to enter the path, took a last second scan of the cabin, and satisfied no one followed, he stepped out and joined the old man. Once in the car and back on the road, he felt more confident about controlling the situation.

If only he felt that same confidence with whatever they would face.

Chapter 40

When the next day dawned, Samuel was there when Mathilda received the report: nearly two-thirds of the resistance had been killed in the battle. When the numbers were spoken, Samuel hung his head. He'd caused this. His actions brought the Seekers and the soldiers. Mathilda dismissed the young boy and slammed her fist against her leg.

"We lost far more than I expected. Our cause has been pushed to its limits. We can no longer hope to counter Mortas with numbers. Our focus must change."

Samuel felt much better after Mathilda cast more healing on him. He no longer felt weak and his mind was clearer.

"We must get the princess. We have no other choice. She was brought here by Mortas, presumably to kill her. We must concentrate everything we have left on that and that alone."

Mathilda nodded. "So, where is she?"

Samuel had no idea. After they were pulled through the seam, Elly and her friend were at the mercy of Mortas.

"She could be anywhere. Does he live in a castle? Is there a place where he's normally found?"

"To the south." It was Char who entered the tent. "He lives in that monstrosity of a castle in the south. He can't stand the colder weather."

"Then we need to go there. Unless you have intelligence that says otherwise."

"And do what?" Mathilda asked, "Just walk in and take her back?"

"Whatever it takes, that's what. The sooner we rescue her, the sooner we end this tyranny. How many more are gonna die?"

"How many are going to die if we go there?"

Samuel breathed deep. "I realize you lost a lot of people here. This will not go forgotten. Their lives are not gone in vain. We will avenge them. We will avenge all of this, but we have to start with Elly."

"I think the old man has a point. She's our only hope. No others are left from the royal family."

Mathilda glared at Char.

"What? You know it. The King and Queen are gone."

"They're dead? Why didn't you tell me?"

"Samuel, I wanted to. Most of the resistance doesn't know yet. They think they're alive. As long as they have that hope, they'll continue to fight. What do you think they'll do when they realize the ones they fight for are no longer living?"

The news struck Samuel to the core. He knew there was a chance they were dead, but he prayed against it. He hoped they lived.

"Are you sure they're dead?"

"Buried them myself. Only Char and I know the truth. It was a few years ago. The Seekers discovered them and we lost the fight."

"And they lost their lives," Char chimed in.

Samuel's world crumbled around him. The hope he felt when he'd crossed the seam was fading fast.

"She's not the only one."

"What do you mean? Who are you talking about?"

Samuel looked into Mathilda's eyes. "Elly. She's not the only one. Remember, there were twins. The boy is safe. At least I think he is. He was in Chicago as well, but with different protectors. I felt it best they were separated in case of…in case of a calamity such as this. The boy, Eric, is alive."

Mathilda took a step back. "You had both of them? And they don't know about each other?"

Samuel shook his head. "I thought it best they were never close. What hope would we have if they were both taken or killed? At least one of them had to live. As long as he is kept safe in the other realm, we still cling to hope."

"Having both would mean so much more. We must get the girl."

THE NEXT DAY, Mathilda led the remaining members of the resistance on the road going south. There were very few dissenters and even fewer who agreed. Still, they began their journey south with close to fifty remaining members, a far cry from the numbers they had only days ago.

Samuel had little to say. His thoughts remained on the loss of the royal family. He did consider the possibility, but it was something he didn't want to imagine as real. But now that it was, the truth was difficult to comprehend.

What did ring true to him more than anything else was the need to rescue Elly. If they could somehow save her from whatever evil Mortas had planned, they could begin the process of restoring the kingdom. When the time was right, he'd have Eric brought over and the two of them could reclaim the throne.

The morning was dreary as dark gray clouds hung overhead. Cold winds blew at their backs, cutting right through the layers of wool on Samuel's back. He longed for his home back in Chicago with the heat at the touch of a button and warm food whenever he wanted it. He laughed at himself, the first jovial moment since the attack, when he thought how easily he was caught up in the trappings of the other world.

"I miss Svengoolie."

"What was that?" Mathilda asked.

"I've grown accustomed to the luxuries of the other world. I'm not a man for this one any longer. What I've seen, what I've experienced… it's amazing. When we are done, I shall return there. I'll share the way with those I trust. The Order needs to have the secret, but I plan on living out the rest of my days there."

"What Order? We're it! I don't know anyone else from the Order other than Phetrix. Everything is wrong. There's been too much destruction wrought by Mortas."

"What about Rhoden? He's of the Order."

"He's the enemy! If he were truly part of the Order, he'd not be part of this!"

"Perhaps. But perhaps we can persuade him to our cause. All of his training can't be undone with a snap. Mortas doesn't have that kind of power. Surely, there's still something good left in him."

"I wouldn't trust him. I've seen what he's done here. I don't know if he crossed the seam, but he's done a lot of terrible things here."

"He has," Samuel replied in a quiet voice. "He's crossed the seam. He's been to the other world."

Suddenly, his plans for a retirement in Chicago took a hit. If Rhoden had the ability to come across the seam, what would stop him from bringing his evil across?

"If we can find the good in him, we need to turn him back to the Order. We'll have to rebuild it. The heirs are key."

Mathilda furrowed her brow. "They are? I mean, I understand what they mean to the people," she said, waving a hand toward the long line of resistance behind them, "But how do they affect the Order?"

"They have the gift."

Mathilda's face registered the shock of the revelation. "They what?"

"As far as I know, they're unaware of it. They know life in Chicago, but nothing else. They have the ability. Both of them."

"This changes everything! They must be brought back. They must come to reclaim their throne!"

"Precisely."

Samuel let the discussion drop. He'd said far more than he intended, but at least now Mathilda understood the enormity of their situation. Restoring the heirs carried a significance that went beyond just rule of law.

Near midday, Mathilda halted the procession. Groups of people huddled together for warmth and to share what meager food they had.

Samuel moved away from the group, sitting by himself to just think about everything. It had been a terrible time back in Chevalon. He didn't miss the rustic life. City living suited him much better. But here, he had a duty. His responsibility lay with the success of their mission and nothing else. Maybe he'd get the chance to live out his life in Chicago.

After an hour of rest, Mathilda got them moving again. Not long after they departed, they came across an old house that was partially burnt. Then a little further on, they passed a small village that was in a similar state.

"The Seekers. Mortas must have commanded them to burn everything as they searched for us," Mathilda said. Samuel could only shake his head. What cruelty did this man not possess?

They left the village behind them and Samuel froze.

"What is it? Do you see a Seeker?"

He wished that were all.

"The seam," he whispered.

"What about it?"

"Someone has crossed. The ward…it's been triggered."

He felt the unmistakable break in the ward he placed at the seam when he left it. Which way? He didn't know. All he knew was that someone had crossed it. Whatever it was, it couldn't be good. Only three people knew how to cross it, and he was one of them.

"Something bad has happened. It had to. I placed a ward at the seam and it's broken. Someone went through."

"Then our time is better spent moving faster. The kingdom's fate is in our hands."

Mathilda yelled back at the resistance behind her. "We must hurry our pace! The time has come for us to act. Let's end the reign of Mortas Frost!"

Chapter 41

Eric wasn't sure what to make of the situation. He couldn't deny the adrenaline-pulsing pull he felt toward being involved in the action. However, he also couldn't deny the fear they held his desire to be involved in check.

He watched Phetrix disappear into the woods with the detective, then turned to the group. His defenders. The woman he'd called mother for most of his life, the life he could remember, looked so different now. Her face had aged just since they arrived at the cabin. He'd always thought she was pretty. She was elegant at times, yet she ran marathons and he'd watched her earn her black belt in Tae Kwon Do. He'd never really thought about the dualities of her life. To him, she was just Mom and what she did was normal.

Fun loving and always in an upbeat mood, the seriousness of her expression now almost made her look like a different person. Her eyes met his as if she felt his gaze. Even now, she offered a reassuring smile and a wink before she finished loading the magazine for her handgun.

She was always there to encourage, to guide, to teach. She was the one who taught him how to shoot his bow with such proficiency. His father taught him hand-to-hand, but never in a serious way. At least, not that he recognized as such. He took Eric hunting and was even more excited than he had been when he brought down his first deer with a well-placed arrow. He handed him the gun to put the deer out of its misery rather than let it die slowly in pain. That had been a hard moment for him. Face to face with a living creature, knowing he had to finish the job, but unsure if he could. When his father sighed and reached for the gun, Eric pulled away. With tears streaming down his face, he pulled the trigger.

Now, he had to wonder about the programs he wasn't allowed to participate in as well as the activities he was encouraged to take. His own martial arts programs, the fencing and sword fighting clubs and lessons. The various academic, science, and leadership clubs he belonged to now felt like preparation for this very moment.

The plan was for Kol, his father, and Alyanna to follow Phetrix in the van and be close to the city when the enemy was located. His mother, Tetrin, and Catron were to stay and prepare to defend the house as well and load the SUV with supplies for a quick getaway. He felt out of place. Everyone bustled doing something important except for him. If he was truly a prince, he didn't want to be the kind that expected others to do for him. He wanted to be a true leader; one who got involved regardless of the task, its difficulty, or its danger.

He walked toward the table. His mother scooped up the three magazines she'd filled and placed them in a pouch she wore on her belt. She looked up and smiled like she had no other cares in the world. "What can I do to help?"

Her smile didn't falter, but he saw a brief fade of the twinkle in her eyes. "Ah, nothing, really. I think we're on track."

"Mom," the word sounded foreign to him. It watered her eyes. "I can help. If this is all to keep me safe, I should be involved in my own defense. What kind of leader would I be if I expected others to fight for me while I did nothing?"

He was vaguely aware the others had stopped to listen. His mother stood and embraced him in a hug that took his breath away. "I love you. You know that, right?"

"I do." Though the words stuck in his throat, he meant them.

Tetrin stepped forward and offered a handgun, butt first. "You know how to use one of these?"

He nodded and reached for it. "Yes." He took the gun, then realized Tetrin was waiting for something. Eric gripped the gun in his right hand, dropped the magazine to make sure it was full, then inserted it and racked the slide to chamber a round. Tetrin nodded his approval and handed him two more magazines.

Catron went outside and moved the SUV to the back side of the cabin. They loaded supplies, then sat around the kitchen table while Tetrin explained the defense of the cabin, should it be necessary.

Tetrin said, "Dina, you and I will take the front."

"Catron, you watch the back."

"I don't think so," she replied before he could continue.

Tetrin sighed. "What's the problem?"

"Don't try that macho crap on me. Try to protect your wife. Keep her safe. I'll not have it."

"I put you there," he said through gritted teeth, "because if we get surrounded, there's no one better to clear a path than you. It has nothing to do with keeping you safe."

They glared at each other for a moment before she said, "So, you put your wife in harm's way. In the most dangerous spot. Guess the honeymoon's over." She spun and went out the back door, leaving her husband shaking his head and Eric and Nadina smiling.

Tetrin turned and caught their expressions. His face reddened. "You got a problem, too?"

"Ah, no," Nadina said. "I'm good."

"No, sir," Eric said. "Where do you want me?"

"You're our back up. Wherever needs filling in, that's where you'll go."

Eric didn't like that and he was sure his expression conveyed his dissatisfaction with the assignment.

Sensing he had another disagreement on his hands, Tetrin whirled and strode off, disappearing through the bedroom door.

"Just do what he says, Eric," his mother said. "If someone does come for us, there will be plenty for all of us to do."

Eric nodded but was determined not to take a back seat to anyone, should the need arise.

"Hey, boy," Tetrin called from the bedroom.

Though he didn't much care for the man's tone or being called boy, Eric opened the door and entered. Without speaking, he stood and watched Tetrin scanning the grounds outside the bedroom window. He motioned for Eric to come. "Okay, I understand your need to be part of this. This is the one spot we don't have eyes. From here you can see the left side of the front yard and all of the side. If they come through the woods, they can get here without being seen if no one is here. You good with this?"

Eric nodded, then thought the gesture required more. "Thank you."

Tetrin nodded. He patted Eric's shoulder and left the room, throwing a, "And stay off the bed," over his shoulder. Eric moved the drapes and took a long pan of the exterior. Then, he closed the drapes, leaving a small gap in the middle. *They won't come*, he thought. How could this Rhoden possibly know where to look?

He pulled up a chair and sat. It promised to be a long wait.

Chapter 42

Speeding a consistent fifteen miles an hour above the posted limit, Grant drove lost in thought. If the old man could locate these invaders from another world—he still didn't believe another world existed—then he decided to call in the troops. Phetrix would be locked up and Grant would then lead the charge to take down the other faction. Once that was done, he'd direct another force to the cabin. Of course, a warning had to be given. Those in the cabin were well armed.

A sound drew him from his reverie. He glanced at his passenger. The old man was reading from an old tattered book. His lips were moving and he could hear his voice, however, he didn't understand the words.

"Hey, what are you doing?"

Phetrix hesitated, closed his eyes, then shut the book and turned his attention toward Grant. "I'm preparing for the upcoming confrontation."

"What's that, like a prayer book or something?"

A thin smile creased the weathered face. "In some respects, yes." He offered nothing more.

Grant changed focus. "How do you expect to find these, ah, invaders?"

"I need to check the wards I placed on the seam."

"But you already know someone crossed, right? That was the alarm you set."

"It gives us a starting point. I doubt they will still be there when we arrive. They will search for the prince. Rhoden will bring strong magic to bear. He will most likely direct his force to the last known place the prince was: the house. He should not be able to track him. I took precautions to hide the trail."

"So, what you're saying is you have no idea where to look."

"What I am saying is I do have an idea where to look. I am not sure they will be there, but it is an idea and a starting point."

The answer did not ease Grant's concerns. Chicago was too big a city to leave finding someone to guesswork. He picked up the radio's microphone to contact dispatch but set it back in its holder. What was he going to say? Has there been any sightings of magical beings? He was already in enough trouble with the boss to ask strange questions.

"You look worried," Phetrix said.

"You think? I mean, come on. It's not every day I have to deal with battling wizards, exiled royalty, and magical creatures."

"Oh, so you have dealt with magic before?"

"What?"

"You said it was not every day that you—"

"No, that was sarcasm. You understand that term, don't you?"

"Of course."

Grant shot an incredulous glance at the old man. That he appeared unruffled by the ordeal annoyed Grant further. This had to be a bad dream. He was going to come awake any second and find he was nestled in his warm, cozy bed.

Phetrix was back to reading and mumbling again. This was nuts. If he dared speak of this to anyone, he'd be relieved from duty and ordered to start psychiatric services immediately. He'd be lucky to get his badge back. The captain would assign him to desk duty until he retired. He might even encourage him to take an early out and find some other line of work.

The Chicago skyline loomed large against the slightly overcast sky. Ten minutes later they entered the city limits. It took another fifteen to reach the site of the seam. They sat and scanned the area for a moment before Phetrix opened the door and stepped out. Grant watched him cross the street, oblivious to the traffic passing him in both directions. He sighed. Better get out before the old guy got run over.

Grant jogged to Phetrix, holding up a hand to stop an oncoming truck. The driver lifted a hand in protest but made no comment and didn't honk the horn. Grant stopped on the other side of the street, but Phetrix continued into the lot. He made hand gestures and Grant could hear him speaking, though the words were lost in the passing traffic.

A spark ignited in midair before fading away like a fourth of July sparkler. Phetrix stood with hands on his hips staring at the empty space. He tried whatever it was he had done again with the same result. Then, he turned to face Grant. The expression of concern carved deep lines into the man's forehead. "Seven crossed. We must go."

Phetrix moved faster than Grant thought the old man capable. They climbed back into the car.

"We need to go to the house immediately. He has been here for more than an hour. We must hurry to catch up to him."

Grant used lights and siren to make the trip arriving six minutes after leaving the seam. The front door had been boarded over. The house looked vacant. Phetrix, despite his age, was out of the car and running before Grant had it in park. He raced for the house and made a sweeping motion with his arm like a third base coach signaling the runner to make a dash for home. Grant approached slower, a hand on the gun and his eyes scanning the area. As far as he could tell, no alternate world characters were near.

Phetrix faced the street and performed the same ritual. Then his face clouded.

"What?" asked Grant.

"If Rhoden was here, he did not use magic."

"You can tell?"

"A residual energy hangs in the air for a short time afterward."

"That's a good thing, isn't it?"

Phetrix did not reply. The deep creases in his forehead took on a darker appearance.

"Well, isn't it a good thing? That means they haven't arrived yet."

"That's the problem. They should have. They have no other way of tracking the prince unless …" He stopped and his face went ashen.

"You're killing me here, man. Unless what?"

"Unless they already know where Eric is."

The words hit Grant like a punch. "But-but, how is that possible?"

"I don't know, but we must hurry." He moved with haste toward the car.

"He'll be safe though, right? I mean, you left him with a lot of firepower."

Phetrix hesitated and locked eyes with Grant. Whatever flickered through the man's eyes did not sit well with Grant. His first thought was, *Uh-oh.* The old man got in without answering him, giving Grant an even tighter knot in his stomach. He got in and started the car.

"What did you do, old man?"

"I had some of them follow after we left and wait for my signal."

Grant lowered his head to the steering wheel in disbelief. "Even after I told you not to?" You're unbelievable."

"If we found Rhoden you would not have had time to organize your men to fight him. I needed a quick response close by."

"Yeah, and how'd that work out for you?"

"We need to go back to the cabin."

Grant pressed down on the accelerator. The car leaped forward. As he maneuvered the first corner, he fished the cell phone from his jacket pocket and punched in the number Nadina gave him. The phone rang out. He swore under his breath and tried to remain calm as he called Nordon. His phone was answered on the first ring.

"Yes?" A note of nervous concern tinged his voice.

"Your wizard friend here messed up. He thinks this Rhoden character is on his way to the cabin."

"Oh no."

"I tried calling your wife, but she doesn't answer." The line went dead. "Hello?" He looked at the screen then deposited the phone in the cup holder and slammed the wheel in disgust.

"Please, Detective Grant. I know you're upset with me, but it's imperative we reach the cabin before Rhoden can capture the prince."

"Yeah, I got it." With siren wailing and lights flashing, Grant sped back the way they'd come, wondering what he'd find when they reached the cabin and whether he should bother calling the Captain.

Chapter 43

In the early morning light, DeWayne slowed to search for his marker. The energy emanating from Rhoden was a force he could feel. The man's eyes were ablaze and the eerie silence from the goon squad had him creeped out. He spotted the dirt track before he saw the white towel.

He pulled to the side of the road and Rhoden swung his now solid black eyes in his direction. DeWayne couldn't prevent the recoil at the sight.

"Is this the place?" Rhoden's voice hissed, resounding all around the van.

"Y-yes. You see that white towel?" He pointed, shocked at how badly his hand shook. "The cabin is up that dirt road to the right. It's back a ways."

"Show me." Rhoden opened the door and stepped out.

"Ah, sure." DeWayne fumbled with the handle before pushing it open. His legs barely held his weight. He was forced to use the van hood for support. "It's right there," he pointed again, hoping his boss would go exploring on his own.

Rhoden started toward the dirt track. "Come."

DeWayne swore under his breath but followed. Rhoden pushed branches back as he followed the track. The first one whipped back, smacking DeWayne in the face. The sudden contact caused him to cry out in surprise. Rhoden pivoted in slow motion. "Shh!"

They traveled for fifteen minutes before Rhoden ducked and motioned for DeWayne to do the same. In the distance, barely visible through the thick trees, was the log cabin.

"This is the place?"

"Ah, yeah, I guess so. It's the only building down this road. They have to be in there."

"For your sake, it had better be a good guess." The black eyes bore into DeWayne as dancing specks of fire flared into a full blaze in the center of the pupil. "Return to the van and send my companions."

"Sh-sure. I should move the van out of sight, too."

Rhoden had already switched his attention back to the cabin. DeWayne backed away, then whirled and ran. He couldn't help himself. Rhoden scared him white. He reached the van and ripped open the door. As one, the six blank faces turned their soulless eyes toward him. The sight reminded him of the old horror flick *Children of the Damned.* An involuntary squeak escaped his lips.

"He-he wants you." He stepped back. Seconds later, they unloaded. DeWayne pointed down the track. "Down there. He's waiting."

They moved toward the trees in pairs, matching steps like an army company on parade. DeWayne watched until they were lost within the foliage. He slammed the sliding door shut, ran around the van, and hopped in. His hand shook so badly that he could not seat the key. He swallowed, closed his eyes, and took several deep breaths before trying again. This time, it worked and the engine turned over.

"Drive away. Just drive away," he said. But he feared Rhoden would hunt him down, and as bad as the man scared him now, he'd hate to become his enemy. He shifted and drove down the road a quarter mile before angling toward the trees. He found a slight depression in the tree line and aimed into it. He exited and found about six feet of the rear was uncovered. It would have to do.

Now what? Stay with the van or follow? He wanted to disappear. He cleared his mind and recalled Rhoden's exact words. No, there were no instructions. Relief flooded over him. His body all but collapsed in on itself as if his bones had gelled.

Whatever was about to happen, he wanted no part. He went back to the van, climbed in through the side door and laid down on the middle seat. DeWayne forced his mind blank and fought the urge to suck his thumb.

A SOFT DING sounded in the cabin. It pinged like a preheated oven. It was as far from an alarm as possible, but its sudden interruption of the silence that had settled over the interior of the cabin sent Tetrin and Catrin into a frenzy.

"Everyone alert," Tetrin called. "We've got company." His head poked through the bedroom door. "Boy, you awake?"

"Yes, sir," he replied.

"Try not to stand right in front of the window. Peek out from a corner so you're not such an easy target."

Eric was annoyed. Not with the brusqueness of the man, but that he had been caught doing exactly what he said. He ducked and moved to the lower corner of the window.

In a softer voice, Tetrin said, "Don't fire unless you absolutely have to, and only then if you have a good target. If they move toward the house, call out."

Eric didn't respond. He wiped his now-sweaty palms on his pant legs and continued to stare out at the surrounding trees. Another tone pinged. A deeper one. "Cat, where's that one?" Tetrin said moving back into the main room.

"Far right."

"I've got it," Tetrin said.

A third chime, higher in tone, had Catrin poking her head in the bedroom. "That's your side, Eric."

He tensed, then straightened as he saw a flash of movement through the branches. "I see them."

"Let them make the first move. Don't waste bullets on difficult shots." He thought she'd gone, but then heard, "You'll be all right. Just stay relaxed. It will take a lot to get into this cabin."

He turned a few seconds later, but she was gone.

Minutes passed like years. He wiped the sweat from his forehead, then realized what a mistake that was and wiped his hand on his pants. At this rate, they'd be soaked through before the first shot was fired. What was taking them so long? The waiting was worse than imagining how the fighting would go. He wanted to stand, to pace, if only to burn up some of the nervous energy.

His thighs groaned from squatting. Eric moved away from the window and stood, stretching his long legs. He pushed aside the curtain and peered out. Something moved right to left. Something big. He tried to follow its path, but it put too much of his face in front of the glass. He moved back.

From the front room, his mother called, "Here they come." A second later the first bullets were fired and the siege was underway.

Chapter 44

Rhoden sent two of his amphoids toward the cabin. He wanted to see the defenses that would be used against them. The two mammoth beasts took a few steps to get going, but once up to speed were difficult to stop.

The two beasts barreled forward, closing the open ground in large thundering strides. The defenders opened up with their strange weapons that shot miniature metal darts. DeWayne had explained about guns and bullets, but Rhoden saw no way the tiny fragments could stop his amphoids. Their hides were tough. Arrows had difficulty penetrating unless fired with astounding accuracy at the face or neck. Even then, it would take several successful strikes to slow or stop the creatures. That was one of the reasons he used them. That, and their inability to ward off his commands.

The beasts plodded on, taking several hits each. To his surprise, the bullets were having an accumulative effect. Both amphoids slowed as they neared the cabin. Then one of them dropped to a knee. It struggled to regain its feet, but as soon as it did, rapid fire drove it to the ground where it collapsed in a heap and did not rise again.

The other one reached the porch. It looked as if it might smash through the door, but as its first step landed on the wooden platform, the door whipped open and a man filled the space. A loud boom resounded over the clearing, standing the beast straight up. A second one drove the amphoid back a step, and a third toppled it off the porch. It landed with a crash that shook the ground, its face no longer recognizable as such.

Astonished by the loss of a third of his force, Rhoden lifted the gun he took from the cop and fired at the cabin. The gun bucked in his hand. He could not tell if any of the tiny missiles struck anything. He kept firing, driving the man back inside the cabin, and then the gun stopped working. He tossed it to the ground in disgust and backed away to regroup his thoughts. Clearly, these people were capable of putting up a solid defense. But, where they might be able to stop the beasts, they still had to contend with him.

Rhoden readied one of his most destructive spells. He had to be careful with the amount of power released. He didn't want to fry or bury the prince. But in the end, as long as he controlled one of the heirs, his death would not be of dire consequence. He unleashed his power bolt, the same one he used to topple castle walls for Mortas. Though he held back some of its brute force, it was still enough to level the cabin.

The unseen power rushed from his fingers, streaking toward the cabin. Rhoden vibrated with excitement and the expectation of the final victory. However, ten feet from the cabin, the bolt hit an invisible wall and was deflected. Shocked to see such a strong defensive ward, Rhoden increased the power until he strained from the effort. Still, the ward held.

He broke off the attack to preserve what energy he had left. This assault was not to be as easy as anticipated. Clearly the ward did not prevent physical forms from passing through, since the amphoid had reached the cabin. Perhaps he needed to be inside the protected area to use his magic. He scanned the structure, searching for the weakest point. He found it. The wall on the left side had no windows.

That was where he needed to be. First, he sent a message to his beasts via the mental connection he had made before they left Chevalon. If he had all four attack, that should serve as distraction enough to allow him to penetrate the barrier.

"HOW MANY MORE DO YOU think are out there?" Dina asked.

Tetrin shook his wild-haired head. "Hope not many. It took a lot of rounds to drop those two." He did a quick peek. "What do you suppose that shimmering was?"

Nadina said, "Someone tried to use magic against us. Phetrix must have set a ward to protect against such things."

"How long do they last?"

"Not sure. I think under enough pressure, it can collapse. Guess we'll just have to wait and see."

"Not for long," Tetrin said. "Here they come again. I see three."

"I think a fourth went left."

"Hear that, Eric?" Catron said. "You got one coming."

"I see him."

Everyone began firing at once, except for Catron.

Eric fired one shot after another in a steady stream. He couldn't be sure if any of his shots were finding the target, but by the way the beast moved, even if they were hits, they had little effect.

The slide locked back. Without taking his eyes off the fast-approaching creature, he dropped it and seated a second. In his haste, he forgot to chamber a round. The first pull on the trigger did nothing. The beast was ten feet away by then.

Eric cocked the hammer, stood, and fired as the beast filled the window frame with its bulk. He raised the gun and squeezed off three rounds into the center of the grotesque face. The shots slowed the beast as it crashed through the glass and wood.

Eric jumped backward. The back of his legs hit the bed and he fell. In one fluid motion he brought his legs up in a backward roll off the bed and to the far side. Though fear crept up his chest and tightened like a metal band, he refused to allow panic to take over.

The beast fell on all four claws. It shook its head and gave a savage roar, then lifted its gaze to Eric. For a moment, neither moved. Then, Eric lifted the gun, sighted, and as the beast scrambled forward, he emptied the magazine into its face. The beast dropped to the floor six inches from Eric.

He was afraid to breathe for fear any sound might wake the creature. With trembling hands he ejected the magazine and slid home his last one. The sounds of battle broke through the haze that filled his mind. He turned to leave the room but thought better of it and went to the shattered window instead. He had a job to do. To protect this side of the cabin.

As he surveyed the grounds, he found no signs of more beasts.

Then, an explosion rocked the cabin. For a moment, all sound ceased, save for the ringing in his ears. Eric shook his head hoping to clear his mind. He turned to face the door. Debris littered the main room floor. A wisp of smoke drifted through the doorway. The deadened *pop, pop, pop* of gunshots filtered through.

Eric took a step toward the door. He needed to be sure his mother was all right. The distinct sound of the shotgun filled the outer room. Before he could take a second step, monstrous arms wrapped around his torso, lifting him from the floor. A strange growling sound surrounded him. He kicked but could not break free. The beast drew him outside through the broken window.

Eric reversed his kicks, trying to connect with the beast, but he had no leverage to get power into the attempts. His arms were pinned tight to his body. The embrace was so tight that drawing breath became difficult.

The beast whirled and in an awkward gait, loped toward the trees. As his body bounced from the lumbering steps, he became aware he still possessed the gun. He twisted his wrist, which hung below the beast's wraparound grip, and angled the barrel backward. The barrel brushed against his thigh, then pressed against something solid. Since he no longer felt it against his leg, he hoped it was the creature's, but with all the movement, he couldn't be sure. Still, it was his only chance. He pulled the trigger.

At first, nothing happened. He didn't feel pain, so either he missed or the beast was immune to pain. He pulled the trigger again. This time, the step on the right side faltered a bit. He pulled the trigger three more times in rapid succession. The beast roared. Something dripped from its maw onto Eric's head. Foul breath blew down his face.

The beast stopped and Eric had a brief moment of hope that it could not go on. Then, he was swept under one arm and cradled like a football. This gave him the opportunity to swing his arm up and aim for the horrid face. Before he could take the shot, the beast's now free arm swept down and clubbed his arm. Instant numbness spread all the way to his shoulder. The gun flew from his deadened grip and all hope fell with it.

The beast took off at a slower pace, limping on one side. Eric swung ineffectual fists at the beast. They entered the woods at the side of the house. It plodded through the trees until they came to the dirt driveway. There it stopped, as if waiting for something.

Eric took the opportunity to renew his escape efforts. He griped one long, scaly finger and attempted to bend it backward. Both hands together barely reached around the digit. He glanced up to see the creature eyeing him. He saw no malice in those black eyes, only an emptiness that reminded him of zombie movies he'd seen.

It reared back its massive head and roared. To Eric it sounded as if it were announcing victory. A minute later, something large crashed through the trees on the opposite side of the track. Another large beast tore through the trees, stopping in front of the first. He was followed by a man that looked like something out of a *Matrix* movie. He was dressed in black with a full-length black cloak. Sweat matted his black hair to his head. He emanated pure evil. His beady eyes showed malice, but something even more frightening. Triumph. Eric guessed this must be Rhoden.

"Ah, you must be the prince. Don't despair. We shall take good care of you for now." He strode with confidence down the driveway. The two beasts followed in single file. He was helpless.

Gunshots still rang in the distance. Despite their best efforts, he had been captured. But the gunshots held hope. Someone was still alive to fight, which meant he could be rescued. He thought about the woman he had called Mom for so many years and prayed she was alive and that she would forgive him for allowing her life's mission to fail.

Chapter 45

Consciousness returned to Nadina in slow increments. First sound, then awareness, followed by memory, fear, then sight. As her eyes opened, she found she was beneath a pile of splintered logs, insulation, and shingles. Filtered light drifted through the collection. As she tried to move, pain came. She winced and halted her efforts to analyze the location.

Something sharp had penetrated her side. She could not see but inched her fingers down until she felt a large wood splinter. She gasped to touch it, then steeled herself to move. Planting palms on the floor, she pushed upward. Whatever was collected on top of her moved, and she had hope that she was not pinned down. As the debris fell away, she became aware of a struggle still being waged above. Her head broke through the clutter in time to see Tetrin being lifted from the floor by one of the beasts and pitched to the side like a rag doll. He struck what was left of the front wall and bounced off, landing in a heap eight feet away.

"No!" screamed Catron. Gunshots followed.

Nadina had to get up and aide her new friend. She shoved hard to her knees. The acute pain in her side caused a gasp. She collapsed to all fours but could not afford to succumb to the pain. She was in the clear and saw Catron, a gun in each hand, firing alternating shots into the approaching beast. The creature showed no signs of being slowed by the bullets. Catron was in trouble.

Nadina got one foot under her and pushed to her feet. Ignoring the wood shard, she searched for her gun. It was nowhere to be seen, but she still had her knife. She drew the six-inch Ka-bar from its sheath and charged.

Over the years on this world, Nadina had taken her mission of protecting the heir, her son, to an extreme level. She'd trained for just such a moment. Back in Chevalon she'd be termed a warrior woman. With that thought, she ran, leaping onto the sofa cushion, then on the upright back, springing into the air. Like an avenging angel, she soared above the beast, landing high on its shoulder. With all her might she plunged the blade into the beast's eye socket. The beast roared back, flailing its massive arm and dislodging Nadina.

She flew eight feet through the air before landing on the floor. She rolled, pushing the splinter in deeper. With a cry of pain and rage, she scrambled to her feet and ran at the beast again. Catron continued to fire until both guns were empty.

The beast whirled in a circle, flinging an arm out to keep anyone from closing on it. Nadina ducked under the arm, hopped on to the kitchen table, and using all her skill and years of training, pivoted into a roundhouse kick that drove the knife all the way into the creature's small brain. It stiffened, wailed, and fell backwards with a loud boom.

Breathing hard, the two women gazed at each other until Catron remembered Tetrin. Her eyes went wide with fright. She dodged past the body and hastened to where her husband had fallen. She cradled his limp body in her arms and sobbed.

Finding breathing painful, Nadina climbed down from the table and staggered into the bedroom in search of Eric. Prayers for his safety raced through her mind, but as she entered the room and spied the gaping hole, she knew they were in vain.

She staggered to the opening, filled her lungs as best she could and shouted, "Eric!" Then, her injury took her down.

Chapter 46

Grant raced down the two-lane road doing more than a hundred. If vehicles ahead of him didn't react in time to the lights and siren to pull over, he swerved into the other lane and hoped oncoming traffic saw him in time to avoid the head-on collision.

Phetrix did not speak. If the speed frightened him, he showed no outward signs. Several attempts to reach Nordon had failed. For now, they were on their own to face whatever was to come.

Still ten miles from the cabin, Grant pulled around a harvester moving way too slow for such a busy road. The move put him on a collision course with a white van. The young black man driving went wide-eyed at the sight but managed to brake and pull over far enough to prevent an accident. Something about the near miss nagged at Grant, but he already had too much on his mind to give it a second thought. With no further sign of traffic in front of him, he pushed the speedometer to one ten.

The phone rang. At this speed, Grant could not afford to be distracted. He handed the phone to Phetrix. "Push the green button and answer it."

Phetrix stared at the phone for a moment, then pushed the button. He looked at the screen.

"Hold it to your ear and say, 'Hello,'" Grant said with annoyance.

"Hello." He listened. Someone's excited voice came through the speaker. "What? Hello."

Grant could take no more. He slowed to eighty and tore the phone from the old man's hand. "This is Grant. Who's this?"

"Nordon. We're at the cabin. It's been destroyed. They have Eric. They'll take him to the seam. You might have passed them."

The nagging thought became a realization and with it came a blast of anger. The white van. The driver was the kid he'd confronted near the seam the day someone blindsided him. He stomped on the brake and was forced to release the phone in order to control the car. The tires squealed in protest as they fought for purchase. The car fishtailed one way. Grant overcorrected and it fishtailed the other way. He swung the wheel back and forth to bleed off the speed until he had control enough to whip the car around and start back to the city.

"Find the phone," he ordered Phetrix. The old man fumbled around on the floorboard until he came up with it. He handed it to Grant. "You still there?"

"Yeah."

"I passed a white van a few miles back. I recognized the man driving it, and—"

"A few miles back?" Nordon interrupted. "If you recognized him, why didn't you turn around then?"

Grant put the phone in a death grip. Through gritted teeth, he said, "I'm going after them now. Are you following to help or you just want to bust my balls?"

"Some of us will follow." The big man's voice softened. "Tetrin's dead, and Dina…" a sob escaped him. "Dina's not doing well. She needs immediate medical care or she'll die, too."

Grant didn't know what to say. "Okay. Do what you have to. We're on it." He disconnected and shoved the pedal to the floor.

As thoughts began to take shape, he picked up the radio. "This is car U-one one seven, Detective Marvin Grant. I'm in distant pursuit of a possible kidnap victim in a white van. No make or license. Extended body with no side windows. Coming into the city from the west, last seen on Route 34. Stop and detain."

"Roger, U-one one seven. Sending it out."

He set the microphone back in its holder and tried to think what else he could do.

DEWAYNE WAS SPOOKED. He couldn't believe the cop hadn't recognized him and started pursuit. He pushed the speed limit for a while, keeping an eye on the mirror. As they approached the city limits, he slowed, not wanting to get stopped.

Rhoden looked asleep in the passenger seat next to him. The two strange beings sat in silence. The boy they called the Prince sat bound and gagged on the floor in the back. His eyes darted around the van. DeWayne imagined he was searching for an out. He felt sorry for the boy. What would be his fate once in the new world? The Prince's eyes caught his in the mirror. *Were they pleading with him?* It didn't matter. He didn't want to see anything happen to the boy, but he wanted it to happen to himself less. He broke contact and concentrated on the road.

They entered the city fifteen minutes later. A minute after that, flashing lights pulled up behind him.

"Uh-oh," he said.

"Problem?" asked Rhoden without opening his eyes. "'Cause you know how much I hate problems."

"Ah, yeah, I understand that, but this is a cop. He wants me to pull over and stop."

"Why would you listen to him?"

"Because he's a cop. If I don't stop, he'll call in backup and we'll have a lot more to deal with."

"As I recall, they weren't much trouble before. Why would now be any different?"

"If they call in more, they may not be able to stop us, but they will certainly be a problem. They'll slow us down and see where the seam is. They might even figure out how to access it and enter your world. They may be nothing more than an annoyance to you, but it's better we deal with them now than lots more later."

"How many of these cops could there possibly be?"

"Thousands."

Rhoden's eyebrows lifted, though he still hadn't opened his eyes. "Indeed? Very well. Pull over and stop."

Up ahead DeWayne noticed a second cop driving straight at them. He angled to the side of the road and braked. The car in front cut across the street to block further progress. The car pursuing stopped twenty feet behind. Two cops got out. The man on the driver's side approached with a hand on his gun. The passenger side cop already had his drawn and approached wide of the van to see both the rear and side doors.

DeWayne lowered the window and waited. Since the van was stolen, he didn't have the proper paperwork, nor did he want to show his license. If Rhoden was going to do anything, he hoped it would be before orders were given.

The driver cop, a tall lean black man made bulkier by a vest, came to the window but stayed far enough away to prevent any fast exits from the van.

"Get out of the van."

"What? Why?" DeWayne said. He glanced down the street and noticed both cops from the backup car had guns drawn and had taken up positions behind the vehicle. This was getting serious.

"Because I said. Get out of the van."

DeWayne glanced at Rhoden. He looked unperturbed by the encounter. In fact, he looked smug, like he knew something no one else did, which was probably true. DeWayne opened the door. "I don't understand," he said to the cop. "I wasn't even speeding."

"This van matches the description of one used in a kidnapping. We're going to check it out with or without your cooperation."

"A kidnapping? For real?" He stepped to the ground.

"You, too." The cop pointed at Rhoden.

To Dewayne's surprise, the man smiled broadly and opened the door. Instead of exiting, he reached a hand toward the second cop and said something. DeWayne couldn't see what happened, but suddenly he heard a shout.

The black cop heard the shout, too. The gun was in his hand in a blink. "On the ground. Now!"

"Okay. Okay. Don't shoot." DeWayne knelt on the ground with hands raised.

"Down on the ground. Face first. Donny, you all right back there? Donny."

Rhoden came around the van. The cop switched targets. Then he was flying backward. He hit the ground and rolled but did not rise. The two cops behind the car began shouting commands. Rhoden ignored them. "Get back in the van," he said to DeWayne.

"But—"

"Now!"

DeWayne did not hesitate. The bullets started flying. He dove inside the van. Despite his fear he couldn't help but peek over the dashboard. Rhoden swung his arms wide. Whatever he was doing either didn't work or he was too slow. Rhoden spun around and stared at the bullet wound in disbelief. A second bullet struck him in the chest and pitched him to the ground. He lifted his head and called out. Seconds later, the sliding door was ripped back and almost off its track. The two remaining beasts ambled out.

One of the creatures moved toward the cops. The other made for Rhoden. The cops barked commands and as the beast increased speed in their direction, they opened fire. The bullets appeared to have little effect. Dewayne watched, mouth agape at the damage that was inflicted with no visible result.

The cops quickly retreated. One dropped an empty magazine and slammed a new one home. Shots were fired non-stop. It was obvious to DeWayne the cops were in a panic. He understood why.

The second beast scooped Rhoden up and carried him to the van. He was placed inside and laid across the middle bench seat. After climbing in after Rhoden, the beast closed the door so hard the van shook.

"Move!" Rhoden shouted with a grimace of pain.

"But what about the other—"

"Go! Now!" he commanded through gritted teeth.

Dewayne didn't hesitate. He shifted into gear and floored the pedal. The van lurched forward. As he pulled away, he caught sight of the beast lifting one of the cops from the ground while the other one moved behind. DeWayne continued to watch the fight in the mirror. One cop went flying. The second cop placed the muzzle of the gun against the back of the beast's skull. It staggered a few steps. The cop kept firing and the beast fell.

DeWayne whipped the van around a corner. He needed to find an alternate route. The detective must have made the connection and put the word out. The van was no longer safe.

"What have they done to me?" Rhoden croaked. "I'm bleeding."

"You've been shot."

"How is this possible?"

"I tried to warn you. The police of this world are deadly. You need a doctor. You want me to take you to a hospital?"

"Get me to the seam."

"The cops will be looking for this van. We should ditch it and find a new ride."

"No," he gasped.

"But—"

"No!" he shouted.

"Okay. You're the boss. But if you don't get those wounds treated, you might die."

Chapter 47

Grant stared at the radio in shock and dismay. If what the dispatcher said was true, the van carrying the prince was stopped and a gun fight ensued. The van got away, but it sounded like the main man, this Rhoden, was wounded. One of the monsters he brought with him was dead also.

"They'll head straight for the seam," Phetrix said. "We must get there before it's too late."

"I hear ya."

Grant picked up the microphone. "This is U-one one seven. Was there any sign of the kidnap victim?"

"Negative, U-one one seven. Officers on scene could not get close enough to verify."

"How long ago did the van leave?"

"Estimation is three minutes."

"Send units to the area around East Lake Street and North Wabash Avenue. The van may be returning to its starting point."

"Roger."

He dropped the mic on the seat and gripped the wheel with both hands. He had a lot more traffic to contend with now.

"Is there a chance?"

"They left the scene three minutes ago and we're almost ten

minutes out from there. The only hope we have is if units can slow them down before they arrive at the seam."

"If Rhoden gets the prince through the seam, he may be able to seal it, preventing me from following."

"Isn't there some sort of magic you can do to stop them?" Grant couldn't believe he'd even asked that question.

"No. I wish there was, but no."

"But isn't there another seam? I saw you enter this world in that parking garage on East Randolph."

"Yes, that is an option, but it will put me miles from where Rhoden enters. I will not be able to catch him before he arrives at the castle."

"Then, I guess it's up to me."

And the car found a new level of speed.

ERIC WORKED HARD against the rope around his wrists. They were bound in front of him. Maybe they didn't know any better, or perhaps it was their way of showing their lack of concern about an attempted escape. During the battle with the cops, he'd been left alone long enough to pull the gag from his mouth and work the rope with his teeth. He'd managed to get the first knot out and loosen the second. He had just enough time to replace the gag before the big goon dropped Rhoden back in the van. Now he had enough wiggle room to get his hands free when the time came. He was not going to make his abduction easy. Of course, if the big goon caught him, there wasn't much he could do to prevent him from pinning him again. If it came to it, Eric knew he could outrun the goon. It was a matter whether he could evade Rhoden's magic.

Rhoden did not look good. He was covered in blood. Eric wished the man would die. That would make everything else easier. He looked at the driver. He might be the only one capable of catching him, but by the fearful look in his eyes, Eric had to believe he didn't want to be here, either. If it came to a confrontation between himself and the driver, Eric vowed the man would take some punishment for his part in the abduction.

Sirens bounced off the downtown buildings, making it difficult to determine where pursuit was, if any. A sudden sharp turn threw him against the side panel. He absorbed the blow on his shoulder and slumped below the seat back to finish his task. With his hands now free, he sat up and began to plan his escape.

He had little hope of getting out through the side and front doors. That left the rear doors. As soon as they slowed, he'd pop the doors and bail. However, the sharp turns kept Eric off balance. In front of him, Rhoden moaned with each change of direction. The goon had one massive paw out to prevent Rhoden from being thrown from the seat.

They rounded another corner on squealing tires. The van rocked. Eric feared it would roll. Then, the driver slammed on the brakes and Eric was on the floor again. This time, however, it was time to move.

"We've got trouble," the driver announced.

Eric didn't wait to see what the trouble was. He glanced once over his shoulder, then lifted the lock, the handle, and shouldered his way outside. The trouble became apparent as soon as his feet touched the street. Flashing lights surrounded them at each end of the street. Eric took one look at the police cars behind him and sprinted toward safety.

Two cops exited their squad car fast. With guns drawn, they shouted commands to Eric.

"Show me your hands!"

"Get on the ground!"

Their voices overlapped, making the individual commands difficult to understand. Eric stopped but stood confused. The cops advanced, guns pointed at him. One yelled and motioned with a hand to get down. Eric knelt and placed his hands behind his head. While one kept him covered, the second pulled cuffs from his belt. However, before he hooked Eric's arm, a roar drew his attention.

His partner shouted commands once more, but this time with more urgency. Eric didn't have to look to see what was coming. He turned to the cop with the cuffs and said, "Run." The cop gave him a quizzical look, then his eyes went wide. Color drained from his face.

He dropped the cuffs and swung his weapon toward the charging bull. Before he could get off a shot, a large arm swept out and back-handed him twenty feet away. He flipped, rolled, came to a stop, and did not move.

His stunned partner screamed and pulled the trigger. But even as the first round struck the beast high in the chest, it lunged forward and scooped Eric off the ground. The cop no longer had a shot.

It turned and ran. The van sped forward as police cars closed in from the opposite direction. The beast followed; its thundering footsteps bouncing Eric hard enough to scramble his thoughts. Ahead, the van bumped over the curb and onto the empty lot. The driver jumped out and ran around to the open sliding door. He reached in and helped Rhoden out and toward the seam.

The beast bounded up behind the van and took Rhoden from DeWayne's grasp. Eric struggled against the bone crushing grip. Six policemen gave chase. Two of them closed and leaped for the beast's back. Like a powerful fullback, the creature slowed but refused to go down.

Rhoden shouted; pain prominent in his voice. Whatever he said or did had no effect on anything. He tried again, this time, forcing a steady cadence. A line appeared six feet off the ground. The beast reached up, snagged the lower lip and pulled, widening the seam. He tossed Eric through. He flew, extending his arms toward the grassy slope. His hands made contact. He held the ground to allow his torso to travel far enough to initiate a roll. He came to his feet, whirled, and searched for the seam.

Eric was in a rustic country setting. Crops filled the land to the right. A thatched roof cottage sat to the left. The sky was a bright blue on this side of the seam, but he had no time to appreciate the difference. A head popped through and dangled in mid-air. It was Rhoden. Eric ran toward him. He leaped, grabbed the lower line, and hoisted upward. Though barely conscious, Rhoden recognized Eric and tried to prevent his escape. Eric drew back a fist and drove it into the man's face. He fell to the ground.

Eric pulled through the seam. With head and shoulders hanging above the ground, he saw the beast battling with the cops. Two of them had taser wires attached, but the current appeared to have little stopping power. Three cops lay face down on the lot, two moving. The third was still. The van driver was cuffed, but another cop, seeing his fellow officers in trouble, left him unattended to join the fray.

In the distance, another police car, this one unmarked, drew to a hasty stop. The detective from the cabin got out, as did Phetrix. Grant pointed at Eric and Phetrix ran around the car toward him.

Eric wiggled to bring more of his weight forward. As the balance tipped and he began to slide forward, something grabbed his ankles and pulled him back. He kicked with frantic desperation. His legs broke free, yet somehow, he was being dragged back into the other world.

He extended an arm toward Phetrix, still forty yards away. "Help!"

Grant kept running, but Phetrix stopped. He began moving his arms in a pattern. Just as Eric thought he had lost the struggle, an invisible force latched on to him. Suddenly, he was the rope and the prize in an all-out magical tug-of-war.

Chapter 48

Grant stopped when he noticed Phetrix was no longer with him. He looked back and found the man doing a strange dance with his arms. The strain on his face made Grant believe the man was having a heart attack. He stepped toward him, but Phetrix waved him on. "Save the boy," he managed through his efforts.

Grant turned toward the seam. Eric hung in the air. Half his body was in sight, half not, like a magician's stage illusion. Beneath the half body, the battle still raged between his brother cops and the huge alien creature. The cops were taking the most damage.

He raced forward. As he came to the side of the beast, he snapped a kick into the side of its leg joint. It buckled. He then whipped his gun into the side of its bulbous head. It appeared stunned. The remaining officers piled on, driving it to the ground.

Grant switched his attention to Eric. The boy was barely holding on. Grant reached up and snagged both arms and pulled. Whatever had hold of him on the other side was every bit as strong.

"You have to climb through to free me," Eric said. All but his hands disappeared for a moment before Grant hauled his head and shoulders back through. "If I let go, can you hold on?"

"I'll try." He grunted with effort. "Just do it. I can't hold on much longer."

Grant stretched his long frame and gripped the lower edge of the seam. Though nothing but air, it had a solid, almost rubbery feel. He pulled. His body felt like it was levitating. He ducked his head, fearing he'd smack it on something hard, but his head poked through the seam. As much as he'd heard about an alternate world, he was still mesmerized that it actually existed.

The land was picturesque. The sky blue and the sun warm. The bad guy stood ten feet away, arms extended toward Eric. Though he wasn't touching him, he somehow had a firm grip. Grant slid his arm through the seam. Hanging a few feet off the ground, he pushed the gun toward the enemy and pulled the trigger. Though the gun bucked in his hand, the lack of sound made him think the gun hadn't fired. However, the reaction from the bad guy told him was mistaken.

He jumped backward and fell. Whatever hold he had on Eric released. Eric fell through the gap, onto what Grant termed the real-world side. He tried to bring the gun on target, but the magic man made a gesture with his arms and shouted something Grant didn't understand. A flare to his left drew his attention. The seam was on fire. No, that wasn't quite right. It looked more like someone was welding. It hit him then. The bad guy was sealing the seam.

As the length narrowed, Grant tried to get off one more shot, but before he pulled the trigger an invisible force smacked him in the head, forcing him back through the seam. He hit the ground on his back. The beast had regained its feet and dove for the seam. It got halfway through before the fire reached it. It bellowed. The scream was cut off as the blaze cut across and through the enormous body.

As the seal closed, the bottom half of the beast fell to the ground. It staggered, disgorging a foul, green spray. Then it twitched, stilled, and fell over.

Phetrix ran up to the prince and helped him to his feet.

"Are you all right?"

"Yes. I'm fine," Eric said, unable to take his eyes from the beast's lower body.

"I'm fine, too," Grant said, getting to his feet. "Thanks for asking." He scanned the air, then put his hand up to touch the now-invisible seam. Glancing at the remains of the beast, he had a second thought and withdrew his hand in a hurry.

"So, what does this mean? Is the seam closed for good?"

Phetrix examined where the seam had been. "Perhaps so. But, if that's the case, we must get to the other seam before it can be sealed as well. Otherwise, we may never be able to cross back. We will not be able to save the princess. Come."

"Hold on a minute," Grant said. "I understand your situation but look around. We've got officers down. An investigation has to be started. My bosses are gonna have a lot of questions. We can't just run off."

"I understand, but this is your concern, not ours. We have an entire world to think about. Whether you take us or not, we have to get to the other seam before it is too late." He motioned to Eric. "Come, Your Majesty. We must leave."

"Now, wait a minute. This is a crime scene. I can't just let you walk away."

"Detective," Phetrix said with steel in his voice. "You've seen what I'm capable of. Do you really think you can stop us? I'd prefer to work with you instead of against you. I need to prevent the seam from being sealed. Once I do that, we can do whatever you need us to. Help us, please."

Grant's face took on a pained expression. He knew what he had to do; what was right to do. But after everything he'd witnessed over the past few days, he'd become a believer in this strange saga. "Where is this other seam?"

"The place where we first met you."

"The parking garage?"

He shrugged. "If that's what you call it."

"That's not far from here." He put his hands on his hips and scanned the area. His fellow officers had the scene under control. Other squad cars and two ambulances arrived. A supervisor would be called out as well. If he was going to leave, it had to be before the supervisor arrived. "All right, but just so you can do what you need to keep the seam open. Then we come back. You'll need to make a statement."

"Whatever you say, Detective."

They moved toward the car. Grant spoke with one of the officers, then jogged after them. Three minutes later, they were driving up the ramp to the third floor of the garage. He pulled into a parking space across from where he first saw the other old guy step off the ledge and disappear.

"Thank you, Detective, for all you have done." Phetrix exited the car.

Eric threw open the rear door and jogged after him. "I'm going with you."

Phetrix spun. "Your Majesty, that is not wise. We've already discussed this. Mortas already has your sister."

"Yeah, a sister I never knew existed." His tone was confrontational.

Phetrix sighed. "Be that as it may, to place you within reach of Mortas would be a huge mistake."

"Be *that* as it may, you can't do this alone."

"I won't be alone. There are people who can help me."

"What's the first thing you're going to do when you get there?"

"What do you mean?"

"Who are you going to see?"

Phetrix started to speak but caught himself.

"Uh-huh. That's what I thought. You're going to find the king and queen, aren't you?"

"Yes. They need to be told about your sister."

"Well, it's about time I met my real parents, don't you think?"

Phetrix glanced at Grant. "Hey, don't get me involved in this family squabble."

"Phetrix, I'm coming with or without your approval."

"Very well, but you follow my orders or I will turn you into a toad and leave you in the swamp."

Phetrix placed his hands on the barrier on the outside edge of the garage and pushed up. He motioned to Eric. "Stand here next to me."

"Hey, wait a minute," Grant said, advancing toward them. "You can't just disappear. There's a lot of questions that still need to be answered. A lot of people saw you with me. They're going to want to know what happened to you. You're putting my butt in a sling."

Phetrix glanced down. "Butt in a sling?"

Eric chuckled. "It's an expression meaning he'll be in trouble."

"Ah!"

"Seriously. You need to give a statement before you go."

"Sorry, Detective. There is no time. Lives are at stake." He spoke some words and the seam appeared. The six-foot wide crease in the air was two feet below the height of the ledge. "Of course, there is one way to ensure we return."

"What's that?"

"Come with us."

"Oh, hell no."

"Go, my boy. Just step directly over the seam. I've got you."

Grant continued. "Get my butt eaten by some strange creature with an unpronounceable name? Unh-uh. No way."

Eric stepped off, fell, and disappeared into thin air. Phetrix turned to look at Grant. "Detective, you know you want to, if only to prove to yourself this was not a dream."

"Dream? This is a nightmare, to be sure."

Phetrix stepped off and was gone.

"A true nightmare with things that'd scare Stephen King into writing romance. I'm talking to myself, here." He walked to the barrier and glanced down. "Well, no bodies. Guess that's a good thing."

"Coming, Detective?"

Grant jumped back and clutched his chest. Phetrix's head floated forty feet above the ground." Are you kidding me right now?" He felt his chest. "Dear God, I think my heart stopped No. Wait. There it is." He glared at Phetrix, who had a wide smile on his face. "You are without a doubt the scariest old guy I've ever met."

Phetrix nodded.

Grant hopped up onto the barrier. "What are you doing? Why are my legs moving without permission? Are you doing this?"

"Not me. This is all you."

"Can't be. I'm not this stupid." He glanced down past the floating head. "This isn't some sick trick to see a black man splattered on the ground, is it?"

"You are perfectly safe, Detective. Just step off and aim next to me."

"Yeah, right."

Eric's head poked through the seam a few feet from Phetrix. "Don't be afraid, Detective Grant. He might lie to you, but I won't."

"That's good. Wait. What?"

Phetrix stuck an arm out and made a sweeping motion while uttering one word. Grant's leg flew out from under him and he became airborne. "You devious son of a …"

He fell through the seam and crashed on the ground. He lay there, afraid to move for a while, before Phetrix closed the seam.

"If you're done resting, Detective, we need to be on our way before one of Mortas's minions discover us."

"That was cruel, even for you." He sat up and took inventory of his long body. "If we ever get back to Chicago, I'm arresting you for assaulting an officer of the law."

"Until then," He extended a hand toward Grant. "We have a kingdom to save." Grant ignored the hand. With an indignant huff, he pushed to his feet and brushed off his clothes. "Now my pants have grass stains."

The three men started off, Phetrix, with a definite purpose and destination to his stride; Eric, taking everything in through wide and wondrous eyes; and Grant, one hand on his gun and head spinning in all directions at once.

Chapter 49

Elly and Shree floundered in the wilderness. Neither girl had experience in the wild, both preferring the concrete and steel of the city far too much to put themselves in such a situation. Now, Elly regretted never joining the Girl Scouts.

"Are you sure we can't eat those?" Shree asked for the third time.

"What if they're poison? We have no way of knowing. We'll have to steal food from someone, I guess."

"But they're red and look delicious!"

"Go ahead, but when you're foaming at the mouth and struggling to breathe, don't come crying to me!"

"Why not? Then you could use your power to make it right!"

Elly shook her head. "If only it were that easy. I have no idea how to control this stuff. We're lucky I was able to do what I did. This entire place is so messed up. I still think it's a dream. There's no way any of this is real."

"Tell that to my arm." Shree let go of the berries dangling from the verdant shrub and the girls followed west to where Elly swore they came from, though they'd been lost in the forest for so long, neither girl was sure of anything.

Elly tried connecting with her power but it remained elusive, taunting her with how close she was. It was frustrating. When she did hold the power, she felt connected to this place, whatever it was, in a deep and profound way. That connection is what she sought. But each time she tried, it stayed out of reach.

Later that afternoon, Shree spotted it first.

"There! Do you see that? Smoke rising from the trees. You think it's a house? Maybe they've got food! It's been so long, I think my stomach is trying to eat itself!"

"We need to be careful no matter what. You heard that guy from before. People are on alert about us. We don't need to get in trouble again. I might not be able to do a thing about it."

They crept closer to the source of the smoke and noticed it was a small thatched roof home with a wooden pen outside.

Shree sighed. "Food. I think I see chickens."

Elly giggled. "Maybe we'll finally get something to eat. It's been days."

They moved closer still, until they were at the edge of the trees. Two men appeared from the home, one heading for the chickens and the other toward a neatly stacked pile of logs. The one that entered the pen hunted for eggs and the other carried an armload of wood inside.

"They're huge! No way am I gonna mess with someone like that!"

"Come on, Shree, we don't have to mess with them. We can ask nicely for something to eat. They didn't look too menacing, right?"

"Are you joking? That dude's head was bigger than a basketball!"

"So? Doesn't mean he's a bad guy."

"Whatever. If you can summon that power, maybe we won't have to worry so much about it."

They stepped from the trees and as soon as they were clear, Elly felt something odd. She stopped, holding her side.

"What is it? What's wrong, Elly?"

"I…I don't know. I feel something…strange. It's like…" She looked down at the half moon scar on her abdomen.

"What in the world?" Shree exclaimed.

The scar glowed, its luminescence clearly visible in the light of day. Then, it winked out and both girls stared at it.

"What…what was that?"

"I feel something different. I don't know what just happened, but something changed, Shree. Something powerful. I can't say what or how or why. It's just…different."

The girls waited for the scar to glow once again, but the moment passed and nothing happened.

Elly still couldn't shake the odd feeling. A sensation stirred within her. It was more powerful than any blast she'd created with the unique power she occasionally wielded. It frightened her yet comforted her in a strange melding of emotions.

"We should probably go."

"But they've got food!"

"I'm sorry, Shree. I just…can't. Not now."

"Ok, I get it. We'll be fine. We have to be, right?"

"Right." They turned to enter the forest again and Elly hoped she was right. They'd find their way back home somehow.

They had to.

Conquest

THE SEAM TRAVELERS BOOK THREE

RAY WENCK
JASON J. NUGENT

CONQUEST

THE SEAM TRAVELERS
BOOK THREE

Chapter 1

Samuel stood on the stony outcrop overlooking the valley below. On the far side of the dark, deep woods stretched out before him was a barely visible black castle, its spires piercing the blue sky.

The home of Mortas Frost.

Samuel wove a spell enhancing his vision as if using binoculars, a unique invention he had the pleasure of trying once at Wrigley Field. Crows cawed and swirled around the black stone, rising like charred wood from the green trees. Flags with a white snowflake on a black field flapped in the breeze. If the forest before them wasn't daunting enough, the immense black walls and sigils of House Frost made them rethink their plans. Samuel shook his head more than once.

"Mathilda, I know we must stop this madness, but the situation seems more dire than I ever imagined. That fortress--if we could even get close enough--seems deadlier than anything I imagined."

Staring off across the forest at the well-defended black walls of Castle Frost, Samuel longed to be back in Chicago, where he at least could hide from his anxieties at home and maybe catch a Cubs game on TV. They had a legitimate chance of taking the division this year and ending the dominance of those pesky redbirds from St. Louis.

"Samuel, I never knew you to cower from a challenge."

"It's not cowering, Mathilda. It's being honest about the situation."

"Aren't you the one who masterminded the entire operation for this very moment?"

Samuel nodded slowly. "Aye. That, I am."

He released the spell and turned away from the dark forest to face the camp behind them. About fifty remaining fighters for the resistance were busy preparing for a battle. They practiced with wooden swords and shields, mimicking the coming fight. But in his mind, no amount of training or skill could prepare for what they would face.

The group was nothing like Samuel envisioned when he put his plan into action. He always hoped there would be a massive groundswell of support for the heirs and they'd outnumber Frost's forces by a good four to one. By the looks of it, they were on the wrong end of that equation. He'd left the resistance in capable hands. How could they have let it come to this?

But inside, he knew the answer. He'd waited too long to make his return. Those loyal to the king were either old or dead. But this was his plan, and whatever the cost, he had to see it through.

"Mathilda, how familiar are you with the forest? Are there dangers I'm unaware of? What sorcery has Rhoden used to fill that land with evil?"

Mathilda shrugged. "I don't know. We've never been this close to the castle before. It wasn't in our best interest to stay near our enemy until now."

Char approached the pair, beads of sweat dotting his forehead.

"This lot's got more work to do before we can even think about attacking Frost, and that's if they stop fighting each other first. I've had to break up at least three fights and it's not even lunchtime yet!" The burly man wiped his forehead and smiled. "But you gotta love their spirit."

Char's smile and the way he spoke reminded Samuel of Joe Madden, the former manager of the Cubs. The man had a way of explaining a terrible situation as though it were nothing at all. Madden seemed like someone Samuel would have enjoyed hanging out with, though he'd never met him. He dispersed the thought. He had to stay focused on the here and now.

Mathilda spoke up. "Char, how long do you think they need before they can safely navigate their way through the forest? We've come all this way to finish what we started. We owe it to them to make sure they're equipped as best as we can."

"Another week? Tomorrow? I'm not sure it'll make much difference. With the two of you using your powers, we should be fine whenever you decide we leave. In truth, I fear the heavy burden for this assault will lie with you two."

Mathilda addressed Samuel. "What do you think? Are you ready for what's to come? Do you think we can make a difference with the forces we have?"

Samuel scratched his chin. The task seemed a bit overwhelming. He didn't like not knowing what to expect once they breached the castle walls, if they even made it that far. But he had to try. The kingdom's existence depended on him fulfilling his duties. He had built this entire network, found a seam to another world, and ferried the heirs away for this very moment. It was time. There was no choice. He anticipated Elly would be inside those walls, afraid, wondering why she was there. He had to save her. Mortas had to be defeated. Everything depended on him. He could not—*would not*--fail his duties.

ONCE AGAIN SAMUEL and Mathilda debated the best possible course of action. The back and forth was endless. Samuel grew tired of her doubting his ability to lead. He had made mistakes in the past, but didn't everyone? No one was perfect, and he'd never claim to be. Better? Maybe. Perfect? Not at all. Of course, mistakes now could cost lives and break the will of the resistance.

"Samuel, when is the time right? When are we going to use what we have and press forward? These fighters have been waiting years for this very moment and you sit idly by, waiting like you don't have a care in the world."

Char grunted.

The three of them were in a large canvas tent in the center of camp. They hid the force amongst the trees on the bluff overlooking the valley in front of Castle Frost. It wasn't ideal, but so far, they'd remained undetected by enemy forces.

It was night and Samuel created a small glowing orb to illuminate the tent. They forbade fires are night, wary of tipping off their location to eagle-eyed scouts at the castle, or worse yet, the Seekers. Even creating the orb was a risk as the use of magic could alert them. Samuel took great pains to hide his power by casting a spell to cover the orb so they wouldn't be discovered. It was a complex maneuver, but one he was grateful for when they found themselves hiding from the Seekers.

"Mathilda, remain calm. If you have forgotten, let me remind you I'm in charge here. All of this is because of me. I have been absent, but you know the reason why. Please spare me the theatrics and trust that I know what I'm doing."

Char shifted his feet and cracked his knuckles.

"I've been with Mathilda for a long time. She knows what she's doing. I've seen how she treats those who dare defy Mortas Frost. She cares about them. Maybe you could learn something from her."

Samuel had enough. "How dare you act as though none of this matters to me? This is not a debate. I care deeply for everyone affected by Mortas. His reign must end! The kingdom will not last as long as he's in charge. The heirs must rule again, or all is lost."

"Why don't we all just leave and go to this Chicago you always speak of?" Char asked.

"Because we—" Samuel had no rebuttal. He knew it wasn't a good idea. Or was it? Honestly, the thought never occurred to him. "Our home is here. We defend it to the last."

Char arched his eyebrow. "But you're so fond of this other place. Why don't we all go and let Mortas rule an empty kingdom? What is the benefit if we all die trying to remove him from power?"

Samuel's silence seemed to placate the man.

"If this all goes badly, maybe we ought to consider an alternate escape plan, where we take our fighters to your Chicago and hide in that world."

Mathilda nodded her approval. "Char's plan makes sense. What do we gain if we all die? Nothing matters if we aren't around for it. Besides, we'll be hunted until the last of us is gone. We'll have no safety if we stay here."

Samuel stood and stretched his old bones. He felt ancient here in the wilderness. His comfortable mattress and easy living in Chicago had made him soft and unfit for this life.

What did they want from him? He'd orchestrated this entire operation for one purpose: to restore the kingdom. He couldn't help falling in love with the place he'd discovered through the seam. It's not like he intended it to happen. There was no way to know what awaited him there. It turned out to be something far greater than he anticipated, and that's what gave credence to Char's suggestion. It might be the way to go instead of losing lives in the plan to depose Mortas Frost. But what of the seam? Could he seal it so Rhoden could never open it again? He wasn't sure.

"I did not come back here to lead refugees into a different dimension. I came here to restore what rightfully belongs. If the time comes and we can no longer fight on, then we can consider this alternate plan. It does not leave this group, understood? Only the three of us will know about it."

He glared at the other two, ready for their arguments, but they made none. His tone must've carried weight. He hoped so. It was another instance of him not anticipating an outcome and it bothered him. He was wiser than that. At least he had been once.

Chapter 2

Nadina woke with blurry vision. She squeezed her eyes tight, then reopened them. It didn't help. She peered through the distortion. She moved to clear her sight, but a sharp, breath-sapping pain erupted in her side. She cried out and rolled into the fetal position, increasing the pain, and froze in place.

She allowed the pain to recede before taking stock of the situation. As long as she didn't move, she could breathe relatively pain free. As slowly as she could, she straightened her legs to a more comfortable and less stressful position.

Her eyes, now tear-filled, did not allow clarity, but memories flooded her mind. There had been a fierce battle. Rhoden and his monstrous minions had attacked. She'd been hurt. She reached for the large chunk of wood that had impaled her, but her fingers found nothing. Taking in a steadying breath, Nadina lifted her head enough to scan her body. The wooden shard was not there. Someone had removed the wood and bandaged her up.

She continued remembering. The cabin had been destroyed. *My God! Tetrin.* An image of him flung lifeless against a wall came to her. Was he dead? What about Catron and Alyanna? Were they still alive? She needed information, and fast, but first she needed to see better. In slow increments, she lifted her hand toward her face and wiped away the blur from her eyes.

Her gaze swept the room. Heavy log walls surrounded her. She was on a rustic, log framed bed. Was she still at the cabin? She fought to bring back more memories, but she couldn't. She blew out a long breath, trying for a calm that would not wash over her rising panic.

She cleared her mind and thought about other things. Nordon. Where was the big man? Fear elevated. Anxiety threatened to cut off her air flow. No. He had to be alive. She could not function without him. She needed him now. Then the breakthrough happened. Eric!

Long and slowly-building, her voice rose to keening level like a whistling tea kettle. The volume increased until her wailing filled the room.

The beast. Rhoden's creation had taken her son. Amidst the pain, the mental anguish, the horror, and the mind-numbing realization she had failed to protect her son, Nadina's body shut down in a sudden collapse.

WHEN NEXT SHE WOKE, the sun was setting. The window shade had been drawn up to allow the day's last light to pour in. Nadina turned her head away from the glare. Her eyes rested on a woman collapsed in a chair. The disheveled form stared at a wall. Nadina strained to see if her chest rose and fell. The unblinking eyes looked lifeless. She called out, but the croak was indecipherable. Swallowing, she tried again.

"Catron!" The woman did not move. "Catron!" Still nothing. *Oh no.* She was dead. As the sorrow built and tears flowed, she sobbed. "Catron!"

This time, the unseeing eyes blinked. The older woman shook her head and trained her eyes on Nadina. In those hollow depths she saw death, a pained soul, and worse. resignation. Catron was ready to die.

She stirred in the chair and swiveled to face Nadina. "So, you live." It was not a question, but a statement, and one that carried disappointment. "How nice for you."

Their eyes locked. Nadina saw a flash of hatred. Though she was sure she knew the answer, she forced the question through her lips. "Tetrin?"

A fiery glare ignited before her eyes softened. She blew out a breath. Her eyes glazed over and grew flat. "Buried."

She stood abruptly. "Thought you were gonna join them. Can't say I cared one way or another."

"I'm sorry, Catron."

"Yeah, you're sorry. Not as sorry as I am." The fire left her body, leaving a slumped, defeated, and frail form.

"You healed me?"

"Guess I did. Took quite a bit of energy. You were in bad shape. Probably still are." She pressed her palms to her back and stretched. "Anyway, they got your boy." Her gaze was challenging, as if to say, *So take that!* "Guess we all lost something important."

The announcement and its cold delivery caused a new flow of tears.

"What about the others?"

"Your man was here. He saw the damage. Saw your condition." She paused to stare at Nadina. A sudden fire raged within those eyes, but she doused it a moment later. Whatever she was going to say vanished with her anger. "Anyway, he was worried about your boy and torn between staying or going. I convinced him to go. Told him I'd take care of you." Catron moved toward the door. "I'll get you healed, and then I'd appreciate it if you leave and don't come back." She exited and closed the door, leaving Nadina to cry alone.

IN THE MORNING, Catron brought in a tray of tea, scones, a fried egg, and a slice of ham. She set it down and studied Nadina. She lifted the blanket and cut away the bandages. The wound was a nasty pucker of angry red skin. Catron looked it over, probing with long, thin fingers. Nadina tried not to wince, but she got the impression Catron was trying to hurt her.

"Looks infected. Might have missed a splinter or two. Wasn't in the best condition to do healing. I don't have any drugs to fight it, but I can do some more healing. At least that will keep the infection from progressing until you can get modern medical attention."

She didn't wait for Nadina to respond. Catron vigorously rubbed her hands together as she spoke her incantations. She hovered her palms over the injured area and a reddish glow filled the space between her hands and Nadina's side. In seconds, a warmth like that of a high-intensity heat lamp filtered down through the layers of skin. As it reached the infection, Nadina stiffened with a wave of pain. She bit her lip and closed her eyes, not wanting to cry out and give Catron the satisfaction of knowing it hurt. Slowly the pain ebbed.

Minutes later, Catron's shoulders slumped and her head drooped. She placed her hands on the bed to steady herself. She exhaled a long, dark breath that looked like smoke releasing from a chimney. Her pupils were hazy. A few more minutes and Catron found the strength to stand unaided.

"There. It's done. While your pain eases, you should eat. I'll find you some clothes, and then I'd like you to leave." She spun and walked from the room without giving Nadina a chance to thank her.

She ate, dressed, and tested her strength as she got out of bed. She still had pain, but nothing so severe as to keep her bed-bound. She exited the bedroom and entered a space of complete chaos and destruction. Most of the front of the cabin was gone. The outside was visible through a gaping, ragged hole. Much of the debris had been cleared away. Catron was sweeping up the smaller pieces.

She stopped to watch as Nadina surveyed the damage. Nadina spotted her purse and weapons on the kitchen counter and made for them. She picked them up along with the keys for Alyanna's car and walked toward the opening. She hesitated. She wanted to say something. To apologize, ask for forgiveness—something. Instead, she silently got in the car and drove away.

Chapter 3

Elly straightened the long brown tunic. The uncomfortable leather shoes were tied tight around her feet. She regretted leaving her own shoes, but they would be a dead giveaway to those searching for her and her friend Shree. Comfort was sacrificed to blend in.

She and Shree were lost. They'd been traveling west, searching for where they'd entered this world, but nothing looked right. Worse yet, she failed every attempt to grab hold of the power she had in this world. Her scar didn't glow anymore and they were alone in the creepy woods.

"Ugh!" Shree called out. Elly turned and giggled. Her friend had stepped in mud and her foot sank ankle deep, completely covered in the thick black mess. "I hate this place! I hate everything about it! Why are we even here? This is so stupid!"

Shree struggled and eventually pulled her foot free with a wet plop.

"Just great. Would you look at that mess? How am I gonna clean it off? I wish we'd never come here!"

Elly's smile faded. She understood her friend all too well. This place was horrible. Nothing was right about it. All she imagined was leaving and finding her way back home. To her parents. To her mom.

"Let me help. It's the least I can do. Your arm is still hurt and I'm the reason you're here." Elly leaned close to scrape off the mud, but

Shree waved her off. She placed a hand on Elly's shoulder and lifted her leg to wipe the mud off with a stick.

"Girl, we're friends. I would've followed you here even if you yelled at me not to. There's no way I'd leave you by yourself when you got those scary dudes coming after you. Friends stick together no matter what. Besides, it wasn't like either of us had a choice in the matter." She finished her task as best she could and tossed the stick away.

Elly blushed, then gave Shree a warm embrace. "I know," she whispered.

They left the safety of the forest and followed what looked like a road. The sun was high in the sky and they were adamant about finding their way home.

Something cried out. They stopped in their tracks. Elly grabbed Shree's hand. The girls scanned the area around them.

Another scream.

"Is it one of those black things?" Elly asked.

"I don't see anything. Do you think we could've missed it?"

The black demon-like creatures were frightening. The last time the girls had encountered them, they were almost killed. Whatever the creatures were, they were nasty and vile. Elly wanted nothing to do with them.

The hideous howl echoed across the land, surrounding them.

"I don't know what that is, and I don't want to find out!" Shree said.

Elly pulled Shree off the road into a nearby ditch. She poked her head above the edge to catch a glimpse of whatever it was that called out to them. Then she saw them.

"Dear God, what are those?"

Shree shuddered. "It's the black things again, isn't it?"

"No. Look. Move slowly. I don't think they saw us."

"They?"

"Shush. Just look."

Slowly, Shree rose next to her. She forced back a yelp and slapped her hand over her mouth.

"Quiet," Elly whispered. "What do you think they are?"

Shree shook her head. "I don't know."

On the road were three creatures that were clearly not human. They had two feet, two arms, and human-like bodies, but their heads were something different. They were giant boulders with black circles for eyes and a large black slit for a mouth. The lack of a noses gave their faces a sinister look. Their heads were covered in patchy green moss with gray rock underneath exposed.

One of them opened its onyx slit into a pit of a mouth and howled loudly. The other two followed suit, all three facing the sky. Their gray rock heads twisted to catch the entire view.

"I think they're looking for something."

Shree tugged Elly's arm. "You think they're looking for those black creatures?"

"Maybe. I honestly have no idea. They could be looking for us. That wizard did want us pretty bad."

"Stupid place. Stupid people. I wish this was all over."

Elly slowly stroked Shree's injured arm. It had healed for the most part, but still gave her fits once in a while.

"It's going to be fine. Together we can face anything."

The creatures drew closer and screamed into the sky. The girls covered their ears to the horrific sound.

"What are they doing?" Shree asked.

"Shush! They'll hear you!"

The creatures stopped, their footsteps falling silent. Elly chanced a look back at the road and one of them noticed her. It raised an arm, pointing a stony gray finger at her, then bellowed loudly. The other two joined the first, and all three narrowed their black hole eyes as they screamed.

"Run, Shree! Come on!"

She pulled her friend's arm, yanking her from their hiding spot. The girls ran into the forest as the creatures took turns shrieking. It was as though they were sending a signal.

Elly looked back and saw the three rock creatures lumbering after them.

"Oh no! Run faster, Shree! They're coming!"

The girls stumbled through thick vegetation. The shoes they'd stolen were terrible and they couldn't run fast. It was probably like running in those stupid dad sandals her father was fond of wearing.

The creatures continued to scream. The sound carried throughout the forest, scaring birds into flight, and silencing all else.

Elly felt her heart thumping in her chest. Blood rushed through her ears. A panicked wave of adrenaline kicked in and she fought against her fears to keep moving away from whatever those things were.

"Elly, watch out!"

Shree's warning came a moment too late. Elly smacked into one of the creatures. It must have heard the call of the three chasing them. It felt like stone. She fought against the grip, but her fists did nothing to dislodge its stony hand.

"No! Get off me!" The other creatures crashed into them and grabbed hold of Shree. Like Elly, she struggled against the thing but made no progress.

"What do you want from us?" Elly cried out.

In response, all four rock creatures howled. The various vocal pitches were disorienting. Fear raced through her body, forcing her heart to beat even harder. The grip tightened. No matter how hard she squirmed, she could not get free.

The creatures howled wildly, growing erratic.

"Shree! Something's happening!"

Her friend didn't reply. The creature holding her clamped a hand over her mouth, leaving just enough room for her to breathe between its thick stone fingers.

Then the creatures stopped and stood as still as statues; their faces to the sky. Then, the unmistakable shriek of the black creatures filled the air.

"Shree!"

Three of the black, demon-like creatures swirled above them, their long black cloaks drifting behind them like ribbons of smoke. They shrieked louder and the rock creatures cried in response. The back and forth between the strange creatures set Elly's nerves on edge.

Then she felt the power.

The sensation was faint at first and she almost missed it. When she recognized what it was, she grasped at it like her life depended on it.

Once firmly in her control, she filled herself with it. The screaming creatures faded from her periphery. The only sensation now was raw power. It had been so long that she wondered if she'd ever touch it again.

Closing her eyes, she let the power consume her. It filled her completElly and she thought she'd burst. With a furious outward push, she forced it away from her in a cataclysmic explosion. She had no control over what it would do. She followed her urge to push outward, forcing a wave of energy bursting from her like a lightning bolt.

The creature holding her exploded in thousands of rocky shards around them. The one holding Shree was damaged and it released her. She fell to the ground, cowering.

Elly pulled in the power once more and again let her rage send it out of her body. A bright flash of light surrounded them. When the light vanished, the rock creatures were diminished to faceless piles of stones.

Overhead, the black demon-like creatures continued to screech. Elly looked upward and was ready to blast them with her anger, but when she tried to grasp the power, it was gone. The sweet sensation was only a memory. She felt its lingering effects but could no longer grasp it.

"Damn it!" she cried out. Losing the power was the worst thing she could imagine. Knowing how powerful she was with it and how desperate she felt without it only intensified the feeling. It was a drug, and she was addicted.

She turned to Shree and helped her up. "Are you ok, Shree?"

The girl coughed but seemed to be no worse for the wear.

"What did you do?"

"I could touch the power again. I don't know what I did, but I got rid of those things." Elly nodded to the piles of rocks on the ground.

"That's wild, Elly! How did you—"

The shrieks above cut her off.

"No time, Shree. Come on. We can't stay here. We gotta keep moving. I don't know if we're ever gonna leave this place, but we can't let those things get us. There has to be someone here who can help."

They rushed deeper into the dense forest to put as much distance between themselves and the flying creatures.

"Nothing's safe around here, Shree. Be careful."

They avoided being spotted by the demon things for the rest of the day. It wasn't easy, but they got far enough away to be out of earshot of the hellish screams.

Chapter 4

Nordon paced. He'd been pacing ever since he'd arrived at the seam. He was two blocks away, unable to get any closer because of the huge police presence. The entire street was closed off. Anyone not involved in the investigation wasn't getting through.

The frustration of not knowing what had happened to Eric was mounting. He wasn't far from storming the crime scene and demanding answers but doing so would involve him in the investigation. He'd be tied up for hours explaining all that had happened and they wouldn't believe much of what he said.

"AHH!" he cried, fists clenched skyward. "I can't take this anymore!"

"Nordon," Alyanna said. "There's nothing you can do. We have to find another way."

He whirled on her. "How? Tell me. How do we get information? How can we save…" He trailed off, his throat constricting, and he whispered hoarsely. "…my son?"

Alyanna took a tentative step forward and placed a hand on the big man's forearm. "Believe me, I know how you feel. But if we are to rescue your son, we need to be smart. We can't just approach and say you want to use the seam to find him. Few, if any of them will believe you. Most will think you're nuts. Regardless, they are angry. They've suffered losses and don't have a clue what it's about. You will be taken in and interrogated for hours, and even if they believe you and let you go, they'll be watching you. You won't be able to move without them on your tail. Is that what you want?"

"No!" he roared. "I don't want that, either. I want to find Eric."

Kol spoke up for the first time since they'd arrived at the seam. "Why don't we try the second seam?"

Mouths agape, Alyanna and Nordon stared at the man. "Second seam?" they asked in unison.

"Yeah. The other one farther down the street. The one Phetrix and I came through."

Alyanna and Nordon exchanged incredulous glances before Nordon exploded. "There's a second seam and you didn't think it important enough to tell us? What do you think I've been doing here for the past hour?"

"That's kind of crucial information for you to keep from us," Alyanna said.

In typical Kol fashion, he shrugged. "I thought you already knew."

Nordon took a threatening step forward, barely able to contain his rage. "If I'd have known about a second seam, do you think I would still be here pacing the street like a caged animal?"

Kol stepped back, suddenly aware of the impending danger. "Ah, I can take you there if you want."

Nordon loomed over the man and Alyanna stepped between them. "That'd be a good idea, Kol. Take us there now."

"Sure. Th-this way."

Nordon slapped his massive palms to his face in disbelief. How could the man be so dense?

Kol led them away from the police barricade and down the street. They walked two blocks, Nordon's already short patience evaporating with each passing step.

"Are you sure you know where you're going?" Alyanna asked.

"Well, I think I do. I mean, I've only been there once, and this world is kind of strange."

"For your sake, I hope you can find it. I don't want to be in your shoes if you get us lost."

Kol shot a nervous glance over his shoulder. Nordon growled.

"I'm pretty sure it's this way."

They walked another fifteen minutes before he said, "Yes. There it is." He pointed.

"A parking garage?" Nordon said. "This other seam is inside a parking garage?"

"I don't know what you call it, but it's where you keep your strange mechanical horses."

Nordon gave him a withering glare and walked toward the structure. "You'd better be right."

They entered and climbed the stairs.

"What floor?" Alyanna asked.

"I don't know," Kol laughed nervously. "We didn't come this way. We walked down the circular road."

Alyanna opened the second floor door and stepped out. "Okay. There's the circular road. Do we go up or down?"

Kol walked to the outer wall and peered over the side. "It's not high enough. We go up."

They made a complete lap. Kol checked again. "Yes. It was about here, but not in this spot." He turned and scanned the garage. "We were next to a tall building made of glass."

"Glass?" Nordon said.

"You mean like that?" Alyanna said, pointing at a high rise office building halfway across the third level.

"I think so!" Kol excitedly jogged toward the building, almost getting run over by a minivan in the process. Nordon grabbed him by the shoulder and yanked him back before damage was done. The middle-age woman driver looked as frightened as Kol, but when she saw Nordon, she punched the gas and sped off, squealing her tires up to the next level.

They stopped and leaned across the wall. "This is the spot," Kol announced.

"You're sure?" asked Nordon.

"Yep. I'm sure."

"Where is it?"

"Ah, I don't know. It seems to me it was in the air between this building and the big one. When Phetrix and I came through, we had to take a long step to stand on top of this ledge."

Nordon and Alyanna exchanged more glances. Alyanna said, "So, what you're telling us is the seam is somewhere out here?" She swept her arm over the wall.

"Yes."

Nordon said, "Great." He folded his arms and leaned against the wall. "Do you know how to open the seam?"

Kol frowned. "Do I look like a wizard?"

Nordon sighed. "Now what?"

Chapter 5

Detective Marvin Grant still didn't believe where he was. "Are you sure this is real? With your little hocus pocus crap, maybe you put me under some crazy spell."

Eric laughed and Phetrix stared with an expression of frustration at the detective.

"I assure you, Detective, this is real. It's more real than you might choose to believe, but real it is."

They'd crossed over dimensions, something Grant still didn't think was possible, and were now walking in a field in the daylight. They were surrounded by trees and hills. At the far end of the field, Grant noticed a small gray shack, but he'd seen worse. He'd lived in worse.

"Come, come. We must hurry. If the princess is here, we have to find her before Mortas does something terrible."

"Yeah, about him. What's his plan for the princess? And him too?" he said, motioning toward Eric.

"Long ago, there was a prophecy about the kingdom. If the heirs had the gift of the power, they'd bring unending peace to the land. Mortas didn't agree. He claimed it was all a lie and led a rebellion against Eric's parents, King Artus and Queen Griselda."

"My parents," Eric whispered. "I still don't believe it."

"It's true. You'll see. Anyway, I discovered both twins held the power and the prophecy was true. At that time, Mortas was planning something terrible. Samuel had already discovered the seam, and we devised a plan for the safety of the kingdom in case anything were to happen. Something did happen, and they were brought into your world, Detective. We kept them apart for their own safety, knowing that if at least one of them was alive, we would be secure."

"Who is this Samuel? How many of you wizards are there?"

"Samuel was my mentor. He's a wise mage. I assume that's what you mean by *wizard*. He taught me how to open these seams and I've kept it to myself for times of emergency."

"How did Mortas get through?" Eric asked.

"Somehow he seduced Rhoden to work on his behalf. Rhoden is a powerful mage poised to rise among the ranks within the Order. However, he fell prey to pride and greed and his quest for powerful magic. He found it in the dark arts. Then Mortas brought him in. After Samuel disappeared, I found Rhoden in my mentor's quarters. He said he was searching for clues as to his whereabouts, but in retrospect, I believe he was stealing Samuel's spells. At the time, I thought nothing of it. Samuel and I trusted him. We never thought he'd turn on us."

"So your world gets all screwed up by betrayal and lies and I gotta pay for it?" Grant asked. He shook his head. "You know what? Your world isn't much different than mine."

Phetrix led them through the muddy fields to the small shack.

"What happened here?" Eric asked. The house was in ruin. There was a giant hole in the roof and the sides were charred.

"Looks like a fire," Grant said. "By the looks of it, not too long ago…maybe a week or two? It's pretty recent." He slowly walked around the perimeter of the house, inspecting it, alert for footprints and any other evidence.

"Seems like only two people were here. But the burn pattern began inside. Maybe there was a cooking catastrophe. Seen it happen too many times in my district."

"I don't think so, Detective," Phetrix said. The mage contemplated and imagined the terrible scene in front of him. "If I know Rhoden, this was the work of Seekers."

"Seekers?" Eric asked.

"Yeah, what the kid said. What are Seekers?"

Phetrix slowly shook his head. "Creatures we fear. Dark, evil phantoms compelled to do the bidding of their master. In Rhoden's hands, they do whatever Mortas wants, which is complete and utter dominance over Chevalon. That's why we're here. To end his evil and put him," he said, pointing to Eric, "back on the throne with his sister. With the twins in charge and the Order to guide you, our world will be restored. Mortas's reign will die. The people deserve better than what they've had."

"I don't understand how I'm part of all this," Eric said quietly. "I mean, none of it feels real. None of this seems like it belongs to me. My world…my reality is different. Don't get me wrong, I want to help people. I want to be part of the solution, but I still don't understand how I fit. I grew up in Chicago. All of this," he said, waving his arms wide, "means nothing to me."

Phetrix cringed. One of his gravest fears about whisking the twins away to the other world was a disconnect with their home. He'd brought it up to Samuel during the initial planning, but the older mage insisted it would not be a problem. Phetrix stared at the problem and wondered how to resolve it.

"Look, kid," Grant chimed in, "this may not be the home you know. But you might be the only hope to whoever lives in this world. I can barely believe this exists either, but here I am, standing next to you and this guy, staring at a burnt house surrounded by some of the most beautiful and peaceful scenery I've ever seen. We aren't in Chicago anymore, but does that mean we're done? You've seen what these people are capable of. If we can end this here with no more loss of life, then we've done good. If what the wizard is telling us is true, you have an obligation to an oppressed people."

Eric slowly walked around the house with his hands clasped behind his back.

"Thank you, Detective. I understand this is a shock to him, but this was the plan all along. It seems we didn't take his feelings about the situation into account. He'll come around. I'm sure of it."

Grant stepped closer to Phetrix. He leaned in and Phetrix could see the red lines streaking Grant's eyes.

"If you've lied to me or this boy, you'll regret ever knowing me. Do I make myself clear?"

Phetrix nodded. "I assure you, there is no deceit in me. Everything I've shared is true."

Eric circled the house several times, muttering words to himself that Phetrix couldn't make out. When the boy was done, he came back to Phetrix and Grant.

"Phetrix, what can we do?"

"The scar on your side."

"The what?" Eric replied. "What about my scar? How'd you know about it?"

"Your sister has an identical one on the opposite side of her abdomen. Does your scar feel different?"

"What do you mean, feel different?"

"Lift your shirt."

"Wait a minute, wizard! This is going too far."

"Detective, this is all part of the truth I've been sharing. It might help you see that I am being honest with you. Eric…your shirt?"

Eric looked to the two men, then lifted his shirt, revealing a half-moon scar on his side.

"See? It's just a scar. Nothing more," Eric said.

"Not exactly. Close your eyes, Eric. Can you feel that? Can you sense the change in this world? There's an energy here that you can touch."

"Wizard! What are you trying to—"

Eric held up a hand and closed his eyes in concentration. After several moments, he opened them wide in shock.

"I…I do feel something different. It's hard to describe. It's like the time I saved my neighbor's kid from being hit by a car. I moved so fast and without thinking and saved her from certain death. No one knew how I did it, not even me. I just made it happen. This strange adrenaline flowed through me. I'd never felt it before, and not since then. What does it mean?"

Phetrix grinned. The boy did know the touch of the power.

"It means you are precisely who I've said you are. Concentrate. I want you to focus on your scar. Focus on the shape of it. Focus on directing your feelings into it. That should channel power into it and open a gateway with your sister."

"A gateway? What kind of nonsense are you spouting?" Grant interjected.

"Detective, let the boy work. This might be our only way of finding Elysonde."

"Elysonde?" Eric asked.

"Your sister. Your twin. She goes by Elly. Now, concentrate! By the looks of this house, we're already behind. We must hurry."

Eric closed his eyes, squinting hard. He breathed deep and his face turned bright red. While the other two watched, the scar flashed white.

"What was that?" Grant cried out, pointing at Eric. "What did you do to him?"

Eric opened his eyes. "I can't do it, Phetrix."

Phetrix smiled. "But, my boy, you already did! Your scar! It lit up. You've tapped into the power. Reach out. Send out the power like a wave, rippling away from you. See if you can find the connection. It'll be like an invisible cord, tying you to Elly. I promise when you feel it, you'll know."

Grant huffed. "This is all a joke. We can track her from here using legitimate ways. I'm a detective, remember? It's my job."

Eric closed his eyes again and the two men watched as he pushed out his hands like thrusting the air around him outward. Phetrix knew that look. He knew the boy had done exactly what was needed. It might not be the cleanest move and would certainly attract the Seekers, but as his first experience harnessing his innate powers, it was a strong start.

Eric's eyes flew open. "I think they're here!"

"Who? Your sister?" Phetrix said.

"No! Look!" Grant said. He directed their attention skyward. Three black ghost-like creatures streaked across the blue sky.

"Seekers," Phetrix muttered. "Eric, they were attracted to your power."

"But I didn't mean to—"

Phetrix waved him off. "It was a necessary risk. Now, prepare for battle."

Chapter 6

Nadina drove back toward Chicago in a trance. She knew she should stop at a hospital but didn't want the hassle of explaining the injury or the loss of time surgery and recovery might take. She had never been to the seam, but Nordon's description gave her an idea of where it might be. She drove, hoping to discover anything that might lead her to Nordon or Eric. Not knowing if they were still alive had her already stressed brain amped up even more.

She made several attempts to call Nordon but it went to voicemail each time.

After a good hour of searching, she realized she had no clue where the seam was and headed home. The house was still a mess from the battle. How many days ago had it been? She couldn't remember. Someone had thought to close the door at least, which prevented looters from stripping the house. It was wedged in place and took some effort to push open, but she got in.

She stood in the front room surveying the damage caused by the fight and the police search of the premises. Had they found the attic security system? Exhausted, she climbed the stairs to their bedroom. The two weapons cases were gone, along with the computers that controlled the security system.

She sat on the bed, unsure what to do. She picked up her cell phone and tried Nordon for the fiftieth time. Still no answer. She tried

Eric and Samuel with the same result. Then she called the police station and asked for Grant. Her first two attempts resulted in no one knowing who he was. The third person informed her of the station he worked out of and gave the number. However, once connected, her request to speak with Grant was met by silence and then whispered words behind a covered receiver before she was transferred to someone else. When she was interrogated about her interest and connection to the detective, she just hung up. Did that mean he was in trouble? Maybe he was missing too. She refused to think about that, since he was with Nordon and they were trying to rescue Eric.

With no place to look and no one else to call, Nadina curled up on the bed and slept.

Chapter 7

Samuel called up spells he knew he'd need for the coming battle. Many had not been used in decades. He wanted to familiarize himself with the words so not to fumble them under stress. The resistance camp had successfully avoided detection, and with his spell to cover spells, he freely used his magic. It had taken time to adjust to Chevalon life, but it was beginning to feel more comfortable as each day passed. He wasn't so sure he liked the familiarity. He'd still rather be in Chicago.

"You silly old man," he grumbled to himself. How easily he was caught in the trappings of the other world. He had a prophecy to see fulfilled before he could ever again set foot in that strange but wonderful world.

It was late afternoon. Char was working with some of the newer recruits and Mathilda taught a small contingent about medical care. They would need to know it whether they wanted to believe her or not.

Swirling his arms to create a large flaming ball, he felt a tug from a distance. It was the pull on the ward he'd left at the seam when he crossed over. He lost his concentration and the flames dissipated into nothing.

"What does this mean?" he said aloud. The wards had been tripped at least five times since he'd been back. With all that activity, he wondered if Mortas was doing as Char had suggested: to leave

Chevalon for the unknown dimension of Chicago. If so, then they had unwittingly unleashed a tyrant into an unsuspecting world, while possibly making their objective in Chevalon that much easier to achieve. Too many loose threads for him to combine made his head hurt.

"Why can't any of this be easy?"

Samuel sat down on a nearby fallen tree, exhausted and sore from working all day. His arms ached and his shirt was soaked with sweat.

"There's one thing both dimensions have in common. The heat!" He chuckled and wiped his brow on his sleeve. Closing his eyes to concentrate on the disturbance he felt from the ward at the seam, Samuel was startled by a horrendous screeching noise from above.

"Seekers," he hissed. "Damn!"

Somehow his magic was detected, even as careful as he'd been.

Circling the trees were two black shadowy creatures. They were long and wispy and moved like strands of ribbon tossed in a storm. They howled and cried out, their senses detecting something unusual.

Him.

Slowly he slid next to a tree. He watched them swirl in the sky. Unworldly screeches echoed across the forest, sure to bring the attention of their masters. Samuel considered blasting them with his power, but if he missed one of them, he'd surely give himself away. The resistance needed him alive, and that was a sure way to make sure he wouldn't be.

To his left he heard someone shouting. Emerging from the brush was Mathilda, her hands glowing bright yellow.

"No, Mathilda! Don't give yourself away!"

She didn't heed his warning and fired a bolt of electricity upwards.

"Fool!" he grumbled. Stepping out into the open, he joined her. If they could dispatch the Seekers quickly, they might have a chance to save the camp.

Samuel conjured the fireball spell again, letting the intense heat fly from his hands upwards to the intended target. His shot went wide right and the Seeker spun in the air. Its ear-splitting scream dropped Samuel to the ground. He rolled to his back, intent on keeping the Seeker in his sights. Streams of yellow electricity screamed upwards from nearby, no doubt Mathilda doing her best to take down one of the Seekers. Samuel focused on the Seeker he'd missed and watched as it darted across the sky. Anticipating its moves, he let loose a massive fireball, knowing he was giving away the camp's location to those at Castle Frost.

The Seeker spun to avoid the fireball, but Samuel expected it and had already released another flame. It bore through the Seeker, burning a hole in its corporeal body. It bellowed loudly and fell to the ground. Samuel jumped to his feet and hesitated, bent at the waist to catch his breath. When he could breathe again, he raced toward where it had fallen.

The Seeker lay on the ground, smoke rising from the hole in its body. Despite the mortal wound, it stubbornly clung to life. When it caught sight of him, it clawed the dirt in an effort to come after him.

"Not today, vile beast!"

Samuel formed another ball of flame and fired it at the Seeker. It struck and incinerated the black creature, its death scream finally going silent.

He bent over, resting his hands on his knees and inhaling deeply. He wasn't prepared for such a battle already and was surprised by how badly his body reacted. Old age and too many bratwursts had taken their toll on him.

"Samuel, are you all right?" Mathilda raced toward him, her hands no longer glowing.

"I'm fine," he replied between shallow breaths.

"What happened? I thought you were hidden from their senses?"

"I don't know. They must've learned how to detect the undetectable. If that's the case, we're in grave danger."

"There were only two of them. Hopefully what we did will not be discovered until we make our move. I think the time for us to act has come. We can't hide out here much longer."

Samuel wanted to argue, but Mathilda was right. Whatever forces they had would have to do. The new recruits would be forced into the fray sooner than he wanted, but there was no other choice. If Elly was inside the castle, they owed it to her and the kingdom to act. They no longer had the luxury of time.

AFTER THE SKIRMISH, Mathilda and Samuel called the camp to a meeting.

Char rounded up all the fighters and made sure they were present for what Samuel insisted was their final directive. Once they were gathered, Samuel used his magic to project his voice so each person could hear him clearly.

"Today you witnessed the presence of two Seekers. With Mathilda's aid, we were able to destroy these vile things."

Several fighters offered up cheers and raised their fists in the air.

"As wonderful as this may seem, it also means we're in danger of being discovered. It's only a matter of time before those within the castle realize we're here. The time has come."

Those who previously applauded their destruction of the Seekers suddenly fell silent as the realization of the impending battle loomed. Death was certain to come for some of them, an unfortunate effect of what must be done.

"I'm ready!" the voice of a young girl in the back called out. "I'm ready to give my life for what's right. Mortas can't defeat us. We won't let him!"

Samuel smiled. Maybe there was hope for them after all, even with their small force.

Soon, others added their support and the camp grew to a wave of anticipation for the difficulties ahead.

"I do not want to mislead you. We go to this battle with death a real possibility for some of us. Our cause is just. The heirs must be saved and restored, or our world will be plunged into darkness."

"It already has been! Something must be done!" an older man called out. Heads nodded their agreement.

"We cannot be certain of anything other than our dedication to this cause," Samuel continued. He'd been building up to this for close to two decades. Knowing that his plan was nearing completion brought a sense of bittersweet victory to him. All the time spent in another dimension, hiding in wait, led to this moment.

"Princess Elysonde must be rescued before Mortas commits an unspeakable evil. The fate of our lands rests with us. Are you ready for what must be done?"

A raucous cheer rose from the group. They were ready. They were committed. They'd need to be. When they faced the terrors Rhoden would unleash in the name of his master, their mettle would be tested. He only hoped it was as firm as it was here and now.

"With the rising sun, we begin our march through the valley. Our path is clear. Our cause is noble. Enjoy this night, as tomorrow brings a danger unlike anything you've ever encountered. Be safe. In the morning, we move."

Gauging by the looks on Mathilda's and Char's faces, Samuel had outdone himself with his speech. The resistance filed out of the assembly with a confidence that Samuel hoped would buoy them during the bleakest times to come.

Chapter 8

DeWayne had been running and hiding since the craziness of the previous two days. He managed to get Rhoden to the seam, but as the cops closed in he knew it was a lost cause. If not for the beast's mayhem that drew the attention of every officer, he might be in jail or dead by now. He slipped away during the battle. As cops were being flung all over the street, he made his way from car to car until he was far enough from the scene to run as fast and hard as he'd ever run in his life.

He had a little of the money he'd cashed in with him, but the majority of it and the coins he'd been given were stashed in the van. He needed it to get out of the city. He had no ride and no home to return to. He couldn't take the chance that the cops didn't know his name. But where could he go? The first night he hid in a homeless community where pitched tents under a bridge offered somewhat of a safe haven. But the way the people watched his every move made him nervous. He feared being mugged and robbed.

Early the next morning he took to the streets again. He walked aimlessly for hours until with a start, he realized he was back in the residential neighborhood where Rhoden had sent his goons to assault the house where the prince was. He stared down the street remembering the battle, the cops, the destruction, the fear. The street looked so peaceful now.

A thought struck him. If everyone was gone or on the run, the house would be empty. There was probably some food. He could shower and get some sleep. The longer he thought about it, the better the idea sounded. His feet were already moving before he decided to go.

He climbed up the front steps, scanning for police who might be staking out the house. No one approached or challenged his presence. The door had been broken in and hung from the hinges. He pushed it open with his foot and listened for movement, prepared to run. There were no voices or sounds of running steps from inside. He poked his head in, scanned the room, and then scanned the street.

DeWayne entered with soft steps, keeping his ears alert for sudden sounds. He crept through the house, checking the dining room and the kitchen. The back door was wide open. He approached, searched the backyard, then closed and locked the door. Next he went upstairs. The three bedrooms were unoccupied. Relieved, he walked downstairs with new confidence and closed the front door. It took some effort, but he managed to wedge it inside the frame. It no longer locked, but that was all right. Anyone trying to get in would make noise.

Feeling more relaxed and somewhat secure, he went through the refrigerator finding ground beef. Burgers! His mouth watered profusely. He ripped open the package and pressed the meat into two massive balls, then flattened them into a large frying pan. As the meat spit and sizzled, he searched for bread, ketchup and mustard, and found a package of American cheese.

He was too hungry to allow the meat to cook beyond medium rare. He slapped cheese on the burgers, placed the oversized patties between slices of bread, and gulped it down. The first bites were so big he had trouble chewing and swallowing. Once the food hit his stomach, he slowed to savor the meal. Afterward, he was spent. He climbed the stairs, took a room on the right, and crashed.

He slept for hours. When he woke, he showered and put on clothes he found hanging in the closet. He went downstairs and ate three bowls of cereal. He sat in the front room and watched TV as he ate. The news was full of stories about the strange events of the past few days. DeWayne scoffed. If they only knew how strange.

He hung out inside all day, enjoying several meals before crashing for the night. He was awakened the next day by the sound of the outer door creaking open. He listened for a few moments to be sure, but when he heard creaking stairs, he knew he was no longer alone. He slid off the bed and hid behind it.

The door to the room opened. He tried not to breathe. It closed a moment later. Was it the police? A looter? Maybe the family who lived there had returned. He had no idea, but his brain worked in overdrive to find a way out.

He heard someone enter the bedroom across the hall. Time crawled by. DeWayne waited, afraid to move and make noise. A short time later, there was a sound he did not recognize. He strained to hear but could not make it out. He pressed to hands and knees, waited, and when no one responded, he got slowly to his feet. Each step took him closer to the door, but he waited longer between them. He pressed his ear to the wood panel. Though not as loud as before, he now knew what he had heard. Whoever had come inside was crying.

He gave it a few more minutes and turned the knob, gritting his teeth at anticipating the door screech. To his relief, the door not only didn't creak, but it was closed.

With careful steps toward the outer edges of the hall and stairs, he proceeded down. He reached the first landing when a voice commanded, "Stop, or I will fire."

Chapter 9

It wasn't quite dark yet, but Elly was done running for the day. Shree looked exhausted too.

"We need to rest. I know it's been a hard day," she said.

"But what about those things chasing us?"

"It's been hours since we last saw them. I think we lost them. If not, I don't know what to do. I can't touch the power. I've been trying but all I get is frustrated."

Shree put her arm around her. "I know. I'm so sorry, Elly. I wish there was something I could do to help."

"Yeah, me too."

The girls found a fallen log and laid large sticks across the top to create a small shelter. It wasn't much, but they'd grown accustomed to close, tight quarters.

"Good thing it's not cold here. Can you imagine what it would be like in the winter?"

Elly giggled. "Yeah, I bet it sucks."

Shree's stomach grumbled and Elly raised an eyebrow.

"Hungry?"

"You know how long it's been since we had something to eat. Can't we go to a city or village? Surely there's got to be a place we can go around here."

"I don't feel safe. This Rhoden dude really wants me dead. Same with his boss man. They've got people everywhere."

Not long ago, the girls found out the hard way just how penetrating the reach of their adversaries was. They had stumbled on a village midday. Smoke rose from the chimneys and farmers were out tending fields and livestock. A few older ladies gave them sideways glances, but no one else seemed to care.

"What do you suppose this place is?" Shree asked. They followed what Elly thought was the main road into the village. It was wide enough for carts, evidenced by the deep ruts in the mud.

"A town or something. If we only had money, maybe we could find somewhere to stay. Like at an inn or something," Elly said.

"Oh God, that would be amazing!"

The girls strolled into the village and stopped at a large grassy square in the middle. Small buildings surrounded the perimeter; most of them shops.

She didn't notice him at first, but later Elly kicked herself for not recognizing the man in black with a snowflake on his chest. He was a loyal guard of Mortas Frost. They'd seen the sigil at the castle before they'd escaped.

The man slunk around the buildings, hiding within the shadows, until he'd crept close enough to apprehend them.

"What the hell, man?" Elly said. Then she noticed the snowflake.

"Shree, run!"

The girls bolted away from him, Elly desperately trying to grasp the power to no avail. Mounting frustration with her lack of skill made her wish she'd never had the power to begin with.

Shree raced ahead, then spun on the man, kicking his legs out from underneath him.

The man struggled to right himself, his foot getting caught in a rut in the hard-packed dirt. Shree stepped forward and planted a kick under his chin and the man dropped.

The girls raced away without turning back. Leaving the village was difficult. Elly knew how badly they needed food and shelter, but it wasn't going to happen. Not at the moment, anyway. The guard had made it clear that even in tiny no-name villages, the bad guys still held the power.

The girls left the village and traveled in the forest afterwards, their only other contact being the rock creatures and the flying demons.

"Shree, I feel something weird."

"Maybe it's hunger. It does all kinds of fun things to a body. Did you know you can only go five days without food?"

"No, it's not that. It's something else. It's like I feel a vibration in the air. It's—" Elly pulled her tunic up. She'd long gotten past modesty with Shree.

Sliding the brown fabric above her thigh, a faint glow shone from underneath. When she uncovered the half-moon scar on her side, both girls gasped.

Its glow was like a burning lightbulb under her skin.

"Why does it do that?" Shree asked.

Elly shook her head, scared out of her mind because her skin illuminated like the bat signal. "I don't know. Am I sick? Maybe something's wrong with me."

"It has to be with your powers, right? Like it's got to be connected somehow."

"Maybe. If so, it's not helping me touch the power."

"Does it hurt?"

Elly shook her head. "Not at all. Actually, it kinda feels…I know this is gonna sound strange, but it's kinda soothing. It's like it calms me. I can't explain why."

"Calming? Girl, that doesn't make any sense. But who am I to question? You're the one with the power. I'm just here for company."

"I don't think so. We're here for a reason. There has to be one."

"Yeah. Because that guy kidnapped us and brought us here. They're under some delusion that you're a princess. If they ever saw you scarf down a meal, they'd think otherwise."

Elly traced her finger along the bright scar. The skin there felt no different than the rest of her, except it glowed. She had no idea why.

Then, as both girls were in awe of the moon, it winked out and left the slightly discolored scar she'd known since she was a little girl.

"Where'd it go?"

"It just vanishes."

"And it doesn't hurt at all?"

"Nope. It's the weirdest thing."

They waited several moments until they grew bored staring at Elly's skin. She covered it with her tunic.

"You know that feeling I had earlier?"

Shree nodded.

"It's gone now. Something isn't right. I don't understand what any of it means, but things are getting weird."

The girls lay down to rest, though Elly's mind wouldn't settle. While Shree finally fell asleep, Elly was awake.

Since their arrival in this strange land, Elly had felt different. The first moment she touched the power and created something with it made her freak out. She kept it in check as much as possible, but when bolts of power and air emanated from her, it was difficult to process.

The glowing scar meant something. It was more than a coincidence that her scar was in the shape of a half moon and lit up like a lamp. As much as she wanted to deny it, maybe what those weird dudes were telling her was true. What if she were a princess, and one with magical powers? But if so, what did that mean about her parents? Did they lie to her? It was a difficult line of questioning, especially after her father's death. That is, if he truly was her father.

The guy Rhoden said she had a brother. Her endless questions kept her awake. She listened to the nocturnal animals and strange forest noises. It was too much for her to rest. She'd be tired the next day, but it couldn't be helped. There was too much going on in her head for her to settle down. Shree would have to take charge. They'd make it.

Sometime during the dark hours of the morning, her scar glowed again, visible under her tunic. But this time, something else happened.

She felt a gentle tugging. She was startled and considered waking Shree, but decided against it, knowing at least one of them would need to be well rested.

Elly stared at her scar. The tug she felt wasn't physical, but from the magic she so desperately wanted to know more about. It called to her, beckoned her west. It was like it was calling her to a specific place.

She wanted to follow the thread before it vanished. Her scar went dark again, but the pull remained, though slightly weaker. She could still follow it, and that was all that mattered. Sleep eluded her the rest of the night. When Shree was finally awakened by the sounds of animals fighting in the distance, Elly was ready to go.

They headed west. Elly was sure they'd find what they needed.

Chapter 10

The tall black man halted, but his body wavered like he would either bolt or faint. "If you take another step, you'll tumble the rest of the way. Back up to the wall and put your hands on top of your head." Nadina waited, finger already squeezing the trigger. "Last chance."

He complied.

As the man backed against the wall, Nadina got a better look at his face. Something was familiar about him. It came to her then. "You're the van driver." He started at the recognition. "Why are you here? Looking for a little revenge from being carjacked?"

"Ah, n-no ma'am."

"Well?"

"I-I just needed a place to crash."

"So you came here? That doesn't make sense. Or maybe you just figured since we were gone, you could waltz right in and clean out the place. Did you take the gun cases?"

His face scrunched in confusion. "Gun cases? No. I never saw any gun cases. I'm not here to rob you. Honestly, I needed a place to sleep, and-and yes, I thought this house was empty. Otherwise I never would have come inside." He added hastily, "I swear. You can see I'm not carrying anything."

Nadina doubted his being here was anything so simple, but she was too tired, too drained, and too defeated to care. With everything she'd been through over the past few days she didn't want to deal with any new problems. And she definitely didn't want to add more bodies to the count. "Go on. Get out of here. Don't come back, or I will shoot you."

The man hesitated, suspecting a trap. She motioned with her gun. "Go. Now." She turned around and walked toward the bedroom. His footsteps pounded fast and hard down the stairs. "And close the door on the way out."

She entered the room and sat on the bed. Her mind whirled, but she forced it blank. As she lay, down a sudden thought fought its way through. Hadn't Grant said a young black man was helping Rhoden?

Nadina bolted up and flew from the room, taking the stairs in huge leaps. She reached the door and yanked, ripping it from the frame. She flung it to the floor, ran outside, and jumped down the front stairs. As soon as her feet touched down she was moving. Left. Right. No sign. Where had he gone? She ran to the corner and scanned the side street. Still no sign of him. The pressure built in her brain. On the verge of exploding, she jogged to the right, to the spot where they'd first encountered the man when Nordon stopped the van and they made their escape.

She had never seen him in the neighborhood before. It couldn't be a coincidence that he was there. He had to be the same man aiding Rhoden. She looked down the alley toward her house, then whipped around to look the other direction. She saw him turning the corner on the next block.

Nadina broke into a run, pushing beyond her limits of speed and remaining endurance. Years of endless training and constant conditioning fueled by the frustration and rage welling deep in her core would not allow her to lose this man. This enemy.

She didn't slow through the turn. The man was thirty yards in front of her. Hearing her approach, he looked back over his shoulder. His eyes widened and he shot off. His long legs gave him an advantage at first, but Nadina was not about to quit. If this was the man helping Rhoden, he had information she needed that might lead her to Eric. The thought of her son choked her up for a moment, but she couldn't allow anything to slow her down. She cleared her mind again and focused on her target.

Briefly the man's lead increased, but it became apparent to Nadina that she was in better shape than he. She kept a steady pace and the gap lessened as the man faltered. She closed within five yards and the man tried to speak.

"You—said—I—could," he huffed and sucked air through a ragged throat, "go."

She pulled up next to him, lifting her gun, and said, "I changed my mind. Now move up against that wall." She pointed to a brick wall. They were in an alley behind a row of commercial buildings.

"I'm not going to make it easy for you to shoot me. If you're gonna kill me, you're gonna have to do it on the run."

The comment angered Nadina. She didn't want to shoot him. At least not yet. But he was going to stop one way or another. She lowered the gun, dashed a few steps in front of him and whirled around, planting a kick into his midsection. The man doubled over, lost his balance, and fell hard. His hands hit first, but he couldn't keep his body up. His knees banged hard on the concrete and he rolled several times, ripping clothes and skin on the debris that had collected on the alley surface. When he stopped, he lay spread eagle and panted hard like he was having a coronary. He was bleeding from several places.

Nadina put her hands on her knees and fought for her own breath. It took a full minute before she could function. She stood upright, placed her hands behind her head, and drew in long, deep breaths until her body no longer demanded huge quantities of air and her racing heart slowed. The man still had not moved other than to suck in air.

A step forward placed her above him. She aimed the gun but his eyes were closed. Sweat and blood coated his face. If not for the ragged breathing, she'd have thought him dead. She cocked the hammer back to get his attention. It did the trick. His eyes flew open and widened to the point of popping, and he rolled on his side, like the move would prevent the bullet from entering him.

"I have some questions for you."

"Okay. Okay. Anything you want. Just please don't kill me."

"Why shouldn't I? You're working for Rhoden, aren't you?" She gave him no chance to reply. "You're just as responsible as he is for my son's capture. You're going to help me find him, or I swear, I'll shoot every joint on your body and leave you here for the rats to finish off."

He cowered under her glare and the ominous bore of the handgun. "Tell me where the seam is." She'd passed through the seam fifteen years ago and hadn't been back since. Everything had happened so fast and the new world was so overwhelming. She had no idea where it could be, and she had searched for it.

"The seam?"

"You heard me. You know exactly what I'm talking about."

"Ah, sure. Okay." He relaxed. "I can tell you."

"No. I need you to show me."

"But I, ah—"

"You have a problem with that?" she inched the gun closer to his head.

"No, No. That's cool. I can show you."

"Then get up."

The man sat up and grimaced. "I'm bleeding."

"Imagine how much more you'll bleed if you don't do what I say."

He got to his feet but not without theatrics. He truly was bleeding. From several places, in fact. But she was beyond caring. This man had helped Rhoden capture her son. She had no sympathy and would show no mercy. He would take her to the seam or feel pain. Lots of pain. And God forgive her, she'd enjoy inflicting it.

Chapter 11

Samuel barely slept at all the night before they were to begin their advance. Far too often his mind wandered to the finer points of life in Chicago that he missed dearly. And something about Char's suggestion nagged at him.

Back in the other world in the land of Chicago, he'd roamed the streets of downtown. Noisy traffic was constant. People pushed their way across the sidewalks. The L screeched overhead. Skyscrapers towered over the buildings on street level. It was a place of confusion and anonymity. He could be in the middle of a crowd and not be seen.

The shops along Michigan Avenue beckoned for attention, though after realizing the money they were asking for their wares was far more than he could spend, he ignored the shiny objects.

The homeless were everywhere. They called out to him for money, though he had little to spare. Once, he gave a dirt-covered woman a ten dollar bill out of pity and watched as she bought a pack of cigarettes from a nearby convenience store. That was the last time he gave in to the needy clambering for his limited funds.

In the midst of the cacophony of downtown Chicago, he often felt uneasy. He lived with a fair amount of nervous energy, expecting to meet his end at any moment by the hand of a random stranger. After discovering Mortas and Rhoden had crossed the seam, he was even more worried they may be after him. He felt confident they didn't know who the twins were, but they would have a better chance of finding him even after he'd altered his appearance.

The resistance was created for one purpose: to defy Mortas Frost and restore the kingdom to the heirs. If the King and Queen were dead, that meant the twins. The last he knew, both were alive. Elly had been taken by Mortas and Eric should be in the hands of his protectors. When Samuel crossed through the seam and traveled north, he knew the reality.

Finding Mathilda and the forces she created was both gratifying and anxiety-inducing. He was thankful they followed a rough version of his plan to build soldiers and hide from the terror unleashed by Frost and Rhoden. The land certainly created a sense of fear and dismay like he'd never known before under the reign of King Artus. It felt like a dark force weighed down on the people and their land.

The resistance created a haven for those seeking a return to normalcy and a safe place to live in the new chaotic order ushered in by Frost. Mathilda did well enough with what little instruction he left behind. There was simply no time for him to oversee the entire operation, not when he was in another dimension doing his best to ensure the heirs were safe. Their disagreements often forced him to back down as he realized Mathilda's investment in their success was far greater than his, another point he didn't anticipate.

More and more, he worried about his own ability to carry out the mission as he continued to find instances when he didn't see the next move.

When he lived in Chicago, he discovered the game of chess. It was similar to a game they played in Chevalon and he enjoyed the strategy involved. Players needed to have foresight of their opponents' schemes in order to counter moves not yet made. It took him a little while to learn the rules, but he persevered while playing against a computer simulation on a tablet. He played against a few people down at Reyes Park, It was a passing phase, and he gave it up in order to focus on his true reason for being in the city.

But when he did play, he had an uncanny ability to guess what his opponent would do at least three moves ahead. It helped him defeat the computer's highest levels and come close to beating some of the best human players he faced at the park.

How he couldn't translate those skills to his true cause flustered him to no end. Several times since he'd been back, he realized how inadequate his foreshadowing of the possible outcomes for Mortas's and Rhoden's actions. It was like he'd been cut off from seeing the options and could only focus on one or two possibilities. When he discovered the missed outcomes, the frustration only mounted.

Perhaps that was part of the reason he slept so terribly.

It was dark outside and Samuel's mind was already exhausted from lack of sleep and constant worry over his own mental state, not to mention the actions of the coming days.

"Calm down, you old man. You've done the best you can," he scolded himself. He wiped his face in a vain attempt to clear the fog from his brain. The only thing he could think of was Char's suggestion.

How terrible would it be to take those willing to leave back across the seam and settle in the new dimension? They didn't all have to go to Chicago. The world was huge and there were plenty of attractive locations for them to live. Why not remove them from the evil and place them somewhere better? He found it amazing and alluring, so why wouldn't they? Why did he get to enjoy it all and they had to remain here? He nearly convinced himself it was the right thing to do.

"But this is home. This is where we belong. This should be our priority. It must be. What I've done over these years is grow this movement in order to destroy Mortas Frost and restore the heirs to their rightful place. All of my work has led to this. We cannot flee when things get tough," he said to the darkness. *But you did, and you want to again. How long are you going to pretend that you aren't going back to Chicago when this is over and live out the rest of your days there?*

Samuel waved the thought away and got out of bed. He stretched, his old bones creaking. Sleep was done for the night. His mind had wandered too far to return to silent rest. Whatever awaited them in the daylight would come soon enough, and his mind had to be ready for anything. Sleep eluded him. Instead he turned to predicting the various outcomes, hoping to avoid missing something like he'd been doing lately.

By the time Mathilda and Char appeared at his tent with the rising sun, he'd been through so many scenarios that he felt confident he'd not missed a thing. If he did, then it was completely random and out of his control. Those problems would always find a way to present themselves, but with enough careful planning, they should weather the storms.

"Are you ready?" Char asked. The large man's gruff voice was strained.

"Yes. There is no other way."

Mathilda nodded. "The resistance has long waited for this day. It's our first step to liberate Chevalon from the evil wrought by Mortas Frost. I don't intend to repeat what happened at our northern camp. We will not back down. With us being so close, once our surprise is sprung, I will not hold back my power. We've got at least four others from the Order within our ranks. I've kept them hidden from the rest, hoping to spare the temptation to turn them in. I know we've all pledged to the heirs, but gold has a way of making one forget their promises."

"We have more from the Order? Here? Why haven't you told me?" Samuel's agitation at not knowing such vital information was obvious.

"I've done much to keep the resistance together in your absence. You didn't need to know everything upon your return."

"I've been back long enough. I should have been informed of a development such as this."

Mathilda shrugged. "Now you know. When the time comes, they will strike with a deadly ferocity. Count on it."

"You need to tell me these things. Anything else you've kept to yourself that might come in handy as we march to our enemy's doorstep?" Samuel smoothed his clothes, missing the sweatshirts and jeans from the other dimension. If they didn't go back to Chicago, maybe he could bring some of his favorite things to this world.

He could tell he had touched a sensitive nerve with Mathilda, but the time for empathy was over. All the information, good or bad, must be dealt with now before they found themselves knee deep in a battle.

Mathilda gritted her teeth. "Nothing more, old man," she hissed.

"Our people are ready. Once we pack up the camp, we're free to move. I'll give the order," Char said. His words broke the tension.

"Good. Let's move quickly, then," Samuel replied. Mathilda scowled at him but followed Char back into the camp.

Samuel wiped his forehead. He didn't like supplanting Mathilda, not after she gave herself over to the resistance like she did, but none of this would be happening if it weren't for him. It was his plan to execute, and he'd do it his way; with modification, of course, but still according to his will. Mathilda had done a marvelous job of opposing Mortas Frost. She'd built a community where people felt safe from the tyranny in the land. They knew what was to come and most were eager to pay the ultimate price if and when the time came. She seemed much more capable to handle those deaths than he did.

Within an hour of their brief meeting, the entire camp was packed up into leather bags and slung across the backs of the members of the resistance. They'd grown in the past couple of days. There were close to seventy fighters now, Char's recruitment efforts in the nearby villages paying off. They'd lost so many up north and Samuel worried they had nothing left to fight with. Seeing these new numbers buoyed his confidence. Knowing there were four other members from the Order hidden amongst their ranks helped too.

He should have known Mortas did not wipe out the Order. They were too well-entrenched in Chevalon to roll over and let him do what he wanted. They had to stay hidden of course, but they were not going to flee. *Like you did?* he asked himself.

But he didn't flee out of cowardice. He left to protect the living assets and secure their future. He didn't run like a coward; he stole away with the most precious commodity left in the land: the heirs. Once restored to rule the land, all the evil and horrific things brought on by Mortas Frost would vanish. The heirs and their ability to work magic like those of the Order were sure portents of the prosperity and peace to come. But first they had to secure them from Mortas's wretched hands.

They had no direct evidence that Elly was in the castle. Their entire operation was based on an educated guess. Even if she wasn't there, they'd take control of Mortas Frost's seat of power, and that would go a long way toward smashing his regime. It was a win no matter what and when Mathilda suggested this course of action on their long march south from the northern stronghold, Samuel at first rejected the idea but then grew to understand her vision. The castle's fall would show everyone that Mortas wasn't invincible. It could create a wave of support from those too frightened to join them before. So much was riding on this operation and if they were to safely secure the princess, it was one step closer to finally overthrowing Mortas.

Chapter 12

They used Alyanna's car. At her insistence, he got in the driver's seat without a seat belt—also her decision. "That'll keep you from crashing the car. Also, you already know you can't outrun me, but if you do try, it won't be me chasing you, but a nine millimeter. You understand?"

He nodded. His skin was ashen.

"Now, take out your ID."

"Huh?"

"You heard me. Take it out or I'll cut it out of your pocket." She produced her knife. It was all the incentive he needed. She took his license out, studied it a moment, then rifled through the wallet. No credit cards but a few hundred dollars in cash. "So DeWayne, is this your bounty for leading Rhoden to my son?"

He didn't answer. She ripped the money from the wallet and pitched it out the window.

"Oh man, I'm cooperating. You didn't have to do that."

"I'm sorry, DeWayne. I'm not myself at the moment. I get that way," her voice escalated and she sat closer, "when people try to kill me and kidnap my family." She was inches from him now. "I'm looking for an excuse to shoot you, so yeah, DeWayne, I had to do it to release some of my pent up anger. Otherwise..." She waggled the gun in front of him. It was for show, yet she hoped he was dumb enough to make a move. He didn't and she sat back.

"Drive."

He started the engine and pulled away from the curb. She kept the ID but tossed the wallet out the window. Fifteen minutes later, the car slowed. Nadina looked around expectantly. "What? Why are you slowing?"

"I assumed you didn't want me to drive up to the police."

She looked down the road. Police cars and other assorted vehicles filled the street. Crime scene tape was stretched out to mark several crime scenes. "Where is the seam?"

He braked and pointed. "In that lot between the two buildings where all the cops are standing."

She had not looked there. From the description she'd been given, she thought it was in a different section of the city. No wonder she hadn't found anything. She sat back in the seat and tried to think, too much pain and anxiety blocked the flow of thought.

"Ah, lady, there's a cop coming."

Nadina looked up four car lengths ahead and saw a female cop approaching. She had one hand on the butt of her weapon and her head lowered to better see the occupants. DeWayne was nervous; perhaps afraid she would turn him in to the police. She should too, but if she did, she'd be cut off from any information he had. "Back out of here and do it slowly so you don't draw attention."

He shifted, but the cop quickened her step and shouted. "Hold it! Stop!" The gun was halfway out of the holster.

DeWayne looked to her for what to do. "Stop. Otherwise she'll get the license and we'll be on the run."

He braked, but clearly did not like the decision.

"Lower the window," the cop said.

DeWayne did.

"What are you doing here?"

Nadina thought quick. "We were heading for that parking garage down the street."

"Okay, then why'd you stop?"

"Sorry. We were just curious. That's a lot of police cars. Can you tell me what happened?"

"No. Let me see some ID." She wiggled her fingers at them.

That wasn't what Nadina wanted, but to refuse was to garner even more attention. She dug out her ID and handed it and DeWayne's across. The no-nonsense officer studied each and squinted back at their faces. A voice crackled over her shoulder mic. She stepped away and responded. Seconds later she handed the licenses back. "I don't want to see you hanging around here again. Understood? This is an active crime scene. Take an alternate route to the garage."

"Yes ma'am," Nadina said.

She stepped back and watched them go. Dwayne backed up, then did a U-turn. Nadina watched the officer in the mirror. To her dismay, the woman took out something from her shirt pocket and made a notation. She had the license plate number and knew their names. She did not want to give her any reason to check up on them further.

DeWayne made the turns and Nadina decided they'd better go to the garage in case the officer followed. It would give her time to think. What if Eric somehow got away? Maybe he was with the police right now. She wished Nordon would answer his phone. She needed his advice, his wisdom, his strength.

She directed DeWayne to enter the parking garage and go up a couple levels. She found a spot where there were other cars and had DeWayne park. She waved her hand in front of him. "Key."

He placed it in her hand. "Now what?"

"Now you stay quiet while I think."

Nadina exited the car. "Stay inside." She walked to the front of the car and paced as her brain raced through scenarios. If the police had Eric, where would they take him? Grant's base station was the most likely place. She needed to find it. What if Eric was injured? He might be in the hospital. Her mind went further. What if Rhoden killed him and dropped him on the side of the road someplace? If Rhoden already had Elysande, did he need Eric too?

No. she couldn't think like that. Eric was still alive. He had to be.

The only solution was to talk to the cops. Before she did, however, she needed to know she had every bit of information DeWayne knew. She faced the car and glared at the man through the windshield. He blanched at the sudden attention, sinking lower in the seat.

She started toward him, wondering the best approach. Nice or violent? She very much wanted to be extremely violent, but unless he believed cooperating was his best chance of survival, he'd clam up and give her nothing.

She opened the door. "DeWayne. We need to talk. Step out here."

He hesitated, shrinking away from her. His face was a study of fear, his expression reaching new levels of horror. "DeWayne. I'm being nice. Don't make me be angry. Please." She had to admit, if the roles were reversed and she heard the menacing tone of her voice, she'd be afraid too. Good. He should be afraid.

She stepped back to allow him room to get out without fear of being attacked. Tentatively he unfolded his long frame out of the car and stood with the open door separating them. Her face twitched. If she felt it, he surely noticed. "Relax," she said more for her benefit than his. "I need to ask you some questions. The only chance you have of getting out of here intact is to tell me everything you know about Rhoden's coming and goings."

"Sure, but all I know is what I already showed you. That was the seam he used. I was supposed to wait for him down the road with a vehicle. I never knew when he was coming. He'd just show up."

Nadina watched his face for tells that he was lying. She was no expert but given his stress level, she thought DeWayne was telling the truth. What other questions could she ask?

"Look, lady, I'm sorry. If I'd have known what that nut job was going to do I never would have agreed to help him."

"Yeah, but you did—and you took money for doing it. Your apology means nothing to me." Her anger was rising again. She fought the urge to backhand him with the handgun. She stepped back from him, no longer feeling in control of her emotions or actions.

DeWayne must have sensed her inner conflict and realized his chance of survival was slim. Taking advantage of her momentary lapse, he charged her. His move took Nadina by surprise. He bowled into her, latching onto the gun and her wrist. His strength was amplified by his desperation. He fought like a demon; like his life depended on it.

Which, in fact, it did.

Nadina was angry that she had allowed her kidnapper to get the upper hand. He used his superior weight to push her back, pinning her against the next car. He leveraged his height to bend her backwards. The gun angled toward her head.

No! This was not going to happen. Nadina regrouped her thoughts and cleared her mind. She had trained for just such a moment.

With all his weight bearing down on her, he had no balance. In a quick move, she slid to the right. His body plunged forward, smacking into the car. She kicked the back of his knee and buckled his leg. As his body lowered, she released the gun with one hand, placed it behind his head, and slammed his face into the roof of the car. His body slackened as his muscles relaxed.

With a hard pull, she ripped the gun from his weakened grip, smashed his head into the door as his body slumped, and aimed at the back of his head. Her hands shook with rage. She became aware of her own whimpering.

The sudden sound of a voice behind her almost made her pull the trigger. "Don't, Dina." She whirled as the large man closed on her. He grabbed her gun hand and pulled it to the side, then engulfed her in an embrace and held her against his chest. "It's okay, my love," Nordon said. "I think he's out."

Chapter 13

The morning passed quietly enough. Elly debated whether she should tell Shree about her experience overnight but decided against it for now. They'd been through a lot and telling her friend they were now following a thread of magic to an unknown destination might be too much. They'd already been heading that way, but now Elly had a reason.

The one thing that did worry her was the possibility that the beacon was from Rhoden. He was clearly skilled with magic. What if he'd found them or sent out some kind of magical radar and discovered them through Elly's use of the power? He could see her attention to the power as a sign to him and pull them toward a trap.

"Shree, we need to rest."

The girls trudged through thick shrubs, branches scratching up their legs under their tunics.

"Yeah, I'm good with that."

They had no water or food and their bodies felt the struggle. Elly still felt the line of power, though she couldn't fully grasp it.

"How do you think we're gonna get home? You think we can find someone to help us?" Shree asked.

"I hope so. This is the way we got here. It has to be the way back, right?"

"It's better than nothing."

After about thirty minutes, they got moving again.

Elly let the invisible pull direct them. She could tell they were getting closer as the day wore on. The intensity of the pull grew as they travelled west. It felt stronger and inescapable. Again, she wondered if it really was Rhoden calling her to him.

Loud crashes in the distances stopped them in their tracks. Something snapped like branches breaking in a storm.

"What's that?" Shree asked.

Elly closed her eyes and focused on the sound. She felt the tug calling her, the line nearly visible to her mind. Then she reached for the power and she touched it. Her mind raced and her heartbeat faster. She touched it! But that was all she could do. She held it carefully like a delicate thread but couldn't do anything more with it. The buffer she felt still prevented her from bending it to her will. When she opened her eyes, Shree was staring at her.

"Where'd you go? I asked you a question and then you fell in a trance or something. Are you all right?"

Elly furrowed her brow. "Yeah. Why are you freaking out? I was trying to touch the power. I wanted to see if I could discover what's making that sound."

"You've been out like fifteen minutes! Whatever's out there has gotten closer and you've just been standing there doing nothing."

"I have? That long? I'm sorry, Shree. I had no idea. Where is that thing now?"

"Beats me. It stopped a few minutes ago. The last I heard, it was coming from over there." She pointed toward the northeast.

"Then we keep going that way," Elly replied, pointing west. If the magical line pulling her could be seen, she knew she was pointing directly at it.

They turned from the source of their fright and remained on the course they'd traveled all day. Shree occasionally turned back in search of the disruption, but whatever it was seemed to pass them by.

"Elly, are you sure this is the way? You'd think we'd be there already."

"I guarantee it. We'll come to it sooner or later."

"How are you so sure? You've never been here before."

"Look up. The sun moves the same as in our world. The cardinal directions are the same. I've been keeping an eye on where the sun is in the sky compared to our location. This is the reverse of where we've come."

"Look at you, you little scout!"

The girls laughed. Elly felt the pull grow even stronger. They were clearly on the right path, whatever it might be.

"It'll be fine, Shree, I promise. I don't intend to get into more trouble. If we stay alert, we'll be fine."

"I hope so. With you not being able to use your power whenever you want, we're at a disadvantage. Hey, has your scar glowed again?"

Elly hesitated. "Nope, not since last time." She hated lying to her friend, but would she understand? Maybe. Or maybe she'd get mad and want to try something else. Elly had to find out what was calling her, whether it was a trap from Rhoden or not.

They traveled for another hour or so before they found shelter for the evening. When they awoke in the morning, both girls were refreshed, a feeling they hadn't had in quite some time. Elly was ready to lead them to their destination, knowing it was close.

They were about half an hour from where they'd spent the night. The birds called to each other in the forest and the sun tried to force its way through gray clouds. Elly's stomach rumbled. She couldn't remember her last meal. Her body was fueled only by adrenaline.

"Elly, I'm so hungry. I don't have much strength. Can't we find a house or something? There's got to be food, right? I'm not made to go days without something to eat."

"I promise you, Shree, we're close to where we need to be."

"I get that you can follow direction based on the sun, but how can you be so confident that we're going to the exact place we need to?"

Elly was done. Her secret had been hidden long enough. She trusted Shree; why not trust her with the truth?

"I know because…" she paused, inhaling deep, "I can feel it."

"What do you mean?" Shree stopped walking and turned to her. "Come on, Elly, what are you saying?"

"I mean I can feel a pull. Something that can touch the power. It's like a beacon. It has been pulling me for a while now. It's been getting stronger and more powerful. We're almost there."

"Why didn't you tell me this before? What if it's a trap or something? You know how badly this Rhoden guy wants us!"

"I know. I should've told you sooner. I've thought about it and don't think it's him. I hope it's not."

"But you aren't sure?"

"No, I'm not." Elly hung her head. "It's just a feeling, I guess. But I don't think it's him."

"Damn, Elly! You gotta trust me with these things! Our lives are at stake here. We're friends!"

"I know. I'm sorry, Shree. I should've said something sooner. It's been nagging at me ever since I felt it. You have every right to know."

Shree shook her head, her hands on her hips. She wiped the sweat off her brow. "Ok, then. What does it feel like?"

Elly let out the deep breath she'd been holding. They were gonna be fine. "I can feel magic leading us this way." She pointed west, the direction they'd been going for a couple days. "It's like a rope or something."

"What do we do if it is Rhoden and he's trying to trap us? You can't do much with your power unless somehow you can grab it again."

"I don't know. I guess as we get closer, we gotta watch out for him. And there's something else, Shree."

The girl scowled at her. "Go on."

"My scar."

"What about it?"

"Two nights ago, it glowed in the middle of the night and the pull was intense. I felt an overwhelming sensation of comfort and safety while it glowed. I know it sounds weird, but I don't think this is Rhoden calling us. It's got to be someone else, someone wanting to help us. What other explanation is there?"

"A feeling? That's what's leading us?"

"Yeah. It has so far."

Shree slowly nodded. "True. I guess we have no other choice, do we?"

"There are always choices. It's up to us to make the right ones."

"I suppose it is. And you're confident this invisible calling isn't harmful to us?"

"I'm pretty sure. If it's the same thing that made my scar glow, then yes, we're safe."

"I hope so. I wanna go home. I wanna get a burger and fries. I wanna sleep in my bed again. I want out of here."

Elly smiled. "Me too. Come on, we're close now. It's not much farther."

Chapter 14

As her body relaxed hearing her husband's familiar voice, the sobs erupted from deep within her core, each one tearing at her soul. He held her until she was cried out. His touch gave her comfort and renewed strength. Even after her tears ceased, she kept her head against his massive chest her to the heavy beat of his heart. The rhythm had a soothing effect. She pushed back, tilting her tear-streaked face upward. He brushed a finger tenderly against her cheek. Though he smiled down at her, no warmth shown in his eyes. That brought her back to the current situation and a hard knot formed in her stomach.

"Eric?" she said, hope still clinging to the word.

His smile faded and the eyes narrowed. He didn't have to answer. She knew the truth. He shook his head.

"We were not in time."

Her legs gave way. If not for being in his arms she would have fallen next to DeWayne.

"I promise, Dina, we will get him back."

"How? We can't get close to the seam and even if we could, how do we open it?"

"We'll find a way."

It was then she became aware of the others standing behind Nordon. She peeked around his huge frame. Kol and Alyanna stood watching. Alyanna nodded. Kol gave an awkward wave.

"This fellow looks familiar," Nordon said.

Nadina turned and looked down at the unconscious man. "He should. He was working with Rhoden. He was the one you carjacked when we escaped the house."

Nordon's eyes hardened. His nostrils flared. He bent and scooped DeWayne's inert body from the ground like he was light as a feather and dangled him from his fingertips.

"Don, I know you want to throttle him, but he may have information we need to get Eric back."

With Herculean effort, arms shaking, he set DeWayne down and pushed him upright against the car, then smacked his face until he stirred. If he was afraid of Nadina, the sight of Nordon standing in front of him must have horrified him. He stammered incessantly like his sanity had fled.

"With one twist of my hand, your neck will snap. You'll cease to exist. The only thing keeping you alive is that you might be useful. Once you stop being useful..." He snapped his fingers. The loud pop was all the image DeWayne needed.

"I'll tell you anything. I swear. Everything I know. I-I just don't know much."

"We'll see about that." Nordon released him. DeWayne slid down the car to the ground and he pulled his knees to his chest and bawled like a reprimanded child.

Nordon and Nadina stepped away and joined Alyanna and Kol. "Do either of you remember how we passed through the seam?"

Alyanna shook her head. "It was so long ago and happened so fast, I barely registered I was in another dimension."

"Kol, you passed through the most recently. What can you tell us?"

Kol said, "I didn't even know those things existed until Phetrix opened the seam and we stepped through. I think you have to be a wizard to make it appear. Do any of you know magic?"

No one responded.

"There has to be a way," Nordon said.

"Did you actually see Rhoden take him through the seam?" asked Nadina.

"No," Nordon said. "We arrived too late. We didn't see Phetrix or the detective, either."

"What if Grant and Phetrix got there in time to save Eric? Where would they go? Do you think Grant would take him to the police station to keep him safe?"

"It's worth checking out," Alyanna said.

"We left the car down the road," Nordon said.

"I've got one here," Nadina pointed.

"Hey!" said Alyanna. "That's my car."

"Yeah. Sorry. It was all that was left at the cabin." She dug out the keys and handed them to her. "You drive. Kol and I will sit in the back with our new friend DeWayne."

Minutes later they were heading back down the street toward Nordon's vehicle. They passed the active crime scene. If anything, the police presence had grown.

"Should we ask one of them where to find Grant?" Nadina said.

"We could just call a station and ask where he is," offered Alyanna. "That way, we can avoid contact with the police."

"Yeah, but I might be able to get more information from someone who's actually on the scene."

They stopped behind Nordon's van and debated the pros and cons of each contact. In the end, Nadina approached one of the periphery cops to see what she could find out. She walked up to a male officer standing guard at crime scene tape stretched across the street.

"I'm sorry, ma'am, but you have to keep clear of this area."

"Not a problem. I just had a question."

"I can't give out any information."

"I don't want any about this. I was wondering if you could tell me where to find Detective Grant?"

The officer eyed her for a long moment before asking, "Do you know Detective Grant?"

"Yes."

The officer hesitated just long enough to give Nadina cause to regret coming forward. "Detective Grant is a very busy man. What is your business with him?"

Red flags unfurled in her mind. "Ah, that's personal."

"Personal, huh? When was the last time you saw Detective Grant?"

Wary now and on guard, Nadina saw the best course was to retreat.

"Never mind. I'll contact him later." She turned to leave, but the officer reached out and snared her arm and spoke into her shoulder mic. "I need some assistance at the northern end with a potential witness."

"Say again," a voice said back.

"Someone asking about Grant."

The excited answer came fast. "Hold them there."

Nadina had seconds to decide what to do and staying wasn't an option. With a quick jerk of her arm she wrenched free, whirled, and took off running.

"Hey! Freeze."

Nadina didn't look back but heard the running steps behind her. Down the street, Nordon reacted with shock at whatever was after her. He jumped into the van. In seconds it was speeding toward her. It drove past her. Squealing tires made her turn her head. Nordon swung the van between her and the pursuit. The sliding door whipped open and Kol's hand reached out.

Nadina grabbed for it, missed, then snagged it on the second try. Kol leveraged her inside and slammed the door, shouting, "Go! Go! Go!"

Nadina fell across a seat as Nordon fed gas and shot down the street. He spun the wheel hard, taking a corner at high speed. The van teetered for a moment, threatening to topple, then bounced down.

"We can't outrun them," Nadina said.

"Where's a wizard when you need one?" Nordon said.

DeWayne bolted past her from the rear seat of the van. Thinking he was trying to escape, she threw her arm out to snag him, but in her awkward position, missed.

Instead, DeWayne stopped behind Nordon's seat and pointed at the windshield. "Take that alley up there to the right."

Nordon glanced back at him.

"Hey! I don't want to get caught by the cops any more than you do. I know this area. Make the turn before they spot you."

Sirens were growing louder.

Nordon glanced at Nadina, who nodded. He slowed to make the turn to avoid slamming into the building to the left of the alley. As he entered, DeWayne said, "Go to the end and turn right. Slow down. It's a tight turn and a dead end."

"What?" Nordon and Nadina said at once.

"Trust me. The only way to outrun them is to hide. They'll be combing the streets but won't look down here."

"You hope."

"Yeah. I also hope the van will fit."

"What?" the chorus asked again.

They reached the end and Nordon leaned forward over the wheel to see what he was turning into. Twenty feet ahead was a brick wall. A large dumpster sat against the wall to the left, making it an even tighter fit. He pounded on the wheel but the angle was bad. He'd cave in the passenger side of the van. He was forced to reverse and try again. Though the side scraped the wall, he managed to pull forward.

"This is a long van," DeWayne said. "Get as close to the wall as you can."

Nordon inched closer as the sirens sounded like they were right on top of them. The van kissed the wall and Nordon shut it down.

"The dumpster is blocking my door."

"Go out the back," DeWayne said.

"Then what?" asked Nadina. "We're trapped in here."

"There's a narrow space between the two buildings behind us. We can slide through there and look for another ride."

"You mean steal one?" Nadina said.

"Well, yeah," answered DeWayne. "Unless you have a better idea."

"I do, actually." She took out her cell phone and made a call. "Where are you?" She listened, then said, "Come and get us when you think it's clear." She spoke to DeWayne. "What are the cross streets through the space?"

"Seventeenth and Madison."

"Look for us at Seventeenth and Madison. We'll wait until you send word you're there and it's clear." She disconnected. "Alyanna is coming for us. Six police cars gave pursuit. She waited for them to pass before leaving. The entire area is being patrolled. We may be here a while."

"Instead of staying in the van where we'll be trapped if they come back here," DeWayne said, "let's get out and stand by the gap. That way, we can run if someone comes."

"Take everything and wipe down the interior," Nordon said. "Don't leave fingerprints."

"What's a fingerprint?" Kol asked.

"A way to identify us," Nadina said. "You don't have to worry about them, but we all do. Wipe all the surfaces around the door with your shirt."

After a hasty job, they exited through the back. Nordon closed the doors and DeWayne said, "I have an idea. Come on, big man. Give me a hand."

DeWayne walked to the dumpster said something to Nordon, who looked from the dumpster to the van, then gave an approving nod. They pushed the dumpster from its place along the wall and maneuvered it behind the van. It covered up to the bottom of the windows.

"It won't fool anyone," Nordon said.

DeWayne lifted both lids and laid them back against the van. "Now it will." The lids concealed the van from a casual glance. If anyone came close, the van would be obvious, but it was better than nothing and might buy them some time.

DeWayne moved to the edge of the alley and peered down to the street. He motioned for them to move, then followed. He led to the narrow space. One look at the size and all eyes swung toward Nordon.

"You should go last," DeWayne said.

"Yeah. Thanks."

Chapter 15

Phetrix, Detective Grant, and Eric rushed into the burned husk of a house in search of shelter from the screaming banshees above.

"Seekers? What the hell are those things?" Grant shouted. He unholstered his gun and clutched it close to his chest.

"That won't do you any good, Detective. They're not harmed by physical means, though they can hurt you."

"Phetrix, what do we do?"

The mage turned to the boy. He saw fear and anxiety in his eyes, but also a bit of the boy's father, King Artus. The determination to do whatever was necessary was etched in him.

"You need to stay safe. I'll deal with them. Detective, if you could make sure the boy sees no harm, I'll prepare to turn these things back."

"How am I gonna protect him if they can't be harmed by anything I do?"

"You're a smart man, Detective. Use your training. Surely they taught you how to avoid danger?"

The seekers screeched above, forcing all three of them to look up.

"I'll handle this. Keep him safe!"

Phetrix ran out of the building shouting to the sky. His only hope was to distract the Seekers enough so they'd trail after him and neglect the prince.

"You were never meant for this! You don't have to follow the evil he's become!" He knew it was pointless to argue with the mindless things, but something about voicing his inner anger made him feel better. The Seekers ignored his plea and circled above the house.

"They must've sensed his power," Phetrix said quietly. Thinking fast, he closed his eyes for a moment to concentrate on the spell Samuel taught him. Seeker screams assaulted his ears, disorienting him. *Focus*, he thought. Focus on the power. Concentrate. What did Samuel teach you?

Phetrix repeated the words in his head, making sure the spell was correct before unleashing the energy around him. Once uncorked, it wouldn't go back and the Seekers would know he was there.

Moving slow and deliberately, Phetrix recited the words aloud. He motioned his hands as though weaving the spell into existence, then he let it fly.

The power radiated outward and covered him, the house, and everything inside, including Detective Grant and Eric.

The Seekers howled as their circular pattern in the sky turned into a convulsive twisting of black bodies. They were lost and confused. His spell had worked! Their senses were severed from trailing the prince, his ability no longer discoverable to them.

Phetrix wiped his brow, the tension of the moment dissipating as the Seekers were in total confusion.

"That should keep you at bay. Go hunt somewhere else!"

The black creatures twisted amongst themselves, screeching wildly like animals that had lost their prey.

One of them broke from the other two and rose in the air. It disengaged from the chaos and moved slowly higher until it stopped. It faced eastward and stared at the horizon for a long time.

"What are you up to?" Phetrix mumbled.

The Seeker screeched a shrill cry and the other two froze in mid-air, then moved to either side of it.

"Oh no! They sense something else!"

Phetrix hesitated, unsure if he should intervene in case it was the princess or let them go. He had one of the heirs safely with him. Would that be enough? Could he restore the kingdom with only Eric? Shouldn't he save the princess too?

Lost in his thoughts, he didn't notice Grant and Eric standing next to him.

"What are they doing?" Grant asked.

"I fear they've come upon the trail of another with the power."

Eric turned to where the Seekers watched.

"I can feel it," he said quietly. "Whatever they sense, I do too. Something is that way. Something with this…this…power."

"Your sister," Phetrix replied in hushed tones. He looked up to the Seekers and back to Eric. "Your power is strong. So is theirs. You both sense Elly."

Eric shook his head. "I still don't know if it's true or not."

"Listen, kid, I'm a skeptic as much as you. But," Grant began, "this is real. Whatever real means in this place, that is. I'm gonna have a hell of a time trying to explain this when I get back."

Silently, the Seekers darted east.

"No!" Phetrix cried. "Leave her be!"

"We can't stop them," Grant said, resting a hand on Phetrix's shoulder. "This won't do anything, right?" He waved his gun in the air.

"No, it will not. Not with them, anyway."

"But it can be an advantage for us. No one here has anything like it, do they?" Eric asked.

Phetrix shook his head. The Seekers looked smaller in the distance. What frightened him more was their silence. They were never silent. Maybe they'd received instructions from Rhoden and lost their minds to his control.

"No, Prince, they do not," he finally said. "Your weapons are foreign to our land. None have defenses against such things."

The Seekers finally flew out of sight and Phetrix felt a sinking feeling deep in his core.

"Can you sense the power that way?" he asked Eric.

"Yeah. Something's pulling me." He pointed to where the Seekers flew. "Do you think it's the same thing?"

"I believe it is. Mortas has outlawed the Order and all users of the power. There are a few left but they're careful and will remain hidden until the time is right."

"Like now. I imagine the right time is now," Grant added.

"You're correct, Detective. Unless they've committed to an assault with their power, they should still be in hiding. That leads me to believe it's Elly. She must've found her connection to the power."

"I wish we had a car," Eric said.

"A chariot?" Phetrix asked.

Grant laughed. "Yeah, something like that. But without such

amenities, I guess we walk, right? I don't suppose you've got a train or something?"

Phetrix didn't quite understand the reference. Eric did and laughed along with Grant.

"Nope, no L here, Detective," Eric replied.

"Letters? How do they help us travel?"

"Wizard, you've got a lot to learn. Maybe we can teach you a few things on the way," Grant said.

"In this world, things from your dimension don't make sense. Come, Eric; lead the way. We must find your sister before the Seekers do."

"What if we don't?"

Grant holstered his gun and turned Eric in the direction they were headed. "You don't wanna know, kid. Some things are better left unsaid."

Chapter 16

Alyanna waited almost an hour before she felt it was safe enough to risk the transfer. DeWayne offered to lead, but Nadina nixed that idea, fearing as soon as he was out the other side, he'd bolt.

"Kol, you'll draw the least attention. Go through first. Act as natural as possible, and if you see a police car, stay calm and ignore it."

Though he nodded, his nervous twitching suggested he was anything but calm. He entered the two-foot-wide space and moved slowly toward the light that was fifty feet away. Once he was halfway through, Nadina went.

DeWayne looked at Nordon and then at the alley, silently weighing his chances of outrunning him.

Nordon patted the gun in his belt. "You might be able to outrun me, but you'll never outrun a bullet."

DeWayne took his turn next.

Nadina saw Kol reach the street. He looked both ways and ran to the right. Nadina didn't know if he was running to the car or running from what he saw. Either way, if he was spotted, he looked guilty of something.

A few feet from the end, Nadina stopped. Moving was slow because of the tightness of the space. She didn't have trouble getting through but wondered about Nordon. What if he got stuck? He would tell her to go, to save herself, but she'd never leave him. Especially not trapped in such a confined space.

At the end, she peered around both brick walls. Alyanna's car was ten feet to the right. No other vehicles were in sight. She exited, stooped low, and moved to the side of the car. She waited for DeWayne to come through. She wanted to be ready in case he took off in the opposite direction.

She took out her gun and held it so he'd see it when he looked out. Though she wouldn't shoot, she wanted him to think she would. She didn't have qualms about shooting the man, especially for his involvement in Rhoden's plan to kill Eric, but the noise was sure to draw every cop in the city.

DeWayne reached the end of the street and peeked. He spotted Nadina, then looked the other way. When he looked back at her she made sure he could clearly see the gun. He looked from the gun to her, then back to the left. Decision made, he stepped out and sprinted the other way. Anger sent a red veil over her eyes. She raised her weapon, took aim, and pressed her fingers to the trigger. However, her common sense returned just in time to prevent the man's death and her possible capture for murder.

DeWayne dodged around the corner and was lost from sight. She sighed and waited for Nordon. Several minutes passed before she was worried enough to go look. She found him still halfway down and not moving.

"Nordon?"

He looked up, panic set in his eyes. "I'm stuck, Dina."

"Stay calm. I'm coming."

"No!" he shouted. "Save yourself. I'll manage."

She gave an inward smile. Just as she thought. He was willing to sacrifice himself for her. Well, she was no different. She'd rather be captured than leave the man she loved. She slid into the gap and made her way toward him.

"No, Dina. You have to go."

"Oh, be quiet, you big lug. I'm not going, so save your breath."

As she closed on him, she studied where he was trapped. His chest, of course, and some of his belly, but everything else was free.

"Did you have trouble before you reached this spot?"

"A little, but I could move. It must be narrower here."

"Step back and try to lean that way."

He did and Nadina pushed on him from her side. No doubt about it. He was stuck. She stepped back. "Are you breathing all right?"

"I can only draw in short breaths."

"Okay. I want you to exhale as much air from your lungs as possible and suck in your stomach."

He did and they tried again. He moved an inch. She stopped when she realized he was out of air and ready to pass out. "Breathe." He drew in fast, short breaths. If she didn't work fast, he'd hyperventilate. If he passed out, she'd never get him out of there.

"Okay. You moved a little that time. We have to try again. If you were moving until you got to this point, you shouldn't have to go too far to get free."

They tried twice more before Nordon could slide backwards on his own. He walked all the way back to the alley.

"It's no good, Dina. You need to go. Get someplace safe. I'll wait for dark and then walk out of here."

"Hush now, Don. Let me think." After a minute she said, "I'm going to have Alyanna drive around the block and stop in front of the alley. We'll meet her down there. You get out first. Once you're in the car, I'll run out, hop in, and we'll be on our way."

He nodded, still exhausted and somewhat spooked from his ordeal. Nadina called Alyanna and told her the new plan. They made their way to the alley's mouth and waited. The car drove up and the back door opened. Nordon walked out and climbed in. Nadina waited for the all clear wave but it didn't come. Instead, she heard, "Cops."

"Go," said Nadina, and she sprinted back down the alley. She reached the corner and glanced back. The car was gone. Her phone vibrated in her pocket. Alyanna said, "It's slowing down. No, it stopped at the alley. The cop is looking down there. Oh no. He's turning. Get out of there now."

Nadina ran for the gap. "Wait for me one block down. I'll exit and run to the right. If you see any cops, drive away. I'll hide and you can pick me up later."

She heard Nordon yell, "No!"

"Tell that big oaf to duck down and follow my directions. I'll be fine." It was difficult to move and talk at the same time in the confined space. Her breathing was getting short like Nordon's had. Behind her the sound of a car door shutting echoed down the walls. She reached the corner, took a quick survey, then darted across the street. She angled toward the far corner and ducked behind the first building. Once there she slowed her pace. She was on a busier street now and didn't want to draw attention. Midway down the block she glanced behind her. No one pursued. She breathed easier. Then a cop car pulled into view on the next cross street where she was supposed to meet Alyanna.

A new wave of panic struck. Had Alyanna been captured? She made a sudden turn into a small boutique. A few customers browsed through the unique clothing. The female employee behind the counter looked up and smiled at her, then went back to scanning purchases. Another woman, this one with spiked fire-engine-red hair and more piercings in her face than Nadina could count, approached.

"Can I help you find anything?" she asked in an Eastern European accent.

"Oh, no thanks. I just wanted to see what you have. Your collection always draws my attention when I walk by, so I decided to come in for a better look."

"Yes, our clothing is quite vibrant. Makes a great statement about the person wearing it." The woman gave her a quick glance up and down. "Though it's not for everyone, I think," she shrugged. "Let me know if you need assistance." Then she whirled and maneuvered through the racks.

Nadina was stunned by the woman's assessment. At first she was angry. Then she looked down. She was drenched in sweat and her clothes were rumpled and dirty. A glance in a full length mirror showed her hair damp and hanging limp. She caught a whiff of a foul odor and raised her arm to sniff. Gross.

She turned to the window and watched from behind a circular clothes rack as the police car drove slowly past. She waited until it had gone down another block before exiting the store. In the doorway, she looked right then left and moved left. She was nearly to the corner when she heard, "Hey you! Stop!" She spun to see the cop she had encountered at the crime scene racing toward her.

A spike of adrenaline hit her and she took off. She rounded the corner, praying Alyanna was still there and not in police custody. She was there and alone, parked in a no parking zone, but the car was facing the wrong way. She sprinted and yelled, "Turn around!" but Alyanna looked at Kol with a confused expression.

Nadina motioned with her hands in circular fashion, but Alyanna did not understand. Nadina saw Alyanna's eyes widened and Nordon point from the back seat. Without looking back, Nadina knew the cop had made the turn.

Nordon flung the rear door open and Alyanna made a half turn in the street. Nadina leaped into the back seat as Nordon clamped his large hands over her body. "Go!" he yelled, and Alyanna swung the car around, cutting off a car coming from the opposite direction. The horn blares, shouts from the driver and the cop, and the excited voices in the car added to the chaos. The door still hung open and the cop reached it before Alyanna could pull away. He hung on and ran alongside.

"Pull over and stop now!"

Alyanna obliged. She hit the brakes. The cop's momentum slammed him into the open door. He let out an "Oof!" and bounded back. Nadina lifted a leg and snapped a kick into his chest, sending him backward. He tripped over the curb and fell on his backside.

Nordon yelled, "Floor it!" and Alyanna pressed the pedal down. She didn't stop at the corner and made a high-speed sharp right turn, catching the open door on the rear bumper of another car. The metallic shriek sent chills through Nadina. The door was slammed shut. Alyanna kept going, but a block later, she was forced to stop at a red light. She tapped a hand on the wheel nervously waiting for the light to change while keeping watch in the mirror.

Nadina was on her knees looking out the rear window. Two blocks down the cop reached the corner. He scanned the road for them. When he spotted them, he spoke into the shoulder-mic and took off in pursuit.

"He spotted us. He's coming," Nadina said.

The light changed and Alyanna sped forward, almost lurching into the car in front of them. "There's too much traffic."

Nordon said, "By now, a dozen cars will be converging on us. We may have to abandon the car."

That statement was met with silence. They advanced two more blocks at a slow speed before catching another light. The tension in the car was palpable. The tight quarters and the nervous sweat steamed the windows and created an odor that made Nordon and Nadina open their windows.

"There he is," Nadina announced. "He's still coming."

The light changed. The car jumped forward as Alyanna cut in front of the car to the left. "If I can get into the left turn lane, I might be able to get some distance."

"I hear sirens," Nordon said. "We have to make a decision. Run or stay?"

Alyanna said, "I did it." But the light for the turn lane was red. In quick fluid motion, her head swung left to right and back again. She punched the gas and the car leaped through the intersection dodging cross traffic.

They could move faster, but if spotted, they'd never outrun a radio.

"We need to get out of the city," Nordon said.

"We can go to my house," Alyanna offered.

"No," Nordon said. "I'm sure that policeman got your license number. They'll know who you are and where you live by now."

"What about our house?" Nadina said. "I was there today. No cops were outside."

"We could try it for now. It would give us a chance to figure out our next move."

Alyanna said, "Do we have any moves left?"

No one answered.

Chapter 17

Samuel wove a spell to protect the resistance fighters from being seen. It was an ancient but effective spell not known by many in the Order. As the oldest living member, he brought a wealth of knowledge to the table; something they'd need as they rebuilt the Order. Mortas had done so much damage because of his greed. King Artus and Queen Griselda were benevolent rulers, as were those before them. No doubt the twins were of the same mold. But Mortas was cruel and angry. He represented a small faction of the kingdom that felt neglected and passed over. Samuel never understood their position. King Artus went to great lengths to represent his entire kingdom and often opened the royal storehouses for those in need. Regardless of the reason, Mortas was in the wrong. His attack signaled a shift in Chevalon society. Samuel intended on rectifying it.

"Hey, old man, are we still protected?" Char asked. Samuel bristled at the comment. Char was a thug, a thick man with a thick head. Most likely he was good for a fight, but he wasn't Samuel's first choice to lead a band of fighters.

"If you're asking about the spell, yes, it's still in effect. We can proceed with full confidence."

"We'd better. This is what's left of the resistance. If we die, the resistance dies."

Samuel swallowed hard. He'd not thought of that before. Their mission was difficult and carried with it many dangers, but to think that this was the last line of defense against Mortas felt like going after his opponent's King with only a rook and a pawn. Those were never great odds.

"We're safe, I promise you. It still wouldn't hurt to move at a steady pace. Though the spell prevents them from seeing us, if we run through here like a herd of elephants, they'll see the trees moving and hear the noise. I can't help that."

Char scrunched his face. "Elephants? What are those?"

Samuel smiled. He'd been so entrenched in the other world he forgot where he was. "They are large animals the size of boulders. Majestic things. One day I hope to see them again."

"Yeah, sure thing." Char turned and went to the head of the line.

The forces were arrayed into three long lines snaking through the forest. They wanted more but Samuel's spell could only cover so much territory before it weakened. He enjoyed a surge of power while back in Chevalon, but it still wasn't enough to blanket them all. The spell was never intended for that.

He heard Char command his troops to slow down and quit making so much noise. He was loud, but at least they were far enough away that those at the castle wouldn't hear them.

Mathilda walked alongside Samuel. "Are you prepared for this? What we do, we do for all the land. We're well past time of hiding our heads in the sand. We may never get another chance like this. I know having the heirs at our side would almost ensure victory, but we're here now and must take what we can."

Samuel nodded, absently looking to the west where he felt the disturbance in the power. Without a doubt, someone had crossed over the seam. He hoped more than anything that it was the heirs. Phetrix was a skilled mage. He would see his mission through, no matter what.

"I agree. We must do what we can. If Elly is in that castle, we'll find her and begin the final purge of Mortas from the land. Cut off the head and the rest will follow."

Mathilda didn't say a word as they moved forward.

The day wore on and grumbling rose up from the troops. They were hungry and tired. They'd crossed nearly half the distance between their previous camp and the castle. They'd be within view of those on the castle walls now if it weren't for Samuel's spell of protection.

Char retreated from the front of the column and approached the two mages.

"Mathilda, Samuel. We must rest. Our people cannot make the trek in one day. I propose we set up camp and preserve our energy for the morning. Then we leave at first light and make our stand at the castle at midday. It might be the last night these people are alive. I'd like them to enjoy it."

"We aren't here for frivolity," Samuel began. "We're here to end tyranny. Do you think evil waits for rest? We must continue."

Mathilda rested a hand on his shoulder. "Char's right. We've asked a lot of our people. The least we can do is offer one more night. Have you ever prepared yourself for death? It takes some people longer than others. We owe them that much."

Samuel wasn't pleased with the delay. If it were up to him, he'd be much farther along than they were now.

"If this is what we've become, then who am I to tell someone they must die without rest?" He stormed away from the pair, clinging to his spell of protection to keep his mind free of anger.

"No fires!" he called back over his shoulder. "I cannot prevent the smoke from being seen. If they want something to eat, it'll have to be raw. We cannot risk it."

Char yelled something at him that he ignored and stalked through the forest until he found a quiet place to rest and regroup.

Though not initially pleased with the delay, his bones felt much better when he sat down. Maybe they did need a reprieve until morning when they'd hopefully be fresh and ready to meet their fate.

Mathilda was right. When had he ever prepared for death? He'd been in difficult situations before, but never one where death was a real possibility. Not that he thought, anyway. Where they were going and with what they had planned, it was more probable than anything else.

He stretched his arms, the muscles in his back aching. *The tension*, he thought. The tension of holding this group together and protecting them. The stress is overcoming you. He imagined seeing a doctor or going to a massage spa in Chicago and how great it felt when someone dug their hands deep into his muscles. A little pain resulted in amazing results. Unfortunately, none of those were nearby.

Moments later, a shout rose up amongst the fighters. Samuel leapt to his feet and gazed back to where they were. Then he heard it. His head whipped up and there they were.

The Seekers.

Four of them had discovered the group and circled overhead, screaming wildly, and making those below tremble with fear.

"Oh no!"

Samuel willed his old body to run through the forest to Char and Mathilda. They were shouting orders to those around them.

"Mathilda! Where are the others from the Order?" Samuel asked. "We need them. Now!" She nodded and ran into the chaos.

"I suppose your spell didn't work on them?" Char asked, pointing upwards.

"It has no effect on their kind. If they were human, sure."

Char grumbled and withdrew his sword. "Then I guess we gotta kill them before they give us away."

"If they've already spotted us, no doubt those in the castle know too. We have no element of surprise. Whether they wanted it or not, our people now have a fight on their hands. A tranquil last night is not to be."

"I blame you!" Char said. "When this is over, we'll have words."

Samuel was taken aback at the man's accusations, but there was no time to deal with it. They were in grave danger. Without other mages to help, he didn't think he had enough power to deal with the four Seekers.

Someone to his left screamed and a Seeker dropped from the sky, crying out as it skimmed through the people. Samuel watched in horror as it tore into a man, shredding his arms and torso into a bloody mess. The Seekers had never done that before. Whatever Mortas did to them made them more dangerous than ever.

"Flee! Run for cover!" Samuel called out.

He let a bolt of lightning fly from his hands, but it missed the Seeker and instead slammed into a tree, splintering it into hundreds of pieces.

The other three Seekers took their cue from the first and dove into the fighters. Samuel couldn't see where they went, but soon balls of fire erupted from the ground and shot upwards.

"Mathilda," he whispered. She must have found the others. "Good. We have a chance. Press on! Char, with me!"

The large man sneered.

"Come, we can do this!"

Finally he followed Samuel as they chased after the first Seeker.

Samuel spotted it through the trees. Waving his hands frantically, he wove a spell to trap it within a force so that it had no choice but to turn around. It slammed into an invisible wall while chasing after a woman, then turned back toward him.

"That's it. Come on, now. Come get me," Samuel growled. Char stood next to him brandishing his sword.

"When it comes at us, I'll bring it down from the air and you strike it in the head."

"My sword will hurt it?"

"Indeed it will."

The Seeker screamed a high-pitched call and homed in on Samuel and his power. As it raced through the air, he prepared himself. He waited for the right moment and impaled it with intense streams of fire. It fell to the ground next to him, writhing and howling from the wounds.

"Now, Char!"

The larger man hesitated.

"Hurry before it gets up!"

Char lunged, piercing its skull with his sword. It groaned deeply, then turned to the side, lifeless.

"That's it! One down, three to go!"

Char smiled. "Let's do this, old man!"

The people nearby witnessing the feat cried out in victory.

"This way!" Samuel shouted, indicating for all to follow him. One of the Seekers was nearby, though the fireballs from the mages did quite a bit of damage.

By the time Samuel arrived, Mathilda and another mage had defeated the Seeker, leaving behind its smoldering body.

Behind them something shrieked, and Samuel twisted around. One of the Seekers had escaped the fray and bolted back into the sky. Smoke trailed from it, but it was alive and it listed side to side, injured and in pain. Bolts of lightning flew in the air after it just missed their mark. It continued to climb higher until it was out of reach.

"Bah! We're doomed for sure!" Char cried out.

"No, but it's not gonna help," Samuel replied.

They turned their attention to the last Seeker. Mathilda had already joined the remaining mages and they quickly dispatched it. Soon the madness was over. The forest fell to an eerie silence. The wounded groaned. Some called for help, and others called on their behalf.

"This was a disaster!" Char said to Samuel. "We won't have enough to fight our way through the castle now! We must retreat!"

Samuel inhaled a deep breath. "Our mission stands. We must continue on and do what we came here for."

Inside, he imagined going back through the seam to the safety of Chicago. Getting lost within the throng of people there seemed much more desirable than what they were about to do.

Chapter 18

DeWayne rounded the corner and sprinted for all he was worth. He gambled the woman would not shoot him. The sound of the shot would bring every cop in the area. Although judging how his body shook, he wasn't as confident as he thought.

He checked for traffic, then crossed the street. His ride was still by the crime scene. He doubted he'd get anywhere near it, so walking was his only mode of transportation for the moment. He'd take a circuitous route back home where his car was parked.

He glanced behind him. The woman was not following. He slowed. He needed to cut down a side street and head in the opposite direction to avoid the cops. His current path took him right back to the seam.

At the next corner, he turned right and stopped. He peeked to make sure no one was tailing him, then shot a longer glance in the other direction. The crime scene area was still abuzz with activity. He was about to move he heard a voice call out.

"Who you running from?"

DeWayne jumped, startled by the voice, then about went skyward when he saw it was a cop. He was so busy checking behind him he never noticed the cop car coming from the cross street.

"Huh? Oh, ah, no one. I was just watching all stuff happening down the street."

The black female officer eyed him. He tried to remain calm, telling himself it was just the suspicious nature of all cops. He hadn't done anything wrong that she knew of.

"You look like you running from someone or part of something shady. Look how you pressed up against that wall, like you a mural."

DeWayne hadn't noticed, but he was stuck to the wall like a flattened cartoon character. He stepped forward, gave the officer a stiff wave, and walked down the street. He tried not to turn around, but the hairs on the back of his neck stiffened. When the car door opened, he thought he might faint. He willed himself not to run, but the urge got stronger with each passing second.

"Hold on there, sport. Let me see some ID."

He stopped and looked over his shoulder. "Huh? Why? I ain't done nothing wrong."

"Maybe not. But then again, maybe so. If you done nothing wrong, showing me your ID shouldn't be a problem." She closed the distance. She was large; built like a body builder. One hand rested on her holster and the other reached out palm up for his ID.

"Ah, sure," DeWayne said, reaching behind him for his wallet. It was then he remembered he no longer had it. That crazy woman took it and pitched it out the window with all his hard-earned money.

"Uh-oh," the cop said. "You look like you just saw a ghost. You almost white. Let me guess. You left your wallet in your other pants?"

"I-I can explain." In one long ramble, he said, "This crazy woman robbed me and took my wallet with my ID. She had a gun. In fact, I think she's the one you been looking for. The one involved in that mess down the street."

The cop froze. Any pretense of a smile was long gone. Her steely-eyed stare bore straight through him. "And what would you know about the mess down the street?"

"Me? Ah, nothing. Nothing at all."

"Then why would you think this woman mugger was involved?"

"I don't, but you guys, the ah, cops were chasing a woman. I just put it together." The response was lame and he knew it. Now she was even more suspicious of him.

"Here's what I'm putting together. You seem to know a lot about something you shouldn't, unless you are involved somehow. If I remember right, and I always do, some of the reports mentioned a tall black man aiding whoever attacked some police officers. What do you have to say to that?"

"Nothing. There's a lot of tall black men in this city. I didn't have anything to do with what's going on down there. I didn't see nothing, I don't know nothing, and don't want no trouble with the law. I was just walking along here and got curious. That's not a crime." He regrouped and the words flowed. "A crazy white woman with a gun took my wallet, my money, and my ID and flung them out the window. I was going back to find my stuff. If I looked suspicious, it's because I was afraid that crazy woman was still around someplace. I ain't never been down there by the seam or seen any battles with strange creatures. Now, can I go try to find my wallet?"

To his surprise, the cop had her gun out and leveled at him. "Turn around and place your hands against that wall."

"What? Why?"

"Do it now." The command reverberated off the walls of the surrounding buildings.

DeWayne obeyed. The policewoman came up behind him, kicked his legs wider apart, then gripped one hand and pulled it behind him. He fought it at first until she leaned against him and shoved his head against the brick. "Don't you resist. I'd hate to have to hurt you."

The cuff bit into his skin. The second one was no better. She patted him down.

"I don't understand. Why you doing this? I ain't done nothing."

"Sometimes it's best to just let people talk. The self-proclaimed innocent say the darndest things."

"I just explained what happened to me."

"Yeah, you did that all right, and then some. If you were never down at the crime scene, how'd you know there was a battle?"

"Everyone knows that."

"Then how did you know it involved creatures?"

DeWayne froze. Had he said that? "That kinda thing gets around. You know, like stories of aliens invading the planet." He thought it was a good response, but she wasn't buying it. "In that case, you won't mind telling your alien story to my boss." She grabbed his arm and led him to the back seat of the cruiser.

Once the policewoman was seated, DeWayne went off. "This is bull! Just another case of police harassment. A black man can't even walk down the street no more without being questioned. I got robbed and no one's chasing her. I'm the one who gets cuffed. I'm suing. I want my lawyer."

"I'll bet you don't even know the name of a lawyer, let alone have one. And if by some chance you do have a lawyer, it just makes me feel all the more righteous about bringing you in, 'cause only the guilty need a lawyer to call when they in trouble."

DeWayne clammed up after that. He started planning his next move. He had valuable information that could be traded for his freedom; information the cops wanted badly. Like who was involved in the battle at the seam, and most importantly, where to find them. Now he just had to work out how not to incriminate himself.

Chapter 19

Elly crouched low, inspecting the field ahead of them. Tall grass swayed in the wind. Thin white clouds streaked across the blue sky. The powerful tug on the magical rope she'd been following led directly across the sea of grass. At the far end of the field, it dipped downward to a valley or just the other side of a hill; she wasn't sure which.

"Come on, girl. Is it safe or not?" Shree asked in a shrill voice. They were growing impatient as they traveled through unknown forests.

Food was scarce, and they'd found barely a handful of berries between them in the past two days. Shree cautioned against trying the bright red berries, recalling a time when she was young and ate something similar off the dark green bush in front of her friend's house in Schaumburg. It took a trip to the ER to pump the toxic contents out of her stomach. Elly considered leaving the berries, but hunger overcame her and she ate anyway. When she didn't immediately fall over in discomfort, Shree picked some too.

But that was far behind them. Now the problem was the vast open field offering little to no cover. They hadn't seen anything for a while, but it still felt scary.

"I think it's safe. I don't know for sure. All I can do is follow my instinct, just like you."

"Yeah, but I don't have the power."

"My powers aren't even accessible to me all the time. It's like there's some kinda block on them or something."

"Then what's your thought on going out there? Think we're good?"

"I guess. If nothing else, at least we'll see the danger coming at us."

"Good enough for me." Shree pulled Elly's hand and they left the cover of the forest for the wide open field.

The grass swished against their tunics. No longer blocked by trees and shrubs, the wind whistled past them. Elly felt exposed, clutching at her tunic like it was a magical cloak.

"Too bad I can't make us invisible or something, right?" she asked.

Shree laughed. "Girl, that would be amazing! I've always wanted to be invisible. Do you know how much fun that would be?"

"Tell me about it! Creeping through the halls at school and listening to what everyone's saying about us…that would rock!"

"Until someone badmouthed one of us and I punched them in the face."

"They wouldn't know who did it. Punch away!"

The girls giggled at the absurd vision. It was a fun moment of escape in a world that wasn't their own.

"Shree, what do you think they're saying?"

"Who?"

Elly swallowed hard. "Our friends. The school. Your parents. All of them. We've been gone for days. What do you think they believe has happened to us?"

"My guess is that my parents called the police, reported me missing, and the police are not doing a damn thing about it. Who cares about some missing black girl? They sure don't."

Elly clicked her tongue. Shree had a point. Back home was full of hate and ugliness, but was this world any different? So far no one gave them grief over skin color, but that wasn't to say prejudice didn't exist. People were ignorant.

"Let's say they do care. Then what? I bet your parents are worried sick! One day you just wind up missing? If I were a parent, it would drive me insane if my child was missing. My mind would go over all the worst possible scenarios."

Shree's face turned down. "Yeah, I guess you're right," she whispered.

"I'm sorry. I don't wanna make you feel bad. I'd be lost out here without you. We'll make it back, and the looks on their faces when we do will be priceless."

"Yeah, sure."

The silence between them grew awkward and uncomfortable. Elly had to break it.

"My parents. My mother has got be so worried about me. With my father dead, she's all alone."

Shree whimpered, forcing the words out. "But what if they aren't your parents? Maybe these people are right about you. So far, everything they've said checks out, right? As strange as all of this is, it's all been true so far. Look at it. You've got a glowy scar on you. You can sometimes channel power. We're in some alternate dimension. It doesn't seem real, but here we are." She spread her arms wide to emphasize her point.

"How can you say they aren't my parents? They've loved me and taken care of me my entire life! If this," she said, mimicking Shree's expression with her arms, "is my reality, I don't want it! My home is Chicago. My home is not here. Nothing about this place calls to me."

"Well, something does," Shree said pointing at Elly's scar. Elly looked down, expecting to see the glow through her tunic, but it wasn't illuminated. She pulled the tunic up to inspect it, but it was still the same reddish color as usual.

"I don't care. I don't belong here. Neither of us do. Our home is far away and I intend to get us back."

"How?"

"We'll figure it out, I suppose. The bond feels stronger, like when you get two magnets close enough and they want to join together."

"Or push apart."

"This is for sure the sticking together kind. I can almost close my eyes and follow the pull to where we need to go. I swear, it's weird."

"I hope it's not some kinda trap. So, if it's your brother…do you think he's cute?"

"Shree!"

The girls giggled again, doing their best to keep the situation light. It was all they could do under such extreme duress.

"I don't know. But…yuck! I can't even…why was that even a question?"

The grin on Shree's face told it all. Like when they had sleepovers as young girls and they'd grow slap-happy from lack of sleep as the night wore on, they'd get goofy and silly. Shree's smile reminded her of the memory that warmed her.

"You gotta find humor in all this, right? It's not just me?"

"No, Shree, it's not. Maybe he is, but that's not for me to worry about. He'd be my brother!"

"No matter what, we gotta be ready for things to change. If what you say is true and not too far this way is a whole new world for you, then these are the last moments we have to live with an old understanding."

"Whoa…what? Where's this coming from? When did you get all philosophical and stuff?"

"I've just been thinking, that's all. What else are we gonna do out here? I've been doing my best not to focus on how crazy all this is. Anything to distract me from realizing we're in a lot of danger has helped me cope. But it's true. Our worlds are about to change more than like going away for college or joining the military. It's heavy stuff, but you got this. You're one of the strongest women I know!"

They stopped and Elly gave her a hug. "I love you, girl. If I had to be lost in a strange world, I'm glad it was with you."

Shree laughed. "Same."

Elly let go and led them west. The strong bond pulled harder now and she didn't think she could resist even if she wanted to. She was certain it led to something good, but there was still a touch of doubt. She couldn't fully trust anything in a world she didn't know.

Chapter 20

They parked one street over and two blocks down from their house and walked in pairs, taking different routes to the house. Nordon went in first to make sure no one was hiding inside to take them into custody. Once Kol and Alyanna arrived, they collapsed around the dining room table. Nordon pressed the broken door back in the frame and shoved a bookcase in front of it to hold it in place.

It had been an emotionally and physically draining day and no one had the energy to speak. Finally, about fifteen minutes after arriving, Nadina said, "I'm taking a shower." She went upstairs.

The hot water beat the stress from her body. As the tension was washed from her, so were her last reserves of energy. After wrapping a towel around herself, Nadina went straight into her bedroom and collapsed on the bed, falling instantly asleep.

The hand clasped over her mouth brought her out from a deep sleep kicking and fighting. A presence near her ear shushed her, then her eyes locked on Nordon's. "Police are outside." She calmed. He released his hand from her face and she sat up. The damp towel from her shower was still wrapped around her. "Get dressed. I'll wake the others."

Before Nordon could open the door, a loud crash from downstairs announced he was too late. "Quickly and quietly, get up to the attic."

Nadina reached the closet first. The attic door was open. "You go first," she said. Despite his size, Nordon was stealthy. He wedged past her and went up the stairs. The creaks of the old wooden stairs were covered by the pounding feet of the invading police. Nadina shut the closet door, arranged the clothes that blocked the door to the attic, and slipped through, closing the door softly behind her.

Voices shouted. Some boomed, "Police!" Others yelled "SWAT!" They had called out the big guns for this takedown. Someone was in their bedroom. She prayed they did not discover the door and that none of them had been at the house during the battle with Rhoden's beasts. Otherwise they already knew about the attic.

Commands were issued. "Get on the floor!" "Hands locked behind your head!" Others were lost in the cacophony of voices shouting. They had Kol and Alyanna. How did they know? Was someone watching the house? She scanned the attic. It offered little in the way of hiding places. If anyone found the attic door, they would be discovered too. They sat on the stairs in the dark, afraid to move, and waited with growing angst.

Nadina slipped into the hastily grabbed clothes. She looked at the mismatched garments and wondered what the red-haired clerk would think about this outfit. Nordon placed reassuring hands on her shoulders.

Kol and Alyanna were questioned. "Is anyone else here? Who slept in that room? The bed's been slept in. Where did they go?" If either responded, the answer was too quiet to be heard. Someone opened the closet door. They'd know their fate in the next five seconds. Clothes hangers scraped against the door. They tensed, ready for battle, but knowing there'd be no fighting trained men with guns.

To their great relief, the closet door closed. Nadina heard the footsteps fade out of the bedroom. Then Kol and Alyanna were led down the stairs. Nordon leaned close and whispered, "I'm going to crawl to the window to see what's going on."

Nadina reached back and grabbed his arm. "No. Let me. I'm lighter. Won't make as much noise."

He nodded and slid to the side of the stair. Nadina scooted past him and crawled along the floor's edge and cut across to the window. She peeled back a corner of the heavy black material glued there to prevent light from showing through to the outside. She peered out the corner of the window.

The streetlight was directly over some of the police cruisers. Kol and Alyanna, hands cuffed behind them, were placed in the back of two different cars and driven away. The remaining cops stood around chatting. One man pointed in several directions, perhaps giving out search grids. Most of the vehicles used in the breech were out of sight. Nadina guessed they were parked on the next block to avoid announcing their presence. The man giving the orders got in his vehicle and drove away.

Most of the others did the same, leaving two men on the street. They walked down the street to an unmarked car and got in but did not drive away. The house was under surveillance. Nadina watched for a few more minutes, then returned to Nordon.

"They took Kol and Alyanna and left two watchers."

Nordon nodded and lowered his head into his palms. Nadina rubbed his back. What did they do now? What could they do? Even if Kol and Alyanna spilled everything they knew, who would believe them? The interrogators would think them insane.

They were out of time, out of companions, and out of options. "Maybe we should surrender," Nordon said through his hands. "Perhaps the police will help us get Eric back."

Nadina thought a moment, then shook her head. "They'd never believe us. Then they'd start investigating us, thinking we had something to do with Eric's disappearance, not to mention Grant's vanishing act. If they think we did something to Grant, we'll never be free to find Eric ourselves. No, Don. If we're to find a way to Eric, it's all on us." She leaned closer and pressed her body to his in a sideways hug.

"I'm going to venture down to see if anyone's still inside."

Nordon looked up, his face contorted with concern.

"Don't worry, my love, I'll be careful."

He squeezed her hand and she stood. Testing the best place for her first step, she opted for the end of the stair. With slow but quiet progress, she reached the attic door and cracked it open. She exited and closed the door, replacing any clothes that moved to cover the entry. The closet door squeaked. She froze and listened. Several minutes passed before she felt confident enough to move into the bedroom. The bedroom door had been left open. Nadina tiptoed to the doorway and poked her head out. Again she froze and listened. If anyone was hiding inside, they were quieter than she.

She crept to the head of the stairs and looked down the worn carpeted path, wondering where to step. The only choice was to the sides. Four steps led to a landing. She took those and squatted to look into the living room. The view she had only showed a third of the way to the front door. Someone had leaned the door against the wall, but it was no longer in the frame. Three more stairs and she sat. She now had a clear line of sight into the living room. No one waited there for her.

She slid stair to stair on her butt until she reached the bottom. Still no movement. From there, she crawled in front of the sofa and peered into the dining room. Empty. Last stop, the kitchen. It made sense that someone would be there. They'd be out of sight and able to hear anyone coming downstairs or through the front door.

Nadina steeled herself, stood, and sidestepped along the dining room wall. The distance to the kitchen door was not long but felt like it took an hour. Once there, she peeked. She didn't see anyone. She was about to take a longer look when she heard something. A footstep? The rear door opened and a female cop entered with a cell phone. She must have stepped outside to make a call.

Nadina ducked back, but her movement was seen.

"Hey!" the cop shouted.

Instead of running, she pivoted and shot her arm out. The police woman came through the door, hand pulling her weapon. Nadina clotheslined her, lifting her feet from the floor. She slammed down hard on the floor, groaned, and rolled, hands clutching the back of her head. Nadina pounced, rolling the stunned woman onto her stomach. She pulled the cuffs free and yanked one hand down at a time. Still dazed by the impact with the floor, the officer gave little resistance. Once cuffed, she stripped the officer of her gun, and shoulder-mic, then undid her belt to remove everything else.

She stood and looked down at her handiwork. God, what had she done? "I'm so sorry." She turned and ran. Upstairs she opened the attic door and called, "Nordon, come now!" By the time he entered the room, she was dressing in jeans and a t-shirt. "Quick, fix the closet to hide the door in case we need it again."

"What happened?"

"Please, just do it. I'll explain later." She pulled on a hoodie. "Pack a duffel with clothes and whatever else you need. Do it fast and meet me downstairs." She opened drawers, pulled out clothes, and stuffed them into her own bag. Then she went through the bathroom taking toiletries. While Nordon finished packing, she ran downstairs.

The policewoman had recovered and was at the rear door. She faced backwards to grip the handle. When she saw Nadina, she said, "No!" As Nadina approached, she stepped forward and planted a kick in her midsection.

Nadina reacted quick. Though the blow landed, she managed to arch backward to avoid much of the force. Her hands caught a foot and pulled, throwing the woman off balance and to the floor.

She leaned on her. "I'm sorry, but we don't have time to be captured. We're searching for our kidnapped son and can't be stopped."

"I don't care," the woman spat. "You're going to jail for a long time. You assaulted a police officer."

Nordon's voice boomed. "So what you're saying is we shouldn't leave a witness?'

That quieted her.

"Nordon, no. We can't. We're not like that. We're not like Rhoden."

"I know, babe. I was pointing out that if we were criminals, we wouldn't have any problem killing a cop."

"You're angry," Nadina said to the woman. "I get that and I understand, but we're trying to save our son."

"Then why didn't you bring it to the police?"

"Believe me, we wanted to. But the truth of the matter is, no one would ever believe our story. I wouldn't believe it if I hadn't lived it myself. Right now, a very bad person has our twins."

Nordon said, "We think they also have your Detective Grant. They may all be dead already, but we have to try."

"Let me loose and I'll help you."

Nadina looked at Nordon, who shrugged. Nadina sighed. "I wish I could trust you, but we can't take the chance. "I'm leaving your things in the dining room. You should be able to free yourself in a few minutes." She stood.

Nordon went outside

"I know it doesn't matter, but we are sorry."

"You're right. It doesn't."

"So be it." She closed the door. Nordon waited in the alley. "Which way?"

He held up car keys. "These are Alyanna's."

"Let's go."

They ran down the alley hoping they had time to reach the car before the policewoman sounded the alarm.

Chapter 21

Phetrix marveled at how well-adjusted Eric was. He hadn't expected as much from him, but his guardians had done a masterful job of preparing him for what was to come. They'd need every advantage if they were going to overthrow Mortas Frost and put an end to his evil.

A day after encountering the Seekers, they came upon a small village. There were only five dwellings clustered close together with another three set far back from the rest. It wasn't much, but it was something.

"Are we good to go there?" Grant asked. He'd grown particularly quiet since the encounter with the Seekers, and Phetrix assumed it was quite an adjustment for the man.

"Perhaps. It's small enough and I don't sense any danger. Food would be welcome right about now. And clothing for you," he said, pointing at Grant. "You give yourself away in those."

"Think they've got White Castle around here?" Eric asked, smiling.

Phetrix furrowed his brow. "Your family castle was white, but it was destroyed. I hear Mortas has raised a black castle not far from here."

Eric huffed.

"Don't sweat it, kid; he missed the joke. I got it, and yeah, I'd love one of those little burgers about now." Grant slapped Eric on the back and the two shared a moment Phetrix didn't understand.

They approached the first house and Phetrix knocked on the door. No one answered. He peered through a crack in the door and grumbled. "Let's try the next one."

The house across from it was just as empty.

"Is this a ghost town?" Eric asked.

"I don't understand," Phetrix replied. "What is a ghost town?"

"It's an abandoned village or town kinda like what we're dealing with here. I think the kid's right," Grant said.

"Jumping to conclusions doesn't help. Considering the time of day, the inhabitants might be out in the fields working."

Grant ran a hand over his head and moved to where he could see more of the surrounding area.

"You make a good point but I still don't think anyone's here. I get the impression they've been gone for some time. Shouldn't there be smoke coming from at least one chimney? Fire used for cooking always makes smoke. Don't people eat around here? Surely someone would have a fire going."

"Detective, you make an excellent observation. The authorities must train you well."

"I did good enough at the academy to pass."

Phetrix didn't understand his reference but it also didn't seem that important. What Grant said about the smoke was alarming.

"I think you may be correct, Detective. The inhabitants must have left their homes for something else."

"Or maybe Mortas Frost had something to do with it," Eric interjected.

Phetrix sighed and looked to the two men. "Your thought holds much more weight. I fear you may be correct."

Grant drifted away from the group, inspecting the rest of the homes. When he got to the last one he whistled for the others to come over. Phetrix and Eric quickly joined him at his side.

"Look in there," he said, opening the door.

Phetrix noticed it first. A man in black armor with a white snowflake on his chest lay on the floor with a sword plunged halfway through his neck. The ground underneath was stained brown from his blood. Next to him lay the bodies of a man and woman, both stabbed multiple times and obviously dead.

"Look at the bodies," Grant asked. Eric covered his mouth and heaved a few times. Phetrix only nodded, the stench of death overpowering.

"The rate of decomposition is such that they haven't been dead for long. My best guess is three days; maybe four. I assume you have bugs here like we do, and they've yet to make their mark."

"Bugs?" Phetrix asked.

"Little tiny creatures that annoy the crap out of you," Eric added.

"Oh, yes. We have plenty."

"If I had to guess," Grant began, "This fella here shot the guy in black. The fatal blow took out his attacker, but whoever was with the soldier took out their anger on these two. I imagine they were only trying to protect their property."

"This is terrible. Has Mortas done this? What would he want with these people?" Eric asked.

Phetrix placed a hand on his shoulder. "He's done so much worse. Every city, town, and village has fallen prey to his ruthless leadership. He demands complete obedience and makes examples of those that refuse, like our friends here. This is what we've come to destroy. This is why you and your sister were whisked away to a different dimension. In our time of despair, we did the only thing we could to preserve the future of Chevalon. I fear we've lost much in the process, but now is the time to fix what's been done. I don't know if your parents are alive, but you and your sister are. You are the promised ones to restore order and remove the blight caused by Mortas."

"That's a lot to hand the kid, don't you think? Days ago he was a normal teenager, worrying about college and girls, and now you make him the savior of a land he knows nothing about?" Grant said. "It's a lot to process. Hell, I know I can't make heads or tails of it. How can you expect him to?"

"No, Grant. I get it. Sort of. I mean, if I'm who he claims I am, shouldn't I fulfill my duty? My parents always taught me to do the right thing. We can't discount the weirdness of all this, but the truth is all around. The seam. The people intent on stopping us. Those crazy demon things. And the power I feel that is leading us east. It has to be real. Everything means I am who he says I am. I can't see any other way."

"Come on, kid, don't let the wizard guy mess with your head. Do you really think it's all true?"

"Don't you? Look," Eric said motioning toward the grotesque display before them. "Doesn't that speak of truth?"

"It tells me the people here are in trouble, but it doesn't say a damn thing about you."

Grant stalked out of the house, leaving Phetrix and Eric alone with the victims.

"Phetrix, how am I to end things? What role do I play in stopping more murders? And my…sister? How does she figure into it?"

Phetrix motioned toward the door. "Maybe we ought to step outside into the fresh air first." They walked away from the house until they could no longer smell the stench. Phetrix cracked his knuckles and continued.

"The prophecies of old spoke of a royal with the power of a mage. If they took the throne, they'd usher in an era of peace unlike anything Chevalon has ever experienced. There are forces who think it is a lie told by the Order to keep the people in line. To see the current rulers as weak. To them, Chevalon needs a new direction. Mortas Frost was the strongest of them all and built a massive following. Founded on lies and treachery, he duped one of the most promising magus of the Order to serve him. Returning you and your sister to your rightful positions as rulers will wipe out all the evil Mortas has done."

"I don't know anything about ruling a kingdom. How am I supposed to defeat them?"

"Your sister," Phetrix whispered. "When the two of you are reunited, your combined powers will make you more powerful than Rhoden or any mage in the kingdom. We have to get you together. The pull you feel is from her. You are trying to reconnect, though you didn't know it."

"It still makes no sense, but if it means I have a chance to finish it, then we have to."

"You sound like a wise ruler already." Phetrix smiled, knowing the burden of convincing Eric of his duties was not his.

"Thanks. Now if only we can get Grant on board."

"I don't believe the detective truly believes what he sees with his own eyes, but he will soon. What choice does he have?"

Phetrix turned and dusted off his clothes. "Detective, are you ready to leave? We have a destiny to fulfill."

"Destiny? What have you gotten me into?"

Phetrix had no answer. He didn't really know.

Chapter 22

It was just the two of them now. Two against the world. Well, actually against two worlds. Nadina stared out the side window as they drove out of the city. The buildings were replaced by houses, then farmland. Though she couldn't see much in the dark, she'd made the trip enough times to have mental pictures of the passing landscape.

They were heading for a cabin on a lake almost two hours from Chicago. She hated being that far away from wherever Eric was, but at the moment it was for the best. By now, the city's entire police force had their description. It was no longer safe for them.

The cabin had been a regular family vacation destination, though they hadn't been for the past four years. Once Eric entered high school, he was too involved in other activities to find the time to go. The owner, Jeb Barkley, was miffed they'd called so late, but they explained they were doing spur-of-the-moment home remodeling and had nowhere else to stay. Though he grumbled, he said, "I'll leave the keys in my mailbox. Swing by and get them, but don't wake me up."

Nadina missed the place. The cabin was on a large parcel of land on a calm, beautiful lake. There they taught Eric how to fish, shoot his bow, and go on long survival hikes. They cooked over an open fire, swam, and boated. Those were good times, certainly better than now. They pulled into the small rural town as dawn rose. Nordon found the house and retrieved the keys. Once back in the car he said, "We should stop somewhere and pick up supplies."

"I don't want to be here that long."

"Agreed, but we'll still need a few things."

"Nordon, if we buy stuff, we'll settle in and won't do anything to find Eric."

He started to counter her concerns but changed his mind. "Okay." He pulled away and turned down Main Street.

She gripped his arm. "Don, I'm sorry. I'm so worried about Eric that I can't think straight."

"It's all right, Dina. We'll find him. You believe that, right?"

She studied his face, then stroked his cheek lightly. "Yes."

They stopped at the lone traffic light. Nadina perked up. "That diner we like opens at six. Why don't we stop there? At least we can have one good meal before we decide what to do."

Nordon smiled. "Sounds good. I'm hungry enough to eat one of their cows."

They parked on the street across from the diner. With almost thirty minutes to kill, they sat in silence holding hands. After a long stretch listening to each other breathing, Nadina said, "Don, do you think he's still alive?"

"Dina, don't."

She choked back a sob.

He pulled her close and stroked her hair. "He's alive. I feel it. I know you do too. We're going to get him back."

"But, then what? What happens if--"

"When," Nordon corrected.

"When we get him back. Which world will he choose?"

"I'm not sure he'll have a choice. If he is the king, he will have to lead his people. I can't blame him. It's what we trained him for. We knew this day would come."

"What do we do?"

He paused, weighing his answer. "We'll do what's right at the moment. It does little good to plan until we know the outcome of this battle. Of course, we may not have a choice. If the police are still looking for us, it might be best to go home."

"I can barely remember that time. We'll be giving up a lot. This world has so much to offer."

"Yes, it does. But it's missing one thing."

"Eric."

"I think our decision has been made."

"Will you be all right with that choice?"

"I'll be all right with whatever we choose as long as you're with me."

Nadina gazed up into the big man's eyes. She placed a hand on his cheek. "I really do love you, Nordon."

He smiled. "And I you."

She kissed him.

Ten minutes later, the open sign lit up in the diner window. They entered and took a booth near the back. They were the only customers. They ordered. Nordon's plate was heaped with enough food for three people. Dina got scrambled eggs and ham with wheat toast but had little appetite. Nordon coaxed her to eat. "You'll need your strength, and who knows when we'll be able to eat again."

She ate, though tasted nothing. As they were cashing out, the small old-fashioned TV behind the counter showed two pictures. Nordon handed the waitress the bill and twenty dollars. Nadina looked up at the screen and gasped, then covered her shock by coughing.

"You all right, sweetie?" the waitress asked as she rang in the ticket.

"Yes, thank you."

As the waitress counted out change, Nadina nudged Nordon and pointed at the TV with her chin. He looked up and his jaw fell open. On the screen were their driver's license photos side by side. The waitress went to give the change, but Nordon wasn't paying any attention. She glanced at where he was staring as the screen changed to the news anchor and the next story.

"Lordy, you look like you seen a ghost."

"Huh? Oh, sorry. Zoned off for a moment." He stuck out his hand and took the change, then handed her back a five for a tip.

"Wow! Nice one. Come back again. Maybe you can teach these farm boys what a real tip looks like." She laughed loudly. The eight customers in the diner looked her way. How many had seen the TV? Of those, how many would make the connection? Nordon turned his head toward the window and walked quickly toward the door.

"Thanks again. You two have a nice day."

"Thank you," Nadina said. They hurried to the car, wanting to get away before anyone noticed the make and color of the car.

"I can't believe it. We're the subjects of a manhunt!" Nadina exclaimed. "What are we going to do?"

"We'll be all right as long as Mr. Barkley doesn't see the story. We may have to move faster than we wanted."

At the end of town, the road forked. Nordon took the wrong one, hoping if anyone was watching they'd inform the local authorities which way they were headed. A few miles out of town, Nordon worked his way back to the right road. Twenty minutes later, they turned down the long dirt road leading to the lake. Five minutes after that, they reached the cabin.

Nordon let Nadina out, then pulled the car around behind the cabin. The road was a long ways off, and no one passing had a view of the cabin, but he didn't want to take a chance. Once he entered, Nadina was sitting on the sofa flicking through the channels, which were few. The news stories were over and nothing else showed.

He set down the duffel bags. "We should be good," Nordon said, "at least until the noon news."

She clicked off the TV and paced. "Tell me again we'll be all right."

"Every journey has obstacles. We'll handle them one at a time as they come. But yes, we'll be all right."

"Police could be on their way here as we speak."

"Stop, Dina. You'll make yourself crazy."

"I'm already crazy. This whole situation has made me nuts."

"We have to relax. That's when we're at our best. Let's start making plans." He pulled out a chair and motioned for her to sit. He joined her at the heavy wooden kitchen table.

"We have no fall back plan," Nadina said. "This was it."

"Then it's time for us to figure out a way to get to the seam and find a way through."

"How?"

"Not sure. But there has to be a way."

"But we'll need someone with magical abilities."

"What about Catron?"

Nadina let the idea run through her mind for a moment. Then she shook her head. "Even if she knows how to open the seam, I doubt she'll help us. She blames us for Tetrin's death. Her last words were 'Don't come back'."

"Well, we are sorta responsible for his death."
"We didn't cause it. Rhoden did."
"Yes, but he was only there because we were."
She had no response.
"I think it's worth a try."

Chapter 23

The fallout from the attack was immediate. Samuel cringed as they walked past the dead and wounded. Fifteen gone. Fifteen souls gave their lives to the cause. On top of that, there were twenty gravely injured.

"Samuel, we can't possibly hope to continue," Char said. He clung by the mage's side as they walked among the shattered remains of the forces. Mathilda had gathered all four of her other mages to attend the wounded. Hopefully they'd be able to save as many as possible through their powers.

"We must. Don't you see? The people cannot let evil win. No matter the cost, Mortas must be defeated."

"The cost? Look around you, mage! The cost has been paid and will continue to be paid. We're too weak now. I didn't think what we had was enough to begin with. Now I'm sure of it."

Samuel turned away from a man with his arm bone protruding through the skin. The man wailed for help and soon one of Mathilda's mages attended to him. He wove a simple spell forcing the man to sleep and went to work on his arm.

"We cannot let this deter us. I know what we face is daunting, but anything worthwhile takes a sacrifice. Everything has a cost."

Char ran a hand through his hair, his lips quivering like he was holding back his thoughts. Samuel was content to let him stew. He'd have to see the truth of their plan. Removing Mortas was paramount. Nothing else mattered. True; their work just grew significantly more difficult, but it didn't make it any less important.

"Char, what we do is for the good of the people. Once this is over, the land can rest at peace once again. Evil cannot win. Ever."

He left the man before there was an argument and carefully watched the faces of the survivors. Many were distraught, and had every right to be. The Seeker ambush came out of nowhere. There was no advance warning and they didn't see them until it was too late.

"Someone should have seen them," he muttered. "How did they see through my spell?" It shouldn't have happened. It was like the Seekers knew where they were. But if that were true, it meant someone on the inside had sent a signal. That couldn't be. Everyone was in danger. Regardless of how it went down, it would devastate their group and the survivors would be left to deal with the aftermath. As much as Samuel wanted to escape through the seam, it was not going to happen. Everything was because of his forethought. He would see it through to the end.

Mathilda found him and reported the latest.

"Samuel, we've lost three more. That's eighteen for sure, and I fear many more will soon die. Once things settle, we may have thirty to forty people able to go on. I can say their resolve has been shaken quite a bit too."

"The number are less than ideal, but we have four mages plus you and myself. That's six powerful weapons. They have none within those walls unless Rhoden is there, but that's still just one mage against six."

"How many more soldiers do you think they have? Mortas has scoured the kingdom to gather as many to his side as possible. He forces them to join, often slaughtering their families if they refuse. His numbers far outweigh ours."

"Then we figure out a way to even it out. We aren't fools!"

"We are if we think what we have left is enough."

Samuel's face burned bright red. He was aware of the situation, as everyone else was, but this was not a time for weak spines. He had long played the game, lulling his opponent into complacency until the time was right to strike. That time was now. Like in a heated chess match, he had to stay steps ahead of his opponent if he expected victory.

"Gather the remaining fighters. I will address them and we will finish what we started."

Mathilda shook her head and walked away, calling out to others to assist her.

Within fifteen minutes, the entire group had assembled nearby. Samuel stood on a fallen tree to gain a better view of what was left. It wasn't encouraging.

"My fellow resistance fighters: despite this setback, we gain no advantage by remaining here to sulk in our defeat. For years I've planned to return when the time was right to oppose and destroy Mortas Frost. The time for evil to end is now." Though he'd been expecting a raucous chorus of agreement, his words were met with silence.

"Don't let this dissuade you from our mission."

"Look around you, mage! We have no one left!" a man called out. A few others agreed and a murmur of dissent trickled through the crowd.

"We have each other. We have six able-bodied mages. We can do this. We can take the castle. It's my firm belief that one of the heirs is inside. If we can free her, we can begin a wave of dissent throughout Chevalon that will crush Mortas for good."

"Six? I've seen more do less!" a woman cried out. She had a point, but the six would have to do.

"Please listen to reason. What comes next will surely test our resolve. We must remain strong at all costs."

Mathilda stood next to him. "Samuel is right. We are outnumbered and overpowered. That means our victory will be that much greater! It means when people of the future talk about this moment, you will be the creators of a new world. They will speak of you in terms unheard of before. You will bring about change. You will restore the land. It is you! Are you prepared for what's to come?"

This time, a few cheers rose up from the crowd. Slowly they grew louder as though a wildfire engulfing brush. Soon, Mathilda had them all crying out for victory. She turned to Samuel with a grin across her face.

"Our forces are ready. Are you?"

Samuel's mouth hung open. What had she done so differently than he? How had she taken charge like this? Because you were gone too long, fool, he reminded himself. These were her people, not his. They never were his. The moment he left through the seam and decided not to stay there, everything had changed. Those left behind, like Mathilda, were forced to figure out how to navigate the growing danger Mortas presented.

It was a move he hadn't seen coming.

Mathilda quickly went into action, calling on others to help the wounded. "You two stay with them. Make them as comfortable as possible. Heal when you can. Be careful but be smart. If you're attacked, use any means necessary to save the people. Got it?" The man and woman she was speaking to nodded and went to work, gathering a few others to help them with the injured.

"That's two less mages for us, but they're needed here," she said to Samuel.

"But moments ago, you were arguing with me about what forces we had left!"

Mathilda grinned. "I was. You were right, though. What we have must do. What choice is there? I suppose dying for freedom is much better than living in fear, don't you think?"

Now it was Samuel's turn to smile. "Exactly."

"If you two are done, I'd like to know how you expect us to continue." Char said. He was more angry and confused than Samuel had ever seen him.

"With resolve and power. We have right on our side. We will win," Samuel replied. Char rolled his eyes and stalked away, clearly not pleased with the answer.

Chapter 24

The twelve o'clock news showed their photos again. Nadina was not immediately recognizable, but there was no mistaking Nordon. He was too big to go unnoticed. The story told that the two were wanted in connection with several assaults on police officers. Anyone with information as to their whereabouts was to call and there was a possible reward.

They shut the TV off and sat back, staring at nothing. Ten minutes later, Nordon got up and went outside. Nadina sprawled on the sofa and closed her eyes. The exhaustion fell upon her like a wrestler, sinking her weight deeper into the cushions. A distant motor roared to life. It took a few moments to register, then panic came and she sat up fast. A car? She got up and ran to the window. No vehicle was in sight, but with all the trees surrounding the cabin, it wasn't surprising.

A thought struck her. It was stupid to wait for a car to arrive instead of getting ready to flee. She whirled around, snatched up both duffel bags, and ran for the door. She bounded down the stairs and around the cabin. She reached the car and patted her pockets. She didn't have the key. She tried the door and thankfully it opened. She tossed the bags onto the back seat then scanned the area for Nordon. It was a bad time for him to take a walk.

A sound came from near the water. She ran down the path as the engine sound grew louder. The vehicle was close. Nadina burst from the trees onto a sandy beach. A small wooden dock jutted out into the lake. At the far end was a little boat with an outboard motor running. Nordon was onboard, bent over looking at something. Her body sagged as the tension melted away, realizing this was the source of the noise.

Nadina walked down the dock and watched Nordon. He stood, wiped his hands on a rag, and turned to the wheel. The engine revved. "That's better," he said to himself. He looked up and saw Nadina. He jumped and clutched at his chest. "Don't sneak up on an old man like that!"

"Sorry. I heard a motor and thought someone was coming for us."

"I just wanted to make sure it runs. It gives us an extra avenue of escape. Want to go for a ride?" His eyes were wide and hopeful, and he seemed excited.

She nodded. "Sure."

"Yeah." He stepped to the side and offered his hand. Nadina took it and stepped down into the boat. Nordon untied the ropes and guided the boat toward the center of the lake. It was peaceful; the water calm. The pale blue surface was reflective. She sat back, closed her eyes, and let the wind sweep her hair back. The air smelled brisk and clean. The sun caressed her face, warming her and making her feel safe.

For the moment her troubles were washed away by the relaxing beauty of her surroundings. The images of those wonderful vacations flashed before her mind's eye. Just herself, Nordon, and Eric. The thought of Eric burst the bubble of her comfort zone. She opened her eyes and reality gave her a cold slap. She sat up. Her muscles tensed and the relaxation from the boat ride drained away.

Nadina glanced up to see Nordon watching her, a grim expression on his rugged face.

"What are we going to do, Don?"

He looked away for a second and refocused on her. "I don't know."

Nadina choked back a sob. "I'm so afraid we'll never see him again." After the words were out, she covered her face and cried.

Nordon idled the engine and sat next to her. He wrapped her in his large, protective arms and rocked. The motion had calmed her in the early days of learning the ways of this new and frightening world, but had little effect now. She cried for several minutes into Nordon's chest before wiping her eyes and pushing back.

"There has to be something we can do."

Nordon released a long, slow breath. "There might be."

That got Nadina's attention. Her eyes cleared. "What?"

"We need a wizard to open the seam, right?"

She nodded, feeling the faintest glimmer of hope. "Yes."

"Well, isn't Catron a sort of wizard? I mean, she might not be in Samuel's or Phetrix's league, but she does use magic."

The excitement grew, then burst like a popped balloon. "Even if she could open the seam, I doubt she would help us. She blames us for Tetrin's death."

"Maybe so, but do you have any better ideas?"

She didn't. "Then let's go now."

"Don't you think we should wait at least a day? Not only to let some of the heat die down, but to replenish our energies. Look at us. We've been through a lot these past few days. I don't know about you, but I'm spent."

"Nordon, I can't wait. I have to do something or I'll explode. We can rest at Catron's."

"If she doesn't shoot us on sight."

She offered a weak smile. "Yeah, there is that."

"All right. Let's head back and pack."

She leaned forward and kissed his cheek. "I love you, Don. I hope you know that."

He smiled, and for the first time since their ordeal began, she saw real warmth in his eyes. "I do and I hope you know the same. Don't worry. We'll get our boy back. And it doesn't matter who his parents are or what his destiny is. We'll be a family again."

Nordon swung the craft around and aimed for the dock. As they neared the wooden structure, Nadina stood and moved to the forward line. In her periphery, she caught a blinking light along the far end of the lake. She turned to look, but whatever it had been was blocked by the trees.

She reached for the first post as Nordon cut the engine and guided the boat forward. She tied off her end while Nordon went aft. With that done she focused her attention on where she'd seen the light and followed the tree line to her left. There! She saw it again. A blinking red light. A second one was close behind.

"Nordon!" she pointed. "Police!"

He stiffened. "We have a few minutes. Start the engine and stay here. I'll get our things."

She hesitated, thinking she was faster and should go, but Nordon was on the dock and running before she could speak.

She turned the key and stood at the helm wondering if they were ever going to catch a break. She watched the progress through the trees, estimating how much time they had before the police swarmed over them. Likely not much. Hurry, Nordon. She was tempted to leap onto the dock and help him.

The cabin door burst open and Nordon lumbered down the steps carrying their duffels. He ran hard, his weight making the dock bob and sway and the wooden planks sag. He tossed the bags down on the deck, then turned and ran.

"Where you going?"

He shouted over his shoulder. "The car!"

The police cars turned down the cabin's driveway, clearly in sight. Three squad cars formed a fast-moving caravan.

"Nordon!" she called.

He was at the car. He turned, saw the approaching cars, and motioned for her to go. "I'll pick you up on the other side!" he shouted and waved for her to go. Before she could tell him no, he was in the car with the door shut. The engine fired up and he shifted.

Untying the lines, she guided the boat away from the dock then opened the throttle. As the boat rose to plane, she turned around to watch Nordon. He was heading straight for the line of cop cars at high speed. A heavy knot formed in her stomach. She turned away from the wheel, praying he would be safe.

The distance closed fast. One car peeled to the side and two cars created a larger blockade. As the deadly game of chicken came within seconds of its explosive conclusion, one police car swerved and Nordon barreled past. The grinding of metal told Nadina he did not escape unscathed, but the car barely slowed as it hit the driveway and sped away. The police cars turned at the same time, blocking each other and giving Nordon a precious extra few seconds' lead. She cheered. "Go, Nordon! Go!"

He disappeared behind the trees. The police cars regrouped and gave chase. Nadina watched the far shoreline for signs of Nordon's progress. She caught a few glimpses, but even though he had a lead, she knew there was no outrunning a radio warning. The police would already be on the air, setting up defenses to corral Nordon. She focused in the distance and spotted a dock. She turned the wheel and steered toward it.

Had the police seen her? Even if not, they'd surely seen Nordon waving his arms at her. How much time did she have? Once she docked, she'd have to carry the two duffels, and they'd slow her down. If necessary, she'd drop them and run. They wouldn't do her any good if she got captured.

She thought about the guns. If she kept one, it increased the chances of a dire outcome. At least in jail she'd be alive. As she closed on her target dock, she wondered if death would be preferable to capture.

Chapter 25

Elly stood on the crest of the hill overlooking the field ahead and cringed.

"What is all that?"

"You don't know?" Shree replied. "Doesn't your power tell you anything about it? Is that what we've been tracking? If so, then I gotta say it's off!"

Spread out before them was a large black-walled castle. From their vantage point, it appeared they were on the backside. The two towers flanking a large wooden drawbridge faced a dark forest. Protruding from the towers were two large black flags with a white snowflake in their centers.

"Maybe he's in there."

"How are we gonna get inside? Just knock on the door?"

Elly shrugged. "I don't know. If that Rhoden dude is in there, that would be a disaster."

"The design on the flags. Didn't the soldiers have a snowflake on their uniforms?"

"Yeah. This place belongs to those fools that brought us here. But if so, why was I pulled here?"

"It has to be that Rhoden guy. I'm sorry, Elly, but looks like you were duped."

She couldn't believe she had been wrong the entire time. Nothing about the bond felt like malice or deceit. Not like she could really distinguish feelings within it, but still; something told her what she felt was right.

"What if…" Elly began in a soft voice. Shree sat with her arms crossed on the ground next to her, waiting for the punchline. "What if this guy that's supposed to be my brother works for Rhoden? What if he's a bad guy too?"

"Girl, I don't even want to think about what that would mean. Honestly, can't we just get back home and leave this mess for these people to clean up?"

Elly liked that idea a lot. They were only on this hill overlooking the castle because she thought she'd been following something important. Getting herself involved in a civil war for a land in a world she knew nothing about wasn't the least bit appealing. She had her own problems.

"Shree, I think it's time we go with your gut. What was I doing, following this thread of power? What did I think would be at the other end? This world isn't ours. My feelings sway back and forth whether we ought to help them or escape to our world." She focused on home; on the busy streets and constant flow of people. The bright lights and tall buildings of one of the world's greatest cities, with endless deep dish pizza options and a passion for sports teams that rarely lived up to expectations was where she wanted to be. No one wanted her dead there.

As she contemplated the benefits of going home, a gnawing deep within her wouldn't let up. She didn't like to see people hurt. The homeless in the streets back home made her sad. Her heart went out to them and she'd often come home broke after giving away all her money. People sometimes needed help whether they asked for it or not. Pride got in the way, but she always felt a connection to those in need and reached out.

"No. This isn't right," Elly whispered.

"Girl, you're not gonna do what I think you're gonna do, are you?"

"What do you mean?"

Shree placed her face in her hands and breathed in deep. When she uncovered, her stern expression took Elly back.

"I know you, Elly. You don't want to go back to Chicago knowing there are people here you can help. You hate to see others suffer. I've been your friend long enough to recognize that look on your face. As much as you wanna go back, you can't do it, can you? Your heart belongs to the needy. I want to go home, Elly, but I ain't leaving your side. We're a team. We stay if you say so. I complain that I want to go home, but you know me. We're staying, aren't we?"

A slow smile crossed Elly's face. Shree was right. Knowing the people of this foreign land needed help dug at her. She would do whatever she could. If they claimed she was a princess, then she'd be the best one she could be. Of course, when they all woke from this crazy nightmare, none of it would matter anyway, if indeed it was all a shared hallucination. She sometimes thought it was.

"We're staying. We'll do what we have to in order to set things straight around here. I have no idea what that is, but we'll figure it out."

They were startled at the pounding of horses running across the field behind them. They spun around in time to find five black clad riders charging toward them. Each soldier wore the dreaded white snowflake on their chests.

"Oh no!" Shree cried. "Elly, can you do something?"

Elly tapped into the power within her but it slipped through her grasp like running water. "Ugh! No, I can't!"

"Then we better run!"

The girls leapt to their feet and ran toward the castle, away from the riders.

The horsemen crossed the open field easily and were soon upon the girls. Two riders swung around to either side, encircling them. The lead rider removed his black helmet to get a better look at the girls.

"You," he finally said to Elly. "You are the escapee! The one Rhoden has been looking for." A grin crept across his face, exposing missing teeth. "He will be most pleased to have you back. Our lord Mortas Frost will reward us well for this."

"Screw you! Screw Rhoden! And screw this Mortas Frost!" Shree yelled out.

"You aren't necessary anymore," the soldier said, nodding to one of his companions. Swiftly, the man slid off his horse, unsheathed his sword, and plunged it into Shree's chest. The girl's eyes widened in shock. Shree fell to her knees clutching the sword and sliced open her hands. The man pulled the bloody blade free.

Elly screamed. "No! What have you done?" She dropped to her friend's side and cradled her in her arms. Shree's eyes darted back and forth, her breathing growing labored.

A fury rose inside Elly. More anger and hate than she'd ever experienced boiled over. This time, the power had no choice but to obey. She unleashed a torrent of hate-fueled energy outward, blindly striking all around her. Screams pierced the air as both man and horse were shredded by her rage, the power striking them and sending extremities flying. She didn't care who they were or what damage she'd done. Her raw emotions were caught up in the blast.

"Shree!" she cried, clutching her friend to her. Blood ran freely from the wound in her back and Elly tried desperately to cover it with her hand, though she knew it was a losing battle. Something else had to be done.

Around her the devastation she wrought was gruesome to behold. Blood and torn flesh covered the ground. The stench in the air was terrible, like grilled rotten meat. Elly covered her mouth and coughed, trying not to disturb Shree in her arms.

"Elly, I hurt," Shree muttered.

"Shh, shh. I know."

Elly closed her eyes and wondered if she could do something with the power. So far, all she could do was send out rough, blunt force when provoked. There had to be a way to channel it into what she wanted; otherwise, what was the use?

Elly ran her hand over the open wound. Shree shrieked as she touched raw flesh. Seeking a connection to the power, Elly dove deep within herself, carefully weaving her way to the power.

Finally she connected with it. Hesitant at first, knowing how fickle the connection could be, she slowly pushed harder until it filled her. Then she concentrated, imagining the power running down her arms and into her fingers and transferring over to Shree, soothing the exposed nerves and stopping the bleeding. She peeked through half-closed eyes to see the bleeding had actually stopped.

"Shree? Shree…are you still with me?" The girl didn't respond but her chest moved slowly up and down.

Closing her eyes again and hoping not to lose the connection, Elly continued her mental exercise and imagined healing the wound like she'd seen in so many movies. She directed the flow of the power into the wound, and instead of forcing raw energy through her body, she directed the flow in a weave back and forth over it, carefully applying herself to the task.

She had no idea how long it took, but eventually she finished and opened her eyes. It was darker outside now. Dusk had fallen across the land and the sun barely poked above the horizon. Men and horses lay motionless around them. Then she saw Shree. She was breathing somewhat normally and the wound on her chest had closed. It still looked painful, but the gaping wound no longer seeped blood. It was a rough fix, but so far, it looked like her work had done the trick.

"Shree, don't die on me. Please don't die."

Elly worried what Shree's parents would say if they never found their daughter. It was then she determined to fight the impending fight ahead of her and return Shree back home as soon as possible. Wounded, maybe; but not dead. It was her duty.

Elly collapsed on the bloody ground next to her friend and smiled, hearing her breathing. She had saved her.

For now.

Chapter 26

Nadina tied off and tossed the duffels on the dock. She climbed up, snagged the bags, and hurried down the dock to shore. She didn't want to go to the road directly in front of the house where she docked. Instead, she traveled along the shoreline and passed three houses before angling toward the road. She checked for oncoming cars but found the road deserted. After a long scan of the area, Nadina spotted a small shack, the kind of shelter built for children awaiting the arrival of a school bus. It was across the street and three houses down from where she stood. She made for it. Most of them were open on the front side. This one was completely enclosed with a door and windows in the front. She wondered if it was locked. It was fall, so school was in session, but it was late afternoon. The kids would either be on the buses heading home or already there. She hoped for the latter.

She tried the doorknob. It turned and the door swung open. Relieved, she stepped inside, closed the door, and ducked below the windows. She had a good view down the road. If either Nordon or the cops came, she'd spot them.

She waited but grew more restless and concerned with each passing minute. Had they captured Nordon? Was he-- she stumbled over the thought--dead? She tried not to be negative, but as time passed, that was the only thing that came to her. If it looked like he couldn't escape, she knew he'd lead them away from her. One of them had to stay safe to continue searching for Eric.

More than a half hour had gone by since she landed. A car approached. She was about to sneak out of her hiding place to check when she caught sight of a truck backing down the driveway of the house behind the shack. She ducked fast, hoping she hadn't been spotted. The truck backed into the road and idled level with the shack. It hesitated, leaving Nadina to believe she'd been discovered. Then, it shifted and drove slowly down the road.

Relieved, she blew out a long breath. The phone buzzed. She patted her pockets. She found it in a front pocket, pulled it out and answered without looking at the screen for the caller ID.

"Hello?"

"Dina."

"Oh, Nordon, thank God. I was so--"

He cut her off. "They've got me boxed in, Dina."

"What? No!"

"Listen to me. I don't have much time. I'm going to toss the phone so they can't get your number. They have me, Dina. There's nothing I can do. I'm going to have to give up. If I hurt a bunch of cops, I'll never get free. Go to Catron. Plead for her to help you.

It's up to you to save Eric. Don't try to find me. I'll be fine. I'll call an attorney and try to get out. Keep your phone so I can contact you. Answer but don't speak until you hear my voice. Hang up if it's not me." Silence. "They're coming. They have me surrounded and about a dozen guns are aimed at me. Dina, I love you with all my heart and soul. Save our son."

With tears streaming, she said, "I love you too, Don. I'll find him. I promise."

But he was already gone. She broke down and cried for a long time, oblivious of the truck coming down the road until the door shut.

In a panic, Nadina looked up as a dirty middle-age woman opened the shack door and poked her head in. "You know this isn't a bus stop, right?" Seeing Nadina's red, moist eyes, the woman softened her tone. "Oh my. Are you all right, dear?"

"I'm sorry. I didn't mean to impose." She bent to pick up the duffels. "I was waiting for a ride. When he didn't show up, I came in here."

"Is he coming?"

Unbidden, the tears welled. She could only shake her head for fear of sobbing again.

"Oh, I'm sorry. Can I do anything for you?"

Nadina shook her head. "No, thank you." She hefted the bags and moved toward the door. The woman backed away and Dina exited. "Sorry for intruding," she said and walked away.

"How far you going?"

That was a good question. "I-I don't know."

"Let me give you a lift."

"But I don't know where I am."

A curious look crossed the woman's face and Nadina hastened a follow up. "We were supposed to be in a cabin. I was dropped off and my friend was going to pick me up, but he's not coming now."

"Just like a man to leave a woman stranded." She opened the passenger door. "Come on. I've got a couple of hours to kill before I have to pick up my daughter from cheerleading. I'll get you as far as I can, or at least to a bus station. Let me guess. Chicago, right?"

"Yes. How'd you know?"

"No offense, but it's easy to tell. Besides, this area isn't all that big. I know almost everyone here."

Nadina climbed in, tossing the duffels in the back. The woman got in and started the engine. "Name's Marge." She stuck out a hand.

"Dina," she accepted it, feeling the hard calloused skin.

"Well, Dina, there's no buses or Ubers in this town. I'll take you as far as the next town. It's about a twenty-minute drive."

"That'd be great. Thank you so much for your kindness."

"Sure. Us gals gotta stick together.

As they reached the corner, two cruisers turned down the street at high speed sans lights and sound. Nonchalantly, Nadina turned and looked out the side window.

"Wonder what's happening," Marge said. "Don't get much activity around here requiring police."

Nadina glanced out the rear window over her shoulder. She had little doubt they were searching for her. Marge braked at the stop sign and watched in her side mirror. The sheriffs' cars slowed then stopped along the lake side of the road. Both deputies got out and jogged toward the water.

Nadina felt she should say something. "Perhaps someone capsized their boat."

"Yeah, that could be it," Marge said, drawing out the words, deep in thought. "Though it seemed like they were looking on land."

Nadina fought to remain calm as the woman turned her penetrating gaze on her. She eyed Nadina for a few moments. "Tell me the truth. Are they looking for you?"

Nadina forced a look of surprise. "Me? Why would they be looking for me?"

"That is the question, isn't it? Just seems funny, you turning up out of the blue, and suddenly the sheriffs are all over the place."

Mouth agape, Nadina stared at her and said, "Hey, if you want to make sure, turn around and ask them. Doesn't matter to me. You're doing me a big favor by driving me. So if you want to take the time to check it out, it's up to you. I'm just along for the ride."

She bluffed, praying Marge wouldn't see through her. She fought to keep her facial muscles from twitching.

Marge turned. For a frightening moment, Nadina thought she was making a U-turn, but she straightened the wheel and drove down the street.

"We've got nice drive ahead of us. Tell me about yourself."

Nadina knew it was a veiled attempt to gather information. Now she regretted giving her real name. She settled back in the seat and began weaving a tale of half-truths, starting with being raised in the country and ending with meeting a man she thought really cared for her, but obviously didn't. She wiped at an imaginary tear as she finished. "This was the first vacation I've been on since my parents died years ago."

Marge didn't respond, other than grunting at the low parts of her made-up life story.

"I mean, there has to be someone out there for me somewhere, doesn't there? That's what they always say, anyway; there's someone for everyone." She looked at Marge as real tears streaked her face. "I don't know why I bother."

Marge's face softened. She patted Nadina's thigh. "You will find someone, and when you do, it'll be magic. Don't give up. It'll happen."

"Thanks, Marge. I needed to hear that." She wiped her face and turned to look out the side window, hoping that would be the end of the woman's suspicions.

Chapter 27

Phetrix worried they'd be late. He had no concept how much time had passed in this dimension but knew with the recent events that they needed to hurry. Losing out on the opportunity to reunite the twins and overpower the evil Mortas wrought was not conducive to their plans. The more frequent Seeker attacks attested to Mortas's far reach with Rhoden's help.

The small group traveled across grassy glens and wooded hilltops. A stream ran through an open field and Grant dropped to his knees, splashing his face.

"Is this water safe to drink?" he asked Phetrix. He thought it an odd question.

"Why wouldn't it be?"

"Diseases. Sickness. Pollution."

"Pollution? Time after time you assail me with odd words."

Eric smiled.

"What is it, Prince?" Phetrix asked.

"These two worlds couldn't be any more different. I mean, I guess this one is kinda like what Earth was a thousand years ago, but..." He cocked his head as Grant sipped greedily from the stream. "But just how did you pass through to our world? Why Earth? Does this seam go to other places?"

It was Phetrix's turn to grin. "There is much to learn, young Prince. Once we're through fulfilling our duties, I will share my knowledge."

"Wait! You mean there's more? You've been to other, um, dimensions?" Grant asked. He rested on the ground and wiped the droplets of water from his face. "I refuse to believe it. All we've been taught is the supremacy of our planet. I'm having a hard time coping, here," he said, nodding. "How am I supposed to believe there's more?"

"Detective, surely you can see how such a possibility exists. Even before we discovered the seam, we held to long-standing beliefs about our place in the cosmos. Observations of the planets and star clusters captivated ancient and current mages alike. Finding the seam created a massive shift in our thinking, but we also understood it needed to be kept a secret. If the wrong people realized it existed, well, you have problems like we do now."

"Then what do we do about it? Can we shut them down somehow?" Eric asked. Both Phetrix and Grant turned to him, speechless.

"Close them?" Grant whispered. "I want to go home. This world doesn't belong to me."

"Prince, if we close them entirely, we lose any chance for future escape. Without them, you'd not be standing here now. It is because the seam exists that we can correct the wrongs we now face."

Eric opened his mouth to speak, then closed it. Phetrix watched as the boy drifted deep in thought, his eyes glazing over as though staring at something far in the distance.

"I don't know, Phetrix. But something has to be done. Can we guard them?"

"That's not a bad idea as long as you can trust the guards," Grant added.

They were silent at the suggestion, all of them unsure about speaking. Phetrix sat on the ground as Grant inspected the area.

"Detective, please don't fret over the land. We're perfectly safe for now."

"Phetrix, look!" Eric called out, startling the mage. He exposed his scar. It was glowing.

"When did that happen?"

"Just now. It tingled."

Grant joined them, crouching and carefully reaching out his hand. "May I?"

"Yeah, go ahead."

Grant gently ran a finger along the scar. "It doesn't feel different than normal skin. It's not puckered like scar tissue. Does it hurt?"

"Not at all. It actually feels kinda cold."

Grant grunted. "What is this, Phetrix?"

"It's the mark. It's how we knew he was the true prince. Your sister," he said, looking directly into Eric's eyes, "has a similar one as I've mentioned before. I'd wager that hers is glowing now also. It bonds the two of you. It's proof you are who you are. It gives hope to those without it."

Eric brushed off the words. "I find it hard to believe something like this means so much. I'm just a kid!"

"You are more than that. Can't you feel it inside?"

Eric closed his eyes, his hand covering the glowing scar. "I feel something. I don't know how to describe it, though."

"If we don't get moving, we'll get stuck in the dark," Grant said.

"The detective is right. We should move on. The castle is not far now. My guess is we'll find what we're looking for there."

They crossed the stream, heading east to what lay beyond.

NOT LONG AFTER the stream was behind them, a deep growl startled the men.

"What's that?" Eric asked.

Grant instinctively unholstered his gun.

Another long, menacing growl greeted them. They froze, searching the trees for the source.

A bush shook. All three spun to their right. Something howled behind them. Phetrix recognized it and tried to remain calm.

"Friends," he said quietly, "I suggest we move this way, but not too fast. Sudden movements will attract it."

"Attract what?" Grant asked.

Eric stood still.

"Prince, it's time to move. You do not want to be here when it emerges from the forest."

"What. Is. It." Grant snarled. He drew his gun, aiming at the bush.

"I doubt your weapon will do much to the creature. They're fast."

"I'm ready to test your doubts. What is it?"

"A frightening beast we call a dread-bear."

"A what?" Eric asked. The boy's face went pale.

"A dread-bear. Similar in appearance and disposition to what you call a grizzly bear, but prone to moments of blind rage. They've not been found this far south in quite some time."

Suddenly the dread-bear rushed out from the brush, eliciting a gasp from Grant. The dread-bear had pitch-black short fur. Its yellowed teeth dripped saliva. Large red eyes burned out of the black face as it snarled at them. It ran on all fours directly at Eric.

"No, Prince!"

Phetrix drew in the power, savoring as it filled him. It was a sensation much different than how it felt through the seam in the other dimension.

He fired a blast of pure white energy at the dread-bear, but something heavy rammed into his back, forcing his shot to sail over the head of the beast. It pinned him to the ground. A gunshot erupted in his ears and the animal's weight flew off him.

Phetrix twisted on the ground in time to face a second dread-bear. It slashed at him with long dark claws, ripping deep gashes into his arms. Phetrix cried out as the dread-bear roared, hot saliva splashing on his face. Eric cried out and Grant yelled something he didn't understand.

Then, in a barrage of gunshots, the dread-bear fell to the ground.

"Phetrix! Your arms!" Eric yelled. The mage had no time to inspect the damage as another dread-bear joined the fray, ripping at the ground and roaring a furious call.

"There's too many of them! I can't hold them off!" Grant screamed. Phetrix felt light-headed and fought hard to concentrate.

The dread-bear roared and snapped at him. He felt the hot breath as the large fangs grazed his arm. Something needed to be done, but he was dazed and couldn't focus on the power. This was normally an easy task, but the searing pain in his arms stole all his attention.

The dread-bear roared and soon they were surrounded by five of the beasts.

"Phetrix, what do we do?" Eric yelled.

"I only have four more bullets before I'm done for! Come on, wizard, what can we do?"

Phetrix closed his eyes and only opened them when a dread-bear howled.

"Eric, Eric. You can do this."

"What? I don't know how to use the power! Are you crazy?"

Phetrix reached out to him and pulled him closer. A dread-bear swiped at him and missed. Grant found a large branch to swing at the beasts, keeping them at a distance.

Blurry eyes and a raging inferno building inside his chest, Phetrix clung desperately to his sanity. He shouldn't be the one in such terrible shape. He was smarter than that! Without his guidance, Grant and Eric were in serious trouble.

Dread-bears circled them, snarling and growling as they dug at the dirt.

"Phetrix, what is it?" Eric asked. Phetrix didn't realize he'd been holding the boy close until Eric unhooked his hands from him.

"The power. You have it." The forced words were difficult to say. His mind threatened to shut down completely.

"Use it. Like a hammer. No finesse. Just smash with it. Feel the energy. Let it out."

Phetrix struggled to make sense of what had happened. Eric stood. Another gunshot sounded. Phetrix fell to the ground, wincing as his raw, exposed arms scraped the dirt. He watched in silent awe as Eric's body glowed like his scar. Even Grant noticed and backed away as far as the dread-bears would let him.

"What's happening to him?" Grant called out. Phetrix said the words in his head, but they failed to escape his lips. He has the power.

Eric pushed his hands outward and two of the dread-bears were thrown backwards. Phetrix smiled.

Grant cheered, though the moment of joy was brief. There were still two dread-bears ready to attack. The creatures circled the men. Eric inhaled. *That's it,* Phetrix thought. *Use the power. Bend it to your will.*

One of the dread-bears lunged at Eric, but the boy failed to attack.

"No!" Phetrix yelled, regretting the sudden movement.

Grant pulled the trigger, felling one of the dread-bears before it could strike Eric. The second one shot past the first and went after Phetrix, bypassing Eric. It swiped at his bloody arms and exposed more of his raw flesh. Intense pain seared through him. Phetrix screamed, his body writhing on the ground. Never had he experienced such a horrifying situation.

Phetrix moaned and the dread-bear snarled, deadly fangs exposed in a show of force. Phetrix watched through blurry eyes how slow it moved as if stalking prey, searching for an opening before preparing for the final, fatal blow.

"Get up, wizard! We don't have the means to stop this!" Grant yelled, though Phetrix didn't know what to say. He struggled with movement, his arms and legs badly.

The last dread-bear snarled and circled them. Eric yelled something and Grant shouted. Phetrix reached inside to grasp the power he'd always known. It felt warm and comforting and completely under his control. His focus returned and he forced the pain away. It was an old trick, but useful when damaged as badly as he was.

Phetrix rose to his feet on wobbly legs. He prepared to strike the final blow. A gunshot erupted. The dread-bear roared and fell to the ground. A large hole in its head leaked blood. It inhaled two final laborious breaths, exhaling long and rattling, and then its chest went still. It was dead at last.

Phetrix let go of the power and fell to the ground in a painful, bloody heap. Eric and Grant rushed to him, hovering like spirits circling the dead.

"Phetrix, are you ok?" Grant asked.

"Don't die on me! I need your guidance if I'm gonna do what you say I am!" Eric added.

Phetrix lost control of his thoughts and words didn't come easy. Searing pain ran through his arms and everything ached.

"Phetrix, come back," he heard Grant say. Then he let go and his world turned black.

Chapter 28

Fifteen minutes later, Marge pulled into a parking lot. "Here you are."

They were parked in front of a bus station. "I can't thank you enough, Marge." She opened the door and jumped out. She stepped on the short running board, reached over the side wall, and lifted the duffels from the bed. Marge was standing near the tailgate. "I wish you luck," she said.

"Thank you and thanks again for the ride. I'll remember your kindness." She stepped forward and embraced the woman. Seconds later she was walking into the station. She kept moving but shot quick glances back over her shoulder. Through the large windows, she spotted Marge still standing there. Then, to her shock and sadness, she saw Marge take out her phone. She tapped the phone three times. 911.

Marge walked toward the driver's door. Nadina had to get out of there. She'd never been in this town and had no idea where to hide. She hurried across the floor and exited the station on the far side of the parking lot. With no idea where she was going, Nadina hustled down the street. She had to get out of sight before Marge realized she was gone. The going was slow with the duffels swinging on each stride.

She'd gone three blocks when she spotted a green sign with a white stick figure reading a book. A library. She turned down the street and found it two blocks down. It was an old single-story brick building. She was so elated she almost didn't notice the building across the street until she was in front of it. The police station was a sister to the library, yet a little shorter. Nadina paused and decided they wouldn't be searching for her yet.

She crossed the street and ran up the four concrete steps. After maneuvering the bags through the door, she asked the librarian behind the front counter if there was a pay phone.

"Well, not anymore," the older woman said with a wide toothy smile. Her name badge said ADELE. "We may be small and in the boonies, but most of us do have cell phones."

"I didn't mean anything by it," Nadina explained in a hurry. "I just need to make a call and don't have a cell phone."

"Oh my," the woman said. She reached under the counter and came up with a large handbag. "I'll tell you what. I'll let you use mine if you swear it's not for anything illegal or to call China or someplace foreign."

"That'd be great, and no, it's nothing illegal. I need to call a cab."

"Oh my," she said again. "No phone and no car. However do you manage?"

"Not very well lately."

"Where are you trying to go?"

"A friend of mine has a cabin off one of the state routes. I'll have to look at a map to remember which one."

"You're not transporting anything bad, are you?" She motioned to the duffels. "No drugs or weapons or a bomb?"

"No," she said with a tense laugh. She picked up her bag and opened it, looking inside first to make sure no guns were showing. she held it up for the woman to see. "Just clothes."

"Oh. Well, that's a relief. Why don't you get on one of the computers and check your route? I'm getting off in fifteen minutes. I'd be happy to take you."

Nadina was stunned. People here were so friendly. That was twice a complete stranger offered her a ride. Of course, the first one hadn't turned out so well, but maybe this one would. Besides, she didn't have a lot of options. "Oh, you're so wonderful. I have to say, though, it might be about forty minutes away."

"It's not like I have anything else to do. Besides, it'll be good to get out of my boring routine." She wrote something on a post-it pad and peeled off the sheet. "Here's the code for the computer. Go check the map and print off the directions."

"Okay. Thanks."

Nadina sat at a computer and followed the instructions to log on to the internet. The search took only five minutes. She found where she was going. It was closer to fifty minutes away. Instead of printing them, she jotted notes, then deleted the search and went back to the front desk.

She sat in the lobby and waited. It was the longest ten minutes of her life. Movement outside drew her attention. Three police cruisers turned onto the street and drove back the way she came from. The hunt was on. Could she stay hidden long enough to make her escape? Finally, Adele walked from behind the desk and a tall black man took her place.

"Ready?"

Nadina nodded.

"I'm out back."

They exited into the rear parking lot to Adele's old brown Chrysler. She didn't move fast, which drove Nadina crazy, and she talked non-stop. They reached the car, but Adele stood on the driver's side and kept blabbing across the roof of the car. Nadina wanted to scream at her but managed to hold her tongue. Adele opened the door and slid inside. Nadina's door was still locked. She rapped lightly on the window and Adele glanced up, surprised. She looked at her like she didn't know her. Then she head-slapped herself. "Oh dear. How senile I'm getting." She reached across the wide bench seat and flicked open the lock.

Nadina reached inside and unlocked the rear door and stashed the bags. She climbed in and pulled the heavy door shut.

"Now, dear, where are we going?"

She gave her the first turns and said, "I was right, it's about forty minutes away." She was afraid if she told her it was closer to an hour she might change her mind.

"Oh, this is so exciting. Like a road trip."

Nadina smiled, though not for long. As soon as they turned onto the main street, Nadina saw local police and sheriffs' cars lining the road. Adele drove slow enough to be going in reverse. She talked faster than she drove. The endless prattle droned on, drowning out the eight-cylinder engine. Several times Nadina thought about asking her to pull over. It might have been slower to walk, but not by much, and at least she'd arrive at her destination with some of her sanity.

Over an hour later as the sun began to set and the night sky flared with bright colors, they reached the long driveway to Catron's cabin. She said goodbye and thanked her profusely, offering to pay her for her time and gas. Adele refused. "My reward will come when I reach heaven." Adele was still talking when Nadina got out, shut the door, and disappeared into the trees that surrounded the property.

She had made it. Now, hopefully Catron wouldn't shoot her.

Chapter 29

The camp was a hive of activity. People moved with a purpose and Samuel marveled at how well trained they all were; even the newer recruits. It was like they had come to the cause prepared just for this.

Char growled direction at a boy who ran off across the field. Then he yelled at a small group that quickly quieted and flew into action.

"What's the plan, mage?" Char asked.

"We leave as soon as everyone's ready. We have no time to waste. The quicker we get to the castle, the faster we end this."

"Or we find our own ends," Char replied.

"I suppose that's true."

Samuel left the man to find Mathilda, who was working her way through the crowd, barking orders and mustering courage.

"Mathilda, how do we look? Think they're ready?"

She spun on him. Her hair stuck to her sweaty forehead. "As ready as ever. Let's do this, Samuel."

"Indeed."

Char called out to someone else, and soon they were in a single long line. Samuel would have no problem protecting them from sight. Their only worry was the Seekers, and they'd deal with them if needed.

"Lead on, Char," Samuel called out. The man yelled something and soon the line snaked forward, away from the wounded.

They trudged through the forest, the late afternoon sun hanging over them. Samuel figured at this pace, they'd arrive at the castle after dark. Maybe they'd use the blackness to get closer without needing his power to cover them.

As the fighters moved on, Samuel felt a growing tension. The people were quiet, yet something about it felt off. He sought Mathilda to discuss the situation.

"Mathilda, are the people worried?"

"Of course they are. Why wouldn't they be? We march to our deaths."

"That's a morbid take. We march to freedom. As they're fond of saying in the other dimension, freedom doesn't come free."

She huffed but said nothing.

"Make sure they're ready when called upon. This is what we've been waiting for all these years."

"Of course. What do you think I've been training them for? They're ready. Scared, but ready."

Samuel looked for an argument but had no response. Mathilda had done so much for the resistance in his absence. Maybe once this was over, he really could go back to Chicago and leave her in charge of the Order. Someone had to rebuild it, and so far, she was the most likely candidate.

The fighters moved ahead, determined in their mission. Still, Samuel couldn't shake his uneasy feeling.

Once the sun went down, Char called a halt to their movement. Samuel found the man to discuss their options. Mathilda joined them.

"Char, how far are we?" Samuel asked.

"Just over that small rise. You can see their fires along the guard towers." He pointed and Samuel followed his lead. Sure enough, small orange fires appeared above them just ahead, glowing in the darkness.

"Are we ready?"

Char wiped his face. "We're as ready as ever."

"You're sure this is the best approach?"

"Mage, it's the only approach. It's the closest we can get to any castle wall without being seen. Once clear of the forest, we'll have to cross fifty strides of open ground. There is one door toward the southwest corner. If we can reach it undetected and your mages can spell or blast it open, we can breech and we'll stand a fighting chance."

Samuel nodded. It was as good as it would get. Their one chance was to get through before being noticed.

"Mathilda, ready?"

"Of course. I've been preparing for this moment a long, long time."

Samuel sighed. She'd never let it rest that he left. Soon, though, she'd focus on something else and he'd be forgotten.

"I want to make one change to your entry plan."

She scoffed and glared at him. He continued undeterred. "I want to split the mages into two groups. You take two and go right, and two will come left with me. We can cover more ground and do more damage, and we also won't have everyone standing in one place where Rhoden can take us out with one spell."

She gave a grudging nod.

"Then let's do this," Samuel said.

"Onward!" Char called out. The soldiers followed without a sound, knowing most would never again see the light of day.

Close to ten minutes into their final push in the dark, a loud crash to their left caught Samuel's attention. There was another crash on the right. Behind them, trees snapped.

"What is this?" Samuel asked.

"Form up around me!" Char called out. The line became an outward facing circle with Mathilda, Samuel, and the four other mages in the center. Char stood next to Samuel, breathing heavy.

Another crash in the trees, and the large stone creatures were upon them. They smashed their way through the brush and headed directly for the group. Shouts rose up, and the mages haphazardly fired bolts of electricity from their hands in a vain attempt to slow the oncoming danger.

"What is this?" Samuel shouted above the bedlam.

"It's another ambush!" Char cried out. "It's like they know exactly what we're doing!"

Samuel spun at the commotion behind him and watched in horror as three soldiers were swiped out of the way by one of the rock creatures. Screams filled the night air. Shouts from the nearby castle added to the madness. Samuel absorbed as much power as he could and waited for the right time to unleash his fury. The rock creatures neared. Stepping out of the way of his companions, Samuel let loose the blast. Three of the creatures shattered. Two others lost arms but still carried on, their one goal to destroy all in their path.

"We cannot stop them!" Char screamed. Soldiers to either side of them broke ranks at the coming beasts, their weapons no match for the rocky beings.

Samuel joined another mage in his attempt to barrel through the creatures and allow a path for escape, but it wasn't enough. He needed to organize the mages for the best effect. He searched for Mathilda but she was nowhere to be seen. Had she been taken down by the rock creatures? Before he could question further, his attention was drawn back to the invading creatures. They swung their arms like large pendulums, blindly striking anything in their path, including one another. It was an inefficient use of their power, but they drove through in unchecked fury.

"Those swords do nothing, Char! We have to retreat! We need to save as many as we can!" Samuel called out.

"You! What's your name?" he asked one of the mages.

"Dorin," the man replied before firing off a lightning bolt that struck one of the rock creatures in the chest and blasted a hole through it.

"Follow Char and give him protection against these things. We need to pull back. Take as many soldiers as possible. Go now!"

Dorin nodded and ran to Char, firing off a constant stream of lightning. Each bolt created a loud peal of thunder and the cacophony grew to an intense level. Samuel felt it in his chest. Loud thumps pushed against his lungs, threatening to knock him over.

"Where the hell is Mathilda?" Samuel cried out. No one replied. They were too busy protecting themselves to notice or care.

Samuel quickly glanced around and two more creatures rushed him. Following Dorin's example, he blasted the things with lightning and felled both. They toppled face down at his feet, shaking the ground.

He noticed the soldiers around him thinning out by falling to the advances of the creatures or following Char. Samuel continued to fire.

All around him the trees shook and the ground vibrated. His heart raced, pounding hard in his chest and threatening to break free. His mouth went dry as he breathed heavy. The drain on him was strong. He had no idea how much longer he'd be able to attack. The creatures seemed to be multiplying. For every one or two he destroyed, three or more appeared. They rushed at the remaining resistance fighters. The main point of retaliation came from Samuel and the unknown female mage to his side. Mathilda was still missing.

"Mage, come on! We have a break in their lines over here!" It was Char. Samuel alerted the mage with him.

"Go. I'll cover you until you're safe."

"What about you? There's too many of them!"

"Just go!" he snarled. She shook her head and raced toward Char.

"Samuel, come on!" he cried out, his voice barely audible over the melee.

Samuel closed his eyes and inhaled deep, filling his lungs until they burned. He opened his eyes and pushed with all his might. A strong force radiated outward from his body, striking down the main line of the creatures around him. The move worked but weakened him considerably. Samuel fell to his knees, gasping for breath. He was too weak to stand and his bones felt like they were liquid. He had nothing left.

Suddenly hands grasped him under his arms and dragged him across the ground. He was vaguely aware worried that it was Frost's men pulling him to certain death. He almost wished it so. The pain in his body consumed him, like thousands of needles poking into his flesh.

"We've got you, mage!" a familiar voice said.

Samuel moved his head slightly and saw Char and another man pulling him away from the ambush to a heavily covered area of brush. The screams of the dying faded and all he heard was the pounding of his blood in his ears.

Mathilda, he thought. *Where was Mathilda? Did they kill her? Was she one of the first to go?*

They'd suffered a terrible loss if she was dead. Then a thought occurred to him that was even more disturbing, and he hoped she was dead instead.

Chapter 30

Nadina stopped at the edge of the clearing and scanned the area. Catron was not in sight. Much of the debris from the front wall of the cabin had been cleared away or stacked to form a makeshift wall. To the right behind and to the side of the cabin was a freshly dug grave. Her heart sank as she thought about Tetrin. Not for the first time, she felt asking Catron for help was a mistake. Although she wanted to walk away, in truth, she had nowhere else to go or anyone else to turn to. Images of Eric and Nordon came to her, fortifying her resolve. She was about to step into the clearing when she heard a voice behind her.

"Thought it might be you."

Nadina jumped and twirled in the air. When her feet touched down, she was sure her heart remained. She instinctively pulled her gun. It was Catron with a shotgun aimed at her.

"Oh! Dear God, you scared me to death."

"That would have been preferable to me shooting you. Thought I told you not to come back."

She started to speak but the words escaped her. Her shoulders sagged. God, she was tired. She holstered the gun. If Catron truly wanted her dead, she'd have pulled the trigger already. "I'm sorry, Catron. The truth is, I have nowhere else to go."

"What happened to the others?" She glanced around, suddenly concerned someone else might be sneaking up on her.

"Captured. The police have all of them."

Catron settled down and lowered the shotgun. "Well, at least they're alive." She cradled the gun and walked past Nadina toward the cabin.

"Catron!" Nadina called. She stopped but did not look back. "I need your help."

"I gave you my husband. Wasn't that enough?" She walked on.

Nadina watched her go. She had no right to ask Catron to help, but if not her, who? She watched as Catron climbed the stairs, each step a greater exertion than the one before. Nadina turned and walked back the way she came.

"Hey!" Catron called after her. "What do you need?"

She felt a flicker of hope and lifted her head. She gazed at the woman standing on the porch.

"If I don't see this through, then Tetrin died for nothing."

Nadina nodded. The burden of guilt rode too heavy on her shoulders. Nadina walked across the clearing and up the stairs. The two women eyed each other, neither having the energy to challenge. Finally, Catron said, "Well, come on in. You can tell me what you need while we eat."

While Catron made a simple meal of venison and corn, Nadina brewed tea. They worked in silence. As they set the meal on the table, the two women stood on opposite sides and held each other's teary gaze. Catron wiped a sleeve across her face, sniffled and said, "Well, let's eat before everything gets all wet."

They sat and filled their plates. Catron chomped a full line across a corncob, wiped her mouth, and said, "Get to it."

Nadina swallowed a mouthful. "Before everyone was captured, we were trying to find a way through the seam to go after Eric and Elly. We realized we needed a magician or someone who at least knew and understood magic."

Catron stopped midway down her next row of kernels. She cocked her head, swallowed, and said, "And you think that's me?"

"I don't know, but you have abilities."

Catron contemplated her words while finishing the row. She set the cob down, wiped her mouth on a paper napkin, and set her elbows on the heavy wooden table. "It's not the same thing as what I do. Sure, elements of magic are involved, but my abilities are limited to the healing arts."

"But it is magic, right?" Nadina said in an excited rush.

"Yes, but an entirely--"

"If you can use magic, you may be able to open the seam. I mean, it's not like offensive spells or healing, but there has to be some correlation, right?" Her tone was hopeful, yet desperate.

Catron studied Nadina with dispassionate eyes.

Nadina reached across the table but stopped short of touching Catron. "Please help me get to my son."

"Even if I offered to help, there's no guarantee I can open this seam."

Nadina nodded. "I know. But how will we know if you don't try?" She felt the tracks of her tears rolling freely down each cheek and made no move to wipe them.

"Do you know where this seam is located?"

"Yes," she blurted. "Yes, I know where they both are."

"Both? There's two?"

Nadina nodded again. "Maybe more; I don't know. But two for sure."

"And you can lead me there?"

"Yes." A sob broke free.

"Where are they?"

"In the city."

"Of course."

"Will you try?"

Catron sighed. "Can I at least finish eating first?"

Chapter 31

Screams pierced the air and startled Elly awake. She hadn't even realized she had fallen asleep. At first she thought it was a firetruck screaming past her window, but then the open skies overhead brought her reality crashing home. She wasn't in Chicago anymore and hadn't been in a long time.

The cries of pain and battle caught her attention again. She pushed herself up from the cold ground and gasped at what she saw in the dancing firelight that brightened the forest.

In the skies in front of the black castle, the black demon-like things were screeching. She saw a horde of creatures that looked like moving rocks pushing their way through the forest toward a group of people. She recognized them and filled with dread. Electricity sparked and balls of fire flew outward from the people. They were fighting them with what appeared to be magic. Was it like hers? If they were fighting the rock creatures too, maybe they could be allies.

"What is all this? Shree! Shree, get up. Something's happening!" Shree had her back to Elly. When her friend didn't move, Elly absently grabbed hold of her arm to shake her awake. When it still didn't work, she turned Shree over. The girl was alive, but barely. The wound on her chest was covered by a thin scab, but tiny rivulets of blood had run and clotted down either side. Her healing seemed to be slowly unraveling. If she didn't get serious help soon, she might lose her friend.

"No!" Elly cried, slamming her fists on the ground.

The fighting grew more intense and Elly feared for her life. She didn't want to be a part of whatever was going on down there.

But she had to do something with Shree. They weren't in a position to travel. Without medical aid, Shree was a dead woman.

Ignoring all the alarms blaring in her head, Elly knew what she had to do. "Shree, I'm gonna leave you for a bit. I'll be back. I promise." Elly held her breath and dragged one of the partial horse carcasses closer to Shree, hoping the animal would block the view of anyone who looked their way. The middle of a blood-soaked grassy field was a terrible place to leave her friend but she had no other option. She could not let Shree die. If it meant giving herself up, Elly would negotiate for her friend's life. It was either try to get help from someone in the castle or let her friend die. There was no choice.

"I'll be back, Shree," she said over her shoulder, and ran off toward the chaos below.

The black creatures were more difficult to spot in the dark sky. Their shrieks were relentless. The trees swayed and snapped in the wake of the rock creatures and the electric sparks that tore through the air. The frightening images ramped up her anxiety and threatened to stall her in her tracks. But then she thought about why she was racing into a war zone and forced the fears to subside. Shree was dying. Someone had to help, even if it was that weirdo Rhoden.

Shouts rose up from the forest as people fought the rock creatures. Shouts of agony and defiance joined together in a chorus of war.

Elly drew closer to the castle and wondered how to get inside. She'd seen the main gate, but surely there was another way in. Soldiers on the ramparts above shouted at her and arrows sliced through the air, nearly striking her.

"Damn it!" she cried. She didn't think they'd attack her. Was she the one they were fighting? If they were opposing Rhoden, then they should be aligned with her. But the chaos of the moment forced her to abandon those thoughts. All she wanted was someone to help her friend.

She carefully moved her way through a narrow stand of trees.

The sounds of death grew louder and more persistent. The madness unfolding in the forest frightened her. If this was why she was brought here, she wasn't sure she wanted to be part of it. People didn't need to die because of her. She was just a teenage girl! She wasn't anything special.

Loud booms like thunder made her shiver. She covered her ears. The ground shook. She wondered if this was what it was like in war when tanks fired on the enemy.

Men and women shouted. The things in the sky were gone. She neared the end of the trees and still hadn't found a way inside. The soldiers stopped firing arrows at her, but she hadn't shown herself since the first volleys.

A shadow darted toward the castle, backlit by the fires blazing across the field from the source of the fighting. She crouched low and hid as best she could along the base of a tree. As the person approached, she realized it was a woman a little older than her mom. She seemed to be fleeing the fight and seeking protection within the trees like Elly had. Swallowing hard and hoping she wasn't making a mistake, Elly came out from her hiding spot and addressed the woman.

"Hello?" she called out.

The startled woman's hands shot out.

"Who are you?" the woman asked, out of breath. Elly noticed a faint glow around her hands. Did she have the power too? Maybe she could help.

"My name is Elly. I'm not here to hurt you. I'm from a land far from here."

"Elly?" the woman said. She smiled warmly. "Are you…the princess?"

Elly didn't know what to say. She had no idea who this woman was. Exposing her true identity hadn't occurred to her, if indeed it were the truth. But if it helped Shree…

"My friend needs help. She's been attacked. She needs a doctor."

"Hmmm. A doctor? Maybe I can help. I'm not a doctor, but I am familiar with certain powers of healing."

The forest in front of the castle exploded as lightning struck the rock creatures. Elly covered her head instinctively.

"Powers?" Elly asked, growing nervous. She'd overplayed her hand. This woman was like Rhoden. She had to be. Elly concentrated, hoping to connect with her own power if needed to protect herself from this woman. She slammed into an invisible wall and couldn't access it. Once again, alarms went off in her head. The woman might be trouble.

"I'm Mathilda. I've been with the resistance working to restore the kingdom to your parents. You are Princess Elysonde, are you not?" The woman stared at her like she was a meal. The hairs stood on the back of Elly's neck. How far could she take this encounter?

"Mathilda? Resistance? What do you know of Rhoden?"

Mathilda smiled. "He works for Mortas Frost. He's a powerful mage that can cross the seam. Have you seen him?"

Elly nodded before she caught herself. She was giving this woman too much information. What if she were here to hurt Elly?

"Can you help my friend? I cannot do anything more for her."

"More? What have you done, girl?"

Elly silently cursed herself. "I only tried to take care of her wounds. Please. She's nearby. If you work for Rhoden…I, I don't care right now; as long as Shree gets help, that's all that matters." Elly couldn't contain herself any longer. Whatever happened would be on her, but so long as Shree got the help she needed, she didn't care.

"Take me to her. I can help. We must hurry. The fighting has grown worse and I don't need you caught up in the mess."

Elly hesitated. She wondered if she was making the right move. Shree's life hung in the balance. Without major healing, she might never recover. This woman…this Mathilda was her only hope.

"Ok. This way." Elly ran away from the castle and back up the small rise toward the scene of the attack. Thunder boomed and lightning streaked through the air. She fell to her knees and Mathilda pulled her up.

"Come on, then. Samuel won't attack you; I can promise that. He's under the impression you're already in the castle. Imagine his surprise when he finds out otherwise."

"Samuel? I don't—"

"Don't worry yourself, child. Take me to your friend. Time is running short."

Elly scrambled back to her feet and they crested the hill to find the bloody mess as she left it with the half-horse carcass hiding Shree.

Mathilda stopped and whistled. "Did you do this?"

Elly hung her head. Murdering people had never been in her scope until she crossed the seam into this strange world. There was always law enforcement to deal with criminals and people who meant harm.

"Yeah," was all she managed to say.

"You are powerful. With training, you could be the most powerful mage in all of Chevalon. I wonder if your brother is as strong."

Elly glanced at her, but Mathilda's attention seemed distant as she pondered the situation. It made Elly's skin crawl. What did Mathilda want with her? Could she trust her?

"My friend," Elly said trying to break the tension. "She's over there. Please hurry!"

Mathilda grunted and rushed to the girl on the ground.

"Did you heal her?" she asked. Her voice shook with the shock of Elly's capabilities.

"I did. I tried to. I have no idea what I'm doing. I can't always use the power. It's like I'm blocked or something."

"Uh-huh," Mathilda said, stroking her chin. "I see. I can help fix that, I think. No matter. That's for another time. What's her name again?"

"Shree."

"Shree? Ok then, let me see what I can do."

Mathilda placed her hands on Shree and Elly watched intently, hoping to learn how to perform the healing. Mathilda wove strands of the power together, something Elly had never thought to do. She saw various shades of yellow braiding together. She'd not seen anything like it. Even when she used the power, she never actually *saw* it; she only felt it leave her and go in a certain direction. The pull that had led her to this place was never visible. Whatever Mathilda was doing must have been for her benefit, so she watched carefully, imprinting the movements into her brain. It felt like how she learned her cheer routines back home.

When she was done, Mathilda sat back on her haunches and wiped her sweaty brow.

"Your swift actions likely saved her. I think she'll be fine, but she needs lots of rest and she's likely not going to get it out here."

Elly looked to the castle. "Can we go there?"

Mathilda smiled. "Yeah, they'll take us in. We'll be in good hands."

"Are you sure? The snowflake. That's Mortas Frost, right? That means Rhoden is with him."

"You are an observant young one, aren't you? That's exactly what it means. Rhoden isn't as bad as you make him out to be. You'll see."

"What? No! He's—"

Mathilda jumped to her feet and wove a spell securing her. Elly struggled against the bond and grew angrier the more it resisted.

"You'll see, little one, you'll see. This whole mess is almost over. How fortuitous it was that you appeared. It seems like Rhoden was right after all; that you would come for your brother. Now as long as he follows the same thread, this will all be over soon."

Elly tried to scream, but the bond held her tight. Silently she apologized over and over to Shree. They had followed a trap after all and as far as she could tell, there was no way out.

Chapter 32

Catron moved with agonizing slowness as she cleared the table and went about gathering items she thought she'd need. Almost an hour later, they left the cabin. Nadina's inner cheek hurt where she'd been gnawing it to curtail her growing impatience.

Catron tossed her the key. "You drive. You know where you're going and it will give me a chance to research and study."

They drove in silence, Nadina trying to coax as much speed from the old truck as possible.

"Old Oscar's like me," Catron said without looking up from her book. "You can't force it to go any faster."

Nadina frowned but eased up on the gas. Her thoughts turned to Nordon. Should she be trying to get him free instead? And what if Catron did open the seam? Could she go alone? She tried to sift through the ever-swirling questions, but the scope of the challenges she faced were too overwhelming.

As they neared the site of the first seam, Nadina noticed increased activity a few blocks from her destination. Television crews stood outside their network vans. Some spoke into cameras while others hastened toward the seam. Police cruisers, ambulances, and fire trucks lined the streets.

"Is all this attention because of you and your people?"

"I don't know," she said, but it couldn't be anything else. She veered to the right, taking the next street over, then slowed as she drew even with the seam on the next block. A parking spot opened on the side of the street and she whipped into it ahead of a news van, earning horn blasts and shouts through the open window. It ceased when Catron turned her head toward them. Nadina couldn't see what Nadina did, but it caused the driver to pale and peel away.

"I'm going to get closer," Nadina said. "I need to know what's happening. You can stay here. I'll be back in a few minutes." She got out and was surprised to see Catron exiting.

"I want to see what I'm dealing with."

The two women walked around the block but a police barricade prevented them from getting across from the lot to the seam. A long line of reporters screamed questions to anyone within the secluded zone. No one answered.

Nadina scanned the street to see the seam, but the building on the side of the lot blocked her view. Thoughts and plans raced through her mind. She snagged Catron's hand. "Come. We'll try the alley."

They turned and hurried back the way they came. She remembered there was a small park directly across from the lot. It didn't go all the way through to the street where they parked, but the alley could take them there. However, before she'd gone three steps into the narrow space, she knew she was wrong. The alley only went partially down.

Still, Nadina continued. All the buildings had rear doors. If she could get inside and go out through the front, they could still have a chance to discover what was going on.

Ahead, a metal door slammed open and two women exited. One paced angrily. The other stopped and lit a cigarette. Nadina got a new plan. As they approached, the pacing woman was venting. "How am I supposed to run a business if the cops won't let my customers down the street? This is wrong. I'm going to sue the city for lost revenue."

The smoker listened and noticed them approaching.

"Hi. I was wondering if we can come in from this way since the street is blocked."

The pacing woman stopped and stared at them. "That depends. If you're here to order something, fine. But if you just want to stand there and gawk at whatever's going on, forget it."

"Well, since you have no customers in here anyway, can't we do both?"

"Yeah, good point."

"In fact, you might be able to make a killing if you go around and tell some of those reporters they can come in if they're willing to pay. Some of them look desperate enough to pay big."

The woman's face lit up. "That's a great idea. Cassie," she said to the other woman, "go around and tell a few at a time we have premium viewing space. Tell them it'll cost twenty bucks a person and they'll get a coffee with the deal."

Cassie looked less than enthusiastic and walked away.

"You two can come in now. I won't charge you, since it was your idea."

They entered a narrow hall that opened into a small café. Nadina walked straight to the window. The lot was off to the left but she had a clear view of most of the space. She pointed. "It's in that lot somewhere." Catron nodded and studied the grounds.

Behind her, the woman cleared her throat to cue them it was time to order. Nadina ordered two black coffees. When the woman balked at her cheap order, Nadina added two scones. She set the mugs and plates on a small round table in front of the window.

They stood for a few moments, then Nadina stiffened and leaned closer to the glass.

"What?" Catron asked.

"It's Nordon. Standing to the left of the seam. And-and all the others, including DeWayne."

"Who's DeWayne?"

"One of the bad guys. They're all handcuffed. The police have them surrounded. A man in a suit is yelling at them. I have to get Don's attention somehow." She looked around, then pulled out a chair and stood on it.

"Hey!" the owner shouted. "Get down."

Nadina ignored her and waved her hands over her head. As frantic as she was waving, Nordon did not see her.

"Maybe I can help." Catron pulled out a chair.

The owner came around the counter, but one glance from Catron stopped her from taking another step. Catron mumbled something as she wove her fingers in the air creating an invisible painting. She swept her fingers toward the window like trying to flick something away. Seconds later, Nordon flinched. The big man towered over everyone. He looked around but his gaze never reached the coffee shop.

Catron tried again. Her actions caused him to step back. A look of concern shone on his rugged face. Nadina wildly waved her hands. As if guided by a laser sight, Nordon swept his gaze slowly toward the coffee house and his head stopped. Several long moments later, his eyes lit with recognition.

Then his face darkened and he shook his head.

Nadina pointed to the right down the street, hoping he'd get the message she was going to the other seam. She tried several times to get him to understand, but Nordon looked perplexed. Behind them the rear door opened and a crowd streamed in, noisy and in a hurry to be the first at the window. They jockeyed for position. Nadina tried once more. This time, Nordon nodded slowly.

Behind Nordon, a cop drawn by Nordon's movements noticed Nadina in the window and spoke into his shoulder mic.

"We've been spotted. Time to go."

They stepped down, but the crowd had grown so thick it was difficult to move. Catron took the lead and plowed forward, forcefully parting the wall of humanity. Once free, they broke into a run and burst through the door. barreling into several camera crews and knocking them down. Angry calls followed them, but they sprinted away. They reached the end of the alley. From behind, they heard, "There they go!"

The chase was on.

They reached the corner and turned toward the truck, but it became apparent to Nadina they would not reach it before being overtaken by the two police in pursuit. She pushed into the next gear and pulled the keys from her pocket. As she ran, she blindly punched the fob to unlock the doors, but she didn't hear the telltale click. With a quick glance down she understood why. The truck was too old to have a keyless opener. She reached the truck, slid the key in and opened her side, but as she climbed in, realized with a start that Catron was no longer with her.

She scanned the street and found her standing on the sidewalk leaning on a tree. Her body convulsed as she gasped for air. The police closed on her. Nadina didn't know what to do. She couldn't risk being caught, but without Catron she would not be able to open the seam. There would be no hope of rescuing Eric.

With the door open, she started the engine and was about to jump back out to save Catron. However, as her foot touched the ground,

Catron stood erect and moved her arms in large circles, wheeling them toward the police. The tree she was leaning on suddenly swayed in an invisible gale of wind. The branches engulfed the two men until they were half covered. Catron turned and fled.

Nadina stood and watched in awe until Catron yelled for her to get in the truck. Before Catron's door was closed, Nadina pulled out onto the street. She fed gas, made a quick right turn, and they were gone.

Nadina made a series of turns, then headed for the parking garage. She found the area where Nordon had told her she could find the second seam and parked. Neither woman spoke, both content with catching their breath. Minutes later, Nadina opened the door and stepped down on shaky legs.

"Where you going?"

"We're here. The second seam."

Catron eyed the area. "Of course it is."

Chapter 33

When Phetrix awoke, the sun blazed overhead. Bright rays warmed his skin. He smelled blood and dirt. Fog settled on his mind and he could not focus on anything. His arm itched, and when he scratched it, an intense bolt of pain ran through his arm and sunk into his chest, making him cry out in agony.

Then he heard footsteps.

"He's alive!"

Grant? Is that Detective Grant? he thought. Soon the man leaned over and peered at him, a wide grin across his dark face.

"Glad to see you back with us, wizard. The kid and I thought for sure you were soon to be dead. We were just discussing how we would get back home with only two bullets and his inability to functionally tap into this power you seem to have."

Eric stood next to him, thin tracks running down his dirty cheeks like he'd been crying.

Phetrix composed himself, preparing for the oncoming pain before he spoke. "I live yet. Healing. I need healing. Maybe…" he paused, waiting for the rising pain to subside. "I need you," he said nodding to Eric.

"Sure! Whatever I can do to help. Just tell me what to do!"

Phetrix closed his eyes. He couldn't exactly heal himself, though he could channel his energy back into himself through the boy in a work-around the Order had discovered eons ago.

"Come here, next to me," Phetrix said slowly. His weak voice made it difficult to speak clearly. Eric dropped to his knees and grasped Phetrix's hand, making the mage recoil in agony. He waited until it dulled enough for him to think again.

"Keep hold of me no matter what," Phetrix mumbled. "Relax your body and clear your mind. When I begin, you will feel warm inside as it moves through you, gathering strength from your energy stores. Don't let go. Hold my other hand."

Eric now held both his hands and completed the circuit.

"Let go? Why would I—"

Phetrix didn't let him finish. Too much was at stake for them to waste time. He channeled a massive amount of energy into Eric's right hand. It coursed through his body, Eric's eyes widening with the sensation. A gasp escaped him and his head rolled back. Phetrix could feel the energy as it exited Eric's left hand and shot back into himself.

The injured mage was forced to concentrate on directing the power. It took an extensive amount of self-control to focus the energy away from their bodies and through another person until it came back to them. It would have been so much easier if they could just wave a hand at their own injuries, but the power didn't work like that. At least not when it came to healing.

Early members of the Order found out the hard way when in battle.

Phetrix focused on a thin line of yellow power; a visual manifestation to help him direct the procedure.

Eric tensed as the power ran through him. Phetrix couldn't think about what it might be doing to the boy. Soon, if it worked like it should, he'd be healed enough to continue and any harm done to Eric could be fixed.

"You're hurting the boy!" Grant cried out. Phetrix ignored the accusation and continued. He felt the wounds slowly closing and the intense burning slowly fading to a dull throbbing. It was working!

Phetrix focused on the worst of his injuries, not bothering with minor cuts and scrapes. He could live with those. Eric's tense grip soon slackened and Phetrix let go.

The boy collapsed next to him and Grant bellowed, "What have you done? He's only a boy!"

Phetrix sat up. Fortunately, nothing hurt too bad.

"Detective," he began with a much stronger voice, "he is fine. Because of his ability with the power, I could channel my energy through him and back into myself. It will take a few moments, but he will recover. I regret using him like that, but as you can see, my injuries were significant." Phetrix held out his arms. Thin red lines crisscrossed against his pale flesh were the only hint of the deep gashes.

"If you've hurt him in some way, I will personally hold you responsible! We aren't in my jurisdiction anymore, and I won't hesitate to act out of line."

"Please, Detective. All is well with the boy. I would never dare injure one of the heirs. They are the sole reason I ever escaped to your dimension and why we are here now."

Grant ran a hand across his head and paced back and forth. He muttered words too low for Phetrix to hear. Slowly Phetrix regained his strength and stood, dusting himself off.

"Where the hell did those things come from?" Grant scolded. A large vein pulsed on his forehead and sweat ran down his face.

"I fear Rhoden has corrupted much. So many things have turned dark and evil since he's been in power. Dread-bears never used to get close to people. They prefer the shadows and solitary living. At least, they used to. Now they roam freely and in larger groups than I've ever seen. Much like the increased number of Seekers, everything seems poised for destruction. If we don't overthrow them, then we've lost Chevalon for good. Our mission must succeed. Our very existence depends on it."

"That's a lot of pressure to dump on a young man like him. Does the girl know?"

"If she's with Samuel, she'll be prepared."

"Then do something for Eric so we can end this nightmare. I never thought I'd miss the gang violence back home, but I cannot take much more of this."

Phetrix stretched his arms and his bones creaked. They were close to confronting Mortas. They were near the end of all the madness that had plagued Chevalon for close to fifteen years. It had taken far too long to get to this point, but at least they were here and ready to do whatever it took to restore order…and possibly restore *the* Order. But first things first.

"Detective, some assistance please?" Phetrix asked. He was still weak. He couldn't stand on his own for very long. He waved Grant over and clung to him for support. To his credit, Grant's strength held firm.

"I'm going to use the same healing spells I used on myself now on him. He'll be up and ready to go in no time. I, however, will require a bit more rest before we can proceed. Healing works with the body to rejuvenate and rebuild itself. My age plays a role in the process. Eric's body is much stronger than mine."

Grant nodded. Phetrix was grateful for him. Though he had no stake in the outcome, he proved to be a valuable asset and ally to their cause. He understood the man's desire to see his mission through, even if it meant crossing the seam to a place he never knew existed.

Waving his hands in a circular motion, Phetrix wove a mild rejuvenating spell and let it settle on Eric. Within moments, the boy stirred. Eric wiped his face with his hands and stretched his arms out wide.

"What happened?" he asked.

"You helped heal me. I am grateful for you. You didn't worry about yourself; only about my welfare, which is a true sign of a worthy ruler if I've ever seen one," Phetrix replied. He strained to smile, a dull ache settling in his bones. It would have to do. He couldn't weaken the boy again for his own sake. Over time, his body would accelerate the healing and the pain would go away.

Phetrix let go of Grant and carefully kneeled next to Eric. "Are you all right? Do you have injuries? I didn't sense it with my power, but I have to be sure. Those dread-bears can be difficult, especially in a pack."

Eric shook his head. "I don't think so. I feel pretty good besides feeling like I'd been shocked or something."

Phetrix grinned. "You are well, then. That's a residual effect of my power channeled through you. It'll pass soon. Thank you again."

Grant leaned over and extended a hand to Eric, pulling him to his feet, and then helped Phetrix.

"Detective, we must be close to the castle now. Eric, can you still feel the pull of the power?"

Eric cocked his head to the side and stared into the distance. "Yeah, it's still there. It's actually kinda…smaller? I'm not sure how best to describe it. The thread doesn't feel as wide but it's much more powerful, if that makes any sense."

"Indeed, it does." Phetrix winced.

"Are you all right? Can I help again?"

Phetrix waved Eric off. "No. I only need time. I won't subject you to that again unless I absolutely have to. What you said about the thread feeling narrower yet more powerful tells me your sister is near."

"And that means the castle, which also means I can soon get the hell out of here and back home," Grant added. "Not that I don't like it here. It's just not home. I will see these people put to justice first. I didn't come here for a joyride."

"Joyride?" Phetrix asked, not understanding the term.

Eric smiled and Grant shook his head. Phetrix let the reference pass. Whatever it was, it wasn't as important as their mission.

"We rest tonight. The boy and I need to recover. At first light we continue our trek. I expect we'll be to our destination before tomorrow's sunset.

"And then we end this evil once and for all."

Chapter 34

Samuel opened his eyes when he felt an overpowering electric pulse through his body. Dorin crouched next to him, his hands on Samuel. The man strained as sweat dripped from his forehead onto Samuel's shirt. It was dark outside and a small orb floated above Dorin's head, giving off enough light to see his task. Owls sounded in the distance and the combat of the day was silent, replaced with the moans of the wounded and the powerful stench of death.

"Where are we?" Samuel muttered. His weak voice sounded wrong in his ears.

"Shh. You've been badly injured. Let me finish," Dorin replied. Another electric wave passed through him, making every hair on his arms stand at attention. Several waves followed, each one jolting life back into Samuel. When he was through, Dorin leaned back and wiped his brow.

"You should be fine. I have to save something for the others. It's only you and me, and I figured if I could heal you, you'd come in handy to heal the rest."

"Where are the other mages?" Samuel croaked. It hurt his throat to speak, but this was important.

"Gone," Char answered. His large face emerged from behind Dorin. "Dead. Missing. It doesn't matter now. All we have are you two."

Samuel closed his eyes and cursed. The Order teetered on extinction. There were now only three members left, as far as he knew. If Rhoden could be turned from his evil ways, maybe they'd have a chance. He had to believe the mage still had good in him. It was impossible to consider the mage no longer held to the honor and duties taught to him since he was a boy. Those lessons had to be inside him.

His thoughts returned to the battle. No. It was too late for Rhoden. He had touched the dark for too long. Anyone who could unleash creatures like those last night to destroy humans was well beyond saving.

That left himself, Phetrix, and Dorin to face Mortas, and he had no idea where Phetrix was.

The entire plan unraveled around him. The resistance movement set in motion when he directed the heirs to the other dimension had collapsed under the pressure from Mortas. Mathilda had done a masterful job with what little resources she had, but in the end, she deserted the cause. Char was loyal, but Samuel doubted his ability to mount a major offensive, especially with their numbers cut to the bone. The attack earlier ravaged them. His stomach turned on itself when he considered what might be left.

The resistance. The heirs. Chevalon's future. Was it all worth it? Had they paid too high a price for their current precarious state of existence?

In answer to the silent question, Char spoke out.

"The odds are not in our favor. It feels like Mortas has won, and we've yet to encounter that evil man. If either of the heirs are inside that castle, our efforts must continue. It's all we have left."

Samuel opened his eyes and slowly pushed himself up. He cleared his head and forced himself to stand. The world spun around him but he fought against the vertigo until it slowed to merely a manageable annoyance.

"I'll do what I can. Our cause is just, but our ability hangs by a thread."

In the dark it was difficult to see the destruction from the attack. Too many voices called for help. Even with night upon them, Samuel saw the bloodstains on the ground and deep crimson streaks running down the bodies of the survivors. He was weak but Dorin had healed him first for a reason.

"Char, help me tend to the wounded."

Char directed him to the nearest soldier. Samuel stumbled but

Char held him up. "You might want to stay close. My legs feel like Jell-O."

"Jell-O? What is that?"

Samuel sighed, realizing the reference meant nothing to the man. "They're weak."

Samuel bent over and placed his hands on the man bleeding out from a nasty wound on his leg. He channeled energy through his hands into the man and followed through his body until he found the wound. Working quickly, he forced the muscle and skin to fuse and made sure arteries and veins were reconnected. Once he was done, he let go. The man stared up at him in amazement.

"Thank you, mage," he uttered.

"It will be some time before you're fully healed. Rest and let your body continue what I've started. Eat something. That will help too."

The man nodded and rubbed his leg where moments ago blood gushed.

"Char, if you would." Samuel held out his hand and the larger man pulled him to his feet. "Let's find another. It might take all night, but we have to try. We cannot let this destroy us. Not now. Not when we're so close."

Samuel found the next nearest injured solider and healed her; a displaced shoulder and broken tibia taking a bit longer to mend.

It continued like that for most of the night; soldier after soldier with serious injuries. He didn't think the line of wounded would ever end, but near sunrise, he met up with Dorin.

"I think we've gotten them all," Dorin said. "I healed fifteen; many with terrible wounds. I thought I lost one, but her heart kicked back in and she's still with us."

"Fifteen? That's all you healed? With the eleven I mended, our force is barely enough to mount any kind of attack. With you and me as the only ones from the Order, I fear our chance of success is not great."

"But there is a chance," Char chimed in. After that, he remained silent, offering support to Samuel when he needed it.

Samuel nodded. "Yes, there is a chance. As long as breath fills my lungs, we have a chance."

"Do we know anything about the heirs? Did you come across Mathilda?" Dorin asked. Dorin was short with long brown hair. Dirt and blood streaked his face. If he hadn't experienced the healing power from him, Samuel would never have guessed he was from the Order. It was not obvious that he wielded magic.

"She was absent from the entire fight. One moment she was next to me; the next she was gone. Throughout the fight I called out, but she never appeared. I'm at a loss," Char said.

"I had hoped to find her, but the longer she's missing, the more I suspect she might be an accomplice to Mortas," Samuel said. It was the first time he'd uttered the words aloud. The shock was obvious on Char's and Dorin's faces.

"You can't possibly accuse her of such an atrocity!" Char said. With as much time as he'd spent with her, Samuel knew it would hit him the hardest.

"What else am I left to consider? When we needed her most, she disappeared. It certainly isn't like her to leave a fight. When we were under attack in the north, she fought back. But something about this feels off. Don't you see it? Mathilda is a powerful mage and she hasn't seen eye to eye with me about how to reclaim our land."

"You were gone a long time," Dorin said with a sharpness in his voice.

Samuel sighed. "I've already explained all of this to—"

"Mathilda," Char interrupted.

"Yes, to Mathilda. I had to leave. Someone needed to watch over the heirs to protect them. They had their own guardians, but none of them had the ability to open a seam, nor did they know where the seams were. It was my sworn duty to protect them. Mathilda came around to my side of things. At least I thought she had."

"But to think just because she left the fight means she's a traitor to the cause is a harsh judgement to make, don't you think?" Char asked.

"I honestly hope it's nothing more than an old man's conjecture. I've seen many things in my lifetime. I base my opinion on my experience."

"Until proven otherwise, I believe she's with us," Dorin said. "She might have a powerful reason to be absent. I would like to know what it is."

"As would I," Samuel added. He didn't want to hammer this out now. They were still outside the castle with the heir possibly inside. He let it drop and scanned those left.

Small clusters of soldiers spoke amongst themselves. Most needed time to fully heal, but they did not have the luxury. If they failed to act now, it only gave Rhoden the opportunity to stall them with yet more monstrosities.

"Gather the forces that are left. We march to the castle immediately. Delay only means we lose for sure."

"Samuel! Are you mad? You know how weak our fighters are. They need time to heal!" Dorin said.

"I agree," Samuel replied, "but we have no more options. This is all we've got. If we let them regroup, we potentially face something worse. We must bring the fight to them before they send others after us and while they think us destroyed."

Char mumbled but stalked off, calling out orders to the raged remnant of the resistance.

Chapter 35

The cold night soon gave way to daylight and the rising sun felt good on Phetrix's face. They had camped under the cover of a small cluster of trees. Normally they'd take turns keeping watch, but all three were exhausted after the dread-bear attack and they risked a night of rest.

Phetrix rose from his uncomfortable position to see Eric and Detective Grant in the distance. They spoke softly so as to not disturb him or share their conversation with him. He stretched his arms and his bones creaked. The pain from the previous day's attack had settled into a dull throb that he could live with. A renewed energy flowed through him and he was ready for the day ahead.

A floral scent descended on his senses and he smiled. It was such a different atmosphere than what he'd experienced through the seam.

Phetrix approached the pair.

"Good morning."

"Phetrix! How are you feeling?" Eric asked.

"Wizard, you look like you slept well," Grant added.

"After all we went through yesterday, my body has responded better than expected. I'm ready for whatever we may face today. Eric, do you still feel the pull?"

The boy nodded. "That's what I was just telling Detective Grant. It's clearly coming from the castle. If this is my sister, she's in there."

"Good, good. Now we must find a way inside and start this reunion."

Grant cracked his knuckles and stretched. He seemed to be restraining his thoughts.

"Detective, I value your opinion. What do you have to contribute?"

"Well, I was wondering how we go about getting ourselves inside a castle undetected. I assume they have guards. What if we lure some out and exchange our clothes? It's not like the kid and I fit in here." To illustrate his point, he waved a hand at the two of them.

"No, you certainly don't belong with those, do you? My garb is much the same." He thought about the proposal for a moment. "I suppose it's the best we have to go on. Let's get closer and figure out how to accomplish this."

The three men left their camp and headed toward the castle in the distance.

Nearly an hour into their travels, Grant stopped.

"Hey, wait a minute. See that?" he asked, pointing through the trees. Three figures in black were gathering wood.

Phetrix wove a spell and held his hands to his eyes to block out what little sunlight shone through the thick trees above. "I don't see the snowflake on their chests, but they could be his men."

"Maybe they don't always wear the sign?" Eric asked.

"It's possible, but even if they aren't his men, we can wear their clothes to gain a semblance of belonging," Grant added.

"Let's proceed with caution. I didn't go through all this only to have the heir find his end at the hands of irritated strangers."

"Gee, thanks. I'd rather not find my end, either!"

Grant led them slowly through the forest, watching each footstep to avoid making noise. The three men gathering wood seemed not to notice them at all. They joked with each other and spoke about someone called Mathilda. Phetrix wondered if it was the same woman he'd met long ago. People and dimensions merged together in his mind and he wasn't sure who was where.

They paused and listened, hoping to discern their plans and how best to overcome them.

"I'm sure she's just gathering more forces or something," one of the men said.

"Yeah, but why not say something?" another asked.

"Maybe she's had enough death. I know I have. What are we gonna do with what little manpower we have left?" the third asked.

"Build a fire and tell Mortas we're at his doorstep," the first replied, earning a chuckle from the other two. He continued. "I have nothing left. My family is gone. No matter what, I'll stay until this is over or we're all dead. We've come too far to turn back now. One day Mortas Frost and his evil mage will see justice. I intend to be there."

The other two grumbled but didn't argue the point. They carried on, stacking small logs into a pile.

Eric and Grant moved a little closer. Phetrix held his breath, worried they'd give themselves away. He waited for the three men to discover them, his heart racing in his chest. *Fools!* he thought. *What are they trying to do?*

He heard commotion behind him and he jumped.

"What the?" he cried out loud. When he turned, it was only a small fox, curious about the stranger before him. He spun around when he heard the three men calling out to him.

"Hey! Who goes there?"

Grant and Eric were hiding and he couldn't find them in the brush. *Great,* he thought. *I'm the one to give us away.*

Phetrix held his arms up. "I mean no harm. I heard something in the forest and saw that it was only friendly folk gathering wood for a fire."

The three men drew their swords and held them pointed at him.

"Are you alone?" one of them asked. He was tall and gaunt with long, stringy red hair matted with leaves. The other two were shorter; one with deep brown hair and the other bald. They were dirty and worn like they'd been in the elements for quite some time.

Phetrix said nothing as he weighed his options.

"I asked you a question," the red-haired man said. "I better hear an answer."

"Whom do you serve?" the bald man asked, earning a stare from his companions.

"Excuse me?" Phetrix replied.

"Whom do you serve? Mortas Frost, or are you one of those royal sympathizers?"

Phetrix's heart pounded. Behind the three men, he caught a glimpse of Grant and Eric. Eric waved to get his attention. Grant tried to wave him away, but the boy didn't pay attention.

Grant snapped a branch and the men spun on them.

"We have more of 'em," the brown haired man said. "Olin, get him!"

The red-haired man, Olin, held his sword to defend against the new intruders. The bald man faced Phetrix.

"What do I do with him?"

The brown-haired man sneered. "If he refuses to talk, run your sword through him. Do you got this, Kenleth?"

The bald man nodded.

"Good. Now we take care of these two."

The brown-haired man joined Olin to face Grant and Eric.

"Kenleth, is it? I do not intend to hurt you. You asked whom I serve. What does it matter?"

"It means everything."

Phetrix looked over Kenleth's shoulder and shuddered as Olin raised his sword at Grant. "No! Please don't hurt him!"

Eric pushed out his hands to move the attackers away but nothing happened. The sword sliced through the air, striking a branch after Grant dove out of the way. When the Detective rolled to a stop, he pulled his gun and pointed it at Olin.

"No, Detective! We don't know yet!"

Phetrix quickly wove a spell that caught Kenleth off-guard. The man's eyes widened in surprise. Phetrix trapped him within the power and pushed him back into a small tree and he fell to the ground.

"A mage!" the brown-haired man cried out. Suddenly Olin pulled back from his attack on Grant. The detective held his weapon with a steady grip, never letting the swordsman out of his sight.

"I ask you one more time," the brown haired man said. "Whom do you serve?"

Phetrix swallowed hard. "I serve the true heir of Chevalon."

"The heirs are dead!" Olin called out.

Phetrix pointed toward Eric. "Then who might that be? Show him. Show him the scar."

Eric shook. "What? No! These guys might want to kill me!"

"If they were Mortas's men, they'd have done so already. Go on, show them."

"Mage, you better be right," Grant called out, still holding his gun pointed at Olin.

Phetrix nodded at Eric, who hesitated with his shirt. "It's ok. go on."

Eric slowly pulled his shirt up and the two men gasped. "It's true!" the brown-haired man said. "The heir…he lives!"

Olin ran closer. "Joelle, can it be? Have we lived long enough to see the return of the prince?"

Joelle shook, visibly moved by the sudden turn of events. "I…I think it is. Quick, check on Kenleth. We have to get back to the camp."

Olin rushed to their fallen man and shook him gently. Phetrix went to the man and bent down, placing a hand on him. Kenleth opened his eyes and reached for his dagger.

"No! No; he's with us," Olin said, holding the man's arm down. "He's with the Order. And we have the heir!"

Kenleth chuckled. "The heir? Yeah, right. We all know it's not true. Mathilda and now Samuel has been telling us stories for years. We're too far into this to turn away now."

"No! Look!" Olin pointed at Eric, who still bared the half-moon scar.

Kenleth covered his mouth. "I never thought I'd see the day…"

"Samuel?" Phetrix asked, catching the name the moment Kenleth uttered it. "You know where Samuel is?"

The two men nodded. "Aye, he's back at the camp. We've been debating our next move. He thinks the heir is inside the castle, but if he's here—"

"My sister?" Eric called out. "I told you, Phetrix! I felt the connection!"

Grant and Eric soon joined with the others in an awkward reunion. Phetrix wiped his hands on his pants and assessed the situation.

"Well, let's not delay. To Samuel! But do not share the news with everyone yet. We don't want to cause a panic," he said, waving his hand outward.

They followed Kenleth to a small camp of ragged soldiers.

"I've seen better forces than this," Grant muttered. "What happened here?"

"We fought dark forces, no doubt directed by Rhoden," Olin said.

"Here we are," Kenleth said. They crossed into the camp and Phetrix could smell the dirty and injured soldiers. Many sat in clusters consoling one another. They approached a large scowling man.

"Char, this is Phetrix and…" he inhaled deep, wiping his brow, "the heir, Prince Erthic."

The large man narrowed his eyes and placed his hands on his hips. "What nonsense is this? And where is the wood?"

"No, he's serious," Joelle added.

"I'm Phetrix, mage of the Order and student of Samuel. He's here, is he not?"

Char glared at him. "Maybe. How do I know you are who you say you are?"

Phetrix nodded to Eric. The boy swallowed hard and looked around. Then slowly he raised his shirt, revealing the half-moon scar once again.

"It's true!" Char cried out. "Come with me now!"

Chapter 36

Elly struggled against the invisible bond. It was a terrible situation, and one she'd experienced before. Fighting the unseen hold on her wouldn't work, but she tried all the same. Going to her death without a fight didn't seem right.

This Mathilda woman duped her. Maybe she actually did heal Shree, but she also ensnared Elly. The woman was clearly powerful in magic, but what side was she on?

Mathilda forced Elly to the castle and levitated Shree. Watching Shree's body hover in the air behind them was a disturbing image.

As they drew closer to the castle, Elly noticed a small iron door she hadn't seen before. Mathilda headed straight for it, glancing toward the still-smoldering forest now and then, as if expecting to find someone she didn't want to see. When they stood before the door, Mathilda slammed a fist on the metal three times. A cover over a small window at eye level slid open and a man's rough voice answered.

"Who goes there?"

"Mathilda, friend and subject to our lord Mortas Frost."

The man paused and called out, "What say you?"

Mathilda sighed. "The Frost always settles at night."

The sliding window slammed closed and a heavy lock was undone from the inside. The iron door swung open slowly to reveal two guards. Their clothes were dirty and they smelled of urine and body odor.

"Mathilda?" one guard said. "I could've sworn you were with those rebels out front. That's the word going round."

"Where's Lord Frost? He needs to see these two immediately."

The guard shot a glance to his partner and Elly realized the second guard only had one eye. Instead of covering the empty socket with a patch, he let it show to all who dared to look. She wanted to scream but was held back by Mathilda's spell.

"Lord Frost is with Rhoden inside. The two have been scheming since your little group decided to knock on the front door. Come this way."

Mathilda huffed and shook her head. She grumbled under her breath. "Morons." Elly waited for the guards to react to her comment, but they never turned back around.

They crossed the castle grounds and climbed black obsidian steps that gleamed under torchlight. They were handed off to other guards and led inside. They snaked their way through dark corridors lined with tapestries showing Mortas overseeing battles. Flaming torches illuminated the scenes depicted forces wearing the snowflake sigil slaughtering their enemies with an image of a white deer on their armor. She sympathized with those soldiers. From what she knew of Mortas, he was an evil, ruthless man like Rhoden.

Every once in a while she caught a glimpse of Shree floating behind her and it freaked her out. Watching someone glide on air wasn't natural.

They turned another corner and entered a large well-lit rectangular room with a black throne at the far end. These walls were lined with large black tapestries depicting the snowflake she associated with Mortas Frost. Three tapestries hung on each side of the room and behind the throne was a large red tapestry with the same white snowflake. Next to the throne was a smaller seat, clearly made to make its occupant feel less significant. At this moment, it was occupied by the mage Rhoden, the man Elly had come to associate with evil.

She tried to grasp the power, but Mathilda's bond had severed her connection. Mathilda forced her and Shree forward until they stood on a pure white stone snowflake embedded in the floor in front of the throne.

"Ah yes, the usurper come to take my throne." Mortas Frost emerged from the shadows and leaned on the throne. He was dressed in black with the ever-present white snowflake on his tunic and a black cloak draped over his shoulders. He eyed her with an excited glee. "I'm so happy to finally meet you." He sat on the black fur seat. "Since you escaped Rhoden's castle, I've been worried about you. The anticipation of when you'd finally arrive was electric." He smiled, but humor didn't reach his cold, hard eyes.

Rhoden leaned forward, his intense gaze pure evil. The man oozed hate. His lips drew tight and eyes narrowed. His devilish sneer made her skin crawl.

"My Lord, under fortunate circumstances, I have secured one of your enemies. The one called Ellysonde, the daughter of Artus and Griselde," Mathilda said. Her voice echoed throughout the chamber.

"You have done well, my friend," Rhoden answered. Mortas glared at him and turned back to Mathilda. Elly made note of the slight, wondering what was going on.

"Thank you, Rhoden. My patience has finally won. I was beginning to think I'd never leave those rebels, but here we are, and with a key to victory within our midst."

Mortas steepled his fingers and carefully inspected Elly. "Who is that?" he asked nodding toward Shree.

"A friend of hers. She was injured by your soldiers. I befriended Ellysonde to gain her trust and offered to heal her. I did the minimum in order to keep the girl alive for now. She's weak and won't last long."

Elly's heart sank and anger burned within her. Her friend was gonna die and she had no recourse. There's no way she'd bring her home dead. Something had to be done. If only she could touch the power once again. The frustration building inside made her furious.

"Good," Mortas said. "She can be disposed of however my soldiers see fit. I'm sure they'd like to have fun before they do." He nodded to the back of the room and two guards with large bellies waddled toward Shree. Mathilda waved a hand and she fell to the floor. One of the guards slung her over his shoulder. His toothless grin sickened Elly.

"Do what you want, but she needs to be dead by morning," Mortas commanded. They carried her off, one of them whistling.

Outrage burned hot within Elly. How dare they treat her friend like that! She fought against the bonds, slamming into them with all her might. The hold on her budged slightly. She looked up, afraid Mathilda or Rhoden had noticed. Rhoden cocked his head as though he felt something and she stopped. There was no need to let him catch on that she might be able to break free. Not yet.

"As for you…" Mortas said, breaking her thoughts. He stepped down from the throne and approached her, extending his hand, and holding her chin. "You will be mine. Until you birth my heir, that is. Once I present our legitimate son to the people, the resistance is dead. They will get their heir, but it will also be mine. The best of both worlds, don't you think?" He smiled and she felt a knot of disgust in her belly. Was this man going to rape her? Suddenly her situation seemed much bleaker than moments before.

Mortas ran a hand through her hair. "You will serve me well. Rhoden, is the brother nearby?" Mortas called over his shoulder. Elly glanced at the mage and he closed his eyes.

"It's hard to tell, my lord, but I do feel his presence. My best guess is he's not far away, though I can't tell where."

Mortas grunted. "It'll have to do. Mathilda, you have done well. You brought my enemies to my doorstep and delivered the heir to me personally. I owe you a debt. You have my gratitude."

He extended a hand toward her, and Elly saw a metallic flash in the light of the torches. Mortas shoved a blade into her stomach and twisted. Mathilda either didn't see it or was caught unaware, trusting him.

Rhoden jumped from his seat. "Mortas! She was our ally! Without her, we wouldn't be where we are! How could you do this?"

Mathilda grasped Mortas's hand. "Lord, why?" she muttered.

"This is not right! She was one of us!" Rhoden screamed. He went to Mathilda and cradled her. Mortas let go of the dagger and the handle protruded from Mathilda's abdomen.

"We cannot have loose threads. She posed a threat to us. I fear her sympathies were compromised. If she turned her back on one group, she will always be a threat. She could do the same to me. Surely you understand, Rhoden."

Fury blazed in Rhoden's eyes. He clearly hadn't expected this betrayal. His body shook and he gently laid Mathilda on the floor, stroking her hair back from her face. "I'm so sorry," he whispered. "It was never meant to be this way."

"Rhoden, don't heal her. She earned what she got. She was nothing more than a pawn for our needs."

Mathilda winced and tried to pull the blade out. "It hurts," she muttered. "Please, Rhoden, I'm loyal."

"Let me help her! She's been our ally for over a decade!" Rhoden screamed, turning up to face Mortas. "She did not betray us!"

"My decision is final. Are you challenging my authority?"

Several guards appeared from nowhere and surrounded them. Elly felt the tension skyrocket. This Mortas guy was evil!

A heavy breathing soldier ran into the room. "Sir, they've mounted a counterattack. What shall we do?" His words rang in Elly's ears and the awkward silence that followed only increased the tension in the room.

"Defend the castle, you moron." He turned to Rhoden. "Unleash the Seekers. Let loose every creature at your disposal. They must all die!"

"But Mathilda! I cannot leave her!"

"So you side with the enemy?"

"I'm not…" she moaned, wincing from the pain, "the enemy. I'm loyal."

Mortas sighed. "Does anyone in here care that my sentence has been passed?"

A large soldier clad in black stepped forward and unsheathed a sword. Elly's eyes widened and Mortas gave a slight nod. The man chopped down with the blade and severed Mathilda's head from her body. The sword clanged on the stone floor. Blood splattered the white snowflake underneath. Rhoden screamed.

"No! Mathilda!" He clung to her lifeless body as the blood ran down his cloak.

"How dare you!" he accused Mortas. "She was loyal!"

Elly noticed the man's hands glow a faint yellow.

"I have made my decision. Now go take care of the rebels. Our work here is almost done. Would you care to meet the same fate?" Mortas said, absently motioning to Mathilda's head. Elly's stomach flipped at the gruesome scene before her. Then she realized she was free. The bond holding her back vanished when Mathilda was killed. The flood of the power rushed into her and filled her to capacity.

In a rage, she let it out.

Chapter 37

In the early morning light, Samuel inspected the rabble before him. What was once a promising group of resistance fighters now was no more than a collection of raiders. He'd been convinced to delay the final assault by an hour to give the men a chance to recover. He still felt the effects of the attack in his bones but had no time to worry about it. They were going to make their way into the castle this day or die trying.

"Char. Dorin. Are the people ready?"

Char spit on the ground and wiped his mouth with his sleeve. "I suppose. Do you have a plan? It's not like we can walk right in."

"No, that we cannot do. However, we could do something else."

Both men stared at him with mouths agape as though he spoke nonsense. To be fair, if he were in their shoes, he'd have done the same.

"What is your proposition, then?" Dorin asked. The man refused to clean himself and dirt caked his face.

"I go alone. No force; nothing. Just me."

"How do you propose to get inside before they kill you?" Char asked.

"I go to the gate. I turn myself in. I'm risking my life in this scenario, but I will get inside. Have you ever heard of the Trojan Horse?"

Both men seemed confused by his question.

"No, of course you haven't." Samuel said. "In any case, it's a tale from long ago, or maybe not so long ago. Who knows, really? The story goes that the Greeks hid themselves inside a wooden horse they offered to the city of Troy. Not suspecting a trap, the Trojans allowed the horse within the city walls, and at night, the soldiers spilled out of the horse and attacked. What I propose is something similar, though without a wooden horse. Just me inside the walls of the castle."

"But Samuel, what if they catch on to who you are? Surely Rhoden won't allow a powerful mage such as yourself to go free," Dorin said.

"This is a terrible idea, mage. If we lose you, we lose direction. This was all your idea, was it not? We cannot risk losing you in such a foolish ploy."

"I have to agree with Char. Without you, that leaves me as the sole mage. How far do you think I can take this group? My powers aren't strong enough to heal them all. You must reconsider."

Samuel knew it was a terrible plan, but his overworked mind had nothing left. A fog descended over his thoughts, making it difficult to see any outcome. He'd played many similar chess matches and each was a loss.

"Then what?" he asked, leaning against a tree. "What do we do? Our numbers are inadequate. We lack strength. We only have the two of us from the Order. For all we know, Mathilda might be inside assisting them."

"Then we wait. Surely something will present itself to us," Dorin said. "Impatience leads to dreadful decisions. We take stock of our resources and we formulate a solid plan."

"But we don't have time! If they dispose of the heir, we're done for!"

"There's always the other one," Char said. His expression didn't change. The seriousness of his tone indicated he truly believed his logic.

"What? No. It's true we only need one, but having both holds so much promise. I will not sacrifice one for the other."

Char shrugged. "Then we wait, like the mage says."

The big man stalked off, throwing his hands in the air.

"He'll cool off. Always does," Dorin said. "I'll do my rounds through the camp. Something comes up, let me know." Samuel nodded and watched the man work among the soldiers. Where did he come from? How did we luck out with this one?

Samuel was drained and ready to collapse. Standing was a struggle, but he was reluctant to let them see his weakness. The people needed to know their leader hadn't given up. Mathilda might be gone, but he was still there. It had been so long since they'd caught a break and now would be a great time for one.

Slowly making his way through the somber camp, Samuel struggled with a plan to breach the castle. It's true they had no evidence that Elly was there. Was he making a mistake by focusing on the castle? The raised banners indicated Mortas was inside, and surely his minion Rhoden was too. Even if Elly was not captive inside, the two responsible for the current state of Chevalon were. Removing them from power was now the sole reason for this band of resistance.

Screams arose from the far end of the camp and immediately Samuel grasped the power. The attack had come to them and the end was now. He hadn't anticipated this, but if that's how Mortas intended to end the resistance, Samuel would make him pay. Death would come, knowing he had fatally wounded Mortas's cause.

Running to the sounds, Samuel prepared to unleash a flurry of electric spikes through the air. He knew Seekers and other monsters awaited him. Whatever it took to save the people would be acceptable to him. When he ran past a group huddled together, the sight made his legs wobble.

"It can't be," he whispered. He fell to his knees, shaking. "It can't be."

Char and Dorin escorted three men toward Samuel, both men grinning from ear to ear.

"Samuel," Phetrix said. "Samuel, are you well?"

"I remember you," the darker skinned man said.

Samuel sobbed. It was too much. When he needed it most, the solution had presented itself.

"Samuel, what's wrong? Let me help," Phetrix said. He stood next to his mentor and placed a hand on his head. Samuel felt the sensation of the healing spell come over him. He waved Phetrix off.

"No, no I'm fine. I just…I didn't think I'd ever…how did you get here?"

Phetrix and Char raised Samuel from the ground. He circled Phetrix in a long embrace. When he let go, he looked at the boy.

"The heir," he said softly. "You are Eric. Prince Erthic. You've come back."

"It was your plan, was it not?" Phetrix asked.

"What the hell is going on?" Grant asked.

Phetrix addressed the man. "Detective, this is Samuel, my mentor. He lived in your dimension for years, subtly keeping tabs on the heirs and their guardians."

The man narrowed his eyes as he inspected Samuel. "You were in the hospital, weren't you? I've seen you in Chicago. So you're like him? You've got powers and such?"

Samuel absently nodded. "I am. Phetrix was my student. But the heir, he's back." Samuel stepped to the boy and held his face in his hands. "You look so much like your mother."

"Umm…thanks?"

"Samuel," Phetrix began, "is Elly here? Eric is quite certain he's been following a thread leading to her. We came here because of its powerful pull."

"The thread? I should've known! Of course it didn't work in the other dimension, but here, it's a natural outpouring of their ability. As long as they live, the thread will call one to the other. Tell me, boy, where is the thread pulling you now?"

Eric pointed toward the castle. "There. I feel it calling me to the castle."

"Are you sure?" Samuel shook him by the shoulders. "Are you positive that's where your sister is?" He let go after he realized what he'd been doing.

"I'm pretty sure. I've felt the pull since I came through the seam. It's like I can see it end within those walls."

Samuel beamed at the boy. "We shall return you to your rightful position on the throne. All these people have been assembled to fight for you. Everyone, please gather around!"

Samuel's excitement overtook his thoughts. Everything he'd been working toward was now coming to fruition. Before him stood the heir!

"Everyone! Hurry!" Samuel called out. When the people encircled them, he hurriedly shared the great news.

"All that we've been waiting for is now here. Behold, I give you the heir, Prince Erthic!" He extended his arms toward the boy, whose face turned bright red. The soldiers cheered wildly, a renewed spirit bolstering their resolve.

Phetrix pulled Samuel to the side. "I wish you would have given us an opportunity to prepare for such an announcement. The boy has barely come to grips with it."

Eric interjected. "It's fine, Phetrix. I know who I am now. I know what it means to everyone. I'm ready to take this challenge."

Phetrix raised an eyebrow at him.

"No, really. I am. How can I deny it?"

"Kid, you don't have to do anything these people say. If you don't feel right, you can always go home."

"Detective Grant, I'm positive. I always felt like I was different. Now I know for sure I am. I was a stranger in a land that did not belong to me."

"But this land does," Samuel said.

Char raised a fist into the air. "The heir has returned! The heir has returned!"

Soon the entire camp joined his chant, drowning out the loud thuds that caught only Samuel's attention.

Chapter 38

Phetrix, Samuel, and Dorin sat away from the rest of the group. Char interrupted them twice regarding protocol for Prince Erthic, and both times earning Samuel's scorn. Phetrix answered his questions, hoping to settle the large man and grow his confidence.

"Phetrix! I've never been so glad to see you. All those years training you and then leaving through the seam has changed me. I see you've grown into your role quite well," Samuel said.

"It has been a long journey and I'm ready to retire back to my mountain cave and live a life of contemplation. I enjoy helping, but the stress has taken its toll on me."

"Do you require healing?" Dorin interjected.

Phetrix waved the man off. "No, no. I'll be fine. I only need this to be over. Yet, our duties as the remnants of the Order are never truly over, are they? Even if I go into isolation, call upon me when I'm needed."

In the natural clearing where they were seated, trees formed a canopy overhead that blocked out the morning sun. Birds chirped noisily and a low hum of chatter from the camp reached them. Phetrix craned his neck in search of Eric and Detective Grant but couldn't find them, so he assumed they were well. Char didn't seem like the kind of man who would let anything happen to them.

"So the boy has felt the pull from his sister?" Samuel asked.

"He has. Ever since we crossed over the seam he's mentioned it. The call brought us here and he claims it comes from the castle. If so, they have Elysonde, and we need to get inside."

"We've been trying to piece that together ourselves," Dorin said. "It was what we were discussing when you appeared."

Phetrix smiled. "Things are certainly different now. The heir is alive and we stand at the foot of Mortas Frost's castle." He let the thought linger a moment and then he remembered something.

"You mentioned Mathilda. Is she here? Has Rhoden done something to her?"

Samuel shook his head. "If only we knew. Once the fighting began, we lost track of her. She didn't engage the enemy and we lost nearly half our forces. Only Dorin and I remain from the Order. It was a terrible battle and the lack of her presence was sorely felt."

Phetrix mulled it over a few moments before proceeding, not knowing what was appropriate with Dorin there. Figuring since the three of them were the last of the Order, he felt it best to begin with brutal honesty.

"Do you think she was a spy? Maybe Rhoden got to her and convinced her to leave our cause?"

Samuel looked to Dorin before answering. "Yes, I do think that's possible and highly likely. She is a powerful mage and we haven't always seen eye to eye. She didn't like me taking over, especially since she took the reins of the Order in my absence."

Phetrix nodded slowly. "I can see that. When last I met her, she acted much how you describe. She resented giving up control of the resistance to someone who'd been gone for a long time. It was personal to her. It could be that she found someone in Rhoden who would stroke her ego and promise great things if she turned traitor."

"I don't understand," Dorin said. "She believed in the return of the heir more than anyone! As long as I've known her, she's been loyal to a fault. Her only concern was to usher in the new heirs and overthrow Mortas Frost. Yeah, she grumbled from time to time, but who doesn't?" His words hung thick in the air.

"Whatever the cause, she must now be seen as an enemy. We cannot trust her unless she proves herself worthy. Until further notice, Mathilda is to be considered a hired hand for Mortas Frost. If we encounter her, proceed with that in mind," Phetrix said. Samuel and Dorin silently nodded.

"You speak truth. We must be vigilant if we're to complete our task," Samuel said.

"So is he really the heir?" Dorin asked. Samuel and Phetrix both offered confused expressions. "I mean, we've waited fifteen years for this moment. I expected a fanfare or something. He's just a boy!"

"I assure you, Dorin, he is the true heir. Along with his sister Elysonde, they are the sole survivors of King Artus and Queen Griselda. Their deaths mean these twins are the rightful rulers. Shouts of acclamation and cheers mean little when faced with such odds as we are. Once this is over, we can enjoy a great feast and the fanfare shall sound," Samuel said. "Until then, we must be careful how we approach the task at hand."

"He has the power," Phetrix blurted out. "He can use it, kind of. With enough training, he can be a powerful mage and the Order might rise from the ashes."

Samuel dragged a finger through the dirt, mindlessly creating a half-moon image.

"There's more," he began. "The scar. The identifying mark. Both of them have it."

Phetrix hadn't known about that. "They do? In the same place?"

"Aye, though they face opposite directions so when they are near, they form one single image. The power they possess grows immensely when they are together. It's part of the reason they had to be kept apart. If by chance they discovered they could wield the power, the energy surge created would've tipped off Rhoden and the Seekers to their whereabouts, even in the other dimension."

"I thought it was to keep at least one of them alive?" Phetrix said.

"Indeed, that was paramount. Having both alive is so much more important for us. Either one alive means hope, and that is a powerful weapon for sure. With both of them alive, we stand a significant chance to defeat Mortas and Rhoden and whatever evil they unleash. That's part of the reason Mortas wanted them both dead. He knew how powerful they could become. True, they've not had training, but we can direct their raw energy as best we can in the upcoming battle."

"But the problem is we only have one of them," Dorin added. "What you say means we need both. How do we make that happen? We're back to our previous problem of getting inside the castle."

Samuel nodded and wiped his hands on his tunic. "That is still our priority. How do we find the princess? Once we reunite her with Eric, we gain the advantage. It's like in chess, when you take the knight and bishop of your opponent while closing in their queen. It's only a matter of time before they run out of moves and you take her too."

Phetrix and Dorin exchanged a confused look. Samuel caught them and snickered. "Gentlemen, if you ever get a chance to move through the seam again, you have to learn how to play. It's a game of skill that demands attention. Always think two to three moves ahead of your opponent and you can often see the solution."

"Any idea what Mortas and Rhoden have planned for their next moves?" Dorin asked.

"I don't know what they have planned, but we've scouted a small recon patrol to the east. We can easily overtake them." The gruff voice startled Phetrix and he spun. Approaching them was the large man Char, and the grin across his face expressed his glee at the news.

"I apologize for interrupting, however one of our scours spotted the patrol not far from here. We can subdue them and go in disguise back to the castle. Once we gain entrance, we have our one chance to end this and tear down the wickedness that's plagued Chevalon for years. The prince thinks it's a good plan. So does that one fella, Grant, is it? What about the rest of you?"

Phetrix stretched his arms and smiled. If Grant saw the wisdom of the plan, there had to be some merit to it. The man had a mind that rivaled many in the Order. If only he possessed the ability to use the power, he'd become a valuable asset to them.

"Samuel, this could be our chance. I think we need to try," Dorin said.

"I agree," Phetrix said. "We can't really walk right into the place, and at least it gives us the uniforms we need. We can add a spell to cover our faces, something I learned from Mathilda. That ought to be enough of a disguise to get inside and find the princess."

"We'll need Eric to go. He can follow the thread to his sister," Samuel said, clearly adding his consent to the plan.

"But what if he's caught? If Mortas then has both heirs, we're finished!" Char added.

The mages turned to him.

"He's right, Samuel. Losing both heirs only dooms us to failure," Phetrix said.

"It's a risk we must take. Everything we've worked for ends now.

One way or another, the final days are upon us. We can go out in a blaze of glory or cower like we've done for years."

A long silence followed his words. Then, one by one they agreed to the plan, Phetrix the last to give his assent to Eric going with the group.

"Char, send your men to the patrol. Be quick about it. I prefer to keep them alive but use whatever means necessary to secure those uniforms. The fate of the kingdom rests on it," Samuel commanded.

"As you wish." Char loped off with a bounce to his step.

The end was coming and Phetrix felt more nervous now than ever before.

Chapter 39

Elly hadn't realized how powerful she was until her anger took over the throne room. Every horrible and terrifying event from the past few days came flooding back and fueled her with destructive power. The death of her father. Their kidnapping. The countless attacks, and Shree now close to death lit her core like a nuclear reactor, the raw power exploding from her. The blast of pure energy sliced through the air in all directions and shook the room like the epicenter of an earthquake. The soldiers around her were sliced in pieces, body parts flung at the walls. Rhoden and Mortas Frost escaped her blast, shielded by an invisible force that they struggled to hold under the force of her attack.

"Be careful with her!" Mortas yelled. "She must be saved. I need her!"

For several intense moments the battle waged with neither side gaining an advantage, but Rhoden was skilled and Elly was not. As her power waned, Rhoden countered her rage with a blast of his own. It lifted her into the air and she crashed to the floor, the impact winding her and making her mind hazy. She knew she was in trouble and reached for the power, but it was cut off. "No," she mumbled into the cold stone floor.

"Rhoden, do not kill her!"

"Much like I asked you not to kill Mathilda?" he snarled.

Elly slowly turned her head to see the two men face to face, Rhoden trying to remain calm and Mortas's cheeks burning bright red.

"You know as well as I that she was an outlier and could not be trusted," Mortas began. "You knew eventually we would have to cut her out of the plan. You knew one day this would come to pass. Do not act as though this is a surprise to you. She brought us the girl and the resistance is ready to die at our doorstep. What other purpose did she have?"

Rhoden's body heaved and he wiped at his cheek. His face shook. Elly could sense he was holding back his rage, but she didn't understand why. He was clearly more powerful than Frost. What kept Rhoden from ripping him to pieces?

"Yes, my Lord. She had served her purpose well."

"It is done, my friend," Mortas said, his tone becoming lighter. He reached out and placed his hand on Rhoden's shoulder. "I know she meant a lot to you, but we must move on. We have her to deal with." Mortas and Rhoden turned to face Elly.

She frantically searched for the power and found nothing but the frustrating wall holding her back. Rhoden moved his hands in the air and she lifted off the floor.

"You will not escape me this time," Mortas said, approaching her. He ignored the dead men lying on the ground around him. Muffled explosions went off in the distance. It reminded Elly of a Fourth of July celebration back home.

Mortas paused and stared into the distance, then spun to face Rhoden. "The Seekers are out?"

Rhoden composed himself. "Yes Lord," was all he managed to say. Though still carrying out the will of Mortas, Elly felt a powerful disconnect between the two men; something she hoped to use to her advantage.

"Good," Mortas replied, his dark eyes fixated on her. Elly shrunk inside though the power held her rigid in front of him. "Do you care to watch the others die? I want you to see what you have done. Had you not left so long ago, none of this would've happened. Don't you see that?"

Elly's mouth twisted in disgust. "My fault?" She was surprised she could speak, figuring that Rhoden secured all of her faculties. From the shock on Mortas's face, he thought the same.

"How is this my fault? I don't even know what the hell is going on!

Only days ago, I lived a good life in the city and now I'm locked up in some weird ass medieval world. I hate this historical period. It's so dirty and boring."

"Mid-evil? Dear girl, I'm the highest level of evil imaginable." A sudden flash replaced Frost's face with a horrifying visage of a burning skull. In a fraction, it winked back out. With the snap of his fingers, all the torches in the hall extinguished. Something wet touched her cheek. She cringed, shrieked, and dropped to the floor. Another snap and the torches relit. Frost stood over her, his tongue extended; a tongue that not only looked wicked but was longer than any she'd ever seen. He slurped it back into his mouth like a strand of spaghetti. A revolting thought occurred to her and she wiped at her cheek. Nausea overwhelmed her. She gagged, but there was so little in her stomach that only phlegm and burning bile came out.

She glanced around the room in search of a safe haven to get away from this evil thing. Her eyes landed on Rhoden. His mouth was agape, evidently as surprised as she was by Frost's display.

Frost took notice. "What, my dear Rhoden? Did you think me without abilities of my own?" His laugh was demonic. He squatted next to Elly. "You and your brother are the cause of this. You will serve me, and when the time has come, you will be useless. Then, like your parents, you will die."

Elly struggled against the invisible hand holding her and found no break in the grip besides having the ability to speak. "You killed my father! How many more do you need to murder? What's your plan anyway? It seems to me you're strong enough to do whatever the hell you want! Why do you need me? Aren't there enough young girls around this place for you to mess with?"

Rhoden waved his hand and she felt the power cover her mouth.

"You've said enough," Rhoden said. Mortas grinned.

"My mage is quite right. I tire of your speech. You are my captive now and my will reigns supreme. You will give me an heir and the rest of Chevalon will fall in line without question. Refuse me and you'll end up like her," he said, pointing to Mathilda's headless body on the ground. "Obey me and you will spend the rest of your days in the dungeons, alive and taken care of."

In her head, Elly screamed at him. No! You will not get away with this! I have to take Shree to her family, you monster! I will never do what you want!

Rhoden turned to Mortas. "Where shall I take her, Lord?"

"To the tower. I want her to see the destruction of those who support her claim to the throne."

I don't have a claim! I'm not from here! The words were a silent scream. None of these people would listen to her and her anger grew.

Mortas sneered as Rhoden led her away. "I will see you soon!" he called.

Rhoden shoved her forward toward a spiral stone staircase in the far left of the room. Soldiers streamed into the room toward Mortas. Elly heard a gasp when they noticed the body on the floor and the dead soldiers around her.

"Just a small setback, but I've handled it. We have something more important to finish. The rebels outside must die. All of them," Mortas began. "What comes next..." His voice trailed off as she climbed the stairs.

Rhoden pushed her forward when she tried to slow down to hear Mortas. "Move!" he commanded. "Nothing there applies to you. Do as you're told and you might live another day."

"I don't want to live another day if it means being his sex slave," she replied, again surprised at the ability to speak.

"He needs a legitimate heir. With you here, you can give it to him. Then everything settles down and the people will see reason. It's what he wants, though I disagree."

"Reason? You call raping a girl and stealing her child reason? Why bother when you already have the kingdom?"

"Shut up and move," he grumbled.

They climbed the last flight of stairs and hurried down a dark corridor. They stopped halfway and Rhoden opened a large wooden door that creaked on its hinges. "In here." He shoved her inside and she nearly fell.

"What are you going to do to me?"

Rhoden sighed. "Stop complaining. You'll be fine for now. If it were up to me, I'd kill you and be done with it. He's making a mistake by keeping you alive. He can get another girl and we claim it's the true heir. The people won't know any different."

"Then do it. Just kill me already. I've had it. My friend is probably going to die and I don't want to be the one telling them it was because you people had some weird fascination with me."

"She very well might be dead now. She's not important. Only you are, to an extent."

"Please! I'll do anything you want. I'll behave. Just please save my friend."

He considered her plea. She held her breath, hoping.

More muffled explosions sounded outside. Distracted, he turned away from her.

"Good. It seems this is the beginning of the end for the rebels. Care to see?" Rhoden led her to the far wall and pulled back a large velvet curtain. Iron bars crisscrossed the window behind it. "You can witness their destruction here. I have work to do. I'll send someone with something to eat. We cannot have you in poor health with your royal duties ahead."

Rhoden wove his hands in the air and Elly opened her mouth to yell at him, but no sound came out.

"Much better," Rhoden said. "It's time to end this."

He spun and left the room, the door slamming shut behind him. Elly fell to the floor. Realizing she could move, she ran to the door. She pulled on the handle, but it didn't budge. She yanked again, wasting her energy trying to free herself, but soon realized it was not going to open.

Stuck in a tower of a castle in a land she'd never heard of, Elly fell to the floor and sobbed, covering her face with her hands. The power was out of reach. No one knew where she was.

And Shree. Her poor friend had paid with her life only for Elly to end up as a prisoner of the most horrid person she'd ever known.

As she succumbed to self-pity, she felt a tingle. She wiped at her face again and lifted her tunic. The scar on her side blazed brighter than ever before and the pull she'd been following slammed into her with a powerful force.

Chapter 40

Samuel marveled at the recent turn of events. It felt like his opponent had exposed his king at the expense of a few pawns and was oblivious to the outcome. He'd take full advantage of the situation until he toppled the king. A few moments spent anticipating what countermoves Mortas might make still yielded nothing significant. They were going into the castle wearing the new uniforms. It was all chance and luck.

Those chosen to go inside were eager and ready, though a bit nervous. Phetrix, Eric, Grant, and Char were selected to infiltrate the castle and secure the princess. Eric agreed quickly, not once arguing for a different plan. Phetrix and Grant had volunteered. Char was hesitant but he soon joined the group.

The four-man patrol was taken quickly with only one injury. Though the arrow pierced the largest man's heart, his uniform was removed with haste to lessen the amount of blood on it. Since it was the largest uniform, Char had to wear it; a delegation that crinkled his nose in disgust.

"Run hunched over," Grant said, "so no one gets a good look at the blood."

Samuel said, "You will all do well. I would like to join you, but I believe staying behind with Dorin and the rest of the group might be in our best interests. We will make the preparations for when you complete your mission. I expect when next we meet, you will have Elly and the end will soon follow."

Phetrix approached him and placed a hand on his shoulder. "Samuel, my friend, all of this is because of you. Your foresight has carried us far. I trust you know what you're doing. We will secure the princess and expose the soft underbelly of Frost's forces. We will not fail."

Samuel was overwhelmed with pride at the mage Phetrix had become. The man was stubborn and clung to higher moral grounds at times, but he was dependable and more like a son than anything else.

"Thank you, Phetrix. I believe in you." The men embraced.

The three surviving prisoners were held in a small pen at the back of the camp. What little information extracted from them helped to get them acquainted enough with their purpose of scouting in the forest and would give the fake scouts the right words to use when attempting to enter the castle. It was a risky proposition but the best plan they had.

Before they left, Samuel approached Eric. "My prince, the possibility of death is high. If Rhoden or Mortas discover your true identity, all is lost. You must remain calm and resolute. I'm asking a lot from you, and it's not with some trepidation on my part. Are you sure you can do this?"

Eric smiled. "I swear I've never been more confident of anything in my life. Something about this place feels right; like I belong even though I know nothing about it. It's weird, but I'm good. I look forward to meeting my sister. We've got a lot to catch up on!"

"Ah, the joy of youth. I wish you well, my prince. We will prepare for the next phase as we hope for your success."

Samuel gave the boy an awkward tap on the shoulder. He didn't know the boy well and wasn't sure how to interact with him yet. Eric laughed and joined the rest of the group heading for the castle.

"Be well, all of you," he called and watched them until they were no longer visible.

"Samuel, the soldiers are ready," Dorin said, breaking his thoughts. The man stood next to Samuel, pretending to look at whatever Samuel was looking at the forest, which at the moment was nothing. He stared blankly, letting his thoughts run wild.

"Good, good. Send a group of men in pursuit. As soon as our people emerge from the trees, the pursuers must be loud and make it look like the guards are being chased. You and I will create a diversion and explode some fireballs against the castle wall. We need to make them believe they're under attack. We must get close enough to engage the enemy when the time is right."

"How will we know?"

Samuel smiled. He'd given Phetrix the order to illuminate the sky with the stag head sigil when they secured the princess. Once that sign appeared, they'd assault the castle. Forced into fighting on two fronts, he hoped to catch Mortas and Rhoden off guard. With the powerful combination of the twins and Phetrix leading the inside attack, Samuel and Dorin would lead the exterior one. It was risky, but the best they had.

"Look to the sky for the stag head. When you see it, it's time. Don't worry; I will be with you."

Dorin's confused expression didn't convey confidence, but the man said nothing about the stag head. "It will be done," he said at last.

"Good, good. Let's gather the forces. It's time to move into position."

As they started through the trees, an explosion rocked the castle grounds and sent a shockwave through the forest.

"What was that?" one of the men said as he felt the rumble under his feet.

Samuel knew immediately. Someone had used magic. Whoever released the power all the way out here was extremely strong. He knew of only two who could've harnessed that much energy. Rhoden or Elysonde. Rhoden wouldn't use the power in his own castle unless forced to do so. The possibility excited Samuel and he hurried his steps. If Elysonde was engaged in battle, he needed to do everything in his power to assist her. They reached the tree line as Char's men were giving a good performance. The four-man team was halfway across the open ground in front of the castle running like their lives depended on it.

Which they did.

Samuel cast a fireball toward the closest wall. Part of the upper wall erupted and crumbled to the ground. Forty paces to the right, Dorin copied the spell. Although less powerful, it was still devastating.

Samuel repeated his spell and after releasing it, turned to watch the progress of the team. They were within twenty running steps of the front gate. Their fate would be determined in seconds.

He moved to get a better view of the gate. If it didn't open for them, he would have to blast it open and pray he didn't take the prince with it. He readied, taking his time to pull the energy from the earth and air. He gathered, let it build, and saw one of the figures stumble and fall. It was the prince. Had he been pierced by an arrow?

Grant ran back for him and helped him up. Eric clutched at his stomach but continued running.

Arrows filled the air, but all appeared to be directed at Char's men. "Don't get too close, you fools," he muttered, knowing he would never be heard. One of the men was struck in the chest and pitched backward, ending the pursuit.

To his relief, a massive metal door opened and the guards slid inside. Now it was up to them.

It was time to withdraw to a safer location. Overhead, the Seekers descended at lightning speed toward the retreating men, their shrieks chilling him to the bone. He had to engage the Seekers or far fewer would enter the trees than would exit.

Chapter 41

Phetrix, Eric, Grant, and the resistance fighter Char ran toward the castle. Eric occasionally swallowed hard and looked around, rattled.

"Stay calm, everyone. If we act out of character, they will notice and the ruse is up," Grant said. "Don't be nervous; they'll catch on. Keep the chatter down and follow Phetrix's lead."

Having the police officer with them turned out to be a good addition and Phetrix was thankful for his help. The skills he possessed from his time in Chicago served him well as they prepared to end the days of Mortas.

"Detective," Phetrix said. "A word before we proceed?"

Eric walked a few steps ahead with Char to give them space.

"I appreciate what you've done up to this point. Your insights are invaluable. Thank you for everything."

Grant smiled and wrung his hands. "It's the least I could do for the kid. I know what's at stake, even if it makes no sense to me. I get it. Besides, how the hell do I get home if I don't help you?" He tapped Phetrix on the arm.

"The moment we're done, I shall return you to your home."

"Thank you, wizard. I'd like that very much."

Halfway to their goal, an explosion rocked the castle, sending smoke billowing from a window. A second later, Eric clutched at his stomach, stumbled, and fell. It wasn't like previous sensations in his side. This one hurt, taking his breath away. What did it mean? Had something bad happened to his sister?

Grant raced back and helped him up. "Are you all right? You didn't get shot, did you?"

"No. I'm not sure what happened. It feels like I was stabbed."

"Can you keep going or do you want to turn back?"

The pain eased a bit but still remained. "No. this may be our only chance. "Let's keep going."

They started running again at a slower pace. The castle loomed closer, but the gates remained closed. On the positive side, they hadn't been shot at.

"Hey guys, we've got company!" Char called out.

Streaking across the sky were two Seekers. They silently patrolled the skies above the castle, guarding it against any mage who dared to attack. They hovered over the castle wall.

"Phetrix, are we safe?" Char asked.

"Yes. They have no reason to suspect us. Their attention is on the trees. They'll know the moment I use my power and come after us. Let's go forward without my powers as long as we can."

Two more Seekers joined the others and Phetrix felt his heart thump in his chest. Seekers were vile and he wasn't sure he'd be able to take them all down. If they somehow found out Eric was there, the situation could turn dire.

Samuel and Dorin unleashed fireballs at the castle wall. They exploded, sending chunks of stone into the air. In an instant, the four Seekers darted toward the origination point. Phetrix hoped Samuel could handle them. There was nothing he could do to help. They approached the gate and one side was open just enough for them to run inside. No one challenged them.

"So far, so good," Grant said once they entered the inner courtyard.

Inside the castle walls, people were busy. A blacksmith and his apprentice worked hard over the hearth, the sound of hammers slamming into steel echoing throughout.

A small group of young soldiers climbed wooden stairs to take positions along the wall under the watchful eye of three men in black armor with the white snowflake on their chests.

Everything seemed normal, which surprised Phetrix. He expected to see them doing horrible things, living up to the terror Mortas inflicted on the land. But instead, they lived like anyone else. It caught him off guard.

"What is it, mage?" Char asked quietly. They stopped as they waited for Phetrix.

"I'm sorry. I thought it would be worse here. But..."

"It's normal?" Eric asked. Phetrix nodded slowly.

"I thought the same thing. We must do this with as few casualties as possible. If we're going to liberate the land, we will need as many people as possible to join our side. Killing them all only makes it worse."

The three men stared in awe at Eric.

"What? I've studied history. I know how this works. I'd rather not be the reason the people turn to Mortas for salvation."

"Kid, you have grown up right before my eyes. If I lived here, I'd follow you for sure. Maybe you ought to come back and run for mayor or something. We need more people like you," Grant said.

"If this goes badly, maybe I'll seek safety through the seam." The smile that followed told Phetrix Eric was committed to the cause. The joke fell flat with Char and Grant, but Phetrix understood.

"Eric, which way do you feel the pull?" Phetrix asked.

Eric closed his eyes and they waited patiently. "That way." He pointed to the main tower to their right.

"Follow me," Phetrix said. The group formed a single file line with Char at the end. They headed for the castle, passing several guards along the way. Each time, Phetrix felt his face flush and his heart race, anticipating they'd see through the ruse. When they passed without a word, he exhaled loudly.

"Hey Phetrix, when I said act normal, I meant to breathe when the enemy walks by," Grant said.

"Let's keep moving," Phetrix replied, not wanting to debate.

They passed a small group of soldiers and one of them called to Eric. "Hey, Marten! When are you going to pay up your debt?"

Eric froze. The disguise spell Phetrix had cast on them to look like the soldiers whose place they'd taken was evidently too good. The others halted as well. Phetrix prepared to cast a spell, but when a Seeker crossed overhead, he held back to wait for the right moment. If he broke the illusion, he had to make sure it was well worth it.

"I'll pay you the money soon," Eric replied. Phetrix winced at the answer. Money was not a term used in this world.

"What?" the guard said.

"He'll pay the gold when he can," Char added.

"Is that so?"

"Come! We have somewhere to be," Phetrix said, trying to get them out of this awkward moment. They were a few steps away when the guard called out to them.

"You don't owe me gold!"

Phetrix felt his chest tighten. They'd made a wrong guess and brought unwanted attention to themselves. If the guard alerted anyone, their disguise was ruined.

Char gave Phetrix a nudge. "Keep going. Don't worry about them for now," he muttered. Phetrix followed his suggestion and they left the soldiers behind.

"I'm sorry. I almost cost us," Eric said.

"Don't think about it. Just keep going," Phetrix replied.

They made it into the castle and entered a large throne room, passing two guards on either side without incident. The room was empty, but a dark red puddle on the floor drew their attention. They approached slowly, all eyes on the drying stain.

"That isn't…" Grant began.

"No," Eric answered quickly. "I think I'd have felt it. I still feel the pull."

"What about that little stumble you took outside? What was that?"

Eric had no answer. At least not one he wanted to voice.

"Which way?" Phetrix asked.

"There," Eric whispered. He pointed at a door, then his finger rose toward the stone ceiling. "I think we go up. In there. It has to be. I feel the pull that way."

Phetrix turned to the rest of the group. "Are you ready?"

Grant and Char gave a quick nod. They opened the door to a winding stone stairway. They passed an empty hallway and continued on. Near the top, Eric stopped. He pointed down a hall. Two guards stood next to a wooden door.

"We will have to subdue those guards," Phetrix said.

"Leave that to me. Char, follow my lead," Grant said.

He approached the guards with Phetrix and Eric behind them.

"We've come to relieve you," Grant said. "We've been told to take over."

"On whose orders?" one of the guards asked. He scowled at them, cracking his knuckles and puffing out his chest.

"On mine," Eric said. Before they could stop him, the boy rushed the guard.

"No!" Grant yelled, but it was too late. The fight had begun.

The guard easily overpowered Eric as he was twice his size and a seasoned fighter, by the look of him. Char and Grant went after the other guard and knocked him to the floor. Char was the same height as the man, and they surprised him.

Phetrix watched the attacks unfold in slow motion, his mind trying to process what was happening. Eric was in trouble. The guard squeezed his neck with both hands and his face turned red. Phetrix pulled his hands back, ready to blast the man with an electric jolt when he was smashed in the back, slammed to the stone floor, and held in place.

"You aren't our men," the person holding him down growled. He took a quick look over his shoulder and realized the guards from outside were with them.

"Mortas will enjoy executing you!'

The other guards raced past him toward Eric, Char, and Grant.

"No!" Phetrix yelled. The time had come for him to expose his power. He would deal with the aftermath. In the moment, it was all he could do.

Phetrix shocked the guard holding him and he jumped back, crying out in pain.

"It's a mage! We have a mage in our midst!" the guard called out.

Phetrix wove a spell and caught the guard in a tight grip so not to harm him. He spun to the others hoping to end the fight before things got worse.

Eric had a knife to his throat and was restrained by the guard. Grant, bleeding from his lip, was held by another guard. Two guards held Char, and he struggled against their hold.

"Make one more move, mage, and the boy dies," the guard said.

"No! Don't!" Phetrix called out. He held out his hands in surrender. "You're making a big mistake. The boy is inconsequential. I'm the one you want, not him."

"Is that so?" He pressed the knife to Eric's throat, a thin red line blooming on his skin.

"No!" Char screamed. He broke from his captors and slammed into the guard, freeing Eric. The boy rolled to the floor and Char ferociously attacked the guard. His former captors joined the fray.

Phetrix was weaving a spell to end the fight when Char cried out in agony. When the guards let up, they saw the reason for Char's scream. A knife stuck out of his belly and his blood was spilling out over the floor. He rolled to the side, clutching the handle. Then one of the guards twisted the blade, making him cry louder.

Grant struggled against his captor and the man stomped on his knee, dropping him to the floor.

"Enough!" Phetrix yelled. He let out a blast of fire that snaked through the air and split into several strands that delved deep into the guards, burning holes in their chests. Smoke rose from the bodies as they toppled over dead. The stench of burned flesh invaded his nostrils. He didn't want to do it, but they had left him no choice.

"Char!" Eric yelled, dropping to the floor beside him. "Phetrix, can you save him?"

Phetrix dropped next to the man and placed his hands on him, weaving a healing spell, but soon let it go. Char was done for.

"I'm sorry, Eric, but he's too far gone. I cannot heal his wounds."

Eric punched the floor. "This is my fault! I should've waited like you said!"

Grant hobbled next to him. "It's just how it is, kid."

"I killed him! He's gonna die because of me!"

Phetrix let the boy grieve. He had nothing else to add at the moment.

"What do we do with him?" Grant asked, directing their attention to the guard Phetrix had immobilized.

"Leave him for now. We may have need of him."

"Kid, come on. We're so close now. We have to keep moving."

"I fear my powers may bring the Seekers our way. Let's get your sister and finish this," Phetrix said.

Eric wiped at his tears and watched as Char took his last breath. He drew the sword that hung at his belt. The weight was off, unlike the balanced swords and foils he used back home.

"I'm so sorry! This shouldn't have happened!"

Grant and Phetrix pulled Eric toward the door.

Chapter 42

It took all three of them to open the heavy wooden door. Phetrix nearly used the power to blast it open when it wouldn't budge, but soon enough it moved. When they stepped through, Eric clung to his side.

"Eric, are you ok?" Phetrix asked and then gasped.

A young frightened girl stared back at them with a small stick in her hand to ward off danger.

Eric held up his hands to calm her down. "Hey, hey, it's ok. We're not here to hurt you. We've come to rescue you."

"The princess," Phetrix whispered. "At last, the heirs," he swallowed hard, choking on the words, "are united."

Grant giggled. He covered his mouth and giggled again, completely out of character. Phetrix wondered if the man had lost his faculties and was no longer capable of rational thought.

"The princess!" Grant blurted out. "We've got the princess!"

Eric seemed just as confused as Phetrix until Grant spoke again.

"We've rescued the princess…in the castle! I hope we're not in the wrong castle."

A smiled crossed Eric's face and even the girl let out a sly smile.

"No way! I should've seen that coming!" Eric added.

Phetrix was thoroughly confused. "I assure you, Detective, we are in the correct castle and this is the princess we've come to rescue."

Grant waved him off and Eric turned back to the girl. "I…I don't even know where to begin." His face scrunched in thought and then he snapped his fingers. "I got it!" Eric pulled his shirt up to reveal the brightly glowing scar on his side. The girl gasped and pointed at it. She exposed her own glowing scar.

Phetrix breathed a sigh of relief.

Grant only nodded.

"Are you my—"

"Your brother?" Eric finished. "That's what I'm told. The weird feeling I've had since I crossed over into this world has drawn me to you. Can you feel it too?"

The girl nodded.

"My name is Eric. I grew up on the southside of Chicago, but apparently I was born here."

"Elly," she replied. "My name is Elly. I was raised in Chicago too. Did we ever meet? What school did you go to?"

Grant coughed into his hand and all eyes turned to him. "I love reunions and stuff, but we better get the hell out of here before more of those guards show up. We've already lost one of our own. Do you think we can fight that many more?"

"Detective, I agree with your plea for haste. We've got what we came for. It's time we take our leave."

"Wait! We can't leave yet," Elly said. "My friend. My best friend came here with me and she's hurt bad. I tried healing her, but my skills aren't that great. She's in the castle somewhere. We have to find her and bring her back with us."

"Back? This is home now," Eric said. "I know who I am now. Don't you?"

"All I know is I wanna go home and Shree needs to come back with me. Her mom is gonna kill me if I don't bring her home."

Grant wiped his face with his hand. "Ok. We find the girl and then we go. Any idea where she is?"

Phetrix beamed with pride at Eric's words. It wouldn't be easy, but they'd have a way forward with him in charge.

"Detective, we cannot waste much time on this endeavor. We can allow a brief foray, but we must keep the heirs safe. Am I clear? Nothing else matters to me and I will do whatever it takes. We have not waited all these years only to lose them in a meaningless search for a friend. Chevalon has its heirs and we have work to do."

"Meaningless? I'm not doing a thing unless we find my friend! You want my help? Help me first." Fire lit her eyes and her jaw was set, ready to take on anyone who denied her.

Eric motioned for them to calm down. "Don't worry, Elly. We'll go after your friend and then we can leave."

Phetrix sighed but agreed to their plan.

Grant led them out of the room and down the hall past the dead bodies with a tinge of guilt as they left Char behind.

"Wizard, can you cast that spell on us again? The one to give some camouflage?"

"Camouflage?" Phetrix asked, unsure what the man asked for.

"The spell to disguise us," Eric added.

"Oh, of course." Phetrix wove the spell, knowing it was powerful enough to attract the Seekers but moved quickly so not to give them enough of a beacon to cling to. When he had finished, they looked like the other soldiers.

"Where do you think she is?" Eric asked.

"The last I saw her, she was in the main hall. I doubt she's there, though. That was hours ago."

"Wizard, do these places have infirmaries? A place where they keep the injured?" Grant asked.

"Normally they do. Most keep them just outside the main building. We should try out there first," Phetrix answered.

"And if she's not there?"

Phetrix shot a sideways glance at Elly before saying, "Then we try the soldiers barracks."

Elly paled at the thought.

Grant led them through busy hallways, ignoring those around them and through the bloody throne room until they were outside in the castle courtyard.

"Can you slow down a bit? My heart is about to explode out of my chest! I just knew someone was going to spot us!" Elly said.

The noise of activity outside the castle pulled Phetrix's attention in all directions. Like Elly, he worried they'd be spotted. A Seeker streaked across the sky and he shivered, half expecting the thing to attack. When it didn't, he let go of the breath he was holding.

"We must proceed with caution, Detective. No sense in bringing unwanted attention to ourselves."

"I know, wizard, but the sooner we find the girl, the sooner we move on from here. This place makes me uncomfortable."

"Is that it over there?" Eric asked. They followed where he pointed toward a building where wounded soldiers came in and out.

"Great job, kid! Come on, then. Let's get her and go."

They took a few steps and a deep voice stopped them in their tracks. Phetrix hadn't heard that voice in ages and a shiver ran up his spine.

"Mage! Welcome to my castle. Where are you taking my future bride?"

The group turned and saw Frost himself with Rhoden at his side. A small retinue of ten or twelve guards flanked them.

"I asked you a question," Mortas snarled, his gaze boring into Phetrix. "And you have my guest with you."

Rhoden swirled his hands in the air and their disguises melted away. "Well done, but you should've known better than to try that trick here. Do you disrespect my powers so much, or are you just that stupid?" Rhoden asked.

Phetrix stiffened.

"Rhoden," he snarled, "we meet again. Has your mind been so poisoned by his lies that you no longer know who you are and who you represent?"

The dark mage sneered. "I represent myself. The Order serves its own as well, or are you too blind to see the truth?"

"Enough of this!" Mortas cried out, his reddened face streaked with bulging veins. "I will not tolerate your bickering. Whatever problems you faced with the Order are done. There is no Order now!"

Phetrix weighed his options. If it weren't for their fool's errand to rescue the injured girl, they'd be out of there already. Nothing he considered seemed plausible. Their only recourse would be to strike hard and before they expected it. He hoped the others were ready.

"Mortas, the Order has come to restore the kingdom to the rightful heirs. You must know your reign cannot last. It never stood a chance. The heirs have come to reclaim what rightfully belongs to them. The people have waited far too long for this day. Now, we prepare to take back what never belonged to you in the first place."

"The heirs?" He scanned the group. "Ah, you have delivered me the prince as well. What a fine gift." He spoke to Rhoden. "Kill all but the girl."

Rhoden wove his hands to expel a furious blast of power when a thunderous roar came from outside the castle that send the ground rumbling. The fear that crossed Mortas's and Rhoden's faces made Phetrix's hair stand on end.

Chapter 43

Elly's blood rushed through her body; her heart pumping hard. *Am I having a heart attack?* she thought. The wild palpitations were unlike anything she'd felt before.

A brother? I have a brother?

The similar glowing scars and their shared experiences growing up in Chicago were coincidences that felt more real to her. Now with both of them facing certain death at the hands of a mad medieval dude, they were dependent on one another for any hope of survival.

She reached in and touched the power, the invisible wall gone.

Yes! she screamed in her head. She filled herself with as much as she could handle, preparing to unleash her anger at Mortas and Rhoden, the two idiots responsible for her situation. Then she heard the roar and felt the rumble underfoot. The shock caused her to release the power before she focused its energy.

"What is that?" she asked.

Phetrix's blank expression scared her. If anyone should know, it would be this wizard guy. Even Mortas and Rhoden appeared frightened by whatever it was. This could not be good.

"My Lord!" a soldier shouted from the ramparts. "An army approaches."

"An army? That's not possible. No one in these lands has an army.

Deal with this rabble, Rhoden. I must see what the fool is talking about."

Using the distraction, Eric rushed to her side. "Are you ok? I can…I can feel you, if that makes sense."

She nodded. She completely understood what he meant. She felt him through the power as well. The invisible pull that directed her through the forest pointed directly at him

"Can you…" She wasn't sure how to phrase it. She called it the power, but would that make sense to him?

"Can you touch the power? Do you have abilities like the wizard?"

Before he could answer, she felt an unseen hand grip her tight, severing her connection to the power.

"Hey! What's going on?"

Rhoden held out a hand toward her and Eric. She noticed Eric was restrained with his arms at his sides just like she was.

"I can't have you free. Your power is too great," Rhoden snarled.

Another loud boom carried through the air, this time followed not only by the vibrating ground, but loud painful screams that caught Mortas's attention. The noise and activity inside the castle rose in an instant.

AS MORTAS DASHED OFF, calling some of the soldiers to follow him, screams pierced the air and shouts of soldiers readying for battle carried across the courtyard.

When he was out of sight, Rhoden turned his attention back to the group. Elly's nerves were on edge. Phetrix and the other guy were confused and didn't seem to know what to do.

"That fool," Rhoden began. "All of this will be mine soon. No matter; none of you will ever live to see it through."

Phetrix circled his hands in the air and a bright light arced outwards. Rhoden wove a shield that glimmered when the energy struck it, but then it radiated outward, slicing through the bodies of the remaining guards.

"You have to be better than that, mage," Rhoden snarled. "I thought you were close to my equal. That little trick is something the girl here can do with no training."

Elly fought against the familiar hold of the power to no use. She was trapped as before. Then she noticed Eric's scar glowing through his shirt and tried to see if hers was as well. By the way she was held with the power, she couldn't make it out, but it felt warm.

The constant booming outside the castle grew louder and more intense. Rhoden took his gaze off them for a moment and the guy with Phetrix charged him.

"Detective! No!" Eric called out. He was too late. The man struck Rhoden and the two of them tumbled to the ground. The man was a flurry of fists. Phetrix broke from his fugue and cast a spell at her and Eric. The grip melted away like snow in the sun.

"We don't have much time!" he called, reaching out for Elly. She gave him her hand and was struck in the back by something heavy, forcing her to the ground.

"None of you move!" a guard called out. Elly turned and saw they were surrounded by ten guards, all dressed in black with the ominous snowflake painted on their chests.

More screams from outside and a fast moving stream of archers climbed to the ramparts. Everything seemed to crawl in slow motion. It was as though Elly was watching a movie and far removed from the actual danger.

The detective struggled on the ground with Rhoden, the mage unable to force the larger man off him. The guards closed in and Phetrix shoved the siblings behind him, guarding them from attack.

"Get back, all of you!" Phetrix cried out.

Rhoden wormed his way out of the detective's grip, and the moment his hands were free, he snared the man with the power. "Stupid man!" he said. "You'll never make it home alive." He twisted his hands and the man cried out in agony, clutching his chest.

Soon more guards arrived and they were surrounded by too many for Elly to count.

"I will mount your heads on the wall for all to see that the resistance is dead!" Rhoden said. He unleashed a bolt of red flame at Phetrix but the mage countered with a line of blue energy. When the strands struck, a loud explosion knocked everyone back several feet.

Elly picked herself off the ground and helped Eric up.

"What are we going to do?" she asked. "Can you use your powers?"

Eric shook his head. He spied a sword on the ground that had fallen from one of the dead soldiers. He picked it up. "But I can use this." He waded forward to attack the soldiers.

Elly closed her eyes in the midst of madness and found the power.

She clung to it, savoring the connection. Then she focused on the glowing half-moon on her side. In her mind, she imagined a tight cord between it and Eric's. She bound them together in a powerful knot and pulled tight. A surge of power so relentless flooded into her and nearly knocked her over. The sensation was like the first time she had touched the power but in a more unique, filling way.

When she opened her eyes, Elly caught Eric staring at her with the widest eyes she'd ever seen. Two bodies lay at his feet, the result of his handiwork.

"What did you do?" he asked.

Rhoden picked himself off the ground and backed away from them. In awe and a tremor of fear, he said, "The prophecies are true. They do wield the power."

She and Eric faced the man. Eric stood holding the sword, blood dripping from the blade. Elly, however, shoved her hands out like throwing a basketball chest pass and Rhoden went airborne. He crashed to the ground twenty feet away.

She scanned the group. Phetrix was still on the ground and didn't move. Elly wondered if the man had died from the blast. The detective moaned and moved slowly on the ground. The soldiers around them had been cut down, mangled and bloody bodies strewn everywhere.

Then the thunderous booms crashed even closer, pulling Elly's attention away from the scene in front of her. It was obvious the defenders were in an all-out pitch battle, evidently not expecting it or being prepared for it. Whoever was trying to get in had to be an ally.

While Eric engaged another soldier with his sword, Elly concentrated on the massive wooden and metal gates. She let the power build and swirl around inside her like campfire smoke. She focused all her concentration and energy on the gate. As she lifted her arms, she let out a war cry.

The large wooden gate exploded. Wood and soldiers flew back and what remained was set ablaze.

"No! It can't be!" Rhoden screamed over the noise. Elly reached for him. She held Rhoden in her hand like a toy and the fierce man fought her grip to no avail.

"Looks like I can do it too," she said, smiling.

Horses raced through the gate. Their riders wore similar garb as the defenders with a different sigil on their breast plates. Still, she feared she had opened the gate to a new and more dangerous foe.

"This can't be happening!"

She turned her eyes to Rhoden, who remained in her grasp. "Oh, it's happening."

"She said they were dead. Both of them!" Rhoden screamed. Elly had no idea what he was talking about, but he didn't like these new invaders. It was all the evidence she needed that whoever they were, she was on their side. She used the power to shut him up.

Soldiers streamed through the flaming gate. They looked like the men inside the castle with black armor and a white image on their chest.

"Are they the same?" she asked Eric, who looked equally confused.

She felt Rhoden fight against her bond and she pulled more of the power from Eric through the bridge she imagined in her mind, reinforcing the wall around Rhoden.

She spotted Shree. The dazed girl staggered across the courtyard in danger of being slain or run down at any second. She started for her. Immediately her control over Rhoden wavered and the man severed the connection, freeing himself.

"No!" Elly cried.

Eric spun. "What is it?"

Rhoden pushed himself back from the group, sliding across the ground. Elly ignored him and ran to her friend. "Shree, I'm here!" Elly called. Shree continued to stagger and seemed lost. "I'm over here!" Elly yelled, but her words were cut off by another explosion. She turned to the gate and her mouth hung open.

Four large creatures that reminded her of wooly mammoths forced their way through. Each one had three riders atop its back; one with heavy leather reigns, one with what looked like a bone horn, and the other with a crossbow. The creatures were dark purple with large tusks to either side of their trunk.

They pulled up short just after entering the gate and raised their trunks high, blowing out horrific screeches through their trunks. Elly and Eric covered their ears.

"What the hell are those?" the detective called out.

Elly had no answer. Eric dropped next to Phetrix and shook the man. "Come on! Wake up. We need you now!"

Elly turned from the creatures and searched for Rhoden. She eventually spotted him running across the courtyard. He forced his hands out and soldiers were flown back from him as he raced away from the fight.

She heard Eric cry out and caught him lifting Phetrix to a sitting position. She saw Shree out of the corner of her eye. A soldier approached her with his sword drawn.

"No!" Elly yelled. She pushed her hand forward and a powerful blue bolt of electricity raced through the air and struck the soldier just before he could end Shree's life. Elly ran and embraced her friend.

"Shree! I can't believe I found you!"

"What's going on?" she replied. Her glassy eyes told Elly she was unaware of her dangerous situation.

Soldiers screamed and arrows flew through the air. The sound of metal clanging against metal was followed by screams of death. The mammoths roared. When they shifted on their feet, a boom sounded and the ground shook.

Phetrix stood with Eric's help. He found new energy when he spied the mammoths. He pointed. In a shocked voice he said, "The White Stag. It can't be. I cannot believe it's real"

The invading soldiers drew closer and Elly realized the marking on their armor wasn't a snowflake, but a deer head.

"Who are they?" she called out over the noise.

Phetrix nearly jumped in the air but Eric held him back. The mage pushed from the boy and stumbled forward.

"Do my eyes deceive me?" He pointed at the largest mammoth and turned to face her and Eric.

"It's your father!"

Chapter 44

If the sight of the mammoth hadn't been shocking enough, the announcement that the grey-haired man with the long scraggly beard was his father all but knocked him off his feet. "My father. You mean, the king?"

"Yes. Yes. The king."

"But I thought he was dead?"

"Obviously not true." The man was as giddy as a school boy.

Elly brought Shree over to Eric. "Eric, this is my best friend, Shree. Shree, this is my brother."

Still dazed, Shree lifted her head in surprise. "Brother? You mean like in the prince?"

"Yep."

"Oh, girl, he's out."

"Shree."

"What? I ain't lying. And he's your brother, so too bad for you."

Elly laughed. Eric blushed. Shree kept eyeing him with a silly grin on her face.

Less than five minutes later, the fighting had ceased. The cacophony slowly settled to a low din.

As they gathered around, the king climbed down from his perch on the mammoth and a raucous cheer erupted. He held up his arms to the crowd and walked toward Phetrix and his group. He embraced the mage. "My old friend. So good to see you again.

"And you, Sire."

The two men stood together silently yet saying so much. Without Phetrix having to ask the question, the king shook his head. "She passed three years ago. It's beyond sad that she didn't live to see this day."

"Or her children again."

At that, the king stiffened. "So, the rumors are true?"

"Yes, Sire." He stepped aside and swept an arm toward Elly and Eric. The two stood dumfounded and nervous. Phetrix waved them forward. King Artus stood on shaky legs as the children he hadn't set eyes on for fifteen years advanced. Tears filled his eyes.

"Erthic and Elysonde, may I present your father, King Artus of Chevalon."

The two glanced nervously from the King to each other, and then Eric knelt. Elly, still unsure, gave a robotic curtsey. The King rushed forward, lifted Eric, and embraced them both. His words were lost in his sobs.

As they stood in that very public private moment, a cheer went up from all inside the castle walls. Shouts of *Long live the King!* and *Long live the heirs!* rose in a crescendo.

Above the cheers, one voice lifted above all others. "How touching. This is quite a reunion. Now I can make sure the entire line is wiped out in one final blow."

Mortas Frost boldly strode into the circle. A hush descended over the masses. Jeers and threats rained down upon him. He held his wickedly confident smile.

"You pathetic fools. You think you've won? Ha!"

King Artus stepped forward and drew his longsword. "You have caused enough death and destruction to these people. It's time your reign ends." He advanced on the man, whose expression never wavered, even when the sword pierced him. King Artus placed a hand on Frost's shoulder and pulled him forward as he ran the blade through his body. Blood bubbled from his lips and ran down his face, yet the smile held true.

Only inches separated them now. Mortas Frost said, "You think this the end? You may have killed the man, but you have released the beast."

King Artus withdrew the sword with slow deliberation, then stepped back. Mortas stood for several seconds before collapsing in a heap. The King stared down on the body and spat. "Your evil is at an end."

He turned as the crowd erupted into even louder cheering. The battle was over and the throne restored to its proper ruler. Fifteen long years had finally resulted in conquest.

A rumbling began, low at first, then shaking the ground. Every eye turned toward the body of Mortas Frost as it rose off the ground. The body was ripped open and fell away to reveal a hideous red and black beast that grew to near twenty feet tall. The massive head had bugged out eyes. Four arms sprouted from the torso, two with claws and the other two with long fingers ending in razor-sharp talons. A whip-like tail snaked around its legs and split into a forked spear.

The demon let out a terrifying roar.

The crowd of people swarmed back, but with so many in such a confined space, there was nowhere to flee. In an instant a barrage of arrows were in the air, most bouncing off the scaly skin. A few men attacked with swords and were quickly dispatched by the four deadly arms that moved in a blur.

Orders were shouted and a defense mounted, but fear struck the hearts of even the stoutest man and it faltered. The demon swept its arms wide, clearing a path and knocking groups of defenders out of the way.

The beast locked on the twins and advanced on them. The king pushed them aside and stood ready to defend. It took a mighty slash in the arm as the blade bit into its skin; black blood erupting. In a flash, as the King tried to pull the blade free, the speared tail whipped around the demon and pierced the King's body. The red and black body convulsed. The tail rose and fell, bouncing the king until he fell to the ground.

Eric and Elly screamed, both dropping to the ground next to their father.

"Watch out!" Phetrix shouted as the tail reversed and shot toward the twins. He cast a spell to deflect the spears, but the force knocked the mage from his feet, dispelling the shield.

The twins raised their heads and locked eyes. The rage within both was palpable. They stood, the glow from their royal birthmarks bright as the sun, blinding all who looked. Without communicating, they locked hands. Adrenaline flooded their bloodstreams. They lifted their arms and unleashed a most furious attack.

The demon was taken by surprise and knocked back but not down. He gathered his own powers and blasted back. The battle raged with the blue-white power of the twins holding back the reddish fire of the beast Mortas Frost.

The twins intensified and stepped forward, and the demon backed away. It screamed a horrifying, earsplitting shriek. The twins continued forward, the power radiating in ever-increasing blinding light. The demon backed away. The fire diminished under the constant onslaught of the twins' unbelievable strength.

Fueled by the rage over the loss of their father, they tapped deeper into their souls, backing the beast up against the castle wall. His own defenses were now just a fine red line in front of his torso.

With a final forward push, the demon's defense failed. Its body vibrated, bouncing off the ground and the castle wall. The beam bore deep into the beast body, melting away the toughened scaly skin. Deeper it pierced, the shrieks of the demon now a constant. In one final violent flash, the body exploded in bits of horrid flesh throughout the grounds.

With the demon destroyed, the twins collapsed, exhausted. Grant and Phetrix ran to them. Phetrix scanned their bodies searching for damage, but to his surprise found none. The twins rolled on the ground, writhing in pain. They could neither rise nor speak.

Several long minutes later, they helped each other to their feet and walked back to where the body of King Artus lay. Their father.

Elly touched his skin and attempted a heal, but she was too weak to draw any energy. She lifted her head to Phetrix. "Please. You're a mage. Heal him." Tears streamed down her face.

Phetrix knelt next to her, his head hanging low. "I'm sorry, child. I can do nothing. He is already gone."

Elly broke down and cried for a man she'd never known. Eric stared at the lifeless body, his own tears also falling free.

Chapter 45

The next few days were a blur, as plans were made for the King's funeral. What had been an event worth celebrating with the removal of Mortas Frost turned into the most sorrowful of occasions.

Phetrix guided Grant back to the seam and saw him safely through. Samuel was seriously wounded in the assault when one of the Seekers broke through and skewered him from behind. His recovery was very much in doubt. In his lucid moments, he informed Phetrix of the ward he'd placed on the seam and that the day after the battle, the alarm sounded. Since Rhoden had not been found, it was assumed the evil mage had made good on his escape.

With the funeral over, the question remained of who would rule the kingdom. It was the hope of the entire kingdom that both twins would stay.

Elly knocked on Eric's bedroom door and entered before he replied. Eric stood at the window gazing out at the castle grounds and beyond.

"Well, brother, what are your plans?"

He turned and gave her a sad smile. "I wish I knew."

"It's a hard choice, and I resent the pressure being put on me. I've given it a lot of thought. I just don't think I'm cut out for this lifestyle. I know it's selfish, but I'm just not that girl."

"I understand. I've been thinking about it myself. Although I didn't know it, I'd been raised with the idea that I would one day rule this land. It's overwhelming and unfair. How do they expect either of us to give up the lives we're accustomed to?"

"They want a decision today so they can make the announcement at dinner."

"Yeah. So I've been told." He slunk away from the window, head down and lost in thought. He shook his head several times. "I don't know if I can do it."

"If neither of us stays, who do you think will rule the kingdom?"

"I haven't the faintest idea. I doubt it's set up with a line of successors like back home. It'd be a shame to have them break out into a civil war to decide who would rule."

"Yeah, especially after all they've been through." She walked toward the door. "Regardless, I'm heading home tomorrow. I have to get Shree back to her family. Detective Grant is going to contact her parents and let them know she is all right. Well, as all right as anyone could be after taking a sword through the chest."

"She doesn't seem to have any complications from the wound."

"No, but she'll always have that scar as a reminder of how close she came to dying."

"Not the greatest souvenir to take back with her."

"Do you think anyone will believe us?" Elly asked.

He laughed and it sounded sincere. "I doubt it. Unless you actually lived it, would you believe it? It might make a good book."

"I'm more a movie girl, myself."

They exchanged smiles.

"Well, I'm going to go see Shree." She paused at the door and gave him a mischievous look. "She has quite a crush on you."

He smiled. "So I've noticed."

"Any reciprocation?"

"Are you a wing woman now?"

"That's what friends do."

"It's not that I don't or might not at some time, but there's still too much to think about right now . Besides, she's from the other world, and that's where she belongs."

"And you don't?"

"I don't know."

"I'll see you later. We have to meet with Phetrix and the royal council to give them our answers."

"I'll see you then."

Elly left and Eric decided to go for a walk through the castle grounds. Everywhere he went he was greeted warmly and offered gifts. It made him uneasy. He didn't want to be worshiped like a king. He'd rather just be himself, Eric, or in this world, Erthic. He thought about his mother and father a lot. He worried about what might have happened to them. Grant vowed to find them and let them know he was alive.

So much to do. So much to think about. He climbed the stairs to the rampart and paced along its lengths, nodding to the guards who now wore the white stag of his family crest.

It was a beautiful land. He liked the rustic quality and the simple lifestyle. He would miss the food and his school, but most of all, he'd miss his parents. He would always think of them as his biological parents, regardless of the truth. They had raised and loved him as their own and deserved his love and respect in return. Before he made such a monumental decision that affected not only his life but theirs, he wanted their council.

He wandered much of the day lost in thought and flipping mental coins. He knew his sister did not want to live here, nor was she interested in being a princess, a queen, or a ruler. He couldn't blame her, but so many people had lost their lives to put his family back on the throne. It was wrong for one of them not to stay.

When the time came for them to meet with the council, his decision was becoming clear.

They were ushered into a room with two empty chairs on one side of a long table. Phetrix and seven other men sat on the other side.

"It has been a long journey for all of us," Phetrix started. "So much has happened and changed that this all feels so strange and rushed. Be that as it may, a decision must be made for the kingdom to move forward and finally know peace."

Eric looked at his sister and smiled. He took her hand. "I know Elly is not interested in ruling. If you knew the world we come from, you'd understand better why that decision is so hard. I too would prefer to live in the world where I was raised. It's what I know and where I feel comfortable. That being said--"

Elly withdrew her hand and interrupted. "Don't speak for me, brother. Like you, I have roots in another world. But I've been thinking.

To be fair, maybe we could co-rule, spelling each other periodically through the year."

Eric's jaw dropped. "Seriously? You'd be willing to do that?"

"Whoa, brother. Don't get too excited. You have to hear me out. I want to graduate from high school. I want to attend college. When I am not in school, I will come and spell you so you may visit our world."

"That would be great, Elly."

"So it's settled," Phetrix said. "One of you will always be here to rule the kingdom." He could barely contain his excitement.

The twins looked at each other, nodded, and said, "Yes."

The council was ecstatic. Words of praise and thanks flowed from them until Phetrix got the group under order.

"That is the best of news. We will do a double coronation."

"Hold on there, mage. Don't rush me. I want to go home first and talk to my mother."

Some of the council members exchanged glances, either because she had called another woman her mother, or they feared if she left she might not come back. Either way, she didn't care.

"Set a day for the coronation and I will return. Someone will have to teach me how to open a seam. My brother will rule until after my graduation in about eight months. I will come back for the summer before heading to college. That will give you a few months in the city. Is that all right?"

Eric smiled. "That's fine."

"Great. I think we can make this work."

With the approval of the council, a date was set. The twins left and walked the grounds.

"What made you change your mind?"

"A lot of things, really. One was my mother. She worked hard to bring up a child that wasn't hers. From what I learned, she was whisked away from this world—her world--and given the task of raising me. She was forced into a marriage for the appearance of having a family just to keep me safe. My father died protecting me. How could I not give some time to this world when they gave up everything for me?"

"I understand. I had the same thoughts."

"The other thing was a man who I did not know giving his life to protect me. Sure, he was my biological father, but he didn't know me. He owed me nothing, yet when that demon struck, he shoved us aside, stood in its path, and died for us. That alone deserves my time and effort. I can never repay him for saving my life. It's just the right thing to do."

Eric nodded.

"But, brother…God, it's so strange to say that…I have something to attend to in the other world. Something that will drive me for the rest of my life until the task is completed."

Eric scrunched his face, trying to discern what it could be.

"If it takes me the rest of my life, I'm going to hunt down Rhoden and kill him."

She delivered the words with such vehemence that Eric took a step back. He started to speak, but she held up a hand to cut him off. "There's nothing to discuss or debate. I've made up my mind. He's going to die for what he's done. End of story."

"I believe you and wish you nothing but success. I don't doubt your determination. What I was going to say was that you should touch base with Grant. He will be a big help to you in your search."

"That's a good idea. Thanks."

They embraced.

Chapter 46

Catron studied the area. She extended an arm, closed her eyes, and stood motionless for several minutes. When she turned back to Nadina, her expression gave away her thoughts.

"What? Can't you find it?"

The other woman sighed. "Oh, it's there, all right. I sense the energy, but it is beyond my capabilities. Someone more powerful than me created this seam."

"So you can't open it?" Nadina's shoulders slumped in defeat.

"Don't get deflated. I need to do some studying."

Nadina perked up, clutching desperately for anything resembling hope. "Is there anything I can do to help?"

"Yeah, I'm going to need coffee. Lots of it and none of that fancy crap. Just good black coffee. While you're at it, buy some food. We might be here for a long time. I have to find the right combination of words and create a potion that will either reveal the seam to me or help me discover it."

"And then you can open it?"

"Hold on there. Don't rush the process. That's just to find exactly where it is. I'll have to start the process all over again to find a way to peel it open."

Nadina sighed but tried to keep her sprits positive. "Okay. I'll be back."

They spent the day and early evening in the car. Nadina stretched out in the truck bed and tried to sleep, but thoughts of Nordon and Eric swirled, keeping her brain too occupied. She gave up, got out, and walked through the garage.

Catron spent her time reading, taking notes, and mixing various herbs and chemicals. So far she had yet to find the proper combination, but she had caused an interesting sparking lightshow beyond the garage wall.

"Well, that was fun," she said, and dumped the rest of the potion over the edge.

As night fell, she closed her book, put away her collection of strange plants, and lowered the seat.

"That's it?"

"For now. I'm going to sleep. When I wake, I'll try again."

"Are you making any progress?"

"Yes."

"So there's still a chance?"

"Perhaps."

"But you *are* making progress, right?"

"In the sense that I'm eliminating possibilities."

"Oh."

Nadina exited the truck to let Catron sleep. She stretched and decided to go to the diner down the street to use the bathroom before they closed. She walked down the sloping garage ramp and stood on the street, sucking in the cool night air. She headed to the right, toward the diner. From somewhere behind her, rapid fire gunshots ripped through the quiet night.

Nadina whirled, ducked, and reached for her gun, only to realize she had left it in the truck. More shots were fired, followed by an explosion. A rolling ball of fire shot into the darkened sky. This was Chicago, so it could be anything, but because it emanated from the area of the first seam sent her running toward the gunshots.

One thought drove her as she streaked down the sidewalk, barely looking as she crossed side streets. What if it was Nordon and Eric returning and the cops were shooting at them? She had to get there. The area was lit not only by the still-burning ball of fire, but by portable lights run by generators the police had set up.

As she came to within a block of the waging gun battle, she slowed and crouched. Nadina moved from car to car parked along the street until she could get a look at the lot. The burning ball turned out to be a torched police car. She saw one cop being dragged from the scene by another officer. Whoever they were fighting was doing damage. She had to get a better look.

She moved on hands and feet until she reached the last parked car in the line. The police had the rest of the road blocked off. She flattened to the ground and alligator crawled to the rear bumper. There she could see into the lot. There was the seam.

And a beast climbing through it to enter this world.

She was relieved to find it was not Nordon and Eric. They would not be commanding beasts. However, Rhoden would. She had to find a way through the seam while it was still open. But how to do so without getting shot or torn to pieces was a question beyond answers; at least for the moment.

The scene was surreal. The beast's head and a lone arm appeared to be suspended in midair. A jagged blue line arced from the hand and carved a long black gash in the cement sidewalk in front of a squad car. Three officers were hunched down behind the vehicle with guns out, hesitant to pop up and fire.

The hand and the beast vanished. Seconds later, the seam winked from existence and took with it any chance of Nadina slipping through to Chevalon.

She stayed behind the car for another ten minutes watching the cops investigate the area around the lot. All held weapons ready for the next attack. On the far side of the small park, a line of television news crews were busy filming. She didn't want any of them to accidently pick her up, so she backed away. The scene resembled what she envisioned a movie set to look like.

When she reached the last car, she stood and walked back to the parking garage. She took the stairs up to the third level. As she exited the stairwell, she saw a bright flash at the far end. It was the area near the second seam. It shocked her and set her sprinting. She rounded the turn and shot up the slope. In front of the truck stood two of the beasts and a man.

She didn't need to be any closer to recognize the man. Rhoden. Her rage spiked and she started toward him. One of the beasts raised its head and spotted her. She stopped in her tracks and dodged between two parked vehicles before Rhoden could see her. Minutes later, the three strode past her hiding place. One of the beasts turned its massive head toward her, silently warning her to stay out of the way.

As they rounded the bend at the end of the ramp, Nadina crawled out and peered after them. Then a new frightening thought came to her and she stood abruptly. "My God! Catron!" She raced up the ramp, stopping at the truck's passenger side. She tried the door. Locked. She peered through the glass, pressing her face flat. The interior was too dark to make anything out. "Catron?" She saw movement. A lighter patch morphed into a very pale face.

"Are they gone?"

Nadina glanced down the ramp. "Yes."

Catron unfolded from the floor where she'd scrunched herself and opened the door. She tried to step out, but whether from her tight quarters or fear, or both, her legs would not hold her. She fell into Nadina's arms.

"I've got you." She held her until Catron grasped the truck bed wall and could support her own weight.

"Well, that was fun."

"What happened?"

"The lights went on the seam was revealed. It peeled down like a banana skin and out stepped this huge beast, like the ones that attacked us back at the cabin. I ducked into the well and tried not to move. I'm still here, so it worked."

"Come on. We have to follow them."

"Oh, do we?"

"Yes." Nadina gave her a hard gaze. "That's the man responsible for killing Tetrin and for my son disappearing into a world I can't get to. He has to answer for his crimes. I will not let him go unpunished." She ran around the truck and hopped into the driver's seat. She started the engine, but Catron still didn't move.

Nadina buttoned down the passenger window. "Are you coming or not?"

Catron hesitated, swaying slightly with indecision, then slid into the seat. Nadina backed from the space and whipped the wheel, squealing the tires. She shot down the ramp. At the bottom she rammed through the barricade arm and stopped. Down the street to the right, a delivery truck was stopped in the middle of the road. As she watched, a man flew through the air and crashed onto the hood of a parked car. The truck moved on. She followed.

"What's the plan here?"

"For now, follow. I want to see where they go. Once we have a location, we can plan how to take him down." She glanced at Catron for her reaction. The woman merely stared out the window and nodded. Evidently, she liked the plan.

Chapter 47

They stayed with the delivery truck through the night. As the sun began its early morning rise, the truck turned off the main road and down a long dirt track. Fearing a trap, Nadina drove past the road a quarter mile and pulled over.

"Stay here if you want, but I'm going to see where they go."

Catron nodded and got out. She slid the seat forward and pulled a pump action shotgun from behind it. She shoved two boxes of shells into her sweater coat pockets and shut the door. "Let's do this." The fear that had held her motionless earlier in the day was now long gone.

Nadina retrieved her handgun from under the seat and slid it into her pants at the small of her back. The two women made their way back to the dirt road. They crouched and looked as far as they could. Seeing no sign of the truck, they moved with caution onto the double track and scanned their perspective sides. Even if they were walking into a trap, Nadina expected to have some warning. The two hulking creatures would not be able to move with much stealth in these woods.

They traveled farther than expected. The road curved enough to keep them guessing about what might lie around the next bend. It forked a mile later.

"Now what?" Catron asked.

Nadina wasn't sure. She bent to examine the ground, but the hard packed dirt and grassy track didn't offer many clues. "How does he know this spot?" Nadina murmured. Had he been there before or was he just guessing? Searching for a safe place to hide? She moved along each trail for a few feet before discovering what looked like a recent tire tread impression. "You can't hide from Rhoden."

She motioned with her head and they took the right fork. A few minutes later, they heard something moving through the trees to their right. They ducked and moved left, stepping into a thicket. They couldn't see the source of the noise, but they were making no effort to be quiet. Trees moved and brush crunched under heavy footsteps. Periodically they caught glimpses of a large creature, but never long enough to identify it.

"Could it be a bear?" Nadina whispered.

Catron gave her a *Seriously?* look.

"Can't be any more absurd than beasts coming from another dimension." Catron was forced to accept the statement with a noncommittal shrug.

"I have a feeling we're close."

Catron nodded. Nadina waited for the creature to move farther away before starting through the woods on the left side of the road. They slowed to a hunter's stalk to avoid being detected. Both women had their weapons in hand and ready. Time passed in slow motion. Soon they arrived at an ancient cabin in a clearing buried deep off the main road. No one would think to look there.

They stopped and crouched low. Seconds later, the front door opened and one of the beasts exited with the body of a man slung over one shoulder. It pounded down the wooden steps and went around the back of the cabin. Minutes later, it reappeared sans body.

"They must have killed the owner of this place to use it as their hideout."

Catron did not respond. A small shed stood to the left of the cabin. The delivery truck stuck out from behind it.

"What are we going to do?" Catron asked.

"Not sure. We need to take Rhoden by surprise before his goons can save him or he can use his magic."

"It has to be when he's alone. Between the two of us we don't have enough fire power to stop both of those beasts."

Nadina nodded her agreement. "We either wait for the right moment or retreat and come back with reinforcements."

"If we leave, he might be gone by the time we get back," Catron said.

"True. We could call the police."

"Could if I had a phone."

Nadina patted her pockets for her own phone. It was gone. Had she dropped it on the ground or left it in the truck? "I don't know what happened to mine."

"Well, we've got three choices. We both stay, we both go, or one stays and one goes."

"I wouldn't feel comfortable leaving you here."

"Okay. Then stay here and cover me."

"Wait," Nadina clutched Catron's arm. "What are you going to do?"

"Make it so they'll still be here when we get back."

Catron handed the shotgun to Nadina and emptied her pockets of the shells. Then, she tiptoed through the woods to the left. In seconds she was out of sight. Nadina scanned along the cabin front. She caught quick movement to the side of the shed. A metallic creak sounded like a gunshot in the quiet environment. She cringed at the noise and lifted the shotgun, ready to defend Catron. To her relief, no one noticed and the cabin remained still.

Minutes later, Catron returned with a handful of wires. "If they leave now, it will be on foot."

Nadina smiled and handed the shotgun back. They took their time returning to the truck, aware the second beast was looming out there somewhere. To their left, something stomped through the woods. They veered away from it.

They exited the woods and saw the truck. Catron deposited the wires in the bed and they got into the cab. Nadina started the engine and bent to look for her missing phone on the floorboard. Something slammed into the truck and rocked it, nearly tipping it on its side.

Nadina jerked up and whipped the back of her head on the steering wheel. Catron and Nadina screamed when they saw the ugly beast outside the driver's side window. As the beast drew back its enormous fist, Nadina shifted and floored the accelerator. The truck shot forward, then halted with a sudden lurch. The beast held tight to the sidewall. It was more powerful than she could've imagined.

She kept the pedal down, spinning the wheels and creating black smoke and the stench of burning rubber. Slowly, the truck began to lift off the road. The beast was going to flip it over.

Catron slid the window at the back of the cab open and pushed the shotgun out. In rapid fire, she pumped and fired three blasts into the beast's face. The truck bounced hard on the ground, tires still spinning. They caught traction and shot forward, whiplashing their necks.

The truck accelerated to ninety and shook like it would fall apart at any second. A hand touched Nadina's arm and she jumped.

"You can slow down now," Catron said.

Nadina shook more than the truck did. She braked and realized she'd been hyperventilating. Her pulse raced and her chest hurt.

"Where did it come from?"

"Evidently, they're stealthier than we expected."

"Evidently."

"Look, I need to regroup. If we're going to deal with these creatures and take Rhoden down, I need to be better prepared. My skills are not offensive, but there are things I can do to slow them down. I need to go back to the cabin and gather what I need and study.

"Take the truck and then come back for me."

"Okay."

On the return trip, Nadina's heartbeat finally returned to normal.

Chapter 48

After dropping Catron off and finding her lost phone under the seat, Nadina drove back toward Chicago. Twenty minutes from her destination, her phone buzzed. She scooped it up. She didn't recognize the number, although it had a Chicago area code. She debated answering it, not wanting to deal with a telemarketer, but then didn't care if it was. She needed someone to vent to. She answered it in a harsh, "What?"

A pause on the other end made her regret her decision. She was about to thumb the disconnect button when a voice came through the speaker.

"Is this Nadina?"

Something about it was familiar. "Who's this?"

"It's Detective Grant."

The name floored her. The truck swerved, almost sending her into the oncoming lane. She slowed to regain control. "Grant. Where have you been? Have you seen my son?"

"Easy now. Take a deep breath and listen. Your son is all right. I just left him."

"Where? Where did you just leave him? And for that matter, why did you leave him?"

"You have to settle down so I can explain."

"I don't have to do any such thing. I want my son. Where is he?"

"Maybe it's best if we meet."

"No!" she raged. She wanted to leap through the phone and throttle Grant. "I need to know now." Her voice cracked and became less intense. "Please." Warm tears streamed down her face. Her vision blurred, but she made no move to clear them, fearing she'd disconnect the call.

"Your son is all right. The danger is over. Let's meet. Come to the station. We can talk there."

"What? No. The police are looking for me."

"They are, but I've already taken steps to clear you and your entire entourage. You'll just have to trust me."

The fury rose again. She strangled the phone. "If this is a trick, I will make you pay. You don't mess with a desperate mother when her child's life is at stake."

"Understood. No tricks. You have my word."

Her voice cracked. "Is he really all right? Promise?"

"Yes."

As she drove, Nadina composed herself. She had to think. If this was a trap, there'd be no way out once she entered the station house. Every fiber in her being screamed at her not to enter, but the one thing that overshadowed all the doubt was the chance to get her son back unharmed

She parked in a lot down the street from the station and left the gun and the keys under the seat. With the door unlocked, she took a chance no one would break in and steal the truck and the gun, but she felt she had no choice. If she was walking into a trap, they'd take the keys. This way, if she made good on an escape, she had a ride waiting; providing it was still there and she could escape.

She entered the building and stood between the two sets of glass doors scanning the lobby and front desk for any clues about what was waiting for her. She got no read from anyone in view. Taking a deep breath, she pulled the door open and approached the front desk.

If the heavyset black man knew who she was, he gave no indication. "How can I help you?" he asked in a steady tone. His dark eyes scanned her.

"I'm here to see Detective Grant."

At the mention of his name, the man's eyebrows shot up. "Ah, yes. He's been expecting you." He picked up a phone. "Your interview is here."

Within seconds, Grant burst from a door and approached. "Good. Glad you decided to come." He took her by the elbow and guided her back through the door. They entered a large boisterous room filled with desks and simultaneous chatter. He led her through another door and down a corridor. Halfway down, he stopped and pressed her shoulders against the wall. Instantly, she was ready to fight. Policeman or not, she would not allow him to take her prisoner. Not with Rhoden still on the loose and her son unaccounted for.

"Relax. Don't fight me. I'm not here to hurt you or your family. I'm trying to get your husband and his friends released."

That calmed her for the moment. He released his hold and continued. "But before I can do that, you have to sit in front of my superiors and give your account of the events leading to this point."

She balked and started to walk away.

"You have to see this from their point of view. It is not only to help you and your family, but to help me as well. I'm in a lot of hot water because of things I've done to help your family. Lives have been lost. Policemen have been killed. More have been injured. They have no explanations for what's going on besides my reports that, frankly, sound like a fantasy story. They think I'm crazy. My career and my life are at stake here. Help me so I can help you. If I'm not cleared, I will have no pull to get your friends released."

"What do you need me to do?"

"Tell the truth. Regardless of how it sounds. Convince them that if not provable, at least the possibility exists."

"What if they don't believe me?"

"That's a reality, but if they get enough of the same story and don't have scientific reasoning, they will have to accept the chance something else—someplace else exists."

"Are they going to lock me up?"

"I honestly don't know."

"What if I refuse or just walk out of here?"

"I wish you wouldn't. This is for both of us and all who have been affected by what your world has unleashed on mine. Help me convince them."

Nadina fought an internal struggle, knowing whatever she chose, she'd lose. After a moment, she nodded and Grant sighed with relief.

"You'll be in the room alone." Nadina balked. "They will not let me be in there. They don't want my presence to affect or alter your testimony. You can do this."

In her mind, this was a waste of time. They were never going to believe her. Still, she allowed Grant to take her to the interview room. He opened the door and stepped aside for her to enter. Seated at a table were seven high-ranking officers. Four men and three women. Nadina found herself praying the women all were mothers.

"I'd like to introduce Nadina. She is volunteering to give testimony."

"You may go, Grant," a white-haired man in the center seat said.

"Nadina, please be seated." The white-haired man continued. "These proceedings are being recorded. For the record, state your full name."

"Nadina Williams." It was not her real name, but in this world they wouldn't know that. It was the name that appeared on her driver's license and marriage certificate.

"Your address, please."

She gave it.

"You understand that what you say here can be used against you in a court of law?"

She nodded and he continued his obscure reading of her Miranda rights.

"Do you wish to have a lawyer present at this time?"

She shook her head.

"For the record, I need you to reply verbally."

"No, not at this time." She emphasized *this*.

"Very well. Let's start with an overall statement of the events leading to the deadly battle in the parking lot on Seventeenth Street. We'll reserve our questions until you're done."

"Very well, but you won't believe me."

A woman at the end of the table leaned forward. "Ms. Williams, we've already seen so much we can't explain. Whatever you say will at least be considered. Please relax and don't leave anything out."

Nadina relaxed a bit and started at the beginning, when she, Nordon, and Eric passed through the seam to this new world. Her story continued for more than two hours concluding with her efforts to find her son. She did not, however, disclose Rhoden's return to this world. She was undecided how best to handle that bit of information, choosing to hold it back in case she needed it later.

Several times during her recitation, she was asked to stop while her interrogators tried to wrap their heads around something she said. For the most part, other than asking for clarification, they held their questions.

When she concluded, she was led from the room by an officer and allowed to use the bathroom. She was then taken to a smaller room where a sandwich, chips, and a soda waited for her. Grant was nowhere in sight, but she assumed he'd be hovering close by.

So far she felt the interview had been going well, if she could ignore the looks of disbelief on their faces.

Thirty minutes later, the officer returned and took her back to the bigger room. The grilling began. She became defensive several times under their constant barrage. They did not go easy on her, calling her story a complete work of fiction. She understood why they'd come to that conclusion, but she stuck to her story, fighting the irritation and anger rising within her.

Three hours later, the white-haired leader looked up and down the line and asked, "Does anyone else have anything to say?"

The woman on the end spoke. "It's a hard story to believe, though much of what you have said makes sense in the context of what occurred. You are either a very strong, very brave woman, or just plain bat-shit crazy. I want to believe this astounding story if only because it makes the explanation of events easier. However, without solid proof of what you say, I don't see how we can accept this tale, regardless of how much truth might be there."

"I did warn you at the beginning that you would not believe me."

Another woman spoke. "Oh, we believe it. We just have assigned other explanations to the events."

"Of course you have."

"You will be held here until we can come to a determination," the white-haired man said.

"Does that mean I'm under arrest?"

"No. It means you're being held for further questioning. However, I must warn you. You've admitted to several crimes that could result in charges being filed against you."

Nadina shook her head and looked away.

"It was a huge mistake coming here. My son's life is in danger and much of this event, as you call it, is still unresolved. I can't find my son if you keep me in here."

"I'm sorry, but that's what is going to happen. We have multiple deaths that need resolution. You have admitted to involvement in an accessory role at the least. At this point, you'd be well advised to retain an attorney."

"You had a gun battle last night with forces you can't describe. There is multiple video of the attack to review. Find another explanation that fits better than mine to explain what you saw. Sometimes things happen that stretch our beliefs to the point of doubt. I can't alter what I know to be true. Can you honestly say that none of you believe in anything that doesn't exist in this world? What about a belief in a supreme being? If you can believe that God walked the earth and now is worshiped by millions, how can you not believe in other unseen and unprovable occurrences? Are there alien beings? There's certainly a lot of unexplained evidence around the world. What about ghosts? Do they exist? Is the other side," she made quotation signs in the air, "or crossing over possible?

"I'm not crazy. This story is real and whatever you decide to believe will not alter what has happened. I did not start this. I only want my son back. If you no longer want us in your world, I have no problem going back to mine."

"That would be the definitive proof we need. To actually witness this seam and what you say is on the other side."

"I would like nothing more than to show you."

"But?"

"Yes, the always present but. I don't have the ability to open the seam. I've been trying so I could search for my son, but," she paused for emphasis, "without a high-level mage, I know of no other way to open the seam."

"Of course not," the white-haired man said with a sufficient amount of skepticism that told Nadina exactly what their findings would be.

Chapter 49

They took Nadina to the bathroom then back to the same room. This time, no meal awaited her. She tried the door only to find it locked. She assumed an armed guard stood on the opposite side. This had been a mistake. She was no longer free to hunt Rhoden or find Eric.

She wondered if Catron had given up on her return. Then she thought about Nordon. Being confined must be driving the big man mad. She thought back on their forced life together. It could have been so much worse. She was fortunate. Nordon had been such a good man. It might not have started as a love story, but it had certainly developed into one.

A short time later, the door opened and Grant walked in with a bag of fast food. He set it down in front of her, nodded to the guard standing in the doorway, and he left, closing the door behind him.

"I'm sorry for what they put you through."

"They don't believe me. They're going to find against me and arrest me. I'll stand trial and lose, because who would ever believe such a wild story?"

"I wish I could say you're wrong."

"No matter what happens to me, I want you to promise to find my son and look after him."

"I would make that promise in a heartbeat, but the chances are I'm gonna go down too."

"Fifteen years I've lived in your world. It took a long time to understand how it works. Despite all we had to overcome, we did. We adjusted and never had a speck of trouble. Now that's all over. In some ways it's a relief, but to spend my life in prison as a result just seems cruel beyond belief."

"Look, I don't have much time. I had to pull some strings to get this. I have a lot to tell you. Then you'll have to choose."

She eyed him. "Go on."

"First of all, your son--in fact, both the heirs--are amazing. They stepped up when needed the most and brought an end to that tyrant Frost."

Nadina perked up at the news. "So, Mortas Frost is gone and my son is well?"

"Yes. More than well." He went on in hurried detail about all that had transpired during his short time in Chevalon. He took a breath and covered Nadina's hands on the table. "Here's the thing. Your son is returning tomorrow, if all goes right."

Nadina reversed his hold and snagged his hands in hers. She squeezed tight and came out of her chair. "Eric's coming home? You're sure?"

"That was the plan when I came through. The idea was to find you and your husband, as well as Elly's mom, and have them all there, kinda like a receiving line."

"Is Elly all right?"

"She's fine, and the other girl, Shree…well, she's better, and she's coming back too."

The joy she felt moments before faded. She sat back down and let go of Grant's hands. "But I'll still be in here, won't I?" Before he could answer, she gripped his hands with urgency. "Promise me you won't bring him here. He can't be arrested for this. He's as much a victim as a part. Please, promise me you'll let him go."

"Well, see, that's where the decision part comes in. Hear me out before you shoot my idea down."

Grant explained his idea, then left her to mull over the pros and cons. She would only have the night to make her choice. On one hand, she risked her son's freedom, but on the other, it could give the interrogators the proof they needed to release them all. It was a huge gamble on her part. Her freedom in exchange for her son's incarceration. She didn't think she could do it, regardless of being free. She was his mother. Perhaps not by blood, but their bonds went so much deeper than DNA. She loved him with all her heart and soul and would do anything in her power to keep him safe.

She was led from the interview room and placed in a holding cell. She lay down on the bench and stared at the ceiling, weighing the impossible decision through the night.

When at last the guard came for her, she was again brought to the small room where Grant was waiting with coffee and donuts. Before she sat, she said, "I'm sorry. I can't do it. I won't risk my son's freedom."

"Then let me present this option. We go through with the plan. Once the seam opens, I'll poke my head in and tell him not to come through until we have the word he's in the clear. That way, if we sense anything amiss, we have Phetrix seal the seam and never open it again. He'll remain free and safe, and the seam will never open again."

"But you're under suspicion as well. Will they allow you to get close to the seam?"

"I'll explain that since I'm from this world I'm less of a flight risk than you are. Besides, other than you, I'm the only one who knows how it works and what to look for."

She sucked in her lower lip and worried at it. "I don't know what to do."

"Come on, Nadina. This will work. We can keep Eric safe from the authorities."

She sat back and searched for a solution she could live with. She sat up. "Am I scheduled to meet with them again?"

"Yes." He checked his watch. "In about fifteen minutes. It won't be an interview. They're going to give their findings and what they intend to do. I'm guessing it will go to a trial. The trial won't take place for a long time. You could be locked up for a year or more if you don't get bail. Since this has to do with the killing of cops, bail is doubtful. This may be the only chance to prove your story. It's certainly the only time we know for sure someone will be crossing."

"Are you going to tell them your idea?"

"Yes. I'll request a few minutes before they address you."

She nodded. "I want to speak to them too."

"I'll arrange it."

He stood to leave.

"Detective, if this fails, remember your promise to look after my son."

"It better not fail. For everyone's sake.

Thirty minutes later, the guard opened the door and she was taken back to the larger room. The same seven people were in the same chairs. Grant was in her seat, but a second one had been added.

White-hair spoke. "Am I to understand this so-called seam will open today?"

"That's what I've been told."

"So, you admit you have no first-hand knowledge of this?"

"That is correct."

"How do we take this as proof?"

"You will see for yourself."

No one spoke.

Nadina became irritated. "Hey, you wanted proof of the existence of another world. Well, here it is. This is my defense. If you're not willing to look for yourself, then you have no right to hold me. This is my chance to clear my name. If you won't take the time to see for yourself and keep an open mind, then you might as well get on with this farce."

The woman on the far side said, "I am intrigued by this opportunity."

"As am I," a man said.

White-hair glanced up and down the row and all heads nodded at him. "Very well. We will delay revealing our findings until after we witness this so-called alternate world."

"Hold on there, big shot."

The room came to a standstill at Nadina's words and tone. "I have some stipulations of my own to add."

"Excuse me? You are in no position to make demands."

"Think again. I'm the only one here who knows the location of the seam."

To his credit, Grant didn't flinch at the lie.

"Not true. The location has been documented. We know exactly where it is."

"No. You know where one seam is. That is not the one they will be using. They know it will be under surveillance by both your people and our enemies. The seam itself may be booby-trapped, but there is a second seam, and if you want to see it, I do have leverage to make demands."

"If this is some ploy to gain your freedom—"

"No. It's my chance to exonerate myself and my family. Cuff me. Have an army of cops surround me. But I want my husband there. It's my understanding that my son's sister will also be coming through with a friend who was kidnapped with her. I want Elly's mother to be there, as well as Elly's friend's parents. They have to be sick with worry. It's only right."

"I'm not going to do that."

"Then you will miss one of the great discoveries of our time. I'd do it just for that reason alone. But then, you're not the one whose freedom may be coming to an end."

They put their heads together and whispered.

Nadina gave them a few minutes. When she could take the delay no further, she said, "Hey. We don't have much time here. We know they're coming today but we don't know when. They move slow in the other world. They don't have the convenience of motorized vehicles. Make your decision and let's get moving. Oh, and one more thing. Once you've seen the proof beyond a shadow of a doubt, we walk away."

"No way. There is still too much to answer for."

"I'm not saying for you to drop the charges. In the end you'll have to anyway. What I'm saying is that we'll be released and not have to remain in jail. You'll know where we are. Put a monitor on me if you want. But that's the deal."

There was more commotion at the head table as they all fought to be heard. Grant stood. "Excuse me." It took a moment for quiet to return. "I have been on this force for a long time. In those many years of service, my record has been stellar. You have called me on the carpet and basically said I'm a liar. My reputation is at stake here, as well as my future in the department. I'm owed the opportunity to remove doubt from your minds. You don't believe my account of what I saw? Fine. But if you deny me this chance to clear my good name, I will wage a war on the front page of every newspaper and media outlet I can until enough people clamor for the truth and you will be forced into explanations that you won't be comfortable giving.

"Now, you may not like what I've just said, but I am owed this opportunity, if only for my excellent service to this department and city.

Make your decision so we can get the wheels in motion and find the answers you need to make an honest and informed decision."

The white-haired man stood abruptly. "Detective Grant, you may have a stellar record, but after what amounts to threatening your superiors, your days in this department may be numbered."

"Why would I want to stay in a department that cannot accept the word of one its officers or give him a chance to defend himself against the most ridiculous charges imaginable? In fact," he said, pulling his badge from his belt, "you can take this worthless piece of scrap metal right now."

"Detective Grant," the woman with the voice of reason said, "Please sit down and let's let cooler heads prevail. I think a vote on the proposal should move things along. I for one agree with the entire plan. It's folly to think they can escape. Should this proof not be what we hoped, they can be returned to cells and charges filed."

A second was offered by one man and another of the females voted for the deal.

In the end, the motion was carried five to two.

Chapter 50

Too much time had passed for Nadina's liking before they started out. Two hours later, she was placed in the back seat of a squad car with her hands were cuffed behind her. She was annoyed about the delay and prayed Eric had not passed through the seam already.

Refusing to give the destination in advance, they were forced to caravan to the parking garage. As they turned in, the radio came to life and White-hair shouted that this was some trick to escape.

Once all the vehicles were inside, orders were given to shut down the garage. Officers were dispatched to all levels to scan for traps or ambushes. With the site secure, the board exited and met in a huddle. After a few minutes, they let Nadina out and she marched to the group.

"We're here. Where is this supposed seam to another world?" White-hair demanded.

"When it opens it will be just beyond that outer wall." Hands still secured behind her back, she jutted her chin.

"There?" one man said. "But that's three stories up in midair."

"Hey, I didn't place them. That's where it is."

"We'll give it an hour," White-hair said.

"No, you'll give it the time it takes," Nadina countered. His glare showed the contempt he felt for her.

Grant came up behind her and unlocked her cuffs, bringing an instant reaction from the group. He said, "Relax. Look around. She's not going anywhere. She's sure not going to vault the wall and fall three stories."

As they waited, Grant went around to the other cars and had the prisoners brought forward. Nadina rushed to Nordon, whose hands were still cuffed, and gave him a strong embrace. Alyanna stood filled with nervous energy, knowing she could be reunited with her daughter. Kol was frozen; shell-shocked by the entire ordeal.

They waited for what felt like an eternity. An hour passed, then two. White-hair--Alyanna had no desire to learn his name--paced and complained. By the time the third hour approached he was out of patience and had the support of three others.

"That's it. I'm calling it. We gave you a fair chance, but it's obviously a ruse."

Nadina was heartbroken. Even if the charges were filed, she hoped to see her son once more. With head hung low, her escort to lead her back to the cruiser.

Kol gagged on words that came out as, "Uh, oh, ook." He bobbed his head toward the outer wall.

Several people turned. Grant said, "Yes."

Nordon said, "Praise the Gods."

Others gasped; some reached for weapons.

A white line that looked like the result of a downed power line sparked to life. As it moved downward, Grant went behind the captives and uncuffed their hands. Once free, Nordon scooped Nadina up in his arms.

A car drove up the ramp. Heads turned to see Shree's mother and father. Alyanna went to their side to welcome them. Neither of them appeared happy.

In a moment, a head popped into view. The wide eyes showed his surprise at seeing a welcoming committee. He ducked back fast. The seam appeared to be closing. Grant was first to react. He ran forward, leaped onto the wall, and jumped for the fast disappearing seam. His fingers grabbed for it and he dangled in midair with nothing but concrete beneath him three floors down.

White-hair shouted, "He's escaping! Stop him!"

The sensible woman shouted at White-hair. "Belay that! Let it play out." She spoke in a commanding voice. He blanched at the tone but did not speak again.

THE NEXT DAY, Phetrix, Eric, Elly, Shree, and a retinue of troops made the long trek to the seam. It took two full days on horseback to reach it. When they arrived, Phetrix handed each of the twins a plain silver ring. "When you're ready to return, put the ring on your index finger, wave in the direction of the seam, and say *Openadus.*"

He made each of them repeat the word several times, then had Elly open the seam. It appeared, reminding them of a zipper. Phetrix poked his head through first. As he pulled back, he wore a strange expression. In a flurry of motion he began to seal the seam. Before he got it closed, Grant's head poked through.

ON THE OPPOSITE side of the seam, Grant's head popped through the gap. Phetrix ceased his spell, leaving barely enough space for Grant's head. "Hey, stop. This is important. If we don't prove you exist, we may all go to prison."

Eric asked, "Is my mom here?"

"Yes, and your dad. Alyanna and Shree's parents too. There's also a host of cops who need to poke their fat heads through the seam to verify the existence of your world."

"I'm not sure I'm comfortable with them knowing about us."

"Hey, this has to happen. Besides, you control the seam. If you don't want people to get in, keep it sealed."

Eric said, "Let them look. They can't hurt us."

Phetrix nodded. "Very well, but no one crosses over to this side."

GRANT SWUNG his legs and landed in a precarious position on top of the wall. Nordon raced forward and snatched him back before he lost his balance.

Once on the floor, Grant clutched at his chest and thanked the big man. He turned to his superiors and said, "Okay, it's open. Now's the time to take a look."

No one was in a hurry to step forward after witnessing Grant's near fall. The woman who supported the trip said, "Oh, for heaven's sake,

I'll go first." They helped her onto the wall and held on from behind. She reached for the seam and pushed her head through.

"Oh! Hi," the woman said.

"Greetings," replied Phetrix.

"Wow. It's pretty here. What is this place?"

"It is called Chevalon."

"Chevalon. Nice." She reached back and pushed a small, flat rectangle through the hole.

"Is that a weapon?" Phetrix asked nervously.

"No," Eric said. "It's called a cell phone. It's used to communicate with others over long distances."

"Is she trying to communicate with someone here?"

"No. She's using it as a camera to take pictures."

The answer confused Phetrix but he made no further comment.

"You must be Eric."

"Yes."

"I've heard a lot about you. So, you're a prince?"

"So they tell me. I've only just found out."

"But you live in Chicago, right?"

"Well, I do for now."

She looked around, then said, "It was nice to meet you."

"And you, as well."

A moment later, a man poked his head through. He looked around and took photos but did not speak. Next came a white-haired man. He looked afraid. "My God. This can't be real."

"It's as real as you or me," Eric said. The man didn't stay long. There was a pause before the next head came, and a longer wait still for the next.

Then Grant returned. "I think we're done exploring. Give us a minute."

Grant jumped back, making a better landing than on his first try. He leaped to the floor feeling lighter than when he first arrived. He felt he'd been vindicated. He approached the group of superiors that held his future in their hands. "Well? Believe me now?"

One of his superiors said, "The cocky attitude isn't helping."

Grant bit back his reply.

After a lengthy, heated debate, White-hair and two others drove off and left the woman, Assistant Chief Peggy Talbot, to give the news. "This has been quite enlightening. We will reconvene back at the station and have a decision for you hopefully by tomorrow. For the moment you are free, but with the stipulation that you will return whenever called."

Nadina nodded. "You have my word."

Talbot offered a hand and Nadina took it. "Quite remarkable." She turned and the rest of the board drove away. One by one, the escorting police cars drove off. A lone car made its way up the ramp and stopped sideways across the drive. Vega, Grant's partner, fresh out of the hospital, walked around the car. "Thought you could use a ride back."

"Very thoughtful of you."

Chapter 51

Elly stepped through first. Before anyone else could move they heard wild squeals of joy from the other dimension. Eric took Shree's hand and helped her through. Shree beamed a wide smile at him. Once on the other side she blew him a kiss.

Eric hesitated, then turned to shake Phetrix's hand. "Thank you for your guidance. I will rely heavily on you in the first few months of my reign."

"Rest assured, the kingdom will still be here when you return."

"I have no doubt."

"You sure you don't want to come?"

The mage held up a hand. "No. I've had my time in your world. I prefer the much slower pace here."

Eric smiled, saluted his retinue, and disappeared through the seam back to his world.

Before he'd taken two steps he was attacked by his mother and father. They hugged, kissed, and cried in an emotional reunion. Grant and Vega stood by an unmarked car watching the proceedings.

The individual groups eventually came together and everyone talked at once. It was a glorious gathering. Shree's parents were still upset that she was gone for so long. They eventually left, wanting to spend some time with their daughter.

Elly spotted Grant and made her way to him. "I've been told Rhoden has escaped to this dimension."

Grant leaned against the car with his arms crossed and waited.

"I'm going to find him."

Grant said nothing.

"I'd appreciate your help to track him down."

He looked at his partner, who shrugged, then finally spoke.

"What's your intent once you find him?"

"Depends."

"On what? I won't get involved in some vigilante revenge thing."

"It depends on you."

"On me?" he laughed. "How so?"

"If you're with me, I'll bring him to justice. If you're not…" she shrugged.

He eyed her, looked at Vega again, then slid a card from his pocket and handed it to her. "Give me a call when you're ready to start looking."

"Give me a day to get settled and I'll be ready."

She nodded her thanks and walked away.

Before they left, they guided Kol back through to his home. The man was so grateful to be back in a world he understood. He collapsed and sobbed.

NADINA AND NORDON invited Alyanna and Elly to a celebration dinner. They pulled into a BBQ place in great spirits. They talked, but though happy to be reunited, a reserved air fell over the table. They all had so many memories, most of them bad.

"Mom," Elly said. "I'm sorry I missed Dad's funeral."

Alyanna tried to smile, but the effort was strained. "It wasn't much of one. With you gone and all the other stuff happening, I didn't do him right."

"Now that I'm back, why don't we plan a memorial service for him?"

She wiped a tear from her eye and took her daughter's hand. "That'd be wonderful. He would like that." She wiped at her eyes again. "He really was a good man."

Trying to give them some privacy, Nadina turned toward Eric. "And what are your plans?"

"Well, I was going to discuss this with you at home, but this is all family anyway." He took a deep breath and began talking. They were both quiet as he spoke. He wasn't sure what to expect, but when his mother hugged him and his father patted him on the back, he knew he'd made the right decision.

When he finished, Elly told her plans. Alyanna was less than pleased but accepted that her daughter would be home most of the year. "So you do plan on graduating and going to college?"

"Yes, but I do owe an obligation to the people of Chevalon. I plan to fulfill that duty."

She hesitated before adding the last part. "I will spend my free time hunting down Rhoden. He has to pay for what he did. I will not rest until I find him."

"Oh, Elly," Alyanna said. "Don't throw your life away chasing after that man."

"Mom, my mind is made up. Dad would still be alive if not for him. I'm doing this."

Nadina and Nordon exchanged glances. Nordon nodded. Nadina said, "If you're serious, we may be able to help." She explained her last encounter with the man. When she was done, Elly's eyes were ablaze with the desire to get started.

"If we wait too long, it'll be harder to find him again."

"If this is the path you've chosen," Alyanna said, "I'll help you."

Elly brightened and she hugged her mother.

After they separated, Nadina drove them home. It felt strange being back there again. Much of the house had been boarded up or given a quick repair. "I think," Nordon said, "since you're going to be gone much of the time, we're going to sell the house."

The news surprised Eric. "Where will you live?"

They exchanged glances and said in unison, "With you."

THREE DAYS later they pulled into the parking garage downtown and parked. A host of people were waiting for them. They greeted everyone and then walked to the ledge where Eric used his ring to open the seam. They took turns stepping through. First Shree and her mother, then Alyanna and Elly, Nadina and Nordon, and finally Grant and Vega.

Eric was surprised to see Vega. He said, "Everyone already thinks Grant's crazy. The way I figure it, this'll give me the proof I need to get him assigned to a desk job."

"Huh. Dream on," Grant replied.

On the Chevalon side, Phetrix sent a royal escort, though he had no idea how many people were attending the coronation.

Vega and Shree's mother were dumbfounded and unable to speak. Two days later they arrived at the castle. Vega said, "Thanks, Grant. Now everyone will think I'm crazy too."

The coronation was a huge event. The castle grounds were packed with spectators and well-wishers. At the insistence of Eric and Elly, the reception was open to all residents of Chevalon. The celebration lasted two full days.

Though Samuel attended the ceremony, his strength had not returned as hoped. He told Phetrix he'd like to finish out his days in Chicago. Phetrix arranged for the transport of his friend and mentor.

The return trip felt longer than the arrival. When they reached the seam, it was a time of goodbyes and more well-wishing. Shree and her mother went first, followed by Alyanna. Eric and Elly embraced.

"I promise I'll be back next summer."

"I'll look forward to seeing you then. And Elly, good luck with your hunt. But please, be careful."

She gave him a playful punch on the arm and laughed. "You're just worried I won't make it back to relieve you."

"Exactly right," he laughed, but inside he was truly concerned for his sister.

She vanished through the seam.

"My old friend," Phetrix said to Samuel. "Take good care of yourself."

"I will, and don't concern yourself with me. I'll be right where I want to be."

They shook hands warmly, but Phetrix doubted he'd ever see Samuel again. Vega went through and helped Samuel cross.

Then it was Grant's turn. He gave both Phetrix and Eric a firm handshake. "Hey, you guys sure do throw a great party. Good luck with this whole king thing."

"Thank you for everything, Detective," Phetrix said.

"Detective Grant, please look out for my sister. I'm afraid her judgement is clouded by her anger. I just found her. I don't want anything to happen to her."

"I'll do my best. I promise."

"Thank you."

As Grant reached for the seam, an electric spark shot him backward. Eric caught him before he landed on the ground. "What the heck was that?"

Eric had no idea and Phetrix looked just as stymied. He scanned the seam for any magic spells or wards but found nothing. He closed and reopened the seam, then peered through. "Seems all right now."

Grant stepped up, cautiously peeked through, then said, "I can't believe they left already. Vega better not be playing games." He stepped through and landed on his feet after a longer drop than he remembered it to be. "Ah, that's more like it. Home, baby. Home." He glanced back as the seam sealed and disappeared, then turned to find Vega. He'd taken several steps before realizing something wasn't right. He stopped and stared around him.

He was supposed to be in the parking garage, but he was in a parking lot. A flat, one-story slab of pavement with a few cars. Then he noticed something else that was strange. Every car in the lot looked to be at least sixty years old. What was going on? This had to be a mistake or a bad dream.

He pivoted slowly, taking in his surroundings. The skyline was wrong too. Something was missing. Entire buildings were gone. The street lights were dimmer, and even the air smelled different.

He walked toward the street. Every car that passed him was a historical vehicle. Was there a car show here? He stopped on the sidewalk and scanned the streets. The shops all had different names. This can't be real. He walked back to where he thought the seam was and tried to find a way back through, but nothing happened.

A squad car pulled over and two cops got out. The men were bookends; one with brown hair and the other blond.

"You got a problem, Mac?"

"Ah, no, Officer."

"Well you looked like you were trying to climb the air."

Unsure what was , Grant said, "I was just playing around." Without thinking, he put his hands on his hips, which pushed his sport coat back to reveal the holstered gun.

Both cops reacted at the same time. "He's got a gun!" They pulled and aimed their guns and shouted commands.

"Whoa, whoa, whoa!" he shouted, raising his hands with palms out. "Easy, I'm no threat. I'm a cop. I'm a cop."

"Don't care what you are! Get down on the ground now before we plug you."

He couldn't believe this was happening but didn't want to get plugged, so he lowered himself flat to the ground. Blond Hair covered him while Brown Hair got behind him and snapped cuffs on his wrists. He then removed Grant's gun and frisked him. He found his wallet and shield. As the two cops looked through the confiscated items, they talked.

"This looks like a real badge," the blond said.

"Yeah, but not one I've ever seen. Says he's a lieutenant at the fourteenth precinct. I don't recall any Grant at the fourteenth."

"Look at that address on his license. Does that even exist?"

Blond squatted in front of Grant. "Where'd you get these forged IDs? You know, it's illegal to impersonate an officer of the law."

"They're not forged. Just drive me down to the fourteenth and they'll vouch for me."

"Hey, this license expires in the year two thousand and twenty-two. How is that possible? You got to pay extra for one that lasts that long?"

"Hell, I doubt he'll even be alive in sixty years. He don't look like no spring chicken."

"What's his birthday say?" Blond said.

"What the—hell, this guy hasn't even been born yet according to this."

"What? Let me look at that. Your math stinks." He counted it off once then used his fingers to try again. "I don't know how much you paid the guy who forged this, but you should get your money back."

"What are you guys talking about? Is this some kind of joke? Did the guys at the station put you up to this?" He hoped it was a prank, but he was starting to get a bad feeling.

"When's your birthday?"

"March third, nineteen eighty-four."

The two men looked at each other. Blond said, "So you won't be born for another twenty-six years? That's pretty good."

"Hey, maybe he's one of those time travelers like in H.G. Wells' *The Time Machine*."

"Yeah, that could be it."

Grant rolled to his side and swung his legs underneath him to sit up. "Wait a minute. Are you telling me this is the year Nineteen Fifty-Eight?"

"Yep, that's what we're saying," Brown Hair said.

"What year did you think it was?" Blond asked.

Grant didn't want to say. They already thought he was crazy. But the words poured out anyway. "Two Thousand Nineteen."

The two men looked at each other and broke out laughing.

Grant saw nothing funny about any of it. His only thought was, *What have I gotten into now?*

Lost

A SEAM TRAVELERS NOVELETTE

Lost:
A Seam Travelers Novelette

Chapter 1

Detective Marvin Grant was lost. Not lost in any traditional sense that a map app wouldn't help, but lost in time, like sixty-one years in the past lost.

He sat in a dingy interview room in the Fourteenth Precinct house staring at the door. He had been on the opposite side of this situation, sweating a perp for an extended time in hopes of wearing him down. Now, he realized just how uncomfortable, thus effective the tact was. His hands were still cuffed although if this was indeed nineteen fifty-eight they hadn't yet learned to put the suspects hands behind his back yet.

The two arresting officers called this an interrogation room. Something else that had changed over time. Nothing looked right. Nothing felt right. This building didn't exist in his time. A new one had been constructed somewhere along the timeline. In the hour he had been allowed to stew his mind kept replaying one specific moment in his attempt to cross through the seam—the electric shock. Whatever it had been, that charge had somehow screwed up the normal function of the seam and messed up the timeline, sending him sixty-one years into the past. He wasn't even alive yet. Hell, his daddy was only two and his mom wasn't born.

The building was small and rundown and the cops wore uniforms that looked stolen from a museum.

Knowing the cause for his predicament didn't help him. Somehow, he had to find a way out of the cuffs, out of the interview room, away from the police station, and back to his own time. Even if he was able to talk his way out of the first three, he had no way of reopening the seam. He was stuck. His only hope was that someone, possibly one of those magic types, missed him and went searching but how would they know where to look?

The door opened and a burly man in a wrinkled white shirt and coffee-stained tie entered the room with his head in a file. His foot bumped the chair opposite Grant, which made him glance up. He stopped and buried his head back in the file. Grant assumed it was his file and that it currently read like a science fiction novel.

He set the file down on the table and placed his hands on the back of the chair. He eyed Grant with a wide smile, then reached into his shirt pocket and withdrew a pack of cigarettes. He tapped one out, slid it into his mouth, then struck a match.

Grant watched with his mouth agape. The man was actually going to smoke in this tiny room. Was that allowed in the fifties? Evidently. The detective drew in a long draw and exhaled the smoke toward the ceiling.

"I have to say, this is a new one. A time traveling detective from the Chicago of the future." He shook his head, pulled out the chair and sat. "You certainly have gone out of your way to make it realistic. Badge, driver's license," he slapped the table causing Grant to jump, "and the gun. Wow! Now that's a piece of workmanship. Did you have it custom made." He leaned forward. "It's a Smith and Wesson but I looked through their catalog and didn't see anything close. Was it expensive? See, that right there tells me you ain't no cop cause a cop could never afford something that nice." He talked around the cigarette. "So, did you steal it?"

Grant sighed.

The detective took another puff and opened the file. "Okay, let's get to this, shall we?"

Grant said, "I'm not sure what to say. There is nothing I can tell you that you'll believe or that will make sense."

The detective snorted. "Got that right?"

"Then let's start with why I'm here. Have a broken any laws?"

The still unidentified detective cocked his head to the side as he studied Grant. "Laws? Hmm! Well, you've got an unregistered handgun. You tried to pass yourself off as a cop. That alone is enough to hold you."

"Just a gag. I have done nothing that warrants arrest. I understand you are curious about me but I was just having some fun."

"Ah, so nothing you said so far is true, eh?"

Grant saw the trap before stepping into it. "What I'm telling you now is the truth. I'm new here and was just out exploring the area. I heard Chicago can be a rough town so I brought some props with me in case someone tried to mug me."

"Mug you? Buddy, a black man in this city is more likely to be the mugger than the muggee."

Grant bristled. This racist cop was close to a thrashing. He reined in his anger. An outburst was not what he needed. He had to find a way out of here then figure out how to get back where he belonged.

Magic. He wished he had never answered the call to that stupid house. He wouldn't be here now. He'd be snuggled up in his nice warm bed and dreaming about, what? magical creatures attacking Chicago?

He cleared his thoughts and leaned over the table. "Sir, I just want to go home. How can I make that happen?"

Chapter 2

Samuel watched as the police loaded the tall black man into the back of the squad car. As soon as he felt the massive expenditure of magic, he rushed to the one location he knew had the capacity to release such an amount. The seam he had discovered, created, and hidden a year ago. To his knowledge no one else knew about the seam. True, he had left the information to create the spell needed to open the seam and the location of one of the two seams hidden in the library back at the castle in Chevalon. If someone had discovered the spell they might have used it but it took great skill to understand the spell and wield the amount of power necessary to accomplish a successful casting.

He didn't recognize the man as anyone from the castle. He certainly wasn't any mage he knew. In fact, he only knew two black mages and both resided in the wizard's tower at the academy of the arts, and neither of them looked like this man.

The man had been arrested and taken away. Although Samuel's curiosity was piqued there was nothing he could do to reach and question the man. He was still learning the ways of this strange land and dared not draw attention to himself. Still, he wanted to know more and the best source might be the seam.

Samuel waited for the police car to drive away then made his way to the site. He cast a veil over the area to conceal his activity. He sensed the magic emanating from the seam but it felt wrong—restricted, as if something held it back. Strange, he thought as he prepared the opening spell and set it free. Other than a small spark nothing happened.

He stared in incomprehension for a moment before he said with a slight tremor in his voice, "Have I forgotten the spell?" The words evoked panic. If he was unable to open the seam he might be stuck in this strange and intimidating world forever. He regrouped, examined the spell in his mind then, sure he had it right, cast it again adding more power than was necessary. The entire seam lit with an electric current then fizzled. The spell had worked and it was right yet the seam did not open. Something was preventing it.

Samuel turned and stared out at the city street the police car had taken. The vehicle was no longer in sight but now he had to find and question the tall black mage. He had to know what the mage had done to the seam. He needed to know why and how to reopen it. Though he had no plans of utilizing the seam it was reassuring to know his escape portal was nearby. He had to get it operational again.

He dispelled the veil and set off down the street in pursuit of his quarry. It promised to be a long and interesting night.

Chapter 3

The pounding on the door had become more insistent. Samuel moved but still weakened from his ordeal in Chevalon his progress was slow. As the pounding took on a more urgent force, Samuel called out, "I'm coming. Give an old man a chance."

Whoever was outside the door must have heard. The knocking ceased and a voice called out, "Hey, ah, wizard man. I need your help."

Samuel did not recognize the voice but the fact he threw out the word wizard so thoughtlessly told him it was someone he knew though not well. He reached the door cast a protection spell and peered through the peephole.

"I, ah, I need to talk to you. It's important," the man said. Though he sounded sincere, Samuel could not see him well enough to allow admittance. He stood too close to the peephole. "Who are you?" he called out.

"Oh, good, you're here. My name is Vega—Detective Vega. I'm partners with Marvin Grant. You know, the tall black guy."

Samuel made the connection and unlocked the door. The man stood gaping at him. "Hi, ah, I'm Vega."

"So you said."

"Yeah, I-I don't know how to say this but I need your like wizardly stuff. Grant is missing. He never came back from, you know, that other place."

Samuel was surprised. The detective was not far behind him and should have crossed through the seam by now. He stepped back. "Come in. and please, stop mentioning that stuff."

"Oh, yeah, sure. Sorry." He moved past Samuel. Samuel peeked down the hall both directions but no one else was in sight. He closed and locked the door and faced his guest.

"Tell me. What's the problem?"

"Well, like I said. Grant never came back. I waited for him for an hour and he never came through. I went up to the seam but just as I touched it there was like this electric current that shot through. It tossed me ten feet away." He held up an amateurish bandage on his left hand. "I burned my hand pretty bad. When I got up the seam was gone."

"It will vanish after a short time of inactivity. It was designed to do that."

"Was it designed to electrocute someone using it? Cause I'm telling you it threw me good. I was dazed for a while."

Samuel studied the man as his mind played through possibilities. He had never heard of or witnessed the seam sending out an electric current. Was it possible that the seam somehow short-circuited? He had to know. "Let me get my coat. I want to see."

As he turned to go, a memory surfaced from a long time ago reminding him it wasn't the first time it had happened. Yet, try as he may, he was unable to bring anymore of the distant memory to focus.

With Vega's help he made it down to street level where the detective had his unmarked police car double parked. They drove to the parking garage. Vega scanned the area to make sure they were alone, while Samuel studied the location of the seam. He still felt the power of the magic. The seam was still there. He exited the car and moved to a spot directly in front of the magic portal. After a quick examination of the seam's integrity, Samuel cast the spell to open the portal. A line of electric current ran around the edges of the seam then shot sparks. The light faded and blinked out leaving the seam hidden and unopen.

Stunned, Samuel had no idea what had happened or what to do to correct the problem. This was something that needed studying and to do that he needed rest to recover his strength. That little bit of magic usage had drained him to a point it was difficult to stand.

Vega slid his arms around Samuel and guided him back to the car. Once inside, Vega turned to him. "Well?"

Samuel shook his head, closed his eyes and laid his head back. "I have no idea. Take me home. I need rest and will try again tomorrow."

"Tomorrow? That might be too late. What if Grant's caught like in between the two worlds? He could be lost forever. Please, sir, you have to help him now."

"Even if I had my full powers, I doubt there is anything to be done. I must study the situation and the history of the spell to find the answer to opening the seam. I have no idea why it has closed. Please. Take me home."

Annoyed at the lack pf progress and effort, Vega slapped the stick into gear and sped out of the garage. He stewed the entire trip starting a sentence twice only to let it sputter and die incomplete. He pulled up the Samuel's apartment building. As Samuel opened the door to get out, Vega said, "I'll be back early in the morning. We have to find him. People at station are beginning to suspect something. He already missed one day of work. If he doesn't show tomorrow he might go on suspension."

"I promise you, detective, I will do my best." He got out and made his way inside. In his apartment, he pulled out an old leatherbound tome with a silver embossed icon displaying a bolt of lightning crossing what appeared to be a polished stick. Magic users knew it as a wand of power but its design was purposeful so as not to draw attention to the contents. Not that seeing the pages helped to discover the story within. The words on the pages were fuzzy and moved leaving anyone without magical ability nauseous and dizzy.

He sat down on the well-worn sofa, placed the book on the table, and stared at it. He did not have the energy to read nor the strength required to open the book and hold the words steady for his perusal.

Samuel laid back and closed his eyes. He had never felt older or closer to the end as he did then. He felt he didn't have much time left on this world. Still, even knowing how close death lurked he could not bring himself to open the tome. With great effort, he lifted his feet and stretched out on the sofa. If he woke tomorrow, he'd read. For now, he needed sleep.

Chapter 4

Grant was tired. By his calculation he was in his third hour of questions. It didn't help that anything he told them was not verifiable. His address did not exist yet. He had no friends to vouch for him and had to do some heavy recall of Chicago history to prevent them from thinking he was a complete loon. He saw no way out of his current situation. Of course, he could tell the truth, that he had been visiting another world and had somehow taken a wrong turn from the year twenty-nineteen to nineteen fifty-eight when he passed through the seam that looked like a slice in a canvas. No, that kind of talk had looney bin written all over it.

The detectives had been playing tag team with him trying to wear him down. Currently, they were out getting lunch and left him to think about whether to *come clean,* as one of his interrogators put it, or spend the night in a cell. Grant was busy concocting a story and was to the point of putting on a display of begging when the lights flickered in his small room.

He glanced at the light as it resumed its function and was returning to his new storyline when the lights winked off and on again.

With a sudden jolt of memory, he stood abruptly knocking over the heavy chair. He remembered being in his precinct house when the same thing happened. Without hesitation, he knew it for what it was—magic. Someone had come to rescue him.

Elated to be getting out, he picked up his jacket from the back of the fallen chair and slid it on. He waited near the door ready to bolt as soon as it opened. However, another jarring thought came to him. They still had his wallet, his badge, and his gun. He couldn't leave without those items. He wasn't sure of the exact name of the space-time thingy but something told him to leave them here in this time might cause some sort of rift that affected the future. He had to find them before he left but where would they be? Which one of the three detectives interviewing him had possession of his things?

The lights steadied and did not flicker again. That made him anxious. "Come on. I know you're out there. Come find me. Hurry."

A commotion reached him full of loud angry and demanding voices. Warnings were given and threats were issued then the lights went out. Grant fought to remain calm. He moved to the side of the door ready to pounce on whoever entered. He didn't want to hurt anyone, especially a fellow cop, despite the way they treated him, but his only hope of returning to his time was to get out of here.

A brilliant flash swept through the gap under the door followed by a booming crack as if lightning had struck the station. Gunshots followed then came a series of thuds. Footsteps scratched at the hallway floor outside the door. Grant tensed, ready to spring. He had no idea who was out there but from his recent experience was certain magic was involved. The question remained if the wielder was friend or foe. He remembered the evil mage Rhoden had escaped to this world. Had he been responsible for the time shift and the sealed seam? Perhaps the wizard was aware of his presence in this timeline and wanted to eliminate anyone who knew of his existence.

He had never fought a mage hand to hand before, but it had to be the same as anyone else. Flesh to flesh, fist to face. Keep striking until the opponent ceased moving. He was good at that having grown up fighting for his survival. He just had to be faster with his hands than the wizard was with his words. A good, hard punch to the throat might counter any magic.

He quieted his breathing though it took great effort. Something crashed. He tried to discern what. Another crash was closer. He knew what it was now. Someone was flinging open the doors along the hall. Whoever was out there was searching for someone. He was sure he knew who.

He crouched wanting to be below eye level when he sprung.

The footfalls stopped outside his door. He knew another door stood directly across from his. He waited.

Whoever was at the door spoke a word Grant did not recognize. Instantly, another crash occurred. Now he was sure it was a magician and his door was next. He steadied himself, drawing in a long breath in anticipation of action.

Though prepared, he was startled by the violence with which the door was ripped open. It crashed loudly, the sound echoing within the small space. Grant flinched wanting to cover his ears but that left him defenseless. He fought through the roaring in his head and waited.

A voice drifted through the din. "I do not know who you are but come out of there now. If you force me to come in, I will assume you are foe rather than friend and will be forced to treat you as such."

"Who-who are you?"

There was a brief pause before an answer came. "We will discuss that once we are away from here. If you are friend you have nothing to fear from me but I need to know what you did to the portal."

"Me? I didn't do anything. It sent me to the wrong place."

Another pause. "Come. The spell I cast will not last much longer."

Grant heard the footsteps recede and made a tentative move toward the door. He did a quick peek. The hallway was hazy as if a fire had been started somewhere. The figure of a man moved steadily away melding with the haze.

Grant hurried out the door and stopped in the squad room. Bodies lay everywhere. Some on the floor, many over desks. To his relief, they appeared to be sleeping. He stopped and looked for the detectives who had been interviewing him. The smokey air made it difficult.

"What are you doing? We must be away now. We have only minutes before the spell wears off."

"I-I understand but I need to find my things."

"They are of no importance. Come."

"No. They are of great importance. I know I can tell you this without it sounding like I'm crazy but, I'm from a different time. The things they took do not belong here and may mess something up in the future. You understand?"

The mage appeared to consider then said, "What things?"

"My badge, my gun, and my wallet."

The mage moved closer so fast Grant barely had time to flinch or raise a hand in defense. "Give me your hand."

Grant hesitated and pulled back.

"Hurry, you fool. We are almost out of time and I will be forced to leave you here."

With caution, Grant lifted a hand. The mage grabbed it, closed his eyes, and muttered something. Grant felt a quick tingle in his hand, then the mage released it. He lifted his hand palm up toward the room and recited some magical words. He moved his hand from right to left across the room until something in one of the desks glowed. "There. Now hurry. I'll be outside."

Grant rushed to the desk and ripped open the top drawer to the right. Inside he found his things. He picked them up and was about to leave when he spotted a holstered .38 revolver. The detective would not wear a weapon inside the interview room. Grant smiled. It was time for payback for the way he'd been treated. He snatched the holster and gun up and ran from the building as someone groaned nearby.

He burst through the door, leaped down the two steps, and found the mage walking nonchalantly out of the parking lot. Grant caught up to him at the street. Without a word, the man turned right and Grant followed a pace behind as he pocketed his badge, wallet and newly acquired gun, then slid his holstered Smith and Wesson .40 over the belt at his side. Just having the weapon made him relax. He had no idea who this man was that he followed but it was better than being locked up. With luck the man had answers and the ability to send him home. For the moment, he followed in silence.

Chapter 5

"Shree, I'm telling you it's him. I have no doubts. I'm going after him." The willowy blonde stood to give pursuit of the man she thought to be Rhoden. Her best friend, Shree, grabbed her arm and yanked her back behind the parked car they had hidden behind when Elly identified their prey as the evil wizard from the other world who had kidnapped them. This was the third sighting since they'd been back less than two days. The other two Rhodens had been wrong as this one most likely was, Shree thought, but her friend was obsessed with finding and punishing the man. Her judgement was clouded.

Not that Shree blamed her. The ordeal the perverse man had put them through had resulted in Shree being seriously injured. If not for the healing skills of the mage Samuel, she might have died in that other world. No, she wanted Rhoden found and punished too, just not spending all her time ducking behind cars as they tracked potential suspects.

"Girl, you had best be certain this time. The last time you almost got us arrested. You're lucky he didn't press charges against you." She released Elly recognizing the futility of talking sense to her by the fire that blazed in her eyes.

"Shree, I know it's him." She stood, eyes scanning the street for her prey. "You coming?"

Shree sighed and stood. "Lead on."

Elly jogged to get within range of the man she thought to be Rhoden. Shree matched her strides but kept back a few yards. They came to a busy corner and Elly strained to find her target. She leaped a few times until she spotted him. "There." She pointed and took off in pursuit.

Shree had an ever growing feeling in the pit of her stomach that this was about to go bad. On the other hand, they had skipped lunch to take up the hunt so it might be her stomach growling.

Elly slowed to a fast walk, her eyes never leaving the man's back.

The distance shortened over the next two blocks, then the man slowed and veered toward the street. He stopped at a car and beeped the door open. Elly saw her chance about to slip away and kicked into a run. He had less than a half block lead but the way she moved that evaporated fast.

Ten yards from her target, a tall black man approached from the other side angling toward her prey. Shree wondered if this was an associate of the man, or if it was Rhoden, one of his minions.

"Jim," the new man said, extending a hand.

"Mason," the target said with enthusiasm. Taking the offered hand in both of his he shook it warmly. "How good to see you. How have you been?"

The exchange took Elly by surprise and two yards away she slowed, stopped, and gawked. Shree almost ran into her.

Mason glanced over Jim's shoulder and spied the girls. "Friends of yours?"

Jim turned. His expression one of confusion. "Can I help you ladies?"

For a moment neither spoke. Elly because she was stymied over being wrong again, and Shree, well, just because the situation was awkward. She was first to respond. "Oh, no, sorry. She thought you were someone else."

Mason said, "By the look on her face I'd say it wasn't someone she liked."

Jim said, "I'm glad it's not me then." He laughed a little nervously.

"Sorry again. We'll just be going." She forcibly turned Elly and walked her away. They reached a corner and Shree pushed her around it then against the wall of a building. "Girl, you gotta get a grip. You're gonna get both of us in trouble."

Before her eyes, Ely's face crumbled. Her eyes watered, her lips quivered, her body shook. “God, what have I become?” she covered her eyes with her hands and leaned forward on Shree’s shoulder.

“Ely, I understand your desire to bring this man down but you are so obsessed that it’s blinding you. You need to take a serious step back. We will find him, I promise, and when we do, we will take him down together. This way is making you crazy which in turn is driving me nuts trying to keep you from doing something stupid. Please. Please. Please, can we do this is a reasonable fashion so we both don’t end up in the nut house?”

Elly nodded her head and wiped her face with her fingers.

“Now, can we please. Please. Please, get something to eat. Following you is like the best diet in the world but does it look like I need a diet? Don’t you dare answer that.”

Elly laughed and the two girls went off to find food.

Chapter 6

To his great surprise and relief, Samuel woke the next morning. He was even more impressed by the fact he felt somewhat refreshed. No, he wasn't at full strength and in fact, doubted he'd ever reach that level again, but at his age and after all he'd been through, breathing was a blessing.

He swung his legs off the sofa, rubbed his face, and stared at the tome siting on the coffee table.

The table's name sparked an interest in having a cup and got up to see to its making. While the coffee brewed, he made himself an egg with toast and sat to enjoy a meal hoping it not only added to his reinvigoration but wasn't his last.

Two hours later, having found two interesting entries in the tome having to do with the creation and closing of a portal, a knock sounded at his door. Sure it was Vega, Samuel spoke a word and made a gesture with his hand and the locks disengaged and the door swung open.

Vega stood there stunned. "Did you just use, ah, you know," he whispered the word, "magic?"

Samuel frowned. "Please come in and close the door, detective."

Vega entered in a burst of nervous energy.

"Any news?"

Vega said, "Huh? Like what? Monsters roaming the streets or Grant's body turning up?"

"Please, detective, try not to be so dramatic. I meant about Grant's missing from work."

"Oh, yeah. I managed to convince the boss that he was missing and might be in trouble. It was all I could think of to keep him from being suspended or fired. They put out a bulletin to the force to be looking for him and one of the other detective teams is beginning an investigation."

Samuel gave that information some thought, then said, "I suppose that's for the best. You and Grant will have to concoct a story if we can get him back."

"If? Oh, please don't say that. We have to find him and he has to be alive."

Samuel nodded, then his eyes clouded over. He had a sudden recollection of being in a police station and putting all those inside asleep but it was only a fragment and he had no idea where it came from. He was sure the scene had never happened, at least not so far in the past, yet the bits he recalled were as vivid as if they just happened.

"Did you find anything?" Vega said, snapping him from the image.

"Yes, I believe I have." He picked up a pad of paper that held his notes. "As the original creator of the portal I alone have complete control over its closure. Should someone else try to do so it will only have a partial effect. The seam will be closed but can be reopened using the proper spell. What I think happened is someone tried to not only close the portal but make it vanish from existence. I am the only one who can make its closure permanent. So, whoever made the attempt did not have the knowledge or me to make it happen. You see, when a wizard creates something, he leaves a small portion of himself within the construct of whatever he created. That makes that creation his. It's like an artist signing a painting, however in this case, that signature has power. It prevents other wizards from destroying what the creator built.

However, the wizard who attempted to vanish the portal had to have great power to do what he did though I suspect it was an accident and the result was not what he intended. Regardless, it still had the same effect. The portal no longer functions until a link to both worlds can be reestablished.

I doubt the spell caster realized his mistake. Still, like I said, his work had the desired effect. To finish the task he needs me, or more exact, a part of me. Something that has my magical essence."

"Such as?"

Samuel smiled. "Oh, my heart, my brain, anything that contains my life force."

"What? So, whoever this is has to kill you to shut the seam down permanently?"

"Yes. Though it's not quite that simple. He would have to kill me at the site of the portal, take out one of my organs and cast the spell while throwing the organ into the seam."

"No disrespect, but you people are nuts."

Samuel smiled again. "I can't say I disagree. There is one thing that may throw a monkey wrench, I believe your term is, into the plan."

"I'm almost afraid to ask."

"If I die before he can get me to the portal." He turned his tired eyes at Vega. "Keep that in mind should he come for me. If it looks like he might succeed, you have to kill me."

"What?" He stood abruptly. "I was wrong, you people aren't nuts, you're completely insane."

"I know it's against everything you have vowed to protect but it may be the only way to get Detective Grant back. You will have to choose. My life for his."

"No. No, I can't do that. You can't ask me to make that choice."

"I'm not asking. I'm telling you what must be done if we can't reopen the portal in time to save your friend."

Vega sat and spread his fingers across his face. "Man, I think I'm the one going insane."

Chapter 7

Grant followed the man several blocks constantly checking behind him for pursuit. By now, the entire station house was awake and searching for not only him but the strange man who walked in and magicked them asleep. He jogged to get next to his savior.

"So, who are you and where are we going?"

"First, I think since I'm the rescuer, I reserve the right to ask the questions. If satisfied I will tell you more. As to the second, we are going someplace safe where we can talk."

"Yeah, okay, safe and talk. I'm onboard with that but can you help me?"

"That depends on the problem and of course, if I believe your story."

Grant frowned and glanced behind him. He spotted a cruiser making its way down the street at a pace that suggested they were looking for someone.

"I think we should duck out of sight for a few minutes. There's a squad car coming up behind us a block back."

If the man heard he showed no sign of concern. He turned into a store that sold clothing geared toward the young and hip of that generation and marched through the center toward the rear. A young female clerk asked if she could help them but with a snap of his finger he sent the now confused woman seeking to assist someone else.

Who was this man with the *Star Wars* power? If he had that much power he was someone to be feared. If it turned out he was the enemy, Grant doubted he'd ever get off a shot.

They exited through the rear door and came out in an alley. The mage walked to the end and stopped at the corner of the building, peering around it. After several seconds, he said, "It's safe now. Let's go. It's not much farther."

They took the connecting street back to N. Western Street heading south. His benefactor appeared to be more cautious now knowing a police cruiser was somewhere ahead. They had taken N. Stave Street from the station, turned on W. Armitage Avenue and made the turn down Western. At least he recognized most of the street names. The area was less populated than in his era and many of the buildings had yet to be built, though a lot of the landmark structures were recognizable and had been there for years.

Four blocks later, having ducked one more patrol car, they arrived at a small, rundown apartment building that Grant was sure no longer stood in his time. It stretched a shaky six stories. This was obviously where the mage lived because he waved to the inattentive man behind the front desk and moved toward the stairs. Grant followed. Though the mage drew little notice, the same wasn't true for Grant. *Seriously, you don't have black people in this dump?*

They stopped on the second floor and moved to the third door on the left. The mage slid a key into the lock, wiggled it a few times, then pushed the door open with a squeal of protest from the hinges.

After Grant entered, the mage glanced up and down the hall before shutting and locking the door.

"Sit over there," he ordered and pointed to a chair that had worn through its upholstery on both arms showing the innards. Grant hesitated, not wanting to be in a defenseless position.

The mage sighed. "Until I determine your friend or foe status, it's best you do as I say. Either go on your own or I'll put you there. I think you know I can do it so save both of us the trouble."

Grant didn't like the man's tone. He didn't like much of anything that was happening but also knew the man was right. He started toward the chair determined not to go easy if whatever was about to happen became confrontational.

He sat, sinking deep into the cushion. He didn't like that either.

Reaction time was going to be slowed as he tried to extricate himself from the sunken position.

The mage moved fast, carrying a wooden chair from the dinette set in what passed for a kitchen. He plopped it down and sat backwards in the chair six feet away. He leaned over the back and glared at Grant.

"Believe me, bud, I've used that same glare a hundred times when interviewing suspects. If you're trying to intimidate me that's not going to work."

"What about this? He twisted his hand so the palm was up then clenched his fist, speaking a word. Suddenly, the air vacated the room and Grant struggled for breath as his throat constricted. He clawed at his throat, then deciding there was little he could do, pulled his gun, and aimed it at the surprised man.

The man released the spell and Grant gasped for breath while trying to keep the weapon aimed at the mage.

"Impressive," the man said. "Most would be too panicked to find a solution. That tells me you're formidable. So, let's remove the threat from the equation." He swept his arm sideways, spoke another word and the gun flew from Grant's hand striking the wall with a resounding thud. It fell to the floor behind a bookcase.

Grant made no effort to reach for the revolver he stole. He didn't want his opponent to know he had backup.

"Now, let's talk. Who are you?"

Grant eyed him thinking about what story to tell. At this point, until he knew more the less he gave away the better. He decided his name wasn't going to alter anything. "My name is Grant."

"Okay, Grant, that's a good start. Tell me what you did to the portal?"

Grant almost snapped his answer but refrained. "Don't know what you're talking about."

The other man frowned. "Now we have a problem. Until I can ascertain your status we can't move forward."

Grant said, "Until I can ascertain *your* status, I agree."

The two men eyed each other though Grant thought his counterpart's eyes did not display anger as much as curiosity. Several moments later, the mage closed his eyes, muttered a few words and held out both palms toward Grant. In a panic, fearing he was about to be attacked magically, he pulled the second gun and aimed at the mage's eye. He waited to feel something from whatever spell had been cast, but if one had been he showed no effects.

The mage opened his eyes and gave a start at the appearance of a second gun. A smile creased his face. "Most formidable indeed. I had not anticipated a second weapon. I thank you for not discharging it." He stood and swept the chair around the proper way and sat. The sudden move had Grant tightening his finger on the trigger. Not knowing the pressure needed to break the trigger like he did his own gun, he was relieved when all bullets stayed in their cylinders.

"I swept you for magic ability, weapons, or totems. Unless your skills or so much greater than mine that you can conceal them, then I am willing to accept you are not an intentional threat. That being the case, let us talk candidly. Why are you here?"

Realizing he still held the gun pointed, Grant lowered the weapon but held it in his lap, barrel pointed forward. "It was not my choice. I left one place expecting to return home and ended up here. I have no idea why."

The mage contemplated Grant's words before speaking. "That is very unusual. Unless you were trying to vanquish the portal it should always send you where you want to go. Once a seam has been established it exists until the creator ends it. It can be concealed but never ended."

"Huh! So what do you think happened?"

"I don't know. Tell me more about where you came from and where you were going."

It was time for cards on the table. "I do come from Chicago just in the future. The year twenty nineteen to be precise. I crossed through the portal into the world of Chevalon to aid some friends who were under attack and held captive."

At that, the mage sat erect and looked concerned. "What friends and what attack?"

"Are you familiar with Chevalon?"

"Yes." He looked like he wanted to say more but kept it to himself.

Grant decided to continue despite the exchange of information not be entirely reciprocal. "I was there to rescue the heirs to the throne at the behest of a wizard named Phetrix."

"Phetrix, you say." It was the most animated Grant had seen the man.

"Yes, do you know him?"

This time the mage answered. "Yes, he was a bit of a protégé of mine. Tell me more."

Grant nodded slowly. This mage was also from Chevalon. "Okay, but then I want some answers. He knew a mage here in Chicago, well not here but the future Chicago. Together they came up with a plan to save these heirs and we crossed through the seam, or portal as you call it."

"What was this mage's name who lived in Chicago?"

"Samuel."

Chapter 8

They finished their lunch of tacos and burritos and were in good spirits. Having just told Elly of her interest in a boy from their class causing her to laugh loudly, spraying some of her pop across the table, Elly went rigid.

A look of panic crossed Shree's face. "Oh my God! Are you all right. Are you choking?"

Elly shook her head and looked at her friend. "Please don't hate me."

"Hate you? Why would I ever hate—oh no. Don't tell me."

Elly nodded. "Shree. He just walked past the window."

"If that's so why aren't you up and running out the door?"

"Cause I made you a promise."

Shree eyed her friend, then sipped at her drink knowing it wouldn't be long. She ignored Ely's sad eyes and her pouty lip.

"Shree, please. Don't make me beg."

"You're hopeless." She checked her phone. "Fine. I release you from your promise but you have to go alone. It's late. I promised my mom I'd be home to help her pack."

Shree's mother had decided after the recent abduction of her daughter, it was time to leave Chicago. "And unlike some people, I keep my promises." She stood. "I'm very worried about you." She leaned over and gave Elly a hug. "If you do this use some sense and don't attack the man. Be careful and don't stay out too late."

Elly crossed her heart but knew better than to say, "I promise."

After one last smile, Shree left.

ELLY BARELY HAD the willpower to stay seated until after Shree was gone. She picked up her phone and called up the picture she had snapped as the man paused in front of the restaurant's front window scanning the street like he was afraid someone was tailing him. It had been the suspicious actions that first drew her attention to him but it was all there in the photo. The build, the hair, the pointed upturned nose, the beady, darting eyes, the menace. It was Rhoden and if she was right, it was better Shree wasn't around to hold her back from what she intended to do to him.

She walked fast and at first made no effort to locate him. He might already be gone anyway. But if he was that paranoid as to be checking behind him, she didn't want to be recognized until close enough to strike.

She fingered the magic knife she had asked Phetrix to create for her. He had balked at the request at first but she was an heir to the throne and was determined. Though the blade was small, only two inches, so it was easy to conceal, when put into action she had but to recite one word, *Extraneous,* and the blade would grow to eight inches and strike true at whatever her target. In this case, she pictured Rhoden's black heart. The blade could not be deflected or prevented from accomplishing its task except by a spell or another defensive magical item.

She increased her pace keeping her head down and her hands in her jacket pocket. Every few steps she lifted her head enough to allow her eyes to scan the sidewalk ahead. The way was crowded with people bustling in and out of the various buildings that made up the famous Chicago skyline. They swarmed in all directions creating a human traffic jam.

Elly wanted to scream for everyone to get out of her way. If they only knew the evil that lurked on their streets they'd move aside in an instant and allow her to end her hunt. Who would ever believe her though? She hardly believed it herself. Her, the cheerleader, the social butterfly, was an heir to the throne of an actual kingdom. It was enough to make her swoon. Too bad no one she knew was ever going to know. She desperately wanted to tell someone, anyone, especially her rival, the snobby Rachel Parsons, whose rich father and richer mother gave her everything she wanted and treated her like a princess. Elly so wanted to show her what real royalty looked like.

With her head down again and no luck locating Rhoden, she slid her phone out and studied the image. He was wearing a long, light brown, all-weather coat. He didn't have a hat but his thick hair stood up and all angles. She glanced up. There. Fifty yards ahead was her target. The man responsible for so much pain and death both in her city and Chevalon. The man involved with overthrowing her family and perhaps killing her mother, not to mention almost killing her foster mother, the woman she had grown up thinking her real mom.

The more she remembered the man's sins and atrocities, the angrier she got and the faster she moved.

Her eyes locked on the back of the light brown coat like a heat seeking missile. She palmed the knife having practiced her attack numerous times for when the moment arose. It was here now and she could barely contain the adrenaline rush or the excitement. At last, Rhoden was going to pay for his crimes. He was going to die.

Chapter 9

"Now that I know what I'm dealing with I need to prepare a spell," Samuel said.

"How long will that take?" Vega asked.

Samuel sighed. "I'm not as young as I once was. I'm not even sure I have the energy left to accomplish the deed. I have no idea where Detective Grant is. Has he been sent to another world? Another time? Or is in in stasis someplace trapped and floating aimlessly. That makes the task more difficult. I may only have enough strength left for one try. It has to be the right one or your friend will be lost forever. On top of that, I don't know who tried to manipulate the portal. To break the spell it will be helpful to know whose magic I am trying to undo."

Vega slumped in his seat defeat already etched on his face.

"I'm sorry. I wish I had better news but the truth is it's going to take as long as it takes. I will give it my best effort but like I said, I may only get the one chance. I want it to be the best I can give."

"Is there anything I can do to help?"

"I wish there was. For now, just let me be to study and build strength. Ah, there's something you can do?"

Vega perked up at the enthusiasm in Samuel's voice.

"Make me an egg sandwich. With cheese I think. The extra protein can't hurt."

Vega gave him a disbelieving look.

"Well, snap to it, sir. You'll find everything you need in the refrigerator."

While Vega cooked, Samuel began putting the pieces together for the spell. It would be more effective if he knew the spellcaster. That thought made him stop. Maybe he did know the spellcaster. Before he continued that line of thought he was struck by another image. He was looking at a man sitting in a worn upholstered chair. The image was fuzzy but it appeared to be a tall, black man. The image began to clear then vanished like a popped bubble.

Samuel was sure he had never seen that image before yet something about the scene was familiar. He puzzled over it for a long while until Vega said, "Yo, earth to Samuel. Come in, Samuel."

Samuel blinked a few times and the image was gone.

"Dude, you asked for this. You should eat it before it gets cold."

Samuel glanced down at the sandwich. Vega had been considerate enough to cut it in half. Samuel picked up a section and nibbled it absently trying to pull the memory forward. He couldn't help but think part of the image was old and some of it new as if it just happened. Why was that?

Something was there on the fringes of his memories. Something important. He pondered what that might be long after the sandwich was consumed. By the time he broke from his deep fugue, Vega was gone. Had the man said where he was going? Had he even said goodbye? Samuel was sure that if either happened, he was unaware. He returned to his work.

Hours later he was ready for a nap. The spell was complete on a generic basis. It needed a few specifics yet. As he moved on weary legs toward the bedroom his overworked mind struggled to come up with a mage of the skill and experience to have caused such havoc to the portal but kept coming up blank. He knew the mages capable of doing the deed but there were few and many had been killed by Mortas Frost during his failed attempt to usurp the throne. Others had been bent to his will. From those he might find the culprit but many of them had died or fled after Frost was killed.

He stretched out on his bed with a pleasurable groan. If any of those swayed to the pull of dark magic had not reverted he might find a formidable opponent in their ranks. However, few if any, ever left the academy towers and fewer still had access to the royal library in the castle.

As he drifted toward sleep one thought popped his eyes open and brought clarity. He was looking at the problem from the wrong side of the portal. Rhoden had escaped Chevalon and was thought to be in this world. Would he have made the attempt? Did he have the skill? He certainly had the power. That made sense. A flicker of excitement ignited more thoughts. Did he have enough knowledge of the man to enhance the spell and make it more focused. He let his mind process the question filtering through the various caches of information he had accumulated during their battles. Yes. He was sure he had enough. Once rested Samuel was sure he could reopen the portal. Then all they had to do was locate Grant. *All,* he scoffed. That may prove to be the most difficult part of the entire process.

Samuel tried to sit up but a heavy weight on his chest forced him down with a gasp. It was difficult to breathe. He tried to take a deep breath but the pain did not allow more than a small inhalation. The pain was severe. He struggled to draw air but the more he tried the tighter the band was across his chest in turn creating more pain. As his vision narrowed and his eyes clouded, his last thought before succumbing was, *too late.*

Chapter 10

Samuel had to clear his throat twice before he was able to speak. "Samuel? You're sure that's the name?"

Grant gave his benefactor a curious look. "Yes. I'm sure. Do you know of him?"

Samuel did the math. Sixty-one years. He was twenty-eight now. That made him eighty-nine. Old but not uncommon for a wizard. How much longer did he have? Where did Grant see him? Chicago or Chevalon? Was he still in Chicago all those years later? When he passed through the portal he had no plans other than exploring and learning and he had certainly absorbed a lot of knowledge in the short time he'd been here. This world was truly incredible and he wanted to learn all he could before returning to his world.

Was that a good thing knowing he lived that long, or bad, knowing at all? If his power and knowledge grew at all he should still have a good forty to fifty more years to live beyond the eighty-nine. He was too flummoxed to think. Was this even possible? He returned Grant's curious stare.

"You know that name," Grant said. "That may be important. It's my understanding that he was the creator of the seam. If you have a way of contacting him maybe he can reopen the seam if only long enough to get me home."

Samuel didn't reply. His mind was working to fast. He was unable to land on just one thought and work through to a solution or even a question. Should he tell this stranger who he was? Was this some elaborate ruse to draw him out? If so, it was masterful because he did not detect any magic. To his knowledge no one else had come through the seam before Grant and after was impossible since the seam was locked down. Or was that the plan. Once they located him in this world perhaps the plan was to keep him here. But who would do such a thing? No one knew he was here. He left without telling anyone where he was going. Unless someone found the spell he secreted away in the castle library, had the ability to read and cast it and the power to control it, no one should have been able to pass through.

He stood and moved to the window where he cast a locate magic spell as he had done on nearly a daily basis since arriving in this great city. Nothing. At least not in the immediate vicinity. If someone was powerful enough to override his spell he might not know. He had to be sure. He whirled around and once again took control of Grant's throat constricting it tighter than his previous assault. He needed the man afraid, to know his death was imminent and but seconds, a mere flick of the wrist away.

The big man rose from his chair, one hand clutching at his throat, the other leveling the gun. Samuel's eyes widened. In his haste, he had forgotten about the second gun. Too late, he adjusted his focus. The explosion came and pain spread throughout his chest. He gasped and bounced off the window, then slid to the floor. The pain was excruciating. A stream of blood streaked down his shirt. It was hard to breathe. He tried to focus but the pain hindered the effort.

Grant knelt next to him pressing on the wound. "Why? Why did you make me do that?"

Samuel held out long enough to cast a spell that both numbed and healed but as his vision slipped away, he feared it was too late.

UNABLE TO KEEP the control she sought Elly increased her pace darting around a corner in pursuit. For a moment, she panicked. He was gone. Then she caught a fleeting glimpse as he ducked into the alley. *Had he seen her?* She hurried to the alley and peeked down its length. Rhoden was nowhere to be seen.

She angled into the mouth of the alley to get an angle to see behind the nearest dumpster. She had to move further to be sure. With no one there she moved faster concerned she had lost him again. Caution was replaced by her desire for speed. Too late she heard the running footsteps behind her. She whirled but they were too close and too many to fend off. The first one hit her. She twisted and used her hands to throw him past and sprawling to the filthy pavement. However, the second one was one her before she had a chance to defend. He planted a shoulder into her stomach like he was making a tackle and drove her backward. He turned her toward the wall. Elly drove her elbows into his back. His steps faltered just before her body slammed into the brick wall.

Stunned, she leaned over the slumped man's shoulder as the third man arrived. He punched her on the side of her face. The blow jarred her causing her vision to spin. As the man holding her attempted to stand, she drove a knee into his chin, snapping his head back. he released her but the first man joined the third and the two managed to subdue her. Elly squirmed and screamed.

"The boss was right," the first man said. "He was being followed."

"Yeah," laughed the third man. "And she's sweet looking. What do we do with her?"

"I know what I'd like to do," the first man said.

"But the boss may want to talk to her first, the third man said.

"Let me go. Help," Elly shouted.

The second man stood still groggy. Elly snapped another kick into his face sending him toppling backward. He shook himself to lose the fog then stood and ran at Ely. She tried to duck away as the punch flew. She dodged a portion but the blow was hard enough to stagger her. His fist hit the wall and he jumped back clutching the injured hand. He screamed obscenities at her. "Oh, I am so gonna hurt you bad." His punch was with his left hand this time and shorter to ensure contact with little pain, at least to him. Elly took the shot on her forehead. Her head smacked into the wall and darkness surrounded her.

Chapter 11

Samuel gasped, sat up involuntarily, then cried out as the pain drove him back down. He panted to control the anguish. He had to admit he was surprised to feel anything again. He gazed around the room. He was alone. The pain was still there but not as debilitating.

He eased to a sitting position with his feet over the edge of the bed inches from the floor. He sat there for several moments until he was sure another wave of agony did not overwhelm him. A tall black man walked toward him.

SAMUEL GASPED and sat up involuntarily, then cried out as the pain drove him back down. He panted to control the anguish. He had to admit he was surprised to feel anything again. He gazed around the room. He was alone. The pain was still there but not as debilitating.

He eased to a sitting position with his feet over the edge of the bed inches from the floor. He sat there for several moments until he was sure another wave of agony did not overwhelm him. A tall black man walked toward him.

"OH, you're up. How do you feel?" he asked. There was something familiar about him but for the moment the fact the man was in his apartment made it difficult to make the connection. The man leaned forward. "Are you sure you should be sitting up? You should be resting. I can't believe your breathing let alone sitting up." He rubbed a large hand over his stubbled face. "Why did you do that? I thought we were communicating. Then you suddenly attacked me."

Samuel was at a loss. He didn't remember doing anything to the man, especially not attack him. If he had, why? The scene was fuzzy and fading. As it vanished from view the man lifted a gun and pointed it at his face.

He didn't understand. What was going on? Was that a dream, a memory, or a vision? There was a lot familiar with the scene but he was having trouble focusing. The pain was returning. He lifted his feet and laid down. Too much was happening. He closed his eyes. He had a lot to sort through and a dread feeling that the clock was running and a life was at stake, other than his.

AS THE MAN closed his eyes and fell back asleep. Grant checked his pulse again. He kept the gun ready in case it was a trick but the man was truly out. He studied the now almost completely healed wound with awe and a little fear. If this man was that powerful what chance did he stand against him should he recover and attack again? Somehow, he had to get through to him and convince him he was not a threat and in fact, needed his help to get home.

He went to the kitchen and retrieved a chair setting it the foot of the bed where he had placed the mage after realizing he wasn't going to die. He leaned back and closed his eyes and pulled up the images of the past few hours.

Grant hadn't known what to do. The man clearly needed a hospital or he'd die. However, if he made the call the gunshot wound had to be reported which got him picked up again and this time no one would come to rescue him. No. It didn't matter. The one person with the power to get him home was dying. No matter what happened, he could not allow the man to die. He raced through the shabby apartment but did not see a phone. They had phones in nineteen fifty-eight, didn't they? Yes, of course they did, however not every house or apartment had one. That meant he had to take the wounded man to the hospital. He thought about where the closest medical center was then realized it hadn't been built yet. His best option was to carry him downstairs and hail a cab. Maybe the guy at the front desk had access to a phone. He had to hurry.

He bent over the body and lifted. The wound no longer appeared to be bleeding. Grant panicked. "Oh no." There was only one reason a bullet wound stopped bleeding on its own. He set the mage down on the sofa and checked for a pulse. To his relief he felt one but to be sure he placed a hand on his diaphragm and felt the slight rise and fall. What was strange was the steady unlabored breathing. That was uncommon to someone with a gunshot wound. There was no gasping, no struggling for air, or moaning or writhing. He looked at peace. No sign of discomfort or pain shown on his face.

Grant tore open the worn pullover shirt to examine the wound. Not only had it stopped bleeding, but the entry wound was scabbing over. How was this possible? Had the mage cast some sort of spell to lessen the damage? Now he wondered if he needed to take the man to the hospital at all. Still, he could not afford to let him die. After careful consideration, he decided to wait but keep a close eye on his condition. If it weakened at all, he vowed to get him to the hospital.

He picked up his two weapons and replaced them. There was another problem. Had anyone heard the shot? This was a different time. People still cared, unlike his time when gunshots were so common they were seldom reported. Not to mention that the man at the front desk had not hidden his disdain at seeing a black man enter his fine, high class apartment building. He wouldn't be surprised to find cruisers already at the front door.

Sure enough, minutes later there came a knock. He waited it out. Another knock was followed by a voice. "Mr. Wise are you all right?"

Grant guessed it was the man at the desk. If he didn't answer he'd surely call the police. He had to convince the man everything was all right. He took a blanket that was draped over the back of the sofa and laid across the mage covering his chest. After making sure any signs of blood were covered he went to the door and opened as a fist descended toward it. Grant stepped back in case the fist was a punch. The desk man stopped abruptly.

"Oh, I, is Mr. Wise here?"

"Yes," Grant said in a whisper. "He's sleeping. He had a long hard day and needs rest. Rest you seem bound on disturbing with all your knocking."

The desk man glanced around Grant but kept his distance. "Oh, ah, sorry. Is he all right?"

The question sounded as if he didn't believe Grant.

"Of course, he's all right? Can't you see? He's right there. Look. He's breathing." He lowered his face to be in the other man's hoping a little intimidation may put an end to the queries. "It's my job to protect him and right now you're bothering his much needed sleep. Do you wish to come in and question his need for rest or are you satisfied that he's all right?"

"Hey," the man said defensively. "I'm just doing my job. Someone reported they thought they heard a gunshot. I'm just—"

"A gunshot," Grant said sounding shocked. "Where?" He pushed forward backing the man up and glancing down the hall looking for any pretend invaders. "Look. There's been some threats against my client. That's why I'm here. It should be over in a few days but if you see or hear anything that might be a danger to Mr. Wise, come and tell me. Please. If I have advance notice it will help me head off any potential problems. Okay?"

The man's eyes had widened during the tale. He nodded enthusiastically. "Yeah. Sure. Anything I can do to help."

Grant nodded. "You're a good man." He stuck out his hand. The other man hesitated, then shook it. Grant held it and gave it a firm squeeze to the point of being uncomfortable. "Thank you for your help keeping Mr. Wise safe." He released the hand, stepped back, and nodded to the man again as he shut the door. He hadn't heard another word from the desk man since but more importantly no cops arrived either.

Grant checked Mr. Wise, he was sure that was a made-up name, then moved him to the bed. Other than the recent few moments, the mage had slept ever since.

Chapter 12

Elly woke with a groan. Her face and her whole head hurt. She came too groggy, unsure of where she was or how she got there. Her arms were strung up over head, suspended from a large spike jutting from a crumbling brick wall. A damp, foul, musty smell permeated the air and assaulted her nostrils. Her shoulders hurt from hanging. She straightened her legs and found she was just able to get her toes on the wet ground to relieve the strain in her arms.

As clarity came so did fear. Able to see the space better now she scanned the room. From the dim light filtering through the small, filthy window, she now saw she was in a basement. A door was in the wall to the right standing slightly askew in the frame as if it wasn't the original door and had been put in place perhaps just to hold her.

She was the only one in the room so took the opportunity to examine her situation more fully and try to find a way out. Though she had some magical ability and lots of power, she had little real experience or knowledge of how to craft that talent into anything useful. She had been so obsessed with getting home to begin her hunt of Rhoden that she ignored the pleas and efforts of both her brother and Phetrix to teach her. That was a mistake.

In truth she had felt lost. The abduction and assault on her had been so personal, so terrifying, she'd been unable to think of anything or that finding and punishing Rhoden. She had foregone any important possible life-saving training to pick up her pursuit. Another mistake. Though she had done some things with magic, she had no idea how other than when she linked with her brother. That was intense raw power like she had never felt before. Any other time it took a desperate situation when either her of Shree's life were at stake or she had been so enraged the magic just sort of happened without her doing anything.

She tried to work up anger now then focused on the rope that bound her hands. Nothing happened. Her mind was too occupied with fear and doubt. She had gone searching for Rhoden wanting to end his life. Now, if it was him that captured her, it was her life in jeopardy.

She cleared her mind, took several deep breaths, and steadied her focus just as the door creaked open and one of the men that attacked her strode in.

"So, princess, you're awake. That's wonderful. The boss was just asking about you." He walked toward her stopping a few feet away. His eyes wandered her body, then he smirked. "He says to be careful, that you're dangerous. I don't see anything to be afraid of."

Elly wanted to say, "Big mistake," but couldn't get her voice to cooperate. It was too dry and a lump seemed to have formed blocking her throat.

He stepped forward and grinned. "You don't look so scary. Boo!" He laughed, put a hand between her breasts and pushed. Her toes lifted from the floor and she swung. Pressure and strain engulfed her shoulders. She tightened her muscles to combat the pain.

She swung back toward him. This time he put both hands on her and pushed harder. Her butt touched the wall. She tried to drag her toes to keep from getting too close to him but he laughed, stepped forward and pushed her again, this time with a squeeze that enraged her. She felt a tingle inside her. She recognized the sensation and smiled inwardly.

As she reached the wall this time, she bent her knees, placed her feet against the wall, and pushed. His eyes widened with shock as he realized he had moved too close. Elly whipped her legs up and slammed into the fool, hitting him with enough force to lift him from the floor and send him flying. He landed in a wet spot and slid back until he struck the wall.

He was stunned for an instant and Elly took advantage of the break to wiggle swing back to the wall. This time as she came forward she used the momentum to slide her hands off the spike. She almost had it on the first attempt but needed a second. She had to hurry. Her abductor was angry, swearing at her, and getting to his feet.

She reached the wall, pushed off hard, and whipped forward straight at the man and his now cocked fist. As he swung, timing her flight, Elly yanked her hands forward with all her strength and the rope slid free. Her legs being longer than the attacker's arm, struck him first. The force plowed him over but at her near parallel position to the floor, and with her hands bound in front of her she was unable to prevent the impact of her landing. She hit the damp ground, bounced, and landed. The air was blasted from her lungs and she lay dazed for precious seconds as the enraged man climbed to his feet.

He stepped forward, his leg back to deliver a violent kick. Elly tightened her muscles and closed her eyes knowing there was nothing she could do to stop the kick from connecting.

"Forzaire!"

The word was followed by a forceful rush of air that lifted the attacker from his feet and slammed him into the wall. His head cracked against the brick and his slackened body fell hard to the floor.

Elly looked at the source of the spell. Her eyes bulged and a roar of fury rushed through her ears and sent a violent shudder throughout her body. Rhoden stood in the doorway eyeing her.

"So, it is you, princess. I'd like to say it's nice to see you again, but it's not." He stepped into the basement followed by the other two she had battled in the alley. "Tell me. Is this a one woman hunt or is your brother, Phetrix, and that old fool Samuel involved as well?"

Ely's fury was too strong and all-encompassing to allow words. Her breaths came in short pants like a bull seeing red.

Rhoden reached out with a hand and an invisible force gripped and lifted her chin. She scrambled to get her feet under her lest he snap her leg from torque to her spine. She stood still not wanting to give him a reason to do further damage.

"Answer me. Are you alone?"

"Yes."

He studied her. "Interesting. I'm not sure if you're lying or not." He released her with a flick of his wrist and she fell back to the floor. "It doesn't matter. If anyone else is here you will be great leverage to get what I want." To the two men he said, "Take her. We're leaving."

One of the men said, "What about Davey?"

Rhoden sneered at the injured minion. "If he's still alive and can walk he comes. If not leave him. And let this be a lesson to you. No one hurts her in anyway. Is that understood?"

The two men nodded quickly, the fear obvious in their eyes and body language.

Rhoden left the room. The shorter of the two men went to check on their partner while the other man scooped Elly up. The shorter man stood and gripped her other arm giving a shake of his head to his partner. Elly took that to mean her attacker was dead. She smiled inwardly. *Good. One down, two to go. Then, I'm coming after you, Rhoden.*

Chapter 13

Samuel woke and spotted Grant slumped in the chair. He studied the man for a moment not wanting to wake him until he came to a decision. He checked his wound. It was almost done healing however the alien projectile was still inside. Eventually, something would have to be done about it, but that had to wait until the current situation was managed.

He ran options and solutions through his mind until ready to have an open discussion with this man from the future, a man who knew him from that time. The thought was incredible but he had to push those contemplations to the side. It was time for action.

Samuel cleared his throat. Grant woke with a start and leaped to his feet, his weapon sweeping the room for enemies. When he turned his focus on Samuel, he stopped and lowered his gun.

Samuel said, "It's time we talked."

"Oh, now it's time? What, did the bullet convince you? Speaking of which, how are you still alive?" He slid the gun into its holster.

Samuel waved off the question. "It's not important. What is, like you said, is getting you back to your time. To do that you need to tell me all you know about Samuel and the portal."

Grant frowned, still annoyed at not getting answers, but he told this strange man everything. Throughout the story the mage did nothing but gaze off and nod. When Grant finished, he wasn't sure if the man was still listening, in a trance, or had fallen asleep.

"That's an incredible story."

"What? You saying you don't believe me?"

The mage raised a hand. "Oh, I believe every word. What's incredible is what apparently lies ahead for me."

It took a moment, but Grant caught on and asked, "For you? What about me?"

"Of course, my friend. I'll do my best to get you back to your time but once back home your story will be over while mine will be only in its early stages. With the knowledge I now possess about the future it will enable me to be better prepared. I must begin to put things in place."

"Well, how about you start by putting me in place."

"Very well. I need to do some research. While I'm doing that I'm famished. Fix me something to eat."

"What am I, your servant?"

"No, you're the man who wants me to return him to his home." With that he scooted off the bed and walked into the front room.

Grant said, "Huh!" and went to fix food.

SAMUEL WOKE with renewed energy and much clarity. He slid out of bed and walked to the bathroom where he reexamined the sore spot in his chest. It hurt and after doing an internal scan mentally, with the help of a spell discovered he had a bullet lodged in his chest. *How had that happened?* No, he now knew he had been shot by the tall black man. A man he now knew was Detective Grant.

The bullet over however long it had been in his body was now breaking down and the lead seeping into his blood stream. He was being poisoned from a wound from perhaps decades ago. He assumed his younger self had placed protective spells over the injury to keep the bullet from doing exactly what it was now, however, since this was all new to him he was unaware that the protection spell was needed. It might already be too late. He had a hard decision to make. Did he expend the necessary energy to reverse the damage to his body, if that was even possible, or did he keep it stored to use saving Grant? In essence, it was his life for Grant's.

Grant apparently was somewhere in the past, his past, and had somehow connected with his younger self. But what had prompted the man to shoot him? That part was still fuzzy. He was getting sharper images but no context. Still, now he had an idea of where to start. The problem was deciphering where in the timeline Grant was.

He went into the living room, sat on the sofa, and opened the tome. He flipped pages searching for a specific spell, actually a series of spells to be cast in succession. To accomplish that however, he had to be at his strongest. Success depended on him being at his very best which again came down to the decision he had to make.

First things first. He had to find Grant. If he was unable to locate him the decision was moot. He couldn't allow that to determine his effort. He had to make an honest attempt to find him. To do otherwise would haunt him for the rest of the little time he had remaining. Once he found Grant he'd let the facts dictate the decision. If Grant could be recovered, well, he had to do his research first.

When Samuel first discovered the path into this world and took up at that time temporary residence in Chicago it was late in nineteen fifty-seven. He tried to recall as much about those early days as possible. First, he sorted through his own memories. The seam then had opened onto a vacant lot, no, not vacant, a parking lot. Years later a parking garage was constructed on the site. It was then, unsure of how the new building might alter the portal, that he created a second backup one down the street a short distance. That way he knew he still had an avenue to travel back to Chevalon as well as an alternate escape route should the need arise, which of course, it did.

Samuel ran through highlights from that first year until he came to his first permanent residence. A shabby apartment in a rundown building in an area that had seen better days. He stopped there and did a mental crossover looking for overlapping similarities between the real memories and the new visions. He found one immediately. When Grant shot him, his younger self had been standing at a window looking out over the scene outside. He recognized the viewpoint. It was from that first apartment.

He tried to recall the exact dates. He had not stayed there long. As best he could remember the times were from September of fifty-seven to June of fifty-nine. Almost two years. That narrowed the gap considerably but still left a lot to sift through. To get Grant back he had to have an exact date.

He closed his eyes and scanned the recent visions. Though many were still fuzzy he was able to narrow the dates down further because of items in the apartment that had been accumulated over time. For the first four months he lived there he had no kitchen table and chairs. He took his meals on the worn sofa that had been left by a previous renter. The scene in the bedroom showed Grant sitting on a kitchen chair. Also, the bed sat up high like it was on frame. For six months he slept on a mattress on the floor. After purchasing a cheap metal frame and box spring, he later added a headboard that another tenant was throwing out. That brought him to March of fifty-eight until June of fifty-nine.

Stuck, he sat forward and began scrolling through the tome again. Then the next revelation hit. The coffee table the book rested on hadn't been acquired until months after the headboard. It had been discarded on the street for trash. Samuel hauled it home, fixed it and set it in its current place. May of fifty-eight. Closer, but still a long way to go. What else had he seen?

Chapter 14

Shree was worried. She had been unable to get Elly on the phone last night and all day today. That was unlike her friend. If she was busy she always sent a quick text saying so. Nothing. They were supposed to meet for their morning workout but Elly never showed. Shree went to her house but as far as she knew, all relatives were still in Chevalon after the coronation celebration since it was their original home, so no one answered. She had nowhere to go for help.

Was she panicking for no reason? Probably, but Elly was so obsessed with finding that creep Rhoden that Shree worried she might do something brash that put her in danger. She wasn't even sure where to start looking.

She returned to the restaurant they ate at the previous day but it was a different crew and no one there remembered seeing her. As she stood on the sidewalk staring anywhere and praying a clue magically appeared, she tried to form her next move. The truth was she didn't have one. Maybe she was overreacting. Any second her cell phone would ring and Elly would have some wild explanation. Yet, somehow, Shree knew her friend was in trouble. Shree might be the only person able to find her, but how? She needed help. Who could she call for assistance? The name came to her immediately. That good looking detective, Grant. If anyone could help it was him. He at least understood the situation having been there himself.

She ubered to the police station and went inside. At the front desk she was stonewalled after asking to see Grant and was told to take a seat.

The officer at the desk gave her a strange look as he left his post and disappeared behind a door. Minutes later a short, stocky, Latino man came out and stood in front of her. She recognized him. He was Grant's partner. She stood and moved toward him but before she could speak, he snatched her arm in a tight grip and led her outside.

"Hey, what's the deal?"

He released her, scanned to see that they were alone, and said, "Why are you here?"

"Why are you so angry?"

He rubbed his face. "I'm not angry. I'm worried. Now, please, why are you here?"

With a sinking feeling, Shree said, "You remember my friend, Ely?"

"Yeah, the princess, right?"

"Yep. That's her. Well, she's missing."

"Missing? Since when?"

"I'm not sure. We were supposed to meet today but she didn't show and is not answering her phone."

"It's important that I know the exact day and time."

"Okay, but I'm not sure. It was sometime between when I left her yesterday about two after eating and this morning. What's going on? Where's Grant?"

"He's missing too."

Shree put a hand to her mouth and said, "Oh no."

"Since you saw her yesterday that means she came through the portal."

"Yeah. You think she might have gone back through?"

"No. Not if it was after two yesterday when you last saw her. The seam is no longer working. It kind of shorted out before Grant made it through."

Shree stared open-mouthed unable to speak. She closed her mouth and tried to think. "So, there's no way they disappeared together."

"I don't see how but after all the crazy stuff I've seen lately who knows. Tell me why you think she's missing. Was someone after her?"

"No, it was more the other way around. She was chasing that Rhoden guy. He's still here someplace. I'm worried she found him or he found her. Will you help me look for her? If this guy found her he's dangerous. She might be in serious trouble."

"Yeah. Maybe this guy has something to do with Grant's disappearance. Show me where you last saw her."

Chapter 15

After feeding them both, Grant cleared the dishes and washed them. Samuel was pouring over books searching for a solution. Though anxious for answers Grant didn't want to disturb him so occupied himself with menial tasks. It was while he was drying the dishes that the idea came to him. Still not wanting to bother the mage he ran through the thought again looking for loopholes. Finding none, he decided he had to speak. "Hey, whatever your name is." He waited for acknowledgment, but he didn't appear to have heard him. He was muttering something to himself. Grant moved closer. "Excuse me. I hate to disturb you, but—"

"Then don't," the mage snapped. Annoyed he said, "What?"

"I was just thinking. I don't want this to sound morose or anything, but if you're alive in two thousand and nineteen will any of what is happening now become a memory?"

"Huh? What?"

"I was thinking. If you plant some sort of memory in your brain now to find Samuel maybe he can help from the other side."

The mage blinked a few times then stood abruptly "Of course. That's brilliant." He scribbled furiously on a piece of paper then held it up. "Here. Hold this chest high and let me look at it and you."

Grant glanced down. It showed today's date, August fifteenth, nineteen fifty-eight.

"Ah, is this going to be enough? You sure he'll know what it means?"

"He'll know."

He focused hard at the sign and said, "This is important, Samuel." He repeated the phrase several times to emphasize the words.

Grant wondered about the use of Samuel's name then thought, "Ah, because you and Samuel are both wizards. I guess all you people know each other."

"Not true but trust me. I know this one."

Something in the way he said that clicked a memory open. "Hey, wasn't Samuel the wizard who first created the seam?"

Distracted and excited, the mage said, "That he was, my boy. That he was."

"And how many other wizards are here in Chicago at this time?"

"None to my knowledge."

Grant made the connection one he should have landed on hours ago. "You're Samuel."

The mage glanced up and smiled. "The same."

"Why didn't you tell me?"

"Well, for several reasons. At first, I didn't know you and wasn't sure I could trust you."

Grant huffed. "Yeah, see where that got you. You got shot."

"Yes. Anyway, later, once I confirmed you knew me from the future, other than learning I was alive, I couldn't risk knowing anything else."

Grant worked his jaw trying to decide whether to tell him something important. What he knew might affect the outcome of whatever plan they came up with. "Here's something you should know."

"No. I can't hear this."

"You have to because it may save us wasted time." Though it was obvious by his distressed look, it was equally as apparent that the man he now knew to be the younger Samuel wanted to know something about his future self. "The battle in Chevalon was fierce. It took a lot out of, ah, you. You were extremely weak and struggling. I think you came back to Chicago to die. It might already be too late."

Samuel collapsed on the sofa a shocked expression making him look pained.

Once the owner of the restaurant became aware that Vega was looking into a missing girl, he was more than cooperative allowing them to scan the security footage from the day before. They found the images of both Shree and Ely. After Shree left, Elly hurried to the door and exited. They backed the video up and Vega saw the moment she perked up at something she spotted outside the window. By the anxious look on her face when she left, she was on the hunt.

As they stood on the sidewalk outside the restaurant, Shree asked, "Now what? She obviously went off to tail whoever she saw walking past. Are there cameras on the street that can help us track her?"

"Yeah, but to see the footage involves a long process which includes filing a formal missing person's report and then convincing the powers that be that we need to see the footage. I have a better idea. I think I know someone who might be able to help."

Chapter 16

Vega knocked on the door. When no one responded he feared the old man had died during the night. He tried again and was about to send Shree for the manager when the door swung open. No one stood near it. Fearful of an assault, he swept Shree behind him, withdrew his gun, and entered with caution.

He found Samuel lying on the sofa. His color had grayed, and he looked near death. He holstered his gun and rushed to him. "What happened? Do you need an ambulance?"

"No. No time. He placed a frail hand on Vega's to stop him from placing the call. "I found him."

"You found Grant? That's great. Where? How?"

"I don't have the energy for lengthy explanations. He is in nineteen fifty-eight and has somehow hooked up with my younger self. I have worked out the details of the spells I need. If I'm guessing what my younger self has in mind it will not require as much strength from me as first thought since he'll be on the other end working from there. I'm just waiting for word from him to know when."

"You mean magically? Can you do that? Send a message across time?"

"Not in the way you're thinking. He is using memories. He creates them and since it's me they enter my mind and I can see them as if I actually lived them."

"Okay, but are you going to be able to do this? You really don't look well."

"I'm dying. Evidently, back in nineteen fifty-eight Grant thought it necessary to shoot me. The details are fuzzy but the bullet is still inside."

"Ah," Shree said, "is Elly with Detective Grant?"

Samuel eyed her seeing her for the first time. "Not to my knowledge."

"I brought her here," Vega said, "because Ely's disappeared and the suspect is Rhoden."

This announcement caused Samuel to sit up which in turn brought about a coughing fit that sprayed blood droplets. "The Princess is missing?" Vega helped him up and Shree ran to get a glass of water.

Samuel said, "I'm sorry but my first duty is to the royal family. I must find her instead of saving Detective Grant." His voice was barely a whisper.

Shree handed him a glass of water and Vega held it as Samuel sipped.

"Please, Samuel, we can do both can't we?"

Samuel appeared to ponder that before saying, "Perhaps there is a way. You see there are some problems with reopening the portal."

"YOU SEE, Grant, I can only keep it open for a short duration. It will be enough to get you through but staying there may be a problem. The only person who can remove the impedance on the portal is the original spell caster."

SAMUEL LOOKED AT VEGA, "since Rhoden is the original spell caster, he must be convinced to remove it. That means you're going to have to find him anyway. Rescue the princess and bring Rhoden to the portal."

"I WILL SEND word to my future self but I suspect that he will have already figured this out. If Rhoden is indeed in your time, he will have to be captured and forced to reverse or dispel the magic he used."

"If he contacts my partner Vega, he will help."

"Good suggestion. I'll make another sign. I just wish there was a way for him to reply."

As Samuel wrote, Grant asked, "So that's it? We just capture Rhoden and get him to reverse the spell?"

Samuel looked up from his writing.

"EVEN WITH BOTH of us working, we can only keep the portal open a limited time. If the spell isn't removed by then the portal will close for good and whoever traveled through it will be sucked back to the previous time."

Vega looked astonished. "So, even if we manage to get him back, he might not be able to stay?"

"That's right. I'm sorry."

"HOW MUCH TIME DO I HAVE?" Grant asked.

"I'm not sure. I'm guessing hours. A lot will depend on the strength of my older self. We will work as hard as we can to give you the time you need to bring Rhoden to the portal."

"What if he refuses to remove the spell?"

"OH, be assured Detective Vega, he will refuse. You have to convince him. However, I have several added notes from over the years that I'm afraid my younger self does not have access to. There are two other ways to assure his cooperation. One, if we can hold the portal open long enough you can throw him through the seam. The magic will be destroyed as will his ability to cast spells. He will not want that to happen and will fight hard to prevent it."

"And the second way?"

"You kill him."

"KILL HIM?" Grant said. "I'd like nothing better but I'm a policeman. I can't just shoot the man unless he's a threat to someone else or to me."

"Consider this. If we can't break his spell there is a real possibility that you will spend the rest of your life in the past. Some other soul will be placed in the body of the baby your parents give birth to. Your life will never be the same. Is that threat enough?"

Grant paused his pacing to give Samuel's words consideration. Rhoden had done horrible, evil things and deserved to die but just outright gunning him down—was he capable of such a cold-blooded act?

"Here, hold these. Let me flash on each then drop the top one. I'll repeat the process until all the signs are gone."

SAMUEL STIFFENED FOR A MOMENT, his eyes going wide then he fell back on the sofa. "Ah! Yes. I knew that. That doesn't leave us much time. Agreed. Rhoden is the key." He blinked, stared at Vega but spoke more to himself. "Oh, Rhoden will be there. He will be drawn to the power of the magic."

"Will Elly be with him?" Shree asked.

"Yes, I expect she will. He will attempt to use her against us. Don't worry child, we'll get her back."

"You okay?" Vega said.

"Yes, and we have to work fast. We have to be in position in two hours."

"Didn't you tell me this Rhoden guy had to kill you and take your heart to destroy the seam?"

"Yes, but that what I have you for." He glanced out the window. "Yes, smart, the sun will be set."

"You get another new memory?"

"Yes. My younger self is smarter than I remember. He is sending me messages." He stood. "There is something very important you have to do. I'll explain as we gather what I'll need. I assume you have a vehicle to take us to the site."

Chapter 17

Rhoden could feel the energy. It was close, he assumed at the portal site but who was trying to access it and from which side of the seam?

He had picked up his other two followers. The injured man in the basement was irretrievable and he didn't want to be short-handed when he confronted whoever might be trying to open the portal. Two of the men controlled the princess. He didn't want to risk her getting away at a crucial time. He planned on using her as leverage to end any further crossings. Once accomplished he would no longer need her. She was going to die tonight. With her gone and the portal sealed forever, he would not be looking over his shoulders as he worked to conquer this world. However, his research indicated to seal the portal permanently he needed the creator, Samuel. All he had to do was kill the feeble old man and cast him into the seam while recasting his spell.

He stopped at the corner, staying to the shadows of a building. A faint glow emanated from the third floor of the parking structure. Someone was here and already working on opening the seam. It had to be Samuel. He turned to his henchmen. "You," he pointed to the burly, unofficial leader of the group, "go around the garage. There's a back entrance. Get up to the third floor unseen and wait for my signal."

"What's the signal?"

Rhoden gave a wicked smile. "When I light up the night with their bodies."

The man looked confused but nodded and ran off. To the second man not holding the princess, he said, "You go up the front ramp but be careful. If they have someone watching they will be there. Get to the end of the ramp of the second floor and wait. I don't want them seeing you too soon."

The man darted across the street.

He glared back at the princess. Her head lulled but he was aware she was at least partially conscious. It was better she was still dazed. She was less of a potential burden or threat. Some princess, he thought. He hated thinking of her with that title. He should be the monarch of Chevalon not this weak woman and her equally as pathetic brother. "Your reign ends tonight, princess. It will be the shortest of any ruler Chevalon has ever had." He looked back at the garage. His men should be in position. He moved forward and rehearsed the needed spells. This was going to be a glorious night.

ELLY WAS BIDING HER TIME. She wanted Rhoden to think she was incapacitated, at least until they got wherever he was heading. From the bits of information gleaned from his discussions with his minions his actions had something to do with the portal. That might mean help was on the way. She just had to pretend a little longer.

For the most part, the two lunkheads assigned to handle her carried her. That meant expended energy which hopefully meant when it was time for her to act, they'd be tired and slow. Since he sent the other two men away once she put her two handlers out of commission it was just her and Rhoden. She didn't know much magic but tried to remember the one Rhoden used in the basement. Could she make it work? Rhoden was stronger and more experienced, but if she took him by surprise, she might get the advantage. From there it was more a matter of pummeling him to death than using spells.

The two men followed their boss across the street and toward the parking garage. She allowed her head to roll back. Through slits she took in the structure noticing a blueish glow somewhere to the rear of one of the floors. Was someone here already? If so, she had to warn them of Rhoden's approach even if it meant giving up her advantage.

They entered the small stairway, their footsteps echoing up the full height. Rhoden turned and hushed his followers. They moved with stealth then. It was up to her to create noise. As they lifted her between them up a step, she reached a foot down and kicked the concrete sending sound upward.

Rhoden whirled and stormed down the two steps he was above them, clutched Ely's jaw, and squeezed. She was unable to hold back the cry of pain. Her eyes flashed open and he glared at her. If you make me hurt you I will enjoy it immensely. Your theatrics will not benefit anyone but will cause you great pain."

He slid his hand to her throat clutched tightly restricting her airflow and spoke several words. Heat filtered through her neck and in an instant she was unable to speak. Something clutched at her vocal cord strangling any sound before it could be uttered.

A wave of panic washed over her. Rhoden smiled at her obvious fear. "Just temporary, princess," he said the word as if spitting it from his mouth, "Your voice will come back shortly. Of course, by then, you will most likely be dead." He smiled and continued up the stairs.

Elly fought to remain calm. Whatever advantage she hoped to have was gone. Worse, she was no longer able to warn those who might be there to help her. She had to relax and think.

One of the goons lifted and tossed her over his shoulder. As he moved up the stairs her head bounced. The tailing goon batted her head back and forth playfully like he was playing solo ping pong. Though it didn't hurt, it was annoying and distracting.

They reached the third floor landing and they all crouched bringing her feet down enough to touch the floor. That gave her an idea. However, before she could implement her plan, something happened out in the garage.

Chapter 18

A fiery current of energy appeared after Samuel had cast his spell. Shree stood to the side holding the tome with instructions to turn to certain pages at specific times. Samuel had instructed her as to when each was to be done to save time. However, he shouted to her now as she had been too mesmerized by the sudden sparking light to do her job.

"Oh! Oh! Yes. Sorry." She turned to the next page.

Samuel glowered at her for a moment then began reading. Done he recited the words and more sparks flew however this time a blueish streak appeared down the center of the fiery area. Samuel felt the energy tearing from his weakened body. He wasn't sure he had enough left for the final spell, but he had to try. The frightened girl flipped the page. As Samuel bent to read it, a bolt of pure energy hit his back driving him off his feet and into a parked car ten feet away.

In an instant the garage became a battle zone. Gunshots erupted from all sections.

Samuel grunted from the effort of staying conscious and crawled behind the car. Shree ran after him her face a mask of the same fear he felt. He had expected Rhoden to make an appearance though he hoped Vega saw him before he got involved. However, to ensure he was protected he wore his cloak with the protective wards repelling magic wound into the fabric and had cast an extra protection spell over the area to make sure Shree was safe. Rhoden's spell had not really touched him but the energy absorbed was released as a concussive force driving him into the car.

Before all the work he had done dissipated, or worse, was dispelled by Rhoden, Samuel had to cast the final spell. However, to do so placed him in the open, an easy target, if not from Rhoden's disruptive magic, then from his henchmen's bullets.

He struggled to his feet, reread the final spell, and said, "Stay here," to Shree. He gathered his remaining strength aware of the pain increasing in his chest and strode toward the portal.

Vega had been taken by surprise. He took up a position at the top of the ramp thinking an assault would come from that direction. He never expected something as simple as them using the stairs. When that mage dude, cast the spell at Samuel, he was unprepared to stop him.

He adjusted and fired twice at the mage driving him back inside the stairwell and the closed door. Almost immediately, shots were directed at him from down the ramp. At least part of the attack was coming from there. However, when bullets chipped away at the concrete near his head, he realized he was in a crossfire. He was facing at least two shooters. If he didn't move, he was dead.

From the other side of the portal, Samuel readied the third spell. He was sure his older, more experienced self had the same three spells working. The problem was the timing. With no real way of telling when the other him started it was guesswork, yet somehow, he felt he was on track. Grant stood anxiously at his side his gun drawn as Samuel had instructed. The blueish streak hung in the middle of the air four feet off the ground and stretched eight feet high. He nodded at Grant who nodded back that he was ready, then began the spell.

Sparks flew, an electric current traced the outline of the seam. For a moment, nothing happened, then the seam sucked outward, then whipped back toward him and exploded. The two men were lifted from their feet and sent sprawling along the grassy noll the portal had been created upon.

She had been unaware of Rhoden slipping from the stairwell the first time. Bullets chased him back and the two men assigned to watch her crouched. The amount of gunfire increased but none seemed directed toward them. Rhoden paused for a second then slipped out of the stairwell again. Elly was sure he was about to create havoc with whoever was out there. Anyone Rhoden fought against was a potential ally for her. It was time to make her move.

With the free man squatting at the door with his back to them and as the man holding her over his shoulder stood, she dug her toes into the concrete floor, pushed as hard as she could, and arced backward.

The sudden shift in momentum sent the man back a step, teetering on the edge of the top stair. Elly slid free. He reached out to grab her, but she backed a step, then snapped a kick into his chest that sent hm tumbling down the concrete steps. Until his partner screamed the man at the door was unaware there was a problem. He turned but Elly kicked him against the door, then launched at him. She slipped her bound hands over his head, then twisted to get behind him. With all her strength she yanked back on the rope pulling it taut against the man's throat.

She walked backward in the confined space to keep him from getting a foothold but as she ran out of room, he pressed her hard against the wall and stood.

She didn't want him to get to his full height. He was much taller than her and keeping the pressure on his neck was hard enough at this level. Instead of allowing his superior height to lift her, she leaped in their air, relaxing the pressure on her opponent, then dropped with all her weight to her knees.

Pain shot up both legs as she hit the hard floor, but the man was yanked backward. His head connected with the wall with a loud thud that echoed down the stairwell. With him stunned, she increased the pressure knowing she didn't have long to finish before he began fighting again. With him bent backward over her body, she pulled with all her might. She wasn't sure how long she held him or how long it took to render him unconscious but she was only going to get one chance. If she went too far, oh well. It's what he got for joining with Rhoden.

When she released him, he made no effort to rise. She rolled him down the stairs where he landed on his partner.

While the pain eased in her knees, she patted her pockets for the knife but as expected it had been confiscated. She worked the rope with her teeth. After a minute making little progress, she scooted to the door to witness the action and locate Rhoden. To her horror, she found him creeping up behind the unaware Samuel.

The old wizard did not look stable. He stood on wobbly legs, facing the seam. With great arm gestures and intricate finger work, he wove a spell she guessed was to open the seam.

Gunshots drew her attention to the right, straight across from the stairwell door. Detective Grant's partner, Vega was crouched behind a car firing in two directions. His opponents had to be the other two goons working with Rhoden.

She had to help. She worked at the ropes feverishly as glared at Rhoden's back. The distance between him and Samuel lessened by the second. She noted in his hand was a glowing, flickering light in the shape of a long knife. A magical blade she guessed created for the sole purpose of killing Samuel before he finished his task. Whatever he was doing, Rhoden did not want him to accomplish it. That meant it was something she wanted to happen.

Working a loop up, Elly could wait no longer. She worked the door open and ran through while still working the knot.

Out of the shadows, a black shape moved. It launched itself at Rhoden, striking him with a massive book. The blow took the mage by surprise but as he fell backward, he swept the blade at the figure. It hissed and sparked as it connected with the book. The two magically items shrieked and repelled from each other. The book went flying while Rhoden had to regain control over the wicked blade. The wielder fell back and tripped over the book. Elly now recognized the attacker as Shree.

Rhoden got to his feet and advanced on Shree. *No, I can't let him kill her.* Elly forgot about untying her hands and just ran.

Samuel, having heard the commotion, gave a flicker of attention toward the combatants, pointed a finger, and a short quick blast of lightning, shot out slamming into Rhoden, sending him sprawling. Shree scrambled backward as Elly reached her. The girl screamed and swung at Elly who took the wild blow on her chest.

"Shree, it's me."

"Oh, my God. Ely. You're safe." She got to her feet and tried to embrace Elly but she dodged, grabbed her hand, and pulled. "Come on. We have to get out of sight." They ran around the closest car and ducked.

Samuel went back to his work. Rhoden got to his feet. The gun fight continued but at a lesser rate of fire.

The roar of a muffled explosion reverberated through the garage.

The seam sucked in then blew out. Samuel lowered his hands, paused a beat, then began again.

Rhoden stirred. Elly watched him. "Do you know what Samuel's trying to do?"

Shree nodded vigorously. "He's trying to reopen the seam. Rhoden tried to seal it."

That was all Elly needed to know. She interrupted further explanation. "We have to give him time to do it." She looked at Shree. That means stopping Rhoden. Can you do it?"

Shree hesitated, then nodded.

"Okay, I'll go straight at him, you try to get around him." Without another word she raced straight at the evil wizard.

Chapter 19

Rhoden focused on Samuel again. The magical knife exploded to life in his hand. He stood and advanced. Elly didn't think he saw her. The longer she went unnoticed the better. Though she feared the damage and pain the knife might cause, her rage and total obsession with destroying Rhoden was so great it overwhelmed caution. She barreled ahead despite the insanity of the thoughtless attack.

Rhoden moved closer and readied the blade high overhead to strike a killing blow.

With a sudden rush of light and power, the seam tore open, like fabric being sliced only this fabric was that of worlds.

The brightness caused Rhoden to throw up his hands to deflect the blinding light. Elly was forced to do the same, now no longer sure where her prey was within the light. As the intensity of the illumination faded and her eyes adjusted, she noted Rhoden had recovered faster, perhaps by some magical means, and was in striking distance of Samuel again. She was not going to get to him in time.

She screamed, "Samuel," but the old mage did not hear. He barely appeared to be standing. The effort to open the seam had taken too much from him. Even if he had heard her call, she doubted he'd be able to stop Rhoden's killing blow. Still, she ran hard if only to get retribution for Samuel.

A body leaned through the seam. It was Grant. He hung above the others as if suspended in mid-air. He saw Samuel, then spotted Rhoden. His arm came up holding a gun. He fired.

The off-balance shot did not strike Rhoden but had been enough to alter the strike and prevent damage to Samuel. The older mage collapsed.

Grant worked to get through the narrow, shrinking space of the seam. Rhoden recovered and, seeing Samuel down, and Grant coming through, changed targets. Just as he readied to plunge the glowing knife into Grant, Elly hit him.

She came in high, drove her still bound hands up under his chin, snapping his head back, and the two of them rolled in a jumble of limbs until they came to a sudden stop at the concrete half wall barrier that surrounded the parking garage.

They recovered at the same time. She noticed the knife was actually a hand carved piece of wood in the shape of a knife. It lay three feet away and no longer glowed as if it had gone dormant. Elly looked up at Rhoden. The rage on his face was so intense it distorted his features into something demonic giving Elly pause, then she allowed her own inner beast loose and her fury surpassed his. With a roar that filled her head, she attacked. She swung her bond hands like a club, but Rhoden blocked and defected it to the side. He punched her on the side of the head, knocking her off balance.

She kicked out catching him under the chin, then dove on top of him.

Grant struggled to get through. The opening appeared to be wide enough, but the energy grabbed at him preventing progress to the other side. With the way open, the younger Samuel could see through the seam to the future side. His older self was down. Concerned with his older self's safety he lost concentration for a moment and the seam closed around Grant who was only halfway through. The detective cried out.

The older Samuel gathered his strength and rose slowly to unsteady legs. His time was ending. He could feel his body dissolving from the inside. But he still had a job to do and would not allow his death to be the reason Rhoden won. He drew in all the energy his weakened body could hold and directed it at the portal. The seam widened and Grant slumped.

Vega appeared out of nowhere and grabbed Grant's arms. He pulled, his partner and friend slid through with grudging slowness. He pulled with all his strength digging his feet into the concrete floor. With no real traction his shoes slipped. He righted himself several times and kept pulling.

Shree joined him getting closer to the seam and wrapping her strong arms around Grant's chest. Together they hauled. Grant moved. Only his legs remained on the other side. Grant stirred and came awake with a start. He had no leverage with which to push but tried to kick his feet loose from the energy grip.

He spotted movement behind Samuel. An armed man lifted a gun. Without concern over what might happen to him, Grant snapped his gun hand free from Vega's grip, aimed, and fired repeatedly until the man went down.

Though the move saved Samuel's life, he lost precious ground being sucked back into the seam. Now his upper torso and head were through and the seam was tightening again.

Vega and Shree took hold again and refocused their efforts. Samuel used the last of his reserves to expand the seam. Just as it looked as if they might succeed, Rhoden appeared again.

Chapter 20

Elly punched, clawed, kicked, and bit, causing a lot of infuriating but minor damage. Rhoden was not that strong nor was he an experienced fighter, but he still had magic and once he managed to get enough space between him and Ely, he used it. The blast hit her in the chest and drove her across the parking spaces and rolling down the ramp.

He stood, retrieved the knife, and seeing he still had time to destroy the seam and everyone around it, spelled the knife back to life. It crackled with eager energy. He advanced, first using another energy bolt to blast both Vega and Shree into the car next to the seam, then he turned his attention toward Samuel who was struggling to stay erect.

Grant who had almost made it through again, raised his arm and fired at Rhoden. The gun spit two rounds before the slide locked back. At least one round struck the evil mage but didn't appear to have any effect.

A beam of light shot through the seam engulfing Rhoden and slowing his progress but the spell faded as the seam narrowed again. This time there was no escaping the death blow Rhoden was about to deliver. He grabbed Samuel's shoulder and plunged the knife deep into his gut. Rhoden laughed loudly, thrilled by his ultimate success. The smile faded as he realized the old man was still standing. More confusing was the lack of pain on the man's face. He glanced down to see the knife had embedded in the cloak. It must have defensive wards imbued within the fabric, he thought. He pulled back on the knife to strike an unprotected area, but the cloak latched on and would not relinquish its hold.

He pulled again with no success. He glanced up to see Samuel was the one smiling now. He raised a hand. On a finger was a large glowing ring. Recognizing it of a source of power, Rhoden released the knife and began a defensive spell but he was too late. The beam of light lifted and threw him back toward the seam. Grant caught his arms and hauled him upward. He had no leverage to do so but used all his considerable strength fueled by the desperation of never returning to his time. Rhoden struggled but was lifted off his feet.

Using Rhoden's body as a counterweight, Grant discovered the closer he moved the evil man toward the seam the more he emerged from it. Just as he thought this might finally work, fire seared his hands. He could smell the charred odor of his flesh. He tried to hold on for as long as he was able, but the pain was too intense. His grip slipped away.

"Noooo!" Elly screamed, racing up the ramp. With all her pent emotions, all her fury, all her desperate desire for revenge and to not fail, and with all the power in her body, she recalled Rhoden's word and shrieked, "Forzaire!" A gust of directed air with the power of a tornado, exploded from her fingers. It was not as powerful as the magic used in concert with her brother to destroy Mortas Frost, but it was the most power she had ever used by herself. Her face was haloed by an amber light. Her hair blew like strands of a whip.

The wind lifted Rhoden and drove him into the seam. He screamed knowing what the end result would be should he pass through without first dispelling the magic he cast on the portal. He gripped the edge of the seam as Grant worked to pry his fingers free. The mage began chanting.

Samuels on both sides of the portal screamed, "Stop him."

Grant punched the mage in the face. Then with all the hostility he ever unleashed went berserk on the man, pummeling his face over and over until it was a bloody mess.

Elly rushed forward, picking up the dagger that now lay at Samuel's feet. As soon as her hands touched the wood the blade ignited. She ran at the seam, leaped, and drove the blade into Rhoden's eye. He shrieked as his face melted. He fell into the seam, and disappeared.

Grant was cast out landing hard but shouting gleefully. "I'm back. I'm back."

Samuel walked forward, staying erect by sure will. As the portal began to close, he spied his younger self.

The younger Samuel said, "You can't die. You're too young."

In a barely audible whisper, the older Samuel said, "Bullet," and pointed at his chest.

The younger mage's eyes widened as understanding came to him. "Hold on. I'll fix it."

As the last of the seam faded, the older mage shouted, "Google and Microsoft." He was unsure if he'd been heard or if his younger self understood the words or their meaning, but his younger self was smarter than he remembered. Then he collapsed.

Chapter 21

Not knowing what else to do for Samuel, Vega called for an ambulance, then he asked for units, and a supervisor. By the time they arrived, Samuel was being carted off. Grant told the EMT's about the bullet in Samuel's chest.

Vega and Grant had already discussed their story. The three dead men in the garage had abducted Grant and were holding him to punish him for arresting one of their friends. They never mentioned the friend's name. The one possible flaw in the story was the discovery that the fourth man was still alive. Elly had only choked him out.

Elly and Shree were told to leave and be with Samuel before the units arrived. They were happy to do so.

A day later, after making a miraculous recovery, Samuel was being driven home by Vega and accompanied by Shree, and Ely. The doctors did not want to release him pending further tests, but he left anyway under a veil that enabled them to pass through the hospital undetected.

They arrived at Samuel's apartment where they met Grant on the sidewalk. Grant and Vega's story held up. The surviving attacker ranted about magic and a blonde girl who they held captive so the magician they worked for could rule the world. He was remanded for a psych eval.

Vega helped Samuel stand. Though recovered he was still weakened from the ordeal and the massive amount of expended energy used keeping the portal from closing. After greeting Grant, Samuel looked at the building with confusion. "Why are we here?"

"What are you talking about? This is your home," Vega said.

"No, it's not."

"Of course, it is. I think we better take you back to the hospital."

Grant looked at the building. "It certainly isn't the one you lived in back in nineteen fifty-eight."

"Look, I know where I live. Here, let me prove it to you. He took out his wallet and showed his ID. The address was across town in a more upscale and exclusive building.

Now Vega and Grant were confused but they took him to the address. Samuel lived in a penthouse. As they entered their jaws dropped.

"Did you do this with magic," Elly asked.

"No. The stock market." He smiled. "I was right. My younger self was smarter than I remembered."

Acknowledgments

With each book I write, I find it harder to find the words to express the gratitude I have for those who make the publishing possible. In this particular title, yeoman's work was done by long time editor and friend, Jodi McDermitt, who was saddled with a deadline that was tough to reach. However, in typical J-Mac fashion, she juggled job, family, her own writing career, and her blossoming stand up comedy act to get the job done right on time. Thank you, Jodi.

I'd also like to thank co-author Jason Nugent for his wisdom and assistance with all things technology. Everyone who knows me will tell you I am not savvy to the ways of the techno-world. I am easily confused and endlessly frustrated by supposedly easy steps to make things work. They never do. There are times when I want to open a seam and join Phetrix in a much simpler world. If not for Jason, this book would still be sitting in my laptop awaiting a miracle.

Lastly, I wish to once more thank the many fans who have taken the chance on a relatively unknown writer. I am rewarded to see so many of you come back for more. It helps to keep an old man's dream alive. Enjoy the journey through the seam.

-Ray

I want to thank my family for their unending support of this crazy thing I do. You are the reason I strive to be better.

I want to thank you the reader for sticking with me. I do hope you enjoy the tales I tell. I've got many more to share!

I want to thank Ray for his knowledge, advice, and for bringing me on board with this project. I've learned so much from you since we first met at a small horror convention that was terrible for sales but great for networking. Thanks for everything. This series has been a fun experience!

Jodi, as usual you rock! Thanks for cleaning up and making sense of this thing we gave you. I appreciate your kind and thoughtful suggestions.

-Jason

About the Author

RAY WENCK

Ray Wenck taught elementary school for 35 years. He was also the chef/owner of DeSimone's Italian Restaurant for more than 25 years. After retiring, he became a lead cook for Hollywood Casinos and the kitchen manager for the Toledo Mud Hens AAA baseball team. Now he spends most of his time writing, doing book tours, and meeting old and new fans and friends around the country.

Ray is the author of twenty-five novels including the Amazon Top 20 post-apocalyptic *Random Survival* series, the paranormal thriller, *Ghost of a Chance*, the mystery/suspense *Danny Roth* series and the ever popular choose your own adventures, *Pick-A-Path: Apocalypse*. A list of his other novels can be viewed at raywenck.com.

His hobbies include reading, hiking, cooking, baseball, and playing the harmonica with any band brave enough to allow him to sit in.

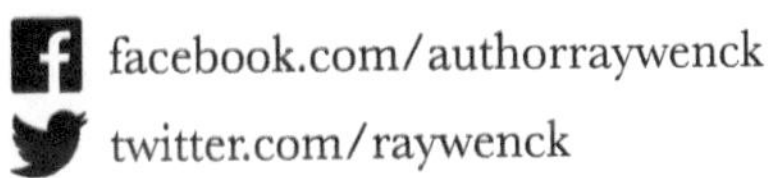

Also by Ray Wenck

Random Survival Series

Random Survival

The Long Search for Home

The Endless Struggle

The Journey to Normal

And Then There'll Be None (Coming Soon)

Danny Roth Series

Teammates

Teamwork

Home Team

Stealing Home

Group Therapy

Double Play

The Dead Series

Tower of the Dead

Island of the Dead

Escaping the Dead

Pick-A-Path Series

Pick-A-Path: Apocalypse 1

Pick-A-Path: Apocalypse 2

Pick-A-Path: Apocalypse 3

Stand Alone Titles

Warriors of the Court

Live to Die Again

Ghost of a Chance

Mischief Magic

Short Stories

The Con

Short Stop (A Danny Roth Short)

Super Me

Co-Authored with Jason J. Nugent

Escape: The Seam Travelers Book One

Capture: The Seam Travelers Book Two

Conquest: The Seam Travelers Book Three

About the Author

JASON J. NUGENT

USA Today Bestselling Author Jason J. Nugent has been a paperboy, pizza maker, dishwasher, restaurant manager, promotional products sales rep, chamber of commerce director, and one time BBQ champion. He has skated with Tony Hawk, had a babysitter with a serial killer brother, and is followed by rapper Chuck D on Twitter. He and his wife share a home in beautiful Southern Illinois with their son, four cats, and one feisty chihuahua.

More information can be found at jasonjnugent.com.

To stay updated with my current projects, please sign up for my email newsletter. You will get regular emails every month and whenever I have a new release.

For doing so, you will get a free story.

facebook.com/jasonjnugentwrites
twitter.com/lailokenri
instagram.com/authorjasonjnugent

Also by Jason J. Nugent

Ceres Horizon

(LitRPG/Gamelit)

Sword of the Moon King

Heart of the Forest

Curse of the Drakku

(Adventure Fantasy)

Curse of the Drakku: Origins (prequel)

The Blood Stone

Dragon's Blood

Bone of the Griffon

The Forgotten Chronicles Trilogy

(Young Adult Sci-Fi)

The Selection

Rise of the Forgotten

The War for Truth

The Seam Travelers Trilogy

(Portal Fantasy Co-Written with thriller author Ray Wenck)

Escape

Capture

Conquest

Short Story Collections

(Almost) Average Anthology

Moments of Darkness

Madness in the Shadows